J·A· JANCE

THREE COMPLETE NOVELS

Until Proven Guilty

Injustice for All

Trial by Fury

WINGS BOOKS

New York • Avenel, New Jersey

This omnibus was originally published in separate volumes under the titles:

Until Proven Guilty, copyright © 1985 by J.A. Jance
Injustice for All, copyright © 1986 by J.A. Jance
Trial by Fury, copyright © 1986 by J.A. Jance

This edition contains the complete and unabridged texts of the original editions. They have been completely reset for this volume.

This 1995 edition is published by Wings Books, distributed by Random House Value Publishing, Inc., 40 Engelhard Avenue, Avenel, New Jersey 07001, by arrangement with Avon Books, the Hearst Corporation.

Random House
New York • Toronto • London • Sydney • Auckland

Printed and bound in the United States of America

Library of Congress Cataloging-in-Publication Data

Jance, Judith A.
    [Novels.   Selections]
    Three complete novels / J.A. Jance.
         p.   cm.
    Originally published in 3 separate volumes (in 1985, 1986) under the same titles as used in the present edition.
    Contents: Until proven guilty — Injustice for all — Trial by fury.
    ISBN 0-517-14764-5
    1. Beaumont, J. P. (Fictitious character)—Fiction.   2. Police—Washington (State)—Seattle—Fiction.   3. Detective and mystery stories, American.   4. Seattle (Wash.)—Fiction.   I. Jance, Judith A. Until proven guilty.   II. Jance, Judith A. Injustice for all.   III. Jance, Judith A. Trial by fury. IV. Title. V. Title: Until proven guilty. VI. Title: Injustice for all. VII. Title: Trial by fury.
PS3560.A44A6   1996
813'.54—dc20   95-23560
                                     CIP

8   7   6   5   4   3   2   1

CONTENTS

Until Proven Guilty

To Jay, Jeanne, and Josh,
and bargain matinees everywhere

CHAPTER 1

She was probably a cute kid once, four maybe five years old. It was hard to tell that now. She was dead. The murder weapon was a pink Holly Hobbie gown. What little was left of it was still twisted around her neck. It wasn't pretty, but murder never is.

Her body had rolled thirty feet down a steep embankment from the roadway, tossed out like so much garbage. She was still tangled in a clump of blackberry bushes when we got there. As far as I could see, there was no sign of a struggle. It looked to me as though she had been dead several hours, but a final determination on that would have to wait for the experts.

My name is Beaumont. I've been around homicide for fifteen years, but that doesn't mean I didn't want to puke. I was careful not to think about my own kids right then. You can't afford to. If you do, you crack up.

My partner, Ron Peters, was the new man on the squad. He had only been up from burglary a couple of months. He was still at the stage where he was long on homicide theory and short on homicide practice. This was his first dead kid, and he wasn't taking it too well. He hadn't come to terms with the idea of a dead child as evidence. That takes time and experience. His face was a pasty shade of gray. I sent him up to the road to talk to the truck driver who had called 911, while I prowled the crime scene along with a small army of arriving officers.

After the pictures, after the measurements, it took the boys from the medical examiner's office a good little while to drag her loose from the blackberry bushes. If you've ever tried picking blackberries, you know it's easy enough to get in but hell on wheels to get back out. By the time they brought out the body bag, I was convinced we weren't going to find anything. We slipped and slid on the steep hillside, without finding so much as a gum wrapper or an old beer can.

I climbed back up and found to my relief that I had waited long enough. The swarm of killer bees that calls itself Seattle's press corps had disappeared with the coroner's wagon. I like reporters almost as much as I like killers, and the less I have to do with them, the better off I am.

Peters' color was a little better than it had been. He was talking with a man named Otis Walker, who was built like an Alaskan grizzly. In the old days people would have said Walker drove a sewage truck. These are the days of sanitary engineers and environmentalists, so Walker told us he drove a sludge truck for the Westside Treatment Center. That may sound like a high-class detox joint, but it isn't. A rose by any other name may smell as sweet, but if it looks like a sewage plant and smells like a sewage plant, that's what I call it.

However, Otis Walker had a heavy, square jaw and a nose that showed signs of more than one serious break. His biceps resembled half-grown trees. I chose not to debate his job title. Despite his fearsome appearance, he was having a tough time talking to Peters. The words stuck in his throat, threatening to choke him.

"You gonna catch that SOB?" he asked me when I appeared over Peters' shoulder. I nodded. "I got a kid of my own at home, you know," he continued, "almost her age. Wears the same kind of gown. Shit!" He stopped and swiped at his face with the back of one meaty paw.

"That's our job," I told him. I wondered what kind of murder this was. The easiest ones to solve are the hardest ones to understand, the husbands and lovers and wives and parents who murder people they ought to cherish instead of kill. The random killers, the ones who pick out a victim at a football game or a grocery store, are easier to comprehend and harder to catch. That's the problem with homicide.

I turned to Peters. "You about done here?"

He nodded. "Pretty much."

Walker pulled himself together. "You guys through with me?"

"For right now," Peters told him, "but don't go out of town without letting us know where to find you. With all this timely-trial crap from the Supreme Court, we may need to get ahold of you in a hurry."

Walker looked dolefully at the blackberry clump halfway down the hill. He shook his head. "I wish I never saw her," he said. "I wish I'da just driven past and never knew she was down there, know what I mean?" He climbed back into the huge blue tractor-trailer and started it, waving half-heartedly as he eased past where Peters and I were standing.

"What now?" Peters asked.

"Not much doing here as far as I can tell. Let's go get something to eat and come back for another look later." The call had come in about eleven in the morning. It was now well after three. I'm one of those guys who has to have breakfast, lunch, and dinner, or I begin to foam at the mouth. I was getting close.

Peters gave me a reproachful look. "How can you think about food? Where are her parents? The medical examiner says she died sometime around nine or nine-thirty. Someone should have come looking for her by now."

"Somebody will come," I assured him. "With any kind of luck it will be after we finish eating." As it turned out, they found us before we even got out of the car in the parking lot at G.G.'s. A marked patrol car pulled up beside ours. The officer rolled down his window. His name was Sanders. I had seen him around the Public Safety Building on occasion.

"What have you got?" I asked him.

"Missing child," he replied. "A girl. Five years old."

"Brown hair, in braids?" I asked him. "Holly Hobbie nightgown, pink?"

He nodded. "The call came in a little over half an hour ago. I went to check it out before calling you guys in. It could have been someone who forgot to come home for lunch."

"She missed lunch, all right," I told him. "And it looks as though we will too. What's the address?"

"Gay Avenue," he answered. "Forty-five forty-three. I'll lead you there."

Peters wheeled out of the parking lot behind the patrol car. "Why the hell didn't someone call us right away?" he muttered. "We could have been there a long time ago."

Peters sometimes reminds me of an Irish Setter—tall, reddish hair, good-looking, loose-jointed, not too bright at times. "Calling us on the radio would have been as good as taking out a full-page ad in the *Post-Intelligencer,*" I told him. "We just got rid of that mob of reporters, remember?"

Peters' jawline hardened, but he said nothing. Our partnership was still new and relatively uneasy. We drove through Magnolia without the fanfare of lights and sirens.

Magnolia is set apart from the rest of Seattle by a combination of waterways and railroad tracks. On this warm day in late April, flowers in well-manicured lawns were just coming into their own. Magnolia is mostly an older, settled, residential neighborhood. Some of the houses are stately mansions with white columns and vast expanses of red brick. I think I had a preconceived notion of the kind of house we were going to, but I was in for a rude awakening. Gay Avenue was anything but gay in every sense of the word.

The patrol car led us to a hidden pocket of poverty just off Government Way a few blocks east of the entrance to Discovery Park. The house at 4543 Gay Avenue was a ramshackle two-story job that had formerly been someone's pride and joy. It had fallen on hard times. Once-white shingles had deteriorated to a grubby gray. Here and there a missing one gaped like a jagged, broken tooth. Two giant stubs of trees gave mute testimony that there had once been a front yard. Yellowed newspapers and old tires littered the weedy grass. It was a perfect example of low-rent squalor plunked down in an otherwise acceptable neighborhood. If I had been one of the neighbors, I would have considered suing whoever owned that eyesore.

At the sound of the cars a band of barefoot, ragtag kids came racing around the house. One pressed a runny nose against Peters' window and stared in at us as though we were gorillas in a zoo. Peters turned to me. "Well?" he asked. "Are we getting out, or are we going to sit here all day?"

I'd rather take a beating than knock on a door and tell some poor unsuspecting soul his kid is dead. I always think about how I'd feel if someone were telling me about Scott or Kelly. There's no way to soften a blow like that. "Don't rush me," I growled. "It's the worst part of this job." I got out and slammed the door.

Sanders came up just then. "What's the name?" I asked him.

"Barstogi. Mother's name is Suzanne. Kid's name is Angela, but they call her Angel."

"Father?"

"I didn't see one. There's some kind of meeting going on in there. Probably ten or twelve people."

Peters ambled up. He glanced at his watch. "What time did you say the call came in?"

"About two forty-five," Sanders answered.

"Five hours after she's dead, somebody finally notices she's missing." Peters' voice was grim.

I pushed open a gate that dangled precariously on one rusty hinge. Gingerly I threaded my way through the debris and climbed some rickety wooden steps. The bottom one was gone altogether. Most of the others were on borrowed time. We stood on a tiny porch with those kids silently staring up at us. None of them said a word. It struck me as odd. I would have expected a barrage of questions from a group like that.

"Don't these kids talk?" I asked Sanders.

He stopped with his hand poised, ready to knock. "Not to me and probably not to you either. I meant to tell you. It seems to be some kind of religious cult. The kids aren't allowed to talk to anyone without permission. Same thing goes for the adults."

He knocked then. Through a broken windowpane in the door we could hear the low murmur of voices inside, but it was a long time before anyone answered.

The woman who opened the door was in her mid to late twenties. She was about five-six or so, solidly built. She had long dishwater-blonde hair that was parted in the middle and pulled back into a long, thick braid that hung halfway to her hips. With a little makeup, a haircut, and some decent clothes she might have been reasonably attractive. As it was, she was a very plain Jane. She looked very worried.

"Did you find her?" she asked.

Sanders didn't answer. Instead he motioned to me. "This is Detective Beaumont, ma'am, and Detective Peters. They'll be the ones helping you now." He backed away from the door as though from the entrance of a cave full of rattlers. He didn't want to be the one to tell her. Peters hovered in the background as well, leaving the ball in my court.

"May we come in, Mrs. Barstogi?" I asked.

She glanced uneasily over her shoulder. She looked as happy to have us on her doorstep as we were to be there. "Well, I don't know . . . ," she began hesitantly, stopping abruptly as someone came up behind the partially opened door.

"I thought I told you to get rid of them, Sister Suzanne." The unseen speaker was a man. His words and tone held the promise of threat.

"I did," she said meekly. "I sent the first one away like you said. There are two more." Before she had looked worried. Now she seemed genuinely frightened.

"Your faith is being tested," he continued severely. "You are failing. Jesus is watching over Angel. You have no need to call on anyone else. Jesus wants you to trust in Him completely. Haven't you learned that yet? Are you still leaning on your own understanding?"

She shrank from the door at his words. I think she would have slammed it in our faces if I hadn't used my old Fuller Brush training and stuck my foot in the way. "We need to talk to you, Mrs. Barstogi. Is there someplace where we can be alone?"

I moved inside and Peters followed. The man who had been standing just out of our line of vision was a heavy-faced, once-muscular man in his late forties who was well on his way to going to seed. He was a little shorter than I am, maybe six-one or so. He was wearing one of those Kmart special leisure suits that went out of style years ago. On his chest hung a gold chain with a heavy gold cross dangling from it. The suit was electric blue. So were his eyes, glinting with the dangerous glitter of someone just barely under control.

He placed himself belligerently between Suzanne and me. "We're all family here," he said. "No one has anything to hide from anyone else. Privacy and pride are Satan's own tools."

"Are you Angela's father?" I asked him.

"Of course not!" he blustered.

"Then I have nothing to say to you." I looked around. The living room was furnished with several period pieces in the Goodwill-reject style. There was an assortment of degenerate chairs and worn couches. The gray carpet was mottled with stains and soil. Seated around the room was a group of women. They could have been sardines from the same can for all you could tell them apart. None of them spoke. All eyes were riveted on the man who stood between Suzanne Barstogi and me.

"Is your husband here, Mrs. Barstogi? Where can we reach him?"

She glanced surreptitiously at the man's face before answering, as if expecting him to tell her what to say or whether or not she should answer at all. "I don't have a husband," she said finally, looking at the floor.

The four of us had been standing in a muddy vestibule, just inside the door. Now Peters moved swiftly around me. He took Suzanne Barstogi's elbow. Before anyone could object, he led her out onto the porch. The man made as if to follow, but I barred his way.

"We are going to talk to her alone," I told him. "If you don't want to end up in jail, you'll stay right here while we do it." I turned and left him there, closing the door behind me.

The children, standing in an ominously quiet group, were still watching. Peters was attempting to shoo them away as I came out the door. He maintained a firm grip on Suzanne's arm. I think he figured she might try to dash back into the house if he let her go.

"Mrs. Barstogi," I said. "When is the last time you saw your daughter?"

"When I put her to bed." Her eyes were wide with fear as she answered. I couldn't tell if it was fear for her daughter or fear of the consequences that would greet her when she returned to the house.

"What time was that?" This, unsurprisingly, was from Peters. I never met anyone so concerned about time.

Suzanne paused uncertainly. "It must have been between three and four."

"In the morning?" Peters asked incredulously.

She nodded. "She fell asleep at church. I carried her in from the car and put her to bed." She spoke as though there were nothing out of the ordinary in the hour.

"What was she wearing?"

"I told the other man all this. Do we have to go over it again?"

"Yes," I answered. "I'm afraid we do."

"She was wearing a pink nightgown, one she got for Christmas last year."

"We'll need you to come downtown," Peters said.

"Now?" she asked.

"Yes, now," I told her. Peters propelled her off the porch. He opened the door and helped her into the car, motioning for me to follow. "I'll drive," he said.

It figured. If he drove, I would have to tell her. I'm not the kind to keep score or hold grudges, but about then I figured Peters owed me one.

I followed her into the backseat. She scrambled as far as she could to the opposite side of the car. She looked like a cornered animal. "Who is that man in the house?" I asked as Peters turned on the ignition. "Is he a relative of yours?"

She shook her head. "That's Pastor Michael Brodie. He's the pastor of our church, Faith Tabernacle. I called him when I couldn't find Angel. He said the best thing for us to do would be to turn it over to the Lord. He brought the others over, and we've been praying ever since. Wherever two or more are gathered together—"

"What time was that?" Peters interrupted. He was beginning to sound like a broken record.

"I got up about eleven and they got here a little before noon," she said. Peters made a sound under his breath. I couldn't hear, but I don't think it was too nice.

"Angel does that," Suzanne continued. "She wakes up before I do. She'll have breakfast and watch TV." She stopped suddenly as though something was just beginning to penetrate. "Why are we going downtown?" It was the moment I had been dreading. There was no way to postpone it further.

"I believe we've found your daughter," I said gently.

"Where is she? Is something the matter?"

"A little girl was found in Discovery Park earlier this morning. I'm afraid it may be Angel. We have to be certain. We need you to identify her."

"Is she dead?" she asked.

I nodded. I deliberately didn't tell her about the gown. I didn't want to dash all hope at once. She needed some time for adjustment. I expected tears, screaming, or wailing. Instead, Suzanne Barstogi heard the words in stunned silence. She closed her eyes and bowed her head.

"It's my fault," she whispered. "It's because I called you. Pastor Michael is right. I'm being punished for my lack of faith."

We were at a stoplight. Peters turned and looked at her. "She was dead long before you called us," he said bluntly. "Your lack of faith had nothing to do with it." The light changed, and we went on.

Suzanne gave no indication that she had heard what Peters said. "I disobeyed, too," she continued. "I snuck upstairs to use the phone so no one would know." She lapsed into silence. We left her to her own thoughts. It seemed the decent thing to do.

By the time we led her up to the slab in the morgue, Suzanne Barstogi was a study in absolute composure. When the attendant pulled back the sheet, she nodded. "I killed her, didn't I?" she said softly to no one in particular. She turned to me. "I'm ready to go home now."

CHAPTER 2

When we brought Suzanne back to Gay Avenue, the place was crawling with people. It seemed to me there were even more Faith Tabernacle people than earlier in the day. Evidence technicians had gone over the house thoroughly, searching for trace evidence, dusting for fingerprints, looking for signs of forced entry or struggle. Everything pointed to the conclusion that Angel Barstogi had left the house willingly, wandering off maybe with someone she knew.

So who did she know? I looked around the room. All these folks, certainly, including Pastor Michael Brodie himself, who was holding court in the living room. He was very angry. His parishioners were walking on eggs for fear of annoying him further, abjectly catering to his every need.

Sergeant Watkins brought us up to speed on the situation. Police procedures notwithstanding, Brodie was accustomed to being in charge. He didn't want anyone talking to his people outside his presence. It was only after Watkins threatened to jail him for obstruction of justice that he finally knuckled under. He sat by the door, still silently intimidating those who filed past him. One by one our detectives took people to separate rooms to record their statements. They were not eager to talk. It was like pulling teeth. We could have used some laughing gas.

Peters and I took our turn in the barrel. The other officers had pretty well finished up with the adults and were going to work on the grungy kids. I took one of the boys, the one who had pressed his nose against the car as Peters and I drove up the first time. We had to walk past Pastor Michael. He shot a withering glance at the kid. The boy seemed to cower under its intensity.

"What's your name?" I asked as we went up the stairs.

"Jeremiah."

"You scared of him?"

He nodded. We went into a bedroom and closed the door. The bed was unmade. I straightened a place for us to sit on the bed, then took a small tape recorder from my pocket.

"Do you know what we're going to do?" He shook his head. "I'm going to ask you some questions and record both the questions and the answers."

"Are you sure it's okay? I mean, we're not supposed to talk to people."

"Why?"

"Pastor Michael says that people on the outside are tools of the devil and that we can catch it from them. It's like chicken pox."

"You won't catch anything from me, Jeremiah. I promise." I switched on the recorder. "My name is Detective J. P. Beaumont. It's five twenty-five p.m. on Thursday, April twenty-eighth. This statement is being taken in reference to Angel Barstogi, deceased. What is your name, please?"

"Jeremiah Mason."

"And are you giving this statement willingly?"

He nodded his head. "You'll have to give your answers aloud," I told him.

"Yes," he whispered.

"Did you know Angel, Angela Barstogi?"

"Yes." His answer was so muted that I didn't know whether or not my recorder would pick it up.

"You'll have to speak a little louder, Jeremiah."

"Yes," he said again.

"When is the last time you saw her?"

"Last night at church. We were playing tag."

"Was there anything unusual about her last night?"

He thought for a moment, then shook his head. "No," he said, remembering the recorder.

"How long have you known Angel?"

"Long time," he replied.

"Were you friends?"

He made a face. "Angel's a girl," he said. Obviously being a girl precluded her being a friend. "Besides," he added, "she's just a little kid."

"Do you know why we're here asking questions?"

"Somebody said it's because Angel's dead."

"That's true. And we're trying to find out who did it. That's my job."

"Pastor Michael says God did it because Angel wouldn't obey the rules."

"What rules?"

"She was all the time talking to people. Even when Pastor Michael got after her, she still did it."

"He got after her?"

"He gave her a licking in church. That's what he always does, but Angel never cried no matter what he did. The other kids knew that if they'd cry he'd stop. Angel wouldn't cry. That made him real mad."

"I'll just bet it did," I said. "And what about you? Did you ever get a licking in church?"

He nodded. "Once for stealing some food from the kitchen after dinner and once for running away."

"Are you afraid you'll get in trouble?"

He nodded again. "Pastor's mad that we're all talking to you."

"How old are you, Jeremiah?"

"Eight." As we spoke, I had noticed a bruise on top of his wrist. A small part of it was visible at the bottom of his sleeve. I pushed the shirt sleeve up, revealing five distinct marks on his arm, a thumb and four fingers.

"How did that happen?"

He shrugged and looked sheepish. "I fell down," he said.

"Where do you live?"

"In Ballard, not far from the church."

"With your parents?"

"With my mom and my stepfather."

"And how does he treat you, your stepfather?"

"All right, I guess."

I could see I had gone beyond what he would tell me. It was one thing to talk about Angela Barstogi. It was quite another to talk about Jeremiah Mason. He could still feel pain. Angel couldn't. "Is there anything you'd like to add?"

He considered. "I'm going to miss Angel," he said, "even if she was a girl."

I reached into my pocket and pulled out a business card with my name and telephone number on it. "If anyone gets after you about today, I want you to call me, understand?" He nodded.

I started toward the door but Jeremiah stopped me. He reached behind a broken-down dresser and pulled out a cup, a child's cup with the ABC's around the top and bottom. The name Angela was written in bright red letters on one side. Gingerly he handed it to me.

"It was hers," he said. "Pastor Michael told her to get rid of it, but she didn't. We hid it." He stopped and stood looking at the cup, shifting uneasily from foot to foot. "Do you think I could keep it?"

Nodding, I returned it to his grubby hand. "I think Angel would like that."

As soon as he had once more concealed the cup, I walked Jeremiah back downstairs. Brodie glared at him as we came past, but he refrained from comment. I guess Sergeant Watkins' threat of jail had carried some weight with Brodie. He had all the earmarks of a bully and a coward, someone who would lord it over those who were weaker than he. I wondered about his frustration at being faced with a tough little kid who refused to cry. I wondered if, by not crying, Angel Barstogi had signed her own death warrant. It was a possibility.

As a homicide detective, however, I'm not allowed to act on mere hunches. I can move only when I have solid evidence that points me in a certain direction. I had a feeling about Michael Brodie, but nothing substantial. Jeremiah's revelations about the "lickings" in Faith Tabernacle gave us a basis for making inquiries, but nothing more.

Slowly the crowd in the house diminished as people filtered out. At last there were only Peters and Brodie and Suzanne and me. We took them into separate rooms.

Suzanne's original numbness was beginning to wear off, but she had a hard time following my questions, to say nothing of answering them. Some things, like the date of her divorce, escaped her completely. She claimed she simply could not remember.

That bothered me. Cops learn to listen to what's said as well as to what isn't; then they combine the two in order to get at the truth. Suzanne was under a lot of stress, but nonetheless there was a lot she wasn't saying. I didn't know why. She was hiding something, that much was certain, but I didn't know what or who she might be protecting. Did Pastor Michael Brodie exert such influence that he could coerce a mother into concealing her own child's murderer? It was a chilling thought, even for someone who has been in this business as long as I have.

We left Gay Avenue around ten o'clock that night. I was starved. It had been a long time since breakfast. We went to the Doghouse, a lowbrow place in my neighborhood that stays open all hours and has fed me more meals than I care to count.

Peters and I don't exactly see eye to eye on food. Peters is an enzyme nut. He eats sprouts and seeds, which may be okay for rabbits, but in my opinion that stuff is hardly fit for human consumption. He avoids sugar and salt. He consumes little red meat and can declaim for hours on the evils of caffeine. In other words, there are times when he can be a real pain in the butt. I don't mind eating with him, but I've thought of carrying earplugs for when he gets on his soapbox.

I, on the other hand, thrive on ordinary, garden-variety, all-American junk food. Karen got the barbecue in the divorce settlement. It went with the house. Since that was the only piece of cooking equipment I had mastered and since barbecuing was unavailable in my downtown high-rise, I converted to restaurants. Other than the department, the Doghouse is my home away from home.

It's at Seventh and Bell, a few blocks from where I live. It's one of those twenty-four-hour places frequented by cops, cabbies, reporters, and other folks who live their lives while most people are asleep. The waitresses wouldn't win beauty pageants but the service is exceptional. The food is plain and plentiful, without an enzyme in sight. Connie, a grandmotherly type with boundless energy, tapped her pencil impatiently as Peters groused about the available selections. She finally pacified him with an order of unbuttered whole wheat toast and some herb tea.

I wolfed down a chili burger with lots of onions and cheese while Peters morosely stirred his tea. "What do you think?" I asked eventually.

"It's got to be some kind of brainwashing," he said. "He's got her hiding something. The question is, what?"

"Beats me." On the way across town we had exchanged information as much as possible. Afterward Peters had become strangely quiet and withdrawn. That's the tough part about breaking in a new partner. There's so much to learn before you can function as a team. Ray Johnson and I had worked together for almost eleven years before he bailed out to become chief of police in Pasco. I had become accustomed to his habits, his way of thinking. It was hard to tell where Ray's ideas left off and mine began.

With Peters it was different. He had a guarded way about him. I was still very much outside the perimeter. After two months of working together I knew almost nothing about his personal life other than the fact that he was divorced. For that matter, he didn't know much about my personal life, either. It's a two-way street.

Peters gave me a long, searching look. "You ever have anything to do with a cult before?" he asked. The question was evidently the tip of an iceberg. There was a lot more lurking beneath the surface than was apparent in his words.

"No," I replied. "First time."

"Lucky for you," he said, returning to his studious examination of the bottom of his teacup. I waited a moment to see if he would continue. He didn't. At last I gave up and changed the subject.

"What's the agenda for tomorrow?"

Before he could answer, a noisy group meandered out of the bar in a flurry of activity. I caught sight of Maxwell Cole at the same time he saw me. He extricated himself from the group and came to our booth. Max is a hulking brute of a man whose handlebar mustache and ponderous girth give him the appearance of an overfed walrus. "Damned if it isn't old J. P." he said, holding out his hand. "Fancy meeting a brother in a dive like this."

I ignored his hand, knowing it would go away. Max's reference was to our fraternity days at the University of Washington. There was no love lost then and even less now. Then we had been rivals for Karen Moffit's affections. I won that round. Karen Moffit became Karen Beaumont, and Maxwell Cole got his nose out of joint. It's ironic that five years after Karen divorced me, I'm still stuck with Maxwell Cole. I'm a bad habit he can't seem to break.

These days he's a columnist for Seattle's morning daily, the *Post-Intelligencer.* His column, "City Beat," serves as a pulpit for Maxwell Cole, self-professed righter of wrongs. He doesn't pretend to be unbiased. He's one of those liberals who always roots for the underdog whether or not it has rabies.

I could handle this self-righteous, pontificating son-of-a-bitch a little better if I hadn't spotted old Maxey Baby down on First Avenue a couple of times, hanging around the porno flicks. I don't think he was down there doing movie reviews. He looked at home there, a regular customer, like me in the McDonald's at Third and Pine.

Cole likes to take on the Seattle Police Department, casting all cops in the role of heavies. I've lost more than one case after he has tried it in the press, noisily waving the flag of the First Amendment all the while. One of his success stories, Harvey Cahill, killed somebody else within a month after Max got him acquitted. By then nobody remembered Cole's bleeding heart. They went gunning for someone to blame. Yours truly took a little gas.

"Still packing a grudge, I see," Max said, carelessly reaching across our table to flick a drooping ash into an unused ashtray. He was oblivious to the fact that he was intruding. I'm sure the idea never crossed his mind.

"I'd say it's a little more serious than a grudge," I allowed slowly. "Antipathy would be closer to the mark."

He turned from me to give Peters a nearsighted once-over, blinking through thick horn-rimmed glasses. "This your new partner? What happened to Ray?"

"Ask the public information officer," I said. "He gets paid for answering your questions. I don't."

Max looked pained. "You know, it doesn't pay to deliberately offend the press. You might need our help someday."

"It's a risk I'm willing to take."

Connie brought the coffeepot and shouldered Max out of the way. She glared meaningfully at his cigarette and removed the offending ashtray. There didn't seem to be any love lost between Connie and Maxwell Cole, either.

"Come on, Max," someone called from the door. "We're waiting on you."

Max paused as if reluctant to abandon the confrontation. He finally sauntered away. Once the door closed behind him, Connie turned back to me. "He writes mean stuff about you," she said, "and he don't tip too good, either."

That made me laugh. "Maybe I'll get even by doing some writing of my own one day," I told her. I had no idea the opportunity would present itself so soon.

Once she left the table, I turned back to Peters. "What the hell does J. P. stand for?" Peters asked.

"Don't ask."

"That bad?"

I nodded. He had the good sense to drop it. Jonas Piedmont Beaumont was my mother's little joke on the world and me too, naming me after her two grandfathers. I first shortened it to initials and then settled for Beau. The initials had stuck with people who'd met me during my university days. I wanted to punch Max in the nose for bringing it up. He once had a nickname too. Maybe I could return the favor.

"Now, what's the next move?" I asked, returning our focus to the business at hand.

Peters looked at his watch. "It's only eleven. What say we go back to the office and sift through whatever statements have been transcribed. That'll tell us who we should hit up tomorrow."

"Maybe we'll have a preliminary medical examiner's report by then too, with any kind of luck."

We went back to the office. For another four hours we pored over the Gay Avenue transcripts. Sergeant Watkins must have moved heaven and earth to have them typed that fast. The pattern was fairly obvious. The adults were noticeably vague about details prior to five or six months ago, although two of them indicated they had previously lived in Chicago. They all gave similar accounts of the last few days leading up to Angel's death. I paid particular attention to the statement from Jeremiah's stepfather, Benjamin Mason. The handprint bruise on that kid's arm hadn't come from a fall. No way. Like Jeremiah, all the children gave every evidence of being scared silly. In his own way, Jeremiah was just as plucky as Angel Barstogi. I hoped he wouldn't have to pay the same kind of price.

We finally called it quits about four a.m., so tired we couldn't make our eyes work anymore. I invited Peters to stay over with me, but he wanted to go on home to Kirkland, out in the suburbs across Lake Washington. He in turn offered me a ride home, but I wanted to walk.

"It'll settle me down so I can sleep."

I walked down Fourth. Most city dwellers avoid deserted streets late at night. They're afraid of being mugged; but then, most people don't pack a loaded .38 Smith and Wesson under their jacket.

Seattle is a deep-water port situated on Elliott Bay in Puget Sound. Huge container and grain ships ply the waters just off the ends of piers that jut out at the foot of steep hills. Although the water isn't more than five blocks from where I live, I seldom smell the ocean. That morning, though, the wind was blowing a storm in across the sound, and the pungent odor of saltwater permeated the air.

I walked with hands shoved in pockets against suddenly chill air. Maxwell Cole came to mind as I walked. He's had it in for me ever since I beat him out with Karen, and for the last twenty-five years of my life it seems like he's always been around, always there to ding me. He was the reporter who covered the shooting when I was just a rookie.

A crazy kid holed up with a gun, and I had to shoot him. He was the only man I ever killed, a boy really, eighteen years old. It tore me up. For weeks afterward I couldn't eat or sleep. All the while my good ole buddy Max, my fraternity brother Max, was playing it to the hilt, interviewing the boy's widowed mother, distraught girlfriend, stunned neighbors, making me sound like a bloodthirsty monster. A departmental review officially exonerated me, but exonerations don't capture headlines. His coverage of that one incident created a killer-cop legend that twenty years of quality police work hasn't dented.

My relationship with Maxwell Cole is anything but cordial, yet, whenever I encounter him in public, he always acts like an old pal has just snubbed him. Old pal hell! As far as I'm concerned, it always takes a monumental effort at self-control just to keep from decking him. I walked into the lobby of my condo, the Royal Crest, feeling some elation that once more I hadn't hit him and given him more fuel for the fire.

The walk had done me good. I was glad to open my apartment door. My place is tiny, a little over eight hundred square feet, with a view that overlooks the city. Lights from Seattle's skyline suffuse my living room with a golden glow, so much so that I often leave the lights off and just sit. Friends have told me it's great light for thinking or screwing. I've done a whole lot more of the former in that room than I have the latter.

Thinking was what I wanted to do right then. I undressed, pulled on a frayed flannel robe, and settled into my easy chair, a tall old-fashioned leather one that I managed to salvage from the debris when I moved out of the house in Sumner.

A sense of quiet settled over me as I gazed out the window. I thought about Angela Barstogi. Angel. Probably was one now. Yesterday morning she had been a living, breathing five-year-old. This morning she was dead. What had made the difference? What had turned her into a homicide statistic?

I thought about the people I had met during the day, turning them over in my mind one by one, trying to get a clear picture of who was involved. I thought about the men whose statements I had read, from Brodie to Jeremiah's stepfather, Benjamin, to Thomas, Amos, and Ezra. They all seemed like dregs to me, seedy characters you'd expect to find living in a halfway house somewhere. They got my hackles up, made me wary.

Thinking about the people involved, assessing them, trying to sort out the relationship—that's how I get on track with a case. And in my mind that's exactly what this was. The beginning of a case, just like any other. What I couldn't have known that morning as the sun began to color the cloud cover outside my living room window was how much Angel Barstogi's murder would change my life.

I thought that after I found her killer, everything would continue as it had before. That was not to be. After poor little Angela Barstogi, nothing would ever be the same.

CHAPTER 3

I dragged myself out of the house at seven-twenty and walked to work, propping my eyes open with a cup of muscle-bound coffee from the McDonald's at Third and Pine. The restaurant mirrors the flavor of the street, and Third Avenue in downtown Seattle is an absolute cross section of life in this country. I love it and hate it.

I feel the same way about the fifth floor of the Seattle Police Department. That's the homicide squad. I've worked homicide for almost fifteen years. I came to the fifth floor with all my illusions intact. I was convinced that murderers were the worst of the bad guys and that capturing killers was the highest calling a police officer could have. It took me a long time to lose that illusion, to figure out that murder isn't the worst crime one human can inflict on another. Maybe part of my disillusionment was just getting older and wiser. I don't know when I stopped viewing it as a sacred charge and started seeing it as a job. I wouldn't be surprised to find that it happened about the time Karen left me. Most of my life went sour about then.

But it also had something to do with the ambitious new cops showing up on the squad, the ones who see homicide as a ticket to bigger and better things, who are more concerned with how their exploits will read in the morning paper than they are about doing the job right. They are plugged full of university credits in law enforcement theory taught by professors who have never dirtied their hands with real blood. I don't like the finished product that shows up on the force or the ones that filter up to the fifth floor, either. I think the feeling is mutual.

All this goes to say that I don't care for too many of the guys there these days. Ray and I had been a breed apart from the others, and it was only after he left that I looked around the floor and found out what was there. Peters is young, but from my observation, he's probably the best of the lot. That is not to be taken as high praise, however, and even now we still hadn't settled into a solid working relationship. Peters arrived a few minutes after I did that morning and dropped a file folder on my desk. It was a preliminary report from the medical examiner's office.

He said nothing when he tossed it in front of me. He stalked away, hands stuffed in his pockets. I didn't have to look at the report to know what was coming. I didn't need a coroner's textbook terms to tell me that Angel Barstogi's last few minutes on this earth were brutal testimony to man's inhumanity to man. If anything, the technical phraseology only made it worse, more dehumanizing.

It said that cause of death was strangulation and that the murder weapon had indeed been the twisted nightgown around her neck. Analysis of stomach contents revealed that she had eaten a hamburger within an hour of time of death. It detailed other injuries—broken bones, bruises, cuts. The medical examiner had removed bits of human tissue and other substances from beneath her fingernails. Surprisingly, she had not been raped. At least she had been spared that indignity. It was a blessing, a very small blessing.

Peters came back and threw a newspaper down in front of me. I don't take a newspaper. It's a personal protest against people like Maxwell Cole. Consequently I hadn't seen the lurid headlines above Angel Barstogi's baby-toothed smile. One thing about newspapers, they never disappoint me. I always expect the worst. I consistently get it.

The preliminary report was still warm in my hand, yet I could have read the same information on the front page and not bothered to go to the office at all. My phone rang before I could say anything to Peters. It was Arlo Hamilton, the public information officer, wanting to know if I had anything for his nine A.M. press briefing.

"Are you shitting me?" I asked him. "Those assholes know everything we do. Maybe they should be giving us the briefing."

"Don't growl at me, Beau. I'm just trying to do my job."

"Me too," I responded, and slammed the receiver down in his ear. "Let's get the hell out of here," I said to Peters, grabbing up both the paper and the file. "This case has just become a media event."

I was pissed off as we headed for the elevator, pissed and looking for somebody to blame. Peters happened to be close at hand.

"What'd you do?" I asked sarcastically. "Pick up the report on the way home and drop it by the newspaper just for fun?"

Peters stopped in midstride and glared at me. "I thought maybe you did. Maxwell Cole isn't an old fraternity buddy of mine."

I looked at the paper again. The byline was indeed Maxwell Cole's. Somehow he had managed to worm his column onto the front page. He's always there, just when I least need him.

I backed off. "If you didn't leak it, and I didn't leak it, then somebody in the medical examiner's office has a big mouth."

Peters looked somewhat mollified, but not totally so.

The Public Safety Building has what are reputed to be the slowest elevators in Seattle, possibly in the Western Hemisphere. We were still in the lobby when Sergeant Watkins nailed us. "Where are you two running off to?" he asked.

He was carrying a folded newspaper under his arm. "You've already read that?" I asked.

"I've read it, Powell's read it, the chief's reading it even as we speak. You'd better come back and brief the captain before you take off. The press is going to be all over this place today."

Captain Powell's office is as private as a glass fishbowl can be. We gave Sergeant Watkins and Powell a verbal rundown of what we knew, including what Jeremiah had told me about Faith Tabernacle and the good Pastor Michael Brodie. Powell took our copy of the preliminary report and read it through. "What was this Brodie character wearing yesterday when you saw him?" Powell asked.

"Blue suit, white shirt, no tie."

"Long sleeves?"

I nodded. The captain continued. "According to this, there were fragments of flesh under her fingernails. If he's our man, there should be scratches showing." You don't get to be captain because you're dumb. Powell rubbed his chin thoughtfully. "Then there's the hamburger, too. Where do you get a hamburger that early in the morning?"

We theorized awhile longer before we finally made our getaway from the fifth floor and picked up a car from the motor pool. The motor pool is

run on a strictly first-come, first-served basis. We were a long way from
first served. The television shows that have the detectives driving the same
high-powered vehicle week after week crack me up. They don't live in the
real world of city budgets. It must be nice. I've grown immune to cars. All
that's important to me is whether or not they run and have enough leg
room. This one ran all right, but the leg room was sorely lacking. That
happens a lot when you're six-three.

Peters drove, but not far. We stopped for breakfast. I washed down
bacon and eggs with coffee while Peters told me about the dangers of
cholesterol and the nitrate preservatives in bacon. I enjoyed the food, not
the accompanying lecture. I missed Ray. He and I shared much the same
vices as far as food was concerned.

Over breakfast we decided to tackle the leak in the medical examiner's
office. A blabbermouth there or in the state crime laboratory could blow
up a case before it ever hit prosecution. We drove up to Harborview Hospital on Capitol Hill and parked behind a car with a bumper sticker that
said, "Have you hugged your medical examiner today?"

Dr. Ralph Baker is in charge. He is a full-fledged physician and also an
elected official. His jurisdiction covers all of King County and includes the
city of Seattle. He glanced balefully up from some papers and looked at his
watch as we were ushered into his cluttered office. "You're late," he
growled. "I expected you half an hour ago."

"We stopped for breakfast."

He grunted. He reached over and picked up a manila folder. Inside was
a folded clipping of the Angel Barstogi article. It had a series of red mark-
ings on it. He sighed. "Some of this is almost verbatim," he said wearily.

"Any ideas?" I asked.

He shrugged. "Two people were on duty last night. Lillian Roberts and
Dan Royden."

"So which one runs off at the mouth?" I asked.

Baker looked at Peters, then nodded in my direction. "That's one of the
things I like about Detective Beaumont. He has such a way with words."
He paused briefly. "You ever hear of the Equal Employment Opportunity
Commission?" he asked.

I nodded. Baker picked up a stray paper clip from his desk and lobbed
it across the room, where it fell expertly into a chipped clear-glass vase that
sat on a bookshelf near the window. From the number of paper clips in it
and the few scattered in close proximity, I guessed catching paper clips was
the vase's sole reason for existence.

The chief medical examiner is a florid Scandinavian with a shock of
white hair. His face flushed a little more violently than usual. "You ever
have an EEOC grievance filed against you?"

I shook my head. He tossed another paper clip into the vase. "I have," he said. "In this state that's tantamount to political suicide. I don't see this job as the end of the line, you know."

As a matter of fact, the thought had never occurred to me. I thought once a medical examiner, always a medical examiner, but that shows how much I know. On the other hand, I suppose it's a short jump from performing autopsies to political office. At least you'd have some preparation for handling the stench of corruption.

I said, "In other words, Lillian Roberts is Deep Throat."

"Maybe she talks in her sleep," he replied. "I'm not making any official accusations, mind you."

Peters had been pretty much left out of the conversation, but now he put two and two together. "You mean Lillian Roberts and Maxwell Cole?"

Another paper clip clinked into the vase. Baker said nothing.

Peters was outraged. "I'd fire her ass."

Baker studied Peters for a moment the way a small child might examine an ant before deliberately crushing it into the sidewalk. "You probably would," he said, "but then, you don't want to be King County Executive, either. Of course," he added, "I'll deny everything if any of this hits the street."

There was no point in sticking around. I had to give Baker credit for letting us know the lay of the land. He could have left us fumbling around in the dark. Besides, I wanted to get Peters out of there before he said something we would both regret. I was afraid his combination of temper and mouth would end up getting us both in trouble. I helped myself to one of Baker's paper clips and made a pretty respectable shot, considering I'd never tried it before. "See you at the polls," I said over my shoulder.

I hurried Peters out the door. He was still blustering in the outer office, but I shushed him until we were outside and climbing into the car.

"Do we let him get away with that?" Peters exploded when I finally let him talk.

"We don't have a whole hell of a lot of choice."

"It's . . ." Peters stopped, totally at a loss for words.

"It's the way it is," I finished for him, "and nothing you or I do is going to change it. We just have to work around it, that's all."

The drive from Capitol Hill to Magnolia was hair-raising. It's common knowledge that police forces are stocked with frustrated juvenile delinquents who have grown up and gone straight, driving like hot rodders and justifying it in their minds because they are finally on the right side of the law. We didn't talk as we drove. I was too busy considering whether or not my Last Will and Testament was up-to-date.

We wheeled onto Gay Avenue. "Oh-oh," I said when I saw Maxwell Cole's rust-colored Volvo parked in front of Suzanne Barstogi's house. Max,

Suzanne, and Michael Brodie were huddled on the front porch, deep in conversation. They broke it off as soon as soon as we pulled up behind the Volvo. Peters didn't recognize the car, but he swore under his breath when he recognized Maxwell's walruslike visage.

Max hurried down the steps toward us as though some trace of the conversation might linger in the ethers of the front porch. He checked his speed and sauntered up to the gate.

"Fancy meeting you here," I said before he had a chance. "What did they do, yank your column back onto the police beat?"

He reddened slightly. "I'm working on the column right now, as a matter of fact."

Suzanne Barstogi came down from the porch and stood near the dangling gate. I ignored her and spoke directly to Maxwell for Suzanne's benefit. "I hope you warned these nice folks that you don't always quote people verbatim." The good pastor came down to stand protectively, or maybe defensively, behind Suzanne.

"Knock it off," Maxwell muttered.

"They know you're the one who plastered Angela all over the front page this morning? I'll bet they think you're a really nice man. You tell 'em what kind of movies you like to watch?"

"I said knock it off!"

"You know," I said, focusing on the bulbous nose supporting his sagging glasses, "I'd like nothing better than to knock it off." Maxwell got my subtle message.

He grabbed open the gate with such force that he wrested it from its last frail hinge. For a long moment he stood there holding the gate in his hand. I think he considered throwing it at me. Instead, he slammed it down and pushed his way past me to clamber into the Volvo. He drove off, leaving a trail of rubber on the asphalt.

"I'll give you that one," Peters grinned.

We turned our attention to Pastor Michael and Suzanne. I've already mentioned that I put in some time as a Fuller Brush salesman. In fact, that's how I worked my way through the University of Washington. I learned a lot about life from a sales manager there. He had a list of trite sayings he would spew with little or no provocation. One that I particularly remember is, "Men change but seldom do they." Those words flashed through my mind as Pastor Michael cordially extended his hand. "I suppose you have some more questions."

My partner shot me a wondering glance. "We certainly do," Peters said.

Brodie gave Suzanne a gentle tap on the shoulder. "Why don't you run along inside with the others." His smile was benevolent. "They can talk to you later if they need to."

Suzanne backed away from him as though she, too, was wary of his change in demeanor. Unconcerned, Brodie picked up the fallen gate and appeared to study the possibility of reattaching it to the fence. There was a long scrape across the back of his hand. Peters saw it the same time I did.

"Will you be conducting the funeral?" I asked, looking for an opening.

"The services," he corrected gently. "In Faith Tabernacle we don't have funerals. Even though the circumstances in this case appear tragic, it is always an occasion for thanksgiving when one of the True Believers is called home to be with our Maker."

"I see," I said unnecessarily. I was trying to reconcile this seemingly soft-spoken, considerate man with the explosively tempered one I had seen the day before. It was inconceivable that the two could be one and the same. Yesterday he had been out of control. Today he was the picture of unctuous self-confidence.

"The Thanksgiving Service will be Sunday at two up on top of Queen Anne. You're welcome to come, if you'd like," he added.

Inconsequential small talk quickly exhausted Peters' patience. "How long have you known Suzanne Barstogi?" he interjected.

There was a slight but definite pause. "Eight or nine years, I suppose," Brodie replied.

"You've known her since before Angel was born?"

Brodie nodded, and Peters continued. "What became of her husband?"

Brodie shook his head sadly. "Andrew slipped away from our flock of True Believers."

"That's why Suzanne divorced him?" I asked.

"Yes." Again there was an almost imperceptible pause. "There can be no marriage with someone outside the Faith."

"Do you have any idea where he is?"

"No, I don't. When someone leaves us, we believe they have died and gone to perdition. No contact with any one of the True Believers is allowed."

"Will anyone try to let him know about Angel? After all, he is her father. He would probably want to be here," Peters suggested.

Brodie looked at Peters as though the detective was a little dense and hadn't quite grasped the finer points of the conversation. "It would be very difficult for someone who is already dead to attend someone else's Thanksgiving Service."

"I see what you mean," I said. Peters' temper was on an upswing again. Maybe control comes with age. I fervently wished Peters could age ten years in about as many minutes.

"How'd you get the scratch on the back of your hand?" Peters asked.

Brodie looked at it. "We've been doing a lot of yard work around the church," he said. "It happened the other day when we were pruning."

A car pulled up just then. A man and three women got out. They walked past us, nodding to Brodie as they picked their way into the house. "We're having a prayer session right now," Brodie explained, backing away from Peters and me. "We're praying for the murderer's immortal soul. It's our way of turning the other cheek."

"Is the whole congregation coming?" Peters asked.

"The ones who aren't working."

"Speaking of working," I said, "what about Benjamin Mason. Does he work?"

Brodie's face went slightly brittle. "He does yard work."

"You know where he is now?"

The pastor shook his head and I handed him a card. "You have him call me when you see him." Brodie took the card without looking at it, then excused himself to go deal with his flock. The purpose of the prayer meeting stuck in my craw. I would have preferred the prayers be for Angel Barstogi or even Suzanne. I didn't think the scumbag who murdered Angela deserved any prayers. I didn't then, and I don't now.

CHAPTER 4

We were standing with the doors open, ready to climb into the car when a voice hailed us. "Yoo-hoo," a woman called. "Over here."

Gay Avenue looks as though it started out to be an alley for another set of streets. Everyone, except the builder of 4543, seemed to understand that. Suzanne Barstogi's house was the only one that fronted on Gay Avenue. All the rest showed reasonably well-kept back doors and backyards. It was one of those backyards, across the street and down one house, to which we were summoned.

A five-foot cedar fence provided an incongruous foundation for a massive wild blackberry bramble. The bush and the fence were like two drunks holding one another up, the resulting wall totally impenetrable. "Over here." It was a quavery, old woman's voice. At the far corner of the fence, the bramble had been cut back enough to allow a wooden gate to open ever so slightly "You are the cops, aren't you?" she asked.

"Yes ma'am," Peters answered. The gate opened a little further, wide enough for us to ease into the opening, but not without picking up a couple of thorny jabs in the process.

Inside, we found ourselves in a weedy yard, facing a diminutive old lady with bright red hair and a spry way about her. She wore old-fashioned glasses with white harlequin frames and narrow lenses. She gave the heavy wooden gate a surprisingly swift shove and padlocked it in one easy motion. "Go on, go on," she said impatiently, motioning us up an overgrown path toward her back door. Peters gave me a slight shrug, then led the way.

"You certainly took long enough over there," she muttered accusingly as we climbed a flight of steps. "I didn't enjoy a single one of my TV programs today because I was watching for you. I was afraid I'd miss you when you left."

We entered through the kitchen. A large gray cat, standing in the sink lapping water from a leaky tap, eyed us speculatively. Our hostess made no effort to chase him out of the sink. "That's Henry, Henry Aldrich. He doesn't talk much but he's good company."

She directed us into a living room. On a blaring black-and-white television set an announcer was gearing up for another episode of "General Hospital." So she had been willing to risk missing her soaps in order to catch us. I gave her credit for making a considerable personal sacrifice.

She settled into an ancient rocking chair, while we attempted to sit on an overstuffed and lumpy couch that had been built with no regard for human anatomy. "Since you're not wearing uniforms, I suppose you young men must be detectives. I'm Sophia Czirski," she announced, "but you can call me Sophie. What can I do for you?"

Peters looked at me helplessly. It was time for him to earn his keep. I shrugged and said nothing. Peters cleared his throat. "I don't know, Mrs. Czirski . . . Sophie. . . . You invited us."

"Oh, that's right. How stupid of me." She wore ill-fitting dentures that rattled and clicked when she spoke. I was afraid they might fall out altogether. Bright red hair gave the illusion that she was much younger than she was in actual fact. Upon close inspection I would have guessed she was pushing the upper end of her seventies. She was tough as old leather, though, and any lapses in thought were only temporary.

"Did you arrest her?"

"Arrest who?" Peters asked.

"Well, Suzanne Barstogi, of course. Her and that phony preacher friend of hers."

"No ma'am," Peters said carefully. "We haven't arrested anyone. This is Detective Beaumont, and I'm Detective Peters."

"Well," she sniffed, "I'm glad you have enough good manners to introduce yourself. What about your friend—Beauchamp, did you say? Can't he talk?"

Peters looked at me and grinned. "Beaumont," he corrected. "No, he's really shy around women. I usually have to do most of the talking."

"You go ahead and ask me anything you like then, Detective Peters. Your friend there can take notes." Obligingly I got out a notebook and a stub of a pencil. Somehow I knew I'd get even; I just didn't know when.

Sophie Czirski didn't require any prompting. "I saw that child outside in February. February, mind you! Without so much as a jacket or a pair of shoes! I could see her, you know." She indicated the living room window, which, from her chair before the television set, offered an unobstructed view of Barstogi's front yard. "I can see everything that goes on there, people coming and going all hours of the day and night. All that stuff about prayer meetings and fellowship. I don't believe it, not for one minute."

"Excuse me for interrupting," said Peters, "but you asked if we had arrested Suzanne Barstogi. Is there some reason you feel she should be under suspicion?"

"Goodness, yes. People who would mistreat a child like they have wouldn't hesitate to kill her. And all the time they pretend to be so holier-than-thou. But they don't fool me, not for a minute."

The gray cat meandered in from the kitchen. He favored us with an insolent look, then leaped to the back of the couch. Once there he stretched out, languidly settling himself directly between Peters and me. I wondered how much gray cat hair would be on my brown jacket and trousers when I stood up. Sophie focused on the cat for a moment, then jumped to her feet.

"Good gracious, talk about manners, now I'm forgetting mine. I haven't even offered you coffee or tea."

I thought about the cat in the sink. "No thanks," I said. "I'm fine."

"I'll have some tea," Peters said agreeably, "but I like the water boiling."

"Absolutely," Sophie said, hurrying into the kitchen. "Tea doesn't steep properly if the water's only lukewarm."

I didn't trust myself to say anything to Peters in her absence. What I did do was check the notes I had taken from the previous day's statements. There was no mention of Sophie Czirski.

She returned a few minutes later with a tray and three chipped but dainty cups and saucers. If she had heard my polite refusal, she ignored it. She passed me a cup and saucer without asking. Peters winked at me behind her back as she placed it in my hand. There was a cat hair floating on the surface of my tea. I discreetly removed it with my spoon once her back was turned.

She settled comfortably into the rocking chair with her own cup. "Now then, what was I saying? Oh yes, I called Child Protective Services right then, that very day. I'm sure they thought I was just a nosy old biddy, although they said they'd look into it. I don't think they ever did, at least not then.

"About a week later I was just finishing watching "Good Morning America" when she came wandering down the street. Henry was outside. She went up to try to pet him, but he doesn't like children. When he wouldn't let her touch him I could see it almost broke her heart. She didn't cry, though. I never did see her cry. She looked so lonesome that I just couldn't help myself. I went to the door, my back door, the one you came in by, and asked her if she'd like to have some cookies and milk.

"She did. She marched right in as if she owned the place." Sophie stopped, put down her cup, and wiped her eyes with a lacy handkerchief. "She talked a blue streak. She called me Soapy." Sophie sniffed noisily and wiped her eyes again. "She loved to talk. She talked about that church her mother goes to, meetings every night until the wee hours. She came to see me every morning for almost two weeks, but she was always careful to be back home before her mother woke up. Can you imagine a mother sleeping until eleven or twelve every single day and leaving that poor little tyke on her own?"

"Did she ever say anything about her father?"

Sophie wrinkled her forehead in thought. "No, she never did. She talked about her mother, and an Uncle Charlie, and that minister fellow. I don't know this Uncle Charlie."

"She talked about Brodie?" Peters asked.

Sophie nodded. "Yes, a lot. She was afraid of him."

"I can't say that I blame her," Peters said.

"One day he drove up while Angela was still here. I never called her Angel. I think that's a terrible name to pin on a little girl. Anyway, she tried to run home, but he caught her coming through the gate. He grabbed her and dragged her home by one arm. The next day she had a cast on it."

"You mean he broke her arm?"

"That's not what they told Child Protective Services. Some young investigator, a snot-nosed kid still wet behind the ears, came out then to look into it. I talked to him, told him what I had seen, but it didn't make any difference. He insisted Angela said she had fallen down. He didn't care that I had seen a handprint on her face or bruises on her arms."

I had been taking notes the whole time. "You said she talked about Uncle Charlie. Who's he?"

Sophie glowered. "How should I know? He's probably from that group. She never came back again after that, wouldn't even wave to me from the yard! I know they killed her though; I'm just as sure of it as I can be. And you can write that down, young man!" Sophie Czirski put down her teacup and wept into her handkerchief.

We sat and waited for her to finish crying. "If only Child Protective Services had listened to me, she wouldn't be dead right now. I have half a mind to call the governor's office and complain."

That seemed like a splendid idea to me. "We had officers in the neighborhood last night, asking questions. I didn't see your name on any of the reports."

"Oh no," she said. "Thursday I have my doctor's appointment; then I go to Bainbridge on the ferry and stay overnight with my son and his family. That's the one night a week I babysit my grandchildren."

We asked more questions, but she could add no more details, at least not then. The doctor's appointment had prevented her from seeing any unusual vehicles the day of the murder. I couldn't help but marvel that so far Maxwell Cole had overlooked Sophie. I hoped that would continue to be the case, but I didn't want to trust to luck.

"Did you happen to notice the Volvo that was at Barstogi's house when we drove up?" I asked as we were getting ready to leave.

"A what? Oh, the brown car. I haven't seen it before."

"It belongs to a reporter. His name is Maxwell Cole."

"Is he the one who wrote the article this morning?"

She was a sharp old dame. Nothing much got past her.

"Yes," I answered. "He was over there talking with Suzanne Barstogi and Brodie when we drove up. If he comes nosing around asking questions, I'd appreciate it if you wouldn't say anything to him. I'd especially like it if he didn't learn any of what you've told us."

For the first time she looked at me as though I might possibly be a member of the human race. "You mean you think this might be important?"

"I'm sure it's important, and I don't want the papers to get ahold of it until after we have a chance to check it out." Unexpectedly, Sophie Czirski started crying again. They seemed to be tears of gratitude that at last someone was taking her seriously, paying attention. I was grateful we had gotten to her first.

"I wouldn't give him the time of day," she said determinedly when the third bout of tears finally abated. She pulled herself together long enough to let us out. We heard her padlock the gate behind us.

It was getting on toward afternoon. The storm that had been hinted on the breeze the night before finally drifted in off the Pacific, kicking up the wind and bringing with it a drenching downpour. Seattle is used to the kind of gentle drizzle that lets people walk in the rain for blocks without an umbrella and without getting wet. This was not that kind of storm. The wind would have gutted any umbrella we had tried to use. We were glad to retreat to the car.

We had barely gotten inside when Peters picked up the preliminary report that had been carelessly dropped in the backseat. He studied it for a few minutes, then handed it to me, pointing at a paragraph close to the bottom. It was something we had missed the first time, and Maxwell Cole evidently hadn't given it any notice either. In her death struggle, Angela's Barstogi's left arm had been broken. Actually a recent fracture had been rebroken. In addition, X rays revealed an old break in her right arm and one on her left leg.

"Must have been a really accident-prone kid," I said sarcastically.

"Right," Peters replied. He was looking at Suzanne Barstogi's house. Like me, he was probably thinking about the living room full of kneeling supplicants. "I'll just bet that asshole's our man."

"Could be," I said. "Sounds more plausible all the time."

"And Suzanne Barstogi's an accessory!" Peters ran his hand over his forehead and hair in a gesture of hopelessness. For a time he was quiet, waging an internal war.

"You ever hear of Broken Springs, Oregon?" he asked at last. It was an off-the-wall question. I thought for a minute, then shook my head without making any connection. He continued. "It's a little place in central Oregon south of The Dalles that's been taken over by a cult. The peons eat long-grain rice and go without, while the swami or whatever the hell he is rides around in one of his thirty or so Cadillacs. My ex-wife and kids are there."

He stopped. For a space there was no sound in the car but the rain slapping the windshield and the roof. I had worked with Peters for the better part of two months without a hint that something like that was in his background. Now he had dropped the whole load at once.

"I'm sorry," I said.

"Me too," he responded bleakly. "I can't understand how it happens, how people put themselves totally under someone else's control. That's the way it is with Suzanne Barstogi. She probably stood right there and watched, maybe even helped." It was a chilling, sobering possibility.

Once more the sound of the rain filled the car. Peters sat hunched over the steering wheel saying nothing, gripping it with such force that his knuckles turned white. The hurt and pain were so thick in the front seat you could almost touch them. "I'll ask Powell to pull you off the case. I think your objectivity is shot to shit."

That jarred him out of his introspection. He sat up and glared at me. "If you so much as try to get me pulled, I'll kick your ass till Sunday, J. P. Beaumont."

"That's fair enough." I could handle him pissed a whole lot better than I could handle him grieving. "Now let's get the hell out of here. I want to go take a look at Faith Tabernacle."

Peters straightened his shoulders and started the car. I wouldn't be surprised if that's not about the time we started being real partners. At least we had taken the gloves off. It was about time.

CHAPTER 5

It was still raining Saturday morning, so I grabbed a bus to the Public Safety Building. The lady Metro driver winked at me. I don't think getting hit on by a lady bus driver is exactly dignified. Besides, I spent too many years with a ring around my finger to know how to handle a pass when I meet one. I consider myself a relatively cool customer. That's why I got off the bus by the back door.

There was a whole stack of messages on my desk. I returned what calls I could. One was from a Tom Stahl. When I tried his number, I discovered it was the telephone company business office. It was closed until Monday. I've had calls from Ma Bell before. It usually means I've neglected to pay my phone bill. I looked in my checkbook. Sure enough, no check showed in April for the March bill. It was nice of Mr. Stahl to remind me! Karen used to handle that. I wadded up the message and pitched it, making a mental note to pay all my bills.

I went over the Sophie material. Who was Uncle Charlie? I pored over the list of Faith Tabernacle members. No Charles or Charlie there, only those quaint biblical names that sounded like they'd just stepped out of the Old Testament. I fed the names into the computer, looking for driver's licenses, vehicle registrations, unpaid traffic fines. There was nothing on any of the names in the state of Washington, except for Brodie. He was the registered owner of a total of five vehicles. Not finding any information is enough to arouse any good detective's suspicions. Who the hell were these people? I fired off another inquiry, this one to Illinois.

Afterward I waited, drumming my fingers on the desk, wondering about Uncle Charlie. No one in Faith Tabernacle had mentioned him. Whoever he was, in or out of the group, he had been important to Angela Barstogi. She had mentioned him to Sophie Czirski when she hadn't mentioned her own father.

I looked up to find Captain Powell perched on the corner of my desk. "How's it going?" he asked.

I guess Powell's all right. He's probably thirty-seven or thirty-eight. He's what I call a young Turk, one of those guys who's on a fast track and plans to make it all the way to the top in a hurry. The best way to handle people like that is to stay out of their way. Their ambition has a way of clobbering anyone who isn't pushing and shoving in the same direction.

"We're plugging," I replied noncommittally.

"What are you finding?"

"We spent a good part of yesterday afternoon around Faith Tabernacle over in Ballard. We didn't get inside. No one was there. The doors were locked, but we spent lots of time with the neighbors."

"And?"

"Pastor Michael Brodie is not well thought of in that neck of the woods. People say odd things go on in Faith Tabernacle, that they sometimes hear children crying."

"Have there been complaints?"

"Peters is checking that out right now. No one has ever been able to get close enough to the kids to talk to them."

Powell rubbed his chin. I'm always about half-suspicious of chin rubbers. It's the same way with deliberate tappers and cleaners of expensive, hand-carved pipes. The gestures are calculated distractions, serving to divert attention from the current topic of discussion.

"Speaking of Peters, how's he working out?"

"He's okay."

"You knew there was some difficulty downstairs. We had to shift him out of property. It was either send him to homicide or bounce him back to walking a beat."

"No, I didn't know that." I might have added that I was outside the departmental gossip mills, but I let it go.

"Captain Howard down there specifically asked for you to be his partner."

"Oh," I said.

"And you think he can handle this case without a problem?"

"Absolutely," I replied. I wasn't about to let on that Peters had told me anything about Broken Springs, Oregon, and losing his family to a cult. I didn't want to risk giving Powell any ammunition about Peters' impartiality. Powell is the kind who might use it. He ambled away from my desk then, no wiser, I hoped, than when he had arrived. I was a little wiser, though. Peters was on our squad without Powell's wanting him there. If the captain was looking for an excuse to bump the newcomer, he wouldn't get any help from me.

Peters showed up a few minutes later. He had checked through 911 records for any complaints from the Ballard area around Faith Tabernacle and come up empty-handed. He looked a little worse for wear, as though he hadn't slept more than a couple of hours.

"You tie one on last night?" I asked.

"No."

"Maybe you should have," I told him.

He didn't take kindly to my remark. "What's the program today?" he asked.

"Let's go downstairs and talk to the crime lab folks. They might have something for us."

The Washington State crime lab is on the second floor of the Public Safety Building. They work for all the law enforcement agencies in Washington, with a number of labs scattered throughout the state. There's a backlog of work, but murder gets priority treatment. Angela Barstogi deserved at least that much. Janice Morraine offered us some acrid coffee that Peters had the good sense to refuse. I didn't. I'm a dog for punishment.

Janice lit a cigarette, and Peters grimaced. I was surprised he didn't launch into an antismoking lecture on the spot. Jan took a long drag on her cigarette, ignoring Peters' pointed disapproval. "What can I do for you?" she asked.

"Have you come up with anything on Angela Barstogi?"

"She had a Big Mac for breakfast, if that's any help."

"As in McDonald's?" Peters asked.

Janice nodded. "She had mustard with whatever she ate. There were traces of mustard under her thumbnails like you'd get from opening one of those little individual packages. You can collect samples, but it'll probably only separate Burger King from McDonald's."

She flicked an ash into an ashtray. Her tone was matter-of-fact. Evidence is evidence. People in this business can't afford to look beyond the evidence to the human suffering involved. If they do, they crack up.

"Did you find anything in her room or in the house?"

"Nothing that appears to be important at the moment. Fingerprints from the room are mostly the girl's and the mother's. There are a few that belong to other children, but no adult prints."

"What makes you say McDonald's?" Peters asked.

"It may not be McDonald's, but it was one of those fast-food joints. Hamburger aside, Baker's office says she was generally malnourished, had been for some time."

Janice reached across me to the end of the table and picked up a folded newspaper. She opened it to the editorial section. "I read this coming in on the bus this morning." She handed me the paper, open to Maxwell Cole's "City Beat" column.

I skimmed through an emotional portrayal of Suzanne Barstogi as a woman of unshakable faith and courage, one who was walking through a time of personal trial supported by her beliefs and the willing help of fellow church members. It spoke eloquently of the group's communal sharing of food and heartbreak. It told in heartrending prose how the congregation as a whole had spent the previous afternoon on its knees praying for the murderer's immortal soul.

Murderers are always the first victims in Maxwell Cole's book, unless the person pulling the trigger happens to be a cop.

I finished reading the column and handed the paper to Peters. "They sound like wonderful people, don't they?" Janice said with just a hint of sarcasm tinging her voice. "Just the kind of people you'd expect to systematically abuse a child for years. The broken bones she had would be consistent with a highly abusive environment. Kids that age don't break bones. They have too much cartilage. Are there other kids stuck in that mess?"

I thought about Jeremiah and how afraid he had been. His fear was not unfounded. I was convinced the bruise on his forearm was not an unusual occurrence. Janice finished her cigarette and rose, dismissing us. "I don't have anything else right now, but I'll call if anything turns up."

"So what now, coach?" Peters asked as we waited in the elevator lobby.

"I vote we go back to Ballard. This time we'll get inside Faith Tabernacle if we have to have a search warrant to do it."

Ballard is a predominantly Scandinavian enclave about five miles from downtown Seattle. It sits across Salmon Bay from Magnolia. You get there by crossing the Ballard Bridge, a drawbridge used to let through sleek sailing vessels as well as stodgy, loaded barges on their way to Alaska. If Magnolia is highbrow, Ballard is lowbrow. If Magnolia is known for its upwardly mobile professionals, Ballard is known for its sturdy blue-collar folks who march along, never quite getting ahead but never falling very far behind either. Ballard is pretty much middle America at its best or worst, depending on your point of view.

Faith Tabernacle was a respectable-enough-looking place situated on the corner of Twenty-fourth and Eightieth N. W. in the Loyal Heights area. It was an older church that gave evidence of some recent renovations, the most jarring of which was a neon sign. New gray shingles sparkled, and surrounding trees had been pruned back with a vengeance. Double doors, new but cheap, stood wide open.

The day before, neighbors had told us that it had originally been a Lutheran church. A steady decline in enrollment and a consolidation of congregations had left it vacant for a number of years until purchase by Michael Brodie's group some six or seven months earlier. Two similarly shaped, parallel buildings had been connected at either end. Half the building was used as a church and half as a parsonage.

The interior of the sanctuary reminded me of a barren medieval church. I'm not a regular visitor of churches, but the ones I have encountered usually have some of the amenities like heat, carpeting, reasonably comfortable pews, that sort of thing. Walking into Faith Tabernacle, the first sensation was one of bone-numbing chill. There was no heat, and the barren concrete floor retained the damp cold from the previous late-spring night. Two banks of rickety benches formed the seating arrangements, with a center aisle between them leading to a raised altar. The benches had no backs on them. If Angel Barstogi had fallen asleep during church, where had Suzanne put her, on a bench or on the cold, bare floor?

At first we thought we were alone, but then a woman emerged from behind a makeshift pulpit. Armed with a scrub brush and a bucket of soapy water, she crawled across the cold surface on hands and knees, diligently scrubbing every inch of the altar, like a buck private preparing for a major inspection.

Peters approached the woman and asked her where we might find Brodie. She motioned with her hand, indicating that she was unable to talk but that we should go through the door on the right of the altar. It led us through a darkened, closetlike room. In the dim light from the doorway behind us we could see a wooden kneeling frame with an open Bible on a stand before it. Other than those two items, the room was empty.

Another door barred the way. I knocked. Beneath my knuckles I found the deep sound of a solid wooden door, not the hollow laminate of the church's front doors. Pastor Michael himself answered my knock. If he was startled to see us, he certainly covered it well. "Come in," he said, stepping back and holding the door. "I was just preparing for this afternoon's service," he said.

I doubt Peters was surprised by what we found there. I wasn't. The room could hardly have been called sumptuous, but it was a long way from the grim, unadorned rooms through which we had entered. The contrast was striking. The place was immaculate. There was none of the dirty clutter of Suzanne Barstogi's house. A well-padded deep brown carpet covered the floor. The two walls that weren't covered with bookshelves were papered in a tasteful grass cloth. A stately mahogany desk with a brass study lamp dominated the room. An open Bible lay in a halo of light the lamp cast on gleaming wood. Pastor Michael snapped the Bible shut as I approached the desk.

"Won't you sit down?" he offered.

We sat. I looked at Peters, grim faced and tense. I wondered how this office compared with the Cadillac-driving swami of Broken Springs, Oregon. Peters was holding himself in check, but just barely. "We wanted to see your church," I said before Peters had a chance to open his mouth. "We thought seeing it might give us some ideas about Angel's death."

Brodie's defenses came up instantly. "Surely you don't think someone in the church had anything to do with it."

"We haven't ruled out anyone so far," Peters commented stiffly, glancing at Brodie's hand. Brodie covered the scratched hand with the other one in a pious and, I thought, highly suspicious, manner. Peters noticed it too.

"How long have you been here?" I asked.

There was the pause—slight, but enough to be noticeable. "Oh, a little over six months, I guess. Before that we met in private homes."

"I see," I said.

"Would you like to see the rest of it?" he asked, rising suddenly. "We have a fellowship hall and a kitchen in addition to my little apartment."

"What's the room we just came through," Peters put in, "the one with the Bible stand in it?"

There was another pause, as if Brodie wanted to consider his words carefully before answering. "That's our Penitent's Room. It's where people can spend time in prayer when they have strayed."

He hustled us out of the study through his apartment, as if anxious to leave the area and the subject matter behind. The apartment was something less than luxurious, but obviously Brodie didn't believe in living in the same kind of squalor deemed appropriate for his flock.

We followed him through the rest of the building. What little of the upstairs that wasn't devoted to parsonage contained several small Sunday School rooms. Downstairs we found a commercial-style kitchen off the fellowship hall. The equipment was polished to a high gloss. The Faith Tabernacle women evidently spent far more time maintaining church facilities than they did their own homes. The fellowship hall was outfitted in the same barren style as the sanctuary. Its only furnishings consisted of two sets of splintery redwood picnic tables pushed together to form two long banks of tables.

When the tour was over, Brodie ushered us back to the Penitent's Room in the best bum's-rush tradition. "I need to go outside to greet people now," he said. "Once the service starts, you will have to leave." He gave a rueful smile lest we think him rude or inhospitable. "It's like a Mormon temple. No one who isn't a True Believer is allowed inside during services."

The lady with the scrub brush was kneeling in front of the little altar in the Penitent's Room, her bucket of soapy water still beside her. She was totally immersed in prayer. We stopped nearby but she never looked up. We went back through the sanctuary under our own steam.

Outside, a little flock of True Believers waited patiently for their shepherd to welcome them to worship. The women, their hair covered with either scarves or hats of some kind, dropped their eyes demurely as we passed. The men nodded without speaking, while the children maintained the same eerie silence we had noticed the day Angel Barstogi died. It was not a joyful gathering.

Jeremiah stood next to a beefy man with a full red beard. He had to be Benjamin Mason. He was a big man who looked like he had spent some time on the working end of a shovel. I walked up to Jeremiah and nodded at him without speaking. There was no sense in getting him in more hot water.

"Are you Mr. Mason?" I asked.

"Yes," he answered, his tone wary, uneasy.

"I'm Detective Beaumont. Did you get a message to call me?"

"Didn't have a phone," he mumbled.

"Mind if we talk to you for a minute?" Reluctantly, he followed us to our car. I thumbed through some notes I'd made from the transcripts. "Brodie says you were working Friday morning?"

He nodded. "That's right."

"And you do yard work. Can you give us a list of places you worked Friday morning?"

"Wait just a minute." Suddenly he came to life. "You've got no right—"

Peters' hand shot out, catching Mason's arm just above the elbow. "You wait a minute, pal. He asked you a civil question. You can answer it here, or we can take you downtown."

"Viewmont," he said. "I was working some houses up at the north end of Viewmont over on Magnolia."

"Anybody see you?"

"Dunno. Usually nobody's home." He mumbled the addresses and I wrote them down.

"Got any I.D. on you?"

His hand shook as he fumbled his wallet out of his hip pocket. When he dragged the battered piece of plastic out of its holder, the license turned out to be an Illinois one, several years out of date. The name on it was C. D. Jason. I felt a jab of excitement.

"What's the C stand for?" I asked.

"Clinton," he answered shortly.

Not Charles, not Chuck, not Charlie, but Clinton. The picture matched, but the names were different. Peters took it from me and examined it. He put it in his pocket. "We'll just take this with us," he said easily.

"But I need it to drive," Mason protested, reaching for it.

"You'd best get yourself a Washington license. Meantime, what did you do to the backs of your hands?"

Mason withdrew his hands and stuffed them in his pockets. Not before I noticed that the backs matched Brodie's, scratch for scratch.

"Let me guess," Peters said. "I'll bet you got those scratches trimming hedges."

"That's right," Mason said. "How'd you know that?"

"Psychic," Peters replied.

Mason or whoever he was scurried into the church like a scared rabbit. Peters said nothing until Mason was out of earshot. He turned to look at the church. "I'd love to get a stick of dynamite and blow this whole pile of shit to kingdom come."

"You'd best not let Powell hear you talk like that. Powell might be looking for an excuse to bust you back to the gang."

Peters gave me a searching look. "You know something I don't know?"

"I don't know anything. I have a suspicious nature."

We spent a couple of hours touring arterials, collecting sample packets of mustard from every fast-food joint we could find that seemed to be within a reasonably close geographical area. It would be strictly blind luck if we happened to get a match, but that sort of thing does happen occasionally. I believe the psychologists call it intermittent reinforcement. It's what keeps bloodhounds like me on the trail. Every once in a while we hit the jackpot. It happens often enough that it keeps us from giving up. We just keep at it.

We carried a picture of Angela Barstogi with us, the one that had been in the newspaper. We asked all the clerks, all the busboys, if anyone remembered a little girl in a pink Holly Hobbie gown. Nobody did.

With the mustard sacked and labeled, we drove over to the Westside Treatment Center. The receptionist was off for the weekend, but we managed to get a list of employees, their schedules, and their phone numbers from a supervisor. We spent the remainder of the afternoon on telephones working our way through the list to no avail. It wasn't that people were uncooperative or reluctant to help. It was just that no one had seen anything. We finally called it a day around seven Saturday night. We were getting nowhere fast.

Peters offered to drive me over to Kirkland and back, to take me to a wonderful health food restaurant he knew. I appreciated the offer, but I was beat. I wanted to be home in my own little apartment with my own little stereo and my own little self. "I'll take a rain check," I told him.

I declined the offer of a ride, too. I didn't want Peters to know that I was going to stop and pick up a Big Mac and an order of fries at the McDonald's at Third and Pine. He had made enough sarcastic remarks about junk food while we were gathering the mustard. I wasn't about to let him know that I am a regular customer at the local Big Mac outlet, that the clerks know me by name and order. It's not that I'm ashamed. It's just that I didn't want to give Peters any more ammunition.

As I stood waiting for my order, I looked around at the stray slice of humanity sitting in those four walls munching Big Macs. There was a genuine bag lady with her multilayered coats. There was a group of young toughs arguing loudly in one corner. In another a couple of long-legged hookers daintily dipped Chicken McNuggets under the watchful eye of a well-dressed pimp.

The clerks took the orders and the money, shoving the food back across the counter with studied disinterest. It was business as usual as far as they were concerned. With all the weirdos hanging around, it was hardly surprising no one had noticed a kid in a nightgown eating a hamburger for breakfast at eight o'clock in the morning.

I went home and let myself into the peace and quiet of my apartment. I mixed myself a generous MacNaughton's. Then I set the table with a place mat and a matching linen napkin. I may like McDonald's, but I won't eat on paper plates in my own home, either. I arranged the hamburger and fries tastefully on the brown-bordered stoneware plate the decorator had assured me was very chic and very masculine. Then I dragged a Tupperware container of radishes and celery out of the fridge.

Those mealtime amenities may seem silly at times, but for three months after I moved out of the house, I ate on nothing but paper plates with plastic forks, knives, and spoons. I was sure Karen would come to her senses and take me back. I was living in a world of miserable, not blissful, ignorance. I kept thinking Karen had divorced me on my own merits, believed that what she said about being a cop's wife was the truth. I hadn't known about the accountant then, the accountant for an egg conglomerate who had come to town looking for an egg-ranch site near Kent or Puyallup. I hadn't known this jerk had walked into the real estate office where Karen had just started working and swept her off her feet.

The day after the divorce was final she married him, and I hired an interior decorator. That's almost five years ago now. He moved Karen, Kelly, and Scott to Cucamonga, California. I guess he's an all-right guy. The kids have never complained to me, and Kelly told me last Christmas that he (his name is Dave) has them put the child support money I send in a special savings account for college. He may be all right, but I hate him, and I eat on real plates with real napkins because I want Karen to know my world didn't end just because she left. At least, it didn't end completely.

I ate, cleared the table, and put the dishes in the dishwasher. I run the dishwasher once a week on Sunday morning whether I need to or not. I made a fresh drink and went to stand on the balcony. It was a chill spring evening, tending more toward winter than summer. Across the street at the Cinerama the ticket holders' line for the nine o'clock show disappeared behind the Fourth and Blanchard Building, a tall, pointed, black glass monstrosity called the Darth Vader Building by locals. For a while I stood there watching and listening, hearing little snatches of conversation and laughter that wafted up to my eleventh-floor perch. Periodically a juggler appeared to entertain those waiting in line. Some people will do anything for money.

I was tempted to mix another drink and stay home to lick my wounds, to bring up all that old family stuff and beat myself over the head with it. It occurred to me, however, that it wouldn't be healthy. At eight fifty-five I put my glass in the sink and rode the elevator downstairs. The ride down was longer than the walk across the street. The last of the line had entered the theater by the time I bought my ticket. I didn't bother to ask what was showing.

It wasn't a good decision. The wife in the movie was getting it on with every Tom, Dick, and Harry in town. Instead of cheering me up, the story rekindled my anger over losing my family.

When I came home, I took myself and a bottle of MacNaughton's to the recliner in my darkened living room, and I didn't quit until we were both gone.

CHAPTER 6

Sunday morning dawned clear and cold. I woke up, still sitting in my chair, nursing a terrific hangover.

Friday and Saturday's storm had blown itself out. The cloud cover that usually keeps Seattle temperatures moderate was missing. The sun had barely come up when banks of fog rolled in. Once the fog burned off, the sun's rays offered no warmth.

Hindsight is so simple. I should have had some premonition my life would change that day. If I had called old Dave, Karen's new husband, and asked him to spare me a few chicken entrails, maybe I could have gotten a seer to give me some advance warning. I wouldn't have been caught quite so off guard. Unfortunately—or perhaps fortunately—Dave and I don't have that kind of relationship. As it was, the morning appeared routine, ordinary, once I'd swallowed enough aspirin to quiet the pounding in my head.

I made breakfast, hoping that food would help. I have mastered the art of microwave bacon and soft-boiled eggs. Then I ran my weekly load of dishes and washed my weekly load of clothes. Anything that has to be ironed goes across the street to the cleaners and laundry. By then I was feeling half human.

After I finished my chores, the week's collection of crossword puzzles was waiting in the hall outside my door. Ida, my next-door neighbor, knows I hate newspapers and love crossword puzzles. She saves them for me all week. On Sunday morning she leaves a little stack outside my door after she finishes with her own paper. I've come to regard the weekly stack of puzzles as a variation on the Easter Bunny theme. It's almost as magical.

Peters has season tickets to the Mariners' games. That particular Sunday, the Yankees were in town. We had decided the day before that I would pull the funeral duty. It's a part of the job that I don't relish, but season tickets are season tickets.

I suppose I should explain why cops go to murder victims' funerals. They go to see who shows up and who doesn't. Statistically most people are murdered by someone they know. Oftentimes a murderer will attend the funeral for fear his not being there will throw suspicion in his direction. Sometimes it works the other way too. The killer is a complete stranger who goes to the funeral because it gives him a feeling of power to be there without anyone knowing who he is, so homicide detectives go to funerals. It comes with the territory.

Brodie had told me that Angela's Thanksgiving Service would be held at Mount Pleasant Cemetery on top of Queen Anne Hill. It struck me as being a little odd. I would have expected them to have a hellfire-and-brimstone sermon in Faith Tabernacle itself. It seemed self-effacing, as though they didn't want to draw attention to the church itself.

I decided to walk to the cemetery. I suppose I could have gone down to the department and checked out a car, but I didn't feel like going anywhere near the department, not even as close as the motor pool.

I got over being a suburban type all at once. I sold my car when I moved to the city. I got my apartment cheap because it didn't come with a parking place. Later I found out why it was cheap. Parking in downtown Seattle costs a fortune. I did the only sensible thing—I learned to love the bus.

Gone were the days of the fifty-five-minute commute. All commuting ever got me was an ulcer, hemorrhoids, and a divorce. Walking isn't all that bad except that having dates without a car has proved to be something of a challenge. The upshot is that I've virtually given up dating except for those rare cliff-dwelling creatures like myself who aren't insulted by an offer of dinner or a movie contingent upon walking to and from. There aren't too many women like that, so my sex life has dwindled. I chum around with some of the lavender-haired ladies from the Royal Crest who are glad to have my friendship but don't make demands on my body or my schedule. Like me, they mostly don't have cars. It's a lifestyle that suits me.

The two-and-a-half-mile trek to Mount Pleasant Cemetery, much of it almost perpendicular, felt good. It finished the job of clearing my head. A chill wind was blowing off Puget Sound, and a few clouds scudded across the sky ahead of the wind. Seattle wouldn't be the Emerald City if it didn't rain on a fairly regular basis.

It wasn't necessary to stop and ask directions at the cemetery office. I could see a little knot of people gathering just over the crest of the bluff. I stationed myself a little apart with my back to a suddenly gray Lake Union. I checked off the arriving players against Brodie's roster.

The True Believers arrived first. It was clear they had been instructed to speak to no one. They came as a group, huddled together near the coffin as a group, and knelt to pray as a group. Suzanne Barstogi, kneeling stoically in the middle of the second row, was accorded no special recognition or position of honor as the mother of the slain child. This was a group Thanksgiving Service, I reminded myself, and Pastor Michael Brodie would not tolerate any individual outpourings of grief that might crack the shell of his little facade.

I had called Brodie earlier and jotted down the names of those he expected to be in attendance. Looking at his flock now, I was able to put some names with faces. Jeremiah, of course, Benjamin Mason/Jason, Ezra, Thomas. There was one more man, but I couldn't recall his name. Other than Suzanne, the women eluded me. They were so drab and so alike, it was impossible to sort them out.

Sophie Czirski was there, her ramrod thinness totally at odds with the pudgy Faith Tabernacle women. She planted herself firmly at the foot of the coffin and glared at the kneeling pastor with open defiance, daring him to question her right to be there. The wind, blowing at her back, periodically made her red hair stand on end. It gave her a wild appearance. If I had been Brodie, I would have thought twice about picking a fight with her.

Maxwell Cole turned up with a long-haired photographer in tow. At Cole's insistence, pictures of the kneeling congregation were taken from every possible angle. His taste is all in his mouth. Sophie watched the proceedings with a malevolent glare. When Cole unwisely asked her to move over so they could get one more picture, she told him in no uncertain words and with considerable volume what he could do with both the photographer and his camera. She didn't budge an inch.

Scattered here and there were a few hangers-on, people who make a habit out of going to funerals, ones who get a kick out of watching as other people's emotions go through a wringer. I looked at them closely, wondering if any of them were named Charlie. After the service I would request a copy of the guest register.

The service itself was just getting under way. The Faith Tabernacle group began singing a tuneless little hymn that no one else seemed to recognize. I moved closer so I could hear what was being said, taking up a position just to Sophie's right at the end of the coffin.

I don't know why I looked up, probably nothing more than good old-fashioned male instinct. Had I paid attention, I would have seen every man in the group staring unabashedly in the same direction. The most beautiful woman I had ever seen stepped over the crest of the hill and strode without hesitation toward Angela Barstogi's coffin.

Even now, thinking about that moment is enough to take my breath away. She was a slender woman, of indeterminate age, wearing a brilliant red dress topped by a short but magnificent fur jacket. Her hair fell in dark, lustrous waves that flowed and blended into the dark fur on her shoulders. Her finely chiseled features might have been carved from tawny marble. Her eyes, gray in the changing sunlight, flashed with an interior storm. For all her beauty, it was plain to see she was very angry. She walked quickly, covering the ground with a long, well-booted gait. She stopped less than two feet from Sophie and bowed her head.

If she was aware of the sensation her appearance caused, she gave no indication of it. She seemed to lose herself completely in the proceedings. Unchecked tears rolled down her cheeks and lost themselves in the deep pile of her coat. In one hand she held a single red rose, not a dark red one, but a bright red one that matched the striking hue of her dress.

I noticed Maxwell Cole sidling toward her. When she raised her head and opened her eyes, he would be at her side. That offended me but I didn't have much room to talk. I was fighting the urge to follow suit. Instead I contented myself with observing her from a distance of several feet. The sun had slipped behind a cloud. When it moved away, her hair came alive with burnished highlights. She was exquisite, beautiful beyond anything I had ever imagined.

Pastor Michael Brodie was just getting into the swing of his message. I looked at him, only to find he too was riveted, his mouth moving mechanically as his eyes devoured every inch and curve of the newcomer's body. I felt an almost uncontrollable urge to leap in front of her and shield her from his gaze. For him to be able to look at her seemed an unbearable violation. The impulse startled me even as it occurred. I am not someone who imagines bedding every piece of desirable flesh that passes in my direction. I'm a healthy, middle-aged, well-adjusted, reasonably disciplined, heterosexual male. This woman's presence rang all my bells.

Brodie droned on and on without my hearing a word of what he said. I thought he would never finish. On the other hand I dreaded the service coming to an end. That would mean she would leave, march back up over the hill and out of my life. My mind scrambled wildly, trying to think of what I could say to delay her, to make her stop so I could at least hear the sound of her voice.

Suddenly there was a chorus of amens. The casket began sinking slowly from view. With the fluid grace of a dancer, the slender woman glided forward and tossed her single rose onto the descending casket. Only then did she brush away the tears that had fallen silently throughout the service.

She turned to find Maxwell Cole directly in her path. The photographer hovered at his elbow. "Excuse me," Max said, "I don't believe we've been introduced."

"No," she replied coldly, looking at his press badge. "I'm sure we haven't. I see no reason to remedy that now."

She stepped to one side as if to walk past him, but he placed himself in her way once more. "I'm a columnist for the *Post-Intelligencer,*" he said lamely. "Would you mind telling me what brought you here?"

"I would mind very much." Her voice was sharp, impatient. Uninvited, I moved swiftly to her side.

"I believe the lady has made it quite clear that she doesn't want to talk to you, Maxey. If I were you I'd beat it." Maxwell Cole looked as though he wanted to throttle me, not only for interfering, but also for bringing up a long-despised college nickname. He looked around, checking to see if anyone else had heard. There was too much potential for ridicule in the situation for him to want to hang around. He backed away, taking the photographer with him. Finally, he turned and followed the True Believers, who were trudging up the hill in a dreary single file that somehow reminded me of the seven dwarfs. All they needed were picks on their shoulders to complete the air of joyless drudgery.

The woman turned to me then. "Thank you," she said, extending her hand. "We certainly haven't been introduced. My name is Anne Corley." She smiled. I was entranced by the sound of her voice, low and vibrant. I almost forgot to take her hand. When I remembered myself and did, I was startled to find her grip surprisingly firm and sure.

"My name is Beaumont, Detective J. P. Beaumont. My friends call me Beau."

"I'm glad to meet you, Detective Beaumont."

"I'm assigned to this case." I continued motioning vaguely in the direction of Angela Barstogi's grave. Some people are repulsed when they find out you're a homicide detective. I more than half expected her to turn away from me in disgust. Instead she gave me a glorious smile.

Sophie Czirski appeared at my elbow. She allowed herself to examine Anne Corley in minute detail before she spoke. "I certainly gave that Maxwell Cole fellow a piece of my mind."

"That you did," I said. "Thank you."

Another smile played around the corners of Anne Corley's lips. "Who, Maxey? I gave him a piece of my mind too. Don't I get any thanks?"

"Yes, of course you do," I said. "Thank you." And then the three of us stood there laughing uproariously as though we had just shared some outrageous joke. When we stopped laughing, Anne Corley introduced herself to Sophie.

"Were you a friend of Angela's too?" Sophie asked, her eyes suddenly filling with tears.

"No," Anne replied. "I never met her. I had a sister who died when I was eight. My mother wouldn't let me attend the funeral. She thought it would upset me. To this day I go to the services whenever I hear of a child dying under unusual circumstances. I always cry. Part of me cries for the child who's gone now, and part of me still cries for Patty."

Sophie took Anne's hand and held it for a moment, her rheumy old eyes behind cat's-eye glasses studying Anne Corley's young gray ones. "There were so few flowers," Sophie said. "Your rose was beautiful and so are you." Sophie turned and walked away with surprising speed for someone her age, her back stiffly unbowed as she climbed the steep hillside.

Anne Corley moved slightly downwind. For the first time I was aware of the delicate scent of her perfume, expensive and intoxicating. She stood next to me, saying nothing but driving my heightened senses into overload.

"Are you still on duty, Mr. Beaumont?" she asked.

I glanced around, dumbfounded to find that the entire funeral party had disappeared. Only Anne Corley and I remained on the windswept hillside. "I guess not, except I need to stop by the cemetery office to pick up a copy of the guest register."

"Do you mind if I tag along? I have a feeling that Maxey may very well be waiting for me in the parking lot."

I looked down at her in absolute amazement. "No," I managed. "I don't mind at all." She took my arm with the calm assurance of someone used to getting whatever she wants. I'd like to pretend that I had the presence of mind to offer my arm to her, but that's not the case. She reached out and rested a featherweight hand on my forearm; then the two of us walked up the hill through the Mount Pleasant Cemetery as though it were the most natural thing in the whole world.

It's ironic to think that Maxwell Cole, a man who had been the bane of my existence for some twenty-odd years, was the catalyst that caused her hand to take my arm. I have a lot to thank Maxwell Cole for. Maybe someday I'll get around to telling him.

CHAPTER 7

Anne Corley stood quietly near the door while an attendant photocopied the guest register for me. I tried not to stare at her while I waited. She smiled as I returned with the copy in hand. "Should I have signed that too?" she asked.

"Shouldn't be necessary," I told her. "I already know you were here."

"What about you? Why are you here?" she demanded.

I explained briefly how killers often present themselves at the funerals of their victims.

"And do you think that's true in this case?"

I shrugged. I thought of Pastor Michael Brodie piously intoning biblical passages over a small casket, of Benjamin Mason/Jason kneeling with his hands clasped in prayer under the flowing beard. "It could be," I answered.

"Oh," she said under her breath. Quickly I folded the piece of paper the attendant had given me and stuffed it into an inside jacket pocket. Out of sight is out of mind.

Back outside, walking toward the tiny parking lot, I noticed a rust-colored Volvo still very much in evidence. Maxwell Cole was observing us over the roof of it. I couldn't help but feel just a little smug. "Where's your car?" I asked Anne.

She nodded in the direction of a bright red Porsche parked at the far end of the lot. "What about yours?"

"I don't have a car," I said, suddenly feeling embarrassed about it. "I walked."

"I probably should have," she said unexpectedly, "but these boots aren't built for walking. Why don't I give you a lift?" The invitation caught me off guard, but not so much that I didn't accept.

We reached her car. She unlocked the door, and I opened it for her. Maxwell Cole followed us at a wary distance. He was approaching the driver's side, jotting down the numbers from the temporary license in the back window. The Porsche was evidently brand-new.

Anne saw him out of the corner of her eye as she turned to ease her way into the leather interior. She smiled again. "Well? Are you coming or not?"

I closed the door behind her and hurried to the rider's side. I came around behind the car, walking directly in front of Maxwell Cole, and climbed into the rider's seat. Max was still standing there, a little to one side, when Anne fired up the powerful engine and rammed the car into reverse. He must have executed a pretty quick sidestep to be sure he was out of the way. I didn't wave to him as we drove by, but I sure as hell wanted to.

I liked this lady, liked her instincts about people and her ability to handle them. She was a lot more than a pretty box of candy.

Anne Corley held the powerful Porsche well in check as she maneuvered the grades, curves, and angles that make Queen Anne Hill an incomprehensible maze for most outsiders. It's a course lots of sports car drivers regard as a Grand Prix training ground. She drove with a confident skill that was careful but hardly sedate.

The fire that had made her gray eyes smolder as she approached Angela Barstogi's grave site had been banked. When she paused at a stop sign and looked at me, they sparkled with intelligence and humor. "Where to?" she asked.

"I live downtown," I said. "Corner of Third and Lenora. How about you?"

"I'm just visiting. I'm staying at the Four Seasons Olympic." That put me in my place. The Four Seasons is absolutely first-class, but then so was the lady.

"Do you have to go home?" she asked after a pause. "Wife and kiddies, or major league baseball on television?"

"Wrong on all counts," I replied. "No wife and kiddies at home. I've got a twelve-inch black and white that I only use to keep tabs on how the media gets things ass-backward. I don't like baseball. I wouldn't go to a live game, to say nothing of watching one on TV."

"You sound like an endangered species to me," she grinned, and we both laughed. "Then what you're saying is that you don't have any pressing reason to go straight home?"

"No."

Her face darkened slightly. I might not have noticed it if my eyes hadn't been glued to her face, drinking in her finely carved profile that could easily have graced the cover of any fashion magazine. A slight frown creased her forehead, then disappeared in far less time than it takes to tell.

"They had a huge potluck after Patty's funeral," she said somberly. "I couldn't go to that, either, so whenever I attend a funeral in Patty's honor, I always treat myself afterward. Care to join me?"

"Sure."

"Where, then?" she asked.

How do you answer that question when you've just met someone and haven't the slightest idea of their likes or dislikes? "I don't know. Where do you want to go?"

She looked at me and laughed. I felt stupid, inadequate, as though I had somehow failed to measure up to her expectations. "I'll tell you what," she said. "I'll choose this time and you choose next time, deal?"

I nodded but I didn't feel any better. My wires were all crossed. I was a gawky kid on his first blind date, which turns out to be with the head cheerleader. I wanted to impress her, although there was nothing to indicate she was in need of being impressed. Like someone who has always lusted after fine china, once he is faced with a Wedgwood plate, does he eat off it or put it away on a shelf? Here I was in a Porsche with the most beautiful woman I had ever seen, and I didn't know what to say or what to do with my hands and feet. I hadn't been that ill at ease in a long time.

She hit Lower Queen Anne, turned left at Mercer, and headed for the freeway, driving easily but purposefully. I didn't ask where we were going. She bypassed downtown and took the exit that put us on Interstate 90. There had been a long silence in the car. I was content to leave it at that.

She had tossed her jacket carelessly in the half-baked backseat they put in Porsches to evade sports car insurance premiums. Her dress was made from some soft fabric that clung to the gentle curves of her body. The neckline, a long V, accentuated her slenderness. In the hollow of her throat lay a pendant, a single jewel suspended on a delicate gold chain. I'm not much of an expert, but real diamonds, especially ones that size, have a way of letting you know they're not fake.

Despite the diamond, despite the fur jacket, despite the car, gradually I stopped being so self-conscious and started enjoying myself.

First Seattle, then the suburban sprawl of Bellevue disappeared behind us. Forested hills rolled by as we climbed toward the Cascades. "Washington is really beautiful," she said while the car sped effortlessly up the wide, curving roadway. We had been quiet for so many minutes that the sound of her voice startled me.

"Have you been here long?" I queried.

"No," she answered. "Not long at all. I just flew into town yesterday."

"I'm not surprised," I laughed. "You couldn't have been around Seattle very long without my knowing it."

She took the Fall City exit and shot me a sidelong glance. "I take that to be a compliment?"

"That's how it was intended."

She said nothing. Somehow I seemed to have offended her. I reverted to adolescence and kept my mouth shut. I was still wondering how to make amends when we pulled into the parking lot at Snoqualmie Falls. Spring runoff was well under way. A thunderous roar of cascading water assailed our ears as we got out of the car.

"This is one of my favorite places," she said. She set off in her long-legged stride toward the viewpoint that overlooks the water, while I followed at a distance.

Snoqualmie in spring is spectacular. Rushing water surges over a sheer basalt cliff into a swirling pool nearly three hundred feet below. The plunging torrent sends a cloud of misty spray back up the wall of the canyon. Mist settled around Anne Corley as she stood on the observation deck. It seemed to bathe her in an otherworldly essence.

The viewpoint was filled with Sunday afternoon tourists, the bermuda-shorted, knobby-kneed, see-America-first variety. The hesitant sunshine of that spring afternoon had brought them out in droves. I didn't miss the contrast between Anne Corley and them, nor did I miss the appreciative men and the covertly wary women. Her delicate beauty swathed in the flowing red dress commanded attention, although she was too engrossed in the water to be aware of it.

When she finally turned away from the falls, she seemed almost surprised to find me standing at her side, as though she had forgotten my existence in her total concentration on the water. She recovered quickly. "Let's eat," she said. "I'm starved."

We followed a flower-lined pathway up to the lodge. Snoqualmie Lodge boasts a fine restaurant, and I certainly couldn't quarrel with the choice. The place does land-office business, however. When I saw the jammed tables and crowded entry, I was sure we would have a long wait. Purposefully, Anne made her way through the crowd and spoke quietly to the hostess. "Why certainly, Mrs. Corley. It will only take a moment," the hostess said.

I stationed myself near the door, hoping we could spend part of the enforced wait outside rather than in the crowded vestibule. Anne made her way back through the crowd. I marveled at the grace and clarity of her movement. People simply melted out of her way. Heads turned to follow her progress. If she had noticed it, acknowledged it, I probably wouldn't have been so impressed, but she was oblivious.

She reached me, took my arm, and guided us back through the crush. By the time we reached the cashier's desk, the hostess was waiting for us, menus in hand. "Right this way, Mrs. Corley."

"How'd you do that?" I asked in whispered admiration as we followed the hostess to a corner table set for two. Her answer was a shrug that told me nothing. Once seated, I pursued it. "Look here, I heard some of the men talking out there. You have to have reservations three weeks in advance to get in this place."

"I do," she said simply. "I called from Phoenix when I knew I'd be coming up for a few weeks. I ate here with friends when I was here a few years ago and fell in love with it. I plan to have dinner here every Sunday afternoon as long as I'm in the area. It's possible to have a standing reservation, you know, if the price is right."

It was my turn to be offended. At least I did an adequate job of faking it. "In other words, when you asked me to choose where I wanted to eat, it was a put-up deal."

"That's right," she agreed mildly just as the waitress arrived with the menu. "Although, if you'd come up with a brilliant suggestion, we could have canceled. Look at that line. I don't think they'd fine me."

Anne ordered a glass of white wine with ice and I ordered Mac-Naughton's and water. Anne picked up her menu, clasping it with long, well-manicured fingers. She wore scarlet nail polish that matched her dress. She gave the menu a cursory glance, then lay it back down.

"You already know what you want?"

"Yes," she said.

"Why don't you order for both of us then."

She did. Prime rib, baked potatoes, steamed broccoli, and carrots julienne. The food was served elegantly, and it was masterfully prepared. Anne ate with a gusto that seemed at odds with her trim figure. I spent the entire salad course trying to think of something intelligent to say. If I'd had any illusions of turning this into a romantic conversation, she squelched them completely when she asked, "Just who was Angela Barstogi?"

The question stunned me. The pleasure of Anne Corley's company had removed all thought of the dead child, of the case, of time itself. It took me a moment to pull my scrambled thoughts together. "Just a kid who ended up living in the wrong time and place," I said lamely.

Anne leveled serious gray eyes on mine, looking at me with the unblinking steadiness of a skilled inquisitor. "Tell me about her," she said.

"You ask that in a very professional manner," I responded. "Are you a reporter?"

"Well, of sorts. I'm a sociologist. I'm working on a book about young victims of violent crimes. I'm not interested in them from the criminological or sensational point of view. I study them in terms of psychosocial considerations."

She was a far cry from the mousy, passive image of a sociologist that I'd formed, more from fiction than from experience. She was like a breath of fresh air. I guessed rich people could decide to do anything they damned well pleased with their lives. She sure didn't live on a sociologist's salary.

I started out to tell her only a little of the Angela Barstogi story, but somehow it all rolled out, from Sophie Czirski's unproved allegations to a Jesus Loves Me poster that had hung above Angela's bed. I hadn't talked about a case that way since Karen left, and never to someone I didn't know. It was a serious breach of discipline in the loose-lips-sink-ships tradition, yet I was unable to check myself. Anne Corley listened quietly, nodding encouragement from time to time.

I finished. We were sipping coffee. She stirred the strong black liquid thoughtfully. "If that's what she had to live with, no matter how she died, she's probably better off."

I don't know what I had expected Anne to say, but that wasn't it. She'd lost her professional demeanor and seemed to be weeping inwardly for Angela Barstogi. Her sadness didn't seem weak, however. There was strength and resilience under Anne Corley's veneer of graceful beauty. It was like finding real wood when you expected particle board.

We left the restaurant within minutes after that. There was no question of lingering over a conversational after-dinner drink. Once more I felt oddly responsible for her abrupt change of mood. It was somehow my fault. That wasn't the only thing that made me uncomfortable. Anne Corley bought my dinner. That had never happened to me before, and I wasn't sure I liked it.

We drove back to Seattle in a subdued mood. I wanted to redeem the evening, but it was obviously beyond recall. She had moved away from me, was grieving for a child she'd never met. No banter, no small talk could bring her back. I congratulated myself for being a social failure. Who goes to dinner with a gorgeous woman and squanders the conversation on murder, child abuse, and other such scintillating stuff? J. P. Beaumont, that's who.

When Anne stopped to let me out in front of the Royal Crest, I half-heartedly asked her up for a drink. She gave me a wilted smile and said, "Some other time," in a voice totally empty of enthusiasm. Dejectedly I watched her drive away. It was clear that whatever interest I had held for her was gone. There was no sense in calling the Four Seasons. I had had one shot at her, and missed. Whatever it was I had lost, it was something I suspected I wanted.

CHAPTER 8

The phone was ringing as I stepped off the elevator. I didn't rush to answer it. I figured whoever it was would call back later. It was still yelling at me after I unlocked the door and turned on the lights.

"Where the hell have you been?" Peters growled before I had a chance to say hello.

"It's none of your goddamned business, actually. It is Sunday, you know."

"I've been trying to get you for a couple of hours. I'll pick you up in ten minutes."

"I don't want to be picked up. I want to go to bed and sulk."

"You're going to the airport. We're meeting someone."

"All right, Peters. Cut the crap. Who are we meeting?"

"A fellow by the name of Andrew Carstogi."

"You mean Barstogi."

"Barstogi is an alias. Andrew Carstogi is Angela's father."

"I'll meet you downstairs," I said.

Peters picked me up in a departmental car, explaining to me as we drove that Carstogi had called in during the funeral. No one could find me, but they had finally located Peters after he came home from watching the Yankees strangle the Mariners.

"How was the funeral?" Peters asked.

The funeral was light-years away. I had gone to the funeral without knowing Anne Corley, and now, five hours later, I had met her and lost her. It had to be some kind of indoor world record for short-lived romance. I shrugged. "Michael Brodie gave quite a performance," I said.

"Faith Tabernacle people were out in force?"

I nodded. "They arrived as a group and left as a group."

"The inquiry came back from Illinois. Drew a blank on everybody—except Brodie and Jason. They show that old license on Clinton Jason, but that's all. I asked them to check him further and to keep looking for the others."

We drove down the Alaskan Way Viaduct, along the waterfront with its trundling ferries and acres of container shipyards punctuated by the red skeletons of upraised cranes. We sped down a canyon of railroad freight cars that towered on either side of the road. The long springtime evening of gray sky and gray sea matched my own dreary outlook. I tried to get Anne Corley off my mind, to focus on Angela Barstogi, the case, anything but a lady driving out of my life in a bright red Porsche.

"Tell me about Angela's father," I said. "What brought him out of the woodwork?"

"There's not much to tell so far. He called the department between two-thirty and three. He had just heard. I don't know how. He raised hell with whoever answered the phone. Said he knew it would happen, that he had tried to stop it. When he said he was catching the next plane out, it sounded like he intended to do bodily harm to Brodie and Suzanne as well. The brass thought we ought to intercept him. Powell wants us to park him someplace downtown where we can keep an eye on him. I had to beat up the airlines to find out what flight he's on."

"I think doing bodily harm to Pastor Michael Brodie is a wonderful idea. What say we miss the plane?"

"Orders are orders," Peters replied.

We rode the automated underground people mover to the United Airlines terminal. We didn't have to wonder who Andrew Carstogi was. An angry young man stumbled through the gate, shedding flight attendants like a wet dog shakes off excess water. He was drunk and spoiling for a fight. I'm sure Carstogi didn't enjoy walking into the welcoming arms of two waiting homicide detectives. The feeling was mutual. It's never fun to be put on the baby-sitting detail, especially when you're dealing with a grieving parent.

Peters and I fell into step on either side of Carstogi. Peters flashed his badge. I thought Carstogi was going to coldcock Peters on the spot.

"What're you guys after me for?" he demanded sluggishly. "My kid is dead. I just got to town."

I thought I'd deflect a little of the anger, calm the troubled waters. "Take it easy. We're here to help."

"You can help me, all right. Just tell me where that asshole Brodie is, that's what you can do." He turned to me with a swaying leer and shook a clenched fist under my nose. "You know where he is? I'll take care of that son-of-a-bitch myself."

Carstogi allowed himself to be guided onto the subway. The security guard eyed us suspiciously as we led him, ranting and raving, through the gate. He hadn't brought any luggage. "Don' need any luggage," he mumbled. "Only came to town to smash his fucking face."

Carstogi balked at the car. "Hey, where're you takin' me? I got my rights. I wanna lawyer."

Peters was losing patience. "Shut up," he said. "You're not under arrest. We're going to try to sober you up."

"Oh," Carstogi replied.

We went to the Doghouse. They have a sign in there that shows all roads leading to the Doghouse the same as signs all over the world tell the distance to that godforsaken end of nowhere called Wall Drug in South Dakota. Connie put us in a corner of the back dining room even though it was closed. She brought me coffee and Peters tea, then asked what Carstogi wanted. He wanted beer. He didn't get it. Peters ordered him bacon and eggs and whole wheat toast served up with a full complement of questions. I thought it commendable that Peters put aside his own personal prejudices and ordered some decent food for Carstogi.

It took a while for food and exhaustion to do their work. When we finally dug under the bluster and bullshit, what we found was a twenty-eight-year-old guy in a world of hurt, a man who lost his wife once and his child twice, all to the same man, he figured, Pastor Michael Brodie.

The story came out slowly. First there had been a series of tent meetings to save souls, of miracles performed before wondering sinners who were prepared to follow the miracle worker to the ends of the earth. Except the miracle worker turned out to have feet of clay. He was into weird stuff like multiple wives and physical punishment for redemption of sins. Anyone who tried to stop him was liable to find himself smitten by the right hand of God. God's right hand turned out to have a mean right hook.

Andrew Carstogi had come to his senses one morning with the crap beaten out of him. It had made a big impression. He had crossed Brodie on the righteousness of physical punishment, on Brodie's requirement that all wives belonged to God's Chosen Prophet first and their husbands second. Brodie hadn't quit until Carstogi was unconscious. If Carstogi had left it at that, it wouldn't have been so bad, but Andrew Carstogi didn't take kindly to being beaten up or losing his wife. He called in the cops and the press.

Chicago is a pretty tolerant place, but once the charges had been made, even though Carstogi had been unable to substantiate them, Faith Tabernacle was held up to ridicule. Experience tells me that the Pastor Michael Brodies of the world can handle almost anything but ridicule.

Carstogi was Disavowed. It's worse than it sounds. In the world of Faith Tabernacle, he ceased to exist. Not only was he no longer a member, he was no longer a husband or father either. He tried to get a court order for custody of Angela. Unfortunately, Suzanne was neither a prostitute nor a drug addict. Later, when Brodie made a killing in a real estate deal on some property the church owned, the whole congregation folded their tents and stole away in the middle of the night. Once they left Chicago the group had as good as fallen off the edge of the earth until a cousin of Carstogi's, a guy in the navy in Bremerton, put two and two together and came up with the connection.

Carstogi finished his story and looked from Peters to me as if we should understand. I still felt there were big chunks missing. "Why do you say he killed her?" I asked.

"He almost killed me," he replied. He had sobered up enough that his words no longer slurred together.

"That's two men going at it. It's a long way from killing a defenseless child."

"You been in the church?" he asked.

"We've been there," Peters replied.

"But during a service?" Carstogi continued doggedly. "Have you been there during a service? If I just coulda gotten that judge to go to a service he woulda given me custody."

"Tell us about the service," Peters suggested.

"You probably won't believe it. Nobody else does."

"Try us," I offered.

He looked at us doubtfully. The sobering process made him more reluctant to talk. "It's like he owns them body and soul. Like it's a contest to see how far they'll jump if he tells them."

"For instance," Peters said.

"If he told them to eat dog shit they'd do it." He said it quickly, with a ring of falsehood.

"That's not really what you're talking about, is it?" Peters' face was a mask that I had a hard time reading myself. Carstogi gave him an appraising look, then shook his head.

Peters followed up on the opening he had made. "You're afraid to tell us for fear you'll end up being prosecuted too, aren't you?"

"It's scary," Carstogi admitted. "I didn't realize until after I got out. You just do what he tells you, what everyone else is doing. It doesn't seem so bad at the time. You don't think that you're hurting someone. The whole time Brodie is there telling you that suffering is the only way those sinners are going to heaven, that you are the chosen instrument of God."

"Shit." Peters got up and left the table. He went into the bar and came back a few minutes later. A distinct odor of gin came with him. Maybe the juniper berries in gin had been promoted to health food status. Because I knew about Broken Springs, Oregon, and Peters' own situation, I could feel for him, but to leave in the middle of an interrogation was inexcusable, to say nothing of drinking on duty.

I made a mental note to climb his frame about it later. I don't like personal considerations to get in the way of doing the job. If you're a professional, that kind of thing doesn't happen. Objectivity is the name of the game. While I was making that little set of mental notes, I should have remembered something they used to say in Sunday School about taking the beam out of your own eye before you start worrying about the mote in somebody else's. But then, I was still very much the professional. J. P. Beaumont hadn't reached his own breaking point yet. It was coming.

Carstogi was exhausted. We put him up in the Warwick, which happens to be at Fourth and Lenora, a half block cornerwise from where I live. It made dropping him off and tucking him in a simple matter. He seemed more than happy for us to stick him in a hotel room and tell him we'd come get him in the morning.

Peters came with me to my apartment. I got out my MacNaughton's and located a dusty gin bottle with enough dregs for a reasonable drink or two. We tried to plan for morning, which by now was already upon us.

"You think he's telling the truth?" I asked Peters.

He nodded. "Sounds like it to me, as far as it goes. He's scared some of the shit is going to roll downhill and he'll end up with charges lodged against him. I'm afraid he'll rabbit on us before we can get him into court."

I had to agree with Peters' assessment. If we went strictly with Carstogi, we would be leaning on a bent reed. "Do you suppose we can use him to bring Suzanne around?"

Peters considered for a moment. "It would be worth a try, although I doubt it'll work. Even considering what she's been through, she won't squeal on that Brodie bastard. That's the mystifying part about brainwashing. She may know he's a killer, but she'll stick to him like glue."

"You could be right," I allowed, "but we have the element of surprise on our side. She has no way of knowing that Andrew Carstogi is in town. Maybe if we brought him over and dumped him on her, it would jar her into slipping. After all, they were together almost ten years. She probably still has some feelings for him."

"It's worth a try," Peters agreed.

We made arrangements to meet at the Warwick at eight. We'd take Carstogi with us to breakfast and then head for Gay Avenue. We'd try to get there before Suzanne had a backup group from Faith Tabernacle. Our best bet was to catch her alone.

Peters left. In the quiet of my apartment, Anne Corley returned to tantalize me. I had managed to keep thoughts of her at a distance while Peters was there, while I was doing my job, but now her presence—or rather the lack of it—filled the place. Considering she had never set foot in my apartment, it seemed odd that it should feel empty without her. Considering I had never laid a glove on her, it was even odder that I should want her so much.

I leaned back in the leather chair and closed my eyes. I must have dozed off. In a dream I opened my door, and she was standing in the hall. She was wearing a filmy red gown, one of those Frederick's of Hollywood jobs with a split up the side. I reached out to draw her into the room. She came close enough to kiss me on the cheek, then slipped out of my grasp and disappeared around the corner of the hall. The hall became a maze. I followed her, turning one corner after another. Every once in a while I caught a fleeting glimpse of the red gown. She stayed elusively out of reach, but all the while I could hear her laughing.

I woke up in a cold sweat. It was just after three. I stumbled off to bed telling myself that there's no fool like an old fool—an old fool with delusions of adequacy.

CHAPTER 9

We were at 4543 Gay Avenue by nine-thirty the next morning. During breakfast we had attempted to explain to Carstogi the importance of bringing Suzanne around. He wasn't wild about seeing her. He still wanted us to take him to Brodie, but sober, he wasn't quite as anxious for a confrontation as he had been the night before.

No one answered our knock, although the doorknob turned in my hand when I tried it. The house was empty. No dirty dishes filled the sink. The beds were made. Someone had gone to a good deal of trouble to clean the place up. We got back in the car and drove to Faith Tabernacle.

Carstogi's reluctance surfaced as we climbed the steps to go inside. Pastor Michael Brodie wielded some residual power that made the younger man, if not downright scared, at least more than a little wary. It's the old talk-is-cheap routine.

The church proper was open but empty. We found Suzanne in the Penitent's Room, kneeling on the stand before the open Bible. Peters and I dropped back while Carstogi approached her.

"Sue?" he asked tentatively. "I'm sorry about Angel. I just heard."

Suzanne didn't so much as look up. There was no sign of recognition or acknowledgment. He stood over her, clenching and unclenching his fists in a combination of nervousness and frustration. A range of emotions played over his face—grief, anger, rejection. He knelt beside her and touched her arm. Her body tensed at the touch but still she didn't look up. "Please, Sue," he pleaded gently. "Come back with me. Let's start over again, away from here, away from all this."

The door to the study swung open and Pastor Michael Brodie charged into the room. He grabbed Carstogi by the collar and hauled him to his feet, shoving him off-balance and away in the same powerful motion.

"Satan is speaking to you through the voice of a devil, Sister! Pray on. Your immortal soul is hanging in the balance."

Carstogi recovered and came back swinging, his face a mask of fury. He was pretty well built in his own right, with the broad shoulders and thick forearms of a construction hand, but Brodie outclassed him all the way around. With the ease of a trained fighter, Brodie fended off first one blow and then another before sending Carstogi crashing against the opposite wall. By then Peters and I moved between them. Peters helped Carstogi to his feet and bodily restrained him. The younger man's nose and lip were bleeding. Brodie may have looked like he had gone to seed, but looks can be deceiving. Carstogi was no match for him.

Brodie turned on me. "Get out," he snarled. "You've no right to bring an infidel into a place of worship."

"She's his wife," I said.

"She's his widow!" he shot back. Brodie lunged toward Suzanne. For a moment I thought he was going to hit her. Instead he knelt in front of her, his face inches from hers. "Do not be tempted to leave off your cleansing. These apparitions are Satan's own instruments, sent to tempt you from the True Way. Shut them out, Sister! Pray without ceasing." He rose, turned on his heel, and returned to the study, locking the door behind him.

Carstogi struggled free from Peters' grasp and rushed toward the door just as it slammed shut in his face. He leaned against it, his shoulders heaving with impotent sobs. Carstogi was no lightweight in the physical department, yet Brodie had disposed of the younger man so easily, he might have been a child. A lot of the power Brodie wielded over the True Believers had to do with sheer brute strength and fear. Fear so strong that he could walk away from a kneeling Suzanne and know she would refuse to speak to us even with her spiritual master out of earshot.

Carstogi swung away from the door and went back to Suzanne. He too knelt before her, cradling her face in his hands. "How could you let him do it? How can you let him get away with it?"

Suzanne Barstogi's eyes were blank. She might have been struck blind. When he let her go, she dropped to the floor like a limp rag doll.

"Come on," Peters said, placing his hand on Carstogi's shoulder. "Let's go. This isn't doing any good."

Carstogi rose to his feet like a sleepwalker. Peters led him outside. A thin mist was falling, and I welcomed it. There was a sense of reality in the rain's touch that was lacking inside the barren waste of Faith Tabernacle.

"You did what you could," Peters was saying to Carstogi.

"I shoulda brought a gun," Carstogi mumbled. "I shoulda brought a goddamned gun."

"It's a good thing you didn't," Peters replied. "Airport security would never have let you out of O'Hare. We need your help. Are you in?"

Carstogi nodded grimly. "What do I do?"

"For one thing, tell us everything you know about what goes on in Faith Tabernacle."

We spirited him back to the Warwick. No way were we going to take him down to the department. The last thing we needed was to give the press a shot at him.

Peters picked up a paper on our way through the lobby. Maxwell Cole's article and picture were the lead items of the local section. The headlines read, SLAIN CHILD BURIED. There was a close-up of Suzanne Barstogi kneeling stoically during Angela's service. According to Max's story, Pastor Michael Brodie was a man of God with enough courage and faith to say hallelujah when one of his flock made off for the Promised Land. Suzanne Barstogi's face reflected total agreement with Brodie's words.

Peters read the article first, then handed it to me. Our charge went into the bathroom. "According to that, Brodie's some kind of latter-day prophet," Peters said.

"I picked up on that too. I can hear our case getting picked apart on page one, can't you?"

Carstogi returned to the room and read the article without comment.

"What was Suzanne doing at church this morning?" I asked.

"It's the start of a Purification Ceremony," he said as he studied the picture. "Did she talk to the cops when it happened?"

I nodded.

"That's why, then," he continued. "True Believers are never supposed to talk to outsiders, especially cops. That's why he threw me out."

"Why doesn't he throw her out?"

Carstogi looked at me incredulously. "Are you kidding? If he kicks a woman out, he loses food stamps, welfare, and medicaid, to say nothing of part of the harem."

"Welfare fraud and sex?" Peters asked. "Is that what all this is about?"

Carstogi flashed with anger. "Of course, you asshole. Did you think this was all salvation and jubilee? I couldn't make that judge back home see it either."

I took the newspaper from Carstogi's hand. "With the likes of Maxwell Cole working for the opposition, we'll be lucky to get anyone to believe it here, either," I said. "What do you know about the good pastor?"

"Brodie's a fighter."

"We picked up on that," Peters observed dryly.

"No, I mean he really was a fighter. Middle heavyweight in Chicago. Local stuff. Never made a national name for himself, but he never lost the moves. The only time I think I can whip him is when I'm juiced." He rubbed his bruised chin ruefully. It occurred to me then that maybe Carstogi was growing on me.

He continued. "When Sue and I started going to Faith Tabernacle, we were having troubles. Too much drinking and not enough money. Not only that, we wanted kids and couldn't seem to have any. Sue went first and then she dragged me along. There were probably fifteen to twenty couples then."

"There aren't that many now," I said.

"No. Most of the men get lopped off one way or another. One of them wound up dead in an alley in Hammond, Indiana. I always thought Brodie did that too, but nobody ever proved it. At first I was really gung ho, especially when Sue turned up pregnant. I thought it was a miracle. Now I'm not so sure, but I loved Angel just the same. I wanted her out of this."

"So who are the five or so who are left?"

"Kiss-asses. The ones who get the same kind of kicks Brodie does."

"We did some checking with the state of Illinois. None of the names check out except for the one named Benjamin." Peters was studying Carstogi closely.

"I never knew their real names, only the Tabernacle ones. I imagine Brodie changed them all by a letter or two, just like he did Suzanne's. Some of the True Believers have records. I know that much."

"You said kicks a minute ago," I put in. "What kind of kicks?"

Carstogi looked from Peters to me. He shrugged. "Go to the ceremony," he said. "That'll tell you everything you need to know."

"You know they don't let outsiders in. What happens?" I asked.

"Last night she probably made a public confession of sin. Talking to the cops is probably the major one. They took her to that room afterward for her to pray for forgiveness. Tonight they'll decide on her punishment. She could be Disavowed, but I doubt that. They'll think of something else."

"What else?" Peters was pressing him.

"Anything that sadistic motherfucker thinks up. Maybe she'll have to stand naked in a freezing room or get whipped in front of the group. He's got a whole bag of tricks." Carstogi's hands were clenched, his eyes sparking with fury. I wanted to puke. It's a cop's job to keep people safe, but how do you protect them from themselves?

Eventually he continued. "Tonight they'll leave her to pray in the church itself rather than in the Penitent's room. In the morning they'll have a celebration."

Peters got up. He paused by where Carstogi was sitting on the bed. "Do you think Brodie killed Angela? You said that last night, and we thought you were just drunk. What about now that you're sober?"

"If she wouldn't do what he said . . ." Carstogi's voice trailed off.

Peters walked to the door with a new sense of purpose. "We need to go down to the department for a while. Will you be all right if we leave you here?"

Carstogi nodded. "I'll be okay."

I followed Peters out. I was a little disturbed by the way he was giving Carstogi the brush-off. "I thought we were supposed to stick with him like glue until we got him back on a plane for Chicago."

Peters ignored the comment. "You ever done any bugging?" he asked.

I stopped. "You're not my type."

"Bugging, you jerk, not buggering. As in wiretapping, eavesdropping, Watergate."

"Oh," I replied. "As a matter of fact, I haven't done any of that either."

Peters favored me with the first genuine grin I could remember, the ear-to-ear variety. We got in the car and he turned up Fourth Avenue, the opposite direction from the Public Safety Building.

"Just where in the hell are we going?" I asked.

"Kirkland. I've got some equipment at the house we'll need to use."

"I take it this is going to be an illegal wiretap as opposed to the court-ordered variety?"

"You catch on fast, Beaumont."

"And you know how to work this illegal equipment?" I asked.

Peters' response was prefaced by a wry face. "How do you think I got the goods on my own wife's missionary?"

"And where do you propose to install this device?"

"I think I can make it fit right under the pulpit itself."

"How long is the tape?"

"Long enough. It's sound activated, so if nothing's going on, it shuts off. It'll get us just what we want." Peters' face was a picture of self-satisfaction.

It sounded like Peters knew what he was doing, but I decided to do a reality exercise, play devil's advocate. "Of course you realize that nothing we get will be admissible in a court of law?"

"Absolutely," he responded, "but it may tell us where to go looking for solid information."

"As in where the bodies are buried." That's what I said aloud. I was thinking about Angel Barstogi and a man left dead in a Hammond, Indiana, alley. It seemed to me that God wouldn't frown on our using a little ingenuity to even the score. God helps those who help themselves. Besides, there was a certain perverse justice in the idea of dredging the truth out of Pastor Michael Brodie's very own sermon. Somehow that seemed fair.

CHAPTER 10

▽

In the final analysis, we weren't able to get it under the pulpit, but we got close enough. Suzanne Barstogi was still in the Penitent's Room when we returned from Kirkland with Peter's tiny sound-activated tape recorder. By this time her knees must have worn out. She was lying prostrate on the floor, sound asleep.

We were alone in the sanctuary. Peters sat down casually on a front bench and attached the recorder under the seat. He handled the equipment with well-practiced competency. As soon as it was concealed, I went past the sleeping Suzanne and knocked on the door to Brodie's study. We had agreed to beard the lion in his den. We wanted to turn up the heat on Pastor Michael Brodie. We could at least give his self-confidence a good shake.

"What are you doing back here?" he demanded in a voice that caused Suzanne to stir and struggle once more to her knees. He looked around, presumably for Carstogi. "What do you want?"

"We want to ask you a few questions about your whereabouts on Thursday morning."

Brodie's florid face twisted. "Are you accusing me . . ." He broke off abruptly. "I was here, at the church, in my study. Are you listening to that heathen's accusations?"

"You mean Carstogi? No, we're just doing our job. Did anyone see you?" I prodded.

"I told you I was here by myself. Nobody saw me. Almighty God is my witness."

"Have you ever been in Hammond, Indiana?" The tone of Peters' question was deceptively mild. He leaned casually, almost insolently, against the entrance to the Penitent's Room.

Brodie's red face went suddenly slack and ashen. He recovered quickly. "What does that have to do with this?"

"Oh, nothing," Peters said. "I was just wondering."

"I know what you're trying to do. Andrew is making trouble. He is a man with a burden of vengeance in his heart. He blames me for his fall from grace. You tell him from me that Jehovah sees into his vile soul. He will rot in hell for his unjust accusations."

"So you claim you were here all Thursday morning, or at least until Suzanne Barstogi called you? Is that right?" I continued.

"That's what I said. Twice." His fists were tight and so was his voice. He was losing control.

"Why did you change her name? Are the others using different names too?"

I could tell that Peters' roundabout questions were having the desired effect. Brodie's eyes shifted uneasily back and forth between Peters and me as if he were watching an invisible tennis ball. We were developing into a team. I liked Peters' way of approaching issues in an off-the-wall manner.

"We're starting new lives with new names," Brodie explained.

"And new wives," Peters added. "What about your name? Did you change yours too, or only the names of your followers?"

"I want you out of here," Brodie ordered. His voice dropped to an ominous whisper. "I want you out of here now!"

Peters uncrossed his legs and stretched. There was no sense of urgency in his movements. He stepped around Suzanne and approached the open Bible, running his finger down the page. "It might be worth your while to go looking for someone who can remember your being here on Thursday morning. Maybe there was a cleaning woman around or a neighbor who saw you."

"Are you threatening me?"

Peters shook his head. "You can call it that if you like. I call it a friendly suggestion."

With that Peters ambled out of the room. I followed, wishing Peters' little recording device had a remote listening capability, because I was sure all hell was going to break loose the moment we were out of earshot.

We made it into the office by one forty-five and found stacks of messages. Tom Stahl had called again. I had left the phone bill payment envelope with the outgoing mail before I left the Royal Crest that morning. I resented his calling me at the office about it, but then, I never was available at home during business hours. I gave the yellow message sheet a toss.

There was a call from Maxwell Cole. I wadded that one up and threw it in the trash along with the first one. Cole had more nerve than a bad tooth to call me for anything. Detectives don't speak to the press. That dubious privilege belongs to the supervisors.

Captain Powell and Sergeant Watkins wanted to talk to Peters or me. We drew straws. Peters lost and took off for Powell's fishbowl. There was one more message, one that intrigued me. It was from a woman who said she would call back around two. There was no name on the message, nor was there a number I could call.

I looked at the clock, drummed my fingers on my desk, then reached for the phone. I had made a mental note of the number on the slip of paper in Anne Corley's back window. I called Motor Vehicles and asked them to get me some information on the Porsche.

Two o'clock was just around the corner. I hauled out a form and started working on a report. I can deal with the creeps. It's the bureaucratic garbage I can't stand. I dictated a brief summary of our activities for the day and put Michael Brodie's and Benjamin Mason/Clinton Jason's names into the FBI hopper. There was an off chance they had a record somewhere, maybe even an outstanding warrant or two. I phoned Hammond, Indiana, to see if Brodie was still under active investigation in the case Carstogi had mentioned.

My phone did not ring at two o'clock. At two-fifteen, though, I looked up to find Anne Corley being led to my desk by Arlo Hamilton, the public information officer, who was grinning like a Cheshire cat. Look what I found, his face seemed to say. Visitors on the fifth floor are kept to a minimum. I think Anne Corley's looks had a whole lot to do with the visitor's badge that was clipped on her jacket. Heads turned in her wake. If there was a grin on Hamilton's face, I'm sure mine mirrored it. No way could I disguise the pleasure and surprise I felt at seeing her again.

"Here you are, Miss Corley," Hamilton was saying as he led her to my desk.

"Thank you very much, Arlo," Anne responded graciously. "I appreciate your help."

"Think nothing of it. The pleasure was all mine." Hamilton looked at me. "I was giving her some information for her book," he explained. "Of course, you know all about that."

"Yes," I said. I did know about the book. "How's it going?" I asked.

She smiled. "Fine. Arlo here has been a world of help."

Anne sat down on a chair beside my desk. For a few moments Hamilton wavered, uncertain whether to go or stay. Finally he made the right choice and left. Anne was wearing a navy blue suit with an innocently ruffled blouse and a daring slit up one side of the skirt. When she crossed her legs, the skirt fell away, revealing a length of well-formed thigh. A few more heads waggled in our direction. The boots she had worn the day before had obscured two of Anne Corley's most notable assets.

"Hello, Beau," she said. Elbows propped on the arms of the chair, she rested her chin on clasped fingers and regarded me with a level, gray-eyed appraisal. "You've been busy."

"Peters and I have had our hands full," I admitted. "Have you had lunch yet?"

She shook her head. I hurried to my feet in hopes I could spirit her out of the building before Peters returned from his debriefing. It didn't work. He caught us in the elevator lobby. There wasn't much I could do but invite him to join us. I'd as soon have bit my tongue, and I could have belted him for not saying a polite no-thank-you. Now I owed him two.

It was still misting out. We walked to a little Italian place in Pioneer Square. Anne was able to talk enzymes knowledgeably enough even though she didn't seem particularly prone to eat them. As a dedicated processor of junk food, I couldn't hold my own in that conversation. She and Peters hit it off, making me more than a little resentful. I was also painfully aware that he was much closer in age to Anne than I was. They chatted amiably and laughed, while I did a slow burn through lunch that had nothing to do with indigestion. Peters was the life of the party. I wanted to choke him.

Toward the end of the meal, he leaned back in his chair and said, "Beau says you're working on a book?" I had made the mistake of mentioning it to him.

Anne gave Peters a clear-eyed look that nonetheless put distance between them. "I come at this through the eyes of the victims. That's the name of my book, *Victims*. How do children become victims, and what happens to them or their families afterward? I had some personal experiences with that sort of thing in my own family. I've made a lifelong study of it."

"You make it sound as though you've been working on this book for quite a while."

"I have," Anne said. "All over the country."

"Making any money at it?" Peters asked. There was a classic cut to her clothing, elegant and expensive. They spoke of style as well as money.

Anne laughed, easily, comfortably. "If I were in it for the money, I'd have quit a long time ago. No, it's strictly a labor of love." The laughter disappeared from her face. She regarded Peters seriously. "Why do you think Angela Barstogi is dead?"

Peters shrugged. "No logical reason; she just is."

The light dawned slowly. I'm not a fast learner. Hearing Anne questioning Peters about the case, I realized that I had been nothing more to Anne Corley than part of her pet research project. It was an ego-bruising realization. I reached for the check, ignoring the fact that neither Anne's nor Peters' coffee cup was empty.

I walked too fast, making it difficult for Anne to keep up. Let her dawdle along with Peters, I fumed. She probably had a whole string of questions to ask him. As for me, I had better things to do with my time than answer questions for some half-baked author. I felt suckered, used. I squirmed a little too. I remembered the previous evening's dinnertime topic. I had shot my mouth off royally, all the time thinking Anne Corley was interested in me when in fact she had only been fishing for information. It would have been easier for me to handle if I had been a rookie. No veteran cop should have been so stupid.

Peters and Anne caught up with me in the elevator lobby on the first floor. Peters excused himself because he had to run an errand. I waited for the notoriously slow elevators, fervently wishing one would come quickly so I could escape Anne Corley's quizzical look.

"Are you angry?" she asked, her question unnervingly direct.

"No," I said quickly, defensively. "Of course not. Why should I be?"

"But you are," she replied.

A bell rang and a door opened. People filed into an elevator, but I didn't. "Yes," I admitted at last. "You're right. I am angry."

"Why?" she asked.

"It's a long story," I answered. "I thought you were . . . Well, I mean I . . ."

"Why aren't you listed in the phone book?" she asked. "I changed my mind about the drink after I dropped you off, but there was no way to call you."

"I'm a homicide detective. We don't have listed numbers." I felt a momentary flash of pleasure that she had tried to call me, but then I remembered her subterfuge and was angry all over again. Another elevator showed up, and I made as if to get on it. She put one hand on my wrist. Her touch nailed my feet to the lobby floor.

"I'm not here about the Barstogi case, Beau," she said. "I came because I wanted to see you."

"Come on, Anne, there's no fool like an old fool. I've been saying that to myself all day. If you want to ask questions, do it aboveboard. Don't play games."

"Will you meet me after work?" she asked.

"Do you want me to bring Peters? We're both working the case." I couldn't resist a dig.

She responded in kind. "Bring a chaperone if you want, but that wasn't what I had in mind."

I swallowed the bait like a starving mackerel. "Where?" I asked.

"Meet me in the lobby of the Four Seasons," she said. "We can have a drink there. About five-thirty."

She turned and walked away. I missed the next elevator fair and square. In fact, I might have stood in the lobby for the rest of the afternoon if Peters hadn't come through and dragged me back to the fifth floor.

The phone on my desk was ringing. "Hello, J. P." Maxwell Cole said. "You didn't return my call."

"You noticed," I observed dryly. "You know I can't talk to you directly. Lay off it."

"Who is she? The car is owned by a law firm in Phoenix, Arizona, and they won't tell me anything."

"I won't tell you anything either, Max. You're barking up the wrong tree."

"Come on, give. You left with her."

"It was strictly social, I can assure you. Had nothing to do with the case, if that's what you're getting at."

"If it was strictly social as you say, tell me who she is."

"Go piss up a rope, Maxey," I told him, and I hung up.

The sole advantage of going to lunch at two-fifteen is there's not a whole hell of a lot of day left when you get back. Maxwell Cole had good sources. The Department of Motor Vehicles gave me the same information he had, the name of a law firm in Phoenix. I called and got a chilly reception from the lady who answered the phone. "Mr. Ames handles Mrs. Corley's affairs," she said, "but I have been instructed to give out no information."

"This is a very serious matter," I said. "I'm investigating a homicide."

"Give me your name, then, and Mr. Ames will get back to you."

"Don't you want the number?"

"No. If you really work for the Seattle Police Department, we'll be able to get your number through information."

My phone rang a few minutes later, and a Ralph Ames introduced himself as Anne Corley's attorney. "You'll have to forgive my receptionist, Detective Beaumont," he said. "Yours was the second call on Mrs. Corley we've had this afternoon. The first one didn't check out."

"Was his name Maxwell Cole?"

"As a matter of fact, it was."

"And he tried to pass himself off as a cop?"

"Well, as an investigator of some kind."

"He's a member of the local press."

"I figured as much," Ralph Ames laughed. "Now, what can I do for you?"

"As I told your receptionist, I'm working on a homicide and—"

"Excuse me for interrupting, Detective Beaumont, but let me guess. You're working on the murder of a young child, and you're trying to figure out why Anne Corley came to the funeral, right?"

"That's exactly right, Mr. Ames."

"She's working on a book. She's been working on it for several years. I get calls like this all the time."

"Yes, she told me about the book," I said, relieved. "Still, I have to check things out. It's my job."

"That's quite all right, Detective Beaumont. This is my job too. Is there anything else I can help you with?"

"No. Nothing I can think of. Thanks."

"Anytime," he said. He hung up.

I waited while Peters finished taking a call from Hammond, Indiana. Yes, Brodie had been investigated in the bludgeoning death of one of his parishioners two years earlier, but he had never been indicted. The case was still open.

There wasn't a whole lot more we could do then, so we took off about four-thirty and went by the Warwick to check on Carstogi. He told us he had made plane reservations for the following morning. Peters went down to the lobby for a telephone huddle with Watkins to see what he thought about Carstogi returning to Chicago. While Peters was out of the room, Carstogi told me he planned to go to a movie that night. There are at least six theaters within walking distance of the Warwick, not counting the porno flicks. I didn't see any reason why he shouldn't go.

As I opened the door to let Peters back into the room, he signaled everything was okay. "You'll keep us posted on how to get in touch with you once you get home?" Peters asked.

"Sure thing," Carstogi said agreeably. He seemed to be in good spirits, all things considered. We left him to his own devices. His close encounter with Michael Brodie's fist had pretty much taken the wind out of his sails.

Peters drove off in his Datsun. I hurried to my apartment and put on a clean shirt; then I caught the free bus back up to the Four Seasons. I didn't tell Peters I was going to meet Anne Corley. I was afraid he'd want to tag along.

CHAPTER 11

Walking into the Four Seasons was like walking into a foreign country. Each marbled floor, gleaming chandelier, polished brass rail, and overstuffed chair belonged to another time and place. It all spelled money. The best Italian marble. The best Irish wool for the carpet. "Anne must be quite at home here," I said to myself.

I wandered through the spacious lobby into the Garden Court. The tables were occupied either by takers of tea in the English tradition or drinkers of booze in the American tradition. Some tables included both. Late-afternoon sun had breached the cloud cover and sparkled through an expanse of arched windows that formed one entire wall of the massive room. Anne Corley was seated at a tiny table in a far corner, her face framed by a halo of sunlight shining through her hair.

Her eyes met mine as I entered the room. I declined the services of the maître d' and made my way to the table. So what if she only wanted to pump me for information? I was willing to trade information for the chance to be with Anne Corley. On the table before her sat two glasses, one with white wine and ice and the other with MacNaughton's and water. Pump away.

"Been here long?" I asked, taking a seat.

She shook her head. The room was crowded. There was a line of people waiting to be seated. "Did you have reservations here too?"

She smiled and nodded. "Reservations make things simpler." She examined my face. "Have you cooled off?"

"I guess. I'm here."

She laughed. "You don't look too happy about it."

I sipped my drink, disturbingly aware of her eyes studying my face. I had the strange sensation that she was burrowing into my mind and decoding the romantic delusions I had manufactured around her. It was at once both pleasant and uncomfortable.

"You didn't bring Peters," she observed.

"No, I decided I could handle the assignment on my own. I'm a big boy now."

"What does a girl have to do to show you that she's interested? Hit you over the head? I find you very attractive, Detective J. P. Beaumont. Is that so hard to believe?"

"Look," I said impatiently. "I told you this afternoon, I don't play games. I'll talk to you about the case as long as what I tell you in no way jeopardizes the investigation. You don't have to pretend I'm some latter-day heartthrob to do it."

She smiled again. "Actually, you sound like a maiden aunt who has just been invited up to see some nonexistent etchings. Let me assure you, my intentions are entirely honorable."

I didn't mean to sound quite so self-righteous. I laughed. "That bad, eh?"

She nodded. The waitress came by with offers of fresh drinks, but Anne waved her away. "I've thought about you all day," she said quietly. "You're really quite pleasant to be with. I realized that after I dropped you off last night."

I could feel a flush creeping up the back of my neck. "That was a compliment," she added. "You're supposed to say thank you."

"Thank you," I murmured.

"You're welcome." Her eyes sparkled with humor. For a time we sat without speaking, listening to the sound of talk and laughter, to the tinkling of leaded glassware that filled the room. It was a companionable silence. I appreciated the fact that neither of us grilled the other about their past. It was enough to be together right then. Eventually she emptied her glass and stood up. "Let's go," she said. "I can only sit around for so long without doing something."

I reached for my wallet, but Anne shook her head. "I already took care of it."

She paused in the lobby long enough to remove a pair of battered Nikes from an Adidas carryall. Her navy pumps disappeared into the cavernous bag.

"Where to?" I asked as she stood up.

"Let's just walk," she replied, and we did. It's unusual for someone with a car to get out and walk like that. We covered the whole of downtown, from Freeway Park to the waterfront. She set a brisk pace and maintained it regardless of the steeply pitched inclines. We walked and talked. She asked nothing about Angela Barstogi, nor did we delve into matters personal. The conversation ranged over a world of topics, from politics to religion, from economics to music. Anne Corley was well read and could hold her own on any number of subjects.

Her mood wasn't as mercurial as it had been the day before. She told wry jokes and laughed at her own punch lines. We wound up at a small Greek restaurant halfway up Queen Anne Hill. We finished dinner about ten-thirty. I bought. My ego needed that hit.

As we left the restaurant, we paused outside to admire a full moon rising behind the Space Needle. She slipped her hand under my arm, her touch both casual and electrifying.

"What now?" she asked.

"A nightcap at my place?" I suggested.

"I'd like that," she replied.

We cut through Seattle Center and walked the seven or eight blocks to my building with her hand still resting on my arm. My mind was doing an inventory of my apartment. How much of a mess was it? Had I picked up the scatter of dirty socks and shirts that often litters the living room? For sure the bed wasn't made. It never is.

The Royal Crest isn't quite as luxurious as its name would imply. We entered the lobby. I tried to look at it through the eyes of a lady with a Porsche. Not that bad, I decided, but it could be better. I was grateful none of my lavender-haired cronies were still in the lobby. Some of them watched the closed-circuit channel twenty-four hours a day, however, and they consider it a sacred charge to know who comes and goes. My bringing home a female visitor would keep the gossip mills running for days.

I pushed open the door and let Anne lead the way into 1106. I didn't turn on the lights. She went straight to the window to look at the downtown skyline. I came to the window and stood beside her. A delicate perfume lingered around her, the same scent that had entranced me the day before at the cemetery. She was as transfixed by the view as I was by her. Her skin reflected back the golden glow of the city lights. The play of light and shadow gave her beauty a haunting quality.

The impulse was more than I could resist. I reached up and ran my finger along her jawline. Her skin was smooth and cool. She made no move away from me. Instead, she turned toward the touch, allowing my finger to retrace its path down her cheek. I felt my throat constrict. "Hello there," I said huskily.

"Hello, yourself," she replied. I took her in my arms and kissed her, feeling her mouth moist and welcoming on mine. I crushed her to me, awed by her response, her willingness.

Self-imposed celibacy is fine as far as it goes, but once you break training, months of deprivation take over. Every sensation is heightened. We
were frantic for release. Each kiss was more demanding than the one
before. Anne didn't shrink before my onslaught. She matched me move for
move, her need as deep and overwhelming as my own.

My hands were trembling with urgency as I fumbled with the top button on her blouse. The ruffled material fell away, revealing the deep hollow
of her throat. I kissed her there and felt her response in a sharp intake of
breath. Two more buttons revealed her breasts, firm and tense with excitement beneath a lacy bra. She pushed my hands away. "Let me do that," she
whispered. With swift, deft movements she undid the remaining buttons
and slipped off the jacket, blouse, skirt, and bra. She returned to my arms
clothed only in the glow from the downtown skyline.

I had removed my tie and jacket, but not the regulation .38 I carry in
a shoulder holster under my left arm. She nestled against my chest. Most
women, encountering the pistol for the first time, express something—
surprise mostly, dismay sometimes, sometimes repulsion. Anne showed
none of these. Her fingers strayed easily across the metal handle, then settled on the small of my back. This time her lips sought mine, sought them,
found them, made them her own.

I put my hand on her chin and pushed her away from me. "I thought
you said your intentions were honorable."

"I thought you said not to play games," she replied matter-of-factly.

I wasn't prepared to argue the point. I kissed her again, letting my
tongue explore at will, learning each corner of her, each curve and crevice.
I could probably get away with saying I took her there in the living room
on the floor, but it wouldn't be the truth. She took me every bit as much
as I took her, maybe more. Her body arched to meet mine, her fingers in
my back spurred me, goaded me. My need and her need melded into one,
and when the climax came, I heard an aching sob escape her lips. I kissed
her cheek. It was wet with tears.

I moved away from her and lay on my side, watching her, "I didn't
mean to make you cry," I said.

She snuggled against me, nestling her back into the curve of my body,
placing my hand so it rested on the sloping fullness of her breast. "I didn't
expect it to be that good. It hasn't been that good in a long time."

We lay like that together, letting the aftermath of our lovemaking
slowly dissolve around us. She lay so still, I thought she had dozed off. My
arm went to sleep. When I tried to move her to one side, she rolled away
from me and stood up. "Do you have a robe I could wear?" she asked.

I dragged two of them out of the closet, one for her and one for me.
Considering we had just made love, it was silly to be self-conscious, but

we both were. The one I gave her was huge when she tied it around her slender frame. She rolled the sleeves up a turn or two so her hands showed. "I offered you a drink," I said. "You want one now?"

All trace of tears was gone. She smiled mischievously. "No thanks, I already have what I came for."

I grabbed her arm and swung her toward me. "Why, you little vixen," I said. "You ought to be ashamed of yourself."

"I'm not," she said. She gave me a glancing kiss, slipping away from me at the same time. I poured a drink for myself and turned on the lights. I watched with some amusement as she padded barefoot around the room, examining my decorator-dictated knickknacks as well as the pictures of Kelly and Scott on the wall in the entryway.

"Your kids?" she asked.

I nodded. "They're both in high school now. They live in California with their mother."

"How long have you been divorced?" she asked.

"Long time. Five years."

"Girlfriends?"

"I'd like to think I've got one now," I said. "What about you?"

She settled cross-legged on the couch, pulling the robe demurely around her. "I'm a widow. My husband died ten years ago." She regarded me seriously. "I've had too much money to be able to tell who my friends are, to say nothing of lovers."

"You're a little young to be a widow."

"I was a lot younger ten years ago." She didn't offer to divulge her age and I didn't ask, although she couldn't have been more than thirty, thirty-two at the outside. She sat there looking off into space. She had a way of mentally going off by herself that I found disconcerting. When she came back to the present she was looking directly into my eyes. "Are you going to ask me to spend the night, or do I have to get dressed and go home?"

I almost choked on a very small sip of MacNaughton's. "Would you like to spend the night?"

"Yes," she replied. She waited for me to finish my drink; then I led her into the bedroom. I squirmed that the bed wasn't made, but she wasn't paying attention to the furniture. She loosened the tie of the robe, letting it fall open. She pulled my hands inside it, wrapping them around her until I could feel the smooth swell of her breasts against my chest.

"Please," she whispered.

We did.

CHAPTER 12

Through a sleepy haze, I sensed someone touching me. It was soft and teasing. I thought I was having one of my famous Beaumont dreams. Then I smelled her hair and felt warm lips on mine.

"What are you doing?" I mumbled.

"I'm getting you up," she whispered softly, her lips nibbling my ear.

"I think I am up."

"Ooh. So you are," she smiled.

I pulled her onto my chest, settled her on me, our bodies blending comfortably. My hands closed on her slender waist. I watched her face, her lips parting as her body caught fire. Her hunger was almost frightening in its intensity. We each made love as we had never made love before. In the quiet that followed, she wept. This time I didn't question her tears. I was grateful for them. This time I thought I knew what they meant.

She was resting on my chest, our heartbeats just then slowing, when the phone rang. It was Captain Powell. He was frantic. "Get your ass down here."

I struggled to see the clock. It was a little before five. "What's up?" I asked. The phone cord tangled in Anne's hair, and I struggled to untangle it and listen at the same time.

"They're dead. Brodie and the woman are dead! Somebody found them both at the church."

I eased away from Anne. "Both of them? Have you called Peters?"

"Yeah. He's on his way."

"Tell him to meet me at the Warwick. I'll go there to check on Carstogi."

"You'd better have him under wraps, Beaumont."

I looked out the bedroom window and could see the silhouette of the Warwick against a gradually graying sky. "Snug as a bug," I said lightly.

"I hope to God you're right," Powell muttered, "for your sake and mine."

Anne Corley was wide awake by the time I hung up the telephone. Wrapped in the voluminous robe, she looked wonderful, with that special glow a woman's skin has after lovemaking. "Good morning," she said, smiling.

I kissed her on the forehead, barely pausing in my headlong rush to the shower. "I've got to hurry."

"Trouble?" she asked.

I nodded. "Emergency call. I need to be out of here in about ten minutes." I left her standing in the bedroom and hurried into the bathroom. By the time I finished showering and shaving I could smell coffee. A steaming cup was waiting for me on the dresser. Anne Corley was back in bed, propped on a pillow, coffee mug in hand. She watched me thoughtfully as I dressed.

"Can you tell me what happened?" she asked.

"No." I planted a quick kiss on her forehead as I sat on the bed to pull on my shoes. "Thanks for the coffee," I added.

"Consider it payment in kind for services rendered." I looked at her, gray eyes alive with laughter over the top of her cup. She had evidently taken no offense at my not telling her what was going on. I appreciated that. "Do you mind if I stay for a while, or do you want me to leave when you do?" she asked.

"Make yourself at home," I said. "Stay as long as you like."

She lay back on the pillows, luxuriating. "Thanks. Any idea when you'll be done?"

"None whatsoever." I shrugged my way into the shoulder holster and pulled on a jacket. I bent over her. She pulled me down on the bed beside her and gave me a lingering kiss. I wanted to crawl back into bed with her and forget the world, the department, everything.

"Thank you," she whispered.

"You're more than welcome." Reluctantly I pulled myself away. There was no mistaking that what had passed between us had been good for both of us. "You're a very special lady," I said as I straightened up to leave.

Euphoria lasted for a little over three minutes. I rode down the elevator in my building, walked the half block to the Warwick, and rode that elevator up to the seventh floor. I knocked on Carstogi's door to no avail. When he didn't answer the third barrage of hammering, I went looking for a night clerk, who used his passkey to let me into the room. Carstogi wasn't there. The bedspread was rumpled, as though someone had lain on top of it to watch TV for a while, but the bed had not been slept in.

I left the room as I found it and returned to the hall, where the night clerk hovered nervously, wringing his hands. He was anxious about adverse publicity. I assured him that whatever had happened was no reflection on the Warwick. Asking him to keep me informed of any developments, I went downstairs to wait for Peters. I had the sickening feeling that we'd been suckered, that Carstogi had played us for a couple of fools.

Peters' Datsun screeched to a stop about the time I hit the plate glass door. He hadn't taken time to go by the department for another car. I gave him a couple of points for that.

"Carstogi's not here," I said, folding my legs into the cramped front seat. "We'd better go straight to Faith Tabernacle."

Two uniformed cops were standing guard when we got there, holding off a horde of media ambulance chasers, to say nothing of neighborhood curiosity seekers. We hadn't discussed it during the drive to Ballard, but I knew that getting the recorder out of Faith Tabernacle undetected was imperative. Whatever was on it would be totally inadmissible as evidence, but it might provide vital information. Information that would lead us to the killer.

We found Suzanne Barstogi near the pulpit at the front of the church. She lay on her left side with one leg half curled beneath her, as though she had been rising and turning toward her assailant when the bullet felled her. She was still wearing the same dowdy dress she had been wearing earlier in the day. It had been ripped from neck to waist. Her bra had been torn in two, exposing overripe breasts. In addition to the bullet hole that punctured her left breast, her upper torso was covered with bloody welts. Before she died, Suzanne Barstogi had been the victim of a brutal beating.

There was little visible impact damage. The bullet had entered cleanly enough, but behind her, where the emerging slug had crashed out of her body, Suzanne Barstogi's lifeblood was splattered and pooled on the pulpit and altar of the Faith Tabernacle.

Peters looked at her for a long time. "He didn't nickel-dime-around, did he?"

No one was in the church with us right then, but they would be soon. Peters quickly retrieved the recorder and put it in his pocket. We found Pastor Michael Brodie in the middle of his study. He was sprawled face-down and naked on the blood-soaked carpet. Peters and I theorized that he had heard noises in the church and come to investigate. Again there was only one bullet hole.

Shooting at such close range doesn't require a tremendous amount of marksmanship, but you've got to be tough. Tough and ruthless. A hand shaking out of control can cause a missed target at even the shortest distance. Then there's always the chance that the victim will make a desperate lunge for the gun and turn it on his attacker. And then there's the mess.

"I would have bet even money that Carstogi wouldn't pull something like this," I said.

"I hate to be the one to break this to you, Beau, but you did bet money. We both did. Our asses are on the line on this one. Your friend Max will see to it. You just hide and watch."

There's an almost religious ceremony in approaching a crime scene. First is the establishment of the scene parameters. In this case, to be on the safe side, we included the entire church. Then come the evidence technicians with their cameras and measurements. They ascertain distances, angles, trajectories. They look for trace evidence that may be helpful later. The secret, of course, is approaching the scene with a slow deliberation that disturbs nothing. This is one place where peons take precedence over rank. Sergeant Watkins paced in the background, observing the technicians' careful, unhurried efforts.

The medical examiner himself, the white-haired Dr. Baker, arrived before the technicians were finished. He made the official pronouncement of death. A double homicide was worthy of his visible, personal touch. Considering the accumulation of people, I was grateful Peters had gotten the chance to stash the recorder when he did.

A uniformed officer told Watkins that the church members were gathering outside and wanted to come in. What should he tell them? The sergeant directed him to assemble them in the fellowship hall, where we could once more begin the interviewing process.

I was a little puzzled when I saw the whole Faith Tabernacle group, as much as I remembered them, file into the room. After all, it was Tuesday morning and presumably some of them should have gone to work. It turned out that they had been scheduled to be there at five o'clock for a celebration breakfast. It was the traditional ending to a successful Purification Ceremony, and would have marked the end of Suzanne Barstogi's ordeal of silence, fasting, and prayer.

Without Brodie's looming presence in the background to enforce silence, it was easier to get people to talk. It was plain that they were shocked by what had happened, and talking seemed to help. They were getting better at it.

The cook, a True Believer named Sarah Norris, had come to church at four to start preparing breakfast, which was due after a prayer session at five. Before early-morning services, she had been in the habit of taking a cup of coffee to Brodie in his study. It was when she took him his coffee that she had found first his body and then Suzanne's.

We were about finished with Sarah when the front-door cop came hurrying into the room. "You'd better come quick. Powell said to call him on a telephone, not the radio, and to make it snappy."

The only phone available at the church was in the study. If Powell didn't want us to use the radio for privacy reasons, the study was no better. We got in Peters' car and drove to the first available pay phone.

"What's up?" I asked as soon as Powell came on the line.

"The night clerk from the Warwick, that's what. He says Carstogi came back and tried to go to his room. He's got him down in the restaurant eating breakfast and wonders what he should do."

"Get a couple of uniformed officers over there to keep him there for as long as it takes us to drive from Ballard."

"They're on their way, but why do I have this sneaking suspicion that you've screwed up, Beaumont?"

"Experience," I told him, and slammed the phone receiver down in his ear. I turned back to the car to see Maxwell Cole's rust-colored Volvo idling behind Peters' Datsun. "Shit."

I climbed into the car. "Sorry," Peters said. "He must have tailed us when we left the church. I didn't see him."

"It's too late now. Drive like hell to the Warwick. Carstogi's in the restaurant having breakfast."

Peters' jaw dropped in surprise. "No shit! Why would he go back there?"

"Beats me, but he did, and we'd better nab him before he gets away. Thank God the night clerk had brains enough to call and let us know." I glanced at Peters, who was looking in the rearview mirror. "Max still on our butt?" I asked.

"Yes."

"We'll just have to lump it. We don't have time to try to throw him off the trail. I don't want Carstogi to slip through our fingers."

"The gun has a way of equalizing things, doesn't it? Yesterday Carstogi was no match for Brodie when they were dealing with fists."

"You've already decided he's our man?"

"Haven't you?" Peters asked.

"No, I haven't. I like to think I'm a better judge of character than that. Carstogi wanted to kill Brodie, but he would have taken Suzanne back in a minute. You heard him yesterday."

"Well, who did it then?" Peters asked. It was a good question. We didn't have an answer by the time we stopped in front of the Warwick. Two patrol cars with flashing lights were outside the hotel, one parked in front of the garage on Fourth and the other at the front door on Lenora. We stopped by the front door.

The clerk met us at the car, the story bubbling out before Peters turned off the engine. "He came up to the desk, said he needed a wake-up call at ten. I didn't want him to go up to his room, so I told him we had a problem with the plumbing and that we'd buy his breakfast in the restaurant while we cleaned up the mess. I didn't know what else to do. I called right away, because you said it was important."

"Thanks," I said. "That was good thinking."

"Where is he now?" Peters asked.

The Volvo stopped across the street. I went back to an officer who was standing near the front door. "Don't let that yahoo in here," I said, pointing at Cole, who was just climbing out of the car.

The dining room at the Warwick is small and intimate. At that hour of the morning it was just filling up with tables of visiting businessmen and conventioneers. Andrew Carstogi had been placed at a small corner table. The hostess watched him nervously from her desk. Peters pulled his gun and put it in his jacket pocket. We approached the table warily.

Carstogi looked up and saw us coming toward him. He grinned and waved at us with an empty fork. "Hi, guys," he said.

"Where have you been?" Peters asked.

Carstogi's grin faded. "Out. Just got back. They told me there's a problem with the room and they're buying me breakfast while they fix it. Good deal."

"Out to where?" Peters continued.

"What is this?" Carstogi asked. "I went to a movie, and I met a girl. There's nothing the matter with that."

"What's her name?" I put in. "Where did you take her?"

"We went to her place. Jesus, how am I supposed to know where it is? What's going on? Why all the questions?"

"How did you get back here?"

"I caught a cab."

"Which one?"

Carstogi stood up. "Okay, I'm not saying another word until you tell me what's going on."

People around us were staring. We were creating a disturbance. "Sit," Peters hissed. We sat.

"We have two brand-new murders," Peters said. "Two homicides at Faith Tabernacle."

The color drained from Andrew Carstogi's face. "Not Suzanne," he whispered.

I nodded. "Suzanne and Brodie both. Sometime during the night. Now tell us, how'd you get back here from wherever you were."

Carstogi opened his mouth to say something and then shut it. Two gigantic tears rolled down his face. He brushed them away with his sleeve. "I caught a cab," he said.

"What kind? Yellow? Graytop?"

"I don't know. Just a cab. It picked me up at her house. I think it was the same cab as last night, but I'm not sure." He looked back and forth from one of us to the other. "It's not true, is it? Tell me it's not true."

"It's true," I said.

"Do you mind if we go through your room?" Peters asked.

Carstogi shook his head mutely. Peters signaled to an officer who had stationed himself next to the hostess's desk. "Have the desk clerk let you into his room to check it out," he instructed. "Let me know if you find anything." The officer hurried away. Carstogi's shoulders heaved with noisy sobs. Peters and I watched, saying nothing. Eventually, he regained control.

"Am I under arrest?" he asked.

"No, but as of now I'm afraid you're the sole suspect."

"But I never went near the church after we left there yesterday. I wouldn't know how to get there."

The officer returned to say that the room was clean. Carstogi looked from one of us to the other. "What's going to happen?" he asked.

I pushed back my chair. "Let's go up to your room and get a statement from you. Do you want an attorney present?"

"I don't need one," he said. "I didn't do it."

I believed him. I just wished that things were always that simple. We led him upstairs and took his statement. Carstogi answered all our questions willingly enough. According to him he had gone to a porno house and had been picked up by a prostitute after the movie.

I don't think Carstogi really grasped that the only thing between him and a first-degree murder charge was a prostitute whose name was Gloria, most assuredly not the name her mommy gave her. He couldn't remember her address, and the description he gave us would have fit half the females in the U.S. Average height, kind of light brown hair, lightish eyes, slim. Carstogi's life was hanging by a slender thread.

We turned off the recorder and stood up to leave. "Are you arresting me?" he asked.

"No, not now, but don't leave here. Stay in the room and don't talk to anyone."

"Okay," he said. "I just can't believe she's dead."

"Believe it," Peters said.

We left the room. "We should book him, Beau," Peters said to me in the hall. "Motive, opportunity. It all adds up. What if he splits?"

"Come on, Peters. We don't have a shred of solid evidence. Nothing more than the fact that he doesn't have an alibi for last night. The girl was probably some hooker off Aurora. You know how easy finding her will be."

"But you intend to look?" Peters regarded me wearily, shaking his head.

"That's right," I answered. We rode down in the elevator without saying anything more.

Maxwell Cole was in the lobby, arguing with the officer stationed at the registration desk, his walruslike face twitching with exasperation. "What's going on, J. P.? This asshole wouldn't spring with any information."

"Good," I said. "Neither will I. Pass the word."

Peters directed one of the uniformed officers to keep an eye on the seventh floor. He nodded and waved.

Cole blustered out of the lobby after us. "I want to know what's going on. Two innocent people have been slaughtered in cold blood. You owe the people of Seattle an explanation."

I turned on him. "I owe the people of Seattle a full day's work for a full day's pay. I don't owe you a fucking thing." The other cop heard this exchange with a poorly concealed grin. "If he gives you any trouble, lock him up," I said as I stalked away.

Peters moved his car to a parking meter and plugged it. We had decided to go up to my apartment and see what kind of fish our hidden recorder might have hooked.

CHAPTER 13

It was only as we rounded the corner of Lenora onto Third that I remembered Anne was in my apartment. My mind had switched tracks completely, and now I didn't know what to do. I decided I'd better call her from the lobby and give her some warning of her impending company.

She seemed pleased to hear my voice. "I'm downstairs," I said. "I'm bringing Peters up with me."

"Who was that?" Peters asked with a conspiratorial grin as we got on the elevator. "Anybody I know?"

"As a matter of fact, you do know her. It's Anne, Anne Corley."

"Why you closemouthed son-of-a-bitch! I got the impression at lunch yesterday that you and she had just met. How long have you been holding out on me?"

The elevator door opened on eight. "Can it!" I snapped as Wanda Jamison got on, coffee cup in hand. She was on her way for a morning coffee klatch with Ida, my next-door neighbor. Wanda and I exchanged idle pleasantries while Peters continued to leer at me over her head.

If I thought Anne would have used the lead time to change out of my robe, I was sadly mistaken. She didn't. I was glad I waited until Ida's door was safely closed before I knocked on my own. Anne opened the door and gave Peters a gracious welcome, as though her being there in a state of relative undress were the most natural thing in the world. She was totally at ease, and Peters was getting a real charge out of my discomfort.

Peters made himself some tea while I paced the confines of my tiny kitchen. "What do you suggest we do with her while we listen to the tape?" he asked.

"I give up." I was long on embarrassment and short on ideas right then. I had told Anne she could stay as long as she liked, but I couldn't have her in the room while Peters and I listened to our illicit tape.

Peters carried his cup into the living room. He took my chair. I sat on the couch next to a cross-legged Anne. It disturbed me to be next to her. I wanted to touch her, but not in front of Peters. I didn't want to soften my image—whatever was left of it.

Peters looked at Anne. "Do you mind if we play a tape?"

Anne contemplated Peters with her direct, gray gaze. "Do you want me to leave? I can go in the other room."

Peters glanced in my direction, then nodded. "I'd appreciate it."

Obligingly, Anne rose. "I'll go get dressed then," she said. Much to my dismay, she leaned over and gave me a familiar peck on the cheek as she went by. The robe fell open, allowing me a fleeting glimpse of flesh and curve.

Once she was out of the room, Peters pointed an accusing finger at me. "You asshole," he said. "If you'd told me yesterday, I never would have tagged along with you to lunch."

I didn't feel like explaining that, yesterday at lunch, I hadn't known either. "Play the tape, Peters," I said wearily. "Just play the tape."

He did.

At first there were indistinguishable noises, openings and closings of doors that weren't followed by sufficient noise to keep the recorder running. Eventually, however, there was a murmur of voices punctuated by coughs and clearings of throats, the sounds of a fitful crowd settling itself. Then Pastor Michael Brodie's voice, stentorian and clear, filled my tiny living room.

"Brethren, we come together this evening as Believers in the one True Faith, as Partakers of the one True Life. We are the chosen generation, a royal priesthood. Are there any here who doubt that we are the People of God?" There was a pause with no answer. Brodie's voice was that of a born orator sounding a call to arms.

"We have come to this place as strangers and pilgrims. There are none of us here who did not once walk in lasciviousness and lust. Our Lord did not come to call the righteous. He came to call the sinners, and those of us who have seen and heard are here, Brothers and Sisters. We are here! Praise God." A chorus of amens echoed on the tape.

"Are we going to have to listen to the whole fucking sermon?" Peters asked.

"Looks that way," I told him.

"We have spoken many times how, in the early days, the Romans were the law of the land. In Romans 7:4 it says, 'Wherefore, my brethren, ye also are become dead to the law by the body of Christ.' Let there be no mistake about it. That means that once we are in Christ, once we have set ourselves firmly on His path, we are dead to the law of the land. We are apart from it. It has nothing to do with us. And when we return to the law of the Romans, the law of the flesh, we turn our backs on The Way, for it is impossible to live in the world of the flesh and the world of the spirit at the same time.

"The scripture goes on to say, 'For when we were in the flesh, the motions of sins, which were by the law, did work in our members to bring forth fruit unto death. But now we are delivered from the law, that being dead wherein we were held; that we should serve in newness of spirit, and not in the oldness of the letter.'

"Did you hear that, Brothers and Sisters? Did you hear that? It says we are delivered from the law. Delivered! Cut loose! Living under the Roman law shackles us, delivers us to death. It is only by living completely and totally in our newness of spirit that we find Life, Life Everlasting." Again we heard the echoing amens.

"He's really tuning up now. Getting into his act."

"Shut up, Peters. I'm trying to listen."

". . . was in this newness of spirit that we made the leap of faith that brought us here to this city. It took courage for each of us to leave the old ways behind. Each of us left friends and family and possessions. We all made sacrifices to be here, trusting that we had found the True Pathway to Christ. In doing so, each of us has taken a vow to lean not on our own understanding. We have sworn to be subject one to another, to submit ourselves to the elders, to humble ourselves under the mighty hand of God that He may exalt us in due time.

"We have found that there are those who would revile us for mortifying our members, who falsely accuse us of evil when in fact we who suffer for righteousness' sake are content and unafraid. There is one of our number here tonight who has brought herself to be purged of sin. In her hour of trial she turned from the teaching and cast herself back into the old ways, turning away from the Law of the Spirit to the carnal law. Sister Suzanne, will you rise and stand before the Brethren."

There was a pause and some audible shuffling in the congregation. "Last night, Sister Suzanne stood before you and confessed her sin, that when Angel, her worldly daughter, was missing, she secretly called the police, bringing the power of the Romans back into our midst.

"We know Jehovah has punished her for this act by taking Angel from her. We know, too, that for breaking her vows she could be Disavowed, cast away from the True Believers in disgrace. Last night she humbled herself before the elders and begged to be allowed to remain. Since yesterday morning at sunrise she has taken no food. She has prostrated herself in prayer at the altar of our Lord, begging His forgiveness, and ours as well.

"Last night, even as she prayed and wept, the elders met to consider her fate. I would like at this time for the elders to come forward." There was a shuffling noise and then quiet. ". . . elders stand before you. Brother Benjamin? Sister Suzanne has submitted herself to the elders for punishment. Have you made a decision?"

I remembered Benjamin's work-hardened muscles. "We have, Pastor Michael." I remembered his voice. It was Jeremiah's stepfather.

"And how do you judge?"

"By the stripes she shall be healed." The people in the room voiced their approval.

"Here it comes," Peters said.

"If our Lord who was without blemish or blame suffered the scourge for our sakes, then it is only right that we who are sinners should follow in His steps. Sister Suzanne, take comfort in the words given to the apostles who suffered and died in the service of our Lord. 'Beloved, think it not strange concerning the fiery trial which is to try you. But rejoice, inasmuch as ye are partakers of Christ's sufferings; that, when his glory shall be revealed, ye may be glad also with exceeding joy.' "

Amens were more fervent now as people were caught up in the spectacle. Even on the tape I could sense their excitement, the shuffling feet, the nervous coughs.

"It is written that 'the time is come that judgment must begin at the house of God: and if it first begin at us, what shall the end be of them that obey not the gospel of God? Wherefore let them that suffer according to the will of God commit the keeping of their souls to him.'

" 'Forasmuch then as Christ hath suffered for us in the flesh, arm yourself likewise with the same mind: for he that hath suffered in the flesh hath ceased from sin.'

"Sister Suzanne, cast all your care upon Him; for He careth for you. It says in First Peter 3:14, 'But and if ye suffer for righteousness' sake, happy are ye: and be not afraid of their terror, neither be troubled.'

"Do you come here willingly, Sister Suzanne?"

"I do."

"I'll just bet," Peters said.

Suzanne's response had been barely audible, but an exultant "Hallelu-jah" sprang from the crowd. Maybe if she had said no, that she had been forced, the ceremony would have been canceled and the True Believers would have been denied their blood lust. A baby cried somewhere in the background and was quickly hushed. So the children were there, watch-ing, listening. I thought of Jeremiah. No wonder he was afraid.

Brodie continued now, his tone no longer that of an orator, but gentler, cajoling, not wanting to frighten Suzanne into backing out at the last minute. "Do you know, too, that those who will smite you do so only as tools of your salvation, bearing you no malice or ill will?"

"I do."

"I think I'm going to puke," Peters said. "She really let them do it to her."

This time there was no sound from the True Believers. They were holding their collective breath in anticipation. This was the sword Brodie wielded over his congregation. Not only had he inflicted bodily punish-ments, he had provided them for the vicarious enjoyment of his followers. Sickened, I resumed listening. Brodie was speaking again, his tone mov-ing, hypnotic, molding her to his will. If Suzanne Barstogi would willingly hurt herself because Brodie asked, would she have resisted beating her own child?

' " 'Being reviled we bless; being persecuted we suffer it.' Will you then, Sister, bless and forgive each of those who stand here tonight to be the instruments of your redemption?"

"Yes." Her answer was nothing more than a whisper. The recorder detected no shifting, no sound from the crowd. They were ready.

"Brother Amos and Brother Ezra, hold her wrists." There was the sound of people moving. "Brother Benjamin, rend her garment." We heard the sound of her dress tearing, the snap of her brassiere, and then, after a pause, the sharp crack of a lash biting into flesh. Reflex made me count the blows, seven in all, each one slow and deliberate. Suzanne made one involuntary cry at the outset. After that she was silent.

The tape went on. There had been an outpouring of amens and hallelu-jahs, but now that was silenced. Brodie was speaking. "Sister Suzanne will spend yet another night in prayer, not in the Penitent's Room, but here, at the altar, where she can feel our Lord's forgiveness. In the morning we shall come again to welcome her return to the fold. Go with God. It is finished."

I heard some murmur of talk as people filed out. The next sound was that of someone weeping. "Suzanne?" Brodie's voice.

She made no response, although the weeping subsided. "Suzanne. Look at me. I have something for you. It'll make it hurt less." A pause, then he continued, his voice soft and cajoling. "Don't try to cover yourself from me, Sister. I've come to minister to your wounds. It's a local anesthetic."

Again the silence. I could imagine him running a fleshy finger across her bleeding breasts, administering some kind of ointment.

"Thank you," Suzanne said softly.

"I want you," he said.

"No, please." There was no audible spoken answer although we heard the sound of the study door closing. I was taken aback. He had asked, and Suzanne had denied him. Even the pastor himself was subject to some rules and prohibitions. It was obvious what kind of additional comfort and forgiveness he had intended to offer.

The tape clicked on and off, running only when there was sufficient sound in the room to sustain it. There was no way to tell how much time elapsed each time the voices stopped and started.

". . . of-a-bitch." The voice was a man's, muffled and indistinct. It sounded as though it might have been coming through a closed door, maybe the study.

I strained to hear. "Turn it up," I said to Peters, and he did.

"Get out!" I could recognize Brodie's voice.

The other man was speaking now. ". . . her alone. She's my wife, not one of your whores."

I heard the familiar menacing tone in Brodie's voice. "You seem to forget, my word is law here." The door slammed. The visitor's hard-soled shoes stormed through the sanctuary. The front door slammed heavily behind him.

Now we could hear the mumble of Suzanne's voice alone. It rose and fell. It was a prayer of some kind, but the words themselves escaped us. It continued for some time, on and off, intermittently reactivating the machine.

Then suddenly, sharply, ". . . t do you want?"

A sharp report of a pistol answered her, followed by the sound of an opening door. We could hear Brodie's voice. "What happened? Suzanne?" A gunshot was his answer too, followed by silence as the machine shut itself off.

The next voice was that of Sarah, the cook: ". . . my God," and the sound of hurrying footsteps. Then came the sound of another door and more footsteps, followed by Peters' voice: "He didn't nickel-dime-around, did he?" The recorder was switched off before anything further was said.

"That was Carstogi!" said Peters, his voice tense with excitement. "It has to be."

"How can you be sure?" I asked. "I don't think it sounds like him at all."

Just then Anne asked permission to return to the living room. She was wearing the same blue suit she had worn the day before, only now her hair was pulled back and fastened in an elaborate knot at the base of her neck. She looked like a ballerina. The similarity wasn't just in looks. I knew that her external beauty concealed the finely tuned, well-conditioned body of a professional dancer.

"Beau, I'm going to take off now," she said, moving toward the door. She nodded to Peters. "Nice to see you again, Ron."

Peters stood up apologetically. "I hope you're not leaving on my account."

She smiled. "No. I have lots to do."

I followed her to the door. "Can you come back tonight? I don't know what time I'll be back, but I can give you a key so you can let yourself in."

"Do you think you can trust me?" She was laughing as she asked the question. I rummaged through the kitchen junk drawer to locate my spare keys.

I handed them to Anne, and she dropped it into her jacket pocket. "Thanks," she said, giving me a quick peck on the cheek.

I walked with her to the elevator lobby, where she turned and kissed me, a full-blown invitational kiss that sent my senses reeling. The elevator door opened. There stood three of my neighbors.

"That wasn't fair," I protested.

"It wasn't, was it?" she agreed. The elevator door closed, and she was gone.

CHAPTER 14

Peters, still intent on the tape, was playing it again as I came back into the room. "So much of what Brodie says sounds like he's quoting directly from the Bible."

"Probably was. Taken out of context and given a forty-degree twist, you can use the Bible to justify almost anything."

Peters' tea was gone. I brought him another cup. We listened to the tape, not once but several times. "There's a clue in here somewhere, if we could just put our fingers on it," Peters said as he switched off the recorder for the last time. He stood up. "I guess we'd better get back over to Faith Tabernacle. The place is probably still crawling with people. Watty will be climbing the walls."

"What about Carstogi?" I asked.

"What about him? I'm sure the trail leads back to him one way or the other."

I remained unconvinced. I said, "Let's get a description of the hooker and put vice on it. Or maybe we could track down that cab."

"You're determined he didn't do it, aren't you? But you're right; we should check it out." Peters glanced down at the tiny machine in his hand. "What about this? Erase it?"

"No, don't. We'll want to listen to it again. If there's something in there that we're missing, maybe we'll catch it next time. Leave it here." I took the recorder from him and placed it in the top drawer of the occasional table beside my leather chair. "That way it won't leak into Cole's hands."

Back at Faith Tabernacle Sergeant Watkins was running the show, directing a small army of officers who scrutinized every inch of the church and took statements from anyone who looked remotely related to the case. At the moment we drove up, Watty was standing next to the front door, supervising a kneeling lab technician who was making a plaster cast of something behind a row of decorative bushes.

"What's up?" Peters asked him.

Watkins glowered at us. "Where the hell have you been?" He went on without waiting for an answer. "We found some tracks here. The footprints have been obliterated, but we should get good casts of the bicycle tires. Someone parked a bike here during the night."

"You think the killer used a bike for his getaway?" I asked, shaking my head.

"You have a better suggestion?" Watty snapped.

I had to admit I didn't have one. "Where's the father?" the sergeant asked.

"He's back at the Warwick. We've got a guard on him."

"A guard!" Watkins exploded. "What I want on him are cuffs and orange coveralls. We've got three people dead so far. We'd better arrest someone pretty goddamned soon."

"Carstogi didn't do it," I said.

"What? Are you his goddamned character witness? I understand he was out all night. Where was he?"

"He doesn't know."

"Doesn't know!"

"He went to the Palace for a sleazy, X-rated movie and got himself picked up by a hooker. He doesn't know where they went. He's from out of town."

Watkins examined my face as though he thought I was a raving lunatic. "That's the shakiest goddamned alibi I've heard this week!" He turned to Peters. "You agree with him, Detective Peters?"

Peters shifted uneasily under his gaze. "No," he said at last. "Beau and I differ on that score. I think Carstogi is our prime suspect."

Watty turned back to me, a look of smug satisfaction spreading over his face. "I'm glad somebody around here has some sense. Majority rules. Now I suggest you get off your ass and nail it down." He walked away.

Peters looked at me for a reaction. "He asked my opinion, Beau." It was part apology and part justification.

"That's why they have two detectives on this case, remember?" We went inside.

The bodies were gone and the crime lab folks were pretty much finished. One of them tossed Peters a bulging manila envelope. "You can cross robbery off the list of motives," he said. "There's seventeen thousand dollars in cash in that baby. It was in a bottom drawer in the study. We're taking it down to the department for safekeeping."

I went into the study. A well-thumbed and much-marked Bible lay open on the desk. I turned some of the pages. The marked passages were all of a vein similar to what we had heard on the tape. Nothing in Brodie's selections spoke of forgiveness or loving one's neighbor, to say nothing of one's enemies. Faith Tabernacle's leader had demanded retribution from his followers, had turned a blind eye on adultery. Someone had learned the lessons well and had given Brodie a taste of his own medicine. "Vengeance is mine" was the message. The Lord was excluded from the equation.

A halfhearted prayer service was continuing in the fellowship hall. The few True Believers who held jobs had not gone to work. Like bewildered sheep they huddled together for warmth, locked in a cell of interminable prayer, waiting for direction. Brodie had told them what to do and when to do it for a long time. Without him they had no idea how to function. I felt sorry for them. At the same time I felt repulsed. They had turned their lives and minds over to a monster masquerading as a messiah.

I saw Jeremiah. I tried to catch his eye in hopes I could get him to come talk to me. I think he saw me, but he studiously ignored me. Already someone had taken up Brodie's mantle and was pulling the strings.

Peters and I hit the street. We went back to Gay Avenue. Like the evidence techs before us, we found nothing. It looked as though no one had been in the house since we had come with Carstogi the day before. As we stepped off the porch to leave, Sophie Czirski hailed us from the concealed gate in her fence.

"Is it true?" she demanded as we approached. "They're both dead?"

"Yes," Peters responded.

"Serves 'em right," she muttered, "both of 'em." Her loose dentures clicked in satisfaction.

"You didn't do it, did you, Sophie?" Peters' question was a joke more than anything, but Sophie's face brightened.

"I didn't," she said. "Wish I had, though. I was right there in the house from "Little House on the Prairie" to the eleven o'clock news. Then I went to bed. No way to prove it, though. Nobody saw me. You want to take me in?"

Peters grinned. "That won't be necessary, but you call us if you see anything strange around here, will you?"

Her red hair bobbed up and down. "I will," she assured us, and we both knew it was true.

We questioned some of the other neighbors and then returned to Faith Tabernacle to canvass that area, looking for leads the whole time. We kept after it all day. For a while it looked as though we were going to come up empty-handed. We were still at it when yellow school buses started discharging passengers in late afternoon. Shortly after that a kid on a bike, probably junior high or so, rode up to where Peters and I were standing.

"You guys detectives?" he asked.

"That's right."

"I saw someone on a bike this morning when I was on my paper route. I usually cut through the church parking lot to get to the house across the street. It's the last one on my route. Someone was just leaving the front of the church. He was in a hurry."

"Did you get a good look at him?"

He shook his head. "It was too dark. I only saw the reflectors on the bike's wheels."

"What time was it?"

Again he shook his head. "I don't know. My dad gets home from work about two—he's a janitor—and he wakes me up. I deliver my papers and go back to bed. That way I can have breakfast with everybody else in the morning. I usually get home around three. This is my last house."

He couldn't give us much more than that. We took his name, address, and phone number and thanked him.

"Nice kid," Peters said as we watched him wheel his bike back down the street.

"He came within an inch of getting himself killed this morning. If he'd seen him, I don't think our killer would've hesitated pulling the trigger again."

About six-thirty we went back to the department to dictate our reports. We finished about an hour later. Peters offered me a ride home, and I accepted. It had been a long day.

The lights were off in the apartment when I came in. I felt a jab of disappointment. I had hoped all day that Anne would be there when I came home. It had been years since someone had been at home waiting to welcome me. I fixed a drink and went to the bedroom to hang up my jacket. Anne was there in my bed, curled up and sound asleep. I beat a hasty retreat to the shower, overwhelmed with gratitude for my good fortune.

Clean-shaven and showered, I slipped into bed beside her. She snuggled against me. When I nuzzled her neck, she stirred. "Good evening, Sleeping Beauty."

She smiled contentedly as my fingers caressed her breast. "Does that make you Prince Charming?"

"Or his grandfather."

She laughed. "You're not that old, are you?"

"I feel that old," I replied. I studied her. She had to be over thirty, but she looked as young as twenty-five. I could feel my body hardening, wanting her, yet I held back, too. Her fingers trailed through the hair on my chest, drumming a tattoo that reverberated through my head.

"You don't feel old to me," she said. The texture of her nipple changed beneath my hand. She pulled her hair to one side, exposing the smooth skin of her bare neck. I kissed her there, feeling her body go taut, her response immediate and palpable. There was an urgency in her kisses, a hungry need that overtook us both. In responding to that need, age was no longer an issue.

Her lovemaking taxed my skill and knowledge, taking me far beyond the gradual experiments Karen and I had evolved together. Anne required nothing less than full satisfaction and gave it as well, her body an exquisitely tuned instrument responding vibrantly to the slightest touch.

It pains me to admit that in things sexual, Anne just flat knew more than I did. Later, as she lay in my arms, satiated and content, I remembered how much she knew and it began to bother me. I began to wonder how she had come to know so much. I began to want to piece together Anne's romantic past. I was rational enough to know it was none of my business, but that didn't stop me. It's a kind of inquisitor mentality that makes me think I've been in this business too long. It also makes me realize what a prude I am. I guess deep down, like most men, I wanted the woman I loved to be a virgin. An adept virgin.

Eventually Anne slipped out of bed. "What do you eat around here?" she asked. "I've seen better-stocked refrigerators in motel rooms."

"I don't cook. I eat out."

"When? I'm starved."

"For what?"

"For food. Any kind."

I thought about the Porsche and the fur jacket. I thought about the Doghouse. I thought about age and sex and money. We were worlds apart, yet I wanted us to end up in the same orbit. "Well, if you're tough enough, I'll introduce you to one of my favorite hangouts. Believe me, reservations won't be necessary."

She took a red sweatsuit out of her Adidas bag. I watched her pull it on, marveling at her sleek, firm body. I drew her to me and zipped up the top. "How do you do that?" I asked.

"Do what?"

"Stay in shape."

"Oh, that," she said laughing. "I jog, I ride, do aerobics, lift weights. Anything else you'd like to know? Measurements, weight?"

"As a matter of fact, I want to know everything."

"For instance," she teased.

"I wrapped my arms around her. "For instance, tell me about your sister, Patty. What happened to her?"

She stiffened in my arms. "No," she said quietly. She moved away. I caught a glimpse of her face as she turned. A curtain had come down over her gray eyes. They were suddenly solemn and distant. "Don't ask me that again." It was a statement, not a request.

I had blundered onto dangerous ground, and I would do well to be more wary in the future. I see that in cops all the time, had seen it in Peters and myself. We can talk about crime in the abstract; just don't bring it too close to home.

Anne reached into her bag, pulling out a brand-new pair of jogging shoes. She held them up for my approval. "I went shopping today," she said in a halfhearted attempt at gaiety. It didn't take.

We walked to dinner. I tried to recapture the evening's earlier, lighter mood without success. Anne had crossed over her solitary bridge and left me alone on the other side. What exactly had she told me about Patty? I wondered. That she had died when Anne was eight? Why, then, did the mere mention of Patty more than twenty years later cause such a reaction?

Connie welcomed us with a knowing wink that set my teeth on edge. It got worse when she brought the menus. She gave Anne an appraising once-over. "I heard you were pretty, honey, but that don't hardly do you justice."

I bit. "How'd you hear that?"

She grinned. "I've got me some confidential sources. The clam strips are good tonight, and we've got liver and onions on the special."

I watched for any hint of disdain as Anne perused the menu. There was none, no hint of snobbishness. She ordered the special, then waited, oblivious to her surroundings, still far removed from me and from the present.

"Hello," I said at length, trying to get her attention. "Where are you?"

"Sorry, I didn't mean to do that."

"It wouldn't be so bad if you'd take me along when you go."

She gave me a searching look. "How did you know I was somewhere else?"

"For one thing, I asked you twice if you wanted a glass of wine."

Connie slung a cup of coffee in my direction and returned with one for Anne when I gave her the high sign. We were halfway through dinner when Maxwell Cole showed up. I thought it was an unfortunate coincidence. I found out later he had been in and out three times earlier in the evening looking for me.

He favored Anne with a deep bow. "What a pleasure to see you again," he oozed, as his cigarette smoke invaded the end of our booth.

Connie came over with an ashtray, which she held out to Max. "This is the no-smoking section, Mr. Cole. If you want to keep that cigarette, you'll have to go over to the next section." Cole ground out the stub.

"I've been on a wild-goose chase," Max said, addressing Anne. "That little Porsche of yours shouldn't be so hard to find, but it seems to have fallen off the face of the earth."

"Why are you looking for my car?" Anne asked.

"I'm not, actually. I've been looking for you. I wanted to ask you some questions about Angela Barstogi's funeral. Are you a relative of hers?"

"Go fuck yourself, Mr. Cole." She said it in such a sweet-tempered tone that at first Max didn't believe his ears. He flushed as he tried to recover his dignity.

"I don't think I said anything offensive," he said.

"Your very presence offends me, Mr. Cole. If you can't stand the heat, you know where they say you can go."

"I could offer a suggestion or two," I added helpfully.

The tips of his walrus mustache shook with rage. "You're going to regret this, J. P. Beaumont. That's the second time today you've taken a hunk out of my skin. I'm gunning for you."

"Sounds like business as usual to me."

Max would have taken a swing at me, but the bartender, who doubles as bouncer, turned up right then. Connie had summoned him soon enough for him to be there when the trouble started. "I wouldn't do that if

I were you, Mr. Cole. I think maybe you'd better go in the other room to cool off." The bartender didn't brook any arguments. He took Cole's upper arm and bodily led him away.

"What's the problem?" Anne asked when they were out of earshot.

"He doesn't like me."

"That's pretty obvious. It's also obvious the feeling's mutual. Why does he call you J. P.?"

I sighed. If we were going to end up in the same orbit, it was time to drag out some of the old war stories, the stuff that made me what I am, and let her take a look at it, warts and all. If that didn't drive her away, maybe she'd return the favor.

"Which do you want first, J. P. or Maxwell Cole?"

"Let's try for J. P."

"I'll have to tell you about my mother first. She was a beauty growing up, but headstrong as they come. She would sneak out of the house at night to date my father. He was a sailor, the first man who asked her out. She was only sixteen. They planned to run away and get married, but he was killed in a motorcycle accident on the navy base over in Bremerton. She didn't know she was pregnant until after he was dead.

"Her parents threw her out, told her they no longer had a daughter. My mother went to the Salvation Army Home for Unwed Mothers in Portland and signed in under the name of Beaumont, my father's hometown in Texas. My first names are Jonas Piedmont, after her two grandfathers. None of her family ever lifted a finger to help us. When she told me where my first and middle names came from, I hated them. I still do. I've gone by Beau most of my life. The initials came up during college. Some of my fraternity brothers figured out it bugged me to be called that. Max never got over it."

"Where's your mother now?"

"She died of breast cancer when I was twenty. She never made up with her parents. They lived here in Seattle the whole time, but I never met them. Didn't want to."

"You loved her very much, didn't you?" Anne commented gently.

It was becoming a very personal conversation. Anne seemed to bring out the lonely side of me, the part that needed to chew over my life with another human being.

"Yes," I said at last, meeting Anne's steady, level gaze. "I loved her. She could have taken an easy way out, given me up for adoption or had an abortion. She didn't though. She never married, either. She said that being in love once was enough for her."

"What about you?" she asked.

"What do you mean?"

"Is once enough for you?"

"Maybe not," I said. It was more a declaration of susceptibility than one of intent.

Anne looked away. "Tell me about Maxwell Cole."

I wasn't quite ready to talk about Karen, but Maxwell Cole led inevitably in that direction. "As I said, we were fraternity brothers together. He started out being Karen's boyfriend. We met at a dance he brought her to, a Christmas formal, and the sparks flew. She broke up with him right after New Year's and started dating me."

"He's a pretty sore loser. Is that the only grudge he's got against you?"

"It's gone beyond the grudge stage," I said grimly. "He's deliberately torpedoed me. When I was a rookie, he almost got me thrown off the force."

"How?"

"There was a kid, a young crazy up on Capitol Hill. He was up there taking potshots at people with a gun. I was the first on the scene. I called to him and told him I was coming in. I thought we could talk it out. As soon as I came around the corner into the alley, he fired at me, hit me in the arm, my left one. The bullet knocked me to the ground. He evidently thought I was dead, because he got up and started walking toward me. I shot him, killed him on the spot.

"Max was just starting on the *P.I.* then. He was a cub reporter, so he wasn't assigned to front-page stuff, but he did a feature on the kid and his family, how the kid had been an emotionally troubled boy who had been shot down in cold blood by a trigger-happy cop with a bullet in his arm. I'm still a killer cop as far as Max is concerned. He brings it up again whenever he has a chance."

"And are you a killer cop?"

"I don't think so. It took months to come to terms with it. I've never had to do it again."

"Would you?"

"Would I what?" I had gotten carried away with the story. Her question brought me back to earth in a hurry. Her eyes were fixed on mine, searching, questioning.

"Would you do it again, given the same circumstance?"

Her gray eyes were serious, her face still and waiting. Here it comes, I thought. The answer to this question is going to blow it. There was no sense in lying. If we were going to be together, I would have to be able to be the real J. P. Beaumont.

"Yes," I said. "Given the same circumstance, where it was either him or me, I would kill again."

Anne stood up abruptly. "Let's go," she said.

CHAPTER 15

The bike washed up with the tide on Wednesday morning. I was still in bed sampling the sensations Anne Corley's body had to offer when Watkins called for me to hit the bricks. He said Peters was on his way from Kirkland. I turned back to Anne. "I have to go," I said.

"Do you have to? Again?" she whispered, her lips moving across the top of my shoulder to the base of my neck. She pulled me to her, guiding me smoothly back into her moist warmth. It would have been easy to stay.

"Yes, goddamnit," I said, pulling away. "I have to. That's what I get for being a cop."

"All right for you," she said, petulantly. She smiled and sat up in bed, the sheets drawn across her naked breasts, watching me as I dressed. It made me feel self-conscious. My body's not that bad for someone my age, but it suffered in comparison to her lithe figure.

"What are you thinking?" I asked, sitting on the bed and leaning over to pull on my shoes and socks.

A man should never ask that kind of question unless he's prepared for the answer. She ran her fingers absentmindedly across my back. "Do you believe in love at first sight?" she asked.

I almost fell off the bed. I turned and looked at her. "Maybe," I said.

She smiled and planted a firm kiss on my shoulder. "I hoped you'd say that," she murmured. I finished tying my shoe and bolted from the room. I was still trying to regain my equilibrium when the bus dropped me at Myrtle Edwards Park, eight blocks from my building.

In Seattle, if you want something named after you, you have to die first. Myrtle Edwards Park is no exception. Myrtle Edwards was a dynamo of a city councilwoman, and the park named in her honor, after she went to the great city council in the sky, trails along the waterfront from Pier Seventy to Pier Ninety-one. It consists of a narrow strip of grass, bicycle and jogging trails, some blackberry bushes, and a rocky shoreline. There is no sandy beach. The waves crash onto a seawall made up of chunks of concrete and rocks, carrying a deadly cargo of stray logs and timbers. Nobody swims in Myrtle Edwards Park, although it is a popular gathering place for noontime joggers and other fitness fanatics.

A squad car was there before me. A park maintenance worker had read a morning newspaper account of the Faith Tabernacle murders. When he saw the bike, a sturdy English three-speed, smashed beyond repair but still a relatively new and fairly expensive one, he called the department. Someone had put him through to Watkins. Not only did he talk to the right person, it even turned out to be the right bike. The tire treads matched the plaster casts taken at Faith Tabernacle.

So how do you find the owner of a bike? It's not like an automobile where everyone has to register and license it. The few who do are mostly those unfortunates who have already been ripped off once and who know there's no other way for them to identify and reclaim a bike if the department happens to get lucky and recover it. In other words, bicycle registration in Seattle is a long way from 100 percent.

Peters and I started at the other end of the question, going to the manufacturer and tracing the serial number to the retail outlet that sold it. The actual store was in my neighborhood, which isn't that unlikely since my neighborhood is a big part of downtown Seattle. The store was a Schuck's, right across the street from the Doghouse. It took Peters and me the better part of two hours of letting our fingers do the walking before we got that far. We ambled into the store about eleven-fifteen, feeling a little smug. A clerk searched through some files before he found what we needed, but twenty minutes later we walked away with a name and address on Queen Anne Hill.

It sounds simple, doesn't it? You apply a little logic, a little common sense, and everything falls right into place. We should have known. Things were going far too smoothly. The house on Galer Street was vacant and had been long enough that weeds were pushing up through a once pristine lawn. There was a For Sale sign with a telephone number on it in the front yard. We took down the number and the address.

We called from a pay phone and were directed to a real estate office on the back side of Queen Anne. Our good fortune continued. The listing agent happened to be in. She remembered the owner well. He had been transferred to London with Western Electric. He had been in a hurry to pack and move. His company bought up the equity in his house, and he had held a gigantic moving sale early in March, unloading everything but the bare essentials. It had been a good sale. A bike might have been one of the items sold. Dead end.

This job is like that. You take a slender lead and do your best with it. Sometimes it pays off, sometimes not. You have to take the good with the bad. We called Watkins to let him know we had come up empty-handed. He told us the preliminary report had come in on the Faith Tabernacle murders. Ballistics tests showed the weapon to be a .38. It was hardly a quantum leap toward identifying the killer. Watkins also said Carstogi had called and wanted to see us.

We went to the Warwick. A detective sat at the end of the seventh-floor hallway. Powell and Watkins were making sure Carstogi didn't go anywhere without an escort.

We knocked. Carstogi opened the door. He looked a little shaken. "Have you seen the paper?" he asked.

"I don't read papers," I said.

Peters shook his head. "I didn't have time."

"Look," Carstogi said bleakly.

Peters read aloud. " 'Police have sequestered the father of Friday's slain child in connection with the subsequent double murder of the child's mother and minister.

" 'Andrew M. Carstogi, being detained in an undisclosed downtown location, arrived in town Sunday evening and was involved in a confrontation at Faith Tabernacle in Ballard during the day on Monday.

" 'The church in the Loyal Heights area was the scene of two gangland-style murders that occurred later that night. Dead are Pastor Michael Brodie, age forty-nine, and his parishioner, Suzanne Barstogi, Carstogi's estranged wife. The woman's age has not been released.

" 'Arlo Hamilton, Seattle Police public information officer, said that detectives are searching for a bicycle that may have been used by the killer in making his escape.

" 'Barstogi and Carstogi, whose exact marital status is unclear, lost their only child, Angela, on Friday. She was the victim of a brutal homicide that occurred in Discovery Park. That incident is still under investigation. No arrests have been made in that slaying and police officials refuse to say whether or not Carstogi is a suspect in either the church murders or the death of the child.

" 'Inquiries in Chicago, former location of Faith Tabernacle, revealed that the group, a fundamentalist sect, left Illinois under a cloud after accusations of physical violence and alleged child abuse. At least one of the violent incidents involved Carstogi, but none of the alleged charges against the group were subsequently proven.

" 'Interviews with Suzanne Barstogi prior to her death gave no hint of any dissatisfaction or disagreement within the Faith Tabernacle organization. She expressed gratitude that the entire congregation had stood by her during the period of the loss of her child.

" 'An unidentified airline employee revealed that Carstogi was a passenger on a flight that arrived at Seattle's Sea-Tac International Airport Sunday night, where he was reported to have been inebriated. He was overheard making threatening statements regarding Brodie. Carstogi allegedly held the minister responsible for the loss of his wife and child.

" 'He reportedly left the airport in the company of two homicide investigators, Detectives Ronald A. Peters and J. P. Beaumont, who are assigned to the murder investigation of Carstogi's daughter.

" 'Funeral arrangements for Brodie and Barstogi are pending with the Mount Pleasant Mortuary, where a spokesman indicated the bodies will probably be returned to Chicago for burial.' "

Peters folded the paper when he finished.

"There's more," said Carstogi. "Look on page seventeen."

Obligingly Peters reopened the paper. "The top corner," Carstogi said.

Peters glanced at me over the top of the paper. "It's Cole's column," he said.

"Read it."

" 'Who is the Lady in Red? The mysterious lady, although that may be a title she doesn't deserve, first appeared in a red dress, driving a red Porsche, and carrying a red rose at the funeral of Angela Barstogi, Seattle's five-year-old murder victim. The lady has since been seen several times in the company of Detective J. P. Beaumont, the homicide investigator assigned to the case.

" 'Seen last in a red sweatsuit in an area restaurant, she became verbally abusive when questioned about her connection to the case. She was accompanied by Detective Beaumont at the time.

" 'Because you, my faithful readers, are the eyes and ears of Seattle, I would appreciate knowing about this lady and why Seattle's finest are keeping her under wraps.' " Peters handed me the paper. Next to the column was a picture of Anne Corley as she had appeared at the funeral, tears streaming unchecked down her face.

"Who is she?" Carstogi asked. "What does she have to do with all this?"

"Nothing," I said. "We've checked her out. She's collecting data for a book on violent crimes with young victims."

"But he says you've been seen together."

"We happened to hit it off, just like you and that girl did the other night, except she's not a professional. Understand?"

Carstogi looked chagrined. "Yeah, I understand."

I was furious at Maxwell Cole. It was one thing to keep my professional life under the bright light of public scrutiny. It was another to expose my personal life, to make my relationship with Anne a topic of casual breakfast conversation.

"I think you'd better hurry up and remember anything you can about that date you had the other night," Peters was saying to Carstogi. "We're looking for a needle in a haystack, but with what you've given us, we don't know what kind of needle or which county the haystack's in." He shook the folded newspaper in Carstogi's direction for emphasis. "Detective Beaumont may not think you're the one who killed Brodie and Suzanne, but he's going to have one hell of a time convincing the rest of us."

"I already told you. Her name was Gloria. That's all I know," Carstogi said, caving in under Peters' implied threat.

"Try to remember where you went." Peters pressed his advantage, finally getting through Carstogi's reluctance to a bedrock of fear beneath.

"I was kind of drunk. I think we drove over a long bridge."

"In a cab, a car?"

"A cab. I think I came back in the same one the next morning."

"Pickup-and-delivery prostitution," Peters muttered. "Where did you go?" he continued. "A motel? A house?"

"It was a house, I guess. I didn't pay much attention. A man came out to the cab and took my money, then Gloria and I went inside, into a bedroom."

"What about the cab?" I asked. "Do you remember anything about it?"

"No. It was blue or maybe gray. The guy chewed gum. He was a big guy, dark hair, kinda oily. That's all I remember."

"Nothing other than that?"

"No." Carstogi shook his head.

I looked at Peters. "What say we take him for a spin and see if he can lead us back to the little love nest?"

"You do that," Peters said. "Drop me at the department. I'll see if vice has been able to dig anything up."

Carstogi came with us reluctantly. There had been some photographers outside the hotel when we went in, and we attempted to avoid them by leaving through the garage. We weren't entirely successful. Maxwell Cole's sidekick from the funeral caught us as Carstogi climbed into the backseat.

Once in the car Carstogi seemed more dazed than anything. "Why does everyone think I did it?" he asked.

"For one thing, your alibi isn't worth a shit," Peters told him. "And the place where the bike was found is well within walking distance of the War- wick. But most important, you're the guy with the motive. Our finding your friend Gloria is probably your one chance to avoid a murder indict- ment. You'd better hope to God we can find her."

"Oh," Carstogi said. From the look on his face, Carstogi was beginning to grasp the seriousness of his situation.

After dropping Peters off, Carstogi and I headed north on Highway 99. Aurora Avenue, as it is called in the city, has its share of flophouses and late-night recreational facilities. Carstogi recognized the Aurora Bridge, but that was all. He had no idea where they had turned off. He and Gloria had apparently played kissyface in the backseat. He said he dozed on the way back, that he didn't remember any landmarks. We wound through the narrow streets around Phinney Ridge and Fremont, to no avail.

"If I could just remember something about that cab," Carstogi said, more to himself than to me.

"I wouldn't count too heavily on that," I countered.

"Why not?"

"Prostitution is illegal in this state. If they say you were with them, they'll blow their little business wide open. I'd guess, from the sound of it, that they're probably a group of freelancers, independents. If we don't get them, the Mafia will."

"You mean they'd lie and say I wasn't with them?"

I looked at Andrew Carstogi with some sympathy. The young man seemed ill-equipped to deal with the real world. "That's exactly what I mean."

Carstogi hunched miserably in the front seat. "But I didn't do it. I would have taken her back. I wanted to kill Brodie, but never Suzanne. I still loved her."

I shook my head at my own stubbornness. "Alibi or no, I believe you."

"Thanks," Carstogi said, his voice crackling over the word.

"It's cold comfort," I acknowledged. "That and fifty cents will get you a cup of coffee."

"Not at the Warwick."

I laughed at his small joke, and he did too. I think he felt a little better when I dropped him off, but I didn't. I figured it wouldn't be long before the room at the Warwick would be traded for somewhat plainer accommodations in the city jail.

CHAPTER 16

I stopped by the Doghouse and had a cup of coffee after I dropped Carstogi at the hotel. I talked with the waitresses, the cashier, the bartender. I asked them all the same thing. Did they know of a gum-chewing cabbie who might be involved in a prostitution ring? No one mentioned anybody right off, but then I didn't expect them to. I had at least gotten the word out. That was worth something.

The apartment was close by. I went up just in case Anne was there. She wasn't, although the subtle fragrance of her perfume lingered in the room. I lingered too, drinking it in. Anne Corley secondhand was better than no Anne Corley at all.

I went back to the department. There was a message on my desk saying that Peters, Watkins, and Powell were having a meeting in Powell's office. I was expected to join them as soon as I returned. I looked at my watch. It was four-forty on Wednesday afternoon. It didn't take a Philadelphia lawyer to figure out what the topic of discussion might be. If we arrested Carstogi right then, he wouldn't stand a chance of getting out before Monday. By the time his seventy-two hours were up, it would be right in the middle of the weekend.

"Where've you been?" Powell growled as I came into the room.

"With Carstogi. We were looking for the place he went night before last."

"I've checked with vice, Beau," Peters said. "Gloria seems to be a popular professional name these days. At least ten have been booked for soliciting in the past three months. How about bringing Carstogi in to look at our pinup collection? Of course, all of them will just jump at the chance to have the book thrown at them one more time."

"I'll bet they will," I said.

"Look," Watkins interjected. "This Gloria story won't hold water and you know it. Why're you so dead set against Carstogi being our suspect?"

"He didn't do it," I insisted.

"Oh, for Chrissakes!" Powell was exasperated. "Whose side are you on, Beaumont? He's got motive, no alibi, physical proximity. What more do you want? I say book him. We'll never get a confession out of him while he's down at the Warwick living in the fucking lap of luxury. What if he blows town while we're standing around arguing about it? Let's get him in here and ask him some bare bones questions."

"What about Brother Benjamin?" I countered. "He lives nearby. Did we get anything back from Illinois on him? What if he had the same kind of beef with Brodie that Carstogi did?"

Watkins shuffled through a sheaf of papers. "Benjamin Mason alias Clinton Jason. Wonderful guy. Ex-junkie, ex-small-time hood. According to this, he stopped being in trouble about the time he hooked up with Brodie. At least there haven't been any arrests since then."

"Is that when he stopped renewing his driver's license?" Peters asked.

Watkins consulted the paper. "Looks that way. How'd you know that?"

Peters shrugged. "Lucky guess," he said.

Powell had been sitting quietly. "Now wait a minute. What's all this about Brother Benjamin? You got anything solid that points to him?"

"We've got as much on him as we do on Carstogi," I said.

"Brother Benjamin didn't have a plane reservation to leave town yesterday. Carstogi did. I want him in here for questioning. Is that clear?" Powell was in no mood for argument.

"It's clear, all right." I could see I was outgunned. "But I think you're making a hell of a mistake."

A newspaper had been lying open on Powell's desk. He picked it up. "Talk about mistakes. Since when do investigators become personally involved with someone from a current case? Maxwell Cole is having a field day. Who is this broad anyway?"

"She's an author," I said maybe a tad too quickly. "She's collecting material for a book. That's why she was at the funeral. It has nothing to do with the investigation."

"Right," Powell said, dragging the word out sarcastically. "If you're going to have a little roll in the hay, I'd suggest you do it a little less publicly."

Peters rose to his feet, placing himself between Powell's words and my flaring temper. "All right, we'll go down and bring him in," he said.

We waited for an elevator. I was still fuming. "You know, Powell does have a point," Peters said. "Maybe you should cool it for a while."

"Mind your own fucking business," I muttered.

We started for the Warwick in silence. In my fifteen years on homicide, I've developed a gut instinct. I know when it's right, and when it isn't. This wasn't. Carstogi wasn't a killer. He didn't have the killer instinct, the solid steel core it takes to pull the trigger. I knew I did. I had done it once. Maybe it takes one to know one.

"Wait," I said. "I want to go see Jeremiah. Before we pick up Carstogi."

Peters clicked his tongue. "You are one stubborn son-of-a-bitch, Beaumont. I'll say that for you." But he headed for Ballard.

The traffic was snarled on Fifteenth. We had to wait for the drawbridge. "You almost blew it on the driver's license thing," I said. "The only way you could put that together was from the sermon on the tape."

"Sorry," Peters said.

I had written Jeremiah's address in my notebook. We found it without difficulty. Jeremiah was sitting on the front steps of a tiny bungalow. He watched us get out of the car.

"Your folks in there?" I asked, approaching the steps where he was sitting.

He shook his head without getting up. I sat down beside him. "I'm here alone," he said.

"How are things?"

He shrugged. "Okay, I guess."

"You been in any more hot water?"

"Probably am now," he said. I knew he meant for talking to us.

"Were your folks both home Monday night?"

"You mean after we left the church?"

I nodded. He continued. "Someone asked me that yesterday. I already told him."

"Tell me, Jeremiah."

"We were maybe the last ones to leave. Mom and I waited in the car for a long time."

"Was your stepfather upset when he came to the car?"

Jeremiah nodded gravely. "He and Mom had a big fight. They yelled at each other."

"What did they fight about?"

"Someone at church."

"What did they say?"

"He called one of the ladies a . . ." He groped for the word. "A whore."

"Which one, do you know?"

"Sister Suzanne."

"Do you know if he left the house again? Later?"

"I don't know. I went to sleep."

Peters had been listening to this exchange. Now he became a part of it. "Does anyone call Benjamin Uncle Charlie? Have you ever heard that?"

Jeremiah shook his head.

"You ever hear of an Uncle Charlie?"

"Only Angel's."

"Does he belong to Faith Tabernacle? Is he a member?"

"No. I never saw him. Angel said he lived far away from here. She said he was nice, that he promised sometime he'd take her for a ride in his van. Some of the other kids thought she made him up."

We asked Jeremiah for more details, but he clammed up. He kept watching the street nervously, as though afraid his folks might drive up any minute. We beat a hasty retreat so they wouldn't see us talking to him. I didn't want them to know we had been there. I didn't want Jeremiah to have to suffer any consequences.

When we got in the car, Peters asked, "Where to?"

"I guess we go pick up Carstogi."

Peters started the motor. "You think Benjamin's voice is the one we heard, not Carstogi's?"

"I don't know what to think," I replied.

Carstogi wasn't surprised to see us. I think he knew it was inevitable. When we came into the room he was sitting on the side of the bed, shoulders hunched, face buried in his hands.

"You'll have to come with us," I said.

Peters brought out the cuffs. Carstogi stood up and pulled away. It was reflex. I caught him by the shoulder and swung him around. "Don't do anything stupid," I warned him. "Things are bad enough for you already."

Carstogi came with us quietly. Peters read him his rights. I didn't have the stomach for it. The public wanted a fall guy, and it was Peters' and my job to provide them with one. We herded him through the booking process. He reminded me of a steer being driven to slaughter, numb with fear and unable or unwilling to help himself. He didn't ask for an attorney.

Once he was dressed in the bright orange jail coveralls, we began to question him. First Peters would grill him and then I would. He sat at the table in the tiny interview room, gazing at the floor while we asked him our questions. His story never varied, but it didn't improve, either. He stuck to it like glue. The questioning process went on for hours. We finally sent him to his cell about nine o'clock. I left right after he did, without saying good night to anyone, including Peters. There was nothing good about it.

I walked my usual path down Fourth. I needed to think, to separate myself from the stifling closeness of the interview room. I didn't like the feeling that I was part of a railroading gang. What we had on Carstogi was totally circumstantial, but I was afraid it might stick. After all, any port in a storm, and Carstogi didn't have much of a cheering section in this part of the world.

What about Brother Benjamin? According to Jeremiah, he wasn't the mysterious Uncle Charlie, but he was certainly a likely suspect with Brodie and Suzanne. The questions circled in my head, but I was too tired to draw any conclusions.

I opened the door to my apartment hoping Anne would be there. I more than half expected that she would be, but she wasn't. I tried calling the Four Seasons and was told Mrs. Corley wasn't taking any calls. That pissed me off. I poured myself a MacNaughton's and settled down to wait. And sulk.

It must have been three drinks later before she called me back. By then I was pretty crabby. "I just now got your message," she said. "Would you like me to come over?"

I felt like saying, Suit yourself. What actually came out of my mouth was, "Sure."

She was there within minutes, greeting me with a quick kiss. I had drunk enough that I resented her lighthearted manner. "What are you so chipper about?" I groused.

"I got a lot done today, that's all. How about you?"

"Same old grind."

We were standing in the entryway. She took the glass from my hand, reached around the corner, and set it on the kitchen counter. Then she took both my hands in hers and placed them behind her back. "Kiss me," she demanded.

I did, reluctantly at first, still trying to hang on to being mad at her. It didn't work. My hunger for her reawakened. I crushed her to my chest as the touch of her lips sent me reeling.

"Marry me," she whispered.

"What?" I asked, thinking I couldn't possibly have heard her right. I pushed her away and held her at arm's length.

"Marry me," she repeated. "Now. We can get the license tomorrow and get married on Sunday."

I examined her face, trying to tell if she was kidding. No hint of merriment twinkled in her gray eyes.

"You mean it, don't you!"

She nodded.

"So soon? We hardly know each other."

"I've just now gotten up my courage. If I give myself any time to think about it, I might back out. Besides, I know all I need to know."

I made the transition from being half drunk to being totally sober in the space of a few seconds. She moved away from me and settled on the couch. I stood for a long time in the doorway, thunderstruck. It was one thing to ask if someone believed in love at first sight, but proposing marriage was something else again.

I come from the old school where men make the first move, do the asking. Not that the thought hadn't crossed my mind. Eventually. After a suitable interval.

"I take it that means no?" she asked softly, misinterpreting my silence for refusal.

Hurrying to her, I sat down next to her and put my arm around her shoulders. "It's just that . . ."

"Please, Beau." She looked up at me, her eyes dark and pleading. "I've never wanted anything more."

We had known each other for barely three days, yet I couldn't conceive of life without her, couldn't imagine denying giving her anything she wanted, including me. I leaned down and kissed her. "Why not? What have I got to lose?"

A smile of gratitude flashed across her face, followed by an impish grin. "Your tie, for starters," she responded airily, kissing me back and fumbling with the knot on my tie. "Your tie and your virtue."

CHAPTER 17

When I woke up, Anne's fingers were tracing a pattern through the hair on my chest. It was morning, and rare Seattle sun streamed in the bedroom window, glinting off the auburn flecks in her dark hair. She was sitting on the bed, fully dressed and smiling.

"It's about time you woke up. Coffee's almost done."

I pulled her to me. "Did I dream it?" I asked, burying my face in a mass of fragrant hair.

"Dream what?" she countered.

"That you asked me to marry you."

"And that you accepted. No, you didn't dream it." She pushed me away. "And now you'd better get up because we're about to have company."

"Company?" I protested, glancing at the clock. "It's only a quarter to seven."

"I told him to be here at seven so we could go to breakfast."

"Told who?"

"Ralph Ames, my attorney. You talked to him on the phone, remember?"

She went to the kitchen, and I ducked into the bathroom, ashamed that she knew I'd been checking on her.

I was shaving when Anne tapped on the bathroom door and brought me a steaming mug of strong coffee. She set it on the counter, then perched on the closed toilet seat to visit in the custom of long married couples. She watched me scrape the stubborn stubble from my chin. "No second thoughts?" I asked, peering at her reflection in the mirror.

She shook her head. "None," she replied. "How about you?"

"I'm not scared if you're not."

A pensive smile touched the corners of her mouth. "I was just like your mother, you know."

I paused, holding the razor next to my jaw. "What do you mean?"

"I thought once was enough."

The phone rang just then. She hurried to answer it, and I heard her direct Ralph Ames into the building. She came back to the bathroom as I was drying my face. She put her arms around my waist, resting her cheek on the back of my shoulder. "I love you, J. P. Beaumont," she said.

Turning to face her, I took her chin in my hands and kissed her. "I love you, too." It was the first time since Karen that I had uttered those words or experienced the feelings that go with them. It amazed me that they came out so easily and felt so right. I kissed her again. A thrill of desire caught me as her lips clung to mine. There was a knock on the door, and she pushed me away.

"Hurry," she said.

When I walked into the living room a few minutes later, a man with a trench coat draped over one arm stood with his back to the room, gazing out at the city. I felt a twinge of jealousy when he turned. He was younger than I by a good ten years, well built, handsome in a dapper sort of way. He was wearing a natty three-piece pinstripe. He extended his hand, and his grip was unexpectedly firm.

"Beau," Anne said, "I'd like you to meet Ralph Ames, my attorney."

I managed a polite enough greeting. "Care for some coffee?" I asked.

Ralph's eyes swung from Anne back to me. "Do we have time? You said we'd grab some breakfast on our way to the courthouse. Then I have a plane to catch."

Seeing my look of consternation, Ames glanced quickly at Anne, who smiled brightly. "We have time."

"But you did say we're going to get the marriage license this morning, didn't you?"

She nodded. "Ralph has agreed to be our witness down at the court-house."

That brought me up short. When had Ralph Ames been scheduled to serve as a witness? Before Anne had popped the question? Before I had accepted? Or had she called him that morning while I was still asleep?

"Great," I said, trying to sound casual.

Anne handed Ames a cup of coffee and motioned him into my leather recliner. "We've got time," she said, returning to the kitchen for two more cups. I settled grudgingly on the couch, determined to be civil. My first halting attempt at conversation wasn't much help.

"What brings you up here, Ralph?" I asked.

His eyes flicked from me to Anne, who curled up on the couch beside me. She shook her head slightly in his direction, and Ames turned back to me. "Anne had some legal matters she wanted me to straighten out for her before the weekend. When she calls, I drop everything and go. I got here yesterday afternoon."

"It must be nice." A trace of sarcasm leaked into my voice. It offended me that Ralph Ames and Anne Corley shared secrets to which J. P. Beau-mont was not privy. Theirs was obviously a long-standing relationship, although I could detect nothing overt to indicate it was anything other than one between a client and a trusted attorney. Trusted retainer, actually. Ames asked a series of pointed, proprietary questions that gave me the distinct impression he was doing a quick background check to see if I measured up.

When it was time to go to breakfast, I led them to the Doghouse. That was pure cussedness on my part. I wanted to drag Ralph Ames someplace where his pinstripe suit would be just a tad out of place. Ames, however, continued to be absolutely amiable. Good-naturedly, he wolfed down the Doghouse's plain breakfast fare.

Throughout the meal, I couldn't shake the sense that I was being examined by some sort of future in-law. It irked me to realize that Ralph Ames knew far more about Anne Corley than I did—that she liked her bacon crisp, for example, or that she preferred hotcakes to toast. J. P. Beaumont was very much the outsider, but I decided I could afford to play catch-up ball.

After breakfast we caught a cab down to the courthouse. I guess I should have been nervous or had some sense of being railroaded, but I didn't. Anne's hand found mine and squeezed it. The radiant happiness on her face was directed at me alone, and it made my heart swell with pride.

We were first in line when the licensing bureau doors opened. I had no idea King County wouldn't take a check for the twenty-six-dollar marriage license fee. Luckily, Ralph had enough cash on him, and he came up with the money. That, combined with his picking up the check for breakfast, made me more than a little testy. As far as I was concerned, he was being far too accommodating.

Ames took a cab to the airport from the courthouse. "Will you be here for the wedding?" Anne asked, as he climbed into the cab.

"That depends on how much work I get done tomorrow," he replied.

Once again the little snippet of private conversation between them made me feel like an interloper. When the cab pulled away, Anne turned back to me. "What are you frowning about?"

"Who, me?" I asked stupidly.

"Yes, you. Who else would I mean?"

"How long have you known him?"

"A long time," she answered. "You're not jealous of him, are you?"

"Maybe a little."

She laughed aloud. "Don't be silly. Ralph is the last person you should be jealous of. He's a good friend, that's all. I wanted him to meet you."

"To check me out? Did I pass inspection?" Even I could hear the annoyance in my voice.

"You wouldn't have a marriage license in your pocket if you hadn't passed. What's the matter with you?"

I shrugged, unwilling to invite further teasing about my jealousy, but making a mental note to remember crisp bacon and pancakes. Anne walked me as far as the department, then struck off on her own up Third Avenue, while I headed for my desk on the fifth floor. There was a note on my desk saying that Peters was in the interview room with Andrew Carstogi, that I should follow suit.

I guess his fellow inmates convinced Carstogi of the error of his ways and had him run up the flag to the public defender's office. By the time I got into the interview room on the fifth floor, Peters and Watkins were there along with a tough-looking female defense attorney. She nodded or shook her head whenever we asked Carstogi a question. Usually I look at this process as a game where we try to get at the truth and the lawyers try to hide it.

Sitting in jail overnight, Carstogi had come up with one additional detail that he had forgotten before. He said he thought the cab company had something to do with the Civil War. After we sent Carstogi back to his cell, we returned to our desks, and I hauled out the yellow pages.

"What's with you today?" Peters asked, thumping into his own chair. "You were late."

I decided to put all my cards on the table at once and get it over with. There's something to be said for shock value. I tossed him the envelope with the marriage license in it. He removed the license, read it, then looked at me incredulously. "You've got to be kidding!"

"Why?"

"Beau, for Chrissakes, what do you know about her? You only met last Sunday."

"She wants me; I want her. What's to know?"

"This is crazy."

"We're getting married Sunday."

"In one week? What's the big hurry? Is she pregnant or something?"

"Look, if you want to come, you're invited. Otherwise, lay off."

Peters was still shaking his head when I turned back to the yellow pages. Halfway through the taxi listings, I found it—the General Grant Cab Company.

We checked out a car from the motor pool and went looking. We found the faded blue cab in a lineup waiting for passengers at Sea-Tac Airport. The driver was chewing a wad of gum when we showed him our badges. His hair looked like he still used Brylcreem. He rolled down the window. "What's up?" he asked.

He didn't want to lose his place in line, so we sat in the cab to ask him our questions. He knew nothing about some hooker named Gloria. He'd never seen Carstogi. We showed him Carstogi's mug shot. Well, maybe he had seen someone like him, but he couldn't remember where or when. We made a note to check out his trip sheets later, but I had an idea that if the driver had been the one who gave Carstogi a ride, it was as a sideline the cab company knew nothing about.

Carstogi's flimsy alibi had just gotten a whole lot flimsier. Peters and I headed back into town. "Where do you want to go? The office?" Peters asked.

"No. Let's go back to my place. I want to listen to that tape."

"Why? Because you still don't think Carstogi did it?"

"Why do you think he did?" I answered Peters' question with a question of my own.

Peters looked thoughtful. "Maybe because I think I would have in his place," he said solemnly. From his tone of voice, it was readily apparent that he wasn't making a joke.

"So you're layering in your own motivations and convicting him? He's innocent until proven guilty, you asshole. That's the way the law works, remember?"

"Who did it, then?" Peters asked. "If Carstogi didn't, who did? The tape shows that whoever the guy was, he'd been around the True Believers long enough to know the rules."

"The guy we heard on the tape knew the ropes, but we don't know for sure he was the one who killed them." We drove silently for a time while I retraced the conversation.

"Maybe we need to go back to Angela Barstogi," I mused aloud. "What I just said about Carstogi is true about Brodie and Suzanne as well."

"What do you mean?"

"We never convicted them, either. Just because they're dead doesn't automatically make them guilty. We never proved anything other than the fact that they had some pretty weird ideas."

Peters clicked his tongue thoughtfully. "I see where you're going. You think the same person may have killed all three of them."

"Having Carstogi here makes it too simple, too easy."

"Maybe so," Peters agreed.

We hurried to my place. I wondered if Anne would be there, but she wasn't. Peters dragged the recorder out of the drawer and turned it on. Personal considerations were forgotten in the charged tension between us. We were ready to listen to the tape from a different point of view.

It was the third time through when it hit me. "Stop," I said. "Run it back just a few turns."

Peters did. For a few moments we heard Suzanne Barstogi's voice raised in solitary prayer, then her abrupt "What do you want?"

"That's it! It can't be Carstogi. She spoke to him."

Peters looked at me, puzzled.

"Remember Monday?" I asked. "She didn't speak to Carstogi, not since he was Disavowed. I don't think she would have broken that rule even if he was holding a gun to her head. She'd be a lot more likely to speak to Benjamin."

"I'll be damned. You could be right, Beau. We'd better take this thing downtown and show it to Watty."

"He's not going to like it. Illegal listening devices are frowned on by the brass."

"We'd better tell him just the same."

A key turned in the lock. Anne Corley hurried into the apartment just as we were getting up to leave. Peters guiltily shoved the recorder into his pocket like a kid caught stealing candy.

"I'm sorry," she said. "I didn't mean to interrupt. I left my watch in the bedroom. I forgot to put it on this morning."

She went into the bedroom and came out fastening the watch. "What about lunch later?" she asked. "We've got lots to talk over."

"We're on our way back to the department right now. Maybe about one-thirty or two."

"Great," she said enthusiastically. "I'll stop by about then."

Anne walked out the lobby door with us. The red Porsche was parked on the street. "Do you need a ride?" she asked, opening the door.

I waved her away. "No thanks."

Peters whistled as the Porsche rounded the corner onto Blanchard. "That's her car?"

"Nice, isn't it."

"Beau, who the hell is she?" I gave him a warning look, just one, and he let it drop.

We took the recording to Sergeant Watkins. As predicted, he was not pleased. He listened to the tape in stolid silence and heard our analysis without comment. "Play it again," he ordered. We went over Monday's confrontation in great detail and heard the tape yet again.

"Taking everything into consideration, you might be right," he allowed reluctantly. "But you're drawing conclusions. None of this has any basis as evidence. It's a damn shame this state can't even spring for voiceprint equipment. So what are you going to do now?"

"Go looking for someone else."

"So look," he said. "Nobody's stopping you. We've got Carstogi locked up until Monday afternoon with what we've got so far. What have you got to lose?"

Peters and I went back to the drawing board. We went over the previous Thursday in minute detail, listening to the initial recorded report of

Angela's disappearance, as well as the statements taken later. We learned nothing new.

We tried Sophie's house. We wanted to know if she had seen a van, the one Jeremiah had told us about. Nobody was home but Henry Aldrich, the cat, and he wasn't talking.

At one-twenty Anne showed up for lunch. We invited Peters, but he claimed to be busy. We left him at his desk and ate in a little Mexican dive at the foot of Cherry. Anne was brimming over with infectious happiness. She had found a minister to marry us and had made arrangements for the ceremony to be held at six a.m. in Myrtle Edwards Park.

"Why there?" I asked. "And why so early?"

She shrugged. "I like it there," she replied, "especially in the morning when it's quiet."

Anne walked me back to the Public Safety Building and kissed me good-bye on the sidewalk, much to the enjoyment of a group of street people gathered around the hot bagel stand outside the front door. "I'll see you when you get off work," she said. "I'll be at your place."

I went up to the fifth floor to find Peters pacing impatiently beside my desk. "Come on," he snapped. "We just hit the jackpot. A grit-truck driver from the Westside Treatment Center saw a black van parked near where Angela was found. He saw it about nine-thirty the morning she died."

"No shit!" We were already on our way to the elevator. "So where has he been all this time?"

"He just got back in town from a fishing trip. He hadn't seen anything about the murder on the news, but someone was talking about it when he went out to pick up a load this afternoon. He called about ten minutes after you left for lunch."

As usual, we had to wait for an elevator, and as usual too, it would have been faster to take the stairs.

Dick Aubrey, the grit-truck driver, turned out to be a wiry, tough little man with a fiery temper and an ever-present cigarette. He had been fishing in Idaho since the previous Friday afternoon.

"I came down the hill around nine-thirty or so, and here's this big black van parked almost in the middle of the friggin' road. I blew my horn at him a couple of times to get his attention."

"Him?" Peters asked. "You could tell it was a him?"

"Oh, sure. He was just starting to climb out of the van. I almost took the door off."

"What did he look like?"

"Big. Straight yellow hair, long. Overweight."

"Would you recognize him if you saw him again?"

"Sure. I got a pretty good look at his face. He was an ugly son-of-a-bitch."

I brought out some glossies of both Pastor Brodie and Brother Benjamin, taken at the funeral. We had purchased them from the P.I. We also showed him Carstogi's mug shots. "Any of these?" I asked.

Aubrey stroked his chin. "Naw. None of these guys. I'm sure of that. This guy was built like a tank. About six-five. Neck like a bull."

"What happened next?" Peters urged.

"Well, I went down to get loaded. You haul two things out of sewage plants, sludge and grit. I do grit. I figured if he was still there when I got ready to leave, I'd call and have him towed away, but by then he was gone. It's a pain in the ass having cars parked on that road. It's too narrow."

We picked Dick Aubrey's brain. He came down to the Public Safety Building and did a composite sketch. With the Identikit sketch in hand, Peters and I went over the names of everyone we had questioned in connection with the case. We were able to put names and faces with every person but one. Angela Barstogi's Uncle Charlie had to be the wild card in the deck.

We took the sketch and went to see Sophie. This time she was home. We walked up to her front door and could hear the television set blaring through the wood. Peters knocked, twice.

"Oh," she said, "are you coming to arrest me?"

Peters laughed. "No, we're here for some help."

We went inside. The cat, inside now, was already on the couch. He took a dim view of sharing it with company.

Peters brought out the sketch Aubrey had made and handed it to Sophie. She held it close to her face, examining it first with the pointed glasses in place and then with them lowered so she could peer over them. She handed it back to Peters.

"Maybe," she said.

"What about a van? Do you remember seeing one of those in the neighborhood?"

She furrowed her brow. "I do, now that you mention it, a black one, but not the last few days. I thought it was part of the group. I saw it a few times, usually in the morning."

"Will you call us if you see it again?" I asked. "Try to get the license number and call us right away."

"I most certainly will, young man," she said. I got the distinct impression Sophie Czirski still didn't approve of me.

We escaped without having tea. We went back to the department and reported to Watkins. We felt like we were making progress. We sent for motor vehicle reports on a list of known sexual offenders in the state of Washington. It's the grunt work, routine things, an expired vehicle license or an unpaid traffic ticket, that often break a case. We left the computer folks to pull together the information we needed.

"Ready to call it a day?" I asked Peters.

"How about stopping by for a drink on the way home. I'll buy."

I glanced surreptitiously at the clock, trying to remember exactly when I had told Anne I'd be home.

"Come on," Peters insisted. "You're not married yet."

I took the bait. "All right," I agreed. "I guess I can stop off for a while."

CHAPTER 18

We went down to F. X. McRory's on Occidental Street. Peters got off on the right foot by buying a bottle of champagne. "All right, you closemouthed bastard," he said, raising his glass, "now that I'm a party to this little romance, you'd better tell me about her."

I didn't need to be asked twice. I hadn't had a chance to tell anyone about Anne. I'm afraid I waxed eloquent. I told him how she had looked at the funeral and about our first dinner at Snoqualmie Falls afterward. I told him about the Porsche and the fur jacket and the Doghouse and the depth and the laughter and the wit and the sudden darknesses, all the things that seemed so contradictory in Anne, and all the things that made me love her.

About that time Captain Powell showed up and, uninvited, took a chair at our table. "What's this I hear about you getting married?"

I looked to Peters for help, but he stared off into space, as innocent as the day is long. "Who is she?" Powell continued.

Taking a deep breath, I said, "her name's Anne Corley. She's the Lady in Red from Maxwell Cole's column."

"Are you shitting me? You said you met her at Angela Barstogi's funeral, last Sunday. What is this, love at first sight? That only happens in the movies."

"It's a shotgun wedding," Peters interjected snidely. I aimed a swift kick at him under the table, but I missed. He grinned at me and motioned to the waitress for what I thought would be our bill. Instead, a second bottle of champagne was delivered, Eastern Onion Style.

It consisted of a singing telegram complete with a down-and-dirty stripper. Only afterward, amid hoots of laughter, did I realize that while we'd been talking, the bar had quietly filled with people from the department. They were all there. Not only Powell, whose frown of disapproval had been replaced by a wide grin, but also the rest of the guys from homicide, Hamilton from public information, and the women from word-processing.

They had a wild assortment of off-color cards, congratulating me for lechery despite my advanced years. It was a rowdy party by any standards. I don't know how Peters managed to arrange it. He must have done it while Anne and I were having lunch.

I had a good time. It was getting late, though, and no one seemed to be in any hurry to leave. I was trying to think of a polite way to abandon ship, when there was a flurry of activity near the front door. My reason for going home early strode toward me, a dazzling smile on her lips. Anne's very presence brightened the room, and it became an engagement party to remember.

Captain Powell came up to be introduced. "Now that I see the lady in question," he grinned, "maybe love at first sight isn't out of the question after all."

Well-wishers came forward for introductions and congratulations. The guests milled around for some time before they gradually began to disappear. At last only the three of us remained—Anne, Peters, and me. Peters looked enormously pleased with himself.

"You sure put one over on me," I said to him. "Thanks."

Anne added her thanks to mine and gave him a peck on the cheek.

"You're welcome," Peters replied.

We left Pioneer Square on foot. Peters said he was going back to the department, while Anne, after producing her pair of Nikes from the ubiquitous Adidas bag, set a swift pace up First Avenue. I found myself hurrying to keep up, wanting to shield her from the human debris around us. "Couldn't we take our constitutional in a better part of town?" I suggested. "First Avenue tends to get a little rough."

"The bums don't bother me," she said, and they didn't. Panhandlers pick out soft touches from blocks away. It's as if they have a radar connection. None of them approached Anne as she marched through them. Something in her carriage, her bearing, moved them away from her. Like the crush of people in Snoqualmie Lodge, the groups of bums opened before and shut behind her while she moved forward unimpeded.

Driving in a car you're not as aware of it, but from Pioneer Square to Seattle Center there's a long, steep grade that tops out at Stewart Street. By the time we reached that point, I was about half winded. Anne set a stiff pace.

"I didn't know I was so far out of shape," I grunted.

Anne was clearly enjoying herself. "You'll just have to get out and walk more," she said.

We walked in silence for a block or two. "Is Ron coming to the wedding?" she asked suddenly.

"Ron? Oh, you mean Peters? I don't know. I invited him."

"I don't think he likes me particularly."

"What makes you say that?"

"During the party I caught him staring at me several times."

"I think he'd like to believe you're after my money, although seeing your car should have taken care of any suspicions on that score. I guess he thinks we're rushing into something. Leaping without looking, that kind of thing."

I caught her by the hand and pulled her back to me. "Why *are* you marrying me? Everybody knows cops make lousy husbands."

She reached up and kissed me on the cheek. "But great lovers. I'm marrying you for your body."

"Anne, you could have any body you wanted. Why me?"

Her eyes, which had been bright and teasing a moment before, softened. "Because you made me remember what it's like to be a woman, Beau. I had forgotten."

I pulled her to me, and we stood clasped in an embrace for a long moment at the corner of First and Virginia. Her answer may not have been good enough for Peters or Powell, but it was for me. At last we resumed walking, both of us quiet and lost in our own private thoughts.

We ran into Ida Newell, my neighbor in the lobby. It was a moment I had been dreading. I was sure by now Ida had monitored Anne's comings and goings on the closed-circuit channel. It was time to make an honest woman of her, I decided. "I'd like you to meet my fiancée, Ida. This is Anne Corley. Ida Newell."

"Fiancée," Ida sniffed. "I'm surprised. I haven't met you before."

"I'm from Arizona," Anne said with an easy smile. "It's been one of those long-distance affairs. I'm very happy to meet you."

That seemed to satisfy Ida. At least she entered her own apartment without further comment. "That was masterful," I murmured gratefully. "You saved my bacon on that one."

Anne smiled. "It'll cost you," she said.

Safety deposit boxes have never been high on my list of priorities. What few trinkets I've kept over the years, I've stowed in various nooks and crannies around my house. I left Anne in the living room and rummaged in my bottom dresser drawer. I found the faded velvet box in its place in the left-hand corner. I felt a lump in my throat as I opened it.

My father was a sailor, a wartime enlistee who probably hadn't learned one end of a ship from the other before he died. The ring he had given to my mother wasn't much, but I'm sure it was the most he could offer his sixteen-year-old sweetheart. I could imagine him proudly making the purchase at some low-life pawnshop in Bremerton. My mother had kept the ring, treasured it. It came to me when she died, and I kept it too. It was my only link with a father whose face I never saw.

I slipped the tiny box into my pocket and returned to Anne. She was sitting on the couch, her head resting on the back of it. "Tired?" I asked.

"A little," she said.

I sat down next to her with my hand on her shoulder, rubbing a knot of stiffness from between her shoulder blades. I cleared my throat. "You know, we had a wonderful engagement party. It's a shame we didn't have a ring."

"We don't need a ring—" she began.

I lay my finger across her lips and silenced her. "Then as we walked, or rather, as we ran home, I remembered that I did have a ring buried among my treasures." I pulled the box from my pocket and opened it. The tiny chip of diamond caught the light and sparkled gamely. "My mother was never married," I explained; "she was always engaged. And now, from one of the longest engagements in history, this ring is going to be part of one of the shortest."

Anne took the ring from the box and held it up to the light. "This was your mother's?"

"Yes."

She gave the ring back to me and held out her hand so I could place it on her finger. It slipped on as easily as if it had been made for her. "Thank you," she said. "You couldn't have given me anything I would have liked more."

We sat on the couch for a long time without speaking or moving. It was enough to be together, my arm around her shoulder, her hand touching mine. That night there was no need in the touching, no desire. We sat side by side, together and content.

"Happy?" I asked.

"Ummmhm," was the answer.

"Let's go to bed," I said, "before we both fall asleep on the couch."

"But it's early," she objected. It was a mild protest, easily overruled.

We undressed quickly but without urgency. Our bodies met beneath the sheets, her skin cool against my greater warmth. I eased her onto her side so her body nestled like a stacked saucer in my own, my hand resting comfortably on the curve of her breast. "Just let me hold you," I murmured into her hair.

It couldn't have been more than eight o'clock, but the previous days of frenetic activity had worn us, fatigued us. Within minutes we both slept. For all the ease of it, we might have been sleeping together like that for years.

CHAPTER 19

Maybe I should start reading the newspapers first thing in the morning. That way I wouldn't get caught flat-footed quite so often. Peters brought me a copy and I read it at my desk with him watching from a few feet away. Maxwell Cole's column pronounced Anne Corley to be a dilettante copper heiress from Arizona.

Max had done some homework. He had dug up a good deal of information. Had Anne Corley not been linked to J. P. Beaumont, I think she would have been pictured sympathetically. Colored by his antipathy for me, however, she became something quite different. Rich, and consequently suspect, Anne Corley was depicted as a character out of a macabre, second-rate movie.

Cole reported as fact that for eleven years, between the ages of eight and nineteen, Anne Corley had been a patient in a mental institution in Arizona. She had been released, only to marry one of the staff psychiatrists, Dr. Milton Corley, a few weeks later. The marriage had caused a storm of controversy and had resulted in Corley's losing his job, in his being virtually discredited. He had committed suicide three years later, leaving a fortune in life insurance to his twenty-two-year-old widow.

Corley's money, combined with that already held in trust for Anne as a result of being her parents' only surviving child, created a formidable wealth. Cole touched on her book, but focused mainly on her wandering the country dropping roses on the caskets of murdered children. It could have been touching. In Cole's hands, Anne became a morbid eccentric, one whose continued sanity was very much in question.

Trembling with rage, I set the newspaper aside. Anne Corley was not a public figure. What Max had written seemed clearly an invasion of privacy, libelous journalism at its worst. My first thought was for Anne. What if she had purchased a paper and was even now reading it alone? How would she feel, seeing her painful past dragged out to be viewed and discussed by a scandal-hungry audience? That was what Cole was pandering to. He was selling newspapers with lurid entertainment rather than information, and he was doing it at Anne's expense.

"How much of it is true?" Peters asked.

It took a couple of seconds to comprehend the implications behind Peters' question. "How the hell should I know?" Angrily I shoved my chair away from the desk, banging it into the divider behind me. I stalked out the door with Peters hot on my heels. We said nothing in the lobby or in the crowded elevator. A couple of people made comment about the previous day's engagement party. It was all I could do to give their greeting a polite acknowledgment.

Once on the street I struck out for the waterfront. Peters picked up the conversation exactly where we'd left off. "You mean she hasn't talked about any of it, at least not to you."

"What's that supposed to mean? That she told all this to Cole and not to me?"

"Seems to me that she would have told you. After all, you are engaged, remember?"

I stopped and turned on him. "Get off my back, will you? I'm your partner. You're not my father confessor."

"But why hasn't she told you? If you had spent eleven years in a mental institution, wouldn't you give your bride-to-be a hint about it, so that if it came up later she wouldn't be surprised?"

"I don't know why she didn't tell me, but it doesn't matter. It's history, Peters. It has nothing to do with now, with the present or with us. Her past is none of my business."

"Why the big rush, then?"

"What's it to you? Why the hell is it any concern of yours?"

"It looks as though she thought if you found out, you'd drop her." He was silent for a minute, backing off a little. He came back at it from another direction. "Did you know she had that much money?"

We resumed walking, our pace a little less furious. "I knew she had some money," I allowed, "quite a bit of it. You don't stay at the Four Seasons on welfare. She said having too much money made it hard to know who her friends were."

"And you think that's why she didn't tell you how much?"

"Maybe," I said, "but I didn't ask her how much, Peters. Don't you understand? I don't have to know everything about her. She doesn't know that much about me, either. That takes time. There'll be time enough for that later."

"Has she shown you any of her book or have you personally seen her working on it?"

"Well, we've discussed it, but . . . No."

"Tell me again why she came to Angela's Barstogi's funeral."

Peters is single-minded. I have to respect that; I am too, usually. The only way to get him to drop it was to tell him what I knew. So I told him about Patty, about how much Anne had loved her, how Patty's death had upset and hurt her, how being unable to attend her sister's funeral as a child was something Anne Corley was doing penance for as an adult. It was a sketchy story at best, lacking the depth of details that would give the story credibility.

"How did she die?"

"I don't know."

We were walking north along the waterfront with a fresh wind blowing in across a gunmetal harbor. Peters listened thoughtfully as I told him what I could. Even as I told the story, I didn't need Peters' help to plug it full of holes.

"Just supposing," Peters suggested, "that she did have something to do with Angela Barstogi's death."

I stopped dead in my tracks. "Now wait a fucking minute."

"You wait a minute, Beaumont. You're too embroiled to see the forest for the trees, but that doesn't mean the rest of us are. All I'm doing is asking questions. If Anne Corley isn't hiding something, it's not going to hurt anything but your pride. Maybe there's a connection between Anne Corley and Uncle Charlie."

"Peters, Anne Corley had nothing to do with Angela Barstogi's death. She wasn't even in town until after the wire services had the story."

"It shouldn't be hard to prove, one way or the other. You owe it to yourself to get to the bottom of this. You can't afford to accept her presence at face value, particularly if she's not being up-front with you. You're a better cop than that."

Unerringly Peters hit the nerve where I was most vulnerable. Cops want to be right, one way or the other. They have to prove themselves over and over. Usually it's less personally important to them. Conflict of interest walked up and smacked me right in the face.

"I'd better ask Powell to pull me from the case," I said.

"Don't be an asshole. That's not necessary, not yet. If we come up with something definite, then it'll be time to bring Watkins and Powell into it.

In the meantime, I think some discreet questions to your old friend
Maxwell Cole are in order."

"Me talk to Cole?"

"No." Peters laughed. "Not you. I will."

"And what am I supposed to do while you do that?"

"Go back over every shred of information we have so far to see if you
can find anything new."

We had reached the Hillclimb, a steep flight of stairs that leads from
the waterfront up through the Public Market and back into the heart of the
city. I felt beaten, defeated. I had turned on her, given tacit approval to
Peters to go ahead and scrutinize Anne's past. Suddenly I was more than a
little afraid of what he might find there.

We climbed the stairs without speaking. The market was jammed with
vegetable and fish merchants setting out their wares. The boisterous activity
was totally at odds with how I felt. We came out of the market at First and
Pike. Peters turned right and started back toward the Public Safety Building.

I stopped. "I'm going to go talk to her," I called after him.

Peters came back. "Why?"

"I have to. I have to give her a chance to tell me. I want to hear it from
her."

"Suit yourself," Peters said with a shrug.

I didn't go directly back to the Royal Crest. Peters' questions hadn't
fallen on deaf ears. Why hadn't she told me? More to the point, what *had*
she told me? Very little, I decided. She had said she had been married
once, but she hadn't mentioned her husband's profession or his subsequent suicide. That's not surprising. Suicide is something that hangs
around forever, dropping load after load of guilt on the living.

Anne had divulged little of her family background, other than bits and
pieces about Patty. And she certainly hadn't mentioned being institutional-
ized; but then, that's hardly something you go around advertising. I know
I wouldn't.

Come to think of it, there was a lot I hadn't told her, either, gory details
in the life and times of J. P. Beaumont. I had touched briefly on my relationship with Karen, but that was all. It was as if Anne and I had an unspoken agreement not to let the past taint our present or our future. On the
one hand, I could rationalize and justify her not telling me her life story.
On the other hand, I was angry about it.

I walked for a long time, trying to think what I would say to her. There
wasn't the smallest part of me that accepted the idea she might have been
responsible for Angela Barstogi's death. I finally turned my steps home-
ward. I stopped and bought a *P.I.* from a vending machine on the corner. I

remembered her reaction when I had asked her about Patty. I had an obligation to be there when she read the article. After all, it was because of me
that she was drawing Maxwell Cole's fire.

The halls in high-rises are less well soundproofed than the apartments.
As I approached my door, I could hear Anne's voice from inside the unit.
That surprised me because I expected her to be there alone. I paused
before fitting my key in the lock. Listening through the door, I could hear
she was on the telephone, that she was finishing a conversation. I turned
my key in the lock and pushed the door open.

I expected to find her on the couch next to the phone. Instead, she was
halfway across the living room, eyes frantic, face ashen. She looked at my
face blankly, with no sign of recognition. All I could think was that she had
laid hands on the article before I got there.

I moved across the room quickly and grasped her by the shoulders. She
was shaking, quivering all over like someone chilled to the bone. "Anne,
Anne. What's wrong? Are you all right?"

For a long second we stood there like that, with me holding her. I
don't think my words registered at all. "What are you doing here?" she
asked.

"I came to check on you. I was afraid you'd read it by yourself. Have
you read it?" She was struggling, trying to escape my grasp. Her eyes stared
blindly into mine. She didn't answer.

"Who was that on the phone?" I demanded. "Who were you talking to?"

My words finally penetrated and she seemed to focus on my face, to
hear what I said. "No one," she stammered. "It was a wrong number."

I shoved her away from me, sending her reeling into the leather chair.
"Don't lie to me, Anne; for God's sake don't lie to me!" I wanted to shake
her, force her to tell me the truth. I started toward the chair, but the look
on her face stopped me. In seconds her face had been transformed. She
might have put on a mask. A calm, cold mask.

"It was business," she said, her voice flat and toneless.

"Yours or mine?"

"Mine," she said.

"Why did you tell me it was a wrong number?"

"I was upset."

I turned back to the couch and sat heavily, the weight of the world
crushing my shoulders. When I looked at her again, she was under control
and so was I, but something was dreadfully wrong. I forced my tone to be
gentle, made the words come slowly, the way you might if you were speaking to someone who didn't know the language. "Was it about the newspaper article?"

She blinked, puzzled. "What article?"

"Maxwell Cole's. In today's paper. It talks about Milton Corley. Tell me about him." I handed her the paper, open to Maxwell Cole's column. She read it quickly, then dropped it in her lap. She looked up at me.

"Why didn't you tell me, Anne? You left me wide open to attack."

Her eyes, fixed on mine, didn't waver. "I didn't think it mattered," she said.

"But it does matter. You should have told me. Yourself."

"What do you want to know?"

"Tell me about Milton Corley. Why did you marry him?" It was not a question I had expected to ask. It was the wounded cry of a jealous suitor, not a professional cop with his mind on his job.

"Because I loved him," she answered.

"Loved him or used him?"

"Used him first, loved him later."

Maybe she was being honest with me after all. "What about J. P. Beaumont? Is it the same with him?"

She raised her hands in a helpless gesture, then dropped them back in her lap. She nodded slowly. "At first I only wanted information."

I felt my heart constrict. "And now?"

"I love you." They were the words I wanted to hear, but I couldn't afford to believe them.

"Why?" The word exploded in the room. "Why do you love me?"

"Because you found the part of me that died when Milton did. I told you that last night."

"You expect me to believe that?"

"Yes. It's the truth."

My gaze faltered under her unblinking one. "Tell me about your book. I want to read it."

"All right," she said. "After I get it back from Ralph. I sent it to Phoenix with him. He's having it typed for me. I have to revise the last chapter."

"Why?"

"I made a mistake."

"What kind of mistake?"

She looked at me as if puzzled. "The kind that shouldn't be made if you're any kind of writer. Why all the questions?"

"I wanted to hear this from you, Anne. You should have told me. I shouldn't have had to read it in the newspaper. It makes you look suspicious."

For several long minutes we sat without speaking. "What about us?" she asked.

"I don't know," I said. "I'll have to give it some thought." I got up to leave. I had touched the personal issue and skirted the basic one. I had to ask. I had to have the answer from Anne Corley's own lips. "Did you have anything to do with Angela Barstogi's death?"

She heard the question without flinching. "So that's what's bothering you," she said in a monotone. She dropped her head in her hands. "No, Beau, I didn't. I was in Arizona. Check with United. Check with anybody."

"Do you know someone named Uncle Charlie?"

She shook her head. I went to the door and stood there uncertainly, my hand on the doorknob. I didn't know whether to leave or apologize. "I didn't think you did, but I'm getting some heat thanks to Maxey. I'd better go back to the office," I said at last. "I've got work to do."

CHAPTER 20

Work was a tonic for me that day. I worked like a fiend. I dove into every statement and every file with absolute concentration, finding comfort in the necessary discipline. Anne had said she had nothing to do with Angela Barstogi. I wanted to prove it to the world and to myself. There was nothing I wanted more than for Peters' suspicions to be dead wrong.

I put in a call to United. They said they'd call back with the information I needed. They did eventually, confirming Anne's arrival in Seattle. It proved the point as far as I was concerned, but the rest of the world needed more convincing. I had to lay hands on Angela Barstogi's killer. That was the only way to clear Anne once and for all. Who the hell was Uncle Charlie, and where was he? How could I find him?

It had been just over a week, but already Angela Barstogi's file was voluminous. I read through it all—statements, medical examiner's report, crime lab report—searching for some key piece that would pull the entire puzzle into focus. I had moved on to the Faith Tabernacle file when Peters came back about four o'clock.

"How's it going?" I asked. It was a natural enough question, but I felt strange after I asked it. I didn't know whether or not Peters would answer me. I didn't know if I wanted him to.

"Maxwell Cole is a jerk," he said. That was no surprise. It was something that found us in wholehearted agreement. Peters peered over my shoulder at the files. "Any luck?"

"Yeah. All bad."

He waited, expectantly, but I didn't volunteer any information. I wanted to see if he would ask. "What did she say?" he inquired finally.

"That she didn't have anything to do with it."

He shook his head. "And that's good enough for you, I suppose?"

"As a matter of fact, it isn't. If it were, I wouldn't be going blind reading these reports, and I wouldn't have called the airlines."

Peters settled on the corner of my desk. "Did you say you met Ralph Ames?" he asked.

"The attorney. Yes, I met him."

"How did he strike you, hotheaded maybe? Prone to fly off the handle?"

"No, just the opposite. Of course, he could be schizo. Who knows?"

"I put a little pressure on Cole. He gave me the name of the girl he talked to in Ames' office. I called right after I left Cole. Ames fired her fifteen minutes before that, for talking to Cole. That surprise you?"

"No. When I tried calling there I went through a screening process. It strikes me that Anne is a valued client."

"Valuable, certainly. The lady's loaded." He paused. "I'm going down there, Beau, to Arizona."

"Why?"

"I've picked up some information, enough to warrant the trip."

I stifled the desire to demand the information, to get Peters in a hammerlock until he came clean. But I knew he was doing his job, holding out on me until he had something concrete. He was right, of course.

"You've told Watty, then?" I could feel my heart pounding in my chest.

"No. I'm going on my own nickel. It's the weekend, and I want to get away from this drizzle. I'm feeling a yen for sunshine."

It took a second or two for me to understand the implication behind what he was saying. Gratitude washed over me like a flood. "Peters, I—"

"Don't thank me, Beau. You may not like what I find."

There was more than a hint of warning in his tone, but I ignored it. I chose to ignore it because I didn't want to hear it. "When's your plane?"

He glanced at his watch. "A little over an hour and a half. Want to take me down and keep the car?" He thought better of it. "Wait a minute. My plane gets in late Sunday evening. That's probably a bad time for you to come pick me up."

"If you're thinking about the wedding, we may go for a stay of execution."

He grinned and tossed me the keys. "Good," he said. "Let's go."

Late Friday afternoon traffic taxed my limited current driving skills. I had gotten out of the habit of fighting the freeway jungle. I had forgotten what it was like. Living downtown had liberated me from the tyranny of Detroit and Japan as well, to say nothing of Standard Oil. Peters winced at a tentative lane change.

"I don't get much practice driving anymore," I explained.

"That's obvious."

I dropped Peters in the departing-passenger lane and drove straight back to town. I didn't know what to think. There was no way to anticipate what I might find at the Royal Crest. My best possible guess was an empty apartment with or without a note.

If Anne Corley did nothing else, she consistently surprised me. She was waiting in the leather chair. A glass of wine was in her hand. A Mac-Naughton's and water sat on the coffee table awaiting my arrival. Anne was wearing a gown, a filmy red gown.

"Hello," she said. "You look surprised to see me."

"I am," I admitted. I examined the gown. I was sure I had seen it before, but I couldn't imagine where. At last it came to me—the hallway dream with Anne disappearing in a maze of corridors. I had dreamed the gown exactly, I realized as the odd sensation of déjà vu settled around me.

"I'm a very determined lady," she said softly. "Anybody else would have thrown in the towel after this morning. You didn't want me to go, did you?"

I sat down on the couch cautiously, tentatively. I tested my drink. "No, I didn't want you to go."

She took a sip of her wine. "You asked me this morning if I'd had anything to do with Angel's death. Does that mean I'm under suspicion?" I nodded. "And I'm being investigated?" I nodded again.

"That first afternoon we were together you said something that made me think Brodie was responsible. Yesterday the newspaper mentioned a man in a black van. Today you seem to think I did it. It reminds me of a game of tag with you standing in the center of a circle and pointing at people, telling them they're it."

"I have to prove they're it," I interjected. "In a court of law, beyond a shadow of doubt. That's a little different from pointing a finger."

"What if you make a mistake?"

"The court decides if they're guilty or innocent. That's not up to me. Where's all this going, Anne?"

She held up a hand to silence me. She was working her way toward something, gradually, circuitously. "How do you feel about those people afterward?"

I laughed, not a laugh so much as a mirthless chuckle. "In the best of all possible worlds, the innocent would go free and the guilty would be punished. In the real world, it doesn't always work that way."

"Supposing . . . ," she started. She paused as if weighing her words. For the first time I noticed a tightness around her mouth. Whatever she was working up to, it was costing her. She had been looking out the window as she spoke, uncharacteristically avoiding my eyes. Now, she turned away from the window, settling her gaze on my face. "Supposing someone was guilty of something but the court set them free. How would you feel about that?"

"If the court sets them free, I have no choice but to respect the court's decision. My feelings have nothing to do with it."

"That's not true, they do!" She jumped up quickly and hurried to the kitchen to replenish the drinks. I watched in fascination. Her movements were jerky, as though she changed her mind several times in the course of the smallest gesture. Where was her purposeful manner, her fluid grace? She came back with the drinks.

"Have you ever been around someone who's retarded?" she asked?

The question was from way out in left field. "No," I replied, "I never have."

"Patty was retarded. I loved her and I didn't mind taking care of her, but she didn't have any control over her bowels. My father hated her for it." Anne stopped abruptly and stood by the coffee table, staring at me as though she expected me to say something. I didn't know what. I reached out and took her hand, drawing her toward the couch.

"I'm sorry," I said. Her body was like a strung bow. I pulled her down beside me, a question formulating itself as I did so. "Who killed Patty?" I asked. I expected her to rebel, to shy away from my hand.

"My father," she whispered. "I saw him do it, but no one would believe me. The coroner ruled it an accident. I tried to tell people, but that's when they started saying I was crazy."

"Who said that, the people you told?"

"Yes," she said quietly. "My mother, her friends."

"And that's when they wouldn't let you go to the funeral?"

A single tear brimmed over the top of her lower lash and started down her cheek. "Yes," she answered. "She wouldn't let me go."

She turned to me for comfort from an old but open wound, burying her head in my chest. Wracking sobs filled the room, the kind of sobs that leave you exhausted without bringing relief. I held her, imagining a helpless eight- or nine-year-old battling alone against injustices perpetrated by adults. Injustice is hard enough to handle as a full-grown man, as a homicide detective. To a child it must have been overwhelming.

I let her cry. There was no point in my saying anything or in attempting to stop her tears before the pent-up emotion had run its course.

At last the sobs subsided and she pulled herself away from me. "I'm sorry," she said. "I never can talk about it without that happening."

"Don't apologize. It's not necessary."

She leaned her head back against my arm and closed her eyes. "I wanted to tell you this morning, but I couldn't. It took me all afternoon to work up to it."

"Thank you," I said, and meant it. I looked at her as she lay with her head thrown back, the strain of the last few hours and moments still painfully etched on her face. She had opened the door a crack and let me see what was inside. It helped me understand her complexity a little and her reticence. I leaned down and kissed away a smudge of tear-stained mascara from her cheek. "Stick with me, kid. We'll make it."

She lifted her head and looked at me. "What makes you say that?"

"I love you, Anne. That's what makes me say it."

The kiss I gave her then was not a brotherly, comforting kind of kiss. I felt the exhilaration you feel after you step off a roller coaster and know you haven't died of it. I wanted to affirm our loving and our living. I wanted to put the ghosts from her past to rest once and for all, and she did too. She responded willingly, hungrily.

The gown was fastened by a single tie. She was naked beneath it, naked, supple, and ready. I slipped out of my own clothes and fell to my knees before her, letting my hands roam freely across her body, letting my tongue pleasure her with promise and torment her with denial. I reveled in the power of control, the feel of her body's aching need awakened at my touch. Several times I brought her to the brink, only to back off, pulling away before she crossed the edge, leaving her writhing, pleading for satisfaction.

"Please, Beau," she begged. "Please."

I drew her to the floor and onto me, my own need no longer held at bay. Her body folded around me and I was home. She gave a muffled moan of pleasure and release. I was complete and so was she.

CHAPTER 21

We napped. There on the floor. Much later, nearly ten, she stirred and awakened me. She snuggled close to me for warmth. "Hungry?" I asked.

"Of course."

"Where would you like to go?" I asked. "I have Peters' car parked downstairs. For a change, wheels come with the invitation."

She laughed. "Uptown, huh?"

"Not exactly, it's a Datsun." She laughed again and got up, picking up the gown from where it had fallen on the couch and tying it deftly around her. It was lovely, but I preferred her without it. I too scrambled to my feet. She stood looking up at me, her eyes momentarily uncertain. I held her close, hoping to stifle all doubt. "Don't worry," I told her. "It'll be all right."

That seemed to give her the reassurance she needed. I followed her into the bedroom. A set of suitcases sat in one corner. She lifted one onto the bed and opened it. "I didn't know if I was moving in or moving out."

The suitcase was filled with clothes on hangers. I picked them up, all of them, and swept them into one end of the closet. "Moving in," I said.

She unpacked quickly with the practiced hand of one who has done it many times. I had never learned to use all the drawers in the obligatory six-drawer dresser, so there was room for her to unpack without my having to shove things around. It seemed as though I had been saving a place for her in my life.

While she showered, I took a lesson from the lady and called for a dinner reservation. Most people who live in Seattle regard the Space Needle as a place visited only by tourists. Not me. It's special enough for a meal there to be an occasion, and it has the added attraction of being within walking distance. I take my kids there for Christmas dinner when they're home for the holidays. The Emerald Suite, the gourmet part of the restaurant on top of the Space Needle, had a last-minute cancellation, so they were able to take us.

When Anne emerged from the shower, I was tying my tie and humming a little tune. I was starting to feel as though the two of us might be on somewhat equal footing. I was conscious of being terrifically happy, and for right then, at least, I was wise enough not to question it.

I had dressed while she unpacked. Now it was my turn to lie on the bed and watch her. She stood indecisively at the closet door for a moment. "What should I wear?"

"We're not going to the Doghouse," I replied.

She chose a muted red dress of delicate silk. Red was her color on any occasion, in any light. Before I met her I had no idea red came in so many different shades. Maxwell Cole had been more correct than he knew when he called her the Lady in Red.

Carefully she selected underwear and put it on. It was a quiet, intimate time together, with her doing things she would usually do alone. She didn't seem disturbed by my presence or by my watching her. In the short period we had been together a bonding had occurred. I had experienced that bonding only once before, with Karen, and then I'd lost it. I was grateful to have it back. I hadn't realized how much I'd missed it.

Anne came to me to zip the dress and to fasten the diamond pendant. "From Milton?" I asked, surprised that there was no pang of jealousy as I asked the question.

"Yes," she said, turning to kiss me. "Thanks."

"Where's your car?" I asked. "Did you bring it along with your clothes?"

She nodded. "It's down on the street."

"We'll have to move it to a lot in the morning, or we'll spend all day feeding parking meters."

"Would you like to take it?" she asked.

I tossed Peters' Datsun keys into the air. "Not on a bet. I don't think I'd better press my luck. I'm just barely qualified for a Datsun. A Porsche would be overkill."

Of course we could have walked, but I drove up to the valet parking attendant. He opened the door with a slight bow in Anne's direction, diplomatically concealing most of his disdain for the battered Datsun.

The old Anne Corley was back. She was delighted and delightful. Everything about the evening pleased her. As the restaurant rotated she asked questions about various landmarks. She ate like a famished puppy and joked with the waiter, who regarded her with a certain awe. We drank champagne and toasted our future. It was a festive, joyous occasion.

The conversation was light, fun-filled nonsense. It was only when the coffee came and we were working our way through two final glasses of wine that she turned serious on me. I knew enough to be wary by now, to tread softly and not force her beyond her own speed.

"Do you want me to tell you about Milton?" she asked softly.

"Only if you want to, only if you think I need to know."

"It's the same version they wrote years ago. He sounds like a monster who took advantage of a young female patient, doesn't he?"

"That's why he lost his job, isn't it?"

"People were only interested in how things looked. No one cared how things really were. It's too much trouble to look beneath the surface."

"But he committed suicide."

"He didn't do it because of his job," she said. "He was dying of cancer. He didn't want to go on. He didn't want to face what was coming. I understand that a lot more now than I did then." She paused. "How old are you, Beau?"

"Forty-two, going on sixty."

"Milton was sixty-three when I married him." She made the statement quietly and waited for my reaction.

"Sixty-three!" I choked on a sip of coffee.

Anne smiled. "I've always gone for older men," she teased. The smile faded from her face, her eyes. "He was the first person who believed me."

I struggled to follow her train of thought. "You mean about Patty?"

She nodded. "I had been locked up in that place for five years when I met him, and he was the very first person who believed me."

"How is that possible?"

"You told me yourself. This isn't the best of all possible worlds, remember? I stayed because my mother had enough money to pay to keep me there. I'd have been pronounced cured and turned loose if we'd been poor."

She watched in silence as the waiter refilled her cup with coffee. "Doctors become omnipotent in places like that. They have the power of life and death over you. The smallest kindness becomes an incredible gift. He took an interest in me. He promised he'd take care of me if I'd have sex with him."

Outrage came boiling to the surface. "When you were thirteen and he was fifty-seven?"

"No. I said I met him then. I was seventeen when it started." She was holding her cup in both hands, looking at me through the steam, using it as a screen to protect her from my sudden flare of anger. "There's no need to be angry," she said. "He kept his part of the bargain, and I kept mine. He saw to it that I got an education, that I had books to read, that I learned things. On weekends he would get me a pass and take me places. He bought me clothes, taught me how to dress, how to wear my hair. I don't have any complaints."

"But Anne . . ."

"When my mother died, I was nineteen. He hired Ancell Ames, Ralph's father, to lay hands on the moneys left in trust for me, money my mother had been appropriating over the years. He got me out of the hospital, and we got married. Everyone believed he married me because of the money. Nobody cared that he had plenty himself. It made a better scandal the other way around." For the first time I heard a trace of bitterness in her voice.

"Did you love him when you married him?"

She shook her head. "That came later. I loved him when he died."

She set down her coffee cup, gray eyes searching mine. "Do you want to know about the money?"

I reached across the table and took her hand. "No," I said, laughing. "I don't want to know about the money. Maybe you should get Ralph to draw up a prenuptial agreement. Would that make you feel better?"

"What's mine is yours," she said.

"Me too," I grinned, "but I think you're getting the short end of the stick."

She sat there looking beautiful and troubled. A lifetime of tragedy had swirled around her and brought her to me. I wanted to free her from all that had gone before, to set her feet firmly on present, solid ground. I took her hand and held it with both my massive paws around her slender fingers. "Considering what you've been through, you have every right to be totally screwed up."

"Maybe you haven't noticed," she replied. "I am totally screwed up."

"So where does all this leave us?" I asked.

"I've talked to Ralph. He's coming back up tomorrow night. I want him to be a witness. What about Peters?"

"He's out of town," I told her, guiltily remembering that I had assured Peters the wedding would be postponed. It was too late to do anything about that, however.

Anne must have seen my hesitation. "You do still want to get married, don't you?"

She sat waiting for my answer; both pain and doubt visible in her face, her eyes. I succumbed.

"I think all my objections have just been overruled," I said. "Would you like to dance?"

She nodded. There was a piano player in the bar, the music soft, old and danceable. I'm a reasonably capable dancer, and Anne flowed with my body. The admiration of those watching was obvious, and I enjoyed it. I wanted to be seen with her; I wanted to be the one who brought Anne Corley to Seattle and kept her there.

We danced until one. I was sleepy when we got back to the apartment. Anne said she was wide-awake and wanted to stay up and rework the last chapter. She wanted to send it with Ralph on Sunday. She also said she planned to jog early in the morning. I kissed her good night in the living room.

"Thanks for a wonderful evening, Anne. All of it."

"It was good, wasn't it?" she agreed.

"Promise we'll have a lifetime of evenings like this."

She didn't answer; she kissed me. "Good night," she murmured with her lips still on mine.

"Good night yourself."

I went to bed and slept the sleep of the just. Peters wouldn't be bringing me any surprises when he came back from Arizona. Anne had finally told me everything.

CHAPTER 22

Freshly shampooed hair, newly dried and fragrant, awakened me on Saturday morning. Anne slipped into bed beside me, her body still warm from a steamy bathroom. "Been out running?" I asked.

"Yes."

She rested her head in the curve of my neck and ran her fingers along the stiff stubble on my jaw.

"What time is it?" I asked, not wanting to turn to see the clock.

"Six," she replied.

"In the morning?" I groaned. "On Saturday? You get up and run at this ungodly hour on Saturday?"

She closed her teeth gently over the muscle on the side of my neck, sending involuntary chills through my body. "What's the matter with being up at this hour?"

"Nothing at all," I said, "now that you put it that way." I rolled over on top of her, pinning her beneath me. "You shouldn't start something you can't finish."

"I can finish it," she replied, placing her hands around the back of my neck and pulling my lips to hers.

What she said actually turned out to be a gross understatement. She was a wild woman, frenzied in her demands for gratification. Had I not known better, firsthand, I might have thought she had gone without for years. She crouched naked astraddle me, plunging herself down on my body with wild abandon, her head thrown back, her face reflecting a fleeting mixture of pain and pleasure. I held back as long as I could, wanting to prolong her enjoyment, but that wasn't enough.

She came back again for more, kissing me, touching me, renewing me until I was able once more to probe inside her, to touch that part of her that had gone for far too long untouched. This time she collapsed on my chest afterward, breath coming in short gasps, her heart thumping wildly from exertion. "Not bad for an old man," I managed.

"Not bad at all," she agreed.

We lay together for a long time, our legs entwined, her head pillowed on my chest. She dozed. We both did. The next thing we knew it was almost eight o'clock. I woke up first, and gave her a gentle slap on the rump. "All right, now it's time to rise and shine," I told her. "We've got to go shopping, and I suppose you're starved. You always are."

"You called that shot," she replied.

I got up and wandered over to the window. The first thing I saw was a diligent meter maid making her way down Third Avenue. "Oops," I gulped. "I'd better run and feed the meter. Where's you car?"

"I already moved it to a lot," she said.

I hurried down to the Datsun and got there as the parking cart was pulling to a stop. "You just made it," the driver said.

Happily I hurried back to Anne. "Saved us ten bucks just now, which I intend to blow on breakfast. I only put half an hour in the meter."

"Where are we going?"

"I've got a friend who left the force to run a jewelry store in Northgate. We're going there for wedding rings. All we have right now is an engagement ring. I'm the old-fashioned type."

"I never would have guessed."

I took her arm and pulled her to me. "Look, young lady, just because we've been having the honeymoon before the wedding, doesn't mean I approve."

She laughed. "I haven't heard any strenuous objections."

We had breakfast before the jewelry store opened and made what plans we could for the day. Ralph Ames' plane was due in at eight fifty-seven, and I thought it only reasonable that we pick him up. I found myself wondering if he was coming as a guest or if his attendance was an official function for which Anne would be billed later. It was none of my business, however, and I didn't ask.

I wished Peters would call. He had left the name of a hotel in Phoenix, and I tried reaching him there but was told he had checked out. I wanted to invite him to the wedding, now that it was on again. He was the only guest from the department I wanted to be there.

The jeweler, Jackson Hall, was a cop until he got ulcers. A partial disability had made him take a second look at the family jewelry business. He had accepted the Northgate branch with good grace if not enthusiasm. He was happy to help us choose matching gold bands, and threw in a set of crystal cocktail glasses as a wedding present.

Jackson sent us to a friend of his in the travel business. In all the rush we had neglected to discuss a honeymoon. Now, with Ralph's plane schedule in hand, we decided on a wedding trip to Victoria on Monday morning. I had plenty of vacation time available, and I figured Powell wouldn't squawk too loud if I used some of it. Through a fluke, a split-level suite with a fireplace was available in the Empress Hotel. We booked it on the spot for Monday and Tuesday nights. We also got a reservation for Monday afternoon's ritual High Tea.

Anne and I gave ourselves a shower that morning and afternoon, not the rubadubdub variety, but the bridal kind. We went from one department store to another, splurging on new sheets, towels, kitchen linens. Anne, long a nomad, had seldom purchased household items. She did it beautifully, her choices impeccable, but also with a childlike wonder and glee that made it seem a springtime Christmas shopping spree. Sometimes I paid, and sometimes she did, but there was no point in quibbling over money. Obviously, we weren't in a position that we would have to worry about the bills.

We dragged our last load of purchases to the car, laughing and cutting up like a couple of kids. The trunk was full and the backseat was rapidly disappearing. "What now?" I asked.

"I'd like you to choose my dress," she said.

For some reason, that touched me, put a lump in my throat. "All right, but you do so at your own risk. I know what I like. I don't know anything about fashion."

"Whatever you like will be fine."

We hopscotched from store to store, with Anne gamely trying on first one dress and then another. Spring dictated pastels, which looked washed out and pale against her strikingly dark hair and tawny complexion. I was going to give it up and marry her in her red jogging suit when a saleswoman brought out a vivid turquoise suit. There was a hint of the Far East in the cut, and the material was a burnished silk. I knew it was right before she ever put it on.

The clerk, pleased to be making some progress, located a delicately feminine blouse and a suitable pair of shoes. When Anne came out of the dressing room, she had fastened her hair on top of her head, with a few tendrils dangling here and there. She was breathtakingly beautiful, and she was mine.

To give the store time to press it, we made arrangements to pick the dress up in an hour. Then we went in search of flowers. I can see how planning for a wedding can take a lifetime. We made decisions together, quickly, and in perfect agreement.

Last but not least, I too was decked out in a new outfit—a suit plucked right off the rack with a matching shirt and tie. It was late afternoon before we finished shopping and staggered back to the apartment. We unloaded the car and left again, this time in search of groceries. Anne had decided to cook a prewedding supper to be served after Ralph's late-evening arrival.

Anne bustled happily in the kitchen while I refrigerated her corsage and two boutonnieres—one for Ames and one for me. By the time I unpacked the rest of our purchases, my linen closet bulged with new additions, and I bagged excess castoffs to take to the Children's Orthopedic Thrift Store on Third Avenue. Already the apartment was showing signs of Anne's presence, her blues and greens softening and diluting the masculine "statement" my decorator had undeniably achieved.

By seven my part of the job was under control. I sat in the living room waiting until it was time to go to the airport. It was then I remembered Andrew Carstogi for the first time that day. He had been so far from my thoughts that his jail cell might have been in Timbuktu. I had been too full of my own plans and concerns to give his problems any consideration.

He came to mind, and I felt a twinge of guilt. It was his pain that was directly responsible for my newfound happiness. I was sorry he was locked up. Our investigation had found nothing that would justify holding him beyond Monday. He would go free that afternoon and return to Chicago and pick up the shattered remnants of his life, having lost a wife, a child, and a week from his life, while I had gained Anne Corley. Life is not fair.

Anne came in from the kitchen, untying the apron we had purchased that afternoon. Already it was soiled with a variety of culinary debris. Stuffed Cornish game hens had gone into the oven along with some scalloped potatoes. A complex salad lurked in the refrigerator. We had chosen an exotic Häagen-Dazs ice cream for dessert.

"Ready to go get Ralph?" she asked.

"Do we have to? Can't I just have you all to myself?"

"Let's go," she said. "If I followed the directions right, the oven will turn off and the food will still be hot when we get back."

"Slave driver," I said, but we headed for the airport.

A magnificent sunset was in progress as we drove south along the Viaduct. The snowcapped Olympics reached skyward over a mirrored sound, while the sky ranged from lavender to orange above us. "I don't know when I've been this happy, Anne. Not for years."

"No second thoughts?"

"Nope."

"I don't have any either."

I laughed. "Do you realize we're getting married on our anniversary? We will have known one another for one whole week tomorrow."

"I think I've known you forever," Anne said softly.

I glanced across the front seat at her, took her hand in mine, and squeezed it. "I think maybe you're right."

I had the usual hassle with airport security over the .38 Smith and Wesson under my jacket. I stuck out like a sore thumb while they verified that I really did have a permit to carry it. Once that was squared away, Anne and I wandered the airport hand in hand, watching planes take off and land, eating caramel corn we bought from the airport candy shop, and griping at one another about ruining our dinner. The passage of time was magic. It seemed to lengthen, but without a sense of waiting. Happiness can do that to you. So can grief.

When Ralph got off the plane, he had a huge box under one arm. It contained long-stemmed red roses, two dozen of them to be exact. I looked at Ralph as a brother-in-law of sorts, which is to say somewhat critically. I watched Anne open the box and wondered crabbily where the hell we would put two dozen roses once we got them home. A mayonnaise jar? Masculine decor isn't long on vases.

I need not have worried, however. In the car Ralph produced another box from a suitcase. He gave it to Anne, with orders that I was to open it when we got to the apartment. The flowers were from him to Anne, but the box was a wedding present to both of us from the firm.

Inside the box was a tall, slender crystal vase. Anne arranged the roses in it and set it on the stereo. Dinner was festive. Ralph was interested in our plans and, to all appearances, more than happy with Anne's decision to marry me.

"She's a wonderful lady," he said to me later in the evening when we were alone in the living room for a few minutes. "She deserves a little happiness out of life, and I've never seen her happier than she is right now."

I felt as though someone had just placed the Good Housekeeping Seal of Approval square in the middle of my forehead. "Thanks, Ralph," I said. "I'm pretty happy myself."

CHAPTER 23

Some days are forever etched in your memory. Three of them come to mind right off the bat—the day my mother died, the day I married Karen, and the day I married Anne Corley. Anne had assured me there was no need to set an alarm, that she would be awake long before five o'clock, and she was. She kissed me and set a cup of coffee on the table beside my bed.

There was no question of fooling around. She was all business. She had finished in the bathroom, leaving it clear for me. I showered and shaved carefully, critically examining myself in the mirror. I hadn't thought about my looks in years, but I was reasonably happy with what I saw. There was a sprinkle of gray around the temples. Anne liked it, said it gave me an air of authority, liked a seasoned anchorman. I managed to put aside my antimedia prejudices long enough to accept that as a compliment. There would have been a lot of gray in the beard if I'd let it grow. The point was, if all the gray didn't matter to Anne, it didn't matter to me.

I wrapped a towel around me and went into the bedroom. Anne stood before the dresser in her slip and bra, piling her hair on top of her head. The result was a gentle framing of her face that reminded me of the late 1890s. It was old-fashioned and attractive.

"You look lovely," I said, running my finger along the soft curve at the top of her lacy slip.

She caught my finger and held it to her lips. "Thank you," she said. "You're not so bad yourself."

I lifted her chin and looked at her. Her eyes were quiet, subdued. "Are you all right?" I asked.

"I'm fine. Just a little nervous."

"I'm a lot more than a little," I told her. That brought a trace of a smile.

Ralph Ames came by the Royal Crest and drove the Datsun. Anne and I took the Porsche. She drove. The minister arrived in a pea green Volkswagen bus. Those were the only three cars in the parking lot at Myrtle Edwards Park when we got there about ten to six. The sun was just putting in an appearance over the hills behind us, while a fresh breeze blew off the water. I worried that Anne might not be warm enough in the shimmering blue suit with its flimsy blouse.

Anne introduced me to the minister. I don't know where she found him. He didn't push any creed, and it may well be that marrying people was his whole ministry. That was okay by me. When the minister asked, "Who giveth this woman?" Ralph stepped forward and said he did. I thought he had a hell of a lot of nerve, but since he was giving her to me, I didn't complain. The ceremony took exactly six minutes. We were in the Four Seasons for breakfast by six-fifteen.

Anne was radiant. I could have slit my throat for not having a camera along, but once more Ralph rode to the rescue. He took pictures of both of us together, and each of us separately. He had even made last-minute arrangements with the hotel for them to produce a tiny three-tiered wedding cake with all the trimmings. It was a nice gesture. It pissed me off. I would have preferred him to be not quite so thoughtful or indispensable.

It was time for Ralph's plane before we finished breakfast. I told Anne I'd take him to the airport in the Datsun. She could take the Porsche back to the apartment, and I'd meet her there later. We rode down the escalator together. The parking attendant brought the Porsche first. I could hardly blame him for that. I opened the door and gave her a hand inside. I leaned down so our heads were even. "I love you, Anne Corley Beaumont," I said.

She smiled. "I love you too." With that, she drove away.

Ralph Ames was standing beside me when I straightened up. "Ready?" he asked. We said little as we drove to the airport. We had nothing in common but Anne. "Did she give you the last chapter to her manuscript?" I asked as we pulled under the airport awning.

He patted his briefcase. "Last chapter? I've got the whole book right here. She's been working on it for so long I can't believe I'm finally going to get a look at it."

"You mean you've never read any of it before? I thought she had already given you everything but the revised last chapter."

"Not before today. I'm planning to take a peek at it on the plane." He dragged his luggage out of the backseat and hustled off toward a waiting skycap with a brief salute to me from beside the car. "Best of luck to you," he said.

I drove back out to the freeway, a little edge of worry gnawing at me. I could have sworn Anne had said the manuscript was already in Phoenix, that was why she couldn't show it to me. Had I somehow misunderstood?

I was halfway back to Seattle when a state patrolman pulled me over. I got out of the car in a huff, ready to show him my I.D. and give him a piece of my mind. I knew damned good and well I hadn't been speeding.

"You J. P. Beaumont?" he asked as he reached the car.

"What of it?"

"We've got an APB out for you. Captain Powell has been trying to get you at home since seven o'clock this morning. Get in. I'll patch you through to Seattle P.D."

I got in, and the patrolman made a connection to the Seattle dispatcher. "Get down here right away. Powell is waiting. He's hot!"

"What the hell do you mean, get down there? I just got married. I'm supposed to be off duty."

"He said to tell you your leave is canceled. He needs you now."

I got out of the patrol car and slammed the door. "Sorry I pulled you over," the patrolman said. "If I'da known the circumstances, I never would have seen you."

"Thanks," I said. "For nothing," I added under my breath.

I drove to the Public Safety Building. Powell was in the fishbowl on the phone as I came in. "What the fuck is going on?" I growled as he hung up.

"We've got another homicide. This one's down in Auburn. It was in the paper this morning."

"I hate to mention this, but I don't work in Auburn. I work for the city of Seattle."

Powell went on as though he hadn't heard me. "A guy came tearing in here at seven o'clock looking for you. He says it's about the Auburn case. He refuses to talk to anyone but you."

"Where is he?"

Powell nodded in the direction of one of the interview rooms. "He's in there. His name is Tom Stahl."

I didn't recognize the name right off the bat, and the slightly built, crewcut young man who paced nervously back and forth in the tiny interview room didn't ring any bells either. From the delicate sway of his hips, I guessed he was a little light in his loafers, one of Seattle's more obvious gays. I let the door slam shut behind me. "I'm Detective Beaumont," I said. "What can I do for you?"

"Everybody connected with this case is getting killed. I'm sure I'm next. When I read the newspaper this morning, I almost had a heart attack. I knew right away it was the same man; I mean, how many Charles Murray Kincaids can there be?" His words came in a breathless lisp.

"What the hell are you talking about?" Stahl had been clutching a newspaper in his hand. Now he dropped it on the table like a hot potato.

"It happened right after I tried to call you, the night before last or yesterday morning, too late to make it into the paper until today. I always read the paper early, before I go to church."

"What happened? For God's sake, make some sense, man." Without meaning to, I was yelling at him. He pushed the paper in my direction and scurried to the far side of the room.

"Read it yourself. I demand some protection."

I read the article. It was simple enough. An Auburn resident, Charles Murray Kincaid, had been found shot to death in an automobile outside his home early Saturday morning. Police were investigating. He had been shot once in the back of the head. There was nothing in the article to explain Tom Stahl's extreme agitation. "So what?" I asked.

"Look at the address." I looked. "It's the same address I gave your wife."

"Now wait a minute," I said, trying to modify my tone. He was obviously frightened. "Let's get this straight. I didn't have a wife until six-fifteen this morning. Why don't you tell me the whole story, from the beginning."

He took a deep breath. "It's about Angela Barstogi," he said. "She ran up a big long-distance bill talking to some guy down in Auburn. Her mother called to complain about the bill. Said she wouldn't pay it because she didn't make the calls. I did some checking. Kincaid had an easy telephone number, 234-5678. It's long-distance from Seattle. Kids called him all the time. As soon as they learned their numbers on "Sesame Street," they'd string numbers together and call him: 1-234-5678. We tried to get him to change his number, vacate it so it would be a disconnect. But he wouldn't. Claimed he loved talking to little kids.

"Anyway, I called one morning to talk to the mother, Mrs. Barstogi. She was asleep, so I ended up talking to Angela. I told her she shouldn't call him anymore, that her mother would have to pay the bill. She said she liked talking to Uncle Charlie on the phone, so when—"

"Wait a minute," I interrupted. "Did you say Uncle Charlie?"

He nodded. "So after I heard she was dead, I tried to call you and tell you, just in case it was important. I only wanted to give you his name and phone number. It's illegal for me to do that, you know. I could be fined and lose my job, but I didn't want to go through security when it was probably nothing. The guys in security don't like me."

"You work for the phone company?" The name came back to me, the messages I had ignored and thrown away. He nodded again.

"When I couldn't reach you at the office, I finally got your unlisted number and called your house. I could be fired for that too."

"My house?"

"Yeah. I called Friday morning. I went to a two-day training session out in Bellevue on Wednesday and Thursday, so I didn't try calling again until I got back to the office on Friday. The woman I talked to said she was your wife, said she'd give you the message. I left Kincaid's name and address with her."

My stomach turned to lead. Just then Powell tapped on the door. "A detective from Auburn is here with their preliminary report. I thought you'd like to talk to him. He says Kincaid drove a black van. You think maybe there's a connection?"

"I'd bet money on it," I said grimly. "Where's the detective?"

"He's taking some stuff down to the crime lab."

I picked up the phone in Powell's office. Some numbers you know by heart. I dialed the crime lab. Janice Morraine answered. I recognized her voice. "Hi, Jan," I said, trying to sound casual. "Beaumont here. Did they bring you a slug from that Auburn case?"

"I think so," she replied.

"Run a comparison with the Faith Tabernacle slugs and call me back." I put down the phone, fighting the urge to heave it across the room.

Powell was looking at me, puzzled. "What have you got, Beaumont?"

"Just a hunch, nothing more."

Tom Stahl came to the door of the interview room. "What next? Protective custody? Do I go, or stay, or what?"

"First we'll need to get a statement. Hang on a minute. You want a cup of coffee?" I couldn't handle being locked up in a small room taking a statement, not when my mind was flying in a dozen different directions.

"Coffee would be fine," he said. "Black."

I walked past my desk on the way to the coffeepot. I stopped and dialed my home number. I got a busy signal. There was a stack of messages on the desk, too. The top one was from Peters, clocked in at seven-twenty that morning. The number was different from the hotel I had tried the previous day.

I dialed and was connected to Peters' room. "Thank God you caught me. I was just heading out to catch a plane. I've booked an earlier flight from Tucson. Where'd they find you?" he asked. "When the operator said your phone was out of order, I took a chance and called the department. They were looking for you. I told them you might be driving the Datsun."

"It worked," I said. "They found me. What have you got?"

There was a distinct pause. "It's not pretty, Beau," he began. "I hope it's not too late. Has she told you about her father?"

"Some," I replied.

"Coroner ruled it a suicide, but Anne swore she'd shot him for killing her sister. That's when her mother had her committed."

My mind scrambled to make sense from what Peters was saying. "Shot him? Anne said she shot her father?" I felt like I was stumbling in the dark.

Peters heard my disbelief. "I came down to Bisbee to check it out. According to records here, Anne's father fell carrying Patty down some stairs. He felt so bad about it he put a bullet in his head two weeks later. Anne insisted she shot him, and she claimed that Patty's death was no accident, that her father had murdered her. Her mother had Anne committed. That's why she spent eleven years in the state hospital."

I could hear the sound of Peters' breathing on the other end of the phone. For the life of me, I couldn't think of anything to say.

"Beau, are you all right?"

After being in the dark, sudden light blinded me. "I've gotta go, Peters," I said. I slammed the phone down in his ear. Powell was coming toward me. I almost knocked him over. "Get somebody to take Stahl's statement," I said over my shoulder.

"Hey, wait a minute. Janice Morraine from the lab tried to get you while you were on your phone," he called after me. "Says to tell you it's a match."

And the rest of my world tumbled down around my ears.

CHAPTER 24

My hands were shaking so badly I could hardly get the key in the ignition. Truths and half-truths chased each other in dizzying circles in my head. Milton Corley had been the first to believe her. That's what she had said. So he was the first to understand that Anne had told the truth about killing her father. The realization sickened me, but I feared the past far less than I did the present.

It was not yet ten o'clock on Sunday morning, and downtown Seattle was virtually deserted. I made short work of the trip to the Royal Crest. She wasn't there. I knew she wouldn't be. The telephone in the bedroom was slightly off the hook. When I hung it up properly, it started working again. How long had the phone been disabled? I wondered. Since last night?

I looked in the closets, in the drawers. The clothes were there; nothing was missing. Then I checked the corner on the other side of the dresser. The Adidas bag was gone. I poured myself a shot of MacNaughton's and sat down in my leather chair. I needed to think.

I tried to remember Friday night. When had we gotten home? What had been said? I remembered going to bed, her saying she wanted to stay up and work on the last chapter so she could send it down to Phoenix with Ralph.

The next thing I remembered was her crawling into bed with me Saturday morning, telling me she had been out for a jog. I had no way of knowing whether or not she had come to bed before that. It had seemed reasonable to assume she had. There had been no cause to question it, but there was no way to prove it, either. There would have been plenty of time for her to drive to Auburn and back between the time I went to sleep and the time I woke up. When had she moved the Porsche to a parking lot?

I waited for the phone to ring, knowing it was unreasonable, knowing she wouldn't call. Where could she be? What was she thinking? Didn't she know I loved her, that I'd find help for her whatever the cost? I waited.

I thought about Pastor Michael Brodie and Suzanne Barstogi blown away in Faith Tabernacle by the same weapon that had killed Charles Murray Kincaid. The same .38. Christ. She must have done that, too. What night was that? Monday? I tried to remember Monday night. She had been here; we had made love. We had made love Saturday morning, too. My stomach rebelled at the thought of her excitement, her need for satisfaction. Had she come to me on the crest of murderous heat that I had misread as passion? I battled to keep breakfast and the MacNaughton's in place. The breakfast, the liquor, and the wedding cake. Jesus.

Had she thought she could get away with it forever, that I would never find out? Or was I next on her list? How long was the list, for that matter? Her father, Brodie, Suzanne, Kincaid? How many more were there? What about Corley? Had Milton Corley really committed suicide, or had he been given a helping hand along the way?

I waited. Peters would be home by four or so. At that point Powell would know and Watkins and the world. An all-points bulletin would go out for Anne Corley Beaumont, wanted for murder, beautiful and highly dangerous. I had to find her before then. I had to be the one to bring her in. The thought of Anne in handcuffs, tossed in the back of a patrol car, was anathema to me.

I waited, watching the time slip by, watching the minute hand move inexorably. I sat for a long, long time, letting my mind wander through the last few days, searching for some hope, some consolation. There was none. I watched the clock without thinking about it, without internalizing the information it was trying to give me. It was two o'clock when I got the message, two o'clock when I realized that at that time one week ago, Angela Barstogi's funeral was just getting under way, and Anne Corley was about to walk into my life.

I jumped to my feet, remembering. She had said she intended to have a standing reservation for Sunday dinner at Snoqualmie Lodge. My nerves were too shot to tackle the phone book myself. I placed a call to the lodge and a hostess answered. "Does Anne Corley have a reservation there for this afternoon?"

There was a pause while she looked. "Yes she does, a reservation for two at three o'clock." I had been holding my breath. I let it out in a long sigh.

"Would you like to leave a message? I'll be glad to give it to her."

"No. No, thank you. I'll catch her later."

I put down the phone. Either she wouldn't show or she was expecting me. It was one or the other. The hostess had said the reservation was for two, not one. I went into the bathroom and splashed cold water on my face. I buried my face in a towel, a soft new towel Anne Corley herself had chosen. I flung it away from me, sending it sailing down the hall. How dare she buy me towels!

I went to the hall closet for my shoulder holster and .38. The holster was there. The gun wasn't.

There was no point in searching the apartment. I knew I had put it away. I always put it away. Anne had taken it. Anne Corley Beaumont, armed, beautiful, and exceedingly dangerous.

I'm qualified to carry a .357 magnum. You get qualified by being an excellent shot. It's a macho symbol I don't need to pack around the department. I keep one, though, in the same bottom drawer where I had kept my mother's engagement ring all those years. I got it out and checked it to make sure it was loaded. I put it in my jacket pocket. A .357 is only good for one thing—killing. I prayed I wouldn't have to use it.

My body ran on automatic pilot. I don't remember getting into the car or driving up Interstate 90 to Fall City. I was doing what I had to do, what was inevitable. It was too painful to do it consciously, so I did it like a sleepwalker. It was like that last night with my mother, wanting her to die and not wanting her to die, wishing her suffering over yet not wanting to lose her. I didn't know whether I should hope for the red Porsche to be there or not. It would hurt either way.

I was trying to readjust my thinking, to turn Anne Corley Beaumont my love into Anne Corley Beaumont my enemy. She would have to be that if I was going to confront her and win. Afterward I could try to salvage what could be salvaged, once she was safe. Locked up and safe.

As it turned out, the Porsche was there, parked directly in front of the restaurant. There was no attempt to conceal her presence. She wanted me to know where she was. I was expected.

I grappled with the realization that Anne had called every shot since I met her. This was no exception. My hand dropped unconsciously to my pocket, checking the .357, making sure it was available. She had outwitted me at every turn. I would have to be wary. She was Mrs. J. P. Beaumont in name only. She was also a ruthless, savvy killer.

The vestibule was crowded. Of course it would be. This was Sunday afternoon. For the first time I realized how foolhardy I had been to attempt this without calling for help, without having a backup. The restaurant was full of innocent bystanders, any one of whom could suffer dire consequences for my going off half-cocked. I eased my way through the crowd to the hostess desk and peered through the dining room.

Anne was there, at a corner table. Our eyes met and held above the heads of the other diners. She motioned for me to come to her.

The hostess appeared then. "Oh," she said, "are you Mr. Beaumont? Mrs. Corley has been expecting you."

"I see her," I said stiffly. "I can find my way."

There was a glass of wine on the table in front of her, and a Mac-Naughton's and water at the place on the other side of the table. She was still wearing the blue suit. The Adidas bag lay in her lap. A lump rose in my throat. It was all I could do to speak. "Hello," I managed.

"Hello, Beau. I'm glad you came."

A thousand questions should have tumbled out one after another. Instead I looked around the room, J. P. Beaumont, the cop, looking over the lay of the land, looking for cover, for trajectories, for who would be hurt in a hail of bullets. "Let me help you, Anne," I pleaded.

"You already have."

My anger blazed to the surface. "I've helped you, all right, led you to three more victims."

She had held my gaze steadily. For the first time she looked down. My hand sought the safety of the .357 in case she reached into the bag. She raised her eyes. "I made a mistake with Brodie and the woman. Even so, they deserved to die."

"Anne! You had no right to judge them. You're not a jury. They were innocent of a capital crime. Child abuse is a felony, but it's not premeditated murder."

"I was evening the score, an eye for an eye." She looked at me defiantly, daring me to take exception to what she said. "I listened to the tape," she continued. "I found it in the table drawer after you and Peters left. It was strange hearing it. Athletes must feel that way when they see an instant replay. I thought there would be something in it that would point to me."

"We'd have been better off if there had been," I said.

It was all coming together now, all the missing pieces. "And the phone call I overheard was from Tom Stahl at the phone company? That's when you discovered your mistake?"

"Yes, but I'm not sorry I killed them, if that's what you mean." There was no hint of remorse about her.

"What did you put in the last chapter, Anne? You told me I couldn't read the book because you had given it to Ralph, but he didn't get the manuscript until this morning. He was planning to read it on the plane."

"I wasn't sure how it would end. I wasn't sure until I saw you walk through the door. I didn't know if you'd come."

"And now you know?"

"Yes, don't you?"

It was like we were playing a game, some private guessing game that had nothing to do with life and death. The people sitting around us had no idea that the attractive couple chatting earnestly in the corner near the window had enough firepower between them to lay waste a roomful of people.

I knew how I was afraid it would end. She was absolutely without fear or compunction. I couldn't let that happen, not at such close quarters, not in a crowd of defenseless Sunday afternoon diners. "Come with me, Anne. Let me take you in. No jury in the country would convict you."

"An insanity plea?" Her voice was full of bitter derision. "You know where they'd send me, don't you? Have you ever been in one of those places? Do you know what goes on?"

"Anne, I'll stick by you. I'll see that you get the help you need. In sickness and in health, remember? That's what we said. This is sickness." I was pleading for my life as well as hers.

"You wouldn't be there at night when the orderlies came. Even Milton couldn't stop that. I had to have an abortion, you know. He paid for it. He didn't cause it, but he couldn't prevent it either."

"What about Milton, Anne? Did he commit suicide?"

"He was scared of what the cancer was doing to him."

"You didn't answer the question."

"No," she said softly. "He didn't commit suicide."

I heard the words and knew they were the truth. "My God, Anne, you told me you loved him."

"I did."

The toll kept rising. I didn't want to know any more, but I was unable to stop the questions. They are too much a part of me, waking and sleeping. "Why your father?"

"The things he did to Patty were terrible, not once, but over and over. I tried to stop him, but my mother wouldn't let me. I should have killed her too, but I never got a chance. I think she knew it. That's why she never let me out. It was only after she died that Milton was able to get me released."

"What about the book?"

"It's a collection. Until now, I was the only one who knew the rest of the story, things that happened after the fact."

"All over the country?"

She nodded. "It happens everywhere," she said.

"How long have you been doing this, Anne? How long have you been a one-woman avenger? How many J. P. Beaumont suckers are there in this world?"

"I've been a widow for ten years," she said.

"And no one's ever caught you?"

"I never wanted to be caught."

The waitress came to take our order. "The gentleman isn't feeling well. We won't be eating after all. If I could just have the bill." She laid a twenty on the table as a tip.

Until she saw the size of the tip, I think the waitress was prepared to be upset. She pocketed the twenty. "Thank you very much," she said, smiling.

The interruption allowed a new train of thought. "Where'd you get the bike? The owner left town in March."

"St. Vincent de Paul's over on Fairview."

"Where'd you keep it?"

"In the parking garage of the building right behind the Royal Crest. It was just one night."

"And you got it out after I fell asleep?"

She nodded.

"What about Kincaid?"

"After the man from the phone company called, I went to Auburn and found his house. He had a black van."

"It could have been the wrong man."

"He wasn't. He confessed. I didn't want to make the same mistake twice." She paused. "Is that all you wanted to know?" she asked.

"Yes," I said. There was nothing else. I knew far more than I wanted to.

"Let's finish this outside, Beau. It's too crowded in here."

With catlike grace, she picked up the Adidas bag and walked outside.

CHAPTER 25

I know how Pharoah felt trying to catch Moses as he disappeared into the Red Sea. Anne Corley Beaumont melted through the vestibule crowd the same way, leaving me pushing and shoving, trying to catch up. When I finally hit the outside door, I made a dash for the Porsche, expecting to see her speeding away. The Porsche sat empty, untouched.

The roar of the falls filled my head. I kept my hand on the gun without drawing it. This could be a trap, I reminded myself. I was dealing with Anne Corley the enemy. She had enough of a head start that she could easily have hidden herself away and be lying in wait. Even then I could have gone back inside and called for help, for a backup, but I didn't. Stubborn, stupid, I thought I could talk to her, persuade her to turn herself in.

Cautiously I made my way around the restaurant. In a heap near one corner of the building I found the blouse, suit, shoes, and discarded Adidas bag. Up the path, heading toward the observation area, I caught a glimpse of red. She had changed into the jogging suit. Any advantage I had because of dress was instantly nullified. With me in my suit and slick-bottomed shoes, she now had an edge. I started running too.

I didn't try for speed. I don't do wind sprints, but I can keep a steady pace for a fair distance. She was running up the path, away from the lodge, toward the hordes of tourists filling the viewpoint and picnic area. I kept my hand on the concealed .357 as I passed a group of picnickers. I didn't want them to raise an alarm, to cause a panic.

I saw her turn down a trail, one that veers steeply down the basalt canyon wall to the pool at the bottom of the falls. I had never been on it. I was sure it was the only way down and the only way back up. Three different times I pushed my way around huffing sets of climbers. Two of them were large groups. The last was a couple, a retired couple, walking by themselves.

"Did you see a woman?" I gasped. "A woman in a red jogging suit?"

"She almost knocked Mabel here down," he said.

I stopped, trying to catch my breath. "Are there any other people down there?"

The man shook his head. "There weren't when we left."

I reached in my pocket and pulled out my badge. "Stand at the head of the trail," I said to him. "Don't let anyone else come down." He looked at me questioningly. I wanted to shock him, galvanize him into action. "She's dangerous, armed and dangerous." I took the .357 from my pocket then, for emphasis, to get his attention. It worked. He grabbed his wife's arm and they hurried up the trail.

I stood for a few moments after they left, slowing my breathing, steadying my nerves. It was more than I could have hoped. We were isolated from the crowd above. I had bought some time. Maybe I could lay hands on her, shake some sense into her, talk her into surrendering. Before reinforcements arrived. Before someone called in a SWAT team.

I stood immobile, listening. Except for the roar of the water, the forest was silent. It was the eye of the hurricane. I was standing like that when the bullet hit me. It caught me full in the left shoulder and spun me into a tree.

The tree kept me from plunging headlong down the side of the canyon. I clung to it for support, my left side numb from shock. The .357 had fallen from my hand. Desperately I looked for it, expecting the next bullet to hit before I could find it. I saw it finally, lying out of reach to one side of the trail.

I looked up to see if I should make a grab for it. Anne was standing in the trail, my short-barreled .38 still pointing in my direction. We looked at one another, both lives hanging in the balance. It couldn't have been more than a second or two in time, but I aged an eternity. Then, with agonizing slowness, she lowered the gun, turned, and disappeared around a curve in the trail.

I let myself slip to the ground. I hoped shock would last a little longer, staving off the pain. I crawled to where the gun had fallen. Once my fingers closed over the butt, I dared breathe again. Slowly I pulled myself to my feet, the world spinning crazily as I did so. I took a tentative step. The movement jarred me, starting shocks of pain pulsing through my body. I gritted my teeth and took another step.

Each movement was excruciating. The bullet, lodged against my broken collarbone, scraped along a nerve at every step. I walked. Slowly and painfully, but I walked. The descent was steep and slippery, the ground wet with slick green moss. Mist from the falls swirled around me like thickening fog. I strained to see. How much of the difficulty in vision was mist? How much was losing consciousness?

My subconscious framed the questions. I answered them aloud. "No. If I pass out, she'll kill me." Pain of realization dulled the pain in my body. I struggled through the last of the trees. There in a clearing, a flat, perpetually wet clearing on the bank of the river, stood Anne Corley Beaumont, her back to the water. The gun was still in her hand, aimed straight at me. She was waiting.

"Drop it," I yelled.

She didn't move. I heard the explosion. A bullet smacked into a tree behind me. I don't know if she thought she heard something off to her left or if some movement caught her eye. She turned slightly, pointing the .38 in that direction. I raised the .357, aimed it, and fired.

I'm a crack shot. I aimed at the .38. I should have hit it, but just as I fired, she lost her footing on the slick moss and fell. I saw the look of surprise and hurt as the slug crashed into her body. The force of the bullet lifted her and spun her to the left, sending her sprawling into the turbulent water. I dropped the .357 and raced toward her, my own pain forgotten.

I reached the bank and saw the torrent fling her against a rock, then pull her away, sending her toward the bank, toward me. I had one chance to catch her before the water dragged her under. I threw myself lengthwise on the bank and grabbed. I caught one leg of the jogging suit. Barely. The force of the current, the deadweight, should have swept her from my grasp. There should have been no strength in my injured shoulder, but fueled by adrenaline, I worked her toward the bank. Inch by inch. At last, shaking with exertion, I dragged her out of the water.

She was coughing and gasping. Blood foamed in the water that erupted from her mouth. I cradled her head in my lap, willing her to live. The coppery smell of death was all around her. I tried to wipe the hair from her mouth, from her eyes. I was crying by then. "Anne, Anne, why?"

She tried to say something. I could barely hear her; the roaring of the water was too loud, the roaring in my ears. I leaned toward her, her lips brushing my ear. "You said . . . ," she whispered, ". . . said given the same . . . the same circumstances . . ." And that was all.

I was still holding her when a Snoqualmie City officer charged into the clearing from the bottom of the path. He was young but his instincts were good. He came on strong, ready to haul me in single-handed. He held his .38 Colt on me and picked up my .357 with his other hand. I tossed him my I.D., letting it fall at his feet.

"Call Captain Powell at homicide, Seattle P.D.," I told him. "Tell him I got her. Don't let anyone who isn't a cop come down that trail."

He left without argument. I lay Anne Corley Beaumont down, closing her eyes, stroking the hair from her forehead one last time. I stood up, feeling the aching chill from my sodden clothes. It was nothing compared to the glacial chill inside. Sudden weakness robbed my legs of strength, forcing me to sit once more. I didn't sit next to Anne. There was nothing more I could do for her.

The officer returned with a couple of blankets. He wrapped one around my shoulders and covered Anne with the other. "Powell says to tell you he's on his way." He looked at me closely. "You need an ambulance."

"No," I said. "I'll wait."

I have no idea how much time passed before I heard the wail of sirens. Peters loped down the trail ahead of Powell and Watkins. How he managed to make connections back from Arizona that fast I'll never know. I was glad to see him. Powell and Watty went to the blanket-covered figure on the edge of the river. Peters came to me. "I'm sorry, Beau," he said.

I felt a sob rising in my throat. It took me by surprise. Peters put his arm on my good shoulder and left it there.

"A week," I said when I could talk again. "I only knew her a week."

"I know," he said.

Powell came over to me then. "The officer says you're hurt." He lifted the blanket and looked for himself; then turned to Watkins. "Get those ambulance people down here now," he ordered. "Have 'em bring a stretcher."

Peters came with me. I was glad to be taken away. I didn't want to be there for the ritual pictures and the measurements. I didn't want to watch as the search for evidence started, as people who knew nothing about Anne Corley or J. P. Beaumont started trying to learn everything about us. They would. That's a homicide detective's job.

Peters pretty much took over. He directed the ambulance to Harborview. The doctors put me under while they removed the slug. When I came back around, Peters was there. I thought he had been there the whole time. It turned out he had gone back to Snoqualmie in the meantime and picked up the Datsun. The city of Snoqualmie had impounded the Porsche, pending completion of its investigation.

The doctor wanted to keep me overnight. I wouldn't hear of it. I wanted to be home. Like an old snakebit hound wanting his own cave under a house, I wanted to go home to lick my wounds. The doctor finally relented only because Peters assured him he would stay with me.

Watkins was waiting in the lobby of the Royal Crest. The building manager had let him in along with someone I didn't know, an eager young man Watty identified as the Snoqualmie homicide detective, Detective Means. Means could hardly restrain himself. He wanted to get started. This was his moment of glory, his first big case. He almost panted with enthusiasm. The whole idea made me weary beyond words.

The doctor had given me the slug. I handed it to Watty, who in turn gave it to Detective Means. "It'll match the ones from Brodie, Suzanne Barstogi, and Kincaid," I said. "It's from my departmental-issue thirty-eight."

We went up to the apartment. I was thirsty. I went to the refrigerator for something to drink. That was how I found the leftover wedding cake, neatly covered in plastic wrap, sitting on the bottom shelf. Peters saw me sag against the cupboard for support. He came and peered over my shoulder. "Jesus," he said.

He scraped it off the plate and ran the garbage disposal. Everybody needs a friend like Ron Peters, especially at a time like that.

We went back into the living room. Means asked the questions. Watkins was there to handle administrative procedures. I was a little surprised Means let Peters and Watkins stay. I expected him to throw his weight around.

He turned on a recorder and read me my rights. "I understand the deceased, Anne Corley, was your fiancée?" he asked.

"No," I said softly. "She was my wife."

CHAPTER 26

Watkins and Means left hours later. I don't know when. Peters walked them down to their cars. He came back and poured a MacNaughton's for me and a gin and tonic for himself. He handed me my drink and an envelope.

"I found it under the front seat of the Datsun."

I held the envelope up and looked at it. My name was written in bold letters on the outside. A small piece of paper fluttered out of it. I caught it in midair. "You'll have to write the last chapter yourself," it said.

I crushed the paper in my fist. "Goddamn her! She knew! She forced my hand!" Peters sat on the couch. "Did you look at it?" I asked.

He nodded. "You probably shouldn't have read it right now." Peters had pulled the plug on both phones in the house, effectively shutting out all unwanted intruders.

I gazed at Seattle's downtown skyline, the golden lights Anne Corley had loved. Or at least seemed to have loved—but then, she seemed to have loved me too. That showed how much I knew. Peters waited quietly, not prying, ready to listen when I was ready to talk. He had gotten a hell of a lot older and wiser in the last few days.

I tossed the wad of paper to Peters. He opened it and reread it.

"We talked about it once, you know," I told him. "She asked me if, given the same circumstances, I'd do it again. When I got her out of the water, that was the last thing she said to me. She repeated what I said, that I'd do it again."

"Do what?"

"Kill. Kill someone in self-defense. I told her I thought I would." My voice broke, tears blurred my vision. Peters got up and took my empty glass to the kitchen. He returned with a full one.

"You were right," he said. "Don't you think Anne knew you would? Don't you think she counted on it?"

"But why? And if she knew, knew it was coming, why the fuck did she marry me?"

Peters shook his head. "I don't know," he said.

For the first time I thought of Ralph Ames. I closed my eyes and shook my head. "What?" Peters asked.

"Ames, her attorney. He'll be back in Phoenix by now. Someone should call him, I guess."

Peters stood up. "What's his number? I'll call."

"Thanks," I said. "I'd better do it myself." The bandage on my chest made it difficult for me to move. Peters reattached the cord to the wall plug and handed me the phone. I got Ames' home number from information. I dialed direct, hoping like hell he wouldn't answer. He did, on the third ring.

"Ralph Ames speaking," he said in his best three-piece-suit diction.

I cleared my throat. "It's Beau, J. P. Beaumont, calling from Seattle. It's about Anne."

"Thank God, I've been trying to call—"

"She's dead, Ralph, I . . ." I interrupted, but I couldn't go on. There was stark silence on the other end of the line.

"Are you all right?" he asked.

I could hear sympathy in his voice, sympathy and concern. "It wasn't a car wreck, Ralph, nothing like that. I shot her. She was trying to kill me."

"There's a plane from Phoenix that gets into Sea-Tac tomorrow morning at ten. Have someone out there to meet me."

"But . . . ," I started to object. He didn't hear me. The receiver clicked in my ear.

I put down the phone. "He's coming up," I told Peters. "He wants someone to meet him at the airport at ten in the morning."

Peters took my glass and gave me a mock salute. "Aye aye, sir," he said. "I'll be there."

The phone rang. I had forgotten to unplug the cord. It was Karen, calling from Cucamonga. "Katy Powell called me an hour ago. I'm sorry, Beau. Are you all right?"

Surprised to hear her voice, I mumbled something unintelligible. I was touched that she had bothered to call.

"The kids don't know what to say. They're sorry too. Do you have someone there with you?"

I looked at Peters. "Yes, I do. My partner. He's staying over."

The conversation fumbled along for another minute or two. When I hung up, Peters looked at me quizzically. "Your ex?"

I nodded.

"It was nice of her to call."

We pulled the plug on the phone before it had a chance to ring again. Peters and I proceeded to get shit-faced drunk. We ran out of gin and Mac-Naughton's about the same time. I passed out in the leather chair. When I woke up the next morning, there was nothing left in the liquor cabinet but a half jug of vermouth. I had a terrible hangover. Anne Corley Beaumont was still dead.

Peters went down to stuff some money in the Datsun's parking meter. I told him I'd break his face if he brought up a newspaper. I didn't want to see what they'd print about Anne and me. Talk is cheap, though, and I don't know if I would have been able to carry out my threat. I was in a good deal of pain. I was grateful the doctor had insisted on giving me a prescription of painkillers. I helped myself to a generous dosage, not only for my shoulder but also for my head. Nothing helped the ache in my heart.

Peters called in sick for the day. It wasn't a lie. Neither of us is a very capable drinker. Without the haze of bourbon, I worried about Ames' arrival. I was sure he meant trouble, that he was flying in to bird-dog the investigation. If the coroner called it justifiable homicide, Ames would still try to see to it that I lost my job. After all, Anne had been one of his prime clients. It was the least he could do.

Peters tried to talk me out of going to the airport, but I insisted. I wanted to get it over with as quickly as possible, like a kid who'd rather have his licking sooner than later. We went down to the lobby. The Datsun was parked across the street. Behind it sat a rust-colored Volvo.

"Goddamn! What the hell is he doing here?"

"Come on, Peters, you didn't expect Max to miss a sideshow like this, did you? I'm surprised he didn't turn up in the emergency room yesterday."

Max crawled out of the Volvo as we crossed the street. "Did you marry her so you wouldn't have to testify against her?"

My fist caught him full in the mouth. A front tooth gave way under my knuckle. Cole fell like a stunned ox. He lay partially on the curb and partially in the street. Hitting him was pure gut reflex. I couldn't help myself. Then I stepped on his glasses. That was deliberate malice. We left him lying there without a second glance.

"Drive like hell," I told Peters. He did. My knuckles bled. I could feel a warm ooze under the bandage on my shoulder.

"You landed a pretty good punch for an invalid," Peters commented. "Remind me not to make you mad when you're not all shot up."

The United flight got in early. We met Ames at the baggage carousel in the basement. He hurried up to me, hand outstretched. "Did you read the last chapter?" he asked without greeting.

"No," I said. "There is no last chapter. She said I'd have to write it myself."

Ames noticed Peters, realizing we weren't alone. His manner changed abruptly, stiffened, withdrew. "I brought the rest of the manuscript back with me," he said. "You'd better read it first. Then we'll talk."

Peters and I read it in the Royal Crest that afternoon. Ames sat to one side, watching us, saying nothing. I had given him the envelope with Anne's note. He looked at it without comment.

We didn't speak as we read. Words could not have lessened the horror. One city after another, one case after another, dates, times, weapons. Anne Corley had been a one-woman avenging angel, striking before the law could, the cases so far-flung, so widely scattered, that no one had ever put the pattern together. The manuscript ended with the death of Charles Murray "Uncle Charlie" Kincaid. There was a handwritten postscript. "I know Beau will keep his word. Love, Anne."

Peters read the note, then got up, took out three glasses, and poured three slugs of vermouth, dividing it evenly three ways.

"Did you know?" I asked Ames, looking at him over my empty glass as the vermouth scorched my throat.

"My job was just to pay the bills as they came in. I never had a clue. Not until I was on the plane going home yesterday," he said. "I tried to call as soon as I got home. There was no answer. I left messages for you at the department. I wanted to warn you, but, as her attorney, I couldn't tell anyone else. I never thought this would happen. She seemed so happy that morning." He ran his hand across his forehead. "It was too late when I left Seattle, Beau. It was too late when you met her."

"Why did she let herself get caught? Why here? Why now?" They were haunting questions, ones I had asked myself over and over all day long.

"She must have wanted to be caught. That's the only thing that makes sense. You were her first connection to the real world since Milton Corley. You made her realize what she'd become."

The room was suddenly too small. I couldn't breathe. I walked to the balcony door, opened it, and went outside. It was late afternoon. The roar of rush hour was just tuning up.

Ames continued, his voice carrying above the noise of the traffic. "Her mother was right to have her committed. She was right, but for the wrong reason. Anne Corley was two different people, Beau. The one is here, on these pages, cold-blooded and ruthless. The other Anne Corley loved you very much." He reached down and pulled a legal-sized packet from his briefcase, the same briefcase from which he had removed the manuscript hours earlier.

"The other Anne Corley is here, in these pages. It's her will, Beaumont. She left you everything. That's why she had me come up on Wednesday. She wanted her will redrawn."

I heard what he said. I drew only one conclusion. I strode back into the room and hauled him to his feet. "Then you did know, you sorry son-of-a-bitch. You knew she was planning something like this."

"No, Beau. Honest to God I didn't. Not until yesterday on the plane, and even then she seemed so happy I never dreamed—"

I shoved him back onto the couch. His head whacked the wall behind him. "Goddamn you," I bellowed. I had to vent my rage on someone. Ralph Ames and Peters were the only ones there.

"If I just could have convinced her to turn herself in, she could have pleaded insanity."

Ames' voice came to me from a long way off. "She had already spent a third of her life in one of those hellholes," he said gently. "She's better off dead."

I made it to the bedroom before the sob racked me. I couldn't argue the point. I knew he was right.

EPILOGUE

We buried Anne Corley Beaumont in her blue silk suit on the bluff of Mount Pleasant Cemetery, as close as we could to Angela Barstogi. She wore the gold wedding band. I put mine in the velvet box along with the engagement ring and put the box back in my bottom drawer.

Ames handled everything. He managed to track down the minister in the pea green Volkswagen to conduct the funeral service. Ralph is nothing if not thoughtful. He squelched the assault charge Maxwell Cole was getting ready to file and handled all the details of both the Snoqualmie investigation and the departmental review. He saw them through to completion, when all charges were dropped and my record at the department had been cleared. He contacted all other jurisdictions, closing the books on other cases involving Anne Corley.

Ralph took me down to the Four Seasons and showed me Anne's suite. Those elegant rooms and I were kindred spirits. Once we had both been full of Anne Corley. Now we were empty. Vacant. There was a difference, though. The rooms were made up, awaiting someone else's arrival. I wasn't. I made Ames take me home.

Peters continued working on the Angela Barstogi case, tying up loose ends. When the final count came in, he discovered Angela had been Kincaid's third victim, all of them picked up by his unusual telephone number. He had a notebook with the names and numbers of children all over the state of Washington. Speaking as a cop, it was lucky for those other kids that Anne killed Kincaid when she did.

I operated in a haze. I developed an infection. For the better part of two weeks, I wasn't connected to what went on around me. It was probably better that way. By the time I rejoined the world, the worst of the difficulties seemed to be over except for figuring out how to go on living without Anne. I wasn't sure I wanted to.

The day I came out of the fog was the day Ames announced we needed to go pick out Anne's headstone. "Where do we have to go?" I asked, thinking about bus schedules.

"I checked on the map," he said. "It's somewhere up Aurora."

We got in the elevator. I pressed Lobby, and he pressed Garage. He led the way. The Porsche was parked in a space on the second level. "I rented it with an option to buy," he explained.

"I can't afford to buy a parking place," I said.

He handed me the keys to the Porsche. "I think we need to have a little talk about your financial position." The results dumbfounded me, the details were staggering. There was something called a marital deduction. The fact that we had been married at the time of Anne's death meant that most of the money went to me without anything going to estate taxes. I had more money than I'd ever know what to do with.

The night before Ames was supposed to fly back to Phoenix, the three of us went to the Doghouse for dinner—Peters, Ames, and me. I was beginning to like the idea of having Ames around, to appreciate being able to ask his advice. A couple came in with two little girls, pretty little things with long brunette hair. I saw Peters' heart go to his sleeve. That's when the idea hit me.

"How are you at interstate custody cases?" I asked Ames.

"I don't usually handle those personally," he said, "but our firm has won more than we've lost."

"And deprogramming?"

"We've handled a couple of those, too," he said.

Peters looked at me then. He was beginning to get my drift. I winked at him. "You know, Ames, unless you've got something really pressing, I think I'd like you to stop by Broken Springs, Oregon, and see if you can pull Peters' two kids out of there."

Ames shrugged. "You're the boss," he said.

I think Anne Corley Beaumont—the Anne I loved—would have approved.

Injustice
for All

To Norman and Evie,
from their "only" child

CHAPTER 1

There's nothing like a woman's scream to bring a man bolt upright in bed. I had been taking a late-afternoon nap in my room when the sound cut through the stormy autumn twilight like a knife.

I threw open the door of my cabin. The woman screamed again, the sound keening up from the narrow patch of beach below the terrace at Rosario Resort. A steep path dropped from my cabin to the beach. I scrambled down it to the water's edge. There I spotted a woman struggling to drag a man's inert form out of the lapping sea.

She wasn't screaming now. Her face was grimly set as she wrestled the dead weight of the man's body. I hurried to help her, grasping him under the arms and pulling him ashore. Dropping to his side, I felt for a pulse. There was none.

He was a man in his mid to late fifties wearing expensive cowboy boots and a checkered cowboy shirt. His belt buckle bore the initials LSL. A deep gash split his forehead.

The woman knelt beside me anxiously, hopefully. When I looked at her and shook my head, her face contorted with grief. She sank to the wet sand beside me. "Can't you do something?" she sobbed.

Again I shook my head. I've worked homicide too many years not to know when it's too late. Footsteps pounded down the steps behind us as people in the bar and dining room hurried to see what had happened. Barney, the bartender, was the first person to reach us.

"Dead?" he asked.

I nodded. "Get those people out of here, every last one of them. And call the sheriff."

With unquestioning obedience Barney bounded up the steps and herded the onlookers back to the terrace some twenty-five feet above us. Beside me the woman's sobs continued unabated. It was a chilly autumn evening to begin with, and we were both soaked to the skin. Gently I took her arm, lifting her away from the lifeless body.

"Come on," I said. "You've got to get out of those wet clothes." She allowed me to pull her to her feet. "Is this your husband?"

She shook her head. "No, a friend."

"Are you staying here at the hotel?" She nodded. "Where's your room?"

"Up by the tennis courts."

She was shaking violently. The tennis courts and her room were a good quarter of a mile away. My cabin was just at the top of the path. "You can dry off and warm up in my room. The sheriff will need to talk to you when he gets here."

Like a dazed but pliant child, she followed me as I half led, half carried her up the path. By the time we reached my room, her teeth chattered convulsively. It could have been cold or shock or a little of both. I pulled her into the bathroom and turned on the water in the shower. "Get out of those wet things," I ordered. "I'll send someone to get you some clothes."

Kneeling in front of her, I fumbled with the sodden laces of her tennis shoes with my own numbed fingers. "What's your name?" I asked.

"Gi . . . Ginger," she stammered through chattering teeth.

"Ginger what?"

"Wa . . . Watkins."

I stood up. Her arms hung limply at her sides. "Can you undress, or do you need help?"

Clumsily she battled a button on her blouse, finally unfastening it. Leaving her on her own, I let myself out of the bathroom. "I'll be outside if you need anything."

Alone in the room, I stripped off my own soaked clothing and tossed the soggy bundle on a chair near the bed. I pulled on a shirt, a sweater, and two pair of socks before I picked up the phone and dialed the desk clerk. "This is Beaumont in Room Thirteen," I said. "Did someone call the sheriff?"

"Yes we did, Mr. Beaumont. The deputy's on his way."

"Have someone stay down on the beach with the body until he gets here. Make sure nothing is moved or disturbed. The woman who found him is here in my room. She was freezing. She's taking a hot shower. Her name is Watkins. Can you send someone to her room for dry clothes? Does she have a husband?"

"There's no Mr. Watkins registered, Mr. Beaumont, but I'll send some-one after the clothes right away."

"She'll need the works, underwear and all."

"I'll take care of it as soon as I can."

"Good," I replied. "And when the deputy comes, be sure he knows she's here with me. Since she's the one who found the body, he'll want to talk to her."

The desk clerk himself brought the clothes, handing them to me apologetically. His nametag labeled him Fred. "I hope I have everything," he said.

I opened the bathroom door wide enough to slip them inside onto the floor before turning back to Fred. "The deputy isn't here yet?"

"There's an accident down by the ferry dock. He can't come until he finishes with that."

"Did the dispatcher call for a detective from Friday Harbor?" I asked.

He shrugged. "I guess, but I don't know for sure. You seem to know about this kind of thing, Mr. Beaumont."

I ought to. I've worked homicide in Seattle for the better part of twenty years.

Fred moved uncertainly toward the door. "I'd better be getting back."

"Who was he?" I asked. Fred looked blank. "The dead man," I per-sisted.

"Oh," he replied. "His name was Sig Larson. He was here with the parole board."

"The parole board!" Cops don't like parole boards. Cops and parole boards work opposite sides of the street. Parole boards let creeps go faster than cops can lock them up. "What's the parole board doing here?"

Fred shrugged. "They came for a three-day workshop. They'll proba-bly cancel now."

I glanced toward the bathroom door where the rush of the shower had ceased. "And her?" I asked.

"She's a member too, as far as I know. Her reservation was made along with all the rest."

"But her husband isn't here?"

"No, she's by herself."

"What about Larson?" Asking questions is a conditioned response in a detective. I asked the question, ignoring that I was more than a hundred miles outside my Seattle jurisdiction. Someone was dead. Who, How, and Why were questions someone needed to ask. It might as well be me.

"His wife is due in on one of tonight's ferries. I don't know which one. She isn't here yet."

I went to the bathroom door and tapped lightly. "I'm going to order a couple of drinks from Room Service. Would you like something?"

"Coffee," was the reply. "Black."

I turned back to Fred. "Did you hear that?"

He nodded.

"Send up a pot of coffee for her and two MacNaughton's and water for me. Barney knows how I like them."

"Will do," the clerk replied, slipping from the room into the deepening darkness.

The door reopened. "I almost forgot. She's supposed to call Homer in Seattle. It's urgent. He said she knew the number."

Fred shut the door again, disappearing for good this time. Still cold, I turned up the thermostat in the room, mulling the turn of events. The lady showering in my bathroom was a married member of the Washington State Parole Board. The dead man on the beach was married too, but not to her, although it was evident there was some connection.

Room Service was on the ball. Coffee and drinks arrived before the bathroom door opened. Ginger Watkins, wearing a pale green dress, stepped barefoot into my room, a huge bath-towel turban wound around her head. She was fairly tall, five-eight or five-nine, with a slender figure, fine bones, and a flawlessly fair complexion. Her eyes were vivid uncut emeralds.

Coming up from the beach, I hadn't noticed she was beautiful. Standing across the room from me, swathed in the gentle light of the dressing room behind her, she took my breath away.

She returned my unabashed stare, and I looked away, embarrassed. "Better?" I managed.

"Yes, but I'm still cold."

I rummaged through the closet and brought out a tweed jacket which I put over her shoulders. I handed her a cup and saucer. "Here's your coffee."

She slipped into one of the two chairs at the table. "I left my wet clothes on the floor," she said.

I pointed to the chair. "There mine are." I poured more coffee. Her hands trembled as she raised the cup to her lips.

"What did you say your name was?"

"Beaumont," I answered. "J. P. Beaumont. My friends call me Beau."

"And I'm Ginger Watkins."

"You told me. The desk clerk said the man's name was Larson. You knew him?"

She nodded somberly, her eyes filling with tears. "Sig," she murmured, her throat working to stifle a sob.

"A friend of yours?"

She nodded again.

"How did you happen to find him? It wasn't much of a day for a walk on the beach."

"We planned to meet down there to talk, after the meeting. I was late. Darrell called. I didn't get there until forty-five minutes after I was supposed to."

"Who's Darrell?" I asked.

She gave me a funny look, as though I had asked a stupid question. "My husband," she answered.

The name sounded familiar, but I didn't put it together right then. I let it go. "Why meet him there? Why not in the lobby or the bar?"

"I told you, we needed to talk."

She set her coffee cup down, got up, and walked away from the table, her arms crossed, her body language closed.

"What about?"

"It was personal," she replied.

That's not a good answer at the beginning of an inquiry into death under unusual circumstances. Accidental drownings in October are unusual. My gut said murder, and murder is very personal. The ties between killer and victim are often of the most intimate kind. "How personal?"

She turned on me suddenly. "You don't have any right to ask me a question like that."

"Someone's going to ask it, sooner or later."

She met my gaze for a long moment before she wavered. "Sig had some business dealings with my family. That's why I needed to talk to him."

"Privately?" I asked. She nodded. "Do you know his wife?"

Her mouth tightened. Her fingers closed tightly on her upper arms. "Yes. I know her."

"What's she like?"

"Mona's a calculating bitch." It was a simple statement spoken with a singular amount of venom.

"I take it you're not friends."

"Hardly." She walked back over to the table and sat down opposite me. "Mona thought Sig and I were having an affair."

"Were you?"

She looked at me, her eyes clear and steady in the glow of the light. "No," she said.

Irate husbands and wives don't always verify their spouses' indiscretions before they rub out a presumed lover. "Is Mona the jealous type? Or Darrell?"

She laughed. "Darrell? Are you kidding? He could care less. Mona called him with the story, and he was afraid it would hit the papers and screw up his campaign."

Suddenly the names shifted into focus. Darrell Watkins, candidate for lieutenant governor. Boy Wonder tackling the longtime incumbent. I whistled. "You mean *the* Darrell Watkins?"

Ginger Watkins peered at me across a cup of coffee. "One and the same," she said softly. "The sonofabitch."

It was no wonder I forgot to give her the message that someone had called.

CHAPTER 2

Deputy Jake Pomeroy arrived about seven. He made a very poor first impression. He was a fat-faced, pimpled kid who looked like he had stepped out of his high school graduation picture into a rumpled deputy sheriff's uniform. Until the detective arrived from Friday Harbor, Deputy Pomeroy was in charge. The deputy considered Sig Larson's death to be the crime of the century on Orcas Island.

He was trolling for suspects. He tossed his first hook in my direction. "Your name's Beaumont, is that correct?" I nodded. "What do you do?"

"Homicide detective. Seattle P.D." I handed him my ID.

He gave me a shrewd, appraising look. "I understand you moved the body. Is that also correct?"

"Yes."

His look became a contemptuous sneer. "Surely you know better than that."

I wanted to slug the officious bastard, but I answered evenly. "We thought he might still be alive."

"When you say 'we,' you mean you and Mrs. Watkins?"

"She found him. I heard her scream."

"And what time was that?" he asked, addressing Ginger.

"A quarter to six," she replied. "I was late."

"Late for what?"

"I was supposed to meet Sig there. At five."

The deputy tapped his front teeth with the eraser of his pencil and eyed her speculatively. "Why?"

"To talk."

His look narrowed. "Wasn't it cold down by the water?"

"We wanted to talk privately."

Pomeroy said nothing as he made a note. "How would you describe your relationship with Mr. Larson?"

"Friends."

"That's all?"

"That's all."

"How long have you known Mr. Beaumont here?"

"We just met. Down on the beach."

She was in my room, wearing my robe, her hair wet from my shower, with my bath towel wrapped around her head. She was also barefoot, because the desk clerk had forgotten to bring her shoes. Jake Pomeroy didn't believe for one minute we were recent acquaintances.

I attempted what must have sounded like a lame explanation. "We were freezing. I was afraid she'd go into shock. Her own room is way up the hill."

Jake gave Ginger an overt leer. "You're sure the two of you never met before this afternoon?"

"I'm sure!" Ginger snapped, a tiny flush marking her delicate cheekbone.

"You did say 'Mrs. Watkins,' isn't that right?" She nodded. "But your husband isn't here with you?" He recast his hook.

"I'm here on parole board business. So was Sig." She was rapidly losing patience.

"Was your husband also a friend of Mr. Larson's?"

The emerald in her eyes gleamed hard and brittle. "They had some business dealings, that's all."

"We'll check this out, of course," he said.

His questions had gone far enough. I resented the insinuations in his clumsy quest for an infidelity motive. "Look, Pomeroy," I told him, "if you want to ask questions about the position of the body, or what time it was, or whether we saw anyone else on the beach, that's fine. But if you're making accusations, you'd better read us our rights and let us call an attorney. If not, I'll shove that gold star where the sun don't shine."

A stunned expression spread over his flabby countenance. He lumbered to his feet. "I'll go back and wait for Detective Huggins."

"You do that."

I banged the door shut behind him and returned to the table. Ginger had unwrapped her turban and was toweling her hair dry. She looked relieved.

I picked up the phone and dialed the desk. "You didn't bring shoes," I growled when Fred answered.

"I didn't? Sorry. I can't do anything about it right now. A whole bunch of people just got here. I have to get them settled."

"Never mind," I told Fred. "I'll get them myself."

Ginger gave me her key. I walked to her room through a lightly falling evening mist. Opening her door, I expected to find the room well ordered and neat. Instead, it was a shambles. The place had been ransacked. I picked up the telephone receiver. Holding it at the top in an effort to disturb as few prints as possible, I called the desk. "Was Mrs. Watkins' room torn apart when you came after her clothes?" I asked.

"Why no, Mr. Beaumont. It was fine."

"It isn't now," I said grimly. "When that detective gets here, send him up."

"He's right here. Want to speak to him?"

"Put him on."

"Hello," a voice mumbled. "This is Detective Huggins."

"I'm Beaumont."

"J. P. Beaumont? Are you shitting me? This is Hal, Hal Huggins. Haven't seen you since I left the force ten years ago. How the hell are you?"

It took me a minute to place the name and the face and the mumbling speech. Hal Huggins had opted for being a big fish in a very small pond when he left Seattle's homicide squad to go to work for the San Juan County Sheriff's Department in Friday Harbor, hiring on as their chief detective. Probably their only detective.

"I'm fine," I replied.

"What are you up to?"

"I was with the woman who discovered the body this afternoon."

"No shit. Pomeroy is lining me up to go talk to her."

"You'd better come to her room first. Have the desk clerk bring you up."

"Okay, we'll be right there. Hey, by the way. There's someone else here you know. I just ran into him in the lobby. Remember Maxwell Cole?"

Does Captain Ahab remember Moby Dick? Cole is a crime columnist for the *Post-Intelligencer*. He's been on my case ever since I beat him out of a college girl friend, packed her off, and married her. As a reporter, he has dogged my career for as long as I've been on the force. Karen and I have been divorced for years, but I'm still stuck with Max. It's like I threw out the baby and ended up having to keep the dirty bathwater.

"Don't tell him I'm here," I cautioned. "What's he doing here anyway? The Sig Larson story?"

"Probably, although he didn't say."

"Don't ask. And don't bring him along."

Fred led Huggins and Pomeroy into Ginger's room. The clerk's mouth gaped. "What happened here? It wasn't like this when I picked up her clothes."

"What time was that?" Huggins asked.

Fred walked around the room as if at a loss for words, examining the debris. "What time?" Huggins repeated.

"Forty-five minutes ago," Fred replied. "No more than that."

Huggins looked at me. "So what's this got to do with the stiff on the beach."

"I took Ginger Watkins to my room to warm up after we left the beach. Fred here," I said, indicating the desk clerk, "came up to get her some dry clothes. Not quite an hour later, I discovered this when I came to pick up a pair of shoes."

"Maybe she trashed it herself."

"No. She's still in my room. It's too cold to be wandering around barefoot."

Huggins glared sorrowfully around the room before turning to Pomeroy. "Call the crime-lab folks, Jake. Have them come take a look. Coroner's got the body, and the beach is covered with water, but they'd better see this all the same." He turned stiffly to me. "Take me to the lady. She can answer questions barefoot. Nobody's taking any shoes out of this room until the lab's done with it."

Pomeroy lingered near the door. "I told you to get, Jake, and I mean it," Huggins growled. Jake got, with the desk clerk right behind him.

Hal and I strolled back toward my room. "You're a little out of your territory, aren't you, Beau?" It was a comment rather than a question, asked without rancor.

"I'm here on vacation, an innocent bystander."

"Pomeroy seems to think otherwise."

"Pomeroy's got a dirty mind."

He chuckled. "How'd you get dragged into this, anyway?"

"I heard a lady scream and went to check it out. I never saw her before six o'clock this evening."

"Pomeroy says if you only met her tonight, how come she's sitting in your room barefoot with a towel around her head, wearing your bathrobe? He told me she had just stepped out of your shower. He thinks you're a hell of a fast worker."

"She was cold, goddammit. I tried to tell him that."

"He's not buying. Envious, I think. Claims she's pretty good looking."

"She is that," I acknowledged.

"What did you say her name is?"

"Ginger Watkins. Her husband's Darrell Watkins."

He stopped short and whistled. "The guy who's running for lieutenant governor against old man Chambers?"

"That's right."

Huggins shook his head. "What did I ever do to deserve this?" he asked plaintively.

"I don't know," I said, "but whatever it was, it must have been pretty bad."

Ginger rose to let us in, a worried frown on her face. "What took so long?" she asked. "I was afraid something had happened to you."

"This is Detective Hal Huggins," I said as he stepped forward, hand extended. "He's from the sheriff's department in Friday Harbor. Hal needs to ask you some questions. Hal, Ginger Watkins."

She offered him a firm handshake, while Hal examined her with care.

"Glad to meet you, Mrs. Watkins, but I'm afraid I have some disturbing news."

Her face darkened. "What?"

"We've just come from your room. The place has been ransacked."

She paled. "Ransacked! When?"

"Between the time the desk clerk picked up your clothes and when I went to get your shoes," I told her.

"But who would do something like that?" she demanded.

"We were hoping you could tell us, Mrs. Watkins." Hal settled himself on the edge of the bed. "Any ideas?"

Ginger shook her head. "None," she said.

"No one else had a key to your room?"

"Sig did. We always kept keys to each other's rooms on trips, as a precaution in case one of us was sick or hurt. I was sick once and he had to break in. It was just a safety precaution."

Huggins looked at her closely. "We'd better go over the whole thing," he said, leaning stiffly against the headboard. "Tell me everything. From the beginning."

CHAPTER 3

Huggins had barely asked his first question when the phone rang. I answered it—the phone, not the question. The voice on the other end of the line was one degree under rude. "I'm told Ginger Watkins is there. Let me speak to her."

"May I say who's calling?"

"No you may not! If she's there, put her on."

I don't like imperious *schmucks*. I fought fire with fire. "Mrs. Watkins is busy at the moment. Can I take a message?"

He fired off a verbal volley. I held the phone away from my ear long enough for the shouting to stop. "Give me your name and number," I told him. "She'll call back."

"I already left one message, damn it. Put her on. Tell her it's Homer."

When I heard his name, I remembered the forgotten message. I hung up the phone, cutting short his tirade. "It was Homer," I told Ginger. "He wants you to call."

Something flickered across her face, but I couldn't tell what. Anger? Fear? She turned her attention back to Huggins. "What were you saying?"

He regarded her with a sad-eyed glower. "I understand you discovered Mr. Larson's body. Now someone has ransacked your room. These incidents may or may not be related. We can't afford to assume they're not." He shifted on the bed, trying to find a more comfortable position. "Isn't it unusual for coworkers to have keys to each other's rooms?"

"Sig and I were close." Huggins waited as though expecting her to say something further. She didn't.

He sighed. "Did you have any valuables in your room? Items of jewelry, something like that?"

She shook her head. "No."

"Anything else of value—cameras, prescription medications?" Again she shook her head. He continued doggedly. "Any paperwork concerning parole board business that might be considered damaging or in some way usable? Maybe something you and Mr. Larson were working on together?"

There was a slight hesitation. "I brought some papers from home. They have nothing to do with work."

"May I ask what they are?"

"I'm filing for divorce on Monday," she said levelly. "I brought the paperwork with me. Sig and I planned to discuss it this evening." Her answer was calm, but her eyes betrayed a turmoil of warring emotions. I noticed it. So did Huggins. "That's why I was late to see Sig," she went on. "Darrell called. Someone told him."

Hal sat up. "You didn't tell him before you left?"

"No." Ginger gave him a wan smile. "It was a surprise."

"Someone told him. Who?"

Ginger shrugged. "I don't know, not for sure."

"Did he mention what time?"

"Sometime today, I know that much."

"Can you guess who it was?"

"Probably Mona."

"Mona?"

"Sig's wife, Mona Larson." The antagonism in Ginger's voice set little alarm bells ringing. Had Sig Larson died in a matrimonial crossfire between his wife and Ginger's husband?

"But how did Mrs. Larson know?"

"I wrote Sig a letter last week, the day I made up my mind. He suggested I not file until after we had a chance to discuss it."

"Why talk it over with him? What did he have to do with it?"

"I told you before, he was my friend. . . . My best friend," she added defiantly. "Why wouldn't I discuss it with him? We weren't having an affair, if that's what you mean." Her denial of an unspoken accusation gave credence to Huggins' line of questioning. Sig's having her room key made it even more plausible.

Hal's disbelief must have showed. She continued. "Our families were involved in a joint venture, a condominium project in Seattle. I didn't want to jeopardize Sig's position."

"Would you have?"

Her smile was caustic. "Evidently not. Homer and Darrell seem to have covered all possible contingencies."

I had sat quietly as long as I could. "Who the hell is Homer?" I demanded.

"Homer Watkins," she replied, her answer permeated with sarcasm. "My illustrious father-in-law."

"I don't know him."

"You haven't missed a thing."

Huggins pulled himself to a sitting position and studied his notes. "How will a divorce go over with the voters?" he asked, approaching from another direction.

Ginger bit her lip. "It won't make much difference. No one will pay any attention. It certainly won't cost him the election." She looked at Huggins closely. "Does Mona know about Sig?" she asked.

"Not yet. We still haven't located her." Huggins sighed. "Let's talk about today, from the beginning."

"I came over on the ferry early this morning," Ginger said.

"Alone?"

She nodded.

"Did you bring your car?"

"No. It's in Anacortes. I didn't think I'd need it."

"What time did you check in?"

"Our meeting started at one. I checked in sometime before that."

"What time did Mr. Larson get here?"

"I don't know. I didn't see him before the meeting. During our afternoon break we arranged to meet on the beach. That's when I gave him my key."

"Do you have a key to his room?"

"No. Mona was coming." Her answer spoke volumes.

"Oh, I see," Huggins said. "Was anyone else aware you planned to meet on the beach?"

Ginger shook her head. "Not as far as I know."

Hal Huggins was meticulous. "You got out of the meeting at four. What did you do then?"

"I went back to my room. I took a nap. Then Darrell called."

"What time?"

"I was almost ready to go meet Sig. It must have been right at five."

"What did he say?"

"He asked me to reconsider."

"And you said?"

"No."

Huggins reminded me of a doctor, probing and poking to find out where it hurts. "Was he upset?"

"He seemed to be. That surprised me. If I didn't know him better, I would have said he was jealous." Her tone was resigned. Ginger Watkins had long since come to terms with her losses, whatever those might be.

"Why wouldn't he be jealous?"

"He's not the type." She gave a half-assed grin, the kind people use to cover their real feelings, to hide something that hurts more than they're willing to admit. Huggins skirted the issue, leaving me wondering what kind of husband wouldn't be jealous of Ginger Watkins.

I had never met the man, but I decided I didn't like Darrell Watkins, candidate for lieutenant governor. As a matter of fact, I was sure I wouldn't vote for him.

"Where did he call from?"

"He didn't say. It could have been anywhere in the state. He's out campaigning."

"You don't keep a copy of his schedule?"

"No."

"Supposing he were jealous. Would he have done something to Sig Larson or maybe hired someone to do it?"

"You mean put out a contract? No, for two reasons. Number one, he wouldn't have the money. Number two, I don't believe he's that much of a hypocrite."

"I see," Huggins said sagely. "You mean he fools around himself?" Ginger's lips trembled. She dropped her gaze and nodded.

Hal's questions had led circuitously to the heart of the matter. I had to give him credit. He made another note. "Watkins is an old, respected name in Seattle. Long on reputation and money both. Supposing Darrell did want to get rid of Sig Larson, why wouldn't he have the money? It only costs a few grand to put out a contract."

"Appearances can be deceiving," she said. "I'm not working gratis, you know."

"Which means?" Hal prompted.

"It means we need the money. Some of Homer's investments haven't turned out so well. The parole board job was designed to help out. Connections are nice. How else do you think someone without a degree could walk into a forty-thousand-dollar-a-year job?" Her voice carried a defensive edge.

The phone rang, and I answered, recognizing Deputy Pomeroy's officious voice. "Detective Huggins," he demanded.

I handed the phone to Hal. He listened for a few seconds before he said, "Keep her at the desk until I get there. And, Jake, if one of those goddamned reporters gets near her before I do, I'll have your badge, understand?"

Hal bolted for the door, then stopped, turning slowly back into the room. "It would be best if you stayed here," he told Ginger. "I'll let you know when you can return to your room."

She nodded. "All right."

"The lab guys'll call when they finish." He strode into the darkness to the sound of steady rain. I closed the door behind him, feeling uncomfortable, not knowing what to say. Ginger Watkins was a stranger I knew far too much about. "Warm enough?" I asked awkwardly.

"I am now." She paused. "I might as well call Homer and get it over with."

"Why call him at all? You can afford to ignore your soon-to-be ex-father-in-law."

She picked up the phone. "Ignoring him is the worst thing you can do to Homer." She dialed the desk to charge the call to her room number, but the desk didn't answer.

"Dial it direct," I told her, and she did.

"You called?" she asked. From across the room I could hear a renewal of his verbal barrage. "What do you want?" She interrupted him bluntly, dealing with rudeness in kind.

There was a long pause while she listened. I watched her. Her hair had dried. Honey-blond waves framed her face. She paced back and forth, tugging on a phone cord that didn't give her quite enough leash.

"I'm not going to change my mind, Homer," she said at last. "I've finally seen through the fog well enough to know what's going on."

Again there was a pause. "When I wanted to do something about it, he couldn't be bothered. Now it's too late. I don't care if he's upset. I'm getting out."

She waited. "That's not true, and you know it. What I do won't make a bit of difference, one way or the other. Besides, why should I care who wins?"

His answer to that question was brief, and she stiffened. "I've found jobs before. I'll find one again." She slammed the phone down, eyes blazing. "That bastard," she muttered.

The phone rang again, and she angrily snatched it off the hook. "Hello!" Sheepishly, she handed me the receiver. "It's for you," she said.

The desk had a message for me from Maxwell Cole. He would be in Room 143. He wanted to talk to me. I put the phone down and turned to Ginger. "Are you all right?" The phone call had genuinely disturbed her.

"I'm fine," she answered without conviction. She walked across the room and stared blindly out the darkened window like a lost, lonely child in need of comforting.

"He threatened to pull your job?"

"It's no idle threat," she returned. "He can do it."

I stood near her, wanting to put an arm around her shoulder and tell her everything would be all right, to give her some of my world-famous Beaumont Bromides. Determinedly she wiped away a tear.

"I'm sorry," she apologized. "I didn't mean to cry."

"You have plenty of reason," I offered.

She looked up at me with a faint smile. "I guess I do. I was thinking about Sig."

"What about him?"

"He gave me back my self-respect," she answered. "Nothing's going to change that. I'll resign if I have to, work as a waitress or a salesclerk, but nobody can take away what Sig Larson gave me." She paused tremulously. "I can't believe he's dead."

Abandoning her attempt to stave off tears, she fell helplessly into my arms, sobbing uncontrollably against my chest. I held her and let her cry, hoping no one was outside my window. Ginger Watkins was, after all, still very much a married lady with a husband who was a well-known statewide political candidate. This would provoke a terrific scandal if it ever hit the press.

I wondered briefly how I had fallen into such a mess. As her sobs subsided, I decided what the hell. Lie back and enjoy it.

CHAPTER 4

Once Ginger regained her composure, I suggested we order dinner from Room Service. It was close to nine. My three-meal-a-day system was going into withdrawal. I ordered two steaks medium-rare. "Some wine?"

She shook her head. "I don't drink."

I ordered two bottles of Perrier. When in Rome, and all that. With her emotional outburst quelled, we waded toward dinner through a mire of meaningless chitchat. "Where are you from?" I asked.

"Centralia. My dad runs the Union 76 station down there."

It was a long way from small-town girl to big-time politics. She readily followed my thoughts. "Good looks help," she said with a smile. "Add some stupidity, and this is what you get."

"What do you mean?"

"I was pregnant when we got married. Homer offered to buy me off, send me to Sweden for an abortion. Darrell only married me because his father was dead set against it. I was a first and last gesture of independence." Her directness was unsettling. I was relieved when Room Service knocked on the door.

Our waiter was a young, local kid with a mouthful of braces and a winning smile. He wore a cutaway coat with a white towel draped casually over one arm. He spread the small round table with a linen cloth and served us with the arch panache of a British butler.

"That kid will go places," I said to Ginger after he bowed his way out of the room.

"At least he seems to enjoy what he's doing," she responded.

I poured two glasses of Perrier and handed her one. "You don't?" I asked.

"I was ready to," she began, "but then after Sig—" She broke off, unable to continue.

"What about Sig?"

"He saved my life," she said. "It's that simple."

"What did he do? Pull you out of a burning car?"

Ginger studied me in silence for a long time. "Something like that," she said quietly. "He got me to quit drinking."

"Drinking?" I'm sure I sounded incredulous.

She picked up the empty Perrier bottle and examined it. "I used to drink vodka, Wolfschmidts, on the rocks."

I grimaced. "We're not talking one drink before dinner."

"I almost died, Mr. Beaumont."

"Beau," I corrected. "My friends call me Beau."

"Beau," she added. "As long as I drank myself into oblivion every night, it didn't matter if Darrell had a steady girl friend down in Olympia when the legislature was in session, or that he was screwing around with some secretary after work. If I drank hard enough and long enough, I could almost forget. Not forgive, just forget.

"Sig was like a father to me. Never laid a glove on me, as far as sex is concerned. He just kept telling me I deserved better."

"He was right," I interjected.

She smiled at me then, green eyes flashing momentarily. "Are you going to take up where Sig left off?"

"At your service." I waved my Perrier glass in a gallant flourish.

Her smile disappeared. "I can't understand why both Homer and Darrell are trying to talk me out of the divorce. Homer never liked me, and Darrell hasn't shown any interest in me for longer than I care to remember."

"Come on, you have to be kidding!"

"Do I?" Her face was devoid of humor.

I groped for a thread of non-threatening conversation. She had said she was pregnant when they married. "You have a child?"

"Had," she corrected. "A girl. Her name was Katy, after my mother. She was almost six months old when I found her dead in her crib. They call it Sudden Infant Death Syndrome, now. Back then it didn't have a name. I blamed myself. The kooks came out of the woodwork, told me

God was punishing me for my sins. It was awful!" She closed her eyes, reliving the pain.

I wanted to say something, but it was a little late to offer condolences.

"That's when I started to drink," she continued as naturally as if she were discussing the weather. "I never got pregnant again. I couldn't sleep. I started having a drink or two in the evening to put me under, to blot out the pain. Eventually I had to drink to live. It's only been since I dried out that I've come to terms with Katy's death, accepted it, allowed myself to grieve. Booze is like that, you know. It buries feelings, keeps you from dealing with them."

The last sentence hit close to home. It was what Peters had told me I was doing, and Ralph Ames, and the chaplain. They told me to stop hiding out in MacNaughton's and come to grips with grief. They said I should cry for Anne Corley and let her go. I wasn't ready.

I veered the conversation away from me and back to Ginger. "Sig helped you do that?"

She nodded. "We were in Shelton doing a series of hearings. Board members travel in pairs, like nuns. One morning I couldn't get out of bed. I had the shakes too bad. That was when Sig broke into my room. He dragged me to my first Alcoholics Anonymous meeting that night. We were scheduled to go home the next morning, but we stayed over. Sig got us rooms in a different motel. It took three days for him to walk me through the DTs. That's when Mona started thinking Sig and I were having an affair."

I looked at Ginger's trim figure and flawless grace. She didn't fit any of the standard stereotypes of a recovering alcoholic. Had she not told me, I never would have suspected.

"I won't go through that again, ever," she continued. "Nothing can be worse than DTs. Sig kept me in the program, talked to me when I got discouraged, kept telling me I was a worthwhile person long before I could see it for myself. I'd be dead by now if it weren't for him."

"He sounds like a hell of a nice guy," I commented.

"He was." She lapsed into silence.

"Do you love Darrell?" It was none of my business, yet I asked anyway. I already knew a great deal about Ginger Watkins, far more than our few hours together warranted, but I wanted to know more. It had nothing to do with Detective J. P. Beaumont. It was Beau, the man, who needed to know.

"I used to," she said softly. "Not anymore."

She met my gaze, then looked down at her plate. "I didn't mean to bore you."

"I'm not bored. What will you do?"

"Live one day at a time. I'll file on Monday, resign from the board if I have to, and go looking for a job."

"What kind of job?"

"Maybe I'll go back to school and get a degree in alcoholism counseling. I'd like to repay Sig Larson."

"Somehow I don't think Sig expected to be repaid."

"No," she agreed, "he didn't. That's why I want to do it." Suddenly she put the brakes on my questioning. "What about you? Who is J. P. Beaumont?"

I gave her an evasive grin. "A homicide cop in the middle of a mid-life crisis, trying to decide what I want to be when I grow up."

"Married?"

"Not anymore."

"Involved?"

I sighed. It was six months later, but the hurt was still there. Not bleeding, but raw nonetheless. "No, I'm footloose and fancy-free."

"You don't sound very footloose," she observed.

"That's very perceptive of you," I said. "You're right." I couldn't match her candor. The kind of open self-revelation that came easily to her eluded me. The telephone jangled a welcome interruption.

"Detective Beaumont?"

"Yes."

"This is Smitty with the crime lab. Could you bring Mrs. Watkins up to take a look around the room?"

"Sure. Find anything?"

"Can't tell." It was a standard answer. "Maybe she can tell us if anything's missing."

"Okay, we'll be right there."

I put down the phone and turned to Ginger. "Traveling time."

She peered in dismay at her stockinged feet. "What about shoes?"

Scrounging the bottom of the closet, I turned up my ancient bedroom slippers. "Put these on. They'll fit like a pair of snowshoes, but it's better than going barefoot."

Ginger stumbled across the room in a trial run. "Not much better," she commented.

The walk to Ginger's room was cold and windy. The rain had stopped. Wispy clouds scudded before a half-moon. Ginger scuffed along, gripping my arm in case she tripped over the out-sized slippers.

"Have you ever been the victim of a break-in before?"

She shook her head. I wanted to warn her, to ease the shock of seeing her things strewn and disheveled by unknown hands. She knew of the break-in from Huggins, but hearing it and seeing it are two different things.

We made it to her room without incident. If Rosario was crawling with reporters, they weren't in evidence. Thank God Huggins had managed to keep Ginger's room out of the limelight. By now members of the Fourth Estate would have filed their stories. They'd be settled in the Vista Lounge, drowning their sorrows or entertaining one another. The Seattle Press Corps Traveling Dog and Pony Show.

Pomeroy opened the door, grunting with displeasure when he saw me.

I ignored him, pushing my way past without any kind of acknowledgment. His face flushed angrily, but he said nothing.

Ginger followed me into the room. She stopped short inside the door, her face blanching, her hands involuntarily covering her mouth.

A man came forward and introduced himself. "I'm Dayton Smith," he said. "Smitty for short. This your room?"

Ginger nodded.

"We've dusted for prints. We'll want your prints and those of any other people known to have been in the room—the desk clerk, maids, Room Service. That's the only way to discover unidentified prints. We'll go down to the lobby after we finish here."

Again Ginger nodded, incapable of speech.

"Look around. Can you see if anything is missing?"

Walking trancelike through the room, Ginger fingered the heap of clothing piled on the floor, sifted through the contents of her makeup case strewn on the counter while those of us in the room watched in silence.

All the officers, with the possible exception of Pomeroy, understood the deep sense of violation a break-in victim feels. Fear, anger, and outrage passed over her face in rapid succession. She knelt beside a scatter of papers dumped near an overturned Gucci briefcase, awkwardly attempting to straighten them. When she finished, I pulled her to her feet.

"Is anything gone?"

She shook her head. "I don't think so."

I looked at Smitty. "No sign of forced entry?"

"No. Whoever came in evidently had a key."

I looked down at Ginger. She was pale and shaking. "Gather what you need," I said. "You can't stay here. We'll have the desk send someone to clean up this mess."

She approached the task purposefully, moving through the room, scooping up nightgown, robe, and shoes from the tangled heap on the floor. She sorted through the things on the counter, placing makeup, hair-brush, and toothbrush in a small case along with her clothing. Pomeroy watched her leeringly from the door. I wanted to kick him.

At last, still wearing my slippers, she turned to me. "I'm ready. Can we go?"

I led her from the room. She sank against me. I supported her willingly, J. P. Beaumont, Good Samaritan in an hour of need.

"Thank you," she whispered.

"You're welcome," I replied, guiltily conscious of savoring the slight pressure of her slender body against mine.

CHAPTER 5

Smitty's partner from the Washington State Crime Lab took Ginger into the hotel kitchen for fingerprinting. I went to the desk where I tackled Fred, demanding another room. "I'm sorry Mr. Beaumont. We're full. We were almost booked before the reporters showed up, and now—"

"Look," I said. "The crime lab's still not done with her room. Besides, she can't go back there. The lock wasn't broken. Whoever got in had a key."

"As I said, we don't have any other rooms."

I turned away from the desk in disgust, only to run headlong into the mustached human walrus who calls himself Maxwell Cole. "Hello, J. P. Why didn't you return my call?"

"Didn't want to, Max. Get out of my way."

"You're being rude," he chided. "I only need to talk to you for a minute."

"What about?" I was pretty sure I knew what Max was after. For once in his life, he surprised me.

"Don Wilson."

"Who the hell is Don Wilson?"

"You remember, Denise Wilson's husband. DeAnn's father. The Lathrop case."

There isn't a cop in Washington State who isn't sickened by the very name. Philip Lathrop sits over on Death Row in Walla Walla, a slime thumbing his nose at the system. Seven years ago, he followed Denise Wilson home from the laundromat and raped her in front of her two-year-old daughter. Denise testified against him, and Lathrop got sent up. He went to prison vowing revenge.

Six years later he was placed in a work/release program. Nobody remembered that the Wilsons lived less than three miles away. He came back to their house one hot July day and finished the job, killing both Denise and DeAnn in a bloody carnage that left hardened detectives puking at the scene. It'll be years before he exhausts the appeals process. It's called a miscarriage of justice!

"What about Don Wilson?" I asked.

"I was to meet him here at four. He never showed."

"So? What does that have to do with me?"

"I wondered if you had seen him. He turns up at parole board hearings, demonstrating, protesting—that kind of thing. He's lobbying for a statewide victim/witness protection program."

"Look, Max, I wouldn't recognize him if I saw him. There hasn't been a protester in sight."

Max blinked at me nearsightedly through thick glasses. "You're sure?"

"Yes, I'm sure, goddammit," I snapped. "Now leave me alone." I was still worrying about Ginger, wondering if there might be a room available somewhere in Eastsound.

Max backed away from me warily. The last time he and I had a confrontation, I loosened a couple of teeth for him.

Just then Ginger returned from the kitchen. She walked past Cole. "I'm done, Beau," she said. "Did you get a room?" It was an innocent question, but I wondered how it would read in the morning edition. As recognition and wonder washed across Max's fat face, I wanted to crawl into a hole.

"Why, Mrs. Watkins, how nice to see you again."

Ginger turned on him coolly. "I don't believe I know you."

"Cole," he said with an affable grin. "Maxwell Cole of the *Post-Intelligencer*. Would you care to comment on Sig Larson's death?"

Her manner changed from cool to frigid. "I would not."

He shrugged and looked at me. "Doesn't hurt to ask."

"Get out of here, Max." I was in no mood to put up with any of his crap.

"Just one more question, Mrs. Watkins. Have you seen Don Wilson today?"

Ginger's reaction was totally out of proportion to the question. "Is . . . he . . . here?" she stammered. Color drained from her face. She groped blindly for my arm.

The change wasn't lost on Max. He stepped toward her, and she shrank against me. "He was supposed to be," Max continued lightly. "We had an interview scheduled at four. He called late this morning. Said something was about to break. I barely had time to get here."

I stepped between Max and Ginger. "Why did he call you? Why not someone else?"

"I've been working on a special piece—".

I took Ginger's arm, cutting him off. "Come on. Let's get out of here."

"But—" Max protested.

"Stay away from her and stay away from me, Max. If you don't, I'll give your dentist and your eye doctor a little more business."

His walrus mouth opened and closed convulsively. They weren't empty words, and he knew it. When Ginger and I left the building, he made no effort to follow.

I led Ginger back to my room and helped her into the chair before I went back to shut and lock the door. "What is it, Ginger?" I asked gently. "Tell me."

"He did it," she said decisively. "It has to be him."

"Who did what?"

"Don Wilson. He killed Sig, I'm sure of it. I had no idea he was here. I never thought—"

"What are you talking about?"

"Don Wilson. He threatened us, both Sig and me. Sig just laughed it off. So did Darrell. No one took it seriously."

"Why did he threaten you? I don't understand."

"We—" She swallowed hard. "Sig and I conducted the hearing that sent Lathrop to that work/release program."

My gut gave a wrench. I remembered the public outcry. There had been talk that the parole board should resign *en masse*. I had been standing next to her. Turning, I moved away, distancing myself. I couldn't help it.

"Please, Beau, it wasn't our fault. We were given incomplete records. We made the decision as best we could with the information at hand." Her voice pleaded for understanding, for me not to abandon her.

"What did Wilson say?" My tone was flat and empty.

"That we'd pay for his wife and daughter. We didn't know, Beau. Can you understand that? There was an administrative foul-up. The rest of Lathrop's records weren't found until much later. We didn't know he had sworn to get even with Denise Wilson. We had no idea where she lived. Washington doesn't keep track of witnesses or victims, not even to protect them."

"When did Wilson threaten you?" I could tell from her voice it was important that I believe her.

"I don't know. Several times. He's always hanging around. In fact, Sig and I were surprised Wilson wasn't here today. He stands outside every meeting, carrying signs, passing out petitions, but I never thought he'd really do it."

"Petitions for what?"

"For a victim/witness protection program."

"But he wasn't here today?"

"No. Sig even mentioned it." I got up and went to the phone. "What are you doing?" she asked.

"I'm calling Huggins. He needs this information." Fred answered. "Is Detective Huggins still around?"

"No," came the reply. "He left in the police boat right after the crime-lab guys took off. He's probably in Friday Harbor by now."

"Call him and tell him to come back," I ordered. "It's urgent."

Fred's response wasn't hopeful. "I doubt he'll want to come back tonight."

"Tell him we've got a suspect. That'll bring him back." I hung up.

Ginger followed me to the door. "Where are you going?" she asked.

"I've got to find Maxwell Cole. You stay here, understand?" She nodded. "Lock the door behind me. Don't let anyone in."

I dashed outside and headed up the path to Room 143. No one answered my knock. I glanced at my watch. It was after eleven. The Vista Lounge was still open. I hurried back toward the main building, a converted mansion that serves as lobby, dining room, and bar. The lounge is a long, narrow room facing Rosario Strait. In its previous life it had been a sun porch. Now it was a posh watering hole.

Maxwell Cole's ample figure slouched on a stool at the end of the bar. He was downing handfuls of salted cracker goldfish and regaling the poor guy next to him with one-sided conversation. I tapped his shoulder.

"Hey, Max. I need to talk to you."

He heaved himself around on the bar stool to face me. "What's this? A change of heart? Decided you can afford to spend some time with your old fraternity buddy after all? Fuck off, J. P. Who needs it?"

He turned away and picked up his beer. I tapped his shoulder again. "I want to talk to you."

Barney is a good bartender. He has a sixth sense for trouble and can spot it before it starts. He ambled down the bar to where Cole was sitting.

"What seems to be the problem?"

"This guy's bothering me," Max whined. "I was sitting here minding my own business."

Barney glanced up at me. "I need to talk to him," I said tersely over Max's head. "About what happened this afternoon."

Max set down his half-empty glass. Barney swept it away and poured the contents into the sink. "After you talk to this gentleman," he said, "I'll buy you another beer."

"Why you—" Max objected.

"You'd better go, fella, before I get upset."

Barney is a beefy former Green Beret who looks as though he could inflict a considerable amount of bodily harm with his bare hands. Max finally scrambled down from the bar stool and reluctantly followed me into the next room, muttering under his breath. Once we were out of earshot of the bar, I turned on him. "You have any pictures of Wilson on you?"

"Hell no. Why should I?"

"Because you just might."

"Maybe one, but it'll cost you."

"How much?"

"An exclusive interview with Ginger Watkins."

"Ginger Watkins is not for sale."

"You say that in a rather proprietary manner, J. P. You got something going with her? I heard what she said about getting a room. She's a married lady, you know. Her husband is big. Very big."

"I want the picture, Max."

"No way."

He was wearing an ugly striped tie, still knotted, but hanging loose around his neck. I grasped it in my fist and lifted him to the tops of his toes. "I'm not on duty, Maxey, so don't tempt me."

"Okay, okay," he sputtered. "It's in my room."

"Go get it and bring it to me. I'll wait in the lobby."

He shambled off. I hurried to the pay phone near the front desk and dialed Peters, my partner, at home, long-distance, collect. I figured that would get his attention. He sounded half-asleep when he answered the phone. "What's up?" he asked when he recognized my voice. "Where are you? And why the hell are you calling me collect?"

"Rosario," I growled. "Send me the bill. Now listen. Remember the Lathrop case? Get down to the department and gather everything you can find on it. A detective from Friday Harbor will be calling for it. I want it ready when he does."

"Just a fucking minute, Beau. Do you know what time it is? It's a long way from Kirkland to the department."

"So move to town. It's not rush hour. It won't take more than twenty minutes to get to Seattle."

"Beau, you're supposed to be on vacation, for chrissake. What's gotten into you?"

"I'm asking a favor, Peters. Please."

"Oh, all right, but I'm gonna remember this. The Lathrop case, you said?"

"Yes, and everything you can find out about the victims' family, particularly Don Wilson, the father."

"Anything else? I'm already awake. Don't you want me to pick up some groceries or a newspaper while I'm at it?"

Maxwell Cole was lumbering toward the building. "Cut the comedy, Peters. This is serious."

"Okay, Beau, okay. I'm on my way."

"Thanks. I owe you one."

"This better count for more than one."

"It does."

CHAPTER 6

I knocked. "Who is it?" Ginger called.

"Me, Beau." I opened the door with my key. Ginger stood near the bed, her face drawn and wary. She glanced at the manila envelope in my hand. "What's that?"

I came inside, shutting and locking the door behind me. I opened the envelope and handed her the picture Maxwell Cole had given me. She looked at Don Wilson's likeness.

"Where'd you get that?"

"Good ol' Max saves the day for a change."

Ginger retreated to a chair in the corner of the room, where she curled up with her legs folded under her and began brushing her hair with a vengeance.

"Huggins is on his way," I told her. "He'll want to go to work on this picture tonight. He'll show it to everyone he can find on or near the ferries, passengers and workers alike. He'll try to get to them while someone still remembers seeing Wilson, either coming over or going back."

Ginger put the brush in her lap. Her voice when she spoke was very small. "Do you think he's still here?"

"I don't know. My gut instinct says yes."

"What can we do?"

"First we talk to Huggins. After that, I don't know."

"Can I stay here, Beau? With you?" Anxious green eyes held mine.

I felt a catch in my throat, remembering the feel of her body against mine as she wept for Sig Larson. "I don't know why not. I'd as soon have you here where I can keep an eye on you. I was going to see if there were any rooms available in Eastsound, but this makes more sense."

She picked up her brush and silently resumed brushing her hair. I called the desk. Fred and I had gone round and round over the room problem one more time after Max gave me the picture. I had pulled rank on him, hoping Detective Beaumont would elicit more action than Mr. Beaumont. No such luck. His tone was somewhat guarded. "Yes, Detective Beaumont. What can I do for you?"

"You have a roll-away bed down there?"

"Yes."

"I want one up here, on the double. Mrs. Watkins will stay here with me. We have reason to believe Larson's killer is still in the area. He may try to reach her next. Don't leak a word of this, is that clear?"

"Yes, sir. I'll deliver it myself. Not even the maids will know. I can pick it up in the morning before I leave."

"And if she has any calls," I continued, "put them on hold and check with me before you put them through."

"I understand."

"When's your shift over?"

"I'm pulling an extra one tonight. I won't get off until eight tomorrow morning."

"All right. Have the roll-away back out of here before you go. I guess that's all."

"Detective Beaumont?"

"Yes."

"Someone said Detective Huggins is just pulling up at the dock."

"Good. See if you can locate any coffee, would you?"

"Sure thing."

When Huggins knocked on the door, he was carrying a tray with a pot of coffee and three cups and saucers. "Somebody handed me this tray. Whatever you've got, Beaumont, it better be good."

"It is, Hal," I assured him. "Believe me."

Ginger poured coffee while I brought Hal up to date and showed him the photograph of Wilson. When I finished, he shook his head sadly. "It's a pisser. The wrong goddamned people get killed. Wilson'll end up on Death Row with Lathrop, and probably beat him to the gallows."

I interrupted Huggins' grim soliloquy. "Look, Hal, I called my partner in Seattle. He's gathering everything Seattle P.D. has on Lathrop and Wilson. It'll be ready when you call. He'll bring it out himself if you ask for him."

"Is he one of the old-timers?" Hal asked. "Somebody I'd remember?"

"No. He's brand-new, but a hell of a nice guy."

"What's his name?"

"Peters. Ron Peters."

He made a note of the name before turning to Ginger. "Can you remember exactly what Wilson said when he threatened you and Mr. Larson?"

Ginger shook her head. "Not the exact words. Just that he'd make us pay, that it wasn't fair for his wife and child to be dead while we were still alive."

"But you didn't think of him this afternoon when you discovered Mr. Larson's body. Why not?"

"I didn't think Wilson was here. If he's around, he's usually out front picketing with all his signs and paraphernalia. I forgot about him completely until that reporter said Wilson didn't show for a meeting."

"Which reporter?"

I answered him. "Max, Maxwell Cole. Wilson called him this morning and set up an interview here at Rosario at four o'clock. Max waited. Wilson never came."

Huggins focused once more on Ginger. "You said you mentioned the threats to your husband. He advised you to disregard them?"

Ginger nodded. "He said the world is full of harmless crazies."

"This one is far from harmless." Huggins sighed, glancing in my direction. "Any ideas, Beaumont?"

There was a quiet tap on the door. When I answered it, Fred stood outside with a roll-away bed. "This is the first I could get away," he said. "It's all right if Detective Huggins knows, isn't it?"

Since the bed was already there, it was too late to debate secrecy. I stepped aside and helped pull the bed over the threshold. He pushed the bed just inside the door, then ducked back into the night. Fearless Fred.

"This is my brainstorm," I said, turning to Huggins. "She stays with me tonight. Without knowing whether Wilson is still on the island, I'm not willing to risk leaving her alone."

He nodded in agreement. "Good thinking. I was going to suggest flying her to Seattle, but I'd prefer having her here in case there are more questions in the morning. The county budget doesn't handle a whole lot of commuting back and forth to the big city."

Huggins stood up. "I'm going, then." He held Wilson's picture up to the light, examining it minutely. "I'll copy this sucker tonight and plaster the island with it tomorrow—the island and every single ferry that stops here. I'll send someone by Wilson's house. It's late. I'd better hit the trail."

I followed him to the door. He turned to me and said in an undertone, "You got a piece on you?"

"It's locked up in a suitcase, but—"

"I'm deputizing you as of right now, Beaumont. I don't want there to be any jurisdictional fuss. Besides, I need you. Get it out, and keep it handy." He poked his head back inside the door. "You're in good hands, Mrs. Watkins. J. P. Beaumont is the best there is."

"You'll give me a swelled head, Hal," I said.

I came back into the room, once more carefully locking the door behind me. I went around the room, double-checking the locks on the windows. Ginger watched me, her eyes gravely following my every move. I took my suitcase from its place in the closet and removed my .38. I put the gun on the bed beside me. Women usually retreat from firearms. Ginger held her ground.

"Are you?" she asked.

"Am I what?"

"The best there is?"

"I don't know about that." I sat looking at my revolver. A gun is a tool, an instrument, until it kills something you love. Then it takes on a life of its own, alien, evil.

"What are you thinking?"

"Nothing," I answered quickly. "Just wool-gathering."

"What happened to your wife?"

"Karen?" I shrugged. "She ran off with a chicken magnate from Cucamonga, California."

"Chicken?"

"Yeah. He was an accountant scouting for a new plant site for an egg conglomerate. Karen was supposed to be selling him real estate."

"He married her?"

"Eventually."

"Kids?"

"Two. A boy and a girl, Scotty and Kelly. They're mostly grown, thriving in California. I see them during the summers." I didn't mention Anne Corley. It was a deliberate oversight.

"Girl friend?"

"None at the moment. Why all the questions?"

"Everyone's been asking me questions all evening. Turnabout is fair play. You said earlier you were having a mid-life crisis How come?"

"Mid-life crises are very trendy these days." I responded with a congenial grin I hoped would derail the question. I didn't want to go into that, to examine motives and lost illusions.

"Will you still be a cop?"

I shrugged. I couldn't imagine being anything else. "Unless you have some other bright idea."

She looked at me seriously, squarely. "You've been hurt too."

"Does it show that much?"

"It shows."

I winced at her direct hit and changed the subject. "You said something earlier that's been bothering me: that you were working because you and Darrell needed the money. How come?"

"We're part of a syndicate that put together a downtown luxury high-rise project, just before the bottom dropped out of the real estate market. Most of our capital—ours, Homer's, and Sig's—has been tied up keeping the project afloat, waiting for the market to turn. Meantime, ready cash is in short supply."

"That's why you and Sig ended up on the parole board?"

She nodded. "Sig was actually well qualified. He knew it from the inside out without ever being either a prisoner or a guard. He did volunteer work at Walla Walla for years. He used to live near there, even started an A.A. group inside. He had every right to be on the board. I was the hanger-on."

Ginger looked at me earnestly. "I tried, though, Beau. Especially after Sig got me dried out. I read everything I could lay my hands on. I did a good job. The Lathrop case was an administrative nightmare." She willed me to believe her. It was important to her that I not lay blame.

"Those things happen," I conceded.

She accepted my remark as a form of absolution. "Thank you," she murmured.

"What will you do if you resign from the board?"

She shrugged. "Something," she replied. "Homer told me tonight he'll see to it that I don't get a penny."

"That's just a threat. He can't get away with it. You have an attorney. He'll see that you get a fair shake."

She laughed. "You don't understand. Homer Watkins' name isn't up in lights. He doesn't make headlines, but he's a mover and shaker in this state. Stone-cold broke, he can still pull enough strings to get anything he wants, including electing his son lieutenant governor. I'll be lucky to get out of the house with the clothes on my back."

"I have an attorney," I offered. "Maybe he could help." I was thinking about Ralph Ames, who even then was preparing for a custody hearing to wrest my partner's two kids out of a religious cult in Broken Springs, Oregon.

Ginger smiled, condescendingly. "How far do you think I'd get paying for an attorney on my own? It takes money to fight the system. I won't have any."

"Ames would do it if I asked him. He's from Arizona. Phoenix. He handles all my personal affairs. Let him take a look at your situation. It wouldn't cost you anything."

A smile flickered around the corner of her mouth. "Beau, listen to me. These are big-time lawyers with big-time staffs. They'd chew up your little guy and spit him out. But thanks. It's kind of you to offer."

"Promise me you'll let Ames look it over first. Talk about the best there is, Ames is it."

Ginger laughed aloud. "All right, all right. If you insist, but he'd better not show up wearing cowboy boots and riding a horse."

CHAPTER 7

I spent some time looking for a delicate way to suggest we get ready for bed. There was no easy way. I finally said it straight out. Ginger retreated into the bathroom to change while I grappled with the Chinese-puzzle roll-away bed. Partial assembly required.

The bed was unfolded and sitting in front of the outside door when Ginger emerged from the bathroom. She wore a jade-colored silk robe with a hint of filmy nightgown underneath. Seeing her, I realized I didn't have a pair of pajamas to my name. I'd been a bachelor so long, my last pair of Christmas pajamas had bitten the dust.

"What are you staring at?" she demanded, one hand on her hip. "Haven't you ever seen a woman in a robe before?"

"Sorry. I was thinking about something else."

I retired to the bathroom to contemplate my dilemma, finally opting for skivvies and no lights. That, of course, presented another problem. No light in a familiar room is one thing, and no light in a city apartment is another. But no light in a strange room where they've never heard of streetlights can be murder on shins, toes, and other unprotected parts of the anatomy. I blundered my way into bed after a bruising game of blindman's bluff.

Settling into the roll-away, I discovered the bed frame formed a rigid hump directly under the small of my back. It was a long way from the king-sized comfort I had grown accustomed to. At last I concluded the bed wasn't any worse than some of the rocks I had slept on just for the hell of it during my hunting and camping phase. This at least had a somewhat higher purpose.

I tossed around a few minutes before dozing off. I had just entered that deep, initial alpha sleep when I heard her say, "Beau?"

Adrenaline pumping, I made a dive for the .38 on the floor beside me. The roll-away tipped up on one corner, pitching me headlong onto the floor in a tangle of sheets, pillow, and blankets. Ginger switched on the bedside lamp.

"What happened?"

"I fell out of bed, goddammit! What's wrong? Did you hear something?"

"No, I was wondering if you were awake."

"I am now," I grumbled. I didn't want to get up. The light still blazed while I sat on the floor clad in a discreet loincloth of sheet. I glared at her, and she started to giggle.

"It's not funny," I muttered.

She nodded, covering her mouth with her hand to contain increasing ripples of laughter. "Yes it is," she gasped at last. "You ought to see yourself."

I looked down. I had to admit that what I could see was pretty funny. The gun had skidded under the bed. No way was I going to crawl around on hands and knees searching for it. With as much dignity as I could muster, I unraveled my legs. At last, wearing the sheet as a toga, I stood on my feet, surveying the debris that had once been a tidy roll-away bed.

"This is a very large bed," Ginger said seriously, stifling her mirth. "It's probably more comfortable than that thing, too." That much was inarguable. I said nothing. "Care to join me?"

"Come on, Ginger. Get serious."

"I am serious." All laughter was gone from her mouth and eyes. "There's plenty of room," she added. "We're consenting adults. We haven't crossed any state lines."

"But you're the wife of the soon-to-be-elected lieutenant governor."

"The soon-to-be-former wife of the soon-to-be-elected lieutenant governor," she corrected with a hint of a smile.

I moved to the far side of the bed and alighted cautiously on the edge of it. I waited for lightning to strike. It didn't.

"Would you like me to call the desk and see if they have any bundling boards?"

I turned on her. "You're making fun of me."

"I can't help it."

Tentatively I slid first one leg, then the other under the covers, clutching the sheet firmly in one hand as a security blanket. I settled warily on my pillow before I turned to look at her. She sat propped up in bed observing me with undisguised interest.

The deep neckline of her gown fell away revealing a firm swell of breast.

"Do you think I'm beautiful?" she asked gravely.

I looked up guiltily, convinced she had caught me peeking. "Of course you're beautiful. Very beautiful."

"Sig used to tell me that. I never knew if I should believe him."

"My God, Ginger! How could you not believe him?"

"I still see a drunk when I look in the mirror." It was a comment made without guile. She wasn't fishing for a compliment: she was attempting to understand, to sort out what was real and what wasn't.

Obviously we weren't going right to sleep. I propped my pillow next to hers, examining her carefully, critically in the golden glow of the bedside lamp behind her. I studied the curve of her forehead, the clear green eyes under delicately arched brows, the fine, straight nose, the gentle pout of her lower lip. "You're not the same person now. I think that's what Sig wanted you to realize."

She drew her knees up and rested her chin on them, musing aloud. "I thought if I once quit drinking, that I'd be good enough, that Darrell would finally pay some attention to me. There are a lot of stories like that in A.A., you know, marriages that bounce back from the brink of disaster. But this is a thirty-six-year-old body. I can't compete with tender blossoms from the secretarial pool."

Silence lengthened between us. Never glib, I could think of nothing to say. But then, I had never before found myself in quite this situation.

"What's the scar on your chest?"

"Huh?" Her question startled me. I looked down as though I had forgotten it was my chest and my scar, the stark white of an incision highlighted against the rest of my skin. "It's from a bullet," I said.

"When did it happen?"

"Last spring sometime," I said carefully. The time, the date, the place are as indelibly inked on my soul as the scar is on my flesh.

"Did you catch him?"

"Who?"

"The man who shot you."

"It was a woman. She's dead."

"Oh."

"Do you mind turning out the lights?" I asked. I didn't want to talk any-more. The conversation was circling too close to my own hurt. It was one thing to help Ginger with hers. Dealing with my own was something else.

The light snapped off. I could feel Ginger settling on her side of the bed. I groped under the bed and located my .38. Once it was within easy reach, I lowered my pillow, resting on it as if it were full of thumbtacks or nails.

"Beau?"

"Yes."

"Could I just lie next to you? I need an arm around me. Someone to hold me."

Tentatively, I held up the covers. She slid across the bed and nestled into the crook of my arm. I inhaled the fragrant perfume of her freshly washed hair. I felt the curve of her hip next to mine, the gentle swell of her breast under a layer of covers. For a long time we were quiet. I think I was holding my breath.

"Beau?"

"Yes."

"What are you thinking?"

"I'm trying to remember which of the Ten Commandments says 'Thou shalt not covet thy neighbor's wife.'"

"Do you?"

"Do I what?"

"Covet me?"

Right then I realized the Garden of Eden was a put-up job. "Yes."

Her hand flitted across my chest, her touch inflaming every strained nerve in my body. She pulled herself up until she lay on my chest, her lips grazing mine.

I was conscious of the tantalizing feel of silk against my skin, the musky odor of a woman's awakening body. She kissed me, cautiously, as though unsure of my response. I wasn't sure either. I waited long enough to be sure lightning still didn't strike, then I pulled her to me, my mouth seeking hers, finding her hungry, willing, eager.

She guided my hand through the cleft in her gown. Her breast was taut and expectant beneath my cupped fingers. I sampled her ear and traced the slender curve of her neck with my teeth and tongue. She gasped, and her body arched as gooseflesh swept across her skin beneath my fingertips.

She slipped from my grasp. I heard her impatiently cast off the silken barrier of gown. My Fruit of the Loom hit the floor as well. Ginger came back to me naked, sleek, and ready. Beyond pleasure, she sought only release.

She slid her body onto mine, moisture finding moisture, need finding need, plunging me deep within her. I grasped her slim waist, raising her, lowering her, hearing her sharp intake of breath each time I probed closer to home, each time I led her to the brink then drew her back, offering and withholding the final gift.

"Now," she whispered. "Please."

When the flood came, it engulfed us both. We surfaced in a quiet pool, spent and out of breath. "That was wonderful," she whispered.

"I'll bet you say that to all the guys," I teased.

She was suddenly subdued. "There's only been one other," she said. "He's never been this good. Ever."

"Flattery will get you everywhere." I drew her into my arms, cradling her head on my shoulder. "Are you going to shut up and go to sleep? It's late. The desk clerk is coming for the goddamn roll-away at eight in the morning."

"I'll be quiet," she said. "I promise."

She snuggled against me. We lay like that for a long time. Her breathing steadied and slowed. I listened as her heart beat next to mine, a thud followed by a smaller echo. Deliberately I tried to slow my breathing, hoping to God I wouldn't snore. Time passed slowly. I stared, sleepless, at the empty space above the bed, wondering how long it takes to learn to sleep double in a double bed, to misquote a familiar song. Probably a long time.

"Beau?"

"What now?"

"I can't do it."

"Do what?"

"Sleep like this. I don't know how to sleep with anyone but Darrell."

I pulled her to me, holding her for a moment in a crushing bear hug. I kissed the top of her forehead, then shoved her playfully toward the other side of the bed. "Go sleep over there, then, spoilsport."

"I'm sorry."

"Don't be. I understand."

And I did understand. Ginger Watkins had been caught up in the need to know she was still alive—a normal phenomenon in the aftermath of death, an instinctive affirmation of survival. If I hadn't been there, she would have found someone else. I just got lucky.

CHAPTER 8

The telephone jarred me awake at seven. "Detective Beaumont? Darrell Watkins is on the phone. He wants to speak to Mrs. Watkins. Should I put him through?"

I felt the unaccustomed warmth of a body snuggled close to mine. It took time to clear my head. I turned, and Ginger stirred, nestling comfortably against me. She had evidently moved there in the middle of the night, our sleeping bodies overcoming our conscious objections. "Sure, that's fine," I said into the phone.

With a noisy clatter I fumbled the phone back into place. "Ginger. Wake up. You've got a call."

Her eyes opened and focused on mine with a look of startled dismay. The phone rang again before she could say anything. I handed it to her.

"Hello?" Ginger said, her voice still thick with sleep. "Oh, hello Darrell." There was a long silence as she listened to what he had to say. Meanwhile, I lay naked under the covers, considering the best way to get to the bathroom while maintaining some degree of modesty.

"No. I haven't changed my mind," she said firmly. That galvanized me to action. I had no intention of eavesdropping on her domestic conversation. I groped on the floor, found the discarded roll-away sheet, and wrapped it around me. With clean clothes from the closet, I withdrew into the bathroom and took a bracing hot shower.

The water pounded me. Despite lack of sleep, I was invigorated, stimulated. Exhaustion, my constant companion for months, dissolved. I was incredibly happy, except for one small cloud on my horizon. Ginger might be remorseful.

I didn't want guilt or regret to tarnish what had happened between us, even if it was nothing more than the survivor's time-honored, near-death screwing syndrome. Maybe that's all it had been for Ginger, but not for me. It had reawakened J. P. Beaumont's lost libido. I was glad to have the old boy back.

Humming under my breath, I emerged from the bathroom. Ginger sat on her side of the bed with her legs tucked under her. She was wearing the lush silk robe.

"Good morning," I said.

"Do you always sing in the shower?"

"Only when I'm happy," I told her.

"I see."

I looked at her, trying to assess the effect of her husband's phone call, hoping for some sign to indicate if she was glad to see me or if she wanted me to drop into a hole someplace. Her face remained inscrutable.

"Is Darrell coming up?" I asked, for want of something better to say.

"He wanted to, but I told him no. He thinks he can talk me into changing my mind. It won't work. I told him I'm staying here the rest of the weekend. I had planned to, anyway. There's no sense in going home just to fight."

"Will they cancel the workshop?"

She smiled mirthlessly. "Not even Trixie Bowdeen has nerve enough to go through with it after what happened to Sig."

"Who's she?"

"Chairman of the parole board."

"You don't like her much, do you."

"No," she responded.

With my hair combed and a splash of after-shave on my face, I surveyed the roll-away with an eye to making it look more like someone had slept in it and less as though a heavyweight wrestling match had occurred. I gathered up the sheets and blankets and started to put it to rights.

"Beau?"

Busy with the bed, I didn't look up when she spoke. "What?"

"Do you think badly of me?"

I abandoned the roll-away. "Think badly of you! Are you kidding? Why should I?"

"Because of last night. I didn't mean to . . . I—"

In two steps I stood beside her. "Look, lady," I said gruffly, placing my hand on her shoulder and giving her a gentle shake. "It's the blind leading the blind. I was worried about how you'd feel this morning, afraid you'd be embarrassed, think I'd taken advantage."

She reached out and took my hand. She kissed the back of it, then turned it over and moved it from her hairline to her chin, guiding my fingers in a slow caress along the curve of her cheek.

"I'm not embarrassed," she said softly. "Greedy, but not embarrassed." She allowed my hand to stray down her neck and invade the soft folds of her robe. She was wearing nothing underneath.

Her robe fell open before me. Our coupling the night before had been in pitch-blackness. Now my eyes feasted hungrily on her body. She was no lithe virgin. Hers was the gentle voluptuousness of a grown woman, with a hint of fullness of breast and hip that follows childbearing. A pale web of stretch marks lingered in mute testimony.

My hand cupped her breast. It changed subtly but perceptibly. The nipple drew erect, the soft flesh taut and warm beneath my fingers. She caught my chin in her hand and turned my face to hers until our lips met. "Please, Beau," she whispered, her mouth against mine.

I shed my clothes on the spot while she lay naked before me, tempting as a pagan sacrifice offered to me alone. My fingers and tongue searched her body, exploring her, demanding admittance. She gave herself freely, opening before me, denying me nothing. She took all I had to give and more, her body arching to meet my every move. A final frenzy left her trembling against my shoulder, my face buried in her hair.

"It wasn't an accident, was it?" she said, when she could talk.

"What wasn't an accident?"

"Last night."

"I don't understand." I was mystified.

"While you showered, I was wondering if last night was an accident or if it could have been that way all along."

I raised up on one elbow to look at her. Her face was serious, contemplative.

Understanding dawned slowly. No one had ever before made love to her like that. Darrell Watkins had never tapped the wellspring of woman in her—not in eighteen years of marriage. I kissed her tenderly. "That's the way it's supposed to be."

"The bastard!" she said fiercely. "The first-class bastard! I'll take him to the cleaners."

I had unwittingly unleashed Hurricane Ginger into the world. "Maybe he doesn't know any better." I inadvertently defended him, and she gave me a shove that sent me sprawling from the bed onto the floor.

"He's been giving it away to everyone else. By God, it's going to cost him." Angry tears appeared on her cheeks.

The phone rang on the other side of the bed. I scrambled to reach it. "This is the desk. Can I come get that roll-away now? I'm almost ready to leave."

I cleared my throat. "Sure. Anytime. The bed's all ready to go." I spoke casually, all the while motioning frantically to Ginger. She hopped out of bed and made a beeline for the bathroom.

"By the way," I continued, stalling for time, "before you come, would you ask the dining room to have my usual table set for two? We'll be down for breakfast in a few minutes. I don't want to wait in a crush of reporters."

"No problem," Fred replied.

I rushed back into my clothes and made the room as presentable as possible. I went so far as to beat an indentation in the pillow on the roll-away. I also did my best to straighten one side of the king-size bed.

Ginger's transformation was speedy. Dressed, brushed, and wearing a subtle cologne, she emerged from the bathroom well before the clerk arrived. She may have worn some makeup other than a dash of pale lipstick, but I couldn't tell for sure. She looked refreshed and beautiful. Smiling, she surveyed my clumsy efforts to conceal our activities. Walking to the far side of the bed, she expertly straightened the bedding.

"Whose reputation are you trying to protect?" she asked.

"All of the above," I told her.

"I see."

The desk clerk knocked. We managed to fold up the roll-away contraption and move it out of the room.

"Hungry?" I asked after Fred was gone.

"Famished," she replied.

"Let's go do it, then," I told her. We walked through a quiet Rosario morning. The only noise was an occasional squawking gull. No one else from her group seemed to be up, although several of the dining room tables were occupied. The hostess led us directly to my preferred table, one by the window overlooking Rosario Strait.

"Morning, folks," said the same cheery waiter who had served us the night before. "What can I get you?"

"The works," I told him. "Eggs over easy, hash browns, toast, juice, coffee."

He looked questioningly at Ginger. "I'll have the same," she said with a smile.

My water glass had a narrow sliver of lemon in it. I speared the lemon with my fork, then offered it to Ginger across the table. Puzzled, she sat holding it.

"What's this for?" she asked.

"To wipe that silly grin off your face," I replied. "People might get suspicious."

She laughed outright, but soon a cloud passed over her face. "I believe," she said thoughtfully, "I'm beginning to understand what Sig meant."

Outside our window the sky directly overhead was blue. As we watched, a thick bank of fog marched toward us, rolling across the water, obscuring the strait beyond the resort's sheltered bay.

We were well into breakfast when, over Ginger's shoulder, I saw an obese but well-groomed woman pause at the dining room entrance, survey the room, then make her way toward us like a frigate under full sail. She wore a heavy layer of makeup. Her fingers were laden with a full contingent of ornate rings. A thick cloud of perfume preceded her.

"Ginger." Her voice had a sharp, schoolmarmish tone. Ginger started instinctively, then composed herself.

"Good morning, Trixie."

The woman stopped next to our table and appraised me disapprovingly. "I went by your room several times last night and this morning, but you weren't there." She paused as if waiting for Ginger to offer some kind of explanation. None was forthcoming.

"Trixie, I'd like you to meet a friend of mine, J. P. Beaumont. Beau, this is Trixie Bowdeen, chairman of the parole board."

"Glad to meet you," I said.

Trixie ignored me. "Have you gotten word that the meeting's canceled?" she asked coldly.

Ginger countered with some ice of her own. "I think that's only appropriate."

Trixie forged on. "We're all leaving this morning. Do you need a ride back to Seattle?"

"No, thanks. I can manage."

"All right." Trixie turned her ponderous bulk and started away. Then she stopped and returned to our table. "Under the circumstances, it's probably best if you don't go to Sig's funeral."

All color seeped from Ginger's cheeks, but she allowed herself no other visible reaction to Trixie's words. "Why not?" Ginger asked.

Her question seemed to take Trixie aback. "Well, considering . . ." Trixie retreated under Ginger's withering gaze, turned, and in a rustle of skirt and nylons, left the room.

Ginger carefully placed her fork on her plate and pushed it away. "Can we go?"

I took one look at her face and knew I'd better get her out of there fast. Trixie Bowdeen had just layered on the straw that broke the camel's back.

CHAPTER 9

The fastest way out of the building was down the back stairs and out past the long, narrow, bowling-alley-shaped indoor pool. By the time we reached the terrace outside, Ginger's sob burst to the surface. She rushed to the guardrail and stood leaning over it, her shoulders heaving, while I stood helplessly to one side with my hands jammed deep in my pockets so I wouldn't reach out to hold her.

I've never seen fog anywhere that quite compares to Orcas Island fog. One moment we stood in the open; the next we were alone in a private world. As the fog swept in, Ginger faded to a shadow. I moved toward her, grasping her hand as the building disappeared behind us. She was still crying, the sound strangely muffled in the uncanny silence.

Pulling her to me, I rocked her against my chest until she quieted. I continued to hold her, but I also glanced over my shoulder to verify we were still invisible to the dining room windows. She drew a ragged breath.

"Are you all right now?"

She nodded. "I am. Really."

"That was an ugly thing for her to do."

"Trixie enjoyed passing along Mona's message." There was a shift in Ginger's voice, a strengthening of resolve. "I've got to resign. Without Sig, I can't stand up to those people. They're all cut from the same cloth."

Ginger broke away from me and moved along the terrace, running her hand disconsolately along the guardrail. I trailed behind her, at a loss for words, wondering what made her think Trixie had served as Mona's emissary.

"The fog feels like velvet," Ginger commented. "I wish I could hide in it forever and never come out."

"That's not the answer."

"Isn't it? When you're drunk you don't feel the hurt."

"What are you going to do?" Her remark had sounded like a threat to start drinking. If she was truly a recovering alcoholic, a drink was the last thing she needed.

"It's okay. Don't worry. I'll go to a meeting. There's one in Eastsound tonight."

"What meeting?"

"An A.A. meeting. Whenever Sig and I were on the road, we went to meetings together. We planned to go to this one tonight. I don't remember where it is."

"Can I come?"

Ginger stopped and faced me, looking deep into my eyes before she shook her head. "It's a closed meeting, Beau, not an open one where everyone is welcome. I'll go by myself. If I'm not going to Sig's funeral, it'll be my private remembrance for him."

She made the statement with absolute conviction. I couldn't help but respect her desire to have a private farewell for the man who had pulled her from the mire. We didn't discuss it again. The subject was closed.

The fog lifted as quickly as it had come. I moved discreetly away from her. "You're one hell of a woman, Ginger Watkins, I'll say that for you." She gave me a halfhearted smile and started toward the building.

"Are you sure you want to go in there? There's probably a whole armload of reporters having breakfast by now. The murder of a public official is big news."

She stopped, considering my words. "Reporters? In there?" She nodded toward the dining room overhead.

"The desk clerk told me last night that some of them stayed over. I know for a fact Maxwell Cole did."

"He was that funny-looking fat man you were talking to in the lobby when I came back from being fingerprinted? The one who was supposed to meet Don Wilson?"

"One and the same."

"Who does he work for?"

"The *P.I.* He writes a crime column."

She paused thoughtfully. "Is that all he's interested in? Crime?"

I couldn't see where the discussion was going. "Why are you asking?"

She grinned impishly. "I told you I'd get Darrell, starting now. I'll file on Monday, but it'll hit the papers Sunday morning. The only reason they want me to reconsider is to keep it quiet until after election day. Believe me, Darrell doesn't want me back. Now, where do I find what's-his-name?"

"Max? Probably under a rock somewhere."

"I mean it, Beau. I want to talk to him."

Hell hath no fury, and all that jazz. I figured Darrell Watkins deserved just about anything Ginger could dish out. "Go on into the Moran Room and wait by the fireplace. I'll see if I can find him and send him there. I'm also going to have your things moved to another room for tonight, if you're going to stay over."

"Why? Can't I stay with you?"

I shook my head. "Discretion is the better part of valor, my dear. You can sleep wherever you damn well please, but you'd better have a separate room with your clothes in it or you'll get us both in a hell of a lot of trouble."

"Oh," she said. "I guess I should've thought of that."

Maxwell Cole was eating breakfast. Talking to him was tough because all I could see was the blob of egg yolk that dangled from one curl of his handlebar mustache. "Ginger Watkins wants to talk to you," I said.

His eyes bulged. "No shit? Where is she?"

"In the Moran Room, just off the lobby, waiting."

Cole lurched to his feet, signaling for the waiter to bring his check. "Hey thanks, J. P. I can't thank you enough."

Max persists in calling me by my initials. My real name is Jonas Piedmont Beaumont. Mother named me after her father and grandfather as a conciliatory gesture after my father died in a motorcycle crash before he and Mother had a chance to tie the knot. It didn't work. Her family never lifted a finger to help us. She raised me totally on her own. They never forgave her, and I've never forgiven them. It's a two-way street.

I shortened my name to initials in high school. In college people started calling me Beau. Except for Max. He picked my initials off a registration form, and he's used them ever since, mostly because he knows it bugs me.

"How about if you drop the 'J. P.' crap, Maxey? That would be one way of thanking me."

With a hangdog expression on his face, Max followed me out of the dining room to the crackling fireplace in the Moran Room. Afterwards I stopped at the desk to reserve a new room for Ginger. Just as I finished, someone walked up behind me and clapped me on the shoulder. It was Peters.

I shook his hand. "Huggins got ahold of you, then?"

"No. I came because a little bird told me." Peters grinned. Then in a lower voice, "What the hell are you doing packing hardware? You're supposed to be on vacation."

"It's a long story," I said.

"I'm sure it is. The ferry was crawling with deputies. They're handing out copies of Wilson's picture to everyone who gets on or off the boat. What's up?"

Peeking around the corner, I could see Ginger and Max in deep conversation. I had noticed a small, glass-walled conference room just off the dining room. I asked to use it. Once inside, with the doors safely closed against unwanted listeners, I told Peters all I knew. Maybe not quite all. I left out a few details. He didn't have any business messing around in my personal life.

Peters shook his head when I finished. "I wouldn't be in Huggins' shoes for all the tea in China. If this thing gets blown out of proportion, lots of political heads could roll. Homer Watkins isn't a lightweight."

"How come you know so much about him?"

"There's enough in the papers that you can piece it together. Your problem is, you only read the crossword puzzles. Crosswords do not informed citizens make."

"Leave me alone. They're nothing but propaganda."

"Let's don't go into that, Beau. I like current events. You like history. I like sprout sandwiches. You like hamburgers. Neither of us is going to change."

I reached for the file folder Peters held in his hand. "Wait a minute. I'm supposed to give this to a Detective Huggins. You're not the investigating officer."

"For God's sake, Peters," I protested. "Don't be an ass. I'm the one who called and asked for it, remember?"

"Captain Powell gave me specific orders that the report goes to Huggins. You're on vacation. Powell doesn't want you screwing around in somebody else's case."

"I'll be a sonofabitch," I said.

Peters ignored my outburst. He had joined forces with the captain and the chaplain to corner me into a "vacation." He, more than the rest, understood my loss. "How're you doing, Beau?" he asked solicitously, changing topics. "You're looking better, like you're getting some rest."

I smiled to myself, considering my total sleep from the night before. I decided against depriving Peters of his illusions. "Sleeping like a baby," I said, grinning.

Huggins showed up about then. He saw us through the plate-glass windows and knocked to be let in. I introduced him to Peters. Within minutes the table was strewn with the grisly contents of the envelope. Maybe Peters couldn't give them to me, but nobody told Huggins not to.

The pictures were there—the senseless slaughter, the bloodied house. Denise Wilson had fought Lathrop. She hadn't died easily. She had battled him through every room before it was over. The pictures sickened me, as did Lathrop's smirking mug shot. There was no picture of Donald Wilson in the file. Without Maxwell Cole's contribution, we would have been up a creek.

"We're screening all the people on the ferries. We'll be talking to employees and guests here today," Huggins told us. "Someone will have seen him. You don't just appear and disappear like that unless you're a goddamned Houdini."

"He's not at his house?" I asked. Huggins shook his head. "Is there any other way to get here besides a ferry?" I continued.

"There are float planes and charter boats. We're checking all of them, but it doesn't look to me as though he has that kind of money. He came over on the ferries, I'm sure of it, and we've got those babies covered."

Peters smiled. "You've heard that old joke going around Seattle, haven't you?"

"What's that?"

"What does a San Juan County police officer use for a squad car? A Washington State Ferry with blinking blue lights."

Huggins glared at him. "Very funny," he said, "but we do a hell of a good job around here."

Every once in a while Peters pulls a stunt that convinces me he's not nearly so old as his years. Then there are times when he's as wise as the old man of the sea.

This wasn't one of those times.

CHAPTER 10

I called Ralph Ames, my attorney in Phoenix. Along with the car, I inherited Ames from Anne Corley. In six months' time, he had become an invaluable friend over and above being my attorney. I called him at home.

"What're you doing?" I asked.

"Cleaning the pool," he replied.

I have little patience with people who own pools or boats. They're both holes you pour money into. Not only that, it's a point of honor to do all the work yourself, from swabbing decks to cleaning filters.

"Did you ever consider hiring someone to do it?"

"No, Beau. I don't jog. Cleaning the pool makes me feel self-righteous."

"To each his own. What are you doing tomorrow?"

"Flying to Portland. Didn't Peters tell you?"

"Tell me what?"

"We have a custody hearing in The Dalles on Tuesday. Keep your fingers crossed."

Peters was at war with his ex-wife. She got religion in a big way and went to live with a cult in Broken Springs, Oregon, taking their two little girls with her. Peters wanted them back. Ames took the case, joining the fray at my request and on my nickel. What's the point in having money if you can't squander it?

"That closemouthed asshole. That's good news."

"So what do you want, Beau? This is my day off. It is Saturday, you know."

"How about flying into Sea-Tac today instead of Portland tomorrow? I'm up on Orcas Island. There's someone here I'd like you to meet. I told her you'd take a look at her situation."

"Which is?"

"Divorce. Messy. With political ramifications. Looks like collusion between her husband and her father-in-law to toss her out without a pot to piss in."

"Are you giving my services away again, Beau?"

"I care enough to send the very best."

He laughed. "All right. I'll see what I can do. Let me call you back."

I gave him the number. As I hung up, Ginger appeared at my elbow. "Who was that?"

"Ames, my attorney from Phoenix, remember? I told you about him. I asked him to come talk to you."

"Here? On Orcas?"

"Sure."

"But you said he was in Phoenix."

"He is. He was coming up tomorrow, anyway. He's trying to get a reservation for this afternoon."

"From Phoenix?"

"If you're going to file on Monday, you need to talk to him tonight or tomorrow."

"How much is it going to cost?"

"Nothing. He'll put it on my bill."

I correctly read the consternation on Ginger's face. "How do you rate?" she asked. "I thought you were just a plain old, ordinary homicide detective. How come you have a high-powered attorney at your beck and call?"

"It's a long story," I said. "I came into a little money."

"A little?" she echoed.

"Some," I conceded.

"I see," Ginger said.

"You done with Cole?" I asked, changing the subject.

"He's one happy reporter." She grinned. "That story will make Darrell's socks roll up and down. It should hit the paper tomorrow."

"What did you say?"

"Enough. I named names. At least a few of them. A private detective had already checked those out. Darrell will come across as an active phi-landerer. Hot stuff."

We left the lobby and walked toward the new room where housekeep-ers had moved Ginger's things. "What do you think Darrell will do?" I asked.

She gave a mirthless laugh. "He'll huddle with Homer and the PR man. The three of them will decide how to play it. Name familiarity is name familiarity. They may get more press if they do an active denial. They'll take a poll and decide."

"That's pretty cold-blooded."

"Um-hum."

"But how are you going to feel with your personal life splashed all over the front page?"

We reached the building where her new room was. Ginger stepped to one side, waiting for me to open the door. The eyes she turned on me were luminously green and deep.

"I just found out about personal," she said softly. "None of that is going in the paper."

There was a tightening in my chest and a catch in my throat. Mr. Macho handles the compliment. I tripped over my own feet and stumbled into the hallway. I found her room, unlocked the door, and handed her the key.

"Are you coming in?"

The invitation was there, written on her face, but I shook my head. "Ames is supposed to call my room. I'd better not."

"Does that mean I can't see you? Have I been a bad girl and you're sending me to my room?" she teased.

"No. Let me see what's happening as far as Ames and Peters are con-cerned. Maybe you and I can go on a picnic."

"Terrific. I'll change into jeans."

"Wait a minute. I said maybe."

She looked both ways, up and down the hall, then gave me a quick kiss on the cheek. "Please."

"Well, all right, now that you put it that way."

Smiling, she disappeared into her room. I returned to mine. I had got-ten a second key for Peters, and he was there waiting when I arrived. "Who's your roommate?" he asked casually as I flopped onto the bed. "Her makeup case is still in the bathroom."

I wasn't any better at sneaking around than Ginger was. I made a stab at semi-full disclosure. "Ginger Watkins stayed here last night. Didn't I tell you?"

Peters' eyes narrowed. "I don't think so."

"There weren't any more rooms, and she couldn't go back to hers. Whoever got in had a key."

"Right." Peters nodded complacently, humoring me.

"We got a roll-away. She's married, for chrissake!"

"Okay, okay," he said. "Have it your way. What's the program?"

"You didn't tell me Ames has a court date in The Dalles."

"Small oversight." Peters grinned. "So we're even. What's going on?"

"I asked Ames to come up here tonight. I'm hoping he can help Ginger with her divorce."

"And you still expect me to fall for that crap about a roll-away bed?" He laughed.

As I threw a pillow at him, the phone rang. It was Ames. "I get into Sea-Tac at five-fifty. Can someone meet me?"

"We'll flip a coin," I told him. "One of us will be there. What airline?"

"United."

"Okay. I'll book rooms here."

"Rooms?"

I glared at Peters. "Peters snores," I growled into the phone. "I sure as hell don't want him in my room, and you won't want him in yours, either. Besides, they've just had a bunch of cancellations. I know rooms are available."

"Rooms," Ames agreed.

Peters and I flipped a coin. He called heads, and it was tails. I figured it was my lucky day. Considering the ferry schedule, he didn't have much time to hang around. I called the desk and reserved two more rooms. Up at the far end of the complex. By the tennis courts. Adjoining.

I was still on the phone when someone knocked. Peters went to the door.

"My name is Ginger Watkins. Is Beau here?"

Peters stepped to one side and rolled his eyes at me once he was behind her. She wore a full-sleeved apricot blouse and a pair of tight-fitting Levi's that did justice to her figure. With a jacket slung nonchalantly over one shoulder, Ginger was a class act all the way.

"This is Detective Ron Peters," I said, "my partner on the force in Seattle."

"I'm pleased to meet you." Her smile of genuine goodwill had its desired effect.

Peters' appraising glance was filled with admiration. "Pleasure's all mine," he murmured.

Ginger turned to me. "Did I leave my calendar here?" she asked. "It isn't in the room, and I checked with the maids. They said they moved everything."

"I haven't seen it. When did you have it last?"

"I don't remember. I may have taken it with me when I went to meet Sig. It's got the address for the meeting tonight. I'm sure someone else can tell me where the meeting is, but I keep all kinds of phone numbers in the calendar. It would be hard to replace."

"Could you have left it in the car in Anacortes?"

She considered that possibility. "No," she said. "I don't think so."

I picked up the phone and called the desk to ask if anyone had turned in the missing calendar. No one had.

"Come on," I said when I got off the phone. "We'll walk Peters to his car. He's just leaving for the airport."

"You are?" she asked. "You barely got here."

"I did," Peters agreed sullenly, "but shore leave just got canceled."

Peters took off in his beat-up blue Datsun. Ginger and I diligently searched the meeting rooms, the dining room, the bar, and the lobby to no avail. The calendar wasn't there.

Rosario is nothing if not a full-service resort. While we were busy, the kitchen packed us a picnic lunch, complete with basket and tablecloth. Ginger's enthusiasm was unrestrained. She practically skipped on her way to the parking lot. A genuine Ford Pinto, white with splotches of rust, was parked next to my bright red Porsche 928. As I went to unlock the rider's side, Ginger assumed I was going to the junker. She started for the rider's side of that one, stopping in dismay when I opened the Porsche.

She came around the Pinto grinning sheepishly. "Isn't this a little high-toned for a homicide cop?"

I placed the picnic basket in the back and helped her inside. "Conspicuous consumption never hurt anybody," I said.

With a switch of the key, the powerful engine turned over. When she was alive, Anne Corley drove the car with casual assurance. I always feel just a little out of my league, as though the car is driving me.

"Have you seen Moran State Park?" I asked. Ginger shook her head. "Why don't we try that? This late in October it isn't crowded."

"You're changing the subject, Beau," she accused.

I feigned innocence. "What do you mean?"

"Tell me about the car," she insisted.

And so I told her about the car. About finding Anne Corley and losing Anne Corley. One by one I pulled the memories out and held them up in the diffused autumn light so Ginger and I could look at them together. We drove and walked and talked. We climbed the stairs in the musty obelisk without really noticing our surroundings. It was my turn to talk and Ginger's to listen.

By the time I finished, we were seated at a picnic table in a patch of dappled sunlight with the food laid out before us. There was a long pause. "You loved her very much, didn't you?" Ginger said at last.

"I didn't think I'd ever get over her."

"But you have?"

"I'm starting to, a little."

"Meaning me?" From someone else, that question might have sounded cynical, but not from Ginger.

I nodded. "Today is the first I've felt like my old self. Peters attributed it to my getting enough sleep."

"That shows how much he knows."

"He's young. What can I tell you?"

"And I'm the first, since Anne Corley?"

"Yes."

"And I was good?" It was a pathetic question. She was looking for the kind of reassurance most women don't need after age eighteen or so.

We were alone in the park. I came around the table and sat behind her, my hands massaging her tight shoulders, rubbing the rigid muscles of her neck. Her body moved under the pressure of my kneading fingers, relaxing as stiffness succumbed to the balm of human touch.

"You were terrific," I whispered in her ear.

She turned to me, two huge teardrops welling in her eyes. "That was stupid. I shouldn't have asked."

She leaned against me, and I continued to rub her neck, feeling her tension soften and disappear.

"No one's ever done that to me before," she said.

"Done what?"

"Rubbed my neck like that."

I kissed her forehead. "All I can say, sweetheart, is you've been married to a first-class bastard."

Unexpectedly, she burst out laughing. I don't think anyone had ever referred to Darrell Watkins in quite those terms in her presence. She turned her neck languidly from side to side like a cat stretching in the sun. "That felt good," she murmured.

We repacked the picnic basket. "Could I stop by your room for a little while before I go? The meeting doesn't start until eight."

"Sure," I said. "By the way, how do you plan to get to that meeting?"

She clapped her hand over her mouth. "I forgot. I don't have my car. I can probably catch a ride with the van that goes to the ferry."

"Don't be silly. Take the Porsche," I said.

"I couldn't do that."

"Oh yes you can."

It was almost our first quarrel, but finally she knuckled under to my superior intellect and judgment. Besides, I had the clinching argument: by taking my car, she wouldn't have to leave nearly so early. She capitulated. Who says women can't be swayed by logic?

And hormones. And expensive toys.

CHAPTER 11

We took a meandering route back to Rosario. At one point we paused, laughing, at a large hand-painted sign on a ninety-degree curve that said, "Slow Duck Crossing."

"Does that mean the ducks are dumb, or are you supposed to slow down?" Ginger asked.

"Possibly a little of both," I observed, braking to negotiate the narrow corner.

A flurry of yellow slips of paper awaited us at the desk. The first, a message from Huggins, was jubilant. A ticket-seller at the Anacortes ferry terminal remembered Don Wilson as a mid-afternoon walk-on passenger. The evidence was speculative and purely circumstantial, but that gave Wilson opportunity. He already had motive.

Huggins' second note was more ominous. Results of the autopsy were in. Larson's cause of death was a blow to the base of the skull with a blunt object. He was dead before he hit the water. The cut on his forehead had occurred after he was dead. The news hit Ginger pretty hard. In addition, her room key had not been found among Sig Larson's personal effects.

A message from Peters said he and Ames were skipping dinner in order to make it back to Orcas. Since the food on the ferries wasn't fit to eat, he advised me to make dinner reservations for after their arrival.

Ginger passed me her own fan-fold of messages, enough to form a formidable canasta hand. Darrell Watkins had called every half-hour. Homer Watkins had called several times. All of the messages, with increasing urgency, said for Ginger to call back.

She returned the calls from my room. I think she wanted the moral support of my presence. She spoke with Darrell first. He had learned of the impending column in the *P.I.* and wanted her to retract it. She was adamant. She would stand by every word of the story as written. He threatened to come up. She told him not to bother, that nothing he could say would make her change her mind.

The call to Homer was much the same. His attempts at brow-beating also came to nothing. I wondered if either of them recognized a subtle shift in her from the day before, an undercurrent of gritty determination. J. P. Beaumont, posing as Professor Henry Higgins, heard the difference and gave himself a little credit.

Nonetheless, the phone calls had a subduing effect on our high spirits. I think we had intended to take advantage of each other's bodies before Ginger left, to recapture the magic of commingled enjoyment to last us until she returned from her meeting. Instead, we sat in my room without even holding hands, talking quietly as the sun went down.

I can't remember now what we talked about. We ranged over a wide variety of topics, finding surprising areas of common interest and knowledge. For someone with little formal education, Ginger was a widely read, challenging conversationalist.

I invited her to join Peters, Ames, and me for dinner after the meeting. She waited until the very last minute to leave for Eastsound, delaying her departure so long that she finally decided to change clothes after the meeting. She was clearly torn between wanting to go to the meeting and wanting to stay with me. I could probably have talked her out of going had I half tried. Out of respect to Sig Larson, I didn't make the attempt.

I walked her to my car. "Be careful," I said. "That's a hot little number."

She smiled. "I've driven one before."

"What time will you be back?"

"Ten. At the latest."

"I'll make reservations for then," I told her.

"Kiss me good-bye?" she asked.

I looked around. The parking lot was deserted. As near as I could tell, all the media types, including Maxwell Cole, had abandoned Rosario on the heels of the rest of the parole board, but years of being a cop have made me paranoid about reporters. I gave her a quick, surreptitious kiss. "Give old Sig a hail and farewell for me too," I said huskily. I had a lot to thank him for.

"I will," she whispered and was gone.

I went into the bar. Barney smiled when he saw me. "Find that calendar yet?" he asked, bringing me a MacNaughton's and water.

"Not yet."

"You get what you needed from that fat slob last night?"

"Yeah," I answered. "Thanks."

"All those yahoos went home this morning," he continued. "They were a bunch of animals, especially that creep, what's-his-name . . . Dole?"

"Cole," I corrected. "And yes, he is a creep."

I drank my drink, aware of how much better I felt. Unburdening myself to Ginger had somehow lifted the pall that had paralyzed me since Anne Corley's death. I set down my empty glass and pushed back the stool.

"Only one?" Barney asked, surprised.

"Later," I told him. "I've got places to go, people to meet."

In actual fact, I went back to my room for the second shower and shave of the day. I dressed carefully. I wanted Ginger to see me at my best, wearing one of the hand-tailored suits Ames had insisted I purchase.

At nine forty-five I went back to the lobby. "Oh there you are," the desk clerk said. "I just this minute had a call for you." He handed me a slip of paper with Homer Watkins' name and number on it.

"He called for me, not Mrs. Watkins?" I asked.

"He was very specific," the clerk assured me. I walked to the pay phone and dialed the number. He answered on the second ring.

"This is Detective Beaumont," I said curtly into the phone.

"It's good of you to call," he said. His voice was smooth as glass, with the resonance of an old-fashioned radio announcer. It was a long way from our first telephone conversation. "I talked to a friend of yours today, a Maxwell Cole. He's under the impression that you have some influence with my daughter-in-law."

"That's correct," I replied. It was also something of an understatement.

"I thought you should be advised that Ginger has been somewhat unstable of late."

"Ginger Watkins' mental health is none of my business," I said.

"I couldn't be happier to hear you say that. She's been under a great deal of stress and can't be held responsible for her actions."

"What are you driving at?" I demanded.

"That's all I wanted to discuss," he said. "I have another call." Having another call on a second or third line constitutes a high-tech version of the brush-off. I put down the phone.

I went into the Moran Room to wait for Ames and Peters. The ferry was due in at nine-thirty, so I expected them at Rosario right around ten. I waited in front of the massive marble fireplace with its cheerful fire.

Ralph Ames was laughing as he came into the lobby. He and Peters were having a good time. I met them at the door. We left word for Ginger, and the three of us went on into the dining room. It was late, and the room was almost empty. We sat at a candlelit table and had a drink.

"You breaking training?" I asked as the waiter handed Peters a gin and tonic.

He raised his glass. "Just this once." He grinned.

We were so busy talking and catching up that I didn't notice the time. At ten-thirty the waiter suggested that if we wanted to eat before the kitchen closed, we'd better place our order. Suddenly I wasn't hungry. I told Peters and Ames to go ahead and order, that I'd wait for Ginger. I excused myself and went to the lobby, where I had the desk clerk call Ginger's room. No answer.

When Fred shook his head, I felt a sickening crunch in my stomach. "Something may have happened to her," I said. "Would you let me check her room?"

After the roll-away bed escapade, he could hardly say I had no business doing so. He put a Back in a Minute sign on the desk, and we hurried to Ginger's room. It was empty, undisturbed.

Back in the Mansion, I checked the dining room. Ames and Peters were happily working their way through salads, but Ginger was nowhere in sight. I went to the pay phone and dialed the sheriff's substation at Eastsound.

The dispatcher answered eventually, her response to my question short and to the point. There had been no reports of any traffic accidents. I tried to fend off rising panic. "Do you know any of the people who go to the Saturday-night A.A. meeting in Eastsound?" I asked.

"Yes, but I can't give out those names. It's confidential."

"Get one of them to call me back, then. It's urgent."

"I'll see what I can do."

I paced the floor in tight circles, trying to hold panic in check. When the phone rang, I pounced on it like a cat attacking a paralyzed mouse.

"My name is James," the voice on the phone drawled. "You wanted to talk to someone from A.A.?"

"Yes, I did. Did you go the meeting tonight?"

"'Course I did. I was one of the speakers."

"Was there a woman there, a woman in a pale orange blouse and Levi's?"

"Sorry, mister, I can't give out that information. Whoever joins our fellowship is strictly confidential. That's why people feel safe in coming."

"You don't understand," I said desperately. "She left here at twenty to eight, going to the meeting. She hasn't come back. All I want to know is whether she made it that far."

There was a long pause. "No," he said.

"No *what?* No, you won't tell me?" I wanted to reach through the phone line and throttle him.

"No, she wasn't there. I woulda remembered someone like that. It was only locals tonight. No visitors."

Cold fear rose in my stomach, my throat. "Thank you," I managed, depressing the switch on the phone. I released it and redialed the substation. The dispatcher was annoyed.

"You'd better get ahold of Huggins over in Friday Harbor. Tell him to call Detective Beaumont. We've got trouble."

Hal called me back within minutes. "What's up?"

"It's Ginger. She's disappeared. She went to a meeting tonight and never got there. I've checked. The meeting was over at nine. She's still not back."

"It's almost eleven!"

"I know," I responded bleakly.

"What kind of car?" he asked.

"A Porsche 928. Red."

He whistled. "No shit? A Porsche? What's the license number?" I gave it to him. "Okay," he added, "I'll be there in half an hour," he said. "Where are you—Rosario?"

"Yes."

"I'll come straight to the docks. I'll call the dispatcher and have her send Pomeroy. I think he's on duty tonight." He paused. "Why'd you let her go by herself, Beau?"

I winced at his implied accusation. I had already asked myself the same question. "She wanted to."

"Oh," he said.

It wasn't a very convincing reason, not then, not now.

With leaden steps I walked back to the dining room to let Ames and Peters know that Ginger Watkins wouldn't be joining us for dinner. Not then. Not ever.

CHAPTER 12

They found the Porsche at seven Sunday morning in the pond by the Slow Duck Crossing sign. I stood to one side, watching the tow truck drag my 928 from the muck. Ginger, still wearing her apricot blouse, lay dead inside.

Huggins opened the door, and water cascaded out, leaving her body slumped over the steering wheel. Pomeroy gave me a half-smirk as I walked over to look inside and make positive identification. I nodded to Hal and walked away as the lab crew surrounded the car.

Peters was down the road, pacing the blacktop. "From the looks of it, she ploughed into the water full throttle and never tried to stop."

He was voicing my own thoughts. I said nothing.

"Is there a chance she passed out?"

"No," I said quickly. "Absolutely not."

Peters eyed me questioningly. "Why not?"

"She didn't drink."

Huggins left the car and came over to where we were standing. "Watkins is on his way," he said. "It'll be a madhouse when he gets here. I understand he's got a whole press entourage."

"Great," I muttered.

"Did you see anything along the road?" Huggins' question was addressed to both Peters and me. Peters pointed. "There's a place back there where she laid down a layer of rubber. Looks like she floorboarded it from a dead stop." The three of us walked back to the place Peters had indicated. Huggins examined the mark, then nodded in agreement. He looked at me.

"Suicide, you think?"

"No way!" I declared vehemently. Huggins and Peters exchanged glances.

"We were going to have dinner," I continued. "She was looking forward to it." My rationale landed with a resounding thud, convincing no one, not even me.

As soon as I saw Darrell Watkins, I recognized him. I had indeed seen pictures of him. Politicians are never as tall or as good-looking as their publicity shots make them seem. Darrell Watkins was no exception. He was three or four inches shorter than I am, maybe five-ten or so. His face boasted classically handsome features topped by dark brown wavy hair, but a hint of potbelly protruded over his belt. A little too much of the good life showed around the edges.

Beside Darrell walked a taller, distinguished-looking man with a shock of white hair. There was a definite family resemblance. Homer Watkins, although pushing seventy, carried himself with the easy grace of an aging athlete. His son might have gone to seed, but not Homer. I looked at them with the kind of curiosity one reserves for snakes in a zoo. They didn't look like evil incarnate, but they had made Ginger Watkins' life hell on earth.

Huggins walked forward to greet them, waving back the crush of newsmen, photographers, and cameras that swirled around them. Ginger would have been offended that the aftermath of her death created a media event that would give her candidate/widower hours of free broadcasting coverage and hundreds of newspaper column-inches all over the state. I thought I was going to be sick.

"Hey, Beau, are you all right?" I had turned my back on the mêlée and was walking away. Peters followed.

"I've got to get out of here," I groaned. "I can't stand this bullshit."

I continued walking. Peters worked his way back through the crowd to redeem his car. I was several hundred yards down the road by the time he caught up with me. He pulled alongside. "Get in, Beau. Don't be a hard-ass." I was too sick at heart to argue.

"The press was handling Watkins with kid gloves," Peters said apropos of nothing.

I glowered at him. "What did you expect?"

Peters shrugged and broke off any further attempt at conversation. In the silence that followed, I tried to come to terms with what had happened. How could Ginger Watkins be the lifeless form slouched in my car? And what could I have done to prevent it? And where the hell was Don Wilson?

Ralph Ames waited for us in the driveway outside the Mansion. "I heard," he said as I dragged myself out of the car. "Is there anything I can do?"

"Not unless you can figure out a way to bring her back." I choked out the words and beat it for my cabin, leaving Peters and Ames standing there together. I didn't want to talk to anybody or hear any mumbled words of sympathy. I didn't have any right to sympathy. That was Darrell Watkins' exclusive territory.

I threw myself across the bed, aware of a faint trace of Ginger Watkins lingering in the bedclothes. I wanted to lock it out of my consciousness, but at the same time I wanted to hold onto it.

There was a gentle tap on the door. Ames came into the room, alone. He sat down on one of the chairs beside the table. For a long time he sat there without speaking. "You can't blame yourself," he said at last.

"Why not? I never should have let her go alone."

"It's not your fault."

I wanted to bellow at him, to rant and rave and vent my anger and frustration. "It is! Don't you see that it is?"

Ames remained unperturbed. "It was an A.A. meeting, is that right?"

"Yes," I said wearily.

"How long had it been since she quit drinking?"

My anger boiled back to the surface. "She wasn't drunk, and she didn't commit suicide. Doesn't anybody understand that, for God's sake?"

He ignored me. "It's possible, Beau. She had lost a good friend the day before—"

"Goddammit, Ames, I'm trying to tell you. Something happened between us. She didn't want to die."

Ames studied me carefully. "I see," he said slowly. He rose to his feet. "I'm sorry, Beau. I didn't know." His quiet understanding rocked me. Hot tears rose in my eyes. I didn't bother to brush them away. Ames paused in the doorway. "It's still not your fault," he added.

The hell it's not, I thought savagely as the door closed behind him. Wilson was here all the time, and I let her walk right into his trap.

I don't know how long I lay on the bed. Long enough to get a grip on myself. Long enough to know that if I walked outside I wouldn't embarrass myself and everyone around me.

I had been awake all night. Exhaustion claimed me, and I slept. In a dream Don Wilson and Philip Lathrop were together, both locked in the same cell. Armed with a gun, I tried to shoot them through iron bars. Each time I pulled the trigger, nothing happened. They laughed and pointed, both of them, together.

I woke in a sweat. Peters was sitting in the chair by the window. Ginger's chair.

"Bad dream?" he asked.

Not answering, I heaved my feet over the edge of the bed and sat there with my face buried in my hands, hoping the whole thing was a nightmare. It wasn't. Ginger Watkins was dead.

"They've released your car," Peters said.

I felt as if I'd been shot. "They've what?"

"Released the Porsche," Peters repeated. "Had it towed into Ernie's Garage in Eastsound."

"That's impossible! Murder was committed in that car. No one should go near it until the crime lab has gone over it with a fine-toothed comb."

"They've gone over it, all right. Not with a fine-toothed comb. The consensus is that she went drinking instead of to her meeting. They're treating it as a DWI, calling it an accident, pending the outcome of the autopsy. They found an empty vodka bottle in the car. The San Juan County Sheriff's Department says it can't afford to be responsible for a car like that. Too valuable."

I got up and went into the bathroom, where I splashed my face with cold water. My square-jawed reflection in the mirror was haggard, drained. When I came out of the bathroom, Peters hadn't moved.

"It wasn't an accident," I said.

"How are we going to prove it?"

It took a few seconds for the meaning of his words to sink in, to understand that I wasn't in it alone, that Peters would help—and so would Ames, for that matter. But even though his "we" eased my burden, the question remained: How would we prove it?

"Drive me to Eastsound," I said. "I want to talk to the mechanic."

"Huggins says he's tops."

"Sure he is. In a backwater like this, you can just bet they've got a top-drawer mechanic. He's probably one step under highway robbery."

We got into Peters' Datsun. He managed to drive us to Eastsound without having to pass the duck pond. "Are you going to tell me what happened?" Peters asked.

"No." My answer was abrupt. "Not now."

Peters deserved better than that. We had been partners for almost a year. He, more than anyone, had seen me through the Anne Corley crisis. I had learned to respect his quiet reserve and to tolerate his health fetishes. In the world of partners, alfalfa sprouts are a small price to pay for someone you can count on.

He didn't take offense. He brought our discussion back to the Porsche. "Huggins says Ernie can dry it out. If he gets to work on it fast enough, he might be able to prevent it from mildewing."

"So by releasing the car, Hal thinks he's doing me a favor?" Peters nodded. "Goddamn him," I said.

Ernie's Garage wasn't tough to find. It's the only one in town. I walked into the clapboard building, wondering for a moment if anyone was there. "Just a sec," an invisible voice called.

A mechanic's dolly wheeled out from under an upraised pickup. On it sat a man with his left leg missing below the knee and his left arm missing below the elbow. Where his hand should have been, a complicated metal gripper was strapped to his arm with a leather gauntlet. The gripper held a small wrench. Ernie Rogers had bright blue eyes, a curly red mustache, and a shiny bald spot on the back of his head. "How'do, mister," he drawled. "What can I do for you?"

"That's my car over there," I said, pointing. The Porsche huddled in a darkened corner of the garage.

"She's a pretty little thing." He clucked sympathetically. "Too bad about what happened."

"Huggins says you can dry it out and get it working. That true?"

He nodded, removing the wrench from its gripper and wiping his metal hand on greasy pants in the typical mechanic's gesture. "It'll cost you," he said. "How long you had 'er?"

"About six months."

"Ever done any major repairs on a Porsche?" Ernie asked. He was still sitting on the dolly, squinting up at me.

"No," I said. "Never have."

"I gotta take the whole damn thing apart, clean it with solvent, dry it, and put it back together."

"How much?"

"Six or seven grand."

In the old days, that's how much I would have spent on a brand-new car. Luckily, these weren't the old days. "How long will it take?"

"Depends on how soon you want me to start. Should do it as soon as possible if you want to save the interior. It'll take time—a couple weeks, maybe. I gotta get the money up front, though. Know what I mean?"

In the old days I never would have had a checking account with ten thousand dollars in it, but Ames had made me open a market-rate account. I pulled the checkbook out of my jacket pocket and wrote out a check for seven thousand dollars, payable to Ernie's Garage. I handed it to him. He looked at it, folded it deftly with one hand, and stuck it in his overall pocket.

"Thanks, Mr. Beaumont. That your phone number on the check in case I need to get ahold of you?"

"Yes. Keep track of your expenses. The insurance company will reimburse me."

Peters and I started toward the door. "I'm sorry about the lady in the car," Ernie said. "She wasn't your wife or anything, was she?"

"No," I said. "We were just friends."

The lie came easily. Ginger had said the same thing about Sig Larson. I wondered if she had told the truth.

CHAPTER 13

Peters stopped at the front desk and bought a paper. He showed me Sig Larson's picture on the front page. "Max's interview with Ginger should be there," I told him.

He flipped through the pages and double-checked the index in the bottom corner of the front page, looking for Cole's City Beat column. "It's not here, Beau," he said. "I looked."

"But he said it would be in today's paper."

"So he lied," Peters said. "What else is new?" Peters sorted through the paper and removed the crossword puzzles, setting them aside for me to work later. "I'm going up to my room to get some rest," he said. "Ames wants to go back to Seattle on the seven-forty ferry tonight. You're welcome to ride along."

"Let me think it over, Peters. I can't quite see the three of us crammed in that Datsun, but—"

"Don't look a gift horse in the mouth," he told me. "It's a hell of a long walk from Anacortes to Seattle."

I accompanied Peters as far as his room. When he went inside, I knocked on Ames' door. Ralph was sprawled on his bed with the contents of a briefcase strewn around him. "Working on Peters' case?" I asked. He nodded. "Are we going to win?"

He looked at me squarely. "Maybe. Maybe not. Our best bet is to work out a negotiated settlement instead of going to court."

"Will they settle?"

He shrugged. "Justice is blind. Money talks. They'll settle if the price is right."

"It pisses me off to think of donating money to that ranting, chanting asshole." It was my money. Although I was willing to do whatever was necessary to buy Peters' kids a chance at a normal childhood, it still made me mad.

Ames regarded me mildly. "You want to bail out?"

"Hell, no. I just don't like that guru making money hand over fist."

Shaking his head, Ames gathered up his papers and shuffled them into a neat stack. "What do you want, Beau?"

I eased myself into the chair by his window, aware that my back hurt. Despite the nap, fatigue railed at me from every muscle in my body. "I want to offer a reward."

"For what?"

"For information leading to the arrest and conviction of the person or persons who murdered Sig Larson."

He picked up a yellow pad and a pen and made several notes in his small, cramped handwriting. "I can do that," he said. "From an anonymous donor, I presume?"

I nodded.

"How much?"

"Five."

"Thousand?"

I nodded again.

"Anything else?"

My mind started to click, like a car that has to be jump-started but runs fine after that. "What are you going to do, once you finish up in Oregon?"

"Go back to Phoenix. Why?"

"You told me I ought to do some investing, remember?"

He nodded. "What do you have in mind?"

"I understand there are a couple of condo projects in trouble in Seattle. Maybe now would be a good time to look into one of those. Would you mind sticking around and researching them?"

"Not as long as you're footing the bill." I got up to leave. "Are you coming back to town tonight?" he asked.

Pausing at the door, I considered my options. Riding with Ames and Peters would be physically uncomfortable but convenient. "No," I said, making up my mind, "I have some thinking to do. I'm better off here, away from everybody."

"And because you think Don Wilson is still on Orcas?"

He caught me red-handed. "So what?" I flared. "I'm on vacation. I can do as I damn well please."

"You don't have any objectivity in this case, Beau."

"Don't lecture me, Ralph. I'm your client, not some half-grown kid." I stormed from the room, slamming the door behind me, knowing he was more than half right.

I headed for the Mansion and the Vista Lounge. I wanted the taste of MacNaughton's in my mouth, the feel of an icy glass in my hand. I almost ran over Maxwell Cole, who was about to climb into the hotel van in front of the building. I was surprised to see him. I thought he was already gone.

"What happened to your column?" I asked sarcastically. "Miss your deadline?"

"Deadline!" he echoed. "If you're talking about the piece I wrote yesterday, the one on Ginger Watkins, I didn't miss the deadline."

"So where is it?" I was looking for someone to bait, and Cole was a likely candidate. His handlebar mustache drooped lopsidedly, making him look more dreary than usual.

"They spiked the son of a bitch. The scoop of the year, and they spiked it!"

"Who did?"

"Beats the shit out of me. One minute it was in, the next minute it was out. My editor isn't talking."

The driver of the van honked. "Hey come on, man. Them ferries don't wait for nothing."

Cole scrambled into the van and settled in an aisle seat. The van pulled out of the gravel drive, leaving me lost in thought. It takes clout to spike a story, a hell of a lot of clout. I wondered who was flexing his muscle, Homer or Darrell, father or son, or father and son. It didn't matter. Whoever it was had robbed Ginger of her meager revenge, her sole token of defiance.

I charged into the lounge. It was deserted except for two slightly tipsy elderly ladies drinking sloe gin fizzes at a table by the arched windows. Barney folded a newspaper and shoved it under the bar as I sat down.

"MacNaughton's?"

I nodded.

"It's too bad about Mrs. Watkins," he commented, placing the drink in front of me. "She seemed like a real nice lady, from what little I saw of her."

"She was." I agreed. I downed the drink and ordered another.

"Too bad about your car, too."

"Cars can be fixed," I said.

He grinned. "I guess old Ernie's in seventh heaven. Heard he's got himself a real-live Porsche to work on."

"You know him?"

"Hell, yes. Went to school together, kindergarten on. Ended up in Vietnam at the same time. Different outfits, though."

"That's where he lost his arm and leg?"

Barney nodded. "He doesn't let it bother him. Goes hunting every year, usually gets an elk. He's got a wife and two kids; another on the way."

"Is he any good?"

Barney grinned. "You'll have to ask his wife about that. He's not my type."

"As a mechanic, asshole. Is he a good mechanic?"

"He's good," Barney said seriously. "He'll put that car of yours back together better than it was before."

"Oh," I said.

A couple came in and sat at the other end of the bar. Barney left me to serve them. I sat there alone, nursing my drink, wondering where to start on a case that was not my case, on a murder that might be suicide or an accident, depending on your point of view.

In Seattle I knew what I'd do—sit down and try to pull together all the details on pieces of paper, set as many pieces of the puzzle on the table as possible, then move them around, trying to find a framework where they would fit.

Barney came back to me. "You want another?" he asked.

I looked at my glass. "Sure. Is that your paper under the bar?"

"It is, but you can have it. I'm done with it."

He pulled it out and laid it in front of me. I recognized Sig Larson's face looking up at me from under a screaming headline. I picked up the paper warily. I don't trust newspapers, don't like them, usually wouldn't be caught dead reading them; but this was different.

This time I was outside the official circle of information, and I needed a starting point. I was going to do something about Ginger Watkins' death, jurisdictions be damned. Sig Larson's death and Ginger's were inextricably linked. I intended to find out how.

I read every word of the laudatory obituary. A retired Eastern Washington wheat farmer, Lars Sigfried Larson had been widely respected. The article mentioned his volunteer work at Walla Walla and his involvement with Babe Ruth Baseball east of the mountains. It mentioned his widow, Mona, as well as his three grown children, married and scattered throughout the West. The funeral would be held in Welton on the banks of the Touchet River on Tuesday at two o'clock. The governor himself was expected to attend.

And so would J. P. Beaumont, I decided. I read on. The family requested that remembrances be sent to A.A. Even in death, Sig Larson didn't duck the issue of sobriety.

I had finished the article and was folding the paper when Peters came in and caught me. "What are you doing?"

"What the hell does it look like I'm doing? I'm trying to fold this god-damned newspaper."

"You haven't been reading it, have you?" Peters' eyes flashed with sly amusement. "You feeling all right, Beau? Maybe a little feverish?"

I stood up and struggled to return the newspaper to its place under the counter. When I flopped back down, Peters' grin faded. "Ames and I are getting ready to take off. Want to have a bite with us before we go?"

I signaled Barney for a new drink. When he set it in front of me, I raised the glass in Peters' direction in a sloppy salute. "Who needs food?"

"You're drinking too much . . ."

I cut him off. "Butt out, Peters."

Without arguing the point, he stalked from the bar. Misery does not necessarily love company. I made short work of that drink and the next one. Detective J. P. Beaumont disappeared with a subsequent dose of Mac-Naughton's. All that remained was me, the man, or whatever bits and pieces were left of him.

"You're hitting it pretty hard, aren't you?" Barney asked, as he delivered my next drink.

"So what?" I returned. He handed me the glass, and I stared morosely into it. I swirled the amber liquid, listening to the crushed ice rustle against the glass.

Gradually, my carefully constructed defenses gave way. Pain leaked from every pore. Ginger's touch had reawakened that part of me that had died with Anne. Now Ginger's death released the grief I had kept so carefully bottled up inside me. It washed across me like a gigantic wave, choking me, drowning me.

The next thing I remember is Barney taking my last drink away and leading me, sobbing, from the bar. He got me as far as the door to my room before I was sick in a bordering flower bed.

It was still light when I staggered out of the bathroom and crawled into bed. I have a dim memory of Barney closing the curtains before he went outside and shut the door behind him.

CHAPTER 14

When I woke up, cold sober, at two o'clock in the morning, I felt painfully alive again. I still hurt, but I had somehow bridged the chasm between the past and the present and was ready to go on. I had Ginger Watkins to thank for that, and there was only one way to repay her.

Ignoring my hangover, I rummaged around for paper, finally locating a fistful of Rosario stationery. I assigned each person a separate sheet of paper—Ginger, Sig, Wilson, Darrell, Homer, Mona. Under each name I noted everything I knew about them: things Ginger had told me, things I had heard from other sources. Maybe there's a better way of sorting out the players than by using paper and pencil, but I've never found one.

If I were keeping score, I'd have to say that Sig Larson dropped a few points in the process. I have an innate suspicion of perfection. Both Ginger's comments and the newspaper's undiluted praise made me wonder if the paragon had feet of clay. Being dead is only part of the qualifications for sainthood. Over and over, I recalled my offhand denial to Ernie, "Just friends," and so was Sig to Ginger. Just friends, right? Like hell.

A twinge of tardy jealousy caused me to turn to Mona Larson's sheet. What about her? Ginger had dismissed her as a calculating bitch. What suspicious wife isn't a calculating bitch, especially if she has some reason, especially from the other woman's point of view?

I could see Mona Larson in my mind's eye, a woman from sturdy farm stock, someone well beyond her middle years who had stood by her man through thick and thin only to see herself losing him to an attractive younger woman. It would give the fruits of her labors a bitter aftertaste.

So, how jealous was Mona Larson? Enough to make her anger public by sending Trixie Bowdeen with the message for Ginger not to attend Sig's funeral. Where had Mona been when she was supposedly en route to Orcas? Huggins had been unable to locate her to notify her of Sig's death. It was an item that merited exploration, but it wasn't top priority. Not that many jealous spouses actually murder their spouses and their spouses' friends.

Friends. There was that word again. Even in private thoughts I tended to gloss over it. *Lover,* then. Ginger and I had been lovers, briefly. And maybe Sig and Ginger had been, too. But if so, Sig was just as bad as Darrell. Ginger hadn't faked her surprise or enjoyment, had she?

No. My ego wouldn't accept that, and no woman could be so unlucky as to have two men as insensitive and unfeeling as Darrell. No. My thoughts chased themselves full-circle. Ginger and Sig could not have been lovers.

What about Homer and Darrell? What did I know of them? Homer and Jethro, I thought. Between them they wielded a large amount of power. With it they had imprisoned Ginger. Neither had wanted to let her go; both had tried to get her to delay the divorce. I recalled Homer's resonant voice on the phone, explaining how erratic Ginger had been, trivializing her motives, warning me to disregard whatever she might say. And all the while Ginger had been dying, or was already dead.

Darrell. What about Darrell, the boozing, whoring scion of an old, established family? A scion who had fallen on hard times, whose wife had to go to work to keep the wolf from the door. I recalled Ginger's response to Hal's question about a contract on Sig's life. No money, she had said. Not no reason, but no money. And no justification, either, since Darrell himself had been screwing around for years. Darrell Watkins, one-man stud service, who never rubbed his wife's neck, who never . . .

I couldn't believe Darrell would have had the nerve to confront Ginger on infidelity. That caliber of double standard is fast approaching extinction. But where had Darrell Watkins been on Saturday night? It would be interesting to know, just for the record.

Ginger. Ginger laughing, crying, stretching her neck as my thumbs massaged the muscles of her shoulders. Ginger's face transformed by a pleasure she had never known or suspected. Remembering that hurt too much, so I stopped.

She had seemed totally carefree as she drove away, waving to me through the window of the Porsche. Respect for Sig had dictated that she go to the meeting and say good-bye, but she would have come back to me, to what I alone had given her. Of that I was sure. Who or what had stopped her? Not suicide. Not booze.

That brought me to the last sheet of paper. Don Wilson. Bereaved husband and father, plunged into the world of political activist, parading his grief on placards and sandwich boards, trying to get someone to listen, attempting to change the system that had robbed him of his wife and child. He had a point, but he had gone after the wrong people.

Why had he agreed to meet Max? Max said something was about to break. What, other than Sig Larson's head? Had the phony interview been a ploy, a device to guarantee press coverage? Maybe Wilson had believed that killing Sig and Ginger would give his cause the public airing necessary to bring it to the top of the silent majority's consciousness. As if they gave a damn.

But it's a long way from political activism to cold-blooded murder, and there was nothing to prove Wilson's conversion—nothing but motive and opportunity.

Wilson had come to Orcas Island. That much we knew—not beyond a shadow of a doubt, but with relative certainty. And, as near as we could tell, he had not left it, at least not by any of the regular routes. He could have hired a boat or a plane, but that was unlikely. It would be too obvious. Besides, Huggins said he had checked all charters and tracked down all private parties who had booked moorage.

Assuming Wilson was still on Orcas, where was he hiding? Did he have an accomplice? Was this the end of it, since Sig and Ginger's decision had placed Lathrop in the work/release program, or was the entire Washington State Parole Board in jeopardy?

Questions. Homicide detectives always have far more questions than they do answers. I analyzed the pieces of paper, pondering each word, poring over each scrap of information until I could have quoted it back verbatim. Hours later, eyes swimming with fatigue, I stumbled to the bed and fell across it, not bothering to undress or pull the covers over me.

Questions continued to buzz in my head. Who had known of the A.A. meeting besides Sig, Ginger, and me? And how would the killer have known she would be in my Porsche?

The human brain is the oldest and best random-access memory. I had almost dozed off when a single word roused me. Calendar. I sat up in bed. The meeting had been noted in her calendar, and the calendar was missing. In fact, it was the only item still unaccounted for in the aftermath of the break-in.

I groped through the darkness for the phone, knocking it to the floor. "What happens to your garbage?" I asked a startled Fred, who answered sleepily on the fourth ring.

It took him a couple of seconds to get his brain in gear. "It goes to the landfill," he mumbled.

"Do you have garbage cans? Dumpsters?"

"Dumpsters, one by each wing, and two here at the Mansion." Fred sounded more awake now. He was gradually becoming accustomed to my middle-of-the-night requests.

"When were they emptied last?"

"Friday afternoon, late. We're on a Monday/Wednesday/Friday schedule."

I banged down the phone and rummaged through my clothes for my most disreputable Levi's and the dung-colored sweater Karen's mother knitted for me the Christmas before we were divorced. I had sworn to wear that sucker out. This would finish the job.

I stopped by the desk and begged a flashlight from Fred. It was cold, and rain was falling as I started my five A.M. assault on Rosario's garbage dumpsters.

Those who think being a detective is romantic ought to try rummaging through three-day-old garbage with a raging hangover, flashlight in hand, in a driving rainstorm. Things happen to apple cores and orange peels and banana skins that can't be described in polite company. If I had known about garbage cans, maybe I would have taken my mother's advice and become a schoolteacher.

I started with the wing where Ginger's original room had been, searching through each carefully fastened black plastic bag. I did the same to the second-wing dumpster, and again found nothing. In terms of garbage, this was lightweight stuff—tissues and soda cans, discarded hairspray cans, and a couple of pornographic magazines. Clean garbage. No calendar.

The last two dumpsters were by the Mansion itself. They contained GARBAGE, foul-smelling foodstuffs that had sat around for several days and gotten surly. I took one whiff and almost gave up, but some of my mother's stubborn determination must have stuck. I dug in and got lucky. At the bottom of the first dumpster, I found it—a leather-bound, gold-embossed executive planner with Ginger Watkins' name imprinted on the front.

Carefully I laid the book to one side and refilled the rancid container. After carrying the calendar back to my room, I stripped to the skin on the rainy porch, leaving my wrecked clothes by the door. I set the calendar on the floor just inside the doorway while I attempted to shower the odor off my body and out of my nose.

I came out of the shower wrapped in a towel and picked up the phone. I dialed Hal's number. On the third ring I realized it was only six o'clock. Homicide is always much more urgent when someone near and dear is dead.

"Guess what?" I asked when he finally answered.

"I give up," Hal mumbled groggily.

"I found Ginger's calendar, the one that was lifted from her room the other night."

"So big fucking deal. Do you know what time it is?"

"It was in the trash, down near the Mansion. You want to come out and pick it up, or should I bring it over to Friday Harbor myself?"

"Beau, give me a break, I didn't get to bed until three."

"Sorry, Hal, but I just found it. I thought you'd want to know."

"I'll pick it up later," he said grudgingly. "But it won't make any difference."

"What do you mean?"

He yawned, fully awake now. "Got the coroner's report just before I went to bed. Said her blood-alcohol reading was point-fifteen. She was dead drunk. Probably passed out cold when she hit the water."

"That's preposterous! It doesn't make sense."

"Of course it makes sense. Blood-alcohol counts don't lie. I'm telling you what they told me. It was an accident, and that's official."

I wanted to argue, but he wasn't having any. "The crime lab dusted for prints, enough to confirm that she was driving."

"You mean you're going to drop it just like that?"

"Look, Beau, we've already got one homicide. We don't need to change a DWI into homicide just for drill."

"But she wasn't drinking. She had nothing before she left here."

"You don't get a point-fifteen reading by osmosis. It was too much for her. The divorce, Sig Larson's death. She was despondent and slipped. It's the classic recovering-alcoholic story. She didn't live long enough to dry out a second time."

Ginger's words rang in my ears. "I won't go through that again. Ever." But I was the only one who had heard her make that categorical statement, the only one who knew that in twenty-four hours she had taken several giant steps beyond grief and found a reason for living.

"What was the time of death? Did they say?"

"Between eight-thirty and nine-thirty, give or take."

"I tell you, Hal, she had nothing to drink before she left here at twenty minutes to eight. How could she get that drunk in such a short time?"

He sighed. "You've been around boozers. With some of them, falling off the wagon is like stepping off a thirty-story building." Hal Huggins didn't budge. Neither did I.

"Do you want this calendar or not?" I demanded.

"I already said I'd come by later this morning and pick it up, but I'm not making any promises."

"Don't patronize me, Hal, goddammit. Will you have it analyzed or not? Don't pick it up just to humor me."

"For cripe's sake. I'll have it analyzed. Good-bye!" The receiver banged in my ear.

I looked at the calendar skulking by the door, its pungent odor invading the room. It made me wonder if I still wanted to be a cop when I grew up. I kept it in the room, odor and all. Considering the phone call, it didn't make much sense to keep it. I might just as well have pitched it outside into the drizzle, but I didn't.

I went to bed and tried to nap, without much luck.

CHAPTER 15

Hal Huggins was in a foul mood when he showed up an hour later. He called me from the lobby. "Bring that goddamned calendar down here and buy me breakfast, Beaumont."

Huggins was seated at a table before a steaming coffee cup when I ventured into the dining room. Grudgingly, he pushed out a chair for me. "I'm not very good company when I don't get my beauty sleep," he growled. "Where the hell is that calendar?"

I handed it to him, wrapped in a Rosario pillowcase.

"What do you expect to find in there?" he asked, nodding toward it.

"Prints, I hope. Especially on last week's pages."

He leaned back in his chair and glowered at me. "Let me ask you this, Beau. Do you think this calendar has anything to do with Sig Larson's death? The break-in occurred after he was already dead."

"No, but—"

"But what?"

"The meeting was listed in there, the one Sig and Ginger planned to attend together."

"Were you awake when you called me this morning?"

"Sure I was awake."

"I told you then and I'll tell you now, Ginger Watkins' death has been ruled accidental. We are not treating it as a possible homicide. Do I make myself clear?"

"Very. So you won't have the calendar analyzed?"

"I'll take it, just for old time's sake, but that's the only reason." Huggins glared at me, his face implacable.

"What are you so pissed about, Hal?"

"I'm pissed because I've got a homicide to work, and I'm shorthanded, and I didn't get enough sleep, and my neck hurts. Any other questions?"

"None that I can think of."

The waiter brought Huggins his food and took my order. Halfway through breakfast, Hal's savage beast seemed somewhat soothed. "You going back today?"

"Probably." Rosario had lost its charm. I wanted to go home and lick my wounds.

"You need a ride?"

"Naw. I can take the shuttle bus."

The waiter brought my coffee and freshly squeezed orange juice. "Find any trace of Wilson?"

Huggins shook his head. "Not yet. Looks like he stepped off the face of the earth once he got on the ferry."

"Maybe he did," I said. "Still no sign of him at his house?"

"Not a trace. King County has round-the-clock surveillance on the place. It doesn't make sense."

"Unless he's dead, too," I suggested.

Huggins' flint-eyed scrutiny honed in on my face. "He might be, at that," he said.

I didn't like the tone, the inflection. "Is that an accusation?" I asked.

"Could be," he allowed, "if I thought vigilante mentality had caught you by the short hairs."

"Look, Hal, I was only trying to help."

He nodded. "I'd hate to think otherwise, Beau."

It sounded like the end of a beautiful friendship. I tried to put the conversation on a less volatile track. "How'd she get the booze, then? It had to come from somewhere. It wasn't in the Porsche when she left here."

"When she left you," he corrected. "She might have gone back to her room and gotten it. She might have bought it on the way."

I was shaking my head before he finished speaking. Huggins' face clouded. "You're sure you never met Ginger Watkins before last Friday?"

"I'm sure," I answered, trying to keep anger out of my voice. From one moment to the next, Huggins and I shifted back and forth to opposite sides, like two kids who can't decide if they're best friends or hate each other's guts.

"Why's it so goddamned important to you that she wasn't drunk?" he demanded.

How does a man answer a question like that without his ego getting in the way? If she was drunk, then I'm not the man I thought I was. A psychiatrist would have a ball with that one. I know she was coming back. She and I had a date to screw our brains out after dinner. That one had a good macho ring to it. I had given her a reason for living. She wouldn't have thrown it all away. That dripped with true missionary fervor.

I said, "It's important to me, that's all."

"My mind's made up; don't confuse me with the facts, right?"

"Something like that."

"Beau—"

"Will you have the calendar analyzed?"

"I told you I will, but—"

"And you'll let me know what you find?"

There was a momentary pause. "I guess." He stirred his coffee uneasily, looking at me over the cup. "It's probably a good thing you're going home today. We might end up stepping on each other's toes."

"I take it that means you're firing me as a San Juan County deputy?"

He nodded. "Yup." He gave me a lopsided grin. "If it's possible to fire someone who's working for free." The tension between us evaporated. Huggins rose, taking his check and the calendar. I snagged the check away from him.

"It's on me, Hal, remember? Your beauty sleep?"

We shook hands. "No hard feelings?" he asked.

"None."

"All right then. I'll be in touch. If I were a betting man, I'd say there won't be a goddamned thing in this sonofabitch." He strode out of the dining room.

It's too bad I didn't take that bet, but hindsight is always twenty/twenty.

I went into the bar because I didn't want to go back to my room. Without Ginger, my room seemed empty. Barney was industriously polishing the mirror.

"Morning," he said to my reflection. "Want a drink?"

"Just coffee," I replied. "I need to think."

He brought a mug and set it in front of me. "On the house," he said, refusing my money. Barney had a sense of when to leave people alone. He said nothing about my making an ass of myself. Instead he returned to his mirror and his Windex.

The question I had asked Hal was far more than rhetorical. He was right, of course. Blood-alcohol readings don't lie. No matter how much I wanted to deny it, Ginger Watkins had been drunk when she ploughed into the water. So where had she gotten the booze? From her room? A liquor store? Where?

"Hey, Barney," I said, "does Orcas Island have a liquor store?"

He grinned. "Hell, no. We're too small. We've got Old Man Baxter, though. He's the official agent. Lives up above Eastsound, about a half-mile beyond Ernie's."

"Did Huggins leave one of Don Wilson's pictures with you?"

"Are you kidding?" He reached under the bar and pulled out a whole handful. "Why, you want some?"

"One," I said. "I only need one." He handed me a picture. I pulled out a pen to write on the back. "Tell me again how to get there."

"Where?"

"Mr. Baxter's."

"Now wait a minute. You come in here, and I give you free coffee. Next thing I know, you want to go see our agent so you can mix your own drinks? No way! I'd lose one of my best customers."

"I promise I won't buy anything," I protested. "I just want to show him this picture."

"Well, in that case. . . . Go past Ernie's. It's the fourth mailbox on the left."

"Thanks, have the desk call me a cab, would you?"

"Why?"

"So I don't have to walk."

"No, I mean why do you want to see Baxter?"

"I want to know if either Ginger Watkins or this man bought something from him Friday or Saturday. Make the call, would you?"

Instead, Barney reached into his pants pocket and extracted a ring of keys. He tossed them across the bar, and I caught them in midair. "What's this?"

"It's the key to an old Chevy pickup parked over by the moorage. You're welcome to use it if you like."

It was a small-town gesture, one that caught me by surprise. When I thought about it, though, there's no such thing as auto theft on Orcas Island. I pocketed the keys. "Thanks, Barney. Appreciate it."

The pickup looked old and decrepit; but ugliness, like beauty, is only skin-deep. The engine ran like a top beneath a rusty hood. I drove into Eastsound, past Ernie's and stopped at the fourth mailbox on the left. The house was a picturesque gray-and-white bungalow that might have been lifted straight off Cape Cod. I knocked on the door.

Mr. Baxter himself opened it. He was a small man with a belly much too large for the rest of him. The living room of the house had been converted into a mini-display room, with a stack of hand-held shopping baskets sitting beside the door. The house had the smell and look of an aging bachelor pad—not much cooking and not enough cleaning.

"Help yourself," he said, motioning me inside.

I pulled Don Wilson's picture out of my pocket. "I didn't come to buy anything," I said. "I was wondering if you'd ever seen this man before."

He peered at the picture, then looked up at me. "You a cop?" he asked. His face was truculent, arms crossed, chin jutting. Mr. Baxter was a short man embattled by a tall world.

Huggins had pulled the plug on my unofficial deputy status. "No," I said. "The woman who died the other night was a friend of mine. I'm trying to find out what happened to her."

"Not from me you won't."

"I'm only asking if you recognize him."

"You ever hear of the confidentiality statute of nineteen and thirty-three?"

"Not that I remember."

"It says no liquor-store clerk tells nobody nothing, excepting of course federal agents checking revenue stamps. We can talk to them."

"All I'm asking is, Did you see him?"

"And if I give out information, they stick me with a high misdemeanor. Nosiree. I'm not talking to nobody."

I could see right off I wasn't going to change his mind. I left. Something made me stop at Ernie's. The doors of the Porsche were wide open, and the insides of the car were scattered all over the garage in a seemingly hopeless jumble. Ernie glanced up as I walked in. He was bent over the engine, a grimy crutch propped under his good arm.

"How'do, Mr. Beaumont. I was just gonna call you."

I figured it was time to jack up the price, now that the car was in pieces and I was a captive audience.

"Why?" I asked.

"You ever have any work done on the linkage?"

I shrugged. "No. Not that I know of."

He hopped away from the car to a nearby tool bench, picked up something in his gripper, and handed it to me. I looked down at two pieces of metal, slightly smaller in diameter than a pencil.

"What's this?"

"That's the throttle linkage cable. Looks to me like it's been cut."

"What does that mean?"

"With that thing cut, Mr. Beaumont, all you have to do is put that baby in motion and you've got a one-way ride."

I looked down at the shiny crimped ends of metal. "It couldn't have broken in the accident?"

He shook his head. "No way."

"Mind if I use your phone?" I asked, keeping my voice calm. It was time for Hal Huggins to eat a little crow.

CHAPTER 16

Hal marched into Ernie's Garage looking thunderous. "What do you mean the linkage was cut?" he stormed.

Ernie pointed him in the direction of the tool bench where the two pieces of cable were once more lying in state. Silently Hal examined them, then he straightened. "How the hell could those crime-lab jokers miss something like this?"

"They were investigating an accident, remember?" I reminded him. "A DWI. Maybe even a suicide."

He glared at me. "That's no excuse."

"So where do we go from here?"

"Damned if I know." Hal settled on a bench near the door. "Not a chance of getting fingerprints now, either," he lamented.

Ernie, back under the hood, peered over his shoulder at Hal, grinning. "Only half as many as there could have been," he said.

Hal didn't bother to acknowledge Ernie's black humor. "Two homicides," he muttered. "Two goddamned homicides in as many days. Do you know how long we usually go up here without a homicide?"

"Did you tell anybody on the way over?"

"Hell, no. I tried to raise Pomeroy to come down to the dock and pick me up. I couldn't find that lard-ass anywhere. Luckily, somebody gave me a ride."

My mind was working. "Then the only people who know are you, Ernie, me, and the murderer."

"That's right. So what?"

"Let's keep it that way."

"What good will that do?" Hal asked.

"It'll give us a chance to investigate without the media breathing down our necks."

Hal nodded, slowly. "That does have some appeal." For a time we sat in silence. "How far could it have been driven like that, Ernie?" Hal asked finally.

Ernie answered without looking up from his work. "A couple hundred feet if the front end was aligned and it was on a straight stretch."

"What gear was it in?"

"Neutral when I got it, but I'm sure the tow-truck driver shifted it so he wouldn't tear up the transmission."

"Can you check with him?"

"Sure."

"And not a word of this to anyone," Hal admonished. "It's important."

Ernie straightened and favored Hal with a sly grin. "Had a feeling it was, or you wouldn't have been here in twenty-five minutes flat. Last time I seen you move that fast was at the Fireman's Picnic when a wasp was after you."

Hal laughed. "I set all-time world records with that sucker on my butt." The camaraderie was small-town stuff, foreign in a nice way.

"Don't worry. I'll keep it quiet." Ernie resumed working on the car, as though we were no longer there.

"What about Wilson?" I asked. "Any sign of him?"

Huggins shook his head. "We're looking, still keeping his house under surveillance, but so far nothing."

We rose and started toward the door; Ernie called after me, "By the way, Mr. Beaumont, maybe it won't cost you the whole seven grand after all."

Hal's eyes widened. "Seven grand?"

"Maybe six and a half." Ernie's head disappeared, dismissing us. Hal looked at me, stunned.

"Six and a half thousand? To fix the car?"

"It's a Porsche," I said. It seemed to me that no further explanation was necessary.

"How much they paying you these days? When I worked Seattle P.D., I was lucky to afford a lube and oil. Matter of fact, I still am. You into graft and corruption?"

"I happened into some money, Hal, that's all."

Hal glowered at me. "Some people have all the luck," he sniffed, walking outside. I followed.

"Where you going?" I asked.

"I'm looking for Pomeroy. He was supposed to come pick me up. I can't drive the goddamned police launch all over the goddamned island."

"Where do you want to go?"

"The duck pond, you asshole. Where else?"

That's how two homicide detectives, one legal and one not, returned to the scene of the crime in a bartender's borrowed pickup. It wasn't much, but it was a whole lot better than walking.

The place where the Porsche had laid down the layer of rubber made better sense now. The car had leaped forward from a dead stop. Even piecing that together didn't give us everything we needed to know. We gave up about mid-afternoon. I took Hal back to his boat.

"What are you going to do now?" he asked.

"Go home, I guess. Hanging around here won't do any good."

He sat in Barney's idling pickup, one hand on the door handle. "We'll get him, Beau. I promise." It was as close as Hal Huggins ever came to making an apology.

"Are you going to warn the rest of the parole board? What if he goes after the whole board, one by one."

Hal looked stricken. "I'll check it out," he agreed. "He could go through them like a dose of salts." He climbed from the pickup and headed for the dock.

Back at Rosario, I packed and checked out of my room. I had the desk clerk call for a float plane. I could have taken the ferry to Anacortes, but without a car, I'd still be a long way from Seattle. A charter pilot could drop me on Lake Union a mile or so from my apartment.

I dragged a newspaper along in the noisy little plane. I suffer from a fear of flying. There's nothing like reading a newspaper to make me forget that I'm scared. Newspapers always piss me off.

The editor opined that the tragic deaths of two members of the Washington State Parole Board over the weekend—one an apparent homicide and the other in a motor vehicle accident—pointed out the high cost of public service. He went on to say that Darrell Watkins was showing great personal courage in continuing to campaign in the face of the loss of his beloved wife.

Bullshit! There was no hint that the beloved wife, now deceased, would have filed for a divorce had she lived to Monday morning. In the editorial, Ginger's and Darrell's life had been a Cinderella story, poor girl marries rich boy and lives happily ever after. As far as Ginger was concerned, the fairy tale had suffered in translation. Somehow I had an idea that Maxwell Cole's interview would never see the light of the day. It wasn't just spiked, it was buried. For good.

The article on Ginger made no mention of drinking. The accident was described as a one-car accident on a narrow road. Darrell Watkins was quoted at some length. "I am going on with the race because I believe Ginger would want me to."

The unmitigated ass! Ginger had been wrong. Darrell Watkins had developed hypocrisy into an art form.

The float plane dropped me at a dock on Lake Union. Without luggage, I could have walked. With luggage, I called a cab. It was early evening when I got home—the city boy glad to be back in familiar territory, with the comforting wail of sirens and the noise of traffic.

My apartment is in the Royal Crest, a condo at Third and Lenora. *Condo* conjures images of swinging singles. There are singles here, all right, mostly retired, who do very little swinging. It's a vertical neighborhood where people bring soup when you're sick and know who comes and goes at all hours. I moved in five years ago on a temporary basis, hoping Karen and I would get back together. We didn't. Five years later, my escape hatch has become home.

In the elevator two people welcomed me back, and on the mat in front of my door I found a stack of crossword puzzles culled from various newspapers and left for me by my next-door neighbor and crony, Ida Newell. Yes, it was very good to be home.

I put my suitcases in the bedroom and looked around the tiny apartment with satisfaction. One of my first concessions to having money was to hire a housekeeper who comes in once every two weeks whether I need it or not. The house smelled of furniture polish and toilet-bowl cleaner. It was a big improvement over the old days when it smelled like a billygoat pen and I needed two hours' notice before I could invite someone up to visit.

The mail was mostly of the bill/occupant variety, although I noticed that some of the occupant stuff was a lot more upscale than occupant mail I used to receive. Somewhere there's a mass-mailing company that knows when you move from one income bracket to another. The whole idea makes me paranoid.

I thumped into my favorite leather chair, a brown monstrosity that gives people with "taste" indigestion. I examined the bill from Rosario with its detail of all calls made from my room. I recognized most of them. Two of the numbers were unfamiliar. One had to be Homer's and the other Darrell's. I chose one at random.

Homer answered on the second ring. I didn't identify myself. "I'm a friend of Ginger's. I was calling to find out about her services."

"In keeping with Darrell's wishes, the services will be private."

"But I wanted—"

"I'm sorry. This is a very difficult time. Darrell wants to maintain a sense of dignity by keeping Ginger's funeral simple. Only family members and close personal friends. I'm sure you understand." He hung up without giving me an opportunity to explain why I thought I qualified as a close personal friend.

Remembering Ginger's description of how Darrell's campaign would handle news of the divorce, I understood all too well. A steering committee had decreed that Ginger's funeral should be handled with classic understatement and simplicity. Not too splashy. That would attract the sympathy vote.

I wanted to gag. Ginger had known news of the divorce wouldn't cost Darrell the election, but she had hoped to sting him with it. Instead, her death would provide the impetus for a come-from-behind victory. I wanted to protest to someone, but I didn't know who.

Restless, I walked two blocks to Avis and rented a car for the next morning. If I was going to make it to a funeral in Welton by two o'clock in the afternoon, I'd have to get an early start. My garage door opener was still with the Porsche on Orcas—probably wrecked, now that it had been wet. I parked the rented Rabbit on the street and went upstairs to get some sleep.

In a dream, Anne Corley and Ginger Watkins were together someplace. It seemed to be some kind of spa. They were both wrapped in thick white towels, with their hair hanging loose and wet. I came into the room. They waved at me and motioned for me to join them, but they were across a large room and between us lay a huge swimming pool. They motioned to me again, and I dove in, clothes and all. I tried to swim toward them, but the current was too swift. It caught me and carried me away, changing from a pool to a river. The dream ended with the sound of both of them laughing.

I awoke drenched with sweat. It was almost four o'clock in the morning. For a while I tried going back to sleep, but it didn't work. Remembering them both together haunted me. At last I got up and made coffee. The city was silent around me—not as silent as Orcas, but silent for the city. As I drank my coffee, I made up my mind that nothing would keep me from showing up at Ginger's funeral to offer my respects.

I consulted the map. I would go east on Interstate 90; but after Sig Larson's funeral, when I came back to Seattle, I would detour south to Centralia and find myself a Union 76 station. Ginger's father lived in Centralia. I was sure he would give me an invitation to the funeral if I explained to him that I was one of Ginger's old friends.

I filled a Thermos with the last of the coffee and headed out. I figured I'd have breakfast somewhere along the way.

CHAPTER 17

The State of Washington is divided into two parts, east of the mountains and west of the mountains. They could just as well be separate countries.

West of the mountains is a fast-track megalopolis that is gradually encroaching on every inch of open space. East of the mountains seems like a chunk of the Midwest that has been transported and reassembled between the Cascades and the Rockies. It contains small towns, large farms, and the kind of vast horizons that brings to mind Robert Goulet's old song, "On a Clear Day You Can See Forever."

Welton is definitely east of the mountains. It's a tiny burg nestled in a hilly curve of the Touchet River, where two Walla Walla County roads meet in a casual Y that doesn't merit so much as a Yield sign, to say nothing of a blinking amber light.

Welton boasts a general store, a Grange Hall, a deserted schoolhouse, five or six dilapidated frame houses, and a double-wide mobile home perched on cement blocks behind the store. The Lutheran church burned down six years ago and has not been replaced. A sign on the light post next to the gas pump announced the schedule for the Walla Walla County Bookmobile. Next to it, another handbill posted notice of Sig Larson's funeral.

The gas jockey at the Texaco Station/General Store, a toothless old geezer named Gus, informed me that Lewis and Clark's party had once camped overnight on the river, supposedly somewhere near where the Grange Hall now stood. As far as he knew, Sig Larson's funeral was the biggest event to hit town since then.

"It isn't ever' day we have this kinda excitement around here," he commented as he scrubbed the rented Rabbit's windshield and checked the oil. "We're gonna shut 'er down and go over to the Hall for the funeral. Least we can do for old Sig, that's for sure."

"He lived around here?"

"Not anymore. Sold out a couple years back when that there wife of his decided Welton warn't good enough. Talked him into one of them highfalutin condanubians over to Lake Chelan. T'was a shame, a dad-gummed shame, if you ask me."

"But he'll be buried here?"

"First wife's buried here, you know. Think the kids had something to do with bringing him back. Son John's a bigwig lawyer down to California. He's the one took it on hisself to see things got done right."

"So Mona's Sig Larson's second wife?"

Gus snorted and spat a brown stream of tobacco juice over his shoulder. "She was already hanging round while Elke—that was Sig's first wife—was dyin' in the hospital over to Spokane."

"I take it you don't like Mona much."

He nodded sagely. "That's for sure," he said. "You can say that again."

Gus wore the logger trademark of mid-calf Levi's held up by a pair of bright red suspenders. Finished with my car, he stood with both thumbs stuck through his suspenders and surveyed the scatter of cars parked haphazardly around the Grange Hall. "Heard the governor hisself is coming. Wonder if ol' Mona'll get herself all gussied up or if she'll show up on that there motorcycle of hern."

Motorcycle! That hardly tallied with the white-haired, displaced-homemaker farm wife I had imagined Sig Larson's widow to be—someone wearing an apron who baked her own bread and canned her own tomatoes.

A mobile television unit bearing a Spokane station's call letters and logo lumbered past us and parked under a tree near the Grange Hall. "Don't that just beat all?" Gus asked. "All them television cameras and ever'thin', just for Old Sig's funeral." He spat again in disbelief.

As we watched, a helicopter dropped noisily from the sky and landed on the weedy playfield of the abandoned schoolhouse next door. Governor Reynolds stepped out, ducking under the blades, accompanied by none other than Homer Watkins himself.

Seeing Homer there was something of a shock. Ginger had implied that highly placed family connections had resulted in her appointment to the parole board, but seeing Homer with the governor brought the reality home.

"I'd better get going," I told Gus. I hurried to the Grange Hall and took an unobtrusive seat in the next-to-last row of ancient folding chairs. From there I could see who came and went without being observed.

I had stopped in Kenniwick and bought a huge bouquet of flowers, which now sat prominently displayed near the foot of Sig Larson's coffin. I had signed the card from "A Friend" and let it go at that. The flowers were a remembrance from Ginger to Sig through me. If Ginger and Sig were flapping around upstairs somewhere, then they both knew what I meant. If they weren't, it didn't matter anyway.

Unlike Lewis and Clark's historic visit, Sig Larson's funeral was immortalized by the press, the same teeming mob that had invaded Orcas Island.

They were joined by troops from Spokane and Tri Cities as well. A full contingent of the Fourth Estate was there, jockeying for position and camera angle, elbowing one another out of the way.

It was simple to divide the guests into two parts: the plainly dressed quiet folk who had probably been lifelong friends and neighbors of Sig and Elke Larson, and the public officials and anxious candidates whose attendance was calculated to pick up a little free publicity over and above the paid political announcements.

The entire front row, on both sides of the aisle, was marked Reserved. As the pianist attempted a frail, halting prelude on an old upright piano, a group of six handsome young people, three couples in their late twenties to early thirties, was ushered to the front row. I surmised they were Sig's children and their spouses. Gus had told me there were two Larson boys and one girl, all married. They sat together on one side of the front row, leaving two places open next to the aisle.

The surviving members of the parole board, five of them, straggled down the aisle behind Trixie Bowdeen like a bunch of dazed sheep. Next came Governor Reynolds and Homer Watkins.

There was some confusion about seating arrangements as they reached the front row. Homer and Governor Reynolds held a hurried, private consultation before both men crossed the aisle to speak solemnly with the young couples. Then they rejoined the parole board.

Darrell Watkins was notable only in his absence.

The room filled quickly, until every chair was taken and people stood two-deep in the back of the room. It was then Mona Larson staged her grand entrance. She wore a black dress with a bold V neckline and a flared skirt over a pair of high-heeled black boots. Her hair, black and glossy, hung straight to her shoulders, with a fringe of bangs that made her look far younger than I had expected. Her tiny waist was encircled by a wide turquoise and silver belt. A weighty squash-blossom necklace with matching earrings completed the ensemble. It wasn't exactly mourning, but it made the point. It was also very striking.

A murmur rustled through the room. Mona strode down the aisle, well aware of the sensation she caused. At the front of the room she paused momentarily to get her bearings, then she turned her back on Sig Larson's children and took the empty seat next to Governor Reynolds. Another flurry of comment whispered through the hall.

From the back of the room it looked more like a shotgun wedding between feuding clans than the funeral of a highly regarded public official. Mona Larson was behaving badly by Welton standards, and it was clear she didn't give a damn.

A minister took his place behind the podium. "Dearly beloved," he intoned, "we are here this afternoon to say good-bye to our dear friend Lars Sigfried Larson . . ." The cameras whirred and the circus got under way.

I don't remember much about the service. As far as I was concerned, I was there on official/unofficial business. I kept my eyes open in case Wilson thought Welton far enough away from Orcas that he could afford to turn up and savor his handiwork. Murderers do that in a kind of cutthroat one-upmanship, but Don Wilson was nowhere to be seen.

At the end of the service, the reverend announced that the Ladies Aid would be serving a potluck lunch, and all were welcome to come back to the hall after interment in the cemetery beyond the school.

The pallbearers hoisted the coffin. Mona Larson, followed by the governor and Sig's children, led a slow procession out of the hall, across the road, and into the cemetery. A man sat smoking on an idled backhoe near the fence, waiting to perform his essential role in the process. Once Sig's coffin was lowered into the grave, Mona turned and left the cemetery alone. Without speaking to or acknowledging anyone, she climbed into one of three waiting limousines and left Welton with an air of regal contempt.

Gus hobbled up next to me. "Ain't she somethin'?" he demanded, with just a hint of awe. "Actin' like she's the dad-gummed Queen of Sheba."

The press corps descended on the food like an army of ravenous ants. I spied Maxwell Cole packing around a paper plate piled high with ham and scalloped potatoes, but I managed to avoid him. The local folks clustered around the Larson children, expressing condolences, relieved now that Mona's abrupt departure had reduced the tension.

Homer Watkins materialized at my elbow. "I understand you're J. P. Beaumont. Aren't you the one I talked to on the phone the night Ginger died?"

I wondered who had squealed on me, but with Max in the room, it wasn't hard to figure it out. "Yes," I said.

"Tragic, tragic," he murmured.

"It is, isn't it," I agreed. "I was a little surprised there was no mention of the impending divorce in the paper."

His eyes hardened. "She told you about that?"

"We talked," I replied noncommittally.

"She wouldn't have gone through with it. She had been under a great deal of stress. I'm sure once things settled down, she would have been fine."

"Fine or quiet?" I asked.

One eyebrow arched. He stepped back half a pace.

"Darrell didn't come?" I asked. The question was more to irk him than to have an answer.

Homer replied nonetheless. "He didn't feel up to it. Good day, Mr. Beaumont. I won't trouble you further."

As people lined up for second and third helpings, Governor Reynolds raised his hand for attention. "I'd like to make an announcement," he said. The media folks abandoned their plates and hustled off in search of equipment. Reynolds moved to the front of the room.

He put on his glasses and read from a prepared text. "This has been a sad occasion for the State of Washington. Sig Larson was a public servant, and he was murdered in the course of that service. He paid with his life. We have reason to believe that his death was related to his being on the parole board. Consequently, as of today, I am placing all members of the parole board under the protection of the Washington State Patrol. That is all."

There was a momentary lull after he finished speaking, then a rush of comment. Reporters attempted to call questions to him from the floor, but he turned away. Reynolds and Homer hurried out of the building. People followed them upstairs and outside, but they dashed to the waiting helicopter without speaking to anyone. With the governor gone, people moved back into the basement, where Trixie Bowdeen assumed the role of spokesman.

"Were you aware the governor was taking this action, Mrs. Bowdeen?"

"Yes," she said. "Each of us has been assigned round-the-clock protection, starting today."

"Is there any idea who the killer or killers might be?"

"No comment."

"How does your husband feel about your having a round-the-clock bodyguard?"

"Fortunately, he's not the jealous type." Trixie Bowdeen flashed what was supposed to be a charming smile. Her quip was greeted by general laughter. I didn't laugh. Governor Reynolds had not specifically mentioned Ginger's death, but I was sure Huggins had notified him regarding the changed status of the investigation. In any event, the protection was probably a good idea.

I left the hall and was halfway across the road when Maxwell Cole called my name. "Hey, J. P."

I turned to find him huffing behind me, carrying a plate of half-consumed pumpkin pie. "What do you want?"

"Any line on Wilson?"

I kept my expression blank. "No," I said. "Nobody's seen him."

"How come Ginger Watkins was driving your car?"

"None of your business," I snarled, walking away. He trotted after me. "I heard her blood-alcohol count was point-fifteen, but she was supposed to be on the wagon."

"Shut up," I said savagely.

He shut up, but only momentarily. "Do you know anything about the governor's victim/witness protection program? Is Reynolds going to drop that idea? That's what Wilson was after."

I stopped in my tracks. "What do you mean?"

Cole looked a little reluctant, as though he had said more than he intended. "Wilson expected an announcement that day at Rosario."

"From the governor's office?"

"That's what he told me on the phone."

"This is the first I've heard anything about an announcement," I said, turning to walk away.

"But, J. P.—"

Ignoring him, I walked back to the gas station where I had left the Rabbit. I climbed in and drove to where two uniformed limo drivers stood smoking under a tree. I rolled down the window. "Did that other driver say where he was taking Mrs. Larson?" I asked.

One looked at the other, who shrugged. "The Red Lion in Pasco, I think," he said. "You know where that is?"

"No," I replied, rolling up the window and putting the Rabbit in gear, "but I'll bet I can find it."

CHAPTER 18

I drove the forty miles into Pasco thinking about Ray Johnson. Ray and I were partners on the homicide squad for eleven years before he took off to become Chief of Police in Pasco. That's what happens to longtime Seattle P.D. folks. They get tired of the rat race and go looking for some one- or two-horse town where they can settle down and not have to look at the slice of life that turns up dead or drunk or both in Seattle's parks and alleys.

Ray had abandoned ship almost ten months earlier, and I had started working with Peters. It takes time to adjust to a new partner, but in the course of that ten months so much had happened that now it seemed Peters and I had been together for years, and Ray Johnson was ancient history.

Ten months is a long time to go without seeing an old friend, and I decided I'd eat a chili-burger and down a whole pot of thick coffee with Ray Johnson before I left town. For old time's sake. Without having Peters lecture me on the evils of the caffeine or red meat.

The sign at the Red Lion in Pasco said, "Welcome Mary Kay." I mistakenly thought Mary Kay was a waitress or barmaid who had returned for a visit.

That shows how wrong you can be.

The Red Lion in Pasco, like Red Lions everywhere, is built on the kind of grand scale that says, "Conventions welcome; all others enter at your own risk." As I drove up, a car pulled out of a parking place directly in front of the lobby. I grabbed the spot, feeling smug. Getting out of the Rabbit, I noticed that the car next to me, and two on the other side of that, were all recent-model pink Cadillacs. They had matching bumper stickers which read, "Ask me about Mary Kay."

Still musing about that, I entered the lobby. A huge banner solved the mystery. Stretched across the lobby, it proclaimed, "Welcome Mary Kay Cosmetics." A regional sales convention was in full swing, and the hotel was thronged with troops of motivated, energetic ladies, all dressed in pink, who periodically burst into disturbingly impromptu choruses of company songs. I should have recognized it as an omen and realized I was headed for trouble.

A harried desk clerk managed to find me a room. Once safely shut away, I picked up the phone and asked for Mona Larson. "I'll ring," the operator told me.

"Hello." The voice was low and husky. For a second I thought I was talking to a man.

"Mona Larson, please," I stammered.

"This is she."

"My name is Beaumont. I'm here investigating a homicide. I need to talk to you."

"How the hell did you find me? That's why I didn't go home. I'm sick of being hounded."

"I'm a detective; that's how I found you. But it's only me. I've ditched the press."

Her tone mellowed a little. "That's a relief. Those bastards have been driving me crazy."

"Would you care to have a drink . . . coffee?"

"I could use a drink. Where are you?"

"In my room. I can meet you in the coffee shop or the bar." Sig Larson didn't drink. Maybe Mona didn't either. It was best to offer the lady a choice.

"All right. It'll take me a few minutes. I'll meet you in the bar. How will I know you?"

"From the looks of the lobby as I came in, I'll probably be the only man in the place."

She laughed. "You'll be the onion in the Mary Kay petunia patch."

She was right. Walking into the Starlight Lounge unnerved me. It was cocktail hour. All the old jokes about salesmen on convention came to mind and did a flip-flop. Saleswomen were just as bad. They sat in groups of twos and threes, giving me a clothes-stripping once-over. Other than the bartender, I was the only man in the room.

I had barely sat down when a woman in her mid-forties sidled up to my table. "Care for a drink?"

I looked around in consternation, hoping she wasn't talking to me. She was. Her face was a paper-smooth mask, eyes shadowed with a disconcerting blend of several different colors. Her lips, darker on the outside than on the inside, made me wonder what a two-toned tube of lipstick looked like.

"Sorry," I answered. "I'm meeting someone."

"Too bad," she said with a wink. She returned to her table while the bartender appeared at my elbow. "Drink, fella?"

"A MacNaughton's and water," I said. He paused to wipe the table. "This is a little weird," I commented under my breath.

He laughed. "You think it's bad now, wait until nine o'clock when they're all on their lips."

The bartender returned to the bar. I sat there, conspicuously alone, waiting for Mona Larson. At Welton she had looked quite bizarre, but now I was anxious to see her. Mona's dramatic clothing would be a welcome contrast to the unrelenting pink, her disdain an antidote to the uncomfortable attention I was receiving at the moment.

Mona rescued me, all right. She had changed her black dress for a black, zippered jumpsuit. Her hair had been pulled up to the top of her head and stuck there with an unlikely comb. A few loose tendrils of hair trailed softly down her neck. Still wearing several pounds of silver and turquoise, she sauntered into the bar with a feline grace that disposed of the pink ladies once and for all.

"Mr. Beaumont?" she asked, extending her hand.

I half rose in greeting. Her handshake was firm, her dark brown eyes straightforward. "Don't bother getting up," she said, sinking gratefully into a low-backed chair opposite me.

"Thanks for saving my bacon," I said.

She glanced around the room disdainfully. "From what? These horny broads?" She turned to me and grinned. "You look like you can take care of yourself."

From what Ginger had said about Mona Larson and from what I had seen at the funeral, I was prepared not to like her, but her manner had a disarming forthrightness about it, and very little of the grieving widow.

"Sorry it took so long," she apologized. "I had a phone call. Are you from Orcas?"

The bartender brought my drink and took her order for Chivas on the rocks while I contemplated my situation. I was in no way from Orcas, and as a Seattle homicide detective, I had no business asking her anything at all.

I took a sip of my drink. "No. I'm from Seattle."

"I didn't know Seattle was involved in the case."

"We are now," I said.

"Do you have a card?"

There are times when I think I'll just stick my little toe in some water. Before I know it, I'm in over my head. I reached into my pocket and pulled out my leather cardholder. I handed her one of my business cards, which she examined without comment and put into a zippered pocket on the leg of her pants. Her fingers were long and slender, but the nails were close-cropped.

"So what do you want to know?"

"How well did you know Ginger Watkins?"

"Well enough."

"What do you mean?"

"We were shirttail relatives. Homer and Sig's first wife were brother and sister. Our families had some business dealings together."

So that was the connection. I had wondered about it.

"Were you and Ginger friends?"

"No."

I waited, hoping she'd expand on the subject. She didn't. "You and Darrell, then?"

"Darrell Watkins is an asshole," Mona said. "He's why I was late. He called from Seattle while I was at the funeral, wanted to explain why he wasn't there. As if I give a rat's ass." She extracted a pack of cigarettes from another zippered pocket. I hurried to offer her a light. She leaned back inhaling.

"Did you know Ginger was going to get a divorce?"

"You bet. I called Darrell to tell him."

"Why?"

She regarded me coolly. "Look, Mr. Beaumont, I played that side of the fence once. You're married to a jerk. Some nice guy sympathizes, listens to you, tells you what a bad deal you've got. First thing you know, you ditch the jerk and marry the nice guy. That's the name of the game, survival of the fittest."

"You think Ginger was trying to pack Sig off?"

She blew a languid cloud of smoke. "Not on purpose. She was so fucked up, she probably didn't know she was doing it. They were nice people, both of them."

I tried reconciling Mona's words with the person who had forbidden Ginger to attend Sig's funeral. It didn't add up. "Why didn't you want Ginger to come to the funeral?"

"Who said?"

"That's what I understood," I replied. "It came from someone, maybe Trixie Bowdeen."

"That cow? All she does is make trouble. She minds everybody else's business. Ginger could have come if she wanted to. It wouldn't have bothered me."

She glanced away from me, angrily swiping a tear. Pain lurked behind Mona Larson's tough exterior, under the brittle wit.

"You loved him very much, didn't you."

She looked at me, her eyes bright with tears. "That's not how they see it in Welton," she said. "I'm the gold digger who married Sig Larson for his money. What a laugh!"

"Did you?" Mona's manner encouraged a direct approach.

She didn't deny it. "There's not much left," she countered.

"The money from the farm?"

"Gone. He left me a mortgaged condo on Lake Chelan, plus my share of the Seattle project, whatever that's worth. I own my Harley free and clear, and that's it, except for my jewelry." She fell silent. I felt sorry for her. Ginger Watkins' calculating bitch wasn't nearly as ruthless, close at hand.

"You work on the Harley yourself?"

She cocked her head. "What made you ask that?"

"Your nails are a whole lot more serviceable than the rest of the nails in this room, like maybe they get a little grease under them on occasion."

"Good guess," she said.

"What do you know about Don Wilson?" I asked, switching topics.

She looked me straight in the eye. "I told him if he called again I'd file a complaint."

"For what?"

"Telephone harassment. I knew all about his wife and kid, but he'd call in the middle of the night, making wild threats. He finally stopped."

"When?"

She thought. "A month or so ago, maybe longer."

"He threatened Sig?"

"Constantly."

"What did he say?"

"That he'd make Sig pay."

"Did Sig do anything about it?"

"Mostly he laughed it off. Initially he tried reasoning with the guy, but you can't talk to someone like that. They won't listen." She paused. "Do you think he did it?" The question was quiet. The noise of the room ebbed and flowed around us.

"It looks like it, at least for now."

She signaled the bartender for a drink. When he brought it, she lit another cigarette. "It's funny. Sig was so glad to get the appointment to the board. He thought, with his experience at Walla Walla, he could help; that he'd make a real contribution." She stopped, words giving way to reflection. It was an awkward silence.

"I understand Sig didn't drink."

She took a sip from her Chivas. "He wanted me to quit, too. There's nothing like a reformed drunk." She gave me a forlorn smile. "I would have, eventually." There was another long pause. She needed comforting and I was at a loss.

"Would you like to have dinner?" I asked at last.

She shook her head. "Not now, maybe later. I have some things I need to do first."

"How long will it take?"

"An hour or so. I'll give you a call when I finish."

She jotted my room number on the back of my card, and returned it to her pocket. We talked a while longer before she got up to leave. She held out her hand. "It was nice meeting you, Detective Beaumont. I'll see you later."

I watched her walk away, striding purposefully out of the room, a lady with places to go and people to see. It was only after she was out of sight that a wave of concern washed over me. I left money on the table and hurried after her, but she was nowhere in sight. I found a house phone and dialed her room. It rang and rang, but there was no answer.

Stopping by the desk, I asked what kind of car Mona Larson had registered. The clerk didn't bother to look at her card. "She's the one with the Harley, mister." He grinned. "Doesn't seem possible someone her size could handle one of those suckers."

I roamed through acres of parking lot to no avail. Finally I went back to my room and tried calling Ray in Pasco. No answer. I tried Mona's room several times as well, but there was still no answer. Giving up, I turned on the movie channel. I don't know when I fell asleep.

CHAPTER 19

A sharp rap on the door jarred me awake. Flipping off the droning television set, I opened the door to find two uniformed police officers standing in the hallway.

"Are you J. P. Beaumont?" the first one asked, stepping uninvited through my open door. He wore gold-rimmed glasses and chewed a cud of gum with unbridled enthusiasm.

"Yes. What do you want?"

The second officer was heavyset: not fat, but with a definite paunch. "You know a lady named Mona Larson?"

"Yes, I do. What's up?"

"When's the last time you saw her?"

"I don't know. What time is it?"

The one in glasses looked at his watch. "Eight-thirty," he said, wrapping the gum around the tip of his tongue and giving it a small, interior pop.

"I saw her about six-thirty. She said she had some things to do."

"Did she say what?"

I shook my head. "No. What's going on?" I kept asking the question, but they disregarded it.

The heavyset one pulled a business card out of his inside jacket pocket and turned it over, examining both sides. I recognized it as one of my own. "Says here you're Detective Beaumont. You here in Pasco on official business?"

A twinge of uneasiness warned me something wasn't right. "No," I said after a pause. "I was at a funeral in Welton this afternoon and decided to spend the night."

"Sig Larson's funeral?" There was an unpleasant undertone to his question.

"Yes. As a matter of fact, it was."

The gum-chewer wandered over to the window. "Mind if we have a look around?"

"No. Yes. What's this all about?" I demanded, getting my back up.

"He asked you nice like," the heavyset one warned. "Now, can we look around or not?"

I retreated to the bed and sat down, more than half angry. Obviously there was some mistake. They had no business pushing me around like a common criminal. I wanted to get to the bottom of whatever it was. "Go ahead," I said, managing to control myself.

Glasses searched the whole room—under the bed, in the closet, in all the drawers, in the bathroom—while Fatso kept an eye on me, all the while fingering his nightstick. "No luggage?" Glasses asked when he finished.

"I didn't plan to spend the night."

"No, I suppose not."

"Are you going to tell me what's going on?" I felt as though I had fallen into a bad dream where things happen and no one tells you why. There wasn't much I could do about it. It was two against one. They were calling the shots.

"You got anyone who'll say where you were between six-thirty and now?"

"I already told you. I've been right here at the hotel, mostly asleep. Now tell me what the fuck is going on!"

Glasses rolled his eyes. "Isn't that what they all say, Willy? I was asleep the whole time. All by myself."

Willy grinned. "That's what they say."

"Now wait just a goddamned minute. You'd better tell me what's happening."

"You want to tell him, Joe?" Willy asked.

"Naw, you go ahead. Since he's so anxious to hear."

"Well sir," Willy said, savoring the words, "it's about this lady we found along the road a little while ago. Victim of a hit-and-run. She had your card in her pocket with a room number written on the back."

"Mona?" I asked. "Is she all right?"

"Didja hear that!" Joe exclaimed. "She's dead as a doornail, and he wants to know if she's all right. You'd better move on over to the wall. Put your hands above your head."

For a second I sat there, too stunned to move. Mona too? I had just had a drink with her, talked to her. We were going to have dinner. Willy took a menacing step toward me. "He said move."

I was in no position to argue. I did as I was told. Willy patted me down. Removing my jacket from a chair, he discovered my shoulder holster underneath. "Why, looky here, Joe." Willy tossed my .38 to Glasses. "Read him his rights." Willy pulled a pair of handcuffs out of his pocket and held them in front of me. "Turn around, buster," he ordered. "You're under arrest."

"What the hell do you clowns think you're doing?"

"Clowns, Joe. You hear that? This renegade big-time cop from Seattle thinks we're a couple of clowns."

"You have the right to remain silent—" Joe began.

"You guys have to be shitting me. Ray Johnson used to be my partner—"

"You have the right to an attorney—"

"And your uncle George sits on the Supreme Court. Right, funny-man?" Willy sneered.

"Anything you say may be held—"

"I said turn around," Willy repeated, his words taking on an ominous edge. I turned. The handcuffs snapped shut behind me. "Did you hear your rights now, Mr. Beaumont?" He gave the cuffs a sharp yank, making sure they were fastened securely.

"I heard them."

"Did you understand them?"

"Yes."

He spun me around so I faced him. "We wouldn't want any question of abrogating your rights, now would we?"

"You asshole—" I began.

He grabbed me by the shoulder and shoved me toward the door. "Where are your car keys?"

"Find them yourself," I snapped.

"Here they are, Willy," Glasses called from the dresser.

"Bring 'em. We'll check out the car on the way." They led me hand-cuffed through the front lobby of the Red Lion, where several dozen women watched in openmouthed wonder.

I've arrested plenty of people in my time, but being arrested was an entirely new and painful experience. Handcuffed wrists in the small of the back make you feel humiliated and trapped and scared and guilty, even if you're not. I wanted to hide my face in my hands, to shield myself from gaping, prying eyes. I couldn't, not with my hands cuffed behind me.

I had parked the Rabbit near the front door. Now it was nowhere to be seen.

"Where is it?" Willy demanded.

"I don't know. It's gone. Somebody moved it."

Glasses and Fatso nodded at each other knowingly. "Sure they did," Willy said. "What kind of car is it?"

"A Rabbit, a red, rented Rabbit."

"Sounds about right," Willy said. "Bring the car, Joe. We'll drive around through the parking lot and see if Mr. Beaumont here can remember where he left it. Musta been driving in his sleep."

Maybe the reason cops hate reporters and vice versa is that we're so much alike. The same kind of questioning minds end up in both profes-sions. The difference lies in what we do with the answers.

It came as no surprise that the same thought process that had brought me to the Red Lion in search of Mona Larson would do the same for a reporter. Fate alone dictated that the reporter should be Maxwell Cole. He arrived just as Willy shoved me into the backseat of a patrol car, blue lights flashing. Cole almost walked past us, but then he spied me. "J. P." he yelped. "Hey, what's going on?"

I prayed we'd leave right then, but we didn't. Joe meandered through the well-lit parking lot, searching for my car. By the time we located the Rabbit in the back row of the lot, a noisy cortege of people had formed behind us. "That's it," I said, nodding toward the Rabbit.

Joe left the patrol car idling and sauntered over to it. Through the open door, I could hear a chorus of questions. Glasses ignored them. He knelt in front of the car and examined the front bumper, then he stopped long enough to peer into all the windows. He hurried back to the patrol car. "Hand me the pliers, Willy."

With my key, Glasses unlocked the door on the rider's side. He used the pliers to lift the latch and open the door. I was grateful for that. At least he wasn't disturbing my evidence. He leaned into the Rabbit, then straightened and came back to the patrol car. "Call for a backup, Willy. Tell them to get someone to impound the car while we drag our friend here off to jail."

"Why? What have you got?"

"Remember the desk clerk told us she was wearing a bunch of Indian jewelry?"

"Yeah."

"Looks like it's all there, and the front end is smashed all to shit."

"That's impossible! I tell you, I've been asleep in my room since seven o'clock."

"We've got you dead to rights, mister," Glasses said.

"I swear I didn't do it."

"Save it for the judge," he said.

We waited in the car interminable minutes until a second patrol car with flashing blue lights and a wailing siren worked its way through the onlookers.

By the time we got to the station, there was a crowd of reporters milling outside, with Maxwell Cole leading the pack. Many of the out-of-town newsies had decided to stay over, thus gaining admittance to the third media event of the day. When Willy opened the door, I didn't want to get out. My mouth was dry; my knees shook, not with fear so much as helpless rage and indignation.

"Get out," Willy commanded.

I didn't, couldn't. Willy grabbed me by the shoulder and bodily pulled me from the car. Again I wanted a shield, a sack, a cloak of invisibility—

anything to lock out the eyes and the cameras and the voices and the nightmare. Willy and Joe herded me into the station and handed me over to a woebegone detective named Barnes.

Barnes struck me as a detective's detective, an old-time cop who used common sense as opposed to some computerized procedural manual. He brought me a Styrofoam cup of bitter coffee. "They read you your rights?" I nodded. Over his voice, in the background, I could hear the demanding questions of the reporters who were laying siege to the Pasco City Police Department.

Barnes cocked his ear as if listening to the uproar outside. "You want to tell me what happened?"

How could I tell him what happened when I didn't know? Mona Larson was dead, but I didn't know how or why or where. "Where do you want me to start?"

"How long did you know Mrs. Larson?"

"I just met her this afternoon."

"At her husband's funeral?"

"No, later, when she came back to the hotel, after the funeral."

"You followed her?" It was a leading question.

"Yes."

"You went to her room?"

"No. I called her, from my room. We met for a drink."

"Why?"

"To talk."

"About?"

"Sig, her husband."

"You knew him, then?"

The questions were getting worse. So were the answers. "No. Not until after he was murdered."

Barnes' eyes glittered with that now-we're-getting-somewhere look. I recognized it. I've used it myself during interrogations. "After?"

"I heard a woman screaming from my room at the Rosario Resort on Orcas Island. I checked it out and found Ginger Watkins with Sig Larson's body. I've been working unofficially with Hal Huggins, the detective from Friday Harbor. Call and ask him. It's the San Juan County Sheriff's Department."

"I probably will give him a call," Barnes said reasonably. "After we finish here. So you met Mrs. Larson for a drink, in the bar?"

"Yes. I think it's called the Star Light Lounge."

"And you talked about?"

"I don't remember exactly . . . her marriage, Welton, her stepchildren. Lots of things. Then she had to leave."

"Did you go with her?"

"No."

"Follow her?"

"No. I told you, I went back to my room for a nap."

"Come on, Detective Beaumont. Let's get to the bottom of this. Did you and Mrs. Larson quarrel about something?" His position solidified. Up till then, I had answered his questions in a warily cooperative fashion, but something in his manner shifted, warning me. Before, I had believed we were on the same side. It was now clear that we weren't.

"Where's Ray Johnson?" I asked.

"The Chief? What business is that of yours?"

"Call him," I said flatly. "Ray and I used to be partners on the force in Seattle."

I could tell my words made some impact. Barnes got up and walked across the room, hands deep in his pockets. "Mrs. Larson was deliberately run down by a man driving a red car. Witnesses saw a Rabbit leaving the scene. Aren't you driving a red Rabbit?"

I didn't answer. He walked back across the room and looked down at me accusingly. "So what have you got against the parole board, Detective Beaumont? Did they let out a crook you thought should have stayed locked up?"

"I'm trying to tell you—"

"You've been on the scene of two recent homicides before this one." He picked up a newspaper that had been lying facedown on his desk. "Not only that, Mrs. Watkins died in your car, a red Porsche. How come you like red so much?"

"Call Ray Johnson, for chrissake! He'll vouch for me."

"The chief is unavailable. He and his wife are celebrating their twenty-fifth wedding anniversary with a second honeymoon in Spokane. I'm not calling him for anybody."

"What about Hal Huggins, the detective over in Friday Harbor?" I struggled to restrain my temper.

Barnes smiled indulgently, as if I were a not-too-bright kid who had screwed up some simple directions. "If you want to call somebody, I'd suggest you call your attorney, not a character witness. You want to use the phone?"

"No, I don't want to use the phone. I want out."

His smile disappeared. "I don't believe you understand, Mr. Beaumont. You're being booked on an open charge of murder."

The words filled the room, sucking out the atmosphere. It was suddenly difficult to breathe. "You're right," I said, caving in, "I want to use the phone." I tried Peters first. No dice. He was in The Dalles, with Ames, for the custody hearing. I didn't know where they were staying.

It's easy to panic in a situation like that, to decide that you're totally isolated and there's no way to get help. I finally dialed Ida Newell's number, collect. Ida, my next-door neighbor, is a retired schoolteacher, the proverbial little old lady in tennis shoes. She collects crossword puzzles for me and mothers me as much as I'll tolerate. It was ten-thirty, but she stays up late to watch the news.

"Why, Beau," she said pleasantly, once the operator connected us. "Where are you?"

I didn't entirely answer that question. "I need your help, Ida. I've got to get in touch with my partner and my attorney. I won't be able to call out after this. Could you please find them and give them a message?"

"Certainly." Thankfully, she didn't ask any questions.

"Their names are Ron Peters and Ralph Ames. They're staying somewhere in The Dalles."

"Where?"

"I don't know."

"Look here, Beau, if you don't know where they're staying, how do you expect me to find them?"

I wanted to bully her to action, but I fought to keep impatience out of my voice. "They'll be at the best hotel or motel in town. Try the phone book, the Yellow Pages."

Ida sounded dubious. "If I find them, what do I say?"

"Have Ames call me." I glanced at Barnes, who nodded reluctantly. I read her the number off the phone.

"That's all?"

"Tell him it's urgent."

"Well, all right."

"Thanks, Ida. You've no idea how much I appreciate this."

I put down the phone. Twenty minutes later, after fingerprints and a mug shot, I was locked up in a cell. Out of deference to my being a police officer, they gave me a private cell.

It was small consolation.

CHAPTER 20

I slept. I don't know how, but I did. Maybe when you're up against something you can do absolutely nothing about, sleep is Mother Nature's balm for the insoluble problem. I slept, blissfully ignorant of what went on around me. Everyone told me about it. Later.

Through the wonders of modern telecommunications, old J. P. Beaumont hit the eleven o'clock news on every major television station in the Pacific Northwest—Spokane, Seattle, Portland, and Boise. The lead story was all about Seattle's rogue cop being booked into Pasco City Jail on an open charge of murder. It made for very splashy journalism and pushed Sig Larson's funeral back to just before Sports.

As far as the press was concerned, my guilt was a foregone conclusion. Not everyone had access to the kind of material Maxwell Cole did. They had to content themselves with only the immediate story. Max sat down and composed an in-depth piece that he transferred by modem to the *P.I.* in downtown Seattle. He dredged it all out of his fertile memory—the kid in the alley when I was a rookie, Anne Corley, Ginger dead in my Porsche. His column would have done the *National Enquirer* proud.

I slept.

Peters saw the story on a Portland station in The Dalles. He dialed Ames' number and found it busy. Ida Newell had just reached Ames at the Papadera Inn, The Dalles' only Best Western motel. Peters came to Ames' room while Ralph was still talking to Ida. Before the news was over, Ames and Peters were checked out of their rooms and driving hell-bent-for-leather to Tri Cities.

I sawed logs. It's called the sleep of the just.

In the bridal suite of Spokane's Ridpath Hotel, Evie Johnson fell asleep while Ray congratulated himself on his performance, not bad for twenty-five years of marriage. He could still hold his own in the bedroom department.

With Evie drowsing contentedly beside him, he switched the TV on low. He'd watch the news for a couple of minutes. He woke Evie scrambling out of bed. She sat up as he pulled on his clothes.

"Where are you going?" she demanded.

"I've gotta go, hon," he said. "You stay here. I'll leave the car so you can come home tomorrow."

"Why? What's wrong?"

"Someone back home lost his marbles and arrested Beau for first-degree murder."

"Can't you call?"

"I can't knock heads over the phone."

By the time Ray was ready, Evie had called the airport and discovered that the last plane for Tri Cities left at ten fifty-five. She dressed quickly, throwing things into the suitcase. "I'll go with you," she told him. "There's no sense in staying here alone."

And still I slept.

San Juan County Sheriff Bill Yates woke Hal Huggins out of a sound sleep. "What the hell is going on?"

"How should I know?"

"I rented a float plane. He'll put you down on the Columbia. Get over to Pasco and find out."

So Hal Huggins, too, began a midnight trek to Tri Cities while I slept on, dreaming I was slicing off one of Maxwell Cole's gaudy ties with a huge pinking shears. No wonder I didn't want to wake up.

Ray hit town first. He came roaring into the jail, waking everybody, including a couple of drunks in the next cell who complained bitterly about being disturbed. "Why the hell didn't someone call me? I could have told you . . ." he shouted over his shoulder as he came down the hall. I could see Barnes hovering at a discreet distance.

"Come on, come on," he growled as the jailer fumbled with the key. "Open up, you nitwit!"

I swung off my cot and slipped into the plastic slippers that had replaced my shoes. I was wearing a bright orange jail jumpsuit that was more than slightly too short in the crotch and, as a consequence, more than moderately uncomfortable.

"Where the hell are his clothes?" Ray rumbled at Barnes. "Go get 'em."

Barnes disappeared down the hall. Ray hurried into the cell as the door opened. "Are you all right, Beau?"

"Sure, Ray. I'm fine. It was a mistake, that's all."

"Why the hell didn't you call me?"

"They said you were celebrating your twenty-fifth anniversary and couldn't be disturbed."

"I'm disturbed, all right! You can bet your ass I'm disturbed!"

Ray hustled me down the hall and into a restroom where Barnes brought me my clothes. "How did you hear about it?" I asked.

"It was on the news. At eleven."

"Where, in Spokane?"

"That's where I saw it, but I'll bet it was all over. You should see the mob of reporters outside right now. The place is crawling."

"Great," I muttered. "That's just great."

He led me into his office, a place not much bigger than the cubbyhole the two of us had shared in the Public Safety Building in Seattle. This one boasted a polished wooden desk, not the institutional gray/green metal of Seattle P.D.

"Where is Evie?" I asked. "I'll bet she's pissed."

Ray grinned. "She was until she found out it was you. She drove back with me. Evangeline always had a soft spot in her heart for you, Beau. There's no accounting for taste. You hungry?" he asked.

Once he reminded me, I was actually far beyond hunger. "Starved," I told him.

He picked up the phone and dialed a number. I heard a phone ringing somewhere outside. "Go pick up a couple of chili-burgers from Marie's," he barked into the phone. "Tell her they're for me, with extra cheese and onions. And make a new pot of coffee. We're going to be a while."

He leaned back in his chair and folded his hands across his gradually widening girth. "What the hell is going on?"

Partway into my story, there was a knock on the door. A pretty young woman entered, carrying two steaming platters of chili-burgers. She left us with them and went out, returning with two freshly brewed cups of coffee. "Thanks, LeAnn," Ray murmured as she set a mug in front of him. LeAnn flashed him a shy smile.

"See there?" He grinned once the door closed behind her. "Around here I get some respect."

The two platters contained burgers smothered with thick chili, melted cheese, and chunks of chopped onions. Ray took a bite, followed by a sip of coffee. "Reminds me of the Doghouse," he said. "Sometimes I really miss that old place."

The Doghouse is a restaurant a few blocks from my condo in Seattle. Ray and I frequented it the whole time we were partners. I go there less often now that Peters and I work together.

I was ravenous. We had barely made a dent in the two platters when we heard a commotion outside. Ray's phone rang. "What is it?" He listened, then held the phone away from his ear and covered the mouthpiece.

"Somebody named Ames. Says he's your attorney."

"Ames! Ida must have found him."

"You want to see him?"

"Sure."

"And a guy named Peters?"

"Him too."

LeAnn opened the door. Ames strode purposefully into the room, talking as he came. "Look here, Chief Johnson, I demand to see my client at once!" Ames stopped abruptly when he spotted me sitting with a plate on top of Ray's desk scarfing down chili-burger as fast as I could shovel. Peters, directly behind Ames, almost rear-ended him.

"What the hell!" Peters exclaimed. The looks on their faces would have been comical if they hadn't been so serious. They had broken speed laws in two states, driving through the night to rescue me from jail, only to find me happily chowing down with the Chief of Police.

I stood up, wiping my mouth with a napkin. "Ralph, I'd like you to meet my former partner, Chief Ray Johnson. Ray, this is Ralph Ames, my attorney, and my new partner, Detective Ron Peters."

"You guys hungry?" Ray asked, indicating the half-consumed chili-burgers. "We could order a couple more. It would only take a minute."

Peters stifled a shudder of disgust and shook his head. Ames said a polite "no thank you" and got straight to the point. "What's going on?"

So I started the story again, from the beginning. I had reached almost the same point where Ames and Peters had made their entrance when the phone rang again. "No lie? He's here?" Ray said. "Send him in."

Hal Huggins came in. Ray showered him with the effusive cordiality one reserves for a late arrival at a class reunion. Once pleasantries were exchanged, the story reverted to square one. I was beginning to wish I had taped it on the first go down so I could turn on a machine and listen to it, rather than repeating it again and again. When I finally finished, there was a long silence.

Huggins spoke first. "I didn't figure him to be that smart," he said.

"Who?" I demanded. Obviously, Huggins knew something the rest of us didn't.

"Wilson. Don Wilson."

"Why him?" Peters asked.

"The calendar," Hal answered. "Ginger Watkins' calendar. Beau found it in a garbage can up at Rosario Sunday night. Wilson's prints are all over it."

"Where'd you get a copy of his prints?" I asked.

"From the F.B.I. Wilson served in the army."

Ray looked dubious. "How'd you get an F.B.I. report back so fast? Those things take months."

"You forget. Parole board members are political appointees. Governor Reynolds placed a call to the White House, and the F.B.I. found his prints in short order."

"So it is Wilson after all," I mused.

"Looks that way," Huggins agreed. "I'm getting a search warrant today." He turned on me. "You're sure he wasn't at the funeral?"

"I'm sure. Believe me, I looked."

Huggins was thinking aloud. "I wonder if we could request any of the television videotape and have someone go over it looking for him."

"Could be," Ray agreed. "Some of them are pretty good about it."

Hal continued. "He had to be there, must have followed you to the Red Lion. He saw you meet Mona Larson and decided to add one more notch to his scorecard. And frame you in the process."

I thought back on my drive into Pasco. I could remember no cars on the road behind me, but I hadn't been looking. I shook my head. "I didn't see any," I said. "But why frame me? It doesn't make sense."

"Muddy the water a little," Huggins suggested. Peters nodded in agreement.

"Had you told anyone that you planned to stay overnight in Pasco?" Ray's homicide instincts were still good, even though he had kicked himself upstairs.

"No. How could I have told someone? I didn't make up my mind until I was almost here and decided to see you."

"Either he followed you or knew where Mona was staying," Peters put in. "How did you find out?"

"I asked one of the limo drivers over in Welton."

"And they told you?"

"They didn't act as if it was any big secret."

The phone rang again. Ray answered. "Put it through," he said. He switched on the speakerphone on his desk.

"Is this Chief Johnson?" a voice asked.

"Yes."

"This is Lee Hawkins. I'm an aide to Governor Reynolds. We're just confirming that you have a suspect in custody in the deaths of Mona and Sig Larson."

"We do not have a suspect."

"But we were told—" There was a pause. "What about Ginger Watkins? We understand her death has been reclassified as a homicide."

"I repeat. We do not have a suspect in custody. In fact, I'll be calling a press conference at seven." Ray paused, turning his chair to consult an old pendulum clock that hung on the wall behind him. In Roman numerals the clock said the time was six-eighteen. "I'll be issuing the Pasco Police Department's official apology to Detective J. P. Beaumont."

"But the paper said—" Hawkins began.

"The paper's wrong," Ray interjected. "They often are, you know. Detective Beaumont is not a suspect in any of the cases, and we have no one else in custody."

"But the governor is ready to announce that he is withdrawing protection from the parole board."

"He's better retract that withdrawal," Ray said into the phone. "In fact, if I were him, I think I'd extend protection to all parole board family members as well."

I waved a hand to get Ray's attention. "Ask him about the victim/witness protection program."

Ray shot me a questioning look, then shrugged. "Someone here is asking about the victim/witness protection program." I mouthed my question to Ray, and he repeated it into the phone. "Someone wants to know when it will be ready."

Hawkins knew exactly what we were talking about. "Tell him not until the next legislative session convenes in January."

"Is that all you need to know?" Ray asked me.

I nodded. Ray put down the phone. "What's that all about?"

"Maxwell Cole said Wilson thought an announcement on that program was imminent."

"Doesn't sound like it to me," Ray replied, getting up and opening the door. "LeAnn, let the members of the press know that I'll be holding a press conference at seven A.M. In the city council chamber."

He turned back inside the room, grinning. "You know," he said, "I think I'm actually going to enjoy this one."

CHAPTER 21

W e did enjoy the press conference. For once we caught the media absolutely flat-footed. When I walked to the podium with Ray, you could have heard a pin drop.

Ray Johnson went straight to the microphones as naturally as if he had been doing it all his life. In ten months he had indeed become a police chief rather than a homicide detective. He was totally at ease.

"Before I issue my statement, I want to introduce you to some guests. On my right is Detective J. P. Beaumont of Seattle P.D. Next to him is Ralph Ames, Mr. Beaumont's personal attorney. Next to him is Detective Hal Huggins of the San Juan County Sheriff's Department.

"What I have to say is short and sweet. The City of Pasco and its Police Department deeply regret that Detective Beaumont here was mistakenly arrested as a suspect in the murder of Mona Larson. We wish to express our sincere apology for any inconvenience this may have caused.

"We are pursuing several leads in the Larson case and are, in fact, working on a major suspect. I repeat, Detective Beaumont is not that suspect. My understanding is that, after consulting his attorney, Detective Beaumont has agreed not to press false-arrest charges against this jurisdiction. However, some legal action may be contemplated. I believe Mr. Ames will be speaking to that issue. Mr. Ames?" He yielded the platform to Ralph.

Ralph Ames looks unassuming. He dresses conservatively and well, but he's a real tiger in negotiations or in court. He stepped to the bank of microphones.

"Thank you, Chief Johnson. Yes, I have advised my client that false-arrest proceedings would be ill-advised. However, in the next few days we will be reviewing all media coverage of my client's arrest to determine whether we have grounds for defamation of character or libel suits in conjunction with media treatment of the incident. It's possible some of the reports were in fact libelous."

Ames sat down, leaving the hall in utter silence. I happened to be looking directly at Maxwell Cole when Ames made his pronouncement. Max blanched visibly, his complexion turning a pukey shade of green.

Ray resumed the microphone. "Any questions?"

There were none immediately. No one was eager to leap into the breach. Eventually, one brave soul near the back tentatively raised his hand. "Do you believe there's a connection between Mona Larson's death and that of her husband?"

I could see Ray's smile coming a mile away. "No comment," he said.

"I understand the governor has now extended State Patrol protection to all family members of the parole board as well as to board members themselves. Is that true?"

"You'll have to ask Governor Reynolds about that."

"Can you tell us why Detective Huggins is here?"

Ray turned to Hal. "Hal," he said, "would you care to answer that?"

We were having a good time. I could see Peters in the back of the room with a broad grin plastered across his face.

"No comment," Hal said.

That got the message across. The reporters could see we were having fun at their expense. There were no more questions.

"Well then," Ray announced, "I guess we're finished."

We left the council chambers together. Back in Ray's office, we couldn't help chortling. We milled around for a few minutes, deciding on the next move. Ames and Peters had been up all night; they were worn out. They wanted to use my room at the Red Lion for a nap. My rented car had been impounded, pending investigation. The crime lab agreed to release it to Avis when they were done with it.

Peters left Ames and me in the station lobby and walked two blocks to get his Datsun. For the first time I noticed how haggard and drawn Ames looked. He was weary beyond words. "You look like hell," I said.

"You wouldn't win any prizes yourself," he returned, his voice cracking with exhaustion, now that his press conference adrenaline had worn off. He flopped down in one of the brown leather waiting-room chairs, resting his head on the wall behind him.

"We lost." His voice was low. I almost didn't hear him. It took a minute for me to realize what he was saying. At last I tumbled. "The custody hearing?"

He nodded. "We got an old-fashioned, dyed-in-the-wool conservative judge who figures only mothers are fit to raise children. No matter what."

I dropped into the chair beside him, chagrined that I hadn't given the custody hearing a moment's thought. I had never seen Ames so down. He's usually the steady one, the eye of the hurricane.

"I'm sorry," I murmured. "How's Peters taking it?" I felt responsible. Peters had pretty much given up the idea of ever getting his kids back until I butted in, encouraged him to fight for them, and told him we'd turn the problem over to Ames. I had watched Peters' hopes rise as the custody hearing neared. Now all that hope had come to nothing.

"Not well," Ames said. He looked at me closely. "Have you ever seen those two girls of his?"

I shook my head. "He was divorced long before we started working together."

"They're cute as buttons, both of them, and they were ecstatic to see him."

"What happens now?"

"I don't know. I need to think about it. The New Dawn attorney made a couple of broad hints, but I'm not sure he's on the level."

Peters pulled up outside and honked. We went out. Ames crawled into the backseat while I slipped into the front with Peters. While we had been involved with the reporters, his face had been animated, alive. Now a morose mask covered his handsome features.

"I'm sorry about the hearing," I said.

He put the car in gear. "Win some, lose some," he said, feigning nonchalance. It didn't work.

"But the girls are all right?" I insisted.

"Sure," he flared. "They can't have shots because shots show a lack of faith. They live on a diet of brown rice and fruit. Milk is a luxury. They have it once a week. On Sundays." Peters' anger played itself out. He fell silent.

"So what do we do now, coach?" I asked, turning to Ames in the backseat.

He shook his head. "I don't know. We took our best shot. I'll have to see what other avenues are open." Ames didn't elaborate, and silence lengthened in the little car.

"Thanks for coming to get me, you guys," I said. "Both of you."

"It's okay," Peters responded. "My turn will come."

Peters and Ames went up to my room to get some sleep. I was wide-awake. I went down to the lobby. On one of the lobby chairs I found an abandoned P.I. Curiosity got the better of me, overcoming my natural aversion to newspapers. I wanted to see what had made Maxwell Cole turn green when Ames mentioned libel suits. By picking up a discarded paper, I could read the column without giving them the satisfaction of paying for it.

Max used the words "rogue cop" over and over. He might have coined the expression himself. The story didn't contain much that was different from the other garbage he's written about me over the years, except for the Mona Larson allegations.

I had a feeling this was one instance where Max's retraction would receive prominent coverage. If I were in his shoes and thought Ralph Ames was coming after me with a libel suit, I'd be looking for cover.

I did pick up one other piece of useful information from reading the newspaper. Ginger Watkins' funeral would be held on Thursday afternoon. No time or place was given, but included in the brief announcement was Ginger Watkins' father's name. He was listed as a resident of Centralia. Tucking that tidbit away in the memory bank, I worked the crossword puzzle in ten minutes flat. For me, that was something of a record.

My presence in the lobby created a continuing stir. Mary Kay ladies sporting May Kay nametags and Mary Kay faces wandered by, staring openly. When I finished the puzzle, I approached the desk and asked if I could use a house phone to bill some calls to my room. The clerk, a sweet young thing with long blond hair, dropped her pen when I announced who I was.

"I'll have to check," she stammered, retreating into a back office. She returned a few minutes later. "Mr. Dixon says that will be fine," she gulped.

I smiled. "If anyone asks, tell them I was framed."

She nodded, wide-eyed, and said, "Thank you." She was so flustered she forgot to tell me to have a nice day.

I gave the hotel operator my room information, and asked Centralia Information for Tom Lander's number.

"The number is 763-4427."

I hung up and dialed. There was no answer. I dialed Information again. I'm a longtime believer in the old phone-factory adage, "Let your fingers do the walking," except mine walk straight to directory assistance. This time I asked for a Union 76 station. Again I dialed.

A man answered, an older man whose voice was deep and whose speech was slow. "Tom's Seventy-six. Tom speaking."

"My name is J. P. Beaumont. I'm a friend of Ginger's. I wanted to let you know how sorry I am."

"Thanks." There was a pause. I could hear him struggling to gain control. "It was your car she was driving, wasn't it?" he asked.

I was surprised that he recognized my name. "That's right," I told him. "I understand the funeral is tomorrow afternoon."

"Yes," he said. "Two o'clock."

"I tried calling Darrell but was told the services will be private. I was sorry to hear that. I'd very much like to attend. Do you think that's possible?"

"Far as I'm concerned. I don't know where those characters get off making it private. Funerals should have lots of people. It shows folks care."

"Where is it? The paper didn't say."

"Two o'clock in the Congregational Church downtown. In the chapel."

"Could I come as your guest?"

"Sure."

"I'll meet you at the church. About one forty-five."

"How will I know you?"

"I'll be able to find you," I told him.

"If anybody tries to stop you, tell 'em Tom Lander said you could come."

The next call was to a florist in the Denny Regrade near my apartment. I ordered a bouquet of flowers for Ginger Watkins from Sig Larson. While I was at it, I called a Pasco florist and ordered flowers for Mona Larson, too. I told the clerk to check with the Pasco Police Department to see where and when they should be sent.

She took my credit-card number and wanted to know what to put on the card.

"Sign the card 'A friend,'" I told her, and let it go at that.

I hoped like hell it would be the last batch of flowers I'd be ordering for a while.

CHAPTER 22

It was pouring rain the morning of Ginger Watkins' funeral, the kind of hard, driving rain that demands umbrellas and confirms for unfortunate tourists that everything they say about Seattle's weather is true.

I rummaged through a closet searching for my one battered umbrella, a fold-up relic with two broken ribs and a bent handle. I hardly ever use it. Seattle's rain is usually no more than a misty drip, a dry drizzle that seldom merits use of what Seattleites fondly refer to as "bumbershoots," otherwise known as umbrellas.

Ames settled into the Westin Hotel. He had work to do and didn't want to be disturbed. Peters went back to the department where one of our Battered Wife/Dead Husband cases was about to come to trial. He spent the day locked up in a series of depositions.

J. P. Beaumont, still on vacation, was left to his own devices. I stopped by to thank Ida Newell for tracking down Ames and Peters.

"I was glad to," she assured me. "Why, the way they wrote you up in the paper was criminal. Are you going to sue them? They deserve it, especially that columnist fellow."

"Ames is looking into it," I told her. "I will if he tells me."

Later, I went to get a haircut. Virgil has been my barber ever since I moved to the city. I've followed him from his first little hole-in-the-wall shop to gradually more prosperous surroundings. Now he's located in an attractive brick rehab on the corner of Third and Vine.

Busy, Virgil waved me into a chair to wait. "It's about time you came in here," he griped. "Saw you on TV, and I says to Betty, I says, wouldn't cha know he'd go and get himself on TV when he needs a haircut? Pray God he doesn't tell who cuts his hair, know what I mean?"

I knew exactly what he meant. I was long overdue. Getting haircuts was one of the things I had neglected in the previous months of malaise.

Virgil finished with a retiree from the Grosvenor House and beckoned me into the chair. "Saved all those articles from the paper for you," he said. "Figured if you was out of town, you might not get 'em, you know?"

"Thanks, Virgil."

"Understand your car got wrecked, too."

"They're working on it up at Orcas. I guess it'll be all right, eventually."

He clipped away, humming a country-western tune under his breath. I know enough about music to know he hummed very badly. When he finished, it was only eleven. I walked over to Seventh and stopped at the Doghouse, more for the company than the coffee. Doghouse regulars greeted me as a celebrity. After all, the idea of a cop gone bad is a real attention-grabber. I sat in a back corner booth and did some serious thinking.

About Sig and Ginger and Mona. I had never met Sig while he was alive, but his death had profoundly affected me. Ginger and Mona I knew briefly, only a matter of hours, before they too were dead. The three deaths plagued me, weighed me down. I kept going back to Mona and Ginger. Different, yes, but both young and vital, and both cut down. Something about the two of them nagged at the back of my mind, but I couldn't put my finger on it. The harder I tried to capture it, the more elusive it became.

The fingerprints accused Don Wilson, but where was he? How was he outmaneuvering all efforts to find him? Was he operating alone or with help? These were questions without answers; or if the answers were there, I couldn't see them.

I ambled back to my apartment and made myself a peanut butter sandwich. Sometimes, out of respect for Peters, I occasionally add sprouts to the peanut butter, but the plastic bag of sprouts in the vegetable drawer of my refrigerator had deteriorated to a vile greenish goo. With the sandwich and a glass of milk, I settled in my recliner and dialed the San Juan County Sheriff's Department.

I more than half expected to be told that Huggins was in Seattle attending a funeral. Instead, he answered.

"Hal? Beau here. You coming to Seattle for Ginger Watkins' funeral?"

"I was going to ask you to go, Beau. I'm up to my neck around here. Think you can swing it?"

"Sure. Homer tried to keep me away, saying Senator Watkins wanted a small, private ceremony, but I got my name on the guest list anyway."

"How'd you manage that?"

"Her father invited me. As his guest."

Hal clicked his tongue. "Homer won't like that." I was sure that was true.

"I take it you've had a couple run-ins with the old man?"

"Like running into a brick wall. I've tried to talk to the husband, and he's stonewalled me at every turn."

"Homer has?"

"Yes, goddammit. Homer."

"Any word on Wilson?"

"Hell no."

"Keep me posted if you hear anything, Hal."

"Sure thing. The search warrant didn't come through yesterday. I'm hoping for this afternoon. And Beau?"

"What?"

"You do the same. If anything turns up at the funeral, give me a call."

I dressed and walked down Fifth to University. The Congregational Church is located at the corner of Sixth and University. The tiny chapel at the south end of the building pinch-hits as a downtown Catholic chapel for weekday noontime business Masses. Ecumenism is alive and well and living in Seattle.

Taking up a position in the lobby of the Park Place building across the street, I watched as people arrived or were dropped off at the church. The first black limo accompanied by two state patrolmen deposited Homer and his illustrious son, Senator Darrell Watkins. The second limo, also with an armed guard, brought Governor Reynolds.

When the third, unattended by official motorcycles dropped off an older, nondescript man who paused uncertainly on the sidewalk, I left my vantage across the street and approached him.

"Are you Tom Lander?" I asked.

"Mr. Beaumont?" he returned, his tone doubtful.

"Yes." Relief passed over his face. We shook hands. He looked down at his old-fashioned suit and dusted an imaginary fleck of lint from his arm.

"Big cities make me nervous," he said uncomfortably.

Homer materialized out of nowhere. "Hello, Tom," he said, elbowing me aside. "They're ready for us now." He scowled at me, trying to place me. "This is a private service, Mr.—"

"Beaumont," I supplied.

"It's all right, Homer," Tom said. "He's with me."

Homer Watkins gave Tom a constrained nod. "Very well," he said, walking stiffly toward the church. Tom Lander and I followed. The chapel couldn't have held more than forty people. An usher showed Tom to a front-row seat, while I took one near the door.

As people came in, I realized Peters would have recognized the political personalities from their pictures. I was an outsider, with no program or scorecard. My only hope of identifying the various guests was to lay hands on the guest book in the vestibule.

I did recognize the parole board, however. Led by Madame Bowdeen, they appeared far more nervous than they had been in Welton. Pressure was taking its toll. Had I been in their shoes, I would have been nervous, too. Looking around, however, I could have assured them with reasonable accuracy that Don Wilson was nowhere to be seen.

A young, bearded minister conducted the service in a smooth, professional way, telling us that Ginger Watkins was a person who had found herself in service to others. His comments made me hope that maybe he had at least a passing acquaintance with the lady.

As the eulogy began, my eyes were drawn to Darrell Watkins' heaving shoulders. He sat in the front row head bowed, silent sobs wracking his body. Next to him Tom Lander reached over and laid a consoling hand across his grieving son-in-law's shoulder.

I can stand anything but hypocrisy. Darrell was making an obvious play for sympathy, and Tom Lander fell for it—comforting the asshole who had screwed around on his daughter the whole time they were married, who had never bothered to give her the smallest satisfaction in lovemaking, who had kept her locked in a confining, stifling marriage, trotting her out on command when his rising political star demanded the display of a pretty wife.

It put a lump in my throat to realize I had given Ginger more pleasure by accident than that whining bastard had in eighteen years of marriage. I didn't hear the rest of the service. I seethed, watching Darrell's bitter, remorseful, crocodile tears. Too little too late. When the pallbearers carried the white coffin out the door, Darrell followed, his face contorted with anguish, supported on one side by Homer and on the other by Tom.

"That son of a bitch," I muttered to myself. I don't think anyone heard me.

Outside, people milled on the sidewalk, waiting for the funeral cortege to form and lead us to Woodlawn Cemetery. I paused as long as I could over the guest book, mentally noting as many names as possible. Then I waited by Tom's limo, expecting to tell him good-bye. Instead, he asked me to come along, to ride to the cemetery with him.

I didn't particularly want to go, but it was hard to refuse the old man. He was so isolated and alone that, in the end, I went.

We rode in silence. I was still seething over the funeral, and Tom seemed lost in thought. I stayed in the car during the graveside ceremony, refusing to be an audience to any more theatrics on Darrell's part. I used the time to jot down as many names as I could remember from the guest book. Once we started downtown, I had myself fairly well in hand.

"What now?" I asked, initiating conversation.

Tom shrugged. "Darrell said I was welcome to come over to the house, but I don't know. I don't feel comfortable with all those mucky-mucks."

"Do you know most of those people?" I asked.

"No."

"How about a cup of coffee before you decide?"

He seemed to welcome the delay. He nodded. "That would be real nice."

The limo driver raised a disapproving eyebrow when I dismissed him, telling him to drop us at the Doghouse. I knew Tom would be far more at home there than in the rarefied atmosphere of the Four Seasons-Olympic or the Westin. He settled gratefully into a booth and smiled when the waitress, calling me by name, brought a coffee pot with the menus.

"I guess even big-city folks can be friendly," he said.

"This is my neighborhood, Tom. I live just a few blocks from here."

We both ordered coffee. I watched Tom shovel three teaspoons of sugar into his cup. "How did you know Ginger?" he asked, stirring absently.

"I only met her the day before she died," I said quietly, "but she helped me, more than I can say. She talked me through a problem I had been avoiding for months. I had to go today. I owed her."

"Ginger was like that," he said. He smiled sadly. "Always ready to help the other guy, always a friend in need. She was the kind of kid who dragged home broken-winged birds and expected me to fix them." He paused. "They mostly died," he added. He stared disconsolately into his cup. "Did you know about the drinking?" he asked.

His question jarred me. "Yes."

"I thought she had beaten it. Sig Larson helped her. What made her start again?"

"I don't know." I didn't have a clue. I ached for him as he pondered Ginger's death. His child's death. Why had she died drunk? Someone had neglected to tell him that her death had been reclassified as a homicide, and I figured it wasn't my place to tell him. That was up to Hal Huggins.

"There was some gossip about them, you know," Tom continued, "Sig and Ginger. But I never put any store in it. Ginger wasn't like that."

"No," I agreed. "I'm sure she wasn't." The topic made me very uneasy. "Did you know she intended to file for a divorce?"

"She wouldn't have," he answered with firm conviction. "She might have threatened, to get Darrell to shape up, but she wouldn't have left him. We Landers hang in there. It's a family tradition."

I wanted to say that Ginger had hung in there more than long enough but I didn't. That would have been kicking him while he was down. Besides, it would have given away too much about Ginger and J. P. Beaumont. Better to let sleeping dogs lie. As far as Tom Lander was concerned, Ginger Watkins and I had been just friends. Nothing more.

"Do you want to go to the house?" I asked.

"Would you come along?" he countered.

He needed an ally, and I was it. "Why not?" I said, rising. "Between the two of us, we should be able to handle that bunch."

We took a cab to the motel where Tom was staying, then we drove to Darrell Watkins' Capitol Hill mansion in a GMC pickup with "Tom's Union 76" emblazoned on the door.

CHAPTER 23

The Watkins mansion sits atop Capitol Hill with a spectacular view of downtown Seattle and Puget Sound. At the base of the hill, Interstate 5 bisects the city. As we rounded the circular driveway and drove past a gurgling fountain, I could imagine Homer and Darrell sipping cocktails and watching the freeway turn to a parking lot each evening as commuters tried to go home.

"Who lives here?" I asked.

"Homer used to," Tom said, "but now he's moved into a condominium."

"This is where Ginger lived, then?"

"For about a year," Tom answered.

The mansion itself was a spacious white colonial, set in a manicured, parklike setting. By the time we arrived, the drive was already teeming with a variety of trendy late-model vehicles. Ginger had described the last few years as a struggle for financial survival. That was why she had gone to work for the parole board. These surroundings gave no hint of encroaching poverty.

"They bought this from Homer?"

Tom shrugged. "Ginger never talked to me about their private affairs. They used to live over there someplace." He gestured down the back of Capitol Hill. "Nice enough place, if you didn't need to find it in the dark."

We rang the bell, setting off a multinote chime. A uniformed maid opened the door. "Yes," she said in a truculent manner designed to frighten off gate-crashers.

"Tom Lander."

"Oh, yes, Mr. Lander." She stepped back, opening the door in welcome. "You're expected."

We entered a foyer with an intricate parquet floor and a magnificent chandelier that hung from a vaulted ceiling far above us. Polished mahogany handrails lined a circular staircase. From behind a closed door to our left came a murmur of voices. "This way, please," the maid told us.

As the door opened, we heard a small burst of laughter from a group of people gathered near a fireplace at the opposite end of an enormous room. To one side an arched doorway led into the dining room where a lavish buffet supper lay spread across a gleaming tabletop.

A scatter of twenty-five or thirty fashionably attired people chatted amiably over drinks and hors d'oeuvres. It would have made a wonderful cocktail party. Any relation to a funeral was purely coincidental.

Our host was nowhere in sight, but Homer broke away from the congenial group and came to meet us, a careful smile displayed on his face. "I'm glad you decided to come, Tom. You too, Mr. Beaumont. Care for a drink?"

"I'll have a beer," Tom said.

"MacNaughton's and water," I answered. Homer nodded to the maid, and she disappeared.

Gravely solicitous, Homer guided Tom toward the fireplace. I trailed behind. "Let me introduce you to some of the folks, Tom. There wasn't enough time at the church."

Several of the names were preceded by "Representative" or "Senator." Clearly this was more a gathering of Darrell's peers than it was one of Ginger's friends. I tried keeping track of names, attempting to remember only those I hadn't already gleaned from the guest book.

Senator George Berry and Representative Dean Rhodes. Ray Johnson always told me that the secret to remembering names was creating colorful word pictures using the names. I had seen him do it for years. I made a stab at it.

Rhodes and Berry. I imagined several roads and saw them intersecting at one giant strawberry. Representative Doris Winters. I covered the strawberry with a giant load of winter snow. Berry, Rhodes, Winters. So far, so good. Representative Larry Vukevich. Shit. Vukevich! Race car driver. Okay. Vukevich racing past the berry. Senator Toshiro Kobayashi. I gave up.

The maid handed me my MacNaughton's. I wandered away from the introductions to a chair beside a leaded-glass window. I needed Peters. He'd know all those people. The room was stifling. I belted that drink and ordered another when the maid walked past again.

The door at the end of the room opened, letting in a welcome rush of cool air. Darrell Watkins—accompanied by a handsome, smiling young brunette—entered the room. Tom's back was to the door. Homer, facing both Darrell and Tom, gave an almost imperceptible shake of his head over Tom's shoulder. Darrell caught the warning and spoke quietly to the woman, who melted smoothly into the crowd.

So this was the tender blossom, the competition Ginger had talked about, already marking her territory and claiming her prize. I downed my second MacNaughton's and sauntered over to where the brunette had settled on a green velvet love seat. She crossed her legs, revealing a rather lengthy stretch of shapely thigh.

"Would you like a drink?" I asked.

She smiled up at me. "Sure. Vodka tonic."

I found the maid and placed the order. "It's for the young woman over there, I forget her name."

"Miss Lacy," the maid supplied helpfully.

"I'll have another MacNaughton's," I said, returning my glass. Casually I meandered back to the sweet young thing on the love seat. "My name's Beau," I said. "You're Miss Lacy?"

"Darlene," she replied, smiling.

"Glad to meet you, Darlene. Mind if I sit down?"

"No." She moved to make room, demurely covering some of the visible thigh. "Are you a lobbyist?" she asked.

"No, I'm a friend of Ginger's."

"Oh," she said, a trifle too quickly.

I don't believe any of Ginger's friends had been expected.

"It's too bad about Ginger," Darlene continued. "I didn't know her personally, but everyone says she was a very nice person."

"She was," I replied.

The maid brought the drinks. Darlene sipped hers, eyes holding mine over the top of her glass.

"What do you do?" I asked.

"I'll go to Olympia in January. I'll be on staff, either with the lieutenant governor's office or the senate. It doesn't matter to me." She laughed. "A job's a job."

Homer caught sight of us sitting together and hastened toward the love seat. "Mr. Beaumont, I didn't mean to ignore you. Would you care for a sandwich, deviled eggs, salad?"

"No, thanks. I was just chatting with Miss Lacy here. She was telling me about her new job. Sounds like a good deal to me." I managed a hollow grin, hoping it adequately expressed my feelings on the subject.

"Have you met Darrell?" Homer asked.

"No," I replied. "Haven't had the pleasure." I took another belt of Mac-Naughton's—for luck, maybe. Or maybe because the room was uncommonly hot and I was very thirsty. I set my empty glass on a polished table and followed Homer to where Darrell was waxing eloquent with the lady from my memory word picture. Snow, I decided fuzzily. That was her name.

Homer caught Darrell's attention. "Darrell, this is Mr. Beaumont. It was his—"

Darrell turned toward me, his smile turning sallow. "Oh yes, Mr. Beaumont. I hope your Porsche isn't ruined."

"No. It'll be fine. It takes time. I wanted to express my condolences," I said.

"Thanks," he said, his face assuming the grieved air that had offended me at the funeral. "So nice of you to stop by." I resisted the temptation to smack that phony look right off his face. Homer steered Representative Snow away from us, leaving Darrell and me together. Darrell signaled the maid for two more drinks. "It's scary," he said, turning back to me. "First Sig, then Ginger, now Mona."

I was sure he knew all about Don Wilson. Considering the family's close ties to the governor's office, that was hardly surprising.

"I hope to God they catch that guy before he gets anyone else," Watkins continued.

"Me too," I said. "We usually do, sooner or later."

He gave me an appraising look. "We? Is Seattle P.D. involved too?" he asked.

"No, not officially. I'm here because Ginger and I were friends." The maid broke in to deliver drinks. My series of MacNaughton's had come in rapid enough succession that I was getting a little buzz.

"I don't recall her mentioning your name." It did my heart good to note the subtle shift in Darrell's manner, a wariness. I was something he didn't expect. How about that! Maybe Ginger had some secrets too, asshole. How d'you like them apples? The thoughts bubbled unspoken through my new glass of MacNaughton's.

"You can't tell about women," I said jokingly. "Ginger and I go back a long way. We ran into each other up at Orcas by accident; but then, life is full of little surprises, right?"

"Right," he replied lamely.

The door opened, and a new trio of people entered. Darrell excused himself to greet them. The room had grown more crowded. There were far more people sipping drinks than had been at the chapel earlier.

The coffee, the MacNaughton's, and the water asserted themselves. Searching for a restroom, I wandered into the kitchen, slipping through the swinging door when a maid carried a new tray of deviled eggs into the dining room.

The kitchen, massive and polished, was a combination of old and new. An ancient walk-in refrigerator covered one wall while, on the other side of the room, a long commercial dishwasher steamed under the hand of a heavyset woman rinsing a tray of plates. On a third wall sat a huge eight-burner range, while the middle of the room held a sleek stainless steel worktable laden with food. The woman looked up from the dishwasher and saw me at the doorway. "Can I help you?" she demanded.

"I'm looking for a restroom."

"No restrooms here," she stated flatly. "Upstairs. On the right."

Chastised, I retreated the way I had come, threading my way through the chatting guests to the foyer and up the stairs. A dizzying trip up the circular stairway convinced me I had had too much to drink. The first likely-looking door I found was locked. I tried the next door. Bingo.

I had already flushed and was splashing my face with cool water in an effort to sober up when I heard voices in the hall outside. I'm sure it never occurred to anyone that a guest might have ventured all the way upstairs in search of a restroom. I opened the door and stepped into the hall. "It looks great, Darrell," a voice was saying from a room farther up the corridor. "The fact that it was private makes it that much better."

"That's what we pay you for, Sam." I recognized Darrell Watkins' voice. "That's what a campaign manager is supposed to do."

"Name familiarity's way up, up five points over last week. That's a tremendous change this late in the campaign. I'd say you have it in the bag."

"I'd better get back downstairs. Leave that paper up here when you go," Darrell said. "We wouldn't want Tom to stumble across it before he leaves."

I was standing outside the door when Darrell Watkins stepped into the hall. He almost ran over me.

"You son of a bitch!" I muttered.

"What are you doing up here?"

"Taking a leak," I said.

"I think maybe you'd better go, Mr. Beaumont."

"I'll go when I'm good and ready, asshole."

Another man appeared behind Darrell, a young blond man in casual clothes who looked as if he had just stepped out of a racquet club advertisement. Behind both of them stood the newly hired Darlene Lacy.

"Who's this, Darrell?" the other man asked.

I answered. "The name's Beaumont, Detective J. P. Beaumont, Seattle P.D." I was riding a boozy wave of moral indignation. "So you ran a poll, did you?" I sneered. "Figured the voters would like it better if you made it look quiet and dignified. That's how Ginger said you'd handle the divorce, too."

"I don't know what you're talking about."

"Oh yes you do. You got the newspapers to bury the story, but Ginger was filing on Monday morning."

"Shut up," Darrell said.

"I won't shut up. How much does it cost to buy the press?"

"You're drunk, Mr. Beaumont. You'd better leave."

"I'm more pissed than I am drunk."

"Get out," he snarled. He moved toward me, reaching out to put a hand on my shoulder.

"Get your hands off me!" I flung him away. What happened next was in slow motion. I reached for him, wanting to grab him by the shoulders and shake his teeth out. Instead, I lost my balance and slipped, shoving him backward toward the stairs. He fell, catching his face on the heavy mahogany ball at the top of the handrail. When he straightened, blood spurted from his nose.

"I said get out!"

"I'm going."

"What's happening up there?" Homer called from below.

Darrell held a hanky to his nose. "Nothing," he replied. "Mr. Beaumont here has had one too many."

I charged down the stairs, shoving my way past Homer in the foyer. The air outside the house was sharp and cold, with a stiff breeze blowing off the water. It cleared the smoke-laden air from my lungs and cut through the haze of MacNaughton's in my head, enough so I was shocked by what I had done. Taking a drunken swing at Darrell Watkins would add credence to the J. P. Beaumont legend—the hotheaded, killer-cop myth promoted by Maxwell Cole and his cohorts.

I took a deep breath of the biting, cold air. "You're not doing a whole hell of a lot to live it down," I told myself aloud.

A horn honked beside me, startling me out of my reverie. Tom Lander's GMC pulled up beside me. Tom leaned over and rolled down the window. "Get in," he ordered.

I did.

"What happened back there?" he asked, putting the pickup in gear.

"I had to get the hell out of there. They were driving me crazy."

"Me too," he said, accepting what I said at face value. "Where to?"

I directed him to my building at Third and Lenora. I didn't invite him up. I was sure he'd be reading all about it in the morning edition, and I didn't feel like doing any explanations beforehand.

"Thanks for coming along," Tom said as I opened the door to get out. "I'm glad at least one of Ginger's friends was there."

Nodding in agreement, I climbed out onto the sidewalk, then I reached back into the truck to shake his hand. "Your daughter was a very special lady, Tom. I'm sorry she's gone."

"Thanks," he said. He drove away without further comment.

Words are never enough in a situation like that. Actions were what was needed. I turned and walked into the lobby of the Royal Crest.

By then I was stone-cold sober.

CHAPTER 24

Friday morning. My last day of vacation, and I was hung over as hell. It seemed like all I had done was drink and go to funerals, a regular busman's holiday. I called Ames to invite him to breakfast. Reluctantly, he agreed.

"I'm very busy, you know," he said crossly as we picked up our menus. "I'm working on the condominium thing, and I'm still negotiating with New Dawn. What do you want?"

"Well," I parried, "as my attorney I thought you ought to know I was in a mild altercation with a Washington State senator last night. Bloodied his nose, probably blacked his eyes. . . . Accidentally," I added.

Ames put down his menu. "This is a joke, right?"

"Wrong. No joke."

"Maybe you'd better tell me about it."

For an answer, I handed him a copy of a newspaper. Ames read silently:

"In a private funeral ceremony attended only by family and close friends, State Senator Darrell Watkins said a tearful farewell to his wife Ginger yesterday afternoon.

"Mrs. Watkins, a member of the Washington State Parole Board, died in a one-vehicle accident on Orcas Island, Saturday, October 25. Her funeral services were delayed to allow fellow board members to travel to Welton for the funeral of another board member, Sig Larson, who was the victim of a homicide the previous day.

"Initially thought to be the underdog against longtime incumbent, Lieutenant Governor Rod Chambers, Sen. Watkins has seen his political base increase even as he has faced personal tragedy. Public-opinion polls now show him running neck and neck with Lt. Governor Chambers.

"A Watkins family spokesman said services for Mrs. Watkins were kept private to avoid a 'sensationalizing press from taking advantage of an unfortunate situation.'

"Senator Watkins, in a terse statement issued late last night, said that he is canceling all campaign appearances for the remainder of the week."

Ames looked up from the paper. "Don't I remember reading that it was his wife's wish that he continue with the campaign? When did you break his nose?"

"Last night. After the funeral. I'll bet he's not a pretty sight this morning."

"No wonder he canceled his public appearances."

"That sorry son of a bitch deliberately staged a 'private ceremony' in order to gain the sympathy vote." I relayed to Ames the conversation I had overheard.

"This the first you've been around politics?" Ames inquired dryly. "That's how it works. Will he bring charges?"

"I don't know. That's why I called you."

"Were there any reporters there at the time?"

"You mean when he fell? Not that I know of."

"I'm surprised they're downplaying it like this. By all rights, you should be plastered all over the front page for the second time this week."

"Maybe I just got lucky," I suggested.

Ames shook his head. "I doubt it. They probably won't go for criminal charges, but my guess is we'll be hearing from their attorneys. They'll sue for damages."

"Wonderful," I mumbled.

"Considering their financial situation, they'd be crazy not to."

"What do you mean?"

Just then the waitress brought our food and put it in front of Ames. He had taken a file folder out of his briefcase. He sighed, put the folder down, and picked up his fork. "You know which of the condominium projects are in trouble, don't you?"

"I wasn't asking about that. You said it wouldn't make sense for them not to sue me."

"Beau, listen to me. I'm trying to explain. The two that are in trouble are Belltown Terrace and Waterview Place. Belltown Terrace is theirs. Scuttlebutt says the project will go on the auction block by the end of the year unless they pick up some new capital. They might go for a fat out-of-court settlement in order to pick up some quick cash."

"Slow down. You're talking about two different things."

"I'm talking money."

"Look, Ralph, if they're going bankrupt, then I'd better not get involved. I didn't realize they were almost to sheriff's-sale time."

Ames looked at me sadly and shook his head. "You haven't been listening."

"Yes, I have. Why would I want to buy a unit from someone who's about to go belly-up? More specifically, why would I want to buy in a building owned by someone who's about to sue me?" Waiting for Ames' answer, I chased a slippery chunk of egg across my plate with a piece of whole-wheat toast. Peters had convinced me to give up white bread, not cholesterol.

"A unit!" Ames exploded. "Who's talking about a unit? I'm talking about the building. You said you wanted to invest. It would be a great write-off. You rent the units for five to seven years; then go in, do some remodeling, and sell them. It's a heck of a good deal."

I put down my toast. I put down my fork. "You were supposed to be looking for a condominium for me to buy."

"The penthouses in Belltown aren't sold. You could live there, but in order to keep our noses clean with the IRS, you'd have to pay rent back to the corporation."

"Ames, I can't buy a whole building."

"Well, not by yourself. I can get you in with a syndicate. I know of one in the market for just this kind of deal, five of you altogether. What do you think?"

I didn't know what to think. I knew my inheritance was considerable, but I still hadn't gotten a handle on the magnitude of it. I kept trying to get my arms around it.

"You do what you think is best," I said to Ames. "You know a hell of a lot more about this stuff than I do, but I can't see myself doing business with Homer and Darrell Watkins, especially after last night."

"Forget last night. We'll be dealing with the bank, not Homer and Dar-rell. The FDIC is ready to eat the bank alive if they don't get out from under this loan. Want to go over the financial papers?"

I shook my head. "That's your job."

Ames patted his mouth with his napkin and returned the file folder to his briefcase. "Very well," he said, rising. "I've got to run. I'm expecting a call from The Dalles."

"How's that going?" I asked.

He shrugged. "I'm not talking. I don't want to get Peters' hopes up, but it's not a dead issue."

He left me in the restaurant. After I paid the bill, I walked down Sec-ond to Belltown Terrace. It was a twenty-story building with a small grassy courtyard setting it back from the street. The sign said "Model Open," so I went inside. A real estate lady came down to meet me. She showed me through the entire project, from the indoor pool and exercise room to the outdoor racquetball court and running track. A gas barbecue grill sat on a small patio near the party room.

I lost the barbecue and also my only form of cooking expertise when Karen and I split up. The number of decent barbecued ribs I'd had since then could be counted on one hand. I decided that if Ames could negoti-ate my way into the building, it might not be such a bad idea.

Taking the woman's card, I promised to call her once I made up my mind. Back on the street, I dealt with the problem of my last day of vaca-tion. The bug was on me. Jurisdictions notwithstanding, I had to do some-thing.

I didn't bother going back to Avis. Considering my track record, they wouldn't be eager to rent me another car. I tried Hertz instead. I drove north on I-5 and took the Lynnwood exit. Using the phone book, I located Don Wilson's address. When I got there, I found that both the front and back doors were secured with police padlocks. Huggins had made the place off-limits. A quick check of the neighborhood showed no surveil-lance vehicles.

Wilson's house was set back by itself on a wooded lot. The nearest neighbor was a good half-block away in a tiny clapboard cottage. I walked to it and knocked. After a time the door inched open the length of a secu-rity chain.

"Yes?" a woman's voice demanded.

I held one of my cards up to the door so she could see it. "I need to ask a couple questions about Mr. Wilson."

"You and everybody else," the woman grumbled, but the door closed long enough for her to unfasten the chain. "What do you want to know?"

The woman was more than middle-aged, with a white apron spread across an ample figure. With an exasperated glare, she pointed her index finger at her ear and made several quick circular gestures.

"What else do you want to know?"

"Crazy enough to kill someone?"

"Wouldn't you be if you was him? You know what happened to his wife and kid."

"When did you last see him?"

"Look," she said, "I'm trying to cook dinner. I don't have all day. I already said this once. Do I have to say it again?"

"It would help," I said.

She sighed. "Well, follow me into the kitchen, then—before I burn it up." Opening the door wide, she motioned me inside. I followed her into a small kitchen where she was peeling vegetables for what looked like a stew. "Last I saw him was Friday morning. He was unloading signs from his car."

"Unloading?"

"That's what I said. Unloading. Packing them into the house."

It struck me as odd. If he was on his way to Orcas to demonstrate, he should have had his signs along. "Why?" I said, more to myself than to the woman.

"How should I know?"

I spent a while longer in the steamy kitchen, but other than stoutly defending Don Wilson's right to go off the deep end, the woman told me nothing more of consequence. I drove back into Seattle with the unsettling feeling that I knew both more and less than I had known before.

By the time I got home, late-afternoon sun had broken through the clouds. I called Peters at the Department.

"How's it going?" I asked.

"I hate depositions," he answered.

"What are you doing tonight?"

"Oh, I don't know. I thought I'd hang around here long enough to wait out the traffic." Friday afternoon rush-hour traffic is worse on Seattle's two floating bridges than it is during the rest of the week, as weekend travelers join regular commuters trying to cross Lake Washington to get to the suburbs and beyond.

"Why don't you stop by and have dinner? Maybe Ames could join us."

"What kind of food?" Peters asked.

I hadn't planned that far in advance. "I don't know."

"Tell you what," Peters offered. "I'll stop by the market and pick up something."

He didn't fool me for a minute. That way he could control the menu. "Sure," I said. "That'll be fine."

Hal Huggins called right after I talked to Peters. "Where've you been? I've been calling all afternoon."

"Out," I said without explanation. "What do you want?"

"We searched Wilson's house," Huggins said. "All his picketing stuff was there—the signs, the brochures, the petitions. Nothing out of the ordinary except one thing."

"What's that?"

"He left a half-chicken thawing on the counter, like he planned to be home in time for dinner. And he didn't leave food out for his cat. By the time we got there, the cat had helped himself to the chicken."

"Smart cat," I said.

"Get serious, Beau. What does that say to you?"

"He didn't expect to be gone long."

"Yeah," Huggins agreed.

We talked a few more minutes before my Call Waiting signal buzzed me to say Peters was downstairs. He carried a box of marinated vegetables, a pound of cooked spinach tortellini, and some fresh sole that he proceeded to bake in my oven. Ames turned us down cold, so it was only Peters and I who sat down to a gourmet dinner overlooking Seattle's nighttime skyline. Peters glanced at his watch as we finished eating.

"I'd be lucky to be home now, even if I left right at five. It takes an hour on Fridays. Longer if there's an accident on the bridge."

"Why don't you move downtown?" I asked.

A shadow crossed his face. "I keep thinking I'll get the girls back. You can't raise kids in the city."

I told him then about what I had seen at Belltown Terrace—the running track, the pool, the facilities. "You could raise kids there," I told him, "and not have to spend half your life commuting in a car."

"I don't have the kids. . . . Probably never will," he replied bitterly. "Besides," he added, "I don't have that kind of money."

Respecting Ames' wishes, I said nothing about continuing negotiations in The Dalles.

Our evening was pleasant. I told Peters about the reception at the Watkins mansion, including my taking a swing at Darrell Watkins. I tried unsuccessfully to recall the names of some of the people there. Vukevich was the only one I could remember for certain. "There was a Representative Snow, I think, and maybe somebody named Lane."

Peters shook his head. The names didn't sound familiar. So much for using word pictures to enhance my memory. You can't teach an old dog new tricks.

CHAPTER 25

Ernie Rogers called at six forty-five Saturday morning. The car was ready; would I like him to bring it to Seattle?

"Sure, but—" I thought about the Porsche and wondered how he'd handle it. Ernie heard the pause and understood it.

"My wife will drive," he said.

"Well, sure. Do you know your way around Seattle?"

"Some."

I gave him directions, describing the electronic gate into the garage on Lenora at the base of the building. "The Genie may not work now that it's been wet."

"It should," Ernie said. "I fixed it. We'll be there early afternoon."

"How will you get back to Orcas?"

"We're going to make a weekend of it. My mother-in-law is keeping the kids. We won't catch the bus back to Anacortes until Monday afternoon. Jenny wants to do some shopping. We thought we'd turn this into a mini-vacation."

"Do you have reservations somewhere?" I asked.

"No, we'll check into a motel after we get to town."

"Do I owe you any more money?" I asked, wondering if I should be prepared to write another check.

"As a matter of fact," he answered, "you'll be getting back some change."

"I'll look for you when you get here," I said. "My parking space is number forty-eight. After you park, come on up to 1106. We'll go to lunch."

"Sounds great."

Peters called from home while I was drinking my second cup of coffee. He was reading his morning paper. "Somebody blabbed about the search warrant. I'll bet Huggins is pissed. The paper names Wilson as the major suspect in both Larson murders. Who's the leak?"

Peter and I had hammered away on Don Wilson's thawing chicken over drinks after dinner. "Does the article mention Ginger Watkins?" I asked.

"Not so far."

"I've gotta go, Peters." I hung up and dialed Hal Huggins' number in Friday Harbor. It was busy and stayed that way. I tried the Sheriff's Department. "I'm sorry. Detective Huggins is unavailable."

"This is Detective Beaumont from Seattle. I'll hold. He'll talk to me."

I was right. Hal came on the line a minute later. "Sorry to keep you waiting, Beau. This place is a zoo. We've got reporters hanging from the ceiling fans. Somebody told them about the search warrant."

"Who?"

"How the hell should I know?"

"Pomeroy, maybe?" I asked. He was my first choice.

"I don't think so. I asked him. He denied it six ways to Sunday. I think he's telling the truth. Musta been somebody else."

A voice spoke to Hal in the background, and I heard his muffled reply. "Hey," he said into the phone. "I've gotta run. The press is eating me alive. I'll let you know if anything breaks."

I put down the phone and sat for a while. Eventually I called Ray in Pasco. He was at home. He sounded glad to hear from me.

"What did they find in the Rabbit?" I asked him after the niceties.

"Not in the Rabbit, on it. Mona's hair, and fibers from her jacket on the front bumper."

"No fingerprints?"

"Yours, smudged. Must have worn gloves."

"Great. Terrific. When's Mona's funeral?"

"It's over. Her brother brought in a bunch of Hell's Angels types from Idaho, cowboys on motorcycles. I went to the service. Except for the brother and his friends, no one was there."

At least I had sent flowers.

I made a late lunch reservation for the Space Needle. It's one of Seattle's best-known tourist attractions. The combination of food and view are unbeatable.

As I hung up the phone after making the reservation, I congratulated myself. It would be the first time I had visited the Space Needle since that night months ago when I went with Anne Corley. Maybe I was finally getting better.

I said a small thank-you to Ginger Watkins wherever she was.

Downtown is deserted on weekends. All the business people are home in the suburbs, mowing lawns and raking leaves. Farther downtown where the stores are, there are still crowds of shoppers, but not up in the Denny Regrade where I live. The flat stretches of the Regrade form a quiet village.

Actually, the Regrade used to be as hilly as the rest of Seattle, but sometime during the early nineteen-hundreds, a city engineer named

R. H. Thompson got carried away with his work and decided to sluice Denny Hill into Puget Sound. He wanted flat, and he got it; only the Depression stopped him before he got started on Queen Anne Hill. That kind of nonsense wouldn't get past environmentalists today, but it did then. Now the Denny Regrade is flat as a pancake.

Expansion from downtown, also stopped by the Depression, left the Regrade as it is today, a neighborhood of condominiums and apartment buildings interspersed with offices and small businesses. New luxury high-rises and flea-bitten hotels coexist in relative harmony.

I opened the door to my solitary lanai and went out to soak up some quiet morning sun. I needed to think.

A couple of things were right at the top of my list. For one, why would the killer have carefully worn gloves to drive my car when he had blatantly left prints all over Ginger's calendar? Of course, he didn't expect the calendar to be found, but still, it was taking a hell of a chance.

And the half-chicken bothered me. My mother was a firm believer in "Waste not, want not." The idea of thawing meat when you had no intention of coming home didn't make sense. And how had he disappeared into thin air? And why had he unpacked all his protest materials before he left for Orcas?

Questions. Always questions with no answers. And reporters buzzing around with their own sets of questions, never having brains enough not to print everything they knew, or thought they knew.

Stymied, I went back inside to shower, shave, and dress. I was ready and waiting when Ernie and Jenny showed up at one-thirty. Jenny Rogers was a smiling woman, several years younger than Ernie. They were a matched set. Her flaming red hair and blue eyes made them look more like brother and sister than husband and wife. She had a pregnant shelf of tummy that could easily have held a coffee cup and saucer.

"Any trouble with the car?" I asked.

Jenny giggled. "Some," she replied.

I looked anxiously at Ernie, afraid something was wrong with the Porsche that he hadn't been able to fix. He grinned. "She had a hard time steering," he explained. "The baby kept getting in the way."

Sports cars are not necessarily built for pregnant drivers.

We decided to walk from my place to Seattle Center. I guess I had never noticed all the curb cuts in the sidewalks. Ernie wheeled along, easily keeping pace with Jenny and me.

They found the Space Needle enchanting. Jenny had never been there, not even on the observation deck. She was delighted with the revolving restaurant, exuberant about the food. Her enjoyment was contagious. We had a great time. Eventually, however, conversation turned to business. Ernie reached in a pocket and pulled out an envelope which he handed to me. In it was a check for five hundred dollars, made out in my name. "What's this?" I asked.

"The job didn't take nearly as long as I thought," he answered. "That's your change."

I remembered Barney at Rosario telling me that Ernie was the best. I had doubted it then, but now I believed it. I'd checked, and couldn't have gotten the work done nearly that fast or cheap anywhere else. Taking a pen, I endorsed the check back to Jenny Rogers and handed it to her.

She was stunned. "Why?" she asked.

"For driving the car back, saving me a day of traveling. And for the baby. Ernie said you wanted to go shopping."

She looked at him quickly, questioning whether she should accept it. He shrugged, and she put the check in her purse.

"Thank you," she said.

Ernie looked uncomfortable. He changed the subject. "Did you see the paper this morning?"

"I didn't see it, but I heard."

"The paper said it's because the parole board let that Lathrop guy out and he killed Wilson's wife."

I shrugged. "Could be," I said.

"Well, they still shouldn't have fired Blia," Jenny said. Ernie shot a quick silencing glance in Jenny's direction. "Well, they shouldn't have," she insisted, with a defiant shake of her head. "It's not fair."

"What's not fair?"

"Blia Vang was a maid working at Rosario who got fired because she lost her keys. They said someone found them and used them to break into Mrs. Watkins' room."

I felt as if I had wandered into a conversation twenty minutes late. "Who's this again?"

"Blia Vang. A friend of ours." Jenny's blue eyes smoldered with indignation. "Somebody stole her keys, so they fired her."

"When?"

Ernie broke in with an explanation. "Blia worked the day that man was murdered. She left her keys on a cart, and someone took them. The hotel claimed she was careless and fired her."

My mind raced. Sig's key to Ginger's room had never been found, but the fact that the maid's keys had been stolen the same day was too much of a coincidence. My gut told me the missing keys were somehow related to the murder.

"Does Hal Huggins know?"

Ernie shrugged. "I don't know. She was too scared to say anything. The manager didn't find out until yesterday. When he did, he fired her on the spot."

"But has Hal talked to her?"

"I doubt it. She took off on the next ferry," Jenny interjected. "She would have been long gone before he knew."

I felt a mounting surge of excitement. Maybe she had seen someone in the hall, someone she could identify. "A material witness can't just walk away. She'll have to tell the authorities what she knows."

"She won't," Jenny said.

"She has to. She could be charged with obstruction of justice."

Jenny gave a sharp laugh. "Try explaining obstruction of justice to a H mong refugee. That's why she ran away. She's scared. She almost died when they took her fingerprints. She won't talk to a cop."

"Does anyone know where she went?"

Jenny and Ernie exchanged glances. "Maybe," Jenny said reluctantly. "But I tell you, she won't talk to you or Hal either. She's scared."

It occurred to me suddenly that Jenny and Ernie Rogers seemed to be far more than casually involved. "Wait a minute. How do you know so much about her?"

Jenny looked shyly at Ernie. He answered with a mildly reproving glare. "We work with the refugees," he explained. "An H mong saved my life while I was in 'Nam. I'm the one who got her the job at Rosario in the first place. I feel pretty bad about it. We both do."

I was like an old, flop-eared hound stumbling across a fresh scent. "Would you help me find her?" I asked, attempting to contain my elation. Their heads shook in silent unison.

"I'll get an interpreter," I argued. "I'd be off duty, no uniform, no badge. This could be important. She may have seen someone or something nobody else saw."

Jenny's manner softened when she understood I believed Blia innocent of any wrongdoing. Ernie remained adamant.

"There might be a reward," I added as a last resort.

"She won't talk to you," Ernie said. "Even if you find her, she won't talk."

"She would if you went along to translate," Jenny suggested. Ernie gave Jenny a black look, but his resistance was weakening. He sat for a long time, looking at me, weighing the pros and cons.

"You're sure she wouldn't get into any trouble?" he asked.

"I guarantee it."

"In that case," Ernie Rogers said gruffly, "I guess it couldn't hurt to talk to her."

CHAPTER 26

I could hardly wait to get home. Jenny had told me there was a possibility Blia Vang was staying with relatives in Seattle. I wanted to start looking for her.

While Ernie waited in the cab, Jenny and I retrieved luggage from the Porsche. In the elevator, Jenny thanked me again for both the money and lunch. It made me uneasy. Being an anonymous benefactor is a hell of a lot easier than looking gratitude in the face.

"Buy something nice for the baby," I said, patting her tummy.

She smiled and stood on tiptoe, leaning over her pregnant belly to give me a peck on the cheek as the elevator door opened to let her off. She gave me the name of a motel near Green Lake in case I needed to get in touch with them.

Back in my apartment I called Detective Henry Wu, a third-generation Seattleite of Chinese extraction. Hank came to homicide from the University of Washington with a major in police science and a minor in Far Eastern studies.

"Hey, Beau," he said, when I told him who was calling. "When you coming back?"

"Monday," I said. "But I need your help today. What do you know about H mong refugees here in town?"

"A very tightly knit group," he replied. "They don't trust outsiders. With good reason, mostly."

"Do you have any friends there?"

"I've got an ear there," he allowed. "Not a friend. Why? What do you need?"

"There's a young woman, used to be a maid up at Rosario. Her name is Blia Vang. They fired her for losing a set of keys. I need to talk to her."

"What about? Is this official police business?"

"More like unofficial police business. Remember old Hal Huggins?"

"Sure."

"He's working a homicide on Orcas. This woman may have a lead for him. She took off before he could talk to her. Rumor has it she's in Seattle, staying with relatives. I've got an interpreter, someone she knows, a fellow named Ernie Rogers. I need to ask her a couple questions. Off the record. No badge, no uniform, nothing. There's even a reward, if that helps."

"Money isn't going to make a hell of a lot of difference if she has to talk to a cop."

"Don't tell her I'm a cop. Say a friend of Ernie Rogers needs to talk to her."

"I'll try," Hank agreed, "but don't hold your breath. Is that all?"

"Well, actually, there's one more thing."

"Shoot."

"My interpreter is in town until four-thirty Monday afternoon. That's when the bus leaves for Anacortes."

"Jesus Christ, Beau! This is Saturday."

"Call somebody. Leave a message. It's important."

"Right," he said sarcastically. "The H mong all have phones and folks to take messages. I'll see what I can do."

"Thanks, Hank. I appreciate it."

I hung up. One of the hardest things about this business is waiting. You put an idea out into the ether, then you wait to see if anything happens. Television detectives notwithstanding, a lot of times nothing does.

On Saturday, nothing happened. I finally got around to unpacking the suitcases I had brought home and stashed in the bedroom without opening. On the table beside my recliner, I discovered the bill from Rosario. Ames had impressed on me the value of saving copies of all bills as potential weapons in future battles with the IRS. I stowed the bill away in a shoe box reserved for that purpose, your basic low-tech-filing system.

I tried Ames. Since it was cocktail hour on Saturday evening, I thought he might be persuaded into coming over. No dice. Claimed he was in the middle of something vital and couldn't take a break. More than a little put out, I walked across the street to the Cinerama and watched the original uncut version of *Oklahoma* for the seventh time.

Afterward, I went home, to bed but not to sleep. Thoughts of Ginger Watkins and Mona Larson haunted me. There was a common denominator, but I couldn't put my finger on it.

It was after three when I fell asleep. The phone rang at six. It was Ames—bright, cheerful, energetic Ames—calling on the security phone from the lobby. "Let me in, Beau. I'm downstairs."

I staggered into the kitchen and started coffee. When I opened the door, Ames bounced into the apartment, brimming over with excitement. "I have the deal put together. The other syndicate members want to know if you're going to buy the penthouse before the purchase of the building, or if you want to rent it back." Words tumbled out in a torrent.

"In that case, you wouldn't be able to buy it outright for five years, but considering the tax write-offs on the building, you needn't worry."

"Wait a goddamned minute here, Ames! Do you mean to tell me you woke me up at six o'clock on Sunday morning because you put a real estate package together?"

Chastised, Ames accepted a proffered cup of coffee. "I had to wait for one guy's plane to land in Japan."

"Which building?" I asked. "The one with the barbecue?"

"Belltown Terrace," he said.

"Okay, that's the one with the grill. What's next?"

"Tomorrow I make them an offer."

I sat down opposite Ames with my own coffee cup. "I have a hard time seeing myself as a real estate magnate."

"It'll grow on you," he assured me, smiling.

"What do I do with this?" I asked, indicating the small apartment that had been my first and only haven after the painful split from Karen and the kids.

"Sell it, or keep it and rent it out. It's up to you."

I remembered when the mortgage on the unit plus the child-support I sent Karen had been an almost insurmountable problem every month. Things had changed. For the better.

I scrambled a couple of eggs while Ames fixed toast. I could summon no enthusiasm for this real-life game of Monopoly. Even though it was theoretically my money, I didn't feel any sense of its belonging to me—or of my belonging to it, for that matter.

"What's wrong, Beau?" he asked, finally noticing my genuine disinterest.

"Mona Larson and Ginger Watkins," I told him.

"What about them, other than the obvious?"

"Something bothers me, and I can't get a handle on it: some common denominator, besides Sig."

"They were both broke," Ames said.

"I beg your pardon?"

"They were both broke," he repeated. "Mortgaged up the yingyang. Belltown didn't work out the way they expected. First the cement strike caught them. When the units finally hit the market, they got clobbered by high interest rates.

"For a long time nothing sold. They all lost a bundle. The whole group mortgaged everything to pay the first segment of the construction loan last year, thinking they could hold out and make the money back through sales. The next segment is due the end of December. There's no way they'll meet it. If they could even pay the interest, they might forestall a sheriff's sale, but after looking at the PDCs, I don't think they can."

"PDCs. What are they?"

"Public Disclosure Commission statements. Elected and appointed state officials fill out financial disclosure forms showing their earnings and holdings . . . that sort of thing. They're a matter of public record. After looking them over, it's clear that the parole board income was keeping both the Larson and Watkins households afloat."

"What about Homer?"

Ames laughed. "He's exempt. He holds no public office. He's always a bridesmaid but never a bride. He's involved in campaigns all over the map, but he's never a candidate himself. I'd guess he's as bad off as everybody else, but he doesn't have to fill out a form saying so."

"Both broke," I mused.

"You have to have pretty deep pockets to be able to weather the kind of financial storm there's been in Seattle's real estate market the last couple of years. My indicators say it's starting to turn around."

"Are mine?"

"Are your what?"

"Are my pockets deep enough?"

Ames laughed again. "They are, Beau. Believe me, you'll do fine. Now, we should take a look at that penthouse. If you're going to buy it separately, I can draw up an earnest-money agreement today."

I rummaged through my wallet and found the business card of the real estate lady at Belltown Terrace. "Call her," I said. "I liked the water view best. Two bedrooms with a den."

Ames seemed startled as he took the card. He had asked for a decision. I don't think he expected one quite that fast. "Just like that?" he asked.

"I looked at it Friday. It has a grill. I'm a sucker for barbecues."

Ames left a short time later, setting off happily on his various missions. At least one Seattle real estate agent was in for a pleasant surprise that Sunday.

Alone, I mulled Ames' information. Broke. Both Ginger and Mona had been dead broke, battling for survival, trying to stay afloat. I found it hard to imagine Ginger living in that palatial estate, running like hell to keep up appearances. In Chelan, Mona and Sig must have been caught on the same kind of treadmill.

Ginger and Mona—both of them married above their station, both young and attractive, and both dead within days of one another, probably at the hands of the same killer. Mona Larson and Ginger Watkins indeed had a lot in common.

Peters' phone call interrupted my reverie. We see each other so little during the week that we have to check in on weekends. Indulging in his favorite vice, current events, he was determined to keep me well informed, whether or not I wanted to be.

"I don't suppose you've read the paper."

"Good hunch."

"Your friend Max has hit an all-time-record low for bad taste, a Death Row telephone interview with Philip Lathrop from Walla Walla. Asked Lathrop what he thought about Wilson knocking off Sig and Mona Larson."

"I don't think I want to hear this," I said.

"Lathrop's comment was, 'It serves 'em right.' "

"That's why I don't read papers," I told Peters.

"Maybe you've got a point," Peters muttered.

Ida Newell dropped off my Sunday collection of crossword puzzles. I was working the second one when the phone rang. It was Hal Huggins. "They found him, Beau."

"Who?"

"Wilson."

"Where? When can I question him?"

"In Prosser. I'm on my way over there right now." Hal hardly sounded jubilant. "But St. Peter's the only one who'll be asking him any questions."

"He's dead? You're kidding! Who found him?"

"A troop of Boy Scouts out cleaning the bank along the Yakima River."

"How long's he been dead?" My mind did a quick geographic review. Prosser was in Benton county, the county next to Pasco where Mona Larson died.

"I don't know, but I'm going over to find out."

"What's the cause of death?"

"Initial report says drowning."

"Drowning?" I repeated.

"I'll find out when I get there."

I heard weariness and frustration in Hal's voice. He had followed a trail of questions, only to be robbed of both his suspect and his answers. To a homicide detective, answers are life's blood.

"Tough break, Hal," I said.

"I know." He paused. "I'd better go." With that, he hung up.

I sat for a long time afterward holding the phone. When a recorded voice threatened me with bodily harm, I returned the receiver to its cradle.

Don Wilson was dead. That finished it, right? Supposedly.

Maybe it did for Hal Huggins. It sounded as if he was buying the whole program.

But I wasn't. Several things demanded consideration: Don Wilson's thawing chicken, his hungry cat, his unpacked protest gear, and an extraneous set of missing keys. All were perplexing loose ends that wouldn't go away, that refused to be tied up in neat little packages.

Loose ends bug me. If they didn't, I guess I'd be in another line of work.

CHAPTER 27

Anyone who's ever been on vacation knows how hard it is to return to work that first day. In my case, the vacation had been the culmination of months of being miserable and disconnected. It felt like I was going back to work after six months rather than a mere two weeks.

Peters spent the day at the courthouse on the dead wife-beater case. Both Peters and I were rooting for the woman, Delphina Sage. Delphina's husband, Rocky, came home drunk one Friday night and beat the crap out of her, same as he did every payday. The only difference was that, the day before, Delphina had bought herself a .22 pistol.

If she had shot him while he was beating her up, it wouldn't have been so bad. We would have called it self-defense and let it go at that. Instead, Delphina waited until Rocky was sound asleep, then plugged him full of holes. From talking to the kids and the neighbors, Peters and I figured Rocky was a bully badly in need of plugging, but Barbara Guffy, King County's chief prosecutor, has a thing about premeditation. She was after a murder conviction.

Peters and I had been working another case just prior to my leaving for Rosario. In two separate but—we believed—related incidents, some jackass had set fire to sleeping transients downtown. Detectives Lindstrom and Davis had one case, while Peters and I had the other. Our victim had died almost immediately, but the other transient still clung stubbornly to life in the burn unit at Harborview Hospital. Both victims remained unidentified.

I was reviewing what little we had to go on when Hank Wu stopped by my desk. "Any luck?" I asked.

He shook his head. "This stuff takes time, Beau. The H mong don't come out of the woodwork and spill their guts just because Henry Wu snaps his finger. What time did you say your interpreter leaves?"

"Today on the four-thirty Greyhound for Anacortes."

"I'd say chances aren't very good."

"Keep after it anyway."

"Sure, glad to." Hank sauntered away from my desk.

Ames had promised to call as soon as he heard anything on the real estate transactions. The penthouse earnest-money agreement called for a March closing date. "That way," Ames had told me with a sly grin, "we'll keep the money in the family."

He called just before lunch, sounding perplexed. "What's the matter, Ames? You sound upset."

"I don't understand. They jumped on the penthouse deal, but they refused to consider the syndicate offer."

"Why?"

"I don't know. Must have come up with another investor who's willing to buy in. That's all I can figure."

"What happened?"

"That's what's so strange. When I talked to the project manager this morning, he was hot on the idea. Said he had to talk to one of the principals. Five minutes later, the deal was off. Just like that. One minute they needed the money; the next minute they didn't. The way they grabbed at that penthouse deal, even with a delayed closing, they don't expect to lose Belltown between now and March."

At Ames' insistence I had studied the project's financial sheet. We were talking big money, several million dollars.

"How can someone come up with that kind of cash in five minutes' time?" I wondered aloud.

"I don't know," Ames told me, "but I intend to find out."

Ames was in no mood to go to lunch. Craving companionship, I tracked down Peters at the courthouse. The two of us walked to a salad bar at Fourth and Madison. He dismissed my questions about Delphina Sage with an impatient shake of his head. "I don't want to talk about it. You do any good this morning?" he asked.

"I went over everything we have on our charbroiled John Doe. This afternoon I thought I'd check to see if Manny and Al's guy up in the burn unit can talk."

"Don't hold your breath," Peters said. "He couldn't last week."

It sounded hopeless to me, and I said as much. "We'll never crack this one. There's nothing to go on. Besides, if bums kill bums, who gives a shit?"

Peters gave me a long, critical look. "We sure as hell won't crack it with that kind of attitude," he responded. "You were supposed to come back from vacation with your enthusiasm back, all pumped up and rarin' to go, remember?"

"Go to hell," I retorted. "What do you think about them finding Wilson?"

"We're talking burning transients, remember?" he reminded me.

"I'm not interested in burning transients. I want to talk about Don Wilson."

"What about him? According to the papers, Hal Huggins has him dead to rights. Left a note and everything. What's there to talk about?"

"A note!" I exclaimed. "Are you serious?"

"Damn it, Beau. When are you going to stop being stubborn and start reading the papers? Yes, a note."

For the first time I felt the smallest prick of annoyance toward Hal Huggins. My phone had worked well enough when he needed my help. So why hadn't he called me with the news of the note? "God damn that Huggins," I grumbled. "What did the paper say?"

"That they found Wilson's body on the banks of the Yakima River just outside Prosser. Said he died of exposure, but that somebody found a suicide note."

"Exposure? Initially they said drowning. Since when is exposure suicide?"

"I'm just telling you what it said in the paper."

"And where did they find the note?"

"The article didn't say."

I left Peters at the table and prowled the restaurant for a pay phone. Locating one in a hallway between the men's and ladies' restrooms, I placed a call to Friday Harbor. Hal Huggins was not in. The woman who answered had no idea when he was expected. I left word for him to call me and went back to Peters.

"Did they say how long he'd been dead?"

Peters shrugged and shook his head. "A couple of days, I guess. At least that's what they implied."

"What about the note?"

"Just that there was one."

I stared morosely into my cup. Peters was fast losing patience. "Look. This Wilson character isn't our case. When are you going to the hospital?"

"Right after lunch, I guess."

He watched me drain my cup. "Know what your problem is, Beau?"

"What?"

"You just don't give a shit about burned-up bums."

"We've been partners too long," I told him.

I drove up to First Hill, Pill Hill as it's called because of all the hospitals. The burn victim in Harborview was in no condition to talk, at least not according to the dogfaced intensive-care nurse who barred my way. She said he had been hit by an infection and wasn't expected to make it.

I went down to Pioneer Square. I walked around talking to people, asking questions. It was tough. All of the drunks were too fuzzy to know who was sitting next to them right then, to say nothing of remembering someone who had been missing from the park bench almost three weeks. In their world, three weeks ago was ancient history.

By four o'clock I was parked outside the Greyhound terminal at Seventh and Stewart as Jenny and Ernie arrived by taxi. Ernie held two suitcases on his lap; Jenny struggled with a collection of shopping bags.

"Want some help?" I asked, coming up behind them.

They both turned. Jenny's face was radiant with that peculiar glow common to pregnant women. Ernie seemed relieved to find someone to help her with the luggage.

"She didn't spend it all," he said, grinning. "But she came real close." He wheeled along beside me as I carried bags and packages into the terminal and checked them onto the proper bus. "You never found Blia?" Ernie asked.

"No, and we've been looking."

"If you find her, I'd still be willing to talk to her, but I hate to miss a full day's work."

"What about a telephone conference call?" I asked. "We could get you, Blia, and me all on the phone together."

Ernie shook his head doubtfully. "You gotta remember that for the H mong, coming to this country is like stepping into a time machine. She was raised one step out of the Stone Age. A telephone conference call is asking too much."

"It was just an idea," I said dismally.

Promptly at four-thirty the bus left for Anacortes. I dropped my company car off at the department and rode a free bus as far as the Westin. I needed to talk. Ames was stuck with me whether he liked it or not.

As it turned out, Ames was glad to see me. "I've been hitting one brick wall after another on the Belltown thing," he complained. "I have some sources here in town, one in particular over at the *Daily Journal of Commerce*. He's mystified, too. Says nobody's acting like there's an outside investor. The real estate community is watching Belltown Terrace because of the sheriff's sale. He doesn't know who bailed them out."

"Well, somebody did," I said, settling onto Ames' bed. "Am I buying the penthouse?"

"If you still want it, considering you'd be buying it from them rather than the syndicate."

I thought about it, but I had been fantasizing about barbecued ribs for three days. My mind was made up. "I want it," I declared.

Ames nodded. "All right." He changed the subject. "Tomorrow I have to go back to The Dalles. They left word this afternoon. I catch an early plane to Portland."

"Want a ride to the airport? My car's back."

He shook his head. "I'll take the hustle bus."

We were ready to discuss our dinner when Peters called. "I figured I'd find you there. I just got out of court. What are you up to?"

"Ames and I are plotting dinner. Care to join us?"

He did. Afterwards, Ames returned to the Westin and Peters dropped by my apartment to chat. Around ten, just as Peters was ready to head home, the phone rang. It was the department. Another transient had been set afire in an alley encampment between First and Western off Cedar. Officers were on the scene. We took Peter's Datsun.

The building at First and Cedar is an office building with a penthouse restaurant on the fifth floor. The narrow alley behind it separates the building from two pay-parking lots. Between them sits a no-man's-land of blackberry bramble eight feet high. A small clearing had been carved beneath the thorny, dense branches with pieces of cardboard for flooring and walls.

Al Lindstrom and Manny Davis were at the scene. We didn't need to ask what was under the blanket in the blackberry clump. Once you've smelled the sweetish odor of charred human flesh, you never forget it.

"Same MO as before," Al told us grimly. "Only it's a woman this time, one of the Regrade regulars. We've got a positive ID. Teresa Smith's her name. Looks like she was sleeping it off here in the brush when someone doused her with gasoline and lit a match." The very fact that someone knew her name gave us a big leg up over the other two cases.

"Who reported it?" I asked.

He gestured toward the building above us. "A guy up there in the bar looked down and saw the fire just as it started. The bartender called 911, but it was too late by the time they got here."

"Did he see anyone?"

"Saw a car drive off. Only headlights and taillights. No make or model."

"So we're not dealing with another transient," Peters commented. It was true. Downtown bums don't drive. They wander, foot-patrol style, throughout the downtown area, hanging out in loosely organized, ever-changing packs.

"How come she was by herself?"

One of the uniformed officers came up as I asked the question. "We found her boyfriend. The food bank up the street was open, and she passed out. The group left her to sleep it off while they went to get food."

A tall, weaving Indian with shoulder-length greasy hair broke free from a scraggly group at the end of the alley. He pushed his way toward us. "Where is she?" he mumbled.

Manny moved to head him off, but the drunk brushed him aside. "Where is she?" he repeated. He stopped in front of me and stood glaring balefully, swaying from side to side.

I brought out my ID and opened it in front of him. I motioned wordlessly toward the heap of blanket. He swung blearily to look where I pointed. When his eyes focused on the blanket, his knees crumpled under him. He sank to the ground, his face contorted with grief, shoulders heaving.

This was an empty hulk of humanity with nothing left to lose, yet I watched as he sustained still another loss. He stank. His hair and clothes were filthy. Blackened toes poked through his duct-taped shoes. But his anguish at the woman's death was real and affecting.

Grief is grief on any scale.

One of the patrolmen knelt beside him. "We've sent for Reverend Laura," he said.

In the old days, Reverend Laura would have gone searching for heathens in Africa or South America. Today, the tall, raw-boned woman is a newly ordained Lutheran minister with a pint-sized church in a former Pike Place tavern. She ministers to downtown's homeless. Wearing her hair in a severe bun and with no makeup adorning her ruddy cheeks, she is both plain and plainspoken, but her every action brims with the milk of human kindness. She appeared within minutes and knelt beside the weeping man, taking his elbow and raising him to his feet.

"Come on, Roger," she said kindly, "let's go to the mission."

"Will you keep him there so we can reach him tomorrow?" I asked.

She nodded. An officer helped her load him into a car. We fanned out, asking questions of all bystanders, interviewing the patrons in Girvan's, including the man who had first reported the incident.

We found nothing, It took us until two A.M. to ascertain we had found nothing. Peters dropped me off at my place. "Why don't you stay here?" I offered. "You can have the bed. I'll sleep on the couch."

"No, thanks," he replied. "I'd better get home."

I'm sure I was sound asleep before he reached the floating bridge.

CHAPTER 28

I woke up Tuesday morning, tired but with a renewed sense of purpose. Roger Bear Claw's grief had catapulted burning transients out of the realm of the inconsequential. Years of discipline took over, bringing focus and motivation. Ginger, Mona, and Wilson were Hal's bailiwick. Teresa Smith and a dead John Doe were mine.

By seven-thirty I was at my desk. Peters stopped by on his way to the courthouse. He dropped a newspaper onto my desk. "Thought you'd want to read Max's column," he said.

It was there in lurid black and white, all about Ginger Watkins' murder. He told the whole story, including the blood-alcohol count, speculating what conversation she and Wilson might have shared over those last few drinks. Columnists speculate with impunity. They also rationalize. Cole's conclusion was that Wilson had taken his own life after destroying those responsible for the deaths of his wife and child. With typical tunnel vision, he ignored the fact that Mona Larson had never served on the parole board.

The moral of the story—and with Max there is always a moral—was couched in snide asides about inept law-enforcement officers. No one was exempt—from the Washington State Patrol and the San Juan County Sheriff's Department to the Pasco City Police. There was, however, one notable omission. J. P. Beaumont's name wasn't mentioned, not once. Evidently Ralph Ames' threat of libel had struck terror in Max's black little heart.

Peters was still there when I finished reading the article. I tossed the paper back to him. "Where the hell does he get his information? Huggins swears there's no leak in his department, but the stuff about the throttle linkage was known only by Huggins, Rogers, me and the killer."

Peters shrugged. "It doesn't really matter, does it? Wilson's dead; the case is closed. Maybe now you can get your mind back on the job. I should be done with the Sage case by noon."

After Peters left, Al, Manny, and I did a quick huddle. "So who's got a grudge against bums?" Manny asked.

"Every taxpaying, law-abiding citizen," Al Lindstrom grumped. Al is a typical hardworking Scandinavian squarehead with a natural aversion to any able-bodied person who beats the system by not holding down a real job.

Al and Manny went to the Pike Place Mission for another talk with Roger Bear Claw, while I was dispatched to Harborview Hospital to check on the surviving John Doe. Before I had a chance to leave my desk, the phone rang. It was Hal Huggins. I tried to check the annoyance in my voice. "It's about time you got around to calling me."

"Lay off, Beau. I'm up to my neck. It's just as well Wilson's dead. The county couldn't afford two first-degree murder trials."

"You're sure Wilson did it? All three of them?"

"Absolutely. Didn't you hear about the note?"

"Vaguely. But exposure? People don't just go out in the woods and wait to die. Besides, it hasn't been cold."

"Who knows? Maybe he fell in some water. That'll do it. Look, Beau, I'm not calling the shots, the coroner is. . . . By the way," he added, "we found his car parked on a side street in Prosser. The note was there."

"How long had it been there."

"I can't tell you that. We're trying to reconstruct Wilson's movements from the time he left Orcas. So far we're not having much luck, but there's no doubt the note is his. The prints check. Handwriting checks. What more do you want?"

"What about the chicken?"

"Oh, for God's sake, Beau, lay off that chicken. Maybe he didn't plan to kill them when he left home; but after he did, he couldn't very well go back without getting caught, not even to eat his chicken or feed his god-damned cat."

"So you're closing the case?" I asked.

"Not completely. As I said, we're still retracing his movements from the time he left Orcas until he showed up in the river."

"How long has he been dead?"

"Old man Scott says two to three days at the most."

"Not 'Calls It Like I Sees 'Em' Scott!"

"That's right. One and the same. He's still Benton County Coroner. He's up for reelection next week."

Only three counties in Washington—King, Pierce, and Whatcom—have medical examiners. All the rest rely on an antiquated county coroner system. Whoever runs for office is elected without any consideration of qualifications. Garfield Scott had earned both his nickname and a permanent place in the Bungler's Hall of Fame when he declared a man dead of a heart attack, only to turn him over and discover a knife still buried in the victim's chest.

"Can't you get another opinion? What if Wilson's been dead longer than that, like since before Mona died?"

"Dammit, Beau. I already told you, I'm not calling the shots. There's an election next week, remember? Scott would never hold still for a second opinion."

I changed the subject. "Who went to Maxwell Cole with Ginger's murder?" I asked.

There was a moment's pause. "I don't have any idea."

"Somebody did," I told him grimly. "It's front-page stuff in this morning's *P.I.*"

"Not anybody from my department, I can tell you that!" Huggins' hackles were up, and so were mine. He attempted to smooth things over. "Thanks for all your help, Beau."

"Think nothing of it," I said. Obviously he didn't.

On my way up to Harborview, I tried to shift gears from one case to another. The same intensive-care nurse stopped me. "He can't talk to you," she snapped. "He's dying."

"Look," I said wearily. "Can he communicate at all?"

"He can nod and shake his head. That's it."

"Even that may tell me something. Someone else died last night, a woman. She never made it as far as the hospital. Without his help, the toll could go higher."

She relented a little. I could see it in the set of her mouth.

"Please," I wheedled, taking advantage of her hesitation. She glared at me, then marched briskly down the hall, her rubber-soled shoes squeaking on the highly polished tile floor. I stood there waiting, uncertain if she was throwing me out or taking it under advisement. She came back a few minutes later carrying a sterilized uniform, booties, and a face mask. Wordlessly, she helped me don compulsory ICU costume.

"You can see him for five minutes. No more."

One look convinced me that Teresa Smith was a hell of a lot better off for dying on the spot. What little was visible of the man's puffy face was fused in a featureless mass of flesh that bore little resemblance to a human being. Tubes went in and out his arms and throat. His breathing was labored.

"He's awake," the nurse said, although I don't know how she knew that. "We call him Mr. Smith."

I stood by the bed, astonished by my revulsion. I'm a homicide cop. I'm supposed to be used to the worst life can dish out. Five minutes left no time for niceties. He was dying. I think he knew it.

"I'm a cop, Mr. Smith. A detective. They'll only let me talk for five minutes. Somebody else got burned last night, up on First Avenue. We think it's the same guy who burned you. Can you help us?"

There was no response. I couldn't tell if he heard me.

"Did you see anyone?"

He nodded, so slightly, that I wasn't sure he had moved.

"Someone you knew?"

This time there was no mistaking it. The mass of flesh moved slightly from side to side. The answer was no.

"One person?"

A minute nod. We were playing hardball Twenty Questions. Every question had to count. There wouldn't be any second chances, not with this Mr. Smith.

"Male?" Another nod. He groaned with the effort.

"Young?"

He nodded again, barely, but his breathing changed. The nurse took me by the arm. "Enough," she said firmly. "He's fallen asleep. You've worn him out."

She led me outside the intensive care unit, where I shed the sterile clothes. "Thank you," I said. She bustled away without acknowledgment. She was a tough old bat, but nobody with the least tendency to a soft heart could work there.

Back in the office I had a despondent Peters on my hands. "They convicted her," he said. "Not Murder One, but a minimum of twenty years for killing that worthless bastard. What the hell ever happened to justice?"

"Sometimes there's no such thing," I told him. "So get to work."

We did. We spent the afternoon with Manny and Al. The information that it was somebody young, probably a kid, constituted the first tiny break in the case. One kid, one young punk, who liked to burn people up. Who was he? Where was he from? Was he black, white, Asian?

Back to questions, always questions. The consensus was that, whoever he was, he wasn't a regular inhabitant of the downtown area. This wasn't your usual drunken brawl over a half-consumed bottle of Big Red. Fights over booze are generally harmless—a little gratuitous bloodshed among friends. This was deliberately malicious. And deadly.

We hit the streets, talking to known gang leaders and toughs. The patrolmen in what the department calls the David Sector of downtown Seattle know most of the street kids by name. They guided us to the various groups, pointing out kids who would talk and kids who liked to throw their weight around. All of them could have gotten gasoline; none of them had cars.

To quote one, a scrawny-looking kid named Spike who wore a black leather vest over a hairless bare chest, "Nobody knew nothin'," although he hinted darkly that there might be a club down at Franklin High with some allegedly vicious initiation rites.

Peters and I drove to Franklin High School in Rainier Valley. The principal, a tall black former Marine, sounded more like a drill sergeant than an educator. He admitted he had some tough kids in his school, but none who would go around setting fire to sleeping drunks, he'd stake his reputation on it. I was inclined to believe him.

Driving back to the department, Peters asked me what I thought. "He seems to know what's going on with those kids," I told him.

"Bullshit," Peters replied. "Nobody ever knows what's going on with a bunch of kids."

We agreed to disagree. It wasn't the first time, and it wouldn't be the last.

I found a note from Henry Wu on my desk. "See me."

Hank sat with his feet propped on his desk reading a copy of the *International News.* "What have you got?"

He put down the paper, a wide smile spreading under his impeccable mustache. "I think I've found her, Beau, in the Stadium Apartments out in Rainier Valley. You know where that is, out on Martin Luther King Way?"

"I think so."

"My source says she lives with her aunt and uncle and some cousins out there. Your interpreter's gone?"

"Yesterday," I said.

I must have sounded ungrateful. Hank bristled. "Look, I moved heaven and earth to get this far. Nobody rushes a grapevine."

"I know. Sorry. It's just that Ernie had to go home." Hank appeared somewhat mollified. "So what do you suggest?" I asked. "Is there anybody on the force who speaks H mong?"

"Even if there was, I wouldn't advise your taking them along, not if you want her to talk."

"What should I do then, go by myself?"

"That guy who left on the bus—Ernie. . . . My source recognized the name, knew who he was. He's evidently widely respected in the Seattle H mong community. It wasn't until I mentioned him that I started getting to first base. My suggestion is that you do whatever it takes to get him back down here."

If you call in an expert, you have to be prepared to take his advice. Henry Wu was the expert. "Thanks, Hank. I'll see what I can do."

I went back to my desk. Peters looked up as I sat down. "What gives?"

"Hank's got a line on the hotel maid from Orcas," I answered. I picked up the phone, ready to call Ernie.

Peters scowled. "Look, Beau, we're already on a case. Two and a half by actual count, if that guy at Harborview is still alive."

I felt like he'd stepped on my toes. "Don't tell me what to do," I snapped. I couldn't very well call Ernie right then, not with Peters peering over my shoulder. We spent the rest of the afternoon circling each other like a squabbling old married couple. By five, we still weren't ready to bury the hatchet.

"You having dinner with Ames?" Peters asked as we waited uneasily for the Public Safety Building's snaillike elevator. I hadn't told him Ames had returned to The Dalles. I didn't tell him then.

"Naw, he's busy," I replied noncommittally.

If Peters was fishing for an invitation to dinner, I didn't bite. We parted company in the lobby, and I walked home to the Royal Crest. I called Ernie right away.

"I think we've found Blia," I said, once he answered the phone. "Could you come down tomorrow if I had a float plane pick you up and take you back?"

"It won't work," he said. "I've got a motor home to overhaul. The Hansens are leaving for Arizona Saturday. I've got that job to do and another due by Friday."

"Nobody else can do it?" I insisted.

"I'm a one-man shop. Without me, nothing happens."

I couldn't very well argue the point. "Call me as soon as you see your way clear," I told him.

"Sure thing," he replied. "Glad to."

Disappointed, I hung up. Outside it was raining a steady fall drizzle. I put on a waterproof jacket and walked to the golden arches at Sixth and Westlake. I picked up a Big Mac and an order of fries to go. Peters would have pitched a fit if he'd glimpsed my evening menu.

Back at the house, I set the table with my good dishes and dined in solitary splendor. Bachelors are allowed their small eccentricities. After dinner I settled into my old-fashioned recliner and let my mind wander.

Maybe the guy who sent us to Franklin had been playing some game of his own, creating a wild-goose chase among the predominantly minority kids there. I was smart enough to recognize that the suggestion played on our own prejudices. Maybe our bum-killing fanatic was to be found at the other end of the spectrum, concealed among the well-heeled kids of Bellevue or the North End.

It was a thought that merited further consideration. Meantime, all we could do was keep looking for that rarest of all birds, the eyewitness.

The discipline of focusing on one issue at a time pushed Ginger and Sig and Mona and Wilson further and further into the background. I had to leave them alone until Ernie could return to Seattle.

For the time being, inconsequential as they might seem, three dead transients took precedence. Harborview Hospital had called the department to say that Mr. Smith was no more. My interview with him had been his very last opportunity to give us any help.

I fell asleep in the chair and didn't wake up until morning. That's something else bachelors can get away with. I'm not sure the good outweighs the bad.

CHAPTER 29

My back was broken when I woke up. In my youth I could sleep all night in a recliner and not have it bother me the next day. Maybe I'm getting old.

I was in the bathroom, my face slathered with shaving cream, when the phone rang. I hurried to answer it, Colgate Instant Shave smearing into the holes of the mouthpiece.

"Did you know?" an unfamiliar voice asked.

"Know what?"

"That Ginger was—" Tom Lander's voice cracked.

I waited while he got hold of himself. "I knew," I said grimly, silently cursing Homer and Darrell Watkins and Hal Huggins and J. P. Beaumont for not having broken the news to Tom earlier.

"Why didn't you tell me? Why did I have to read it in the paper?"

I didn't have an answer. I had known he wasn't told, but I had shut the knowledge out of my mind.

"Was it Wilson?" he continued doggedly.

"That's what Hal Huggins thinks," I countered.

"What do you think?" he demanded.

"I don't know." It was an honest answer.

"You could have told me."

"I expected Homer or Darrell would do that."

"They didn't."

I felt like I owed him something, but not enough to lapse into idle speculation about thawing chickens and hungry cats and extra keys. "Look, Tom, I'm following up on some leads. I'll be in touch if I find anything out, okay?"

"Why should I believe you?"

"No reason," I answered. "Because I asked."

"All right," he agreed reluctantly. "But was she really drunk, or was that just part of the story?"

"Her blood-alcohol count showed she had been drinking, enough to be drunk."

"Oh," he said, disappointment thick in his voice.

"Why, Tom? What does it matter?"

"It's personal," he replied and hung up.

I went to the bathroom and finished shaving, thinking about Maxwell Cole. I couldn't help wondering how he had gotten his information, particularly since Huggins was so sure it hadn't come through his department. I decided to pay a call on Max, for old time's sake. I called the P.I. He wasn't in and wasn't expected before ten.

I checked the phone book. Bingo. Maxwell Cole. It gave a Queen Anne phone number but no address. I dialed. He sounded groggy.

"Hello, Max. This is Beaumont. I want to talk to you."

"To me? How come?"

"Just a couple of questions. Can I come over?"

"I guess."

"Good. What's the address?"

He gave me a number on Bigelow North, an old-fashioned street strewn with fallen chestnuts and mounds of moldering leaves. The house was an eighteen-nineties gingerbread type set among aging trees and crowned with leaded glass gable windows. It surprised me. I had always figured Max for the swinging hot tub and cocktails type. This hardly fit that image.

I pulled up and parked. Before I could get out of the car, Max blustered out the front door and down the walk. He heaved himself into the Porsche.

"What are you doing here?" he demanded.

"You invited me, remember?"

"I was asleep. Let's go someplace for coffee." We drove to an upstairs coffee-and-croissant place on top of Queen Anne Hill. "So what do you want?" Max asked, once we settled at a table.

"I want to know where you got your information on Ginger Watkins."

Wariness crept over his flabby face. "Why do you want to know?"

"I do, that's all."

"My sources are confidential."

"You'd be forced to tell, under oath."

"There won't be a trial. Wilson's dead."

"Did Wilson tell you about Ginger? Were you in touch with him after that day on Orcas?"

Max shook his head. "Don't try to trick me, J. P. Why do you want to know? Huggins says the case is closed. He's satisfied Wilson did it."

"Who set up the meeting on Orcas? Was it Wilson?"

Max nodded.

"What did he say?"

"That something big was going to break, that it would be announced during the parole board retreat. He thought it should go in the special feature I was doing on him."

"Did he say what this 'something big' was?"

"He didn't. I thought it would be about the Victim/Witness Protection Program. That's what he was working on, but nobody's mentioned it since. He must have had his wires crossed."

"Did you ever publish it? The feature, I mean?"

Max looked stunned to think that I had missed a word of his deathless prose. "I used some of it in the column after Wilson died, but not much. I was still pissed at him for dragging me all the way to Orcas and then missing the interview."

"Was it Pomeroy?" I asked in a feint-and-thrust maneuver designed to throw him off guard. It didn't work.

"I'm not talking," Max returned stubbornly. "I already told you that." I wasn't able to get any more out of him. We finished coffee, and I took him home.

I turned up at the department around ten. Peters, glancing up from a stack of papers, glared at me. "What'd you do? Forget to set your alarm?"

I didn't answer. I sat down at my desk, hoping to reshuffle my priorities and get the two John Does and Teresa Smith back on top of the desk. Don Wilson, the wild card, refused to go away.

"I talked to Hal," I said to Peters as I passed his desk. "Old Man Scott swears up and down Wilson was dead two to three days at most. If that's true, how come he floated to the surface? That usually takes five days to a week."

"Current," Peters offered helpfully. "The current could have washed him up on shore without him necessarily floating to the surface."

"I wish Baker could take a look at him." Dr. Howard Baker is King County's crackerjack medical examiner. Nothing gets by him. Dr. Baker is no coroner, but then King County isn't Benton County, either. "Why the hell couldn't Wilson have died inside King County? It would simplify my life."

"Wish in one hand, shit in the other, and see which hand gets full first." Peters' comment was philosophical. I love it when he lectures me in parables.

Just then Peters' phone rang. He listened briefly, then slammed down the receiver and jumped to his feet. "Come on," he said. "We've gotta go."

"Where?"

"Manny and Al are down in Pioneer Square. They may have a lead in the transient case."

That effectively put the cap on Ginger and Sig and Mona and Wilson. I followed Peters through the fifth-floor maze and out of the building. Pioneer Square is only a few blocks from the department, down the hill, off James.

As the name implies it's an old neighborhood made up of stately old buildings whose insides have been gutted and brought up to code. Gentrification has brought new tenants—law firms, trendy shoppes, and tiny espresso bars. The only glitch is that the new tenants haven't quite convinced the old ones, the bums, that they don't live there anymore. The merchants and the bums are constantly at war to see who controls the turf.

Peters and I walked down the hill. Manny and Al were in the Elliott Bay Bookstore, downstairs in the book-lined espresso bar. With them was a young woman in tennis shoes and a ponytail. She might have been any well-built teenager poured into a tank top and tightly fitting jeans, nipples protruding under the knit material. She looked like a teenager until you saw her close up. Her face was still attractive, but it showed signs of excessive wear.

Periodically she popped a bubble with a wad of gum, but she kept a nervous watch on a flashily dressed black man two tables away. He sat with both arms folded across his chest, silently observing the proceedings.

"So nothing happened," she was saying as Peters and I approached the table. "It washed off. He never lit the match, but I told Lawrence I'll bet it's the same guy. When I heard it on the news, I told him." She nodded toward the man I assumed to be Lawrence. "He said I could tell."

Al motioned us into two empty chairs while Manny spoke earnestly to the girl. "These are Detectives Peters and Beaumont," he explained. "They're working the case with us. Would you be willing to do a composite drawing, Sandra?"

She glanced questioningly toward Lawrence. He nodded. Evidently, anything that damaged the merchandise was bad for business. It didn't make sense to let someone set fire to the stable.

"Yes," she answered.

"This was three nights ago?"

I think she forgot she was talking to a cop. She gave Manny a bat of her long lashes as she answered. "Yes."

"And there were two of them?"

"Yes."

"Black or white?"

"White."

"Blond? Brunet?"

"One of each."

"How tall?

"I don't pay much attention. I mean, it's not important, you know? Maybe six feet or so."

"How old?"

"Twenty. Maybe younger."

"And they both paid?"

"I charge extra for two." Lawrence shifted uneasily in his chair, but I don't think Sandra noticed. At least he didn't tell her to shut up.

"Where did you go?"

"To a room at The Gaslight up on Aurora."

"So what happened?"

"Nothing. . . . Nothing kinky," she added. "Not even both together. But while the second one was getting it up, the first one pulled a bottle out of his coat pocket and poured something on me. It smelled terrible. It burned my eyes.

"The second one started yelling, 'What are you crazy?' and the first one said 'Just having a little fun.' I jumped up to call Lawrence, but one of them knocked me down, and they took off. The second guy didn't even get his shirt and shoes on. I followed them to the door, screaming like mad. They drove off before Lawrence could catch them."

"You're sure it was gasoline he poured on you?"

"Yeah. From one of those screw-top Coke bottles. Lawrence said if they'da lit a match I'da died."

Manny nodded. "It's true," he said. Sandra swallowed hard. I wondered how old she was. Probably no more than seventeen, although she looked half again that old.

"After that woman died, Lawrence said I could tell. He said this was one time we'd better cooperate."

Manny nodded again, encouragingly. "Lawrence is absolutely right," he agreed. "What kind of car was it?"

"White. One of those little foreign cars like maybe a Toyota or a Datsun. I don't know which."

"What year?"

She shrugged. "But it had some of those university parking stickers in the window. We watch for those. They're usually bad news."

Lawrence stood and motioned toward the door. Sandra caught the signal and rose obediently. "I gotta go."

"Can we call you for the composite?" Manny asked.

She nodded. "Lawrence knows how to get ahold of me."

Lawrence made a quick exit with the girl trailing behind him on an invisible leash.

"I'll just bet he does, the son of a bitch," Al Lindstrom muttered under his breath. "That makes me sick."

Manny glared at his partner. "Don't look a gift horse in the mouth, Al. We get paid for solving murders, not for busting hookers and pimps. She's the best thing that's happened to us all week."

CHAPTER 30

I felt like a goddamned rubber band. Teresa and friends bubbled to the surface while Ginger and friends receded. The four of us went to lunch—Manny, Al, Peters, and I. Manny was high as a kite, while Al was still pissed, speculating that Lawrence made more than all four of us put together. Well, three of us, anyway. I wasn't talking.

Other than comparing notes on what Sandra had said, there wasn't much to do until she completed the composite. We agreed that since Manny had done most of the talking with Sandra, he should make the next contact and set up the appointment. There was no sense in causing Lawrence to be any more squirrelly than he already was.

The idea that the car was a white Datsun or Toyota with a university sticker was some help, but not much. There are literally thousands of cars registered at the U Dub, as locals refer to the University of Washington. We figured somebody should contact the campus police and ask for a preliminary list.

Seattle P.D. and the campus police get along fairly well. As law-enforcement officers, campus cops suffer from a severely restricted sphere of influence. They do a lot of PR work within the confines of their narrow jurisdiction, keeping a lid on anything that might offend the tender sensibilities of well-heeled alumni. Peters and I were to brief them on the current situation. We figured they'd be overjoyed to be involved in a real crime that didn't involve property theft.

As soon as lunch was over, we split up the act. Manny and Al headed for the medical examiner's office to pick up the preliminary report on the Harborview John Doe. Dental charts were our only possible means of identification. There sure as hell wouldn't be any fingerprints. Peters and I were supposed to go to the university. About ten to one, we stopped by the department to pick up a car, but Margie Robles, our clerk, caught us before we got away.

"There you are!" she exclaimed. "I've been looking all over for you."

"Why? What's up?"

"Somebody named Ames. He's called three times so far. For you or Detective Peters."

"Why would he call me?" Peters wondered.

"Did he leave a number?" I asked.

"Not the last time. Said you should meet him at the airport at one forty-five. Both of you. Here's the flight number." She handed me a yellow slip of paper.

Once she was out of earshot, Peters turned on me.

"What's this about? More footwork for Hal Huggins?"

"I guess," I said.

He glowered at me. "We'd better not take a company car, then. We can just barely make it." He angrily strode toward the door with me right on his tail. I had an idea Ames wasn't calling about Ginger and friends. He had been in The Dalles, negotiating with New Dawn. If he had sprung the kids, it would be a kindness to give Peters some advance warning, but if he hadn't . . . I wasn't about to make that kind of mistake. I let Peters stay pissed.

The Datsun was parked in a cheapo monthly garage at the bottom of James. Peters ground it into gear and angrily fishtailed us out of the parking stall. "You've got more nerve than a bad tooth. We shouldn't work an unauthorized case during regular hours. You'll get us both in trouble."

I said nothing. It was pure luck that got us to Sea-Tac without a speeding citation. The parking garage was crammed to the gills. We searched through three levels before we finally spotted a little old lady vacating a spot. Peters beat two other cars to it. We were inside the terminal by one thirty-five. Naturally we had to hassle with the security guards over our weapons.

By the time we reached the gate, Northwest Orient Flight 106 from Portland was already parked in place at the jet bridge. Passengers were disembarking. I saw Ames first. He was packing one kid on his hip and dragging the other along by the hand. The girl Ames was carrying spotted Peters. "Daddy, Daddy," she squalled.

Peters whirled toward her, a look of stunned amazement on his face. As he stood glued to the floor, unable to move, the girl who was walking broke loose from Ames' grip and raced for Peters' knees. She hit him with a full flying tackle that almost toppled him. Meantime, the kid Ames was carrying set up such a howl, he had no choice but to set her on the floor and let her run too.

Peters sank to the floor, buried under a flurry of bawling kids. I moved to where Ames, looking inordinately proud, was attempting to smooth the wrinkles from his usually immaculate jacket. What appeared to be the better part of a Tootsie Roll was stuck to his silk tie.

I grabbed his hand and pumped it. "How the hell did you pull it off?"

"You've just funded their mother on a five-year mission to Nicarugua. No children allowed, of course."

"Of course," I said.

"Fully deductible," he added.

"Of course." With Ames in charge I should have known the solution would be fully deductible. Peters gradually emerged from the mêlée and came over to Ames and me, one child in each arm. They were cute little imps, five and six years old with baby teeth, long dark hair, thick lashes, and brown eyes.

Peters was more than a little choked up. "I don't know what to say," he blurted.

"How about introducing me?"

"This is Heather," he said, indicating the smaller one, "and this is Tracie. My friend, Detective Beaumont."

"Beau," I corrected.

The smaller of the two regarded me seriously. "Hello. Mommy says my name is Joy and she's Truth." She pointed at her sister. They had evidently lived under different names in Broken Springs, Oregon.

"I like Heather better," I said.

We stood there awkwardly, bottling up the hallway, not knowing what to say or do. It was a moment that could have become maudlin, given half a chance, but Ames took charge. He herded us down the hallway like a bunch of errant sheep, leaving us long enough to pick up luggage. When he rejoined us, he carried only his own suitcase and a briefcase.

322 ▼ Injustice for All

"What about them?" I asked, indicating the girls.

"New Dawn's attorney told me I could have them this morning, as is, take it or leave it. I took it. I decided we could get them clothes once they got here."

One glance at Peters told me Ames had made the right choice. You can always buy new clothes. I doubted he would have gotten a second crack at the kids.

We crowded into the Datsun for the trip back to Seattle. Peters sat in the backseat with the girls. I drove while Ames attempted to clean the chocolate off his tie.

"I guess you're taking the rest of the afternoon off?" I asked.

Peters grinned. "Looks that way. I can't believe you did it!" he said to Ames.

I could believe it, all right. I counted on Ames to smooth it over so Peters would never know exactly how it happened. It would be better for him to believe that his ex-wife had experienced a sudden change of heart. There was no need to tell him certain amounts of money had changed hands.

I got out at the department, and Ames assumed the driver's seat. I tracked down Captain Larry Powell and told him that Peters was gone for the day, explaining that his kids had come home unexpectedly. Powell was glad to hear it, but he didn't press for details. I didn't volunteer any, either.

Once Peters dropped me at the department, I checked out a car and drove to the university. Driving there, I suddenly recalled an old undergraduate pastime that had been called Bum Bashing in my day. It involved dragging home a bum on one pretext or another and then beating the crap out of him once he was there. Of course, back in the old days, I couldn't remember anyone's ever dying of it. Obviously the current generation had elevated the sport from intramural to semipro. By actual count we had three victims dead. My hope was that Sandra's encounter had been with the same bunch and that we could somehow nail them.

As I expected, the officer of the day, Joseph Randolph, was more than happy to help me. He listened carefully as I explained the problem, then left me in a waiting room while he went to work on it. Forty minutes later, he called me back into his office. With a triumphant grin, he handed me a huge computer printout that must have weighed ten pounds.

"Here it is," he said. "Every single car that's registered on campus this quarter—make and license number."

I could tell he was proud of getting it for us so fast. I hated to burst his bubble. "Can you break it down by make and model?" I asked.

His face fell. "I don't know when we could schedule that much computer time."

I took the whole list back to the department. Manny, Al, and I divided it three ways and began weeding through it. By quitting time, we had found 73 Datsuns and 51 Toyotas. No colors. We called it a job and went home. That's one thing about this kind of work. When you're looking for a needle in the haystack, you don't have to do it all at once. Both the needle and the haystack will stay right there and wait until the next day.

I called Peters at home to find out how things were going. They had just come in from buying bedroom furniture. He said he'd decided to take the rest of the week off. It would take that long to get the girls registered for school and locate a baby-sitter. I told him not to worry, since sorting through the vehicle list would probably take the better part of a week.

Ames turned up, wearing a clean tie and jacket. The two of us went out for a celebratory dinner, co-conspirators congratulating each other behind Peters' back. With the kids in Peters' custody and the major real estate deal canceled, Ames planned to return to Arizona on Saturday. I was sorry to hear it. It cost me money, but I enjoyed having Ames around. I supposed, however, that he did have other clients.

"You making any progress on the Watkins case?" he asked as we left Rosselini's Four Ten Restaurant to walk home.

I shook my head. "Huggins is sure Wilson did it. Since it isn't my case, I don't have much to say about it."

Ames looked thoughtful. "I can't help but think that the murders and the project might be related."

"How's that?"

"I'm not sure. It's just a thought."

We walked together as far as Fourth and Lenora, then split up. I went up to my apartment, mulling Ames' words along with thawing chickens, hungry cats, and extra keys.

CHAPTER 31

Once more I had a face full of shaving cream when the phone rang. It was Peters looking for a good pediatrician. In order to register the girls for school, they had to have a complete set of vaccinations. New Dawn believed in prayer, not science. As I tried to keep shaving cream out of the receiver, I considered growing a full beard.

I returned to the bathroom and had barely put razor to chin when the phone rang again. I jumped and left a good-sized nick. I'm sure I sounded exasperated when I answered. "Is this Detective Beaumont?" The voice was female, sultry, and dripping with the honeyed accents of the Deep South.

"Yes," I answered tentatively.

"My name's Colleen Borden with Armour Life Insurance." I steeled myself for the inevitable pitch. Various estate planners and financial advisors had crawled out of the woodwork ever since my windfall. "Ah'd like to make an appointment with you."

"I'm not interested in any life insurance. I'm going to live forever." It was the line that had given me the most luck in getting rid of pushy bastards.

"Ah'm not tryin' to sell you somethin,' Mr. Beaumont." She sounded clearly affronted. "Ah'm not a salesman. Ah'm a claims inspector."

That caught my attention. "A claims inspector?"

"Yes. Ah investigate death claims."

"Whose claim are you investigating?"

"That's why Ah want to see you. Ah'll be comin' to town tomorrow and wondered if maybe we could get together for dinner, say at the Westin, the Palm Court, at six."

"How will I know you?"

"The reservation will be in my name."

She hung up. I spent the next few minutes taking the phone apart and prying Colgate Instant Shave out of the holes with a toothpick. A death-claim inspector. I wondered which one. There were any number of deaths in need of inspecting.

I finished my shave on the third try. I was almost late by then. I hit the elevator with a tiny piece of tissue stemming the flow of blood on my chin.

Manny and Al were hard at work on the list when I got to my desk. I settled down with my portion of it, wishing Peters were there to lighten the load. Manny took off about eleven to oversee Sandra's composite drawing, while Al and I grappled with the list until our eyes burned.

Manny came back about two, practically walking on air. He had two drawings. Each pictured a clean-cut, ordinary-looking kid. It gets me when a cold-blooded killer looks like the kid next door or maybe even *is* the kid next door.

But it wasn't the drawings that had Manny excited. Sandra had come up with one other tiny scrap of information. The white car had carried a bumper sticker. She couldn't remember the whole thing, just that some of the letters had been funny, maybe backwards or upside down. The only one she remembered for sure was a K, and maybe a backwards E.

A frat rat! From a house with *kappa* in it and maybe a *sigma*. Sandra, bless her little heart of gold, had saved our eyesight. Instead of having to go through the computer printout listing every car on campus, she had narrowed our investigation to the much smaller world of sororities and fraternities. A quick consultation with Ma Bell's Yellow Pages told us the university boasted only ten Greek houses with *kappa* in their names.

Manny, Al, and I drove to what we call Never Never Land in two separate cars. If Seattle is a liberal egg, then the University of Washington is the yolk, although the kids there now are far more conservative than the students of, say, the sixties or seventies. They still do drugs, and they still live in an aura of permissiveness where some students literally get away with murder, but it's a hell of a lot better than it used to be.

We didn't notify the campus police. It wasn't necessary. Greek Row isn't on campus proper.

Parking places are at a premium. We finally parked in front of two separate fire hydrants on Seventeenth NE. Manny and Al took one side of the street, and I took the other, wishing the whole time that Peters were there to back me up instead of sitting in a doctor's office somewhere waiting to have his kids vaccinated for polio, tetanus, typhoid, and God knows what else.

I was the one who got lucky, if you can call it that. Kappa Sigma Epsilon at 4747 Seventeenth NE was a white, New England-style building. I remembered it as an old-line, socially prominent Eastern fraternity. Like fraternities in general, it had fallen on hard times. The paint was chipped and peeling, and a couple of broken windows were patched with plywood.

I knocked and waited. Finally a wide-eyed kid answered the door. I pulled out the two sketches. "I wondered if you could help me. Do you recognize either of these guys?"

He looked at the pictures, then back at me. "You a cop?" he asked.

I pulled out my ID. Five years ago, a kid at the university wouldn't have given me the time of day. That's what I expected now. I was wrong.

He nodded, pointing. "That's Howard Rayburn. The other's Vince Farley. Howie's upstairs. Want me to get him?"

Sometimes you make a decision that you spend the rest of your life regretting, playing it back over and over; wondering, if you had done something differently, would disaster have been averted. At that moment in the vestibule of Kappa Sigma Epsilon I made one of those bad decisions.

I didn't know what I was up against, and I didn't want to go in without a backup. "No, thanks," I said. "I'll be right back." I hurried to the grass median and waited until I saw Manny coming back down a sidewalk. I motioned for him to come. He in turn called Al.

"What have you got?" Manny demanded.

"Looks like they both live there. Only one is home."

"Want me to radio for more units?" Al asked. I nodded. He loped off toward their car. I motioned Manny to cover the back door, while I returned to the front porch. This time I didn't bother to knock. I met the same kid, coming down the stairs.

"I told Howie you were here," he said helpfully.

It was the worst thing he could have done, but I hadn't told him not to. "What room?" I said, taking the stairs three at a time.

"Turn left. Third door on the left."

I drew my .38 as I dashed down the hall. The third door on the left was ajar. I tapped on it, but there was no answer. I pushed the door open, but nothing happened. Cautiously I looked inside. No one was there. A dresser drawer sat open with half its contents spilled onto the floor. Someone had left the room in a hell of a hurry.

I flew back down the hall to the vestibule at the bottom of the stairs. The same kid was still standing there. When he saw my Smith and Wesson, his jaw dropped.

"Did he come this way?" I demanded.

Incapable of speech, he shook his head.

"Is there another way down from up there?"

He nodded dumbly.

"For chrissake talk to me! Where is it?"

"The fire escape comes out down by the kitchen."

I raced in the direction he pointed. I came to the backdoor and looked outside long enough to see Manny crouched behind a dumpster. I turned around and almost ran over the kid who had trailed behind me down the hall.

"If he didn't get out here, where else could he be? Is there a basement?"

This time he pointed to a darkened stairway leading down from the kitchen. I heard wailing sirens as backup units charged through traffic. Sprinting to the bottom of the stairs, I paused on a musty landing before dashing down a narrow hall. I checked rooms as I went—laundry room, boiler room, bicycle room, poolroom. All of them were empty.

If Howie hadn't made a run for it before Manny got to the dumpster, he was still hiding somewhere in the building. The question was Where.

I had started up the stairs to begin a systematic, room-to-room search when I remembered chapter rooms. Every fraternity had one—at least they used to—a secret room hidden somewhere in the house, where the whole fraternity gathered for formal meetings and initiations. I went back to the poolroom. One wall curved in a semicircle.

"Where's the chapter room?" I snapped. "There?"

The boy nodded.

"Where's the entrance?"

He opened the door to a seemingly small closet which became a black-walled stucco room, an Aeolian cave for initiation rites. He pointed toward a small door. I motioned him away from it and knocked. No answer. I tried the doorknob. It turned in my hand. I pushed the door open, but stayed outside.

"Howie?" I asked into the blackened room.

There was no answer, but I could sense another person's presence. Maybe I could smell his terror, hear his heart thumping. I knew he was there.

"Police, Howie. We know you're in there. Give yourself up."

Still there was no answer.

"Come on out, Howie. We know all about you and Vince. It's no use."

I heard a half-sob. "I didn't do it." His voice was a choked whisper. "I made him leave, but he said I was an accessory after the fact."

"Come on out, Howie. We can talk about it later."

I stood with one eye closed, hoping to adjust my vision to the deeper darkness of the other room. It didn't help.

There is no silence quite as stark as that between hunter and hunted. The two of us were alone in a frozen universe. The small click of a released safety catch shattered the silence.

"Throw it down," I commanded. "Come out with your hands up."

Instead, Howard Rayburn, age nineteen, put the gun to his head and blew his brains out.

CHAPTER 32

I was sick as I walked through the process. Howie Rayburn was almost the same age as my own son, Scott. The media showed up outside, including the ubiquitous Maxwell Cole. I stumbled across him when I went outside with the medical examiner's team.

He waved to me, but I ignored him. It's a double standard. No one had been particularly interested when Teresa Smith burned to death. She wasn't as newsworthy as someone who might have lit the match. I returned to the building without acknowledging him.

Nobody could tell us where Vince Farley was. We sealed off both Rayburn's and Farley's rooms until Al came back with search warrants. By late afternoon we knew more about Vince Farley than we wanted. His father owned a string of racetracks all over the Southwest. Vince was flunking out of school. He kept a little scrapbook. We found clippings, not only of the three incidents in Seattle, but also one from Iowa City, Iowa. Same MO. Vince Farley himself was nowhere to be found.

Howard Rayburn's mother, a widow, showed up. She appeared to be a nice lady—shocked, disbelieving, grieving, hurt. Al talked to her; I didn't. Couldn't.

The afternoon turned sunny, the blue clarity of the sky mocking what was going on below. We worked the rest of the afternoon. It was dark before we got back downtown and started writing reports; midnight before I came home and took a long shower, trying to wash away the day's filth. I fell into bed but couldn't sleep. I finally got up and administered a bottle of medicinal MacNaughton's. It worked; I slept.

I stumbled to my desk at eight the next morning—sick, hung over, exhausted. Peters called to touch bases. "You guys got a line on Farley?" he asked.

"Not yet." I sighed wearily. "We've got a dragnet out, but it hasn't turned up anything. We heard rumors late last night that he might have crossed into Canada. His mother is divorced and lives in Toronto."

"That means extradition?"

"Fat chance, right?"

"Right," Peters echoed. "So what are you doing today?"

"We'll be back at the U, interviewing fraternity brothers. We didn't get to all of them last night."

And that's what we did. All day long. Back downtown late in the afternoon, we tried to put some international tracers on Vince Farley. Still no luck. We heard through the grapevine that his father's attorney was raising hell with the Chief about his son's name being plastered all over the media. It was the age-old story. Poor little rich kid fucks up, and Daddy's attorneys ride to the rescue.

I got back to my apartment about five-thirty. I sat down in the chair long enough to take off my shoes. I made the mistake of leaning back, intending to rest my eyes a minute. The next thing I knew, it was six-thirty and the phone jangled me awake.

"Hello," I mumbled into the phone.

"Detective Beaumont, am Ah to understand you're standin' me up?" An angry Southern belle is anything but sultry.

"I'm sorry," I stammered. "I'll be right there."

"Ah've already been waitin' a whole half-hour."

"No, really, I'm only a couple of minutes away."

The Palm Court maître d' greeted me with a knowing smile. "You must be Mr. Beaumont. Right this way, please."

I had been far too preoccupied during the preceding thirty-six hours to give Ms. Colleen Borden from Armour Life Insurance Company any thought. Had I done so, I'm sure I wouldn't have pictured a platinum blonde in her late forties with an hourglass figure and a crimson smile. Her hair was pulled back ballerina-style and covered with a broad, brimmed fedora. A well-cut lavender dress, softly draped, showed her figure to good advantage. At the base of her throat lay a gleaming diamond pendant. Her eyes were a startling shade of violet, set in a timeless face.

The waiter held my chair. I slipped into it while she gave me a shrewdly appraising once-over. "Well now," she drawled, "Ah don't believe anybody told me you were quite this cute, Detective Beaumont. Seein' you in the flesh maybe Ah'm not so mad at you for fallin' asleep."

It wasn't how I had expected our conversation to start. I mumbled an apology. She held up her hand. "No, now Ah don't want to hear another word about it. We'll just have ourselves a little drink and a little dinner. Then, if you still feel like apologizin', maybe we can work somethin' out." She gave me a sly grin. I would have had to be blind, deaf, and dumb not to have known what she meant.

I put a bland smile on my face and ordered a hair-of-the-dog Mac-Naughton's. "What can I do for you?"

330 ▼ Injustice for All

She took a long sip of Southern Comfort. "Mah daddy owns Armour Life Insurance Company," she drawled. "And his daddy owned it before that. We're not very big, but we're solid."

She paused and gave me a dazzling smile. "Years ago, Daddy called me into his office. He doesn't have any sons, you see, and he says, 'Cody.' That's what he calls me. 'Cody, Ah want you to come into the business so you'll know how to run it when the time comes, but Ah don't want you out sellin' none o' this stuff. That's too hard a life for a little lady. What Ah'd like you to do is make sure that when we pay a claim it's on the up and up.' And that's what Ah've been doin' ever since."

"What does this have to do with me?"

Instead of answering my question, she motioned to a waiter who hovered in the background. "You decided what you want?" she asked. "Ah do believe Ah'll have the pheasant. Ah just love pheasant." Without looking, I nodded, and she ordered two of them. She turned back to me, the smile once more in place.

"Why do you suppose Homer and Darrell Watkins turned you down when you made them such a right tolerable offer?"

With that, any notion that Colleen Borden was a lightweight went right out the window.

"Ames says they found another investor."

"Ralph Ames is your attorney, the one who was handlin' your deal?"

"Yes."

"Do you have any idea where that man is?"

"Ames? Why, no. He said he'd head back to Phoenix tomorrow, but I don't know where he's been today."

"Ah've hung around here all day long, hopin' to run into him, left him messages. He hasn't returned a single call, not one."

"That's not like him," I said contritely, as though both Ames and I had been remiss. "Have you tried in the last few minutes?"

"Ah left word that he should join us." As if on cue, the maître d' hurried to our table. "Excuse me, Miss Borden. There's a gentleman outside who says his name is Mr. Ames. Should I show him in?"

"Oh, by all means. Do have him come in."

There was a flurry of activity around our table as a third place was set. Ames followed the maître d' uncertainly, as though not sure what to expect. I stood to introduce them. It was comical to see. Ames fell into those violet eyes and never knew what hit him.

"Ah'm very pleased to make your acquaintance, Mr. Ames," Cody drawled. "Ah've been doin' my very best to find you all day long."

"I'm sorry to be so difficult," Ames apologized. "I've been out in Kirkland helping a friend of ours. I was actually . . ." Ames paused and cleared his throat. "Interviewing baby-sitters. He has to have one by Monday, you know."

Colleen nodded seriously, as though she understood perfectly.

"And then," Ames continued, Colleen's undivided attention making him babble, "once we got the girls registered for school, we had to take them shopping for clothes, shoes, lunch pails, bedding, everything."

I burst out laughing. The very idea of Ralph Ames, attorney extraordinaire, interviewing nannies and dragging tykes through Nordstroms and The Bon on a full-scale shopping marathon struck my funnybone, especially since he was so dead serious about it. Colleen took offense at my laughter. That moment sealed Ralph Ames' fate.

"Mr. Beaumont, Ah think it's perfectly wonderful that Mr. Ames has been helpin' his friend, and Ah don't see any reason for you to be laughin' at him."

Ames turned an interesting shade of red and took a long sip of the Southern Comfort that Colleen had ordered for him. By the time we were into the main course—three pheasants instead of two—Colleen Borden knew as much about Peters' custody fight as confidentiality would allow.

Then, just when I thought we were never going back to Armour Life Insurance Company, Colleen delicately laid down her fork, turned her violet-eyed charm full on Ames, and said softly, "Supposin' we get down to business."

Cody Borden was the consummate iron fist in a velvet glove. "To begin with, Ah've talked to Hal Huggins. He's a nice man, but Ah don't believe he's ever been involved in an insurance case of this magnitude." She blinked a long blink with her very long eyelashes. "You see," she drawled, "we're talkin' about three million dollars altogether."

"Insurance fraud!" Ames exclaimed. "A buy/sell agreement funded with life insurance. Why didn't I think of that?" Ames came on-line without missing a beat.

Colleen smiled at him. "That's right, sweetie. Five hundred thousand apiece, with a five hundred thousand accidental-death benefit."

Ames' accountant mentality took over. He whistled. "That would be plenty to get them out of the woods. When would the claim be paid?"

"Well, now," Colleen murmured, "that all depends, doesn't it? Two to three weeks if everythin's in order. Much longer than that if there's a problem."

"Three weeks would be in time to ward off the sheriff's sale."

Colleen nodded. "These policies are all well beyond the contestable period. We'll be payin' the claims, regardless. Ah just want to be sure in my own mind that we're not payin' good money to a murderer."

She removed a sheaf of papers from a slender briefcase, handing them to Ames rather than me. Swiftly he skimmed through them. "It's essentially a buy/sell arrangement," he explained to me a few minutes later, "with all proceeds going to the surviving partners."

"And the surviving partners are?" I asked.

"Why, Darrell Watkins and his daddy, of course," Colleen answered sweetly.

"Have you talked to Hal Huggins about this?" I demanded.

"He's got it stuck in his craw that somebody named Wilson did it. But in talkin' to him, Ah kept comin' up with your name, Mr. Beaumont. And then, when Ah started looking into the Belltown Terrace situation, Ah saw your name again." She smiled. "Seemed like too much of a coincidence to me, wouldn't you say?"

Ames had been studying the papers throughout this exchange. He looked around as though waking from a long sleep. "If both surviving beneficiaries were implicated in the deaths of the other partners, what would happen?"

Colleen smiled again. "Why, sweetie, if someone proves that, the proceeds go to the insured's next of kin."

Dinner wasn't over. I believe we had dessert and coffee, but I bowed out of the conversation. I sat there thinking about Mona Larson's brother from Idaho and Sig Larson's three kids and Ginger Watkins' father, Tom Lander.

Maybe Hal Huggins was buying the Don Wilson story, but I wasn't. Cody's idea made perfect sense. Darrell and Homer could knock off the others, frame Wilson, and use the three million to bail themselves out of the hole. Greed for motive rather than revenge.

I made up my mind on the spot that, if Hal Huggins wouldn't do something about it officially, then I would unofficially.

I left the table with Ames and Colleen still huddled over a sheaf of papers. I had the distinct impression, however, that they wouldn't stick to business forever.

CHAPTER 33

al Huggins didn't answer either at home or at the office when I got back from the Westin. Why should he? After all, it was Friday night. As far as Hal was concerned, he had solved three murders that week. He was probably out celebrating.

I tried again the next morning, as soon as I woke up. Woke him, too. "What's going on?" he muttered, half asleep.

"Did you talk to Colleen Borden?"

"That dingey broad? Yes, I talked to her. Goddamned insurance companies are all alike—do anything to avoid paying a claim. All they want to do is take your money; then, as soon as somebody dies—"

"Hal," I interrupted, "did you listen to her? I think she's onto something."

"Look here, Beau," Huggins bristled. "I'm telling you once and for all. Wilson did it. We've got motive, opportunity, witnesses that place him near the scene, fingerprints on a confession. What the hell do you want?"

"I want to nail the guilty party."

"You know, Beau, I keep wondering why you're so involved. I heard you were up nosing around Wilson's house the other day. This isn't your case, remember?"

"Are you going to investigate Colleen Borden's allegations or not?"

"The case is closed as far as my office is concerned."

"My mind's made up, don't confuse me with the facts. Didn't you tell me that once? Does it have anything to do with the fact that Tuesday is election day and Darrell Watkins is a major political candidate? Did the sheriff tell you to stifle?"

"Go fuck yourself," Huggins replied, hanging up.

I got Ernie Rogers' home number from the Directory Assistance. "It's Saturday. What time are you coming over?" I asked, once I got him on the phone.

Ernie sounded surprised. "I didn't think you still needed me. I thought the case was closed. That's what the paper said."

"It may be closed there," I returned grimly. "It isn't here. How long will it take you to get to Seattle?"

"I'll check the ferry schedule and call you back."

"Screw the ferry schedule. Charter a float plane. I'll pay for it. Get here as soon as you can. Have him land at the Lake Union dock. I'll pick you up."

He called back a little while later to say that the soonest he could arrive would be one o'clock. It was almost ten. I had three hours to do what I needed to do.

I had kept one of Don Wilson's pictures. I needed to assemble a few others for a rogue's gallery. While I was at it, I decided to kill two birds with one stone.

Directory Assistance gave me Darrell Watkins' campaign headquarters. A quavery-voiced old lady answered the phone. "Do you have access to Mr. Watkins' calendar?" I asked.

"Certainly," she responded. "It's right here on the wall above my head. That way we all know what's going on at all times. Of course, he's canceled everything now that his wife . . ." Her voice trailed off.

"I know. I was wondering about some appearances during the last couple of weeks." I was playing liar's poker and doing my best to sound casual, unhurried. "I'm writing an article about Mr. Watkins. My records show he was in Vancouver and Longview on the eighteenth, and Chehalis, Centralia, and Olympia on the nineteenth. Is that correct?"

"I don't know where you got that," she snorted. "He was scheduled to be in Bellingham and Everett on the eighteenth and nineteenth."

There was a catch of excitement in my throat. Everett is a short hop from Anacortes and the ferry to Orcas.

"Is that all you wanted?" she demanded impatiently.

"Do you have any brochures with his picture?"

"Certainly. We could send you a whole packet. Are you interested in doorbelling?"

"No. All I need is one brochure. Can I pick it up?"

"Our campaign headquarters is at the corner of Denny and First North."

"Good," I said. "I'll be right over."

Getting a picture of Homer Watkins proved somewhat more difficult. Not impossible. I finally managed to dredge one out of a newspaper file. It was several years old and dated from Homer's tenure as president of the Washington Athletic Club. It was good enough for my purposes.

I stopped by the department and sifted through the collection of pictures we keep on hand to build montages for witnesses to use when they're trying to identify a suspect. You can't just hand them a picture and say, "Is this the one?" You have to give them a batch of pictures and say, "Do you see anyone you recognize?"

Ernie was true to his word. The float plane pulled up to the dock on Lake Union right at one. The pilot said he'd have lunch and then come back to the plane. Ernie had left his wheel chair at home. Assisted by a steel crutch, he hopped from the plane to the Porsche. Once inside, Ernie and I took off for Rainier Valley.

The Porsche created quite a stir among some kids playing a spirited game of soccer in the parking lot of the Stadium Apartments, a low-income housing complex on Martin Luther King Way. From the way he had put the Porsche back together, it was clear Ernie Rogers was a top-drawer mechanic, but his skill with language dumbfounded me. The kids broke up their game and admiringly surrounded the car, giving us a thumbs-up greeting. Within moments Ernie was speaking to them in a language I had never heard before. They responded by enthusiastically directing us to a building near the back of the complex.

People with two good legs never notice stairways. We were directed to a set of dingy stairs thick with the stale odor of boiled rice, rancid cooking oil, and old fish. Ernie turned around, sat down, handed me his crutch, then made his way up the steps on his butt without a word of complaint. We located the correct apartment number and knocked on a flimsy, hollow door.

It opened slowly, revealing an old woman, gray-haired and tiny, who peered cautiously up at us. Ernie spoke to her rapidly but softly in the same musical language he had used on the children outside. Her face brightened, and she favored him with a benign smile. A slight inclination of her head motioned us into the room.

It was empty except for one derelict chair and a floor covering of woven mats. I had the feeling that, moments before we entered, the room had teemed with people. Now it contained only two, the old woman and a venerable old man with white hair and a twisted driftwood walking stick. He sat regally on the only chair—a cane-backed wooden one that leaned slightly to one side. He nodded to Ernie, and spoke to the old woman who disappeared and returned with a folding chair for Ernie. The old man spoke again, addressing Ernie, who turned to me.

"He wants to know if Blia is in trouble."

"No," I answered. "We're looking for the man who stole her keys."

The old man studied me closely as Ernie translated. "The hotel didn't believe her when she said someone stole them."

"I do," I told him. When Ernie translated, the old man nodded sagely.

"He wants to know what you want with Blia."

I reached into my coat pocket and removed the packet of pictures. I handed them directly to the old man. "I want to show her these. One of those men may have been the one who stole her keys. Maybe she'll recognize him."

The old man examined the pictures minutely in the dim light of the curtained window, then he spoke quickly to the old woman who shuffled from the room. Moments later she returned, leading a shy young woman with waist-length jet-black hair. The younger woman seemed reluctant, but the old woman prodded her forward. When Blia saw Ernie, her face brightened. She moved forward more willingly.

The woman led Blia to the old man, who handed her the pictures. "Ask her if she saw any of those men at Rosario the day she lost her keys."

Ernie translated. The girl walked to the curtained window and studied the pictures. I held my breath as she leafed through them one by one. It was possible she had seen nothing, would recognize no one. Suddenly she stopped. She handed one of them back to Ernie, who passed it to me.

The face in the picture was that of Homer Watkins.

I'm sure my face betrayed the impact the picture had on me. I had expected it to be Darrell Watkins, wanted it to be him so badly I could taste it. There are very good reasons why neither doctors nor detectives should work on cases too close to home. It warps perspective.

I looked up. Everyone in the room was staring at me. "Ask her when she saw him," I said to Ernie.

He translated for her, then turned to me with Blia's long response. "She was cleaning her last room. Someone had checked in and then changed his mind. The desk wanted the room recleaned because they thought they could rent it again. When she came out of the room, he was standing by her cart. A few minutes later she realized her keys were missing."

"Can she remember exactly what time it was?"

"Late. After dark. Around seven o'clock." Blia hadn't moved from her place near the window. She watched me warily, gauging my reactions to each translation.

"Tell her thank you," I said. "And tell her there's a reward. Someone will be in touch with her next week to arrange it. He will be authorized to pay her five thousand dollars, but she may have to testify in court."

Ernie looked at me quickly before he translated. He spoke for a long time. Blia's face changed several times, mirroring surprise, joy, doubt, and, finally, after the old man spoke sternly, agreement.

"She'll testify," Ernie said. "If you need it."

The old woman showed us out of the apartment. "Five thousand dollars is a lot of money," Ernie said as he bumped his way down the stairs. "Where'd it come from?"

"Beats me," I replied. We were both quiet after that until we were in the car and halfway back downtown. "Whose picture?" Ernie asked.

"Not the guy I expected," I said.

"You can't tell me who, though?"

"No, I'd better not." He accepted my refusal good-naturedly. I felt obliged to explain. "If word leaks out before we're ready on this one—"

"Forget it," he said. "It's no big deal."

We stopped at the Doghouse for coffee before I took him back to the plane. Once the float plane was airborne above Lake Union, I went home.

There was no sense in calling Huggins. His mind was made up. And there was no sense in calling Peters. His hands were full. I called the Westin and was told Mr. Ames had changed his mind. He hadn't checked out, after all. I left a message saying that I would need him in Seattle during the week and that he shouldn't leave without checking with me first. I had a feeling Ames' virtue was no longer intact.

I settled into my recliner. I'm not one of the trendy types who sits in a half-lotus position to do his thinking. My legs would stick permanently. A recliner and a steaming cup of strong coffee are all I need to get the creative juices flowing.

The ball was definitely back in my court. What I had to do more than anything was think it through. There was far too much at stake to go off half-cocked.

Homer. Blia Vang had fingered Homer. He had been at Rosario that Friday afternoon, and no one had known it. So he had gotten the keys and then let Wilson into Ginger's room to get the calendar? That didn't make sense, but that was the way it looked.

I tried to put myself back in that Friday afternoon, to remember all the events in the exact order in which they had occurred. It can be done. It's a process very much like a self-induced hypnotic trance. Or a time machine.

The parole board meeting got out at four. Ginger and Sig were supposed to meet at five, but Darrell called and held Ginger up, made her late. By the time she reached the rendezvous, Sig Larson was dead.

Homer Watkins and Don Wilson, an unholy alliance. Unless . . . Something Blia Vang had said jumped out at me.

Someone had rented a room at Rosario and then changed his mind. Who? And what about Darrell Watkins' campaign appearances in Everett and Bellingham?

The thought had no more than crossed my mind when I was out of my chair, emptying my cup in the sink and shrugging my way into the shoulder holster.

Either Homer and Darrell were in it together, or Darrell was next on the list.

CHAPTER 34

The Porsche loves to get on the freeway and go. I headed north to Everett, driving directly to the offices of the *Everett Herald.* It's a small-town paper. The receptionist, a bored teenager, was happy to have some company.

I flashed my badge at her, and she bustled around, finding me what I needed—all papers from the two-week period prior to October eighteenth. I located the information I wanted, eventually. Buried among wedding announcements, Pop Warner football scores, and pre-holiday church bazaars was an article detailing Darrell Watkins' campaign swing through Bellingham and Everett. He was to address the Bellingham Rotary and Jaycees on Friday afternoon and a League of Women Voters convention at the Everett Holiday Inn Friday evening. Saturday morning he was scheduled to be the keynote speaker at a Merchant's Fair breakfast.

Thanking the receptionist for her help, I drove to the Holiday Inn. I didn't mess around with the desk clerk. I asked to speak directly to the manager. He was an eager Young Turk, fresh out of school with a degree in hotel management. His nametag pegged him as Mr. Young, which seemed entirely appropriate.

"What can I do for you?" he asked, after minutely examining my identification.

"I'd like to see your guest register for the night of October eighteenth."

"This is, of course, highly irregular."

"Mr. Young," I said firmly, "I'm attempting to prevent another homicide. There's not much time."

"Can't this wait until Monday when I could check with my superiors in Seattle?"

"No. Someone else could be dead by then." Youth can often be intimidated by a steady, middle-aged stare. It worked like a charm.

"Oh, all right. I don't see how it could hurt."

There were lots of registration slips. Many of the women had registered separately, even though they were staying in the same room—a variation on the female penchant for separate checks. I thumbed through them carefully. I was close to the bottom before I found the one I wanted, a slip that read Darrell Watkins. I jotted down the license number of the car, an '81 Audi.

Mr. Young had stood peering over my shoulder the whole time. "Did you find what you needed?" he asked.

"Yes. Can you make me a copy of this?" I showed him the slip.

"This is nuts. I shouldn't have shown it to you in the first place without a court order. Now you want me to make you a copy?"

"By the time I can get a court order," I said, "the killer may strike again. The score is four to nothing right now. The killer's winning."

He made me a copy. "One more question," I said as he handed me the paper. "Who on your catering staff handled the League of Women Voters convention?"

"That would have been Sue Carleton."

"Is she here?"

He sighed, exasperated. "She's upstairs."

Sue Carleton turned out to be a heavyset dame in her middle years. I had a feeling she had come up through the ranks—without a degree in hotel management but with a healthy regard for and an easy ability to work with other people. She had a pleasant manner and a sparkling sense of humor.

"What can I do for you, Detective Beaumont?" she asked.

"I wanted to talk to you about the League of Women Voters."

"They were awful." She smiled. "Too many chiefs and not enough Indians. I almost lost my mind."

"I wanted to ask you about one of the speakers, Darrell Watkins."

"That jerk. He was late. I had to pay my people overtime because they didn't finish on time."

"What happened?"

"He was supposed to speak at the beginning of the program. He didn't show up until nine when they were almost finished. They let him give his whole speech anyway. I was livid."

I stood. "That's all I needed to know. Did he offer any explanation?"

"Car trouble, I think. Does this help?"

"You'd better believe it. Thanks."

Galloping out of the Holiday Inn, I sped north to Anacortes, hoping I'd hit the ferry schedule right. No such luck. A ferry was just pulling away from the dock as I drove up to the ticket booth. There was nothing to do but cool my heels and wait for the next one.

It was possible Darrell could have been on Orcas with Homer at the time Ginger's room was broken into and still have made it back to Everett by nine. If, that is, he had better luck with the ferries than I did.

Once on Orcas, I drove straight to Rosario without notifying Huggins. I wanted to get in, verify the information, and get back out—without arousing attention.

It was Saturday evening. A laughing crowd was grouped around the massive fireplace in the Moran Room, and a clutch of people stood in front of the desk, waiting to register. The overtaxed desk clerk was far too busy to help me right then.

I went into the Vista Lounge. Barney was at his station. He glanced up and waved as I walked past. I had no more than taken a seat on a stool at the end of the bar when he brought me a MacNaughton's and water.

"That's pretty good," I said as he set the drink in front of me.

He grinned. "I don't do much, but I'm good at what I do."

Someone signaled for a beer. Barney drew one from the tap, delivered it, then came back to me. "So what's up? You get your car back all right?"

I nodded. "Ernie did a great job. I'm up here looking for some answers," I told him.

"What kind?"

"I need to see the guest register for the eighteenth. . . . Quietly," I added.

"Unofficially?" I nodded, and he grinned. "I might be able to help. Did you see the lady at the desk?"

"Just a glimpse. She was busy."

"We're engaged," he said proudly. "Tell me what you want. She'll get it for you."

Another customer summoned him. When he returned, he stood in front of me, vigorously polishing the bar. "What are you looking for?" he asked.

"At least one room was rented twice that day. Someone checked in, changed his mind, and checked back out. I need a copy of any registration slips on rooms that were rented twice that day."

He gave me a sly wink. "Looking for somebody sneaking around, eh?" He glanced at my glass. "You want another?"

"No. I'd better switch to coffee. It's a long drive."

"You're not staying over? We've got rooms."

I shook my head. I drank a couple of cups of coffee and ate a hamburger while I waited. It was almost an hour before Barney's fiancée delivered the goods. There were three rooms that had been rented twice on the eighteenth. Using a lighted hurricane lamp from one of the tables, I studied the copies Barney gave me. Five of the six names didn't ring any bells. Three of them had actually spent the night. The other two were probably respectably married people sneaking an illicit afternoon without their lawfully wedded husbands and wives.

The last name stopped me cold. Don Lacy. The address was in Burien. I wrote it down, 12823 S. 124th. The clincher was that the car was a 1981

Audi, the same make and model listed on Darrell Watkins' guest registration at the Holiday Inn. Naturally the license numbers didn't match. What a surprise! Don Lacy and Darrell Watkins had to be one and the same.

I left the lounge and walked to the last wing of the hotel where Ginger's original room had been. The room registered to Lacy was right next door to Ginger's. When Darrell had been talking to her, pleading with her not to divorce him, he had been directly on the other side of a narrow wallboard partition, not calling long-distance from somewhere on the mainland.

Hurrying back to my car, I barely had time to catch the last ferry to Anacortes. I sat by one of the huge windows, staring at glass that reflected the bright lights inside the boat rather than the midnight water outside.

My mind jumped to a dozen different conclusions. Wilson, Homer, and Darrell all had to be involved together. Somehow. All three of them had been at Orcas that afternoon. Funny how both Darrell and Homer had neglected to mention it. The question remained, Were they in it together, or was one covering for the other?

I wanted to be the one to find the answers. I owed Ginger that much, but I wasn't working with a full contingent of soldiers. I didn't have all the resources of Seattle P.D. standing behind me, backing me up. I suppose I could have called Huggins and insisted he reopen the case, but I didn't. Pride, I guess. I wanted to nail the case down with a fistful of incontrovertible evidence before I called for reinforcements.

My mother used to say, "Pride goeth before a fall." It's true.

By the time I reached Anacortes, I had a game plan mapped out in my mind.

It was almost two in the morning when I hit Seattle. I drove straight through town and took the Sea-Tac exit to Burien. The address on S. 124th street wasn't hard to find. A silver Audi was parked in the driveway. I drove home.

Once in the house, I went searching for the phone book. I looked under Lacy, Darlene, 12823 S. 124th Street. That answered a lot of questions. I put the phone book away and went to bed.

Ames woke me Sunday morning. According to my count, that was two Sundays in a row. He wondered if I would care to join Cody and him for brunch at the Westin. Ames sounded smug. He couldn't quite conceal his lack of disappointment when I said no. Ames had never struck me as much of a ladies man. He was proud of what he regarded as a personal conquest.

I wasn't the kind of guy to tell him that he had been duck soup for someone like Colleen Borden, and she was far too much of a lady to tell him herself. I left his delusions of adequacy intact.

"Too much to do, Ames, sorry. But I'll want to talk to you later today or tomorrow about some of the reward money."

"Okay," he said. "But if you don't reach me in my room, you might try Cody's."

"Right," I said.

I waited until ten o'clock before I called Janice Morraine at home. She's a criminalist in Seattle's Washington State Patrol Crime Lab. Over the months, she and I had become friends. I couldn't call the crime lab directly to ask for help. I didn't have an official case number.

"How are you at handwriting analysis?"

"So-so," she answered.

"How about trading breakfast for an off-the-record opinion."

She laughed. "Smooth talker," she said.

We went to an omelet house at the bottom of East Madison, right on Lake Washington. There, amid the early-afternoon Sunday brunch crowd, she smoked one cigarette after another and compared the two signatures from copies of the guest-registration forms. She studied them in silence for several long minutes, leaving me to sip my coffee and stare at the top of her head bent over the papers in total concentration. At last she looked up at me.

"You know I'm not the final word," she said. I nodded. "But in my opinion, they were signed by the same person."

"That's what I thought."

"Is this *the* Darrell Watkins?" she asked, pointing at his signature. I nodded again. "If this is something bad, you'd better not just take my word for it," she warned.

"I won't."

"And we haven't had this conversation?"

"How did you guess? Now, what do you want to eat?"

We each had huge omelets with crisp hash browns and thick, jam-covered toast. As far as I was concerned, it was a celebration. I was getting closer and closer to nailing those bastards. Nothing definite. Strictly circumstantial, but closer nonetheless.

Darrell Watkins, Homer Watkins, and the deceased Don Wilson. Gradually I was closing in on the truth.

Hurrying back to my apartment, I pawed through the receipt shoebox until I found my bill from Rosario. The long-distance phone calls were there—time, duration, phone numbers, and charges. Thank God for computer printouts.

I saw the problem immediately. How could Homer have been seen by Blia Vang at seven o'clock Friday night, less than an hour after he had phoned my room and left word for Ginger to call? Her answering call to

Seattle was right there on my bill, dialed direct from my room. The time on the printout said seven-forty. The call from Orcas to Seattle had lasted six minutes.

Settling into my recliner, I studied the list of phone calls with minute care. Again on Saturday, there were calls to Seattle numbers, one to Homer in the early evening and one to Peters much later.

I didn't bother to work the crossword puzzles Ida Newell had dropped outside my door. I sat there and wondered why Blia Vang had lied to me, or if she hadn't, how had Homer Watkins managed to be in two places at once.

CHAPTER 35

Monday morning I woke up early and waited until six before I called Ray Johnson in Pasco. Evie answered the phone. "Just a minute, Beau. Ray's in the shower." Evie and I chatted amiably until Ray came on the phone.

"How the hell are you?" he boomed.

"I need your help, Ray."

"Sure thing. What's up?"

"Remember that morning when we were all there in your office and the governor's office called?"

"I remember. Just before the press conference. They wanted to make sure we had you safely under lock and key."

"Do you happen to remember the man's name? The governor's aide?"

Ray Johnson is an encyclopedia of names. Once he hears one, he doesn't forget it. When he left Seattle for Pasco, I felt as though I had lost my right arm. I had come to depend on him to remember names for both of us.

"Just a minute now," he said. "Hold on and it'll come to me. Something to do with a bird. Hawk . . . Hawkins. That's it, I'm almost sure. What do you need him for? I thought the case was all sewed up."

"Except for a couple of loose ends," I said.

By ten to eight I was suffering from a serious case of twenty-four-minute flu. I called the Department at eight. Peters wasn't in yet. Margie took the call.

"I'm not feeling well, Marge," I said, doing my best to sound feeble.

"I hope it's not stomach flu," Margie sympathized. "That's going around. My kids were both down with it last week and missed two whole days of school."

By five after eight, I was in the Porsche heading south on the freeway, feeling much better. It was a miracle. As I drove toward Olympia, my mother's words came back to me. "One thing about Jonas, he doesn't let good sense stand in the way of what he wants."

My mother's twenty-five-year-old words still held the ring of prophecy. What I was doing didn't make good sense. J. P. Beaumont, good sense to the contrary, was turning up the heat under Homer and Darrell Watkins, attempting to smoke them into the open. It was best not to use a direct attack.

I parked as close as I could to the governor's office on the governmental campus and walked in as big as life. I asked the doe-eyed young receptionist for Mr. Hawkins.

"Do you have an appointment?" she asked.

"No," I said, flashing my ID in her direction. "But I'm sure he'll see me just the same."

I was right. Within five minutes I was shown into Lee Hawkins' office. I handed him my City of Seattle business card which he examined with some care.

"Weren't you the one—"

"Who was mistakenly arrested in Pasco?" I supplied helpfully. "Yes, I am."

He nodded. "I thought so. The name looked familiar. What can I do for you?" He dropped my card onto his desk.

"I'm actually here about the Washington State Victim/Witness Protection Program."

"I see."

"What's going on with that?"

"Well, we've been involved in negotiations with the Senate and House Judiciary Committees. There's no question that the program will cost money, although the governor's office supports the idea wholeheartedly." He paused and looked at me. "Is this on or off the record?"

"Off."

"We've about ironed out all resistance. We're hoping it'll be presented as a joint bill early next session."

"No announcement will be made prior to that?"

"That would be premature, Mr. Beaumont."

"And no announcement was planned for the parole board retreat on Orcas?"

"Absolutely not."

Just in case my message hadn't gotten through, I added one final hook. "That's funny. Don Wilson was sure there would be an announcement at Orcas."

Lee Hawkins smiled. "He must have been mistaken."

"Of course," I replied. "Thanks." I left and drove straight back to Seattle. If somebody called to check on my health, the invalid should be at home, in bed. And if somebody took the bait, the fisherman should be hanging onto the other end of the pole for dear life.

Predictably, the phone was ringing as I got off the elevator. It was Peters. "Where the hell have you been? You're supposed to be sick."

"I needed some medicine," I lied. "How're the girls?"

"They're in school. The baby-sitter Ames hired will pick Heather up after kindergarten. Tracie can walk home by herself. Mrs. Keen—that's the baby-sitter's name—will stay until I get home tonight. Do you have everything you need? Yogurt, or maybe some Pepto-Bismol?"

"Everything, thanks. I'm much better. What are you doing?"

"Manny and Al are trying to negotiate a peace treaty with the feds to extradite Farley from Canada."

"Good luck." I was glad I wouldn't be there to fight and lose the opening rounds of the paperwork war. I've seen more than one crook hole up across the border, hiding out in plain sight behind a mountain of red tape.

"Get well," Peters said. "See you tomorrow."

I fixed a pot of coffee, sat down, and put my feet up. The next caller was Ames, totally focused on business. "What about the reward money?"

"Never mind. The witness may have lied to me. We'll have to see."

"Okay," Ames said agreeably. "Whatever you say."

"How's Cody?" I couldn't resist catching him off base. Ames was trying with some difficulty to concentrate on work. His obvious confusion was laughable.

He hesitated, half switching gears, attempting to maintain his dignity. "She's working today. I don't know doing what." He paused again, scrambling for what to say next. "I guess, as long as I'm here, I'll go ahead and mother-hen the penthouse deal. Are you going to do any customizing?"

I hadn't thought about it. "What do you suggest?"

Ames sighed. "I'll get a couple of decorators to take a look and see what they say."

"Just one thing, Ames."

"What's that?"

"Wherever I go, my recliner goes."

"Right," he said.

He hung up. I poured myself a cup of coffee. And waited. It was the calm before the storm. I was convinced the storm was coming. Who would call, Darrell or Homer? I figured it was a toss-up.

When the phone finally rang at four that afternoon, it was a delivery boy bringing flowers. I buzzed him into the building and opened the door without even bothering to check the peekhole. The crime prevention unit would have drummed me off the force.

"Hello, Detective Beaumont," Darrell Watkins said easily. "I've got a gun. You're coming with me." He raised a snub-nosed .38 from behind the box of flowers.

He lifted my Smith and Wesson out of its holster and dropped it into a jacket pocket, all the while keeping me covered.

"I understand you were making inquiries about the Victim/Witness Protection Program."

"That's right."

"Was your interest personal or professional?"

"Both."

"Since that's a program I'm interested in, too, I thought maybe we should get together and talk. Where's your car?"

"In the garage."

"Let's go."

He directed me to the Watkins mansion on Capitol Hill. I walked ahead of him to the house and pushed the door open, half expecting to find Homer waiting inside, but the entryway was empty, the house itself quiet.

I stepped over the threshold, tensing as I realized we were alone, hoping I could catch him off guard, take him by surprise.

Instead, something hit me behind my right ear. I went down like a sack of potatoes.

The cold woke me. I opened my eyes, thinking I'd gone blind. I could see nothing. I struggled to move, and ran my nose into my knee. It startled me to find my knee jammed directly in front of my face. It shouldn't have been there. I tried moving my fingers and felt my feet. Slowly it started making sense. I was tied, trussed in a fetal position, with my hands and feet fastened together at my ankles.

I was also stark naked.

It's tough getting your bearings in pitch darkness. Under me were what seemed to be wooden slats. A humming motor clicked off, followed by ominous silence.

I was trapped in a refrigerator waiting to die.

Rocking painfully on the small of my back, I tried rolling as far as I could in one direction, hoping to find a door and figure out a way to open it. I rolled until I encountered a smooth, hard surface. Before I could ascertain whether it was door or wall, a door at the other end of the compartment jerked open. A single light bulb next to the door snapped on, momentarily blinding me.

When I could see, Darrell Watkins was standing over me. "My, my. Aren't we clever. I didn't think you'd wake up before I got back. I had to take your car downtown and park it on Third Avenue. In the bus zone. By now it's being towed at owner's expense. It'll take days to find it."

"You're crazy."

"Maybe," he said agreeably. "But smart."

"Is this how Wilson died of exposure?"

He nodded. "I let him hang around long enough for the drug to get out of his system, then I sprayed him with cold water. Worked like a charm. I never had to tie him up. I'm afraid your rope burns will show."

I wanted to keep him talking. I gauged the distance between us, wondering if I could roll against his legs with enough strength to knock him down.

"You met him on the ferry?"

"He met me on the car deck so I could give him a copy of the governor's proclamation."

"But there was no proclamation."

Watkins shrugged. "Don Wilson didn't know that. He got in the car, I gave him one little prick with this, and he went night-night."

He held up a hypo, the needle glinting in the light from the bulb near the door. I made a tentative roll toward him. He laughed and stepped away. "None of that," he said.

"Wilson went off the ferry in your car?"

"That's right. Out cold on the floor of the backseat. I put him in the trunk later. He slept like a baby until Sunday when I finally got him back to Seattle. I had plenty of time to see Sig Larson."

"And kill him?"

He grinned. "That too." He sobered suddenly. "You puzzle me, Detective Beaumont. As far as I can tell, you're the only one who doesn't believe Wilson did it. How come?"

"Gut instinct. Wilson left a chicken thawing at home, and he didn't feed his cat. Looked like he planned to come back."

"He did. You think you're pretty smart, don't you! Guess that's why you're there and I'm here, right?" He laughed—the maniacal laughter of someone losing his grip. "Except for that, I was good, though, wasn't I? Framed Wilson every step of the way, that poor, stupid bastard. He wanted to make headlines."

"You're the one who called him to Orcas?"

He nodded, grinning. "You bet. I even arranged for that reporter to do a series on him. That was brilliant."

His words reeked of ugly truth. "You've been planning this for a long time."

"Months. This was my last chance before the sheriff's sale. After that it would have been too late."

"Mona too?"

"Mona too."

"How did you know she was at the Red Lion?"

"My father. I told him I wanted to explain why I couldn't go to Sig's funeral. I was waiting. When you drove up, I decided to use your car. That was masterful, don't you think?"

"You did it for the money?"

"Money isn't everything, but it helps. I'll need every penny to get back on even ground."

"You think you'll get away with it?"

"Absolutely!"

"How did you get Ginger drunk?"

He laughed. "You should have seen her face. She was real surprised to see me. I was waiting just outside the gate. I almost missed her because she was driving a different car. Your car. How come?"

I ignored his question and repeated my own. "How'd you get her drunk?"

"A hose, a soft plastic hose. That was for Tom's benefit. She promised him she'd never drink again. Little Miss Perfect. Shoved it down her throat and poured the booze through it. She was already unconscious. It worked, too. Did you see old Tom at the funeral?"

"What about the calendar. Did you take it?" If I was going to die, it would at least be *with* some answers.

"Sure. I had to put Wilson's fingerprints on something while he was passed out in the back of the car."

Far away, through the chill, I heard the chime of the doorbell. Darrell jumped as though shot. I tried to call for help. He covered the distance between us in one long step. A hand clamped over my mouth, and a needle pricked my arm.

The lights went out, literally and figuratively.

CHAPTER 36

When I awakened again, my fingers and toes were numb. Trying not to succumb to panic, I moved them as much as possible, hoping to force circulation back into them. There was a gag in my mouth with sticky tape holding it in place.

The humming motor clicked off. In the subsequent silence, I could hear another person's breathing.

I strained to listen. The roaring beat of my own heart threatened to drown out the shallow sound. The person was sleeping a sleep very close to the big one. Painting with effort, I rocked toward the sound. Four painful rocks away, I encountered another naked body, bound and trussed as I was, with legs as hairy as my own. Another man. For some unaccountable reason, that made me feel better.

Positioning my back against his, I tried to jar him awake. He stirred a little, but immediately resumed his shallow breathing. Again I attempted to shake him. Exertion caused beads of sweat to pop out on my body. I was aware of further heat loss as cold, dry air met perspiration.

Painfully I scooted around until my feet were in his face. I kicked him, and his breathing changed. He was awake now, whoever he was. Some circulation had returned to my fingers and toes. I felt for the tape that covered his mouth. Grasping a corner of it between my thumbs and forefingers, I rolled away from him, taking the tape with me.

It took long, precious minutes to roll back again and reposition myself to remove the cloth material that had been stuffed into his mouth behind the tape. "Thank you," he choked once the gag was out. I recognized the voice.

Homer Watkins lay on the wooden slats beside me.

He had not yet mastered the fundamentals of movement in our condition. I rolled around until my face was against his fingers. His first numbed attempts at grasping the tape on my gag didn't work. It took numerous tries before he was at last able to hold the tape while I rolled away. Then I maneuvered my way back so he could remove the gag.

"Who are you?" he asked as soon as I could speak.

"Beaumont," I answered. "What time is it?"

"I don't know. It was morning when he put me in here. He kept me up all night, raving. He's crazy."

"We'll discuss that later. Let's get out of here first before we die of cold or suffocation. Can you untie me?"

We struggled in the dark, our fingers too numb and clumsy to know what they were about. Time passed, I don't know how much. Finally I gave up in defeat. "Stay here," I ordered. "I'm going to find a bottle to break."

I remembered seeing a wine rack, but in the struggle to free us, I had become disoriented. I rocked back and forth across the confines of our prison, searching for the rack, my muscles screaming at the unaccustomed position. After what seemed like hours, I finally bumped up against the stack of corked bottles.

Deliberately breaking a bottle seems easy, but not if your hands and feet are tied together. The adult male body has long since lost the newborn limberness which allows a baby to suck its toes. Each movement was an agony, each failure unbearable. I wanted desperately to break the bottle in the farthest corner of our cage. There's an atavistic fear of bleeding to death in the dark. I didn't want to roll blindly and helplessly on broken glass.

At last I managed to return to Homer with a jagged shard from a bottle. "You do me," I said. "If anybody gets cut, it'll be me."

Fortunately, the insides of our wrists were tied together. The cuts and slices in my flesh, though painful and bloody, were also superficial. As Homer sawed at my restraints I asked him questions. The exercise served two purposes. It gave me some answers, and it took both our minds off the sticky blood that accompanied his work.

"Why did you go to Rosario that Friday?"

"Darlene said she thought that's where Darrell went. I was worried about him. He was upset."

"Why?"

"God knows he had no right to be jealous, but he couldn't believe she'd go ahead and divorce him."

"You took the maid's keys and broke into Ginger's room?"

"Someone had already been there. The room was a mess. I panicked."

"But I talked to you. Ginger called you back."

"When she didn't return my call at first, I was afraid he might have killed her too."

"Ginger called you in Seattle. I have the phone number on my bill."

"I have a phone in the car. I forwarded calls there."

A long silence ensued between us, with only the scraping of glass on the fibrous rope filling the emptiness left by the stilled motor. "Why didn't you turn him in?"

He waited a long time to answer me. "When they said it was Wilson, I believed it, wanted to believe it."

"It wasn't."

"I know," he said hollowly.

Eventually, after what seemed an eternity, the rope parted. My hands and feet were freed.

To my complete frustration, I wasn't instantly able to straighten up and walk to the light switch. My muscles were too cramped and stiff. I lurched across the wooden slats, crawling awkwardly on my knees, dreading the broken glass, groping blindly for the elusive switch I knew was there. Eventually I found it.

The sudden light from the single 40-watt light was dazzling. I found the thermostat and turned the refrigeration unit off, then I cut through Homer's bonds. Movement returned slowly. Even then, it didn't do us a hell of a lot of good: there was no latch inside the refrigerator door, only a smooth, seemingly impenetrable metal surface.

I turned from the door to Homer. "How long have you known for sure?"

"Since last night. I wouldn't let myself believe it. I never saw him in a jealous rage before."

"Jealous rage hell!" I said harshly, stripping away Homer's last vestige of justification. "He's after money, the insurance. He set it up to frame Wilson for the first three. You can bet he has some plan so it will look like J. P. Beaumont did away with you."

Homer swayed dangerously. I caught him and broke his fall. "He would, wouldn't he! He'd kill me too." Homer Watkins sank the rest of the way to the floor. You don't fake the kind of shock that spread across his face. Seeing it told me once and for all that Homer was innocent. Darrell Watkins had acted alone.

The naked old man, diminished, squatted brokenly on his haunches, a picture of abject defeat. I looked down, thinking to help him to his feet. In looking down, I saw our way out.

Our cell's wooden slats were actually the tops of pallets, wooden lathing on frames of sturdy two-by-fours. "Get up, Homer, quick," I urged, grasping him by the wrist and pulling him to his feet.

The pallets were about three and a half feet square. I picked one up, hefted it, stood it on edge. With both of us swinging in concert, we could use it as a battering ram. The latches on the outside of the door couldn't hold forever under that kind of treatment.

I explained the plan. "If the door opens and he's outside, chances are he'll have a weapon. Keep swinging, and hope we can hit him."

We took a first tentative swing at the door. The noise of the blow seemed deafening. We waited, breathless, expecting Darrell to charge through the door. Nothing happened. We swung again. Again nothing happened.

"All right," I said, "here goes. Swing together in rhythm. Back and forth. Eventually we'll build momentum."

I didn't tell Homer my other worry, that our air would run out and we'd suffocate before we ever broke through to the outside. At least we'd die warm.

Swing, blam. Swing, blam. Swing, blam. Obviously the house was empty, or the noise would have aroused a response. Swing, blam. Swing, blam. Swing, blam. The metal dented as the inside of the door crushed against an outer shell. Swing, blam. Swing, blam. Swing, blam. The door shuddered each time we hit it, giving way under every blow. Swing, blam. Swing, blam. Swing, blam. As the hinges crumbled, momentum carried us into the kitchen. We were out. We were free. We weren't going to die.

At least not then, and not in a refrigerator.

The kitchen was dark. It was night. Homer crossed the floor and switched on a light. A clock over the sink said nine o'clock. "What night?" I asked.

"Tuesday," he said. "Election night." The strength that had sustained him as we battered the door ebbed away. he leaned heavily against the stainless steel table in the center of the room. "What are you going to do?" he asked.

I gave the first answer that came to mind. It had no bearing on the question he was really asking. "I'm going to find some clothes."

There is something implacably sane about insanity. I found all our clothes, both Homer's and mine, in a dirty-clothes hamper in the laundry room. Where else? It was as though Darrell expected a maid to appear and wash them for him, maybe even dispose of the corpses in his refrigerator—a kind of macabre *noblesse oblige*. Darrell Watkins was no more accustomed to living without money than I was used to living with it.

Homer was still leaning against the table when I returned to the kitchen. He hadn't moved. "What are you going to do?" he asked again, his voice a plaintive monotone.

I countered with another question. "Where is he?"

"The victory party."

"Where?"

Homer took the clothes I handed him. "I won't tell," he said stubbornly. "I'll show you. Will you arrest him?"

"If I can."

"Don't," he said.

I was bent over, tying my shoe, convinced I had misunderstood him. "What did you say?"

"Don't arrest him. Put him out of his misery. He's a mad dog."

I knew what he was asking and why. I shook my head. "I'm an officer of the law, Homer. I can't do that."

My .38 had been in its holster at the bottom of the clothes hamper. I checked it now, making sure it was loaded, that it wasn't jammed. "Will he be armed?"

"No." Homer stopped speaking abruptly and stood examining his shoes as though unsure which shoe went on what foot. "I can't say," he resumed at last. "He's killed four people so far. What do I know?"

A phone hung on the kitchen wall. I had seen it the moment the light came on, but I waited to use it until we were both dressed. Homer's dignity had suffered enough.

While I waited, I washed the dried blood from my hands and wrists. When Homer finally finished tying his shoelaces, I picked up the phone and dialed the department. It was late, after nine, but I knew Peters would be there. We were partners. He would be working, trying to find me.

"Beau!" he exclaimed, relief evident in his voice. "Where the hell are you?"

Quickly I gave him the address. "Come as fast as you can. Bring a couple squad cars with you, but no sirens, understand?"

"Right," he replied without question.

Homer had disappeared from the kitchen while I talked on the phone. He returned now, wearing a heavy jacket over his suit. He still looked cold and pale. "Are you warming up?" I asked.

He nodded. "I'm coming with you." He was determined.

"You can't," I said. "It's too dangerous. It would be better if you stayed here."

"No. I know where he'll be. Maybe I can talk him into giving up."

It was remotely possible. "Where's the party?" I asked.

"Will you take me along?"

I relented. "Oh, all right. Now where are we going?"

"The Trade Center," Homer replied.

"Shit!" I remembered seeing live election-night coverage from the Muni-League party in previous years. It was usually held in the Seattle Trade Center. The candidates and their campaign workers would gather there, winners and losers alike, to watch the returns. There would be throngs of people, drunk and sober, television cameras, bands, lights, reporters. It would be chaos—the last place any cop in his right mind wants to go after a crazed killer.

Peters and four uniformed patrolmen arrived within minutes. The three of us—Peters, Homer, and I—rode in a squad car to the Trade Center at Elliott and Clay.

"Let me talk to him," Homer insisted as we made our way through traffic. "Maybe I can get him to surrender."

My initial reaction was to say no out of hand. We're not in this business to risk civilian lives. Peters, however, assumed the role of devil's advocate. "It's going to be a madhouse in there. If Homer can get him to come quietly, it could prevent wholesale bloodshed."

Spending well over twenty-four hours in cold storage had put me in a mood to listen to sweet reason. "All right," I agreed. "So how do we handle it?"

Homer let out his breath as though he had been holding it. "I'll lead the way to our spot. We're usually on the first floor, near the escalator. Give me a minute or so to find him."

It was better than no plan at all.

We approached the Trade Center with lights flashing but no sirens. Not wanting to broadcast a warning, we maintained radio silence. Surprising him was our only chance. Alerting the world could create a riot.

Once there, Peters designated an officer to assume command outside the center. He deployed men to cover all building and parking-garage entrances. It was an empty gesture. We all knew that if panic ensued, no one would be able to tell Darrell Watkins from hundreds of other terrified partygoers crushing through the doors, racing to get outside.

Peters and I paused for a moment outside the door, giving Homer a head start in crossing the crowded room. "Are you sure you're okay?" Peters asked.

"Yeah. I'm all right."

"I'll go first," he said. "You follow."

"No deal, asshole," I told him. "You've got a couple little kids to raise. No fucking way you're sticking me with that job."

Before Peters had a chance to object, I pushed my way in front of him, following Homer Watkins into a wall-to-wall throng of people.

CHAPTER 37

Afterwards, there were conflicting stories. A woman said she saw Homer Watkins walk up to Darrell, pull a gun out of his jacket, and try to shoot him. Others said there was a struggle, the gun went off, and Homer fell mortally wounded.

I heard the report of a pistol and a woman's scream. Time froze. The sea of people turned as one man, moving toward the disturbance and away from it at the same time, surging forward and back, closing ranks. I fought my way through, moving in slow motion, flinging people aside, only to have others blunder into my path.

"Out of the way. Police!" Peters roared behind me, but the crowd became denser, more compact. Absolutely silent, and compact. To this day, I don't know if that silence existed anywhere but in my mind. It ceased when I reached the escalators.

People coming down screamed and swirled back up the moving stairs, attempting to escape the carnage below. They encountered a wall of people above them who stood unable to move, transfixed by fear.

I saw Darrell Watkins as he broke and ran. Gun in hand, he dashed up the escalator three and four steps at a time, plunging over people, pushing them aside.

Delayed pandemonium erupted through the crowd as I touched the rail of the down escalator. Maybe the noise was there the whole time and I only just then heard it. Clearing the way with my drawn .38, I charged up the downward treadmill, desperate to reach the top. My only hope was to drive him farther up into the building. Away from the crowds. Away from doors that would lead him outside.

Peters must have been only one or two steps behind me at the outset, but the crowd caught him in a crushing wave of panic and carried him back toward the door with them. I paused and turned briefly at the top of the stairs, hoping he was with me. He wasn't.

It would be Darrell Watkins and J. P. Beaumont. Alone.

The Trade Center is made up of a soaring atrium, with a ground floor and two layers of shops arranged around circling balconies under a huge skylight. Watkins charged up the second escalator. On the second level the crowd had thinned. I raced across the landing to the up escalator and followed, watching in dismay as he disappeared around a corner and down a hall before I reached the next level.

He was halfway down the long corridor when I turned the corner in hot pursuit. "Stop or I'll shoot," I shouted.

I paused to fire, but he was out of range. My slug ponged harmlessly off the wall behind him. I ducked my chin into my chest and sprinted down the corridor after him as he vanished into a stairwell. Gasping for breath, I flung open the fire door. I stood on a concrete landing, listening to the echo of retreating footsteps. For one heart-stopping moment, I thought they were going down. Then a gust of fresh air rushed down the stairwell into my face, followed by the warning shriek of an alarm on an opened emergency exit.

He had gone to the roof.

I crept up the stairs. It could be a trap. He might have opened and shut the outside door to trick me. Maybe he was lying in wait around the blind corner of the stairs, ready to blast me into oblivion. I held my breath as I rounded the turn. He wasn't there. The stairs leading to the emergency exit were empty.

Below I heard the wail of sirens as ambulances and emergency vehicles raced to the scene. They would set up a command post and summon the Emergency Response Team, trying to position them to negotiate a surrender or, as a last resort, to fire off a clean shot. Peters would direct officers through the building, evacuating the crowd, securing first one area and then another.

But all that was happening in another world, far below us. Out on the roof, Darrell Watkins was waiting. For me.

I pushed open the heavy door. Over the wail of the alarm, I heard a bullet whine past the door's metal frame above my head. That was his second shot. I counted, wondering subconsciously what kind of a gun Homer had smuggled into his jacket. How many bullets? Did Darrell have four more shots, or seven? And did he have another gun of his own?

Standing in what amounted to a metal bunker at the top of the stairwell, I was better off trying to draw his fire and exhaust his ammunition while I could use the heavy door as armor between us. Each bullet he expended was one less available to slaughter innocent bystanders. Or me.

I yanked the alarm wire off the wall, silencing its bloodcurdling screech. In the sudden quiet that followed, a surprising calm settled over me. He was trapped. His only way out was past me. If I could drive him to a frenzy, force him to attack me in the open, maybe I could end it.

The irony struck me with the force of a physical blow. Darrell Watkins and J. P. Beaumont, men who had possessed the same woman, were locked in mortal combat.

I remembered Homer's hopeless pronouncement in the kitchen. "Put him out of his misery." I was tempted! God, was I tempted! But shooting was too easy, too good for him. I wanted him to live to know his loss, to pay a price, to suffer humiliation and defeat, to live out his days with Philip Lathrop as his lifelong companion. They deserved each other.

I would take him alive. I steeled myself to use every weapon at my disposal.

Somehow Ginger Watkins would forgive me. I opened the door a crack so he could hear me.

"She was a hell of a lay," I called into the night.

"What?"

"Ginger. She was one hell of a lay," I taunted. "Too bad you didn't know how good she was."

Another bullet whined off the metal door. That was three.

"You lying son of a bitch!"

"What's the matter. Can't take a dose of your own medicine? She was hot stuff, Darrell," I continued, soft enough so he had to strain to hear me. "She was so hungry. You never gave her what she wanted. She needed a man to take her, to make her know she was a woman."

I waited, silence brittle between us, hoping another bullet would crash into the wall near my head. Nothing happened. He was across the roof from me, crouched out of range behind a small fenced terrace outlined in a sudden splash of moonlight. Needing to draw his fire, I opened the door and spun around toward the back of the rooftop box that formed the top of the stairwell.

It worked. Too well. A slug ripped into my upper left arm, spinning me against the wall. Searing pain came quickly, making it hard to talk, to concentrate. How many bullets was that now, four or five?

"You couldn't handle that, could you?" I rasped through gritted teeth. "You had to have young ones like Darlene, girls you could impress with money if not performance. Ginger had been empty so long I couldn't fill her up."

"Liar," he said.

"Just because you couldn't get it up for her didn't mean nobody could."

"No," he croaked, his voice a hoarse, broken whisper. "It's not true."

"It is, too. Ask me. Ask Sig. Didn't he tell you? He could have."

"Maybe with him, not you." His voice rose dangerously. A tongue of flame spewed from his pistol in the darkness. The shot whistled harmlessly away into the night sky. Five or six? Let there be only six bullets, I prayed, not nine.

"I can prove it. How about the stretch marks from Katy? Remember those, or had it been so long since you looked at her that you forgot?"

I waited to see if he would reply. There was nothing. No response. "She'd have been stupid to divorce you," I continued. "She should have just screwed around behind your back. That would have been fair."

Several separate shots peppered the wall of the stairwell, followed by silence. For a long time we remained motionless, frozen in place, him across the fenced balcony and me behind the stairwell, a sticky stream of blood oozing through my jacket sleeve. I couldn't tell for sure if he had emptied the bullet chamber. Or if he had another gun.

It was time to play Russian roulette.

I stepped into the open. If he had only one shot left, he could squander it on me. Whether or not he got me, Darrell Watkins was finished.

"I always knew she was fucking around. She had to be."

"Is that why you killed her, Darrell, or was it the money?"

He raised up, his form outlined on the other side of the terrace. "Both," he said simply. "She was going to divorce me." He spoke with the wonder of a philosopher contemplating life's fundamental mysteries. He seemed quiet, subdued.

"Drop the gun, Darrell."

"I won the election. Did you know that?"

"Put your hands on your head. You're under arrest."

My words were a catalyst, spurring him to action. With an enraged roar, he vaulted over the fence, charging at me like a wounded bull. He landed on the terrace.

Except it wasn't a terrace at all.

It was the skylight.

The glass shattered. With an agonizing screech, he plunged out of sight, crashing into the mêlée of television cameras and milling people three stories below.

I walked over to the jagged hole and looked down. Far below, Darrell's crumpled body lay in a broken heap, seeping blood on the red brick floor. Around him television cameras hummed, fighting for focus and position, recording live footage for the people staying up late to watch election-night returns. Viewers would have their full recommended daily dose of blood and guts before they fell asleep. In living color.

The door behind me flew open. Peters burst onto the rooftop, his .38 glinting in the moonlight. "Are you all right?" he demanded.

"I am now."

CHAPTER 38

We went to Peters' house in Kirkland the following Sunday for dinner. My left arm was in a sling. Cody Borden insisted she knew just what I needed. She would cook Southern for us—Southern Fried Chicken, black-eyed peas, and cornbread. She bustled around Peters' kitchen with Peters serving as cook's helper. She wore stiletto heels. One of Peters' oversized aprons was cinched tightly around her tiny waist. She looked better than any middle-aged woman has a right to look.

Peters was catering to the invalid. I had been off work the rest of the week, recuperating. In the interim, Peters, Cody, and Ames had joined forces to spoil me rotten.

Ames, content for once to let Cody out of his sight, sat on a couch with Heather and Tracie cuddled on either side of him. He was teaching them the Pledge of Allegiance. They had never learned it while they lived with New Dawn in Broken Springs, Oregon. At Greenwood School in Kirkland, they were required to memorize it.

I listened on the sidelines. Uncle Ralph, as they called Ames, showed infinite patience. It was funny that the man who inspired stark terror in the heart of Maxwell Cole was meek as a lamb with those two little ankle-biters. They had him wrapped around their fingers.

It was a quiet family setting, as American as apple pie. I sat in an easy chair across from them, my arm safe from squirming little bodies, sipping a MacNaughton's. Physically, I remained in the room, but my thoughts roamed far afield.

Had Homer Watkins lived, things would have been different. Since there were no surviving partners, however, Armour Life would pay the insurance proceeds to each person's next of kin.

Tom Lander had put his 76 Station on the market. He planned to buy a motor home and hit the road. Sig's children had been notified and were in the process of filing a claim. No one had yet been able to locate Mona's brother, but Cody said she was working on it. Cody said it would be only a matter of days before death benefits owing them were paid.

As far as we could tell, Homer had no surviving kin, and his attorney said that his will left everything he owned to Children's Orthopedic Hospital.

I understood Blia Vang had used her reward money to make a down payment on a small house with room for a large garden. Ames was handling those details, including getting Blia hired on in the Westin laundry. Blia's whole family—aunt, uncle, and cousins—would be moving out of the low-income housing development and into a place of their own.

I didn't go to Homer and Darrell's double funeral. I sent flowers to Homer, not Darrell. The funeral was widely attended. And televised.

Thinking about Ginger still hurt, but Anne Corley's pain was a little more remote. I had Ginger to thank for that. She had helped me say good-bye to Anne, to move beyond that chapter in my life. Without her, I don't know how long it would have taken to get back on track.

I returned to Peters' living room in time to hear the girls repeating in singsong unison: "One nation, under God, invisible, with liverty injustice for all."

"And justice for all," Ames corrected gently.

I took a long sip of MacNaughtons. Thinking about Ginger and Mona and Sig and Homer, I wondered if the girls hadn't gotten it right the first time.

Trial by Fury

To Will,
who used to be the strong, silent type

CHAPTER 1

I was hung over as hell when Detective Ron Peters and I hit the crime scene at ten after eight on a gray and rainy Seattle Monday morning. Peters, my partner on Seattle P.D.'s homicide squad, was quick to point out that it could have been worse. At least I had some hope of getting better. The black man lying behind the dumpster at the Lower Queen Anne Bailey's Foods didn't.

He was dead. Had been for some time. The sickish odor of decaying flesh was thick in the air.

Partially wrapped in a tarp, he lay propped against the loading dock, the whole weight of his body resting on his shoulders, his broad head twisted unnaturally to one side.

The human neck is engineered to turn back and forth and up and down in a multitude of combinations. This wasn't one of them. I didn't need the medical examiner's officer to tell me his neck was broken, but it would require an autopsy to determine if a broken neck was actually the cause of death.

Fortunately, the medical examiner wasn't far behind us. Old Doc Baker, his full head of white hair wet and plastered flat on his head, turned up with a squad of youthful technicians. Baker supervises departmental picture-taking and oversees the initial handling of the corpse.

Crime-scene etiquette comes with its own peculiar pecking order. In phase one, the medical examiner reigns supreme. Baker barked orders that sent people scurrying in all directions while Peters and I stood in the doorway of the loading dock trying to keep out of both the way and the rain.

The store manager, with a name tag identifying him as Curt, came to stand beside us. He chewed vigorously on a hangnail. "This is real bad for business," he said to no one in particular, although Peters and I were the only people within earshot. "Corporate isn't going to like it at all!"

I turned to him, snapping open my departmental ID. "Detective J. P. Beaumont," I told him. "Homicide, Seattle P.D. Is this man anyone you recognize?" I motioned in the direction of the dead man.

It was a long shot, checking to see if Curt recognized the victim, but it didn't hurt to ask. Every once in a while we get lucky. Someone says sure, he knows the victim, and provides us with a complete name and address. Having that kind of information gives us a big leg up at the beginning of an investigation, but it doesn't happen often. And it didn't happen then.

Curt shook his head mournfully. "No. Never saw him before. But it's still bad for business. Just wait till this hits the papers."

"Optimist," Peters muttered to me under his breath. To Curt, he said, "Who found him?"

"Produce boy. He's upstairs in my office."

"Can we talk to him?"

"He's still pretty shook up. Just a kid, you know."

We followed Curt through the store, deserted except for a few anxious employees who watched our progress down an aisle stacked high with canned goods. At the front of the store, he led us through a door and up a steep flight of steps to a messy cubbyhole that served as Curt's office. From the debris and litter scattered on the table, it was clear the room doubled as an employee lunchroom.

The produce boy was just exactly that, a boy, a kid barely out of high school to look at him. He sat by a scarred wooden desk with his tie loosened and his head resting on his arms. When he raised his head to look at us, a distinctly greenish pallor colored his face. The name tag on his blue apron pocket said *Frank*.

"How's it going, Frank?" I asked, flashing my ID.

He shook his head. "Not so good. I've never seen anybody dead before."

"How'd you find him?"

"The lettuce," he said.

"Lettuce?"

"Not lettuce exactly. The produce trimmings. I was taking them out to the dumpster in a lettuce crate. That's when I saw him."

"What time?"

"After seven sometime. Don't know exactly. I don't wear a watch."

"And you didn't move him or touch him in any way?"

"Are you kidding? I dropped the crate and lost my cookies. Right there on the loading dock. Then I ran like hell."

"What time?" Peters asked, turning to the manager.

"Twenty after seven. I checked when I dialed 911."

We asked the full quota of questions, but there was nothing either Frank or his boss could add to what they'd already told us. Finally, thanking them for their help, we left the office and returned to where Doc Baker was still throwing his considerable weight around.

"What's it look like?" I asked when he heaved himself to his feet, motioned the techs to pack up the body, and came over to where Peters and I were standing.

"Death by hanging from the looks of it," he said. "Rope burns around his neck. That's probably how it got broken. I'll be able to tell you for sure after the autopsy."

"When will you do it?" Peters asked.

Baker scowled. "Don't rush me. This afternoon, probably. We have another one scheduled for this morning. What was it, a full moon over the weekend?"

Peters shook his head. "You've got it wrong, Doc. According to what I read, rapes and robberies go up during a full moon, not murders."

Baker gave Peters another sour look. They never really hit it off. Baker didn't have much patience with Peters' photographic memory for everything he'd read, and Peters regarded Baker as a pretentious old fart. Young detectives who hang around long enough, however, eventually figure out that Howard Baker is a very *wise* old fart.

Keeping out of the cross fire, I asked, "What's the approximate time of death?"

"Off the top of my head, I'd say he's been dead two days or so. I'll have more exact information later."

Over the years, I've learned to rely on Doc Baker's educated guesses. He may be a pompous son of a bitch at times, but autopsy findings tend to verify his "top of the head" theories. I'm willing to give credit where credit is due.

We watched as technicians carefully placed paper bags over the victim's hands to protect any trace of evidence that might have remained on his skin or under his fingernails. As they wrestled with the body, I realized this was a big man, well over six feet tall. He must have been in his late thirties or early forties. His close-cropped, wiry hair was lightly sprinkled with gray.

"Any identification?" Peters asked.

Doc Baker, observing his technicians, appeared to be lost in thought. There was a long pause before he answered. "No. No identification. Nothing. Plucked clean as a chicken. Watch and rings are gone, although he evidently wore both. No wallet. They even took his clothes, every stitch."

Baker paused and looked at me, one bushy eyebrow raised questioningly. "Robbery, maybe?"

"Maybe," I said.

Once the body was loaded, the next wave of technicians moved into the picture. The crime scene investigators from the Washington State Patrol's crime lab took over the territory. The rain had solidified into a steady downpour, but the team tackled the dumpster in hopes of finding some clue that would help identify the victim.

Peters turned to me. "We'd better get busy, too," he said.

My hangover hadn't improved, but I knew better than to expect Peters to give me a break in that regard. He's a man who doesn't drink very much, and he doesn't have a whole hell of a lot of patience with people who do.

We walked across the lot to where uniformed officers had cordoned off the area. Just beyond the group of banked patrol cars, Arlo Hamilton, Seattle P.D.'s public information officer, held forth for a group of reporter types. He raised a hand to momentarily silence further questions. Extricating himself from the group, he walked over to Peters and me.

"Any idea who it is?" Arlo asked.

"None whatsoever," Peters answered.

Hamilton turned back to the reporters. "That's it. No further information at this time. The autopsy is scheduled for this afternoon." There was general groaning and grumbling as the reporters dispersed. Hamilton came back to us, shaking his head. "I got called in twice over the weekend. Here we go again, first thing Monday morning."

"Doc Baker says it must have been a full moon," Peters told Hamilton with a sarcastic grin.

"Right," Hamilton replied, then strode away.

We stopped in the drizzly parking lot and looked around. Two sides of Bailey's Foods face Seattle Center. A third side is bounded by the backs of businesses that front on First Avenue North, while the fourth side is lined with backs of apartments and businesses that front on Mercer. There was nothing to do but hit the bricks with our standard question: Had anyone seen or heard anything unusual over the weekend?

The answer was no. Time and again. Everywhere we went, from little old retired ladies to a burly night watchman who was pissed as hell at being awakened out of a sound sleep. They all told the same story. No one had heard any unusual noises. Well, maybe it had been a little extra noisy Friday and Saturday nights, but that was to be expected. After all, the state high school basketball championships were being played in the Coliseum. Aside from that, there was nothing out of the ordinary. No strange vehicles. No strange noises. Business as usual.

Except for one dead man with a broken neck. He had evidently crept into the parking lot like fog. On little cat feet.

Who he was or where he'd come from, nobody seemed to know. Or care.

CHAPTER 2

An army travels on its belly. J. P. Beaumont can go only so far on an empty stomach. On a good day. My endurance is reduced in direct proportion to the amount of Mac-Naughton's consumed the night before—in this case, far too much.

By noon we had worked our way through most of the businesses and several almost deserted apartment buildings on Lower Queen Anne. Famished, I called a halt.

"We'll come back later, after people get home from work. How about breakfast?"

Peters shrugged. "It's up to you."

Leading the way to the Mecca Cafe, I ordered a full breakfast and conned a sympathetic waitress out of a pair of aspirin. Peters ordered herb tea. Tea, but no sympathy.

"You drink too much, Beau," he said.

"Lay off," I told him.

"I won't lay off. You were fine when you left the house. What happened?"

I had spent Sunday afternoon helping Peters reassemble a second-hand swing set for his daughters, Heather and Tracie. The girls had supervised from the sidelines. They're cute little kids, both of them. They were underfoot and in the way, but being around them made me realize once more exactly what I'd lost. I had finished the evening at the Dog House, my home-away-from-home hangout in downtown Seattle, crying over spilt milk and singing solos with the organist. Cold sober I don't sing. I know better.

"Guess I got to feeling sorry for myself," I mumbled.

"Sorry!" Peters exclaimed. "What the hell for? You're set. You wouldn't have to work another day in your life if you weren't so god-damned stubborn."

"Sure, I'm set. Now that it's too late."

"Too late?" Peters echoed.

"Too late for me and my kids. Did I build the swing set for my own kids? No way. I was working nights as a security guard, trying to make ends meet. Karen had to ask a neighbor to help her put it up. No Little League games, no school programs. Now I've got both money and time, and where the hell are my kids? In California with Karen and their step-father."

I dunked a piece of toast in my egg yolk and waited to see if Peters would jump me for eating eggs, too. He was quiet for a moment, stirring his tea thoughtfully. "Maybe you should join a health club, play racketball, get involved in something besides work."

"And maybe you should give up Homicide and go in for family counseling," I retorted. On that relatively unfriendly note, we left the Mecca and went back to work.

After lunch we spent some time in the Seattle Center Administration Office and got the names of all the security people who had worked Friday's games. It was nice to have a list of phone numbers to work from for a change. They let us use a couple of empty desks and phones. We sat right there and worked our way through the list. For all the good it did us. None of the security guards could remember anything unusual, either.

When we left there, we finished our canvass of the neighborhood as much as possible considering the time of day, eventually returning to the car in the Bailey's Foods parking lot. A man wearing a faded red flannel shirt over khaki pants and topped by a dingy Mariners baseball cap was leaving a nasty note under the windshield wiper.

"This your car?" he asked.

"Belongs to the mayor," Peters said, unlocking the driver's door.

"City cars park free on city streets," the man continued plaintively. "Not on private property. Was gonna have you towed."

"Look," Peters explained, "we're with Homicide. We're working a case. Didn't the store manager tell you?"

"Got nothin' to do with the store. Parking's separate. Good for half an hour, while you shop. That's it. You gonna pay me or not?"

Peters glowered. "We're here on official business."

"Me, too," the man whined. "My boss says collect. I collect. From every car. You included."

I reached into my pocket. "How much?"

"Two bucks." The man glanced triumphantly at Peters, who climbed into the driver's seat, slamming the door behind him. I waited while the man counted out my change.

"You work over the weekend?" I asked.

"Me? I work every day. I've got four lots here on Queen Anne Hill that I check seven days a week, part-time. Keeps me in cigarettes and beer. Know what I mean?"

I nodded. "Did you tow any cars from here over the weekend?"

He lifted his grimy baseball cap and scratched his head. Peters had started the car. Impatiently, he rolled down the window. "Coming or not?" he demanded.

"In a minute," I told him. I returned to the parking attendant. "Well?"

"What's it worth to you?" he asked.

I had no intention of putting a parking attendant on the city payroll as an informant. "How about if I don't let my partner here run over your toes on the way out?"

Glancing at Peters, who sat there gunning the motor, the attendant mulled the idea, then reached into a pocket and retrieved a tattered notebook. He flipped through several pencil-smudged pages before stopping and holding the notebook at arm's length.

"Yup, three of them Friday night, four on Saturday, and one on Sunday. Sunday's real slow."

"Where to?" I asked.

He stuffed the notebook back in his pocket. "Like I said. That'll cost you."

It's a wonder some people are smart enough to get out of bed in the morning. He was standing directly in front of a green-and-white sign that said "Violators will be towed. At owner's risk and expense. Lincoln Towing."

"That's okay," I said. "We'll figure it out."

"It's about time," Peters grumbled when I finally got into the car. "Where to?"

"Lincoln Towing," I told him. "Over on Fairview. They towed eight cars out of the lot over the weekend. Maybe one of them belongs to the victim."

Peters put the car in gear, shaking his head in disbelief. "Come off it, Beau. Doc Baker said he was dumped here. After he died. Why would his car be left in the lot?"

"Humor me. Unless you've got a better idea."

He didn't. We drove through what Seattlites jokingly refer to as the Mercer Mess, a city planner's worst nightmare of how to stall traffic getting off and on a freeway. It's a tangle of one-way streets that circle this way and that without any clear direction.

Lincoln Towing actually sits directly in front of traffic exiting Interstate 5 and coming into the city. At the Fairview stoplight, Lincoln Towing's Toe Truck, a tow truck fitted out as a gigantic foot complete with bright pink toes four feet tall, may very well be the first sight some visitors see as they drop off the freeway to enter Seattle.

Lincoln's Toe Truck lends a whimsical bit of humor. As long as you're not one of Lincoln Towing's unwilling customers. Then it's no laughing matter.

The man who got out of a taxi and stomped his way into the Lincoln Towing office directly ahead of us wasn't laughing. He was ready to knock heads.

"What the hell do you mean towing me from a church parking lot! It isn't Sunday. I was just having breakfast down the street."

A girl with a wholesome, scrubbed appearance greeted his tirade with a sympathetic smile. "The lot is clearly marked, sir. It's private property. We've been directed to tow all unauthorized vehicles."

He blustered and fumed, but he paid. By the time he got his keys back, it was probably one of the most expensive breakfasts of his life. He stormed out of the office. The clerk, who had continued to be perfectly polite and noncommittally sympathetic the whole time she was taking his money, turned to us. "May I help you?"

I opened my ID and placed it on the counter in front of her along with the list of license plate numbers from our surly parking lot attendant. "We understand you towed these cars over the weekend. They're all from the Bailey's Foods lot on Queen Anne Hill."

She picked up the list and looked it over. "What about them?"

"Could you check them against your records. See if there was anything unusual about any of them?"

She went to a computer terminal and typed the license numbers into it. A few minutes later she returned to the counter, shaking her head. "Nothing out of the ordinary about any of them, except one."

"Which one?"

"A Buick. It came in early Saturday morning."

"What about it?"

"It's still here."

"That's unusual?"

She smiled. "Sure. Most of them are like that guy who just left. They get here by taxi half an hour to an hour after the car. They can't wait to bail it out."

"But the Buick's still here, and that's unusual?"

"Not that unusual," she replied. "Sometimes you run into a drunk who takes a couple of days to sober up and figure out where he left the car. That's probably what happened here."

"Which Buick?" I asked.

She pointed. "The blue one. The Century. Over in the corner."

"Mind if we take a look?"

"I don't know why not." She shrugged and called over the intercom for someone to escort us. A young fellow in green Lincoln Towing coveralls led us to the car. We peered in through the windows. An athletic bag sat on the floor of the back seat. An airline identification tag was still attached to the handle. It was turned in the wrong direction for us to read it.

"Would it be possible for you to open it up so we could see the name on that tag?"

"Well . . ." The young man hesitated.

"It could be important," I urged. "Something may have happened to the driver."

He glanced from me to the window of the office over my shoulder. "Okay by me," he said.

He opened the front car door, reached in, and unlocked the back. Using a pen rather than a finger, and careful to touch only the smallest corner of the name tag, I flipped it over. The name Darwin Ridley was written in heavy felt-tipped pen along with an address and telephone number in Seattle's south end.

I read them to Peters, who jotted them down. Nothing in the car appeared to have been disturbed.

"Thanks," I said to the Lincoln Towing guy and backed out of the car.

"No problem," he said, then hurried away.

Peters scowled at the name and address. "So what now? Motor Vehicles?"

I nodded. "And check Missing Persons."

Peters shook his head. "I still think you're way out in left field. Dead men don't drive. Remember? Why would the car turn up in the same parking place as the corpse? It doesn't make sense."

"The car's been here since Saturday morning. Nobody's come to claim it. Something may have happened to the owner, even if it isn't our victim."

"All right, all right. No use arguing."

"Besides," I said, "you've got nothing better to do this afternoon."

We returned to Lincoln Towing's office and dropped off a card, asking the clerk to please notify us if anyone came to pick up the Buick. Then we headed for the Public Safety Building, where Peters went to check with Missing Persons while I dialed the S.P.D. communications center for a registration check from the Department of Motor Vehicles. I also put through an inquiry to the Department of Licensing on a driver's license issued to Darwin Ridley.

I've reluctantly come to appreciate the value of computers in police work. By the time Peters finished with Missing Persons, I knew via computer link that the Buick was registered to Darwin T. Ridley and his wife Joanna. The address on the name tag and the address on the vehicle registration were the same.

Peters, shaking his head, came to sit on the edge of my desk, his arms folded obstinately across his chest. "Missing Persons's got nothing. What a surprise!"

Margie, our clerk, appeared from nowhere. "Did you guys pick up your messages?"

She had us dead to rights. We shook our heads in silent, sheepish unison. "So what else is new? The medical examiner's office called and said they've finished the autopsy. You can go by and pick up preliminary results if you want."

"Or even if we don't want, right?" Peters asked.

"Right," she answered.

We headed out for the medical examiner's office. It's located at the base of Harborview Medical Center, one of several medical facilities in the neighborhood that have caused Seattle locals to unofficially revise First Hill's name to Pill Hill.

Doc Baker's receptionist led us into his office. As usual, we found him tossing paper clips into his battered vase. He paused long enough to push a file across his desk.

Peters picked it up and thumbed through it. "Death by hanging?"

Baker nodded. "Rope burns around his wrists and ankles. I'd say somebody hog-tied that poor son of a bitch and lynched him. Hanged by the neck until dead."

"You make it sound like an execution."

Baker tossed another paper clip into the vase. "It was, with someone other than the state of Washington doing the job—judge, jury, and executioner."

"Time of death?"

"Two o'clock Saturday morning, give or take."

"Any identifying marks?"

He sent another paper clip flying. This one bounced off the side of the vase and fell to the floor. "Shit!" Baker bent over to retrieve it. "Not so as you'd notice," he continued. He tried again. This time it landed in the vase with a satisfying clink. "Surgical scar on his left knee that would be consistent with a sports injury of some kind."

"Nothing else?"

"Nothing. Not even dental work. Didn't have a single filling in his head."

"Got good checkups, right up until he died."

Baker glowered at Peters. "That's pretty unusual for a man his age."

"And what's that?" I asked.

"How old? Oh, thirty-nine, forty. Right around there."

"Anything else?"

"Last meal must have been about noon. We're working on stomach contents."

"Drugs?"

"Morphine, as a matter of fact. Not a lethal dose, but enough to knock him colder than a wedge."

"A junkie, then?"

Baker shook his head. "No way. We found only the one puncture, in his buttocks. Very difficult to self-administer, if you ask me. No other needle marks."

"How much did he weigh?" I asked, thinking of the driver's license information in the notebook I carried in my pocket. I didn't pull it out and look at it though, for fear of tipping my hand prematurely.

"Two twenty. Six foot four. Big guy."

"Anything else?" I asked.

Baker lobbed another paper clip into the vase. "The killer took his time. Hanging victims don't come out squeaky clean. This guy was hosed down before somebody wrapped him up in the tarp."

"Any identification on the tarp?"

"Sure, Beau, the tarp had a goddamned serial number on it! What do you think?"

I shrugged. "It could happen."

"One more thing," Baker added. "We found some flakes in his hair."

"Dandruff?" Peters asked.

Baker glowered. "Blue flakes. We're sending them down to the crime lab. It could be from whatever the noose was tied off to."

We'd pretty much worn out our welcome with Baker. "Great," I said, getting up. "Let us know if you find out anything more. We'll do the same."

I led the way. Once outside the building I paused long enough to take the notebook out of my jacket pocket and check my notes. Darwin Ridley's weight was listed as two ten and his height was listed as six four.

"Well?" Peters asked.

"It's possible. Weight is off by ten pounds, but lots of folks fudge on weight by a pound or two."

"So what do we do?" Peters glanced at his watch. "We can either go by that address down in Rainier Valley, or we can go back up to Queen Anne and see if any of the residents are home now. Can't do both. Tracie and Heather have a dental appointment right after work."

"Cavities?" I asked.

"Two each. No perfect checkups in our family. I'll need to be on the Evergreen Point Bridge by four-thirty to beat the worst of the rush."

By working in Seattle and living on the east side of Lake Washington in Kirkland, Peters seemed to spend the better part of half his life parked on the floating bridges, going in one direction or the other. It was almost three o'clock.

"Let's go back to Queen Anne and see if we can find out anything more. I can check Ridley out by myself after you leave."

Peters scratched his head. "You know, every time you say that name, it seems like it's one I should recognize, but I just can't place it."

"Ridley?"

He nodded. "It'll come to me eventually."

We walked back to the car. Little patches of midafternoon sun had broken through the clouds and rain. It felt almost like spring as we once more tackled the questioning process on Queen Anne Hill. A few more people were home, but it didn't do us much good. They hadn't heard or seen anything unusual, either.

It was frustrating but certainly not unexpected. I decided a long time ago that only people with a very high tolerance for frustration survive as homicide detectives.

I've worked Homicide the better part of twenty years. I must qualify.

CHAPTER 3

Peters bailed out of the office at about four-fifteen. Taking kids to dentists was one part of parenthood I had brains enough not to envy. I completed our share of paper work and handed it over to Margie for typing.

I decided to walk back to my apartment and take my own car down to Rainier Valley to check on Darwin Ridley. People who know Seattle only from television weather reports assume we live under unfailingly gray and dreary skies. The network weather reports never mention that our clouds often burn off during the day, giving us balmy, springlike afternoons, while the rest of the country remains frozen in the grip of winter.

This was one of those afternoons. If it hadn't been for the departmental issue .38 in my shoulder holster, I would have stripped off my jacket and slung it over my arm as I sauntered down a noisy Third Avenue. From either side of the street and from below it as well came the rumbling sounds of construction, the jackhammer racket of a city changing and growing. Harried pedestrians bustled past, blind and deaf to the process.

I entered the lobby of the Royal Crest and experienced a twinge of regret. Within weeks I'd be moving into a new place at Second and Broad, leaving behind the apartment that had been my haven ever since the divorce. Maybe being over forty makes the prospect of change, even change for the better, extremely uncomfortable.

It was rush hour. Honking horns told me that traffic was heavy everywhere, including the usually free-moving Fourth Avenue. It didn't make sense for me to leave my apartment and jump into the fray. I wasn't in that much of a hurry.

Instead, I made a pot of coffee and flopped into my ancient leather recliner, a relic from my first marriage, and the only stick of furniture I had managed to salvage from the house in Sumner when Karen threw me out. The recliner was brown and stained and scarred with years of use—ugly but honest. I had served notice to the interior designer working with me on the new place that where I went, so did the recliner.

With a steaming mug of coffee for company, I settled back to mull the Bailey's Foods case and try to get a handle on it. Being a detective with Homicide is very much like playing chess with a dozen opponents. The game requires anticipating all the moves, yours and the other players' as well, without ever getting a clear look at the board or knowing exactly who all the players are.

Was Darwin Ridley the dead man? A routine check of police records had turned up nothing but a couple of unpaid parking tickets. Ridley appeared to be a fairly law-abiding man. The name and address in Rainier Valley provided a very slender lead. Only the slimmest circumstantial evidence suggested we were on the right track. My first move was simple: Ascertain whether or not Darwin Ridley was alive. If he was, that was that, and we could go barking up another tree.

If lightning did strike, however, and it turned out Ridley was our victim, then the game would become infinitely more complicated.

Grieving families must be handled with utmost care, for two reasons. First, the sudden violent death of a loved one is possibly the worst shock a family ever withstands. Survivors are faced with a totally unanticipated death that leaves them with a lifetime of unresolved feelings and unsaid good-byes.

The second reason isn't nearly as poignant. The killer may very well be lurking among those grieving relatives and friends. Most homicide victims are murdered by someone they know rather than by a total stranger. Separating real grief from phony grief is an art form in its own right.

So I sat there waiting for the traffic to die down and puzzling about an unidentified man by a grocery store dumpster who would never get the chance to flaunt his set of perfect teeth in some old folks' home. And about a towed Buick Century, sitting forgotten in a corner of the Lincoln Towing lot. And about a man named Darwin Ridley, who was either dead or alive. By six o'clock, I was ready to find out which.

My Porsche was happy to be let out of the garage, but it protested being held to city speed limits. Or maybe it only seemed that way because I was hearing the call of the open road myself and wanted to be on a freeway going somewhere. Anywhere.

I found Ridley's house with no trouble, a neat, old-fashioned brick Tudor, situated near Lake Washington but minus the high-priced view. There was a two-car carport attached to the house. In it, shining in the glow of an outdoor light, sat a sporty bronze-and-cream Mustang GT. The other half of the carport was empty. Early evening dusk revealed a well-tended front yard, trimmed by a manicured hedge. Several lighted windows in the house indicated someone was home. Pulling into the carport, I parked behind the Mustang.

The house looked peaceful enough, so much so that I almost dreaded ringing the bell. Whatever the outcome, having a homicide detective pay a call tends to disrupt a family's ordinary evening routine. I more than half wished Darwin Ridley himself would open the door.

He didn't.

Instead, an attractive black woman, still puffing with exertion, came to the door. Her hair was held back by a purple sweat band. A fine film of perspiration beaded her upper lip.

She flung open the door angrily, as if expecting someone she knew but wasn't too happy with. Then, seeing a stranger, she slammed it almost shut.

"Yes?" she asked guardedly through the crack.

"I'm Detective Beaumont, Seattle P.D." I held my ID up to the open slit of door. "Are you Joanna Ridley?"

There were long, brilliantly colored fingernails on the hand that took my ID into the house and then passed it back to me without opening the door further. "What do you want?"

"I was hoping to speak to your husband."

"He's not here."

"Do you know when he'll be back?"

"No."

She wasn't exactly brimming over with spontaneous information. "Could I speak with you then, Mrs. Ridley?"

Reluctantly, she inched the door open a little wider. In the glow from the porch light, she looked up at me defiantly, her full lips pursed, eyes smouldering. Her hair was pulled back from a high, delicately curved forehead. I was struck by her resemblance to that classic bust of Nefertiti I had seen when it came through Seattle with the King Tut exhibit years ago.

Joanna Ridley was an exotic beauty, with wide-set eyes glowing under magenta-shaded lids. Her look of absolute disdain brought me back to earth in a hurry.

"Why do you want to talk to me?" Her arch tone was almost a physical slap in the face.

"We're conducting an investigation, Mrs. Ridley. It's important that I talk to you."

"I suppose you want to come in?"

"Yes."

She stepped aside to allow me inside. My gaze had been riveted to her face. It was only when I looked down to gauge the step from the porch up into the house that I realized one of her hands rested on a wildly protruding tummy. Joanna Ridley was more than slightly pregnant. She was very pregnant.

She wore a huge pink sweatshirt that hung almost to her knees. An arrow pointed downward from the neck, and the word *Baby* was emblazoned across the appropriate spot. Her legs, what I could see of them, were well-shaped and encased in a pair of shiny, royal blue leotards. Joanna Ridley was the complete technicolor lady.

Padding barefoot ahead of me, she led the way into the living room. A rubber exercise mat lay in the middle of the floor. On the VCR a group of blurred aerobic exercisers were frozen in midair. She switched off the VCR and the screen went blank. I wondered if unborn babies liked aerobics, if they were willing or unwilling participants in America's latest health-nut fad.

Joanna Ridley spun around to face me. Her question was terse. "What do you want?"

"Do you have any idea how we could reach your husband?"

"No."

"Has he been gone long?"

Some of the defiance left her face. Awkwardly, she squatted down beside the exercise mat, folded it, picked it up, and wrestled it behind the couch. Once more her hand returned unconsciously, protectively to the swell of baby in her abdomen. I got the distinct impression she was avoiding the question.

"A couple of days," she said evasively.

"How long?" I insisted.

"I saw him last Friday morning, at breakfast, before he left for school. He's a teacher. A coach for Mercer Island High School."

"He's been gone since Friday and you haven't reported him missing?"

She shrugged. "He lost."

"I beg your pardon?"

"The game. The Islanders lost Friday night. The first round of the championship. He'll come home when he's good and ready."

"He does that? Just disappears?"

She nodded. "When they win, he celebrates. When they lose, it's gloom and doom. He hides out afterward. He usually doesn't miss school, though," she added.

"He did today?"

Joanna Ridley turned her back on me and walked to the couch. She sat down, curling her legs under her in a way that should have been impossible for someone in such an advanced stage of pregnancy. Maybe doing aerobics does make a difference. Uninvited, I helped myself to a chair.

She took a deep breath. "They called looking for him. Left a message on the machine. I didn't return the call."

There was a brief silence between us while I wondered exactly how pregnant she was and whether the female reproductive system would withstand the shock my intuition told me was coming. If Darwin Ridley was missing, had been since Friday, I had a feeling I knew where he was, and I didn't know how she'd take it.

Looking for a way to delay or soften the blow, I cleared my throat. "As I said, Mrs. Ridley, we're conducting an investigation. Would you happen to have a recent photograph of your husband?"

Despite her bulging center of gravity, Joanna Ridley gracefully eased her way off the couch. She left the room and returned a few moments later carrying an eight-by-ten gilt-framed photograph, which she handed to me. Staring back at me was a good-looking middle-aged man with a sprinkle of gray in his curly hair. His mouth was set in a wide grin. With perfect teeth.

"It's a good picture," I said.

She took it back from me and examined it closely herself, as though she hadn't looked at it for a long time. "It is, isn't it."

"Did your husband ever have any kind of surgery?"

She looked at me thoughtfully, considering before she answered. "On his knee," she said at last. "An old football injury."

"Right or left?"

"Left." Suddenly, she seemed to lose all patience with me and my apparently inane questions. "Are you going to tell me what's going on?"

"Mrs. Ridley, I'm sorry to have to say this, and at this point let me stress that we're not sure, but we have reason to believe your husband may be the homicide victim who was found on Queen Anne Hill early this morning."

Her slender fingers tightened around the picture frame, gripping it until the knuckles showed light against the darker skin. She stepped backward, sinking heavily onto the couch.

I hurried on. "We need someone to make a positive identification. This afternoon we discovered that over the weekend your husband's car was towed away from the same parking lot in which the victim was found."

"You think he's dead?" She choked over the last word.

"As I said, Mrs. Ridley. We're not sure. From looking at the picture, I'd say it was the same man, but that doesn't constitute a positive identification. There's certainly a strong resemblance."

She leaned back against the couch, resting her head on the wall behind her, closing her eyes. Her breathing quickened. I was afraid she was going to faint. Alarmed, I got up and went to her.

"Are you all right, Mrs. Ridley? Can I get you something? A glass of water? Something stronger?"

She looked up at me through eyes bright with tears. "Where is he?"

"The medical examiner's office. Harborview Medical Center."

"And you came to take me there?"

I nodded. "If you're up to going. You could send someone else—a relative, a close friend. A person in your condition . . ."

She stood up abruptly. "I'll go."

"You're sure it won't be too hard on you?"

"I said I'll go," she repeated.

She paused by the door long enough to pull on a pair of leg warmers and some short boots. She draped a long yellow wool shawl over her shoulders. "I'm ready," she said.

Outside, I helped her into my car. Sports cars are not built with pregnant ladies in mind, whether or not they do aerobics. There was absolute silence between us during the drive to Harborview. She asked no questions; I offered no information. What could I say?

A brand new, peach-fuzzed night tech in Doc Baker's office came out of the back as we entered. "What can I do for you?"

"I'm Detective Beaumont. Seattle P.D. I believe we have a tentative identification on the Queen Anne victim."

"Great!" He glanced at Joanna Ridley's somber face. She stood there silently, biting her lower lip. He curbed some of his youthful enthusiasm. "Sure thing," he said. "If you'll wait here for a couple of minutes . . ."

He disappeared down a short hallway. I offered Joanna a chair, which she refused. Instead, she walked over to the doorway and stood peering out. Harborview Medical Center sits on the flank of First Hill. Even from the ground floor she could look down at the city spread out below and beyond the early evening hazy glow of parking lot lights. Eventually, the tech came back for us.

"Right this way, miss," he said. I winced. He wasn't going to win any prizes for diplomacy, or for observation either, for that matter.

He led us down the same hallway and stopped in front of a swinging laboratory door. He pushed it open and held it for her to enter. Joanna seemed to falter. I didn't blame her. Eventually, she got a grip on herself and went inside. I followed her, with the tech bringing up the rear.

A sheet-draped figure lay on a gurney in the far corner of the room. "This way, please," the tech said.

Joanna Ridley didn't move. She seemed frozen to the spot. I stepped to her side and took hold of an arm, just above the elbow. Gently, I led her forward.

The tech moved to the head of the gurney and held up a corner of the sheet far enough to expose the still face beneath it. In the quiet room, Joanna gave a sudden, sharp intake of breath and turned away.

"I need to lie down," she said.

CHAPTER 4

I led Joanna Ridley into a small, private waiting room and helped her lie down on a dilapidated couch. The tech brought a glass of water. "Is she going to be all right?" he asked nervously. "I can call somebody down from Emergency."

Glancing back at her, I saw tears streaming down her face. She didn't need a doctor or a whole roomful of people. "No," I told him. "She'll be okay. I'll let you know if she needs help."

The tech backed out of the room. I set the water down on a table without offering any to her. She didn't need plain water, either.

For several long minutes, I waited for her sobs to become quiet. Eventually, they did, a little. "Mrs. Ridley," I asked gently, "is there anything I can do to help? Someone I can call?"

Her sobs intensified into an anguished wail. "How could this happen when the baby . . ."

She broke off suddenly, and my adrenaline started pumping. "The baby! Is it coming now? Should I call a doctor?"

Joanna shook her head. "My baby's not even born yet, and his father's . . ." She stopped again, unable to continue.

My own relief was so great, I walked to the table and helped myself to her glass of water, all of it, before I spoke, offering what comfort I could. "It'll be all right. You'll see. Really, isn't there someone I can call?"

Her sobbing ceased abruptly. Raising herself up on one elbow, she glared at me angrily. In her eyes I was something less than an unfeeling clod. "You don't understand. My baby's father is dead."

Unfortunately, I did understand, all too well. I knew far better than she did what was ahead for both her and her baby. From personal experience. Except my mother hadn't had so much as a marriage certificate to back her up when I was born. Society was a hell of a lot less permissive back in the forties.

"My mother did it," I said quietly. "You can, too."

She looked at me silently for a long moment, assimilating what I had said. Then, before she could respond, the technician burst into the room. "Dr. Baker's on the phone. He wants to talk to you, Detective Beaumont." The tech bounded back out of the room with me right behind him. "He wants to know who it was," he said over his shoulder.

"How the hell did he find out?"

"He told me to call if we came up with something."

"What do you mean *we?*" I fumed.

He led me into another office, picked up a telephone receiver, and held it toward me. I snatched it from his hand.

"Beaumont," I growled into the phone.

"Understand you've got a positive ID. Good work, Beau. That was quick. What have you got?"

"Who the fuck do you think you are, calling me to the phone like this? I just barely found out myself. All I know so far is a name and address."

"Well, get on with it for chrissakes."

"Look, Baker. That poor woman just learned her husband's dead. I'll start asking questions when I'm damn good and ready."

"Don't be a prima donna, Beau. Give me what you have."

"Like hell!"

I flung the receiver at the startled tech, who stared at me dumbfounded. I hurried back down the hall to the room where Joanna Ridley waited. The phone rang again, but I didn't pause long enough to hear what the tech said to his irate boss. Besides, I was sure Baker's next phone call would be to either Captain Powell or Sergeant Watkins.

Hustling back into the waiting room, I startled Joanna Ridley, who was dabbing at her eyes with a tissue. There was no time to waste in idle explanations. "Come on," I said, helping her up. "Let's get out of here."

"Where are we going?"

"I'll take you home. We've got to go now, before we're overrun with cops and reporters."

The tech had followed me. We ran into him head-on in the doorway. He was carrying a metal clipboard and had a pen poised to take down information. "Detective Beaumont, you can't leave."

"Oh, yeah? Watch me!"

"But I need some information . . ."

"You'll have it when I'm damn good and ready."

"What's going on?" Joanna managed as I hurried her, half-resisting, out the door and down the hallway.

"This place is going to be crawling with officers and reporters in about two minutes flat."

The technician trailed behind us, whimpering like a scolded puppy. "But Dr. Baker says . . ."

"Piss on Doc Baker. You had no business calling him! Now get out of here."

I helped Joanna into the car and slammed the door behind her for emphasis. The technician was still standing with his mouth open and clipboard in hand when I fishtailed the Porsche out of the parking lot and onto the street.

Dodging through a series of side streets, I paused at a stop sign on Boren, signaling for a right-hand turn, planning to drive Joanna Ridley back down to her home in Rainier Valley to talk to her there.

"I don't want to go home," she said.

Surprised, I glanced in her direction. She seemed under control. "Are you sure? I'm going to have to ask you some questions. It might be easier."

A marked patrol car, red lights flashing, raced past us on Boren. Obviously, Baker had sounded the alarm and troops were out in force to pull J. P. Beaumont back into line. I waited until the car turned off toward Harborview before I eased the Porsche out into the intersection and turned left.

"I understand what you did back there," Joanna said quietly. "Thanks."

"No problem."

I wondered where to take her. Obviously, we couldn't go to the department, and my own apartment was a bad idea as well. I settled on the only logical answer, the Dog House.

The Dog House is actually a Seattle institution. It's a twenty-four-hour restaurant three blocks from my apartment that's been in business for more than fifty years. I've needed almost daily help from both McDonald's and the Dog House kitchen to survive my reluctant return to bachelorhood.

You'll notice I said the kitchen. The bar at the Dog House is a different story.

Steering clear of the scene of my previous night's solo performance, I took Joanna Ridley through the main part of the restaurant and into the back dining room. It was closed, but I knew Wanda would let us sit there undisturbed.

She brought two cups of coffee at the same time she brought menus. Joanna accepted coffee without comment, but she refused my offer of food. Groping for a way to start the conversation, I asked what I hoped was an innocuous question. "When's the baby due?"

It wasn't nearly innocuous enough. Just that quickly tears appeared in the corners of her eyes. "Two weeks," she managed. She wiped the tears away and then sat looking at me, her luminous dark eyes searching my face. "Is it true what you said, that your mother raised you alone?"

I nodded. "My father died before I was born. My parents weren't married."

She lowered her gaze and bit her lip. Her voice was almost a whisper. "Are you saying that'll make it easier, that we were married?"

"It'll be better for the baby," I returned. "Believe me, I know what I'm talking about."

Wanda poked her head in the doorway to see if we were going to order anything besides coffee. I waved her away. I decided I'd offer Joanna Ridley food again later, if either of us had the stomach for it, but now was the time to ask questions, to begin assembling the pieces of the puzzle.

"Mrs. Ridley," I began.

"Joanna," she corrected.

"Joanna, this will probably be painful, but I have to start somewhere. Do you know if your husband was in any kind of difficulty?"

"Difficulty? What do you mean?"

"Gambling, maybe?" Even high school teams and coaches get dragged into gambling scams on occasion.

Joanna shook her head, and I continued. "Drugs? One way or another, most crimes in this country are connected to the drug trade."

"No," she replied tersely, her face stony.

"Was he under any kind of medical treatment?"

"No. He was perfectly healthy."

"You're sure he wasn't taking any medication?"

Again she shook her head. "Darwin never used drugs of any kind. He was opposed to them."

"The medical examiner found morphine in his bloodstream. You've no idea where it could have come from?"

"I told you. He didn't use drugs, not even aspirin. Is that what killed him, the morphine?"

It was my turn to shake my head while I considered how to tell her. "He died of a broken neck," I said softly. "Somebody tied a rope around his neck and hung him."

Joanna's eyes widened. "Dear God!" She pushed her chair back so hard it clattered against the wall. Dodging her way through empty chairs and tables, she stopped only when she reached the far corner of the room. She leaned against the two walls, sobbing incoherently.

I followed, standing helplessly behind her, not knowing if I should leave her alone or reach out to comfort her. Finally, I placed one hand on her shoulder. She shuddered as if my hand had burned her and shrugged it away.

She turned on me then like a wounded animal, eyes blazing. "It'll always be like that, won't it! We're accepted as long as we're smart enough to know our place, but cross that line, and niggers are only good for hanging!"

"Joanna, I . . ."

She pushed her way past me, returned to our table, and grabbed up her shawl. Just as suddenly as the outburst had come, it subsided. Her face went slack. "Take me home," she said wearily. "There are people I need to call."

I dropped money on the table for the coffee and trailed her outside. When I caught up, Joanna was standing by the Porsche, fingering the door handle. "Since when do cops drive Porsches," she asked when I walked up to open her car door.

"When they inherit them," I replied. I helped her into the car and closed the door behind her.

Sliding into the driver's seat, I glanced in her direction before I started the engine. She sat with her head resting against the carseat, her long, slender neck stretched taut, eyes closed, her face impassive. That unconscious pose elicited once more the striking similarity between Joanna Ridley and that ancient Egyptian queen, but this was no time to tell her how beautiful she was. Joanna Ridley was in no condition to hear it.

"I didn't finish asking all my questions," I said, starting the car and putting it in gear.

"Ask them tomorrow. I'm worn out."

"Somebody will come stay with you? You shouldn't be alone."

She nodded. "I'll call someone."

We drove through the city. It was early, not more than eight o'clock or so, but it seemed much later. I felt incredibly tired. Joanna Ridley wasn't the only one who was worn out. She just had a hell of a lot better reason.

I drove back to her place and pulled up in front of her house. "Would you like me to come in with you?" I asked. "I could stay until someone comes over."

"Don't bother," she said. "I can take care of myself."

I started to get out to open the door for her, but she opened it herself, struggled out of the low-slung seat, and was inside the house before I knew what had hit me. I sat there like a jerk and watched her go.

It wasn't until I turned the car around that I noticed the light in the carport was out. I couldn't remember her switching it off when we left the house, but she must have. As a precaution, I waited in the car with my hand on the door handle long enough to see her pick up a phone, dial, and begin talking.

She'll be all right, I said to myself as I put the car in gear and drove up the street. What Joanna Ridley needed right then was family and friends, people who cared about her and would give her the strength and courage to pick up the pieces and go on with her life. What she didn't need was an aging police watchdog with a penchant for finding bogeymen under every light switch.

Right that minute Joanna Ridley needed J. P. Beaumont like she needed a hole in her head.

CHAPTER 5

One of the drawbacks of living in the Royal Crest is the lack of soundproofing. I can hear my phone ringing the moment the elevator door opens. It's always a horse race to see if I can unlock the door and grab the phone before whoever's calling gives up. My attorney keeps suggesting I get an answering machine, but I'm too old-fashioned. And too stubborn.

Detective Peters was still on the phone when I picked it up. He was hot.

"God damn it, Beau. What the hell are you up to now? I've had calls from Watty and Captain Powell, both. They're ready to tear you apart. Me, too. They demanded I tell them what *we* had. Remember me? I'm your partner."

"Hold up, Peters. It's not my fault."

"Not your fault! I heard you told Doc Baker to piss up a rope."

"Not in those exact words."

"Jesus H. Christ, Beau. What's going on?"

"It's Ridley, all right."

That stopped Peters cold. "No shit! The basketball coach? I remembered where I'd heard the name while I was stuck on the bridge, but there was no way to get hold of you. Who identified him?"

"His wife. He'd been missing since Friday, but she didn't report it. Thought he was sulking over losing the game. She figured he'd come home eventually."

Peters gave his customary, long, low whistle. "Have you sealed the car?"

"Not yet. I just dropped Joanna Ridley back at her house."

"Should I come on in? That Buick shouldn't sit outside any longer than it already has."

I glanced at my watch. It was nine o'clock and I was tired, but there was a lot of merit in what Peters said. Every effort has to be made to preserve evidence. "What about your girls?"

"Mrs. Edwards is here. The kids are asleep, and Mrs. Edwards is watching television." Mrs. Edwards was Peters' live-in housekeeper/babysitter. "I'll meet you at Lincoln Towing in twenty minutes."

As an old Fuller Brush salesman, I recognize an assumed closed trap when I see one. Not do you want to meet me, but when will you meet me.

I needed to hit my second wind pretty damn soon. I was going to need it. Peters is a hell of a lot younger than I am, and he's disgustingly immune to vices of any kind. Including booze. I avoided my recliner. I didn't dare sit down and get comfortable for fear I wouldn't get back up. Instead, I made a cursory pass at the refrigerator in a vain search for food before driving to Lincoln Towing's Fairview lot.

I waited outside the lot itself, watching the eager beaver fleet of tow trucks come and go. Peters must have flown low across the bridge. He was there in far less than twenty minutes. His first question nailed me good. "Did you have her sign a voluntary search form?"

"You can't expect me to remember everything," I told him. He glared at me in reply, and we went inside together.

The night clerk wasn't thrilled at the added paperwork involved in our securing Ridley's Buick. She did it, though. Once the car had been towed to the secured processing room at Fifth and Cherry, I was ready to call it a day.

"No way," Peters said, opening the passenger door on my Porsche and climbing inside. "I'm not letting you out of my sight until we've mended some fences along the way, starting with the medical examiner's office."

We found the same night tech sound asleep in the employee's lounge. The bell over the front door didn't faze him. He awoke with a start when I gave his shoulder a rough shake. "I thought you wanted information," I told him.

He stumbled sleepily to his feet and went in search of his clipboard. I couldn't help wondering if Doc Baker knew his baby tech took a little evening nap on company time. Eventually, the tech returned relatively awake and prepared to take down my information.

I filled in as many blanks on his form as I could, based on what information I had gleaned from Joanna Ridley. It consisted of the usual—name, address, phone number, next of kin—enough to clear the medical examiner's office of one of its prime responsibilities: Identification of the victim.

As Peters and I left the office, I paused in the doorway. "By the way, you might want to call Doc Baker with that now. He's probably waiting to hear from you." The tech didn't look eager to pick up the phone to call Doc Baker's home number.

"You ever hear of winning friends and influencing people, Beau?" Peters asked as we walked outside.

"I don't like people who sleep on the job. Where to next?"

If I had any delusions of going home right then, Peters put a stop to them with what he said next. "We'd better check in with the department and let them know what's up. Officially."

We were ready to climb into the car. I looked at him across the roof of the Porsche. "What the hell happened to you, Peters? You used to be a lot more flexible, remember? You didn't always do things by the book."

He grinned at me. "Two and a half years of hanging around with J. P. Beaumont. That's what happened. Somebody in this outfit has to go by the book, or we'll both get our asses fired."

Back on the fifth floor of the Public Safety Building we sorted through our individual fanfolds of messages.

"Call," Peters said. "Five bucks says I take it."

"You're on."

"Full house." Triumphantly, Peters turned his messages face up on the desk. Three from Sergeant Watkins, two from Captain Powell. "See there?"

"Read 'em and weep," I told him, turning over my own—four of a kind, all from Captain Lawrence Powell. With a grimace of disgust, Peters slapped a five-dollar bill on the desk in front of me.

One of the other detectives sauntered over to our cubicle. "I don't know what you two have been up to, but people are gunning for you. I'd lay low if I were you."

We never had a fighting chance of lying low. We were right in the middle of writing our reports when Sergeant Watkins showed up in a stained sweat suit and worn running shoes. He hadn't bothered to dress for the occasion. He ignored Peters and came straight after me.

"You interested in the Officer Friendly program in Seattle Public Schools?" he demanded. "By the time Doc Baker finishes with you, that may be the only job in the department you're qualified for."

"Doc Baker was out of line," I returned. "So was his tech. They had no business demanding information before I had a chance to question the individual."

"*Doctor* Baker," Watty corrected, enunciating every syllable clearly to be sure I understood his meaning. "Doctor Baker happens to be the King County medical examiner, and don't you forget it."

He glanced down at the forms we were working on. He sighed and headed for his desk, still growling at us over his shoulder. "When you finish those reports, you could just as well bring them by so I can see what you've got."

It was eleven by the time we were perched on the front of Watty's desk, waiting while he scanned our reports.

"A high school basketball coach. Holy shit! I'd better get Arlo Hamilton on this right away. Can you two be here for a press briefing at eight tomorrow morning?"

We both nodded. Unlike crooks, cops don't get time off for good behavior. By the time I drove Peters back to his Datsun at Lincoln Towing, I could barely hold my head up.

"You satisfied?" I asked. "Is everything by the book now?"

"As much as it's going to be," Peters replied mildly. "What do you want to do tomorrow? Go to Ridley's house or stop by the school?"

"The house first," I answered. "We'd better get that voluntary search form before this gets any deeper."

Peters rolled his eyes and grinned. "Wonders will never cease."

I drove back to Third and Lenora and put the Porsche to bed in its assigned place in the parking garage. I walked onto the elevator only because it would have been too much trouble to get down on my knees and crawl. A phone was ringing when the elevator door opened. It's always my phone.

"Hello," I snarled into it.

"Don't sound so happy to hear from me." It was Ralph Ames, my attorney, calling from Phoenix. Ralph Ames' law firm, and more importantly, Ralph's personal attention, had been a gift to me from the same lady who left me the Porsche. I'm not one of his more dependable clients.

"I understand you didn't make your closing interview this afternoon."

"Damn it, Ralph. I got busy here and completely forgot about it. Can we reset it?"

"No sweat," Ralph told me cheerfully. "Only you'll have to swear on a stack of Bibles that you'll show up this time."

"I swear. Just let me know when it is."

When I got off the phone I was careful to steer clear of any hair of the dog. I figured I'd need to be on my toes early and long the next day. A clear head was essential. I fell into bed, but by then I was too wound up to sleep.

My mind slipped into overdrive and busily tried to sift through all the information it had received that day. So far the only person firmly fixed in my memory bank was Joanna Ridley. What was it she had said when she blew up at me there in the waiting room? Something about crossing a line. What line had Darwin Ridley crossed? And why had it been fatal? That was one of the tough questions I'd have to ask his widow the next day.

It was late when I finally drifted off. I was still awake when the last of the serious drinkers left Palmer's Tavern across the street. It seemed like only minutes later when I surfaced in a dream with Anne Corley.

She never changes in my dreams. She's always young and beautiful and vibrant, and she's always wearing that same, tantalizing red dress.

In the dream, I'm always so glad to see her it's pathetic. She smiles and reaches out to take my hand. Over the months I've learned to force myself awake then, to propel myself out of the dream before it has a chance to turn ugly.

I awoke shaking and dripping with sweat. I know better than to try to sleep again after one of those dreams. I always return to that same instant like some crazy broken record.

Instead, I stumbled out of bed, took a long hot shower, shaved, and dressed. I was at the Dog House ordering breakfast by five-thirty, along with a generous slice of Seattle's colorful cast of late-night/early-morning characters.

I appropriated the discarded remains of a newspaper from the table next to me. I ignored the news as I always do. Daily doses of news are bad for me. Instead, I worked *The New York Times* crossword puzzle over coffee, bacon, and eggs.

It's one way to take your mind off your troubles.

CHAPTER 6

The murder of a prominent man is always news. The murder of a winning high school coach is news with a capital N. The department's conference room was jammed to the gills for the promised briefing, with the attendees nothing short of a *Who's Who* in Seattle media, from television reporters to print pukes. Including Maxwell Cole, my all-time least favorite newspaper columnist.

Max is part of a long-running rivalry that dates back to college days. His position as crime columnist for the *Seattle Post-Intelligencer* has kept us at odds for as long as I've been with Seattle P.D. He has a way of getting under my skin. And staying there.

Arlo Hamilton, Seattle P.D.'s public information officer, is a reasonable sort, but I could see he was losing patience as Max asked questions that were nothing less than an ill-disguised tirade—the media busily manufacturing news to suit themselves.

"One of my sources stated that Mr. Ridley was . . ." He paused for dramatic effect and consulted a small notebook. "I believe the word he used was *lynched*. Doesn't that sort of take you back to the Old South? Is it possible this homicide was racially motivated?"

"As I said before, Mr. Cole, at this time we have no motive in this crime. The exact cause of death is being withheld pending investigation."

"But wouldn't you say lynching is a step backward to the Ku Klux Klan mentality of the sixties?"

"I wouldn't say anything of the kind."

"You're ruling out race as a possible motive, then?"

I was glad Arlo was running the press conference instead of me. About then I would have told Max to fuck off. Hamilton managed to remain unruffled. "We are investigating all possibilities at this time. No potential lead will be ignored, racial or otherwise."

Arlo glanced around the room, hoping to shut Max down by calling on someone else. Max blithely launched into another question.

"Two years ago, during the height of the Neo-Nazi scare, there was talk of creating an all-white preserve here in Washington. Could this action be connected with one of those groups?"

"As you know, Mr. Cole, members of those groups were apprehended, tried, and found guilty of numerous crimes. Those who didn't die during the initial siege of their headquarters are in prison for long terms. I don't think we need worry that Mr. Ridley's death is part of a Neo-Nazi plot. Any other questions?"

Fortunately, someone else raised his hand, and Hamilton gratefully acknowledged him. "Were police officers in attendance at the basketball championships in Seattle Center Friday night?"

Hamilton nodded.

"The Mayor's office has been concerned about special event security at the Center. Has security been beefed up?"

"Yes, it has. The horse patrol was there as well as several officers patrolling the grounds on foot. None of them saw anything out of line."

"You're saying that it wasn't a lack of security?"

"Look, you guys, give me a break. Don't read between the lines. We had numerous officers at the Center, but until we know exactly what happened, I can't say whether it was a security problem or not."

It was clear the newshounds had Arlo's scent. There was no need for Peters and me to hang around for the bloodletting. I reached over and tapped Peters on the shoulder. "Let's get out of here."

He followed me to the door. I didn't notice that Maxwell Cole had trailed after us until he showed up at the elevator lobby. Everything about Max is big, from the layer of flab that spills over the top of his belt buckle up to and including his ego. He wears a waxed, handlebar mustache that tends to be littered with bits and pieces of his most recent meal—egg yolk in this particular case.

"How's it going, J. P.? You two working this one? I saw you hanging around the briefing room."

"Look, Max, we've got a long day ahead of us. Get lost."

"Come on, J. P. Give an old fraternity brother a break. All I need is an angle. Race would be dynamite. It would bust this town wide open."

I try not to deal with Maxwell Cole in anything but absolute contempt. Lesser insults go straight over his head. "We're booked up already, Max. We don't need you to start a race war just to keep us busy."

The elevator door slipped open. We got on and left him standing there in the hallway. "Think he got it?" Peters asked once the door closed.

"Beats the hell out of me."

We went on down to the garage and checked out a car. The first order of business had to be the voluntary search form from Joanna Ridley. That would enable the crime lab to go to work on Darwin Ridley's Buick.

Several cars were parked on the street outside Joanna Ridley's house, including an immense old Lincoln. I led the way to the door and rang the bell. A tall but stoop-shouldered black man opened the door and peered down at us through gold-rimmed glasses. "What can I do for you gentlemen?" he asked.

"We're with Seattle P.D.," I said, offering him my ID. "We're here to speak to Mrs. Ridley."

"Joanna's not feelin' too well."

Joanna Ridley appeared in a doorway behind him, wearing a flowing blue caftan. Her eyes were swollen, and she wore no trace of makeup. She looked haggard, as though she hadn't slept well, either. "It's all right, Daddy," she said. "I'll see them."

The old man stepped to one side, allowing us to enter the house. The living room was filled with nine or ten people, all of them involved in various conversations that ceased as Joanna led us through the gathering to a small study that opened off the living room. She closed the door behind us, effectively shutting out the group of mourners gathered to comfort her.

"Mrs. Ridley, this is my partner, Detective Ron Peters. We brought along a form we need you to sign so we can search your husband's car." I extracted the folded form from my jacket pocket and handed it to her. I watched as her eyes skimmed the lines.

"It'll save us the time and effort of getting a search warrant," I explained.

A scatter of pens and pencils lay on the desk. Without hesitation, she put the paper on the desk, located a pen that worked, and scrawled her name across the bottom of the form.

"Will that do?" she asked, handing it back to me.

"For a start. We also need to ask some questions, if you don't mind." She took the chair behind the desk. Peters and I sat on a couch facing her. With determined effort, Joanna Ridley managed to retain her composure.

"To begin with, you told me yesterday that, as far as you knew, your husband had no drug or gambling connections. Had you noticed anything unusual in your husband's patterns? Any threats? What about money difficulties?"

She shook her head in answer to each question.

"Any unusual telephone calls, things he might not have shared with you?"

There was the slightest flicker of something in Joanna's expression, a momentary waver, before she once more shook her head. A detective lives and dies by his wits and by his powers of observation. There was enough of a change in her expression that I noted it, but there was no clue, no hint, as to what lay behind it. I tried following up in the same vein, hoping for some sort of clarification.

"Anyone with a grudge against him?"

This time, when she answered, her face remained totally impassive. "Not that I know of."

"How long had you two been married?" Peters asked.

"Fifteen years." Peters' question came from left field. It moved away from the murder and into the personal, into the mire of Joanna Ridley's private loss and grief. She blinked back tears.

"And this is your first child?"

She swallowed. "We tried, for a long time. The doctors said we'd never have children."

"How long did your husband teach at Mercer Island?"

She took a deep breath. "Twelve years. He taught social studies at Franklin before that. He was assistant basketball coach at Mercer Island for eight years, head coach for the last two."

"Didn't they win state last year?" Peters asked. "Seems like I remember reading that."

Peters' memory never fails to impress me. He impressed Joanna Ridley, too.

She gave him a bittersweet smile. "That's true, but people said it was only a holdover from the previous year, the previous coach. Darwin wanted to do it again this year so he could prove . . ." She stopped abruptly, unable to continue.

"I know this is painful for you," Peters sympathized. "But it's important that we put all the pieces together. You told Detective Beaumont here that you last saw your husband Friday morning at breakfast?"

She nodded. "That's right."

"You didn't go to the game?"

"I don't like basketball."

"You didn't attend his games?"

"Our work lives were separate. I stayed away from his career, and he stayed away from mine."

"What do you do?"

"I'm a flight attendant for United. On maternity leave."

"Joanna," I cut in, "something you said last night has been bothering me, something about crossing a line. What did you mean?"

Joanna Ridley was not a practiced liar. She hesitated for only the briefest moment, but caution and wariness were evident in her answer. "Blacks go only so far before they hit the wall. It was okay to come from Rainier Valley and go to Mercer Island as assistant coach, but not head coach."

"There were problems, racial problems?"

"Some."

"And you think your husband's death may be racially motivated."

"Don't you?" she asked in return.

I could tell she was concealing something, hiding what she really meant behind her curt answers, her troubled gaze. Finally, biting her lip, she dropped her eyes and sat looking down at the bulge of baby in her lap.

At last she looked back up at us. "Is that all?" she asked. "My guests are waiting."

It wasn't all. It was a hell of a long way from being all, but we had reached an impasse, a place beyond which progress was impossible until Peters and I had more to go on.

"For the time being," I said, rising. Peters followed. I handed her my card. "Here's my name and numbers. Call if you remember something else you think we need to know."

She took it from my hand and dropped it onto the desk without looking at it. Her expression said that I shouldn't hold my breath.

When she made no offer to get up, I said, "We can find our way out." She nodded, and we left.

"We said something that pissed her off," Peters mused as we climbed into the car. "I don't know exactly what it was."

"She lied," I told him.

"I know, but why?"

"There must have been phone calls, or at least, one call. And then later, when I asked her about what she said last night. That was all a smoke screen."

Peters nodded. "I thought as much."

There was a brief silence in the car. In my mind's eye I played back the entire conversation, trying to recall each nuance, every inflection. Peters was doing the same thing.

"Something else bothered me," Peters said.

"What's that?"

"The part about her not going to the games, not liking basketball."

"Karen wasn't wild about homicide," I said. "Wives aren't required to adore whatever it is their husbands do."

"Point taken. So what now? Run a routine check on her?"

"Sounds reasonable."

"By the way," Peters added, "how come you didn't mention she was pregnant last night?"

"Didn't I?"

"No."

"I must be getting old. The mind's going."

Peters chuckled, and there was another short silence. "I hope she's not the one," he said at last. "She seems like such a nice lady."

"Appearances can be deceiving," I said.

I felt Peters' sharp, appraising look. "Ain't that the truth!" he said.
I didn't answer. Didn't need to. Anne Corley had taught me that much.
In spades.

CHAPTER 7

We took the signed search form back to the Public Safety Building and hand-carried it through the process. Once it had crossed all required desks and swum upstream through all necessary channels, we followed the State Patrol's criminalists into the processing room.

Over the years, you get used to the unexpected. When you're dealing with homicide, there's no telling what'll turn up in the victim's vehicle—the murder weapon, incriminating evidence, perhaps even another victim. That's happened to me more than once.

Peters and I had already seen what was in the car itself, but we were most curious about what might be hidden out of sight in the trunk. We were prepared for anything, except for what we found—a trunkful of Girl Scout cookies. Fifteen boxes in all.

We weren't the only ones who were surprised. It set the guy from the crime lab on his ass as well. "I'll be damned!" he said.

He conducted a quick inventory: Five Mints, three Carmel Delights, three Peanut Butter Patties, two Lemon Creams, and two Short Bread. The entire selection. If there was a hidden message concealed in the variety of cookies, the pattern eluded us.

On the other hand, the contents of the athletic bag turned out to be quite revealing—sweats, a clean shirt, a change of underwear and socks, toothbrush, toothpaste, and a bottle of Chaps. Darwin Ridley had intended to smell good, if not during the game, then certainly after it. And it appeared that he had planned to spend the night away from home regardless of whether or not the Islanders won.

We left the lab tech to his detail work. Peters and I drove across the floating bridge to Mercer Island. During the early years of Seattle, there was a group of visionaries who had wanted to turn Mercer Island into a vast park to benefit the whole city. That idea was squelched on the premise that no one in his right mind would travel that far for a picnic. Now, depending on rush hour traffic, Mercer Island is one of Seattle's closest suburbs. It's also one of the poshest.

Mercer Island High School is tucked back into the island's interior. On that particular day, it was a hotbed of activity. A whole contingent of reporters had beaten us to the punch. They hovered in eddying groups, hoping to capture a newsworthy comment from a grief-stricken team member or student. News vehicles occupied every visitor parking place as well as a good portion of the fire lane.

Peters and I parked a block or so away on the street and walked. We located the principal's office from the crowd milling around the door, both inside and out. A harried clerk stood behind a counter, attempting to maintain some semblance of order. Peters and I shoved our way through the mob, many of whom we recognized from the early morning press conference.

"We need to see the principal," Peters said brusquely to the clerk when we finally reached the counter.

"You and everybody else," she replied sarcastically.

He handed her the leather wallet containing his ID. She took off her glasses to examine it and then gave it back. She replaced her glasses, settling them firmly on her face. "All right. Let me check with Mr. Browning."

She disappeared into an inner office and returned moments later. "He'll see you now," she announced.

The only thing big about Ned Browning was his voice, which rumbled from an incongruously diminutive chest. His elfin features smacked of Santa Claus. His handshake, however, was that of a born wrestler.

"You're here about Mr. Ridley's death?" We nodded. Obviously, Ned Browning wasn't one to beat around the bush. "I'm sure you understand what an effect this terrible loss has had on our student body today." He spoke with the measured cadence of an old-time educator, one used to having his listeners' undivided attention. Or else.

"I considered dismissing school entirely when we first were notified of the situation. It's difficult to know what's the best thing to do in a case like this."

He paused and rubbed his chin, staring fixedly at us.

"Not canceling school was probably a good idea," I said. "It's best to keep things as close to normal as possible."

My comment was greeted with all the enthusiasm Ned Browning might have given an unfortunate truant's overused alibi. He ignored it totally. He continued speaking as though I'd never opened my mouth.

"The trouble is, this team has faced a similar problem once before. Some of these boys were already playing varsity ball when their previous coach, Mr. Altman, died of a heart attack.

"Of course, that was last year. It happened during the summer. It wasn't a situation like this where he was here one day and gone the next. We had the benefit of some adjustment time before school started in the fall. Not only that, Mr. Ridley had worked with the team for several years as the assistant coach. There was enough continuity so they were able to put together a winning team. They won the state championship last year. Were you aware of that?"

Peters and I nodded in unison. Browning went on. "I've sequestered the entire team as well as the squad of cheerleaders in Mr. Ridley's classroom. Of all the students, they're probably the ones who are most upset. They're the ones who worked most closely with him.

"Our guidance counselor, Mrs. Wynn, is with them. I thought it best to keep them together and isolated for fear some of your friends out in the other room would get hold of them." Ned Browning nodded slightly in the direction of the outer office. All of his actions were understated, self-contained.

"Believe me, Mr. Browning, those jerks out there are anything but friends. If we could talk with each member of the team . . ."

Browning cut me off in mid-sentence. "They're not there for your convenience, Mr. . . ."

"Beaumont," I supplied. "Detective Beaumont."

"Thank you, Detective Beaumont. These are adolescents who have suffered a severe loss. I've assembled them for the purpose of enabling them to begin working through their grief. It's the idea of peer group self-help. I won't tolerate any manipulation by you or anyone else. Is that clear, Mr. Beaumont?"

There was no Santa Claus twinkle in Ned Browning's eyes. They were sharp and hard. He meant what he said. I couldn't help feeling some real respect for this little guy, doing the best he knew for the benefit of those kids. I wondered if they appreciated him.

"Mr. Browning," Peters broke in, "neither Detective Beaumont nor I have any intention of manipulating your students, but we do need to interview them, all of them. It's the only way we'll get some idea of what happened Friday night."

For a time Browning considered what Peters had said. Finally, making up his mind, he nodded. "Very well. I'll take you there, but you must understand that the well-being of these young people is my first priority."

He rose. His full height wasn't more than five foot seven. "This way," he said. He led us out through a back door, avoiding the crowd surrounding the front counter. What had been Darwin Ridley's classroom was at the end of a long, polished corridor. Browning stopped before the closed door.

"What did you say your names are again?"

"Beaumont," I said. "Detectives Beaumont and Peters."

He ushered us inside. The room was hushed. There must have been twenty or so people in the room, standing or sitting in groups of two or three, some of them talking quietly, some weeping openly. The group was made up mostly of boys with five or six girls thrown into the mix. All of the faces reflected a combination of shock, grief, horror, and disbelief.

In the far corner of the room, a woman in her mid-thirties stood with one comforting hand on the heaving shoulders of a silently weeping girl. Browning gestured to the woman. She gave the girl a reassuring pat and walked toward us.

"This is Mrs. Wynn, one of our guidance counselors. She's also the advisor to the cheerleading squad. Candace, these are Detectives Beaumont and Peters from Seattle P.D. They need to interview those students who were at the game Friday."

Candace Wynn had a boyish figure and a headful of softly curling auburn hair. An impudent cluster of freckles spattered across her nose. Those freckles were at odds with the hostile, blue-eyed gaze that she turned on us.

"That's absolutely out of the question!"

"Candace, of course we will cooperate fully with the authorities in this matter."

"But Ned . . ." she began.

"That, however, does not mean we will allow any exploitation. My position on the media remains unchanged, but we have an obligation to teach these young people their civic responsibility."

The previous exchange had been conducted in such undertones that I doubt any of the kids had overheard a single sentence. Browning raised his hand for attention. His was a small but totally commanding presence. The students listened to his oddly stilted remarks with rapt concentration.

"My intention was that you should gather here and not be disturbed. However, I have brought with me two detectives from the Seattle Police Department. They are investigating Coach Ridley's death. It's important that we work with them. All of us. They have asked to spend time with you today, to discuss anything you may have seen or heard in the course of the game at the Coliseum Friday night."

He paused to clear his throat. A whisper rustled through the room. "We at this school have all suffered a severe loss. Those of you in this room, the ones who were most closely connected with Coach Ridley, are bound to suffer the most. Grief is natural. We all feel it, but it's important that we put that grief to a constructive use.

"Mrs. Wynn will be here throughout the interview process. I urge you to cooperate as much as possible. Helping these men discover who perpetrated this terrible crime is perhaps the only practical outlet for what we're feeling today. Detective Beaumont?"

I stepped forward, expecting to be introduced, but Browning continued. "Before you begin asking your questions, Detective Beaumont, I think it only fair that the students be allowed to ask some of you. All day long we've been subjected to a barrage of rumors. It would do us a tremendous service if we had some idea of what's really going on.".

I'd been snookered before, but let me tell you, Ned Browning did it up brown.

Where, oh where, was Arlo Hamilton when I needed him?

CHAPTER 8

I've never faced a tougher audience. Browning was right. Those kids were hurting and needed answers. As a group they had taken a closer look at death than most kids their age. Adolescents aren't accustomed to encountering human mortality on a regular basis. Two times in as many years is pretty damn regular.

They needed to know when Darwin Ridley had died, and how. Evidently, some helpful soul had spread the word that Ridley was despondent over the loss of the game and had committed suicide on account of it. The asshole who laid that ugly trip on those poor kids should have been strangled.

I answered their questions as best I could, fudging a little when necessary. I knew what would happen as soon as they stepped out of Ned Browning's artificial cocoon and the media started chewing them to bits. The principal stayed long enough to hear my introductory remarks, then left when Peters and I started our routine questioning process.

It took all afternoon to work our way through the group, one at a time. It was a case of patient prodding. The kids were understandably hesitant to talk to us. Candace Wynn, the guidance counselor, hovered anxiously on the sidelines.

Peters was a lot more understanding about that than I was. I had no patience with what I viewed as a direct impediment to our conducting a thorough investigation. As a consequence, we split the room by sex. I talked to the boys, the team members, and Peters dealt with the girls, the cheerleaders—helpless chicks to Mrs. Wynn's clucking mother hen. At least it kept her out of my hair.

Surprisingly, in spite of all that, we did get a few answers fairly early on. One of the first team members I interviewed was a gangly kid named Bob Payson, captain of the basketball team. I asked him if he had noticed anything unusual about Darwin Ridley's behavior the night of the game.

Payson didn't hesitate for a moment. "It was like he was real worried or upset or something."

"He was preoccupied?" I asked.

Payson nodded.

"Before the game? After it? During?"

"The whole time," Payson answered. "He was waiting at the gate when the team bus got there."

"The gate?"

"To Seattle Center. The team buses all stop at that gate there on Republican."

"Across from Bailey's Foods?"

Payson nodded. "That's right."

"He didn't ride on the bus with the team?"

"That was weird, too. Always before he rode the bus, but not this time."

My ears pricked up at that. Something out of the ordinary. Something different in the victim's way of doing things the night of the murder. Most human beings are creatures of habit. They don't like change, they actively resist it wherever possible. A change in Darwin Ridley's behavior the night he died might well be connected to his murder.

"So he didn't ride the bus, and he seemed worried when you saw him?"

"Yeah. He was looking up and down the street like he was waiting for someone. He told us to go on in and suit up, that he'd be inside in a minute."

"Was he?"

"No. He didn't come in for a long time. In fact, he got to the dressing room just before we had to go out and warm up. He didn't even have time to give us our pep talk."

"That was unusual?"

"You'd better believe it."

"He was a good coach?"

"The best."

"So what happened during the game?"

"We were leading by two points at halftime. He talked to us then, told us we were doing great." Payson paused.

"And then?" I prompted.

He frowned. "Just before time to go back on court, someone came to the door and talked to him."

"Did you see who it was?"

"No. They knocked. He opened the door and talked through the crack to whoever it was. After they left, he went over and sat down on one of the benches. He told us to go on, that he'd be out in a minute. He looked real upset."

"There wasn't anyone in the hallway when you went out?"

"No. At least I didn't see anybody."

"And did he come right out?"

"I don't know exactly when, but it was after the half started."

"That was unusual?"

"I told you. Coach Ridley was a good coach. He never missed part of a game before that, as far as I know."

"What about after the game?"

"We were pissed."

"Why?"

"The ref made a bad call in the last two seconds. They won by two points. On free throws."

Payson was suddenly quiet. He sat there fingering the intertwined *M* and *I* emblazoned in white felt on his maroon letterman's jacket. He seemed close to tears.

"What is it?" I asked.

"He just walked off. I couldn't believe it. He never said anything to us. Not good game. Not nice try. Nothing. Not even a word about the bad call. It was like he couldn't wait for the game to be over so he could be rid of us."

Payson was quiet again. There was more to his silence than just grief over the death of someone close to him. It wasn't an end of innocence, because I'm not so sure innocence exists anymore. But it was the end of something else—of youthful hero-worship, maybe—and the beginning of a realization of betrayal. It's hell growing up.

"He didn't even leave us the damn cookies," Payson managed.

"Cookies?" I almost choked on the word. "Did you say cookies?"

Payson grinned sheepishly and swiped at his eyes. "Girl Scout cookies. Pretty stupid, huh? But it was a tradition. Every member of the team got his own personal box of cookies after the first game in the tournament—win or lose, it didn't matter."

I hadn't expected an answer to the Girl Scout cookie question this early in the investigation. "Why Girl Scout cookies?" I asked.

"Coach Altman, our first coach. His wife was a Girl Scout leader, and he always brought cookies. Coach Ridley said he was going to do the same thing. And he did, last year. I guess this time he just forgot."

"He didn't forget," I said.

Bob Payson's eyes lit up. "He didn't?"

"The trunk of his car was full of Girl Scout cookies. Something kept him from giving them to you, but he didn't forget." It was small enough comfort, but Payson seemed to appreciate it.

Embarrassed, he mopped a tear from his face. "Knowing that makes me feel better and worse, both. How come?"

I shook my head. "Beats me," I said. "Can you think of anything else, Bob?"

"No. Can I go now?"

"Sure," I said, "you've been a big help. Thanks."

As Payson got up, I glanced across the room to where Peters was talking to one of the cheerleaders. She had broken down completely. She had buried her face in her arms and was sobbing uncontrollably. Candace Wynn patted her shoulder and gently straightened the girl's hair.

All other eyes in the room turned warily toward the weeping girl. Raw emotion can be pretty tough to take, especially when everyone is feeling much the same thing, but only one or two have nerve enough to express those feelings.

The counselor leaned down and spoke into the girl's ear. She quieted some, and I went on to the next boy on the team. Peters finished with the cheerleading squad long before I had worked my way through the team. In the course of the interviews it became apparent to me why Bob Payson was captain. None of the other boys was either as observant or as articulate as Bob had been. They told me more or less the same things he had, but without some of the telling details.

By three o'clock, parents began arriving to take their kids home. I could see Ned Browning's handiwork in that as well. One way or another, he was going to make sure the likes of Maxwell Cole didn't lay hands on any of his "young people" as long as they were in the school's care and keeping.

Unfortunately, I knew the news media a little more intimately than Ned Browning did. I guessed, and rightly so, that reporters would make arrangements to snag the students at home if they couldn't reach them at school. Had Ned and I discussed the matter, I could have told him so.

By the time the last of the students had left, Peters and I were wiped slick. As usual, we had worked straight through lunch and then some. Candace Wynn looked like she'd been pulled through a wringer, too. We invited her to join us for coffee at Denny's, a suggestion she accepted readily. It wasn't totally gentlemanly behavior on our part, though. We still hadn't interviewed her.

I waited politely until she had swallowed a sip or two of coffee before I tackled her. "Mrs. Wynn," I began.

"Call me Andi," she said. "I hate my name."

"Andi, then. Were you at the game?"

She nodded and smiled. "Where the cheerleaders go, there go I."

"Can you tell us anything about that night, anything odd or unusual that you might have noticed about Mr. Ridley."

Her eyes clouded. "You'll have to bear with me," she said. "We were good friends. It's hard to . . ."

"We understand that," Peters interjected. "Your point of view might be just that much different from the kids', though, that you could give us some additional insight."

She sighed. "I knew him a long time. I never saw him as upset as he was that night."

"Any idea why?"

"No. I tried to talk to him about it during halftime, but he just cut me off."

"Are you the one who came to the dressing-room door?"

Andi gave me an appraising look, as though surprised that I knew about that. She nodded. "He said he couldn't talk, that he was busy with the team. He shut me out completely."

"What about after the team left the dressing room? Did you see him talking with anyone in the hallway? Something or someone made him late for the second half."

"I knew he was late, but I didn't see anyone with him."

"Could he have been sick? Did he say anything to you?"

"No."

"Did you talk to him after the game at all?"

"I left during the third quarter. My mother's sick. I had to go see her. I was late getting back."

"So you never talked to him again, after those few words at the dressing room door."

"No." She choked on the word. "Something was wrong. He looked terrible. If only I . . ." She stopped.

"If only you what?"

"If only I could have helped him." She pushed her coffee cup away and got up quickly. "I'm going," she said. "Before I embarrass myself."

"We appreciate your help, Andi," Peters said.

"It's the least I can do."

We watched her drive out of the parking lot in a little red Chevy Luv with a bumper sticker that said she'd rather be sailing. As she pulled onto the access road, Peters said, apropos of nothing, "How many women do you know who drive pickups?"

I shrugged. "Not many, but it figures. She's a guidance counselor. My high school counselor at Ballard wore GI boots and drove a Sherman tank."

Peters laughed. "Come on now, Beau. Mrs. Wynn isn't that bad. I think she's cute. And she really seems to care about those kids."

On our way back to the Public Safety Building, Peters and I compared notes from our respective interviews. The cheerleading squad had been able to tell Peters very little that the team hadn't already told me, except they said Darwin Ridley had been five minutes late coming into the game after halftime.

The cheerleaders had taken a short break at the beginning of the third quarter, and they had followed Darwin Ridley onto the court. None of them were able to tell who or what had delayed him between the dressing room and the basketball court.

It wasn't much of a lead, but it was something. It gave us another little sliver of the picture. It didn't tell us what exactly had gone awry in Darwin Ridley's life that last day of his existence, but it was further testimony that something had been sadly amiss.

All we had to do was find out what it was. Piece of cake, right?

Sure. We do it all the time.

CHAPTER 9

I could probably get away with saying that I went to Bailey's after work that day because I'm a dedicated cop who doesn't leave a single stone unturned. I could claim that once I'm on a case, I work it one hundred percent of the time. I could say it, but it wouldn't be true.

The visit to the store was necessary because I was out of coffee. And MacNaughton's. And the state liquor store is right across the street from Bailey's parking lot.

So much for dedication.

To my credit, I did have my mind on the case. In fact, I was mentally going back over Bob Payson's interview, word for word, trying to see if there were any additional bits and pieces that could be pulled from what he had told me. I was so lost in thought, that I almost ran over the poor kid.

"Would you like to buy some Girl Scout cookies?"

The girl standing in front of two cartons of cookies was around eleven or twelve years old. She had a mop of bright red curls that could have come straight from Little Orphan Annie. She also had an award-winning smile. I'm a sucker for a smile. I stopped and reached for my wallet.

"How much are they?"

"Two fifty a box."

"And what kinds do you have?"

She gave me the complete rundown. I took two boxes of Mints and handed her a twenty. She rummaged in a ragged manila envelope for change.

"Do you sell here often?" I asked.

"I'm here every day after school. My mom brings me over. I earn my way to camp by selling cookies."

I felt my heartbeat quicken. Adrenaline does that. It's got nothing to do with heart disease. "Were you here last week?"

Handing me my change, she nodded. "All last week and all this week. It's a good place."

"You're serious about this, aren't you?"

"I've signed up to sell one thousand boxes. That way my mom doesn't have to pay to send me to camp."

She finished speaking and turned away from me to ask someone else. I had already bought. She couldn't afford to waste time with me at the expense of other potential paying customers. She homed in on a little old lady coming out of the store, carrying a cloth shopping bag filled with groceries.

"Did you save me some?" the woman asked, handing over the correct change.

"Right here," the girl replied, picking up an orange box and tucking it inside the woman's shopping bag. With the transaction complete, she turned back to me.

I took a wild stab in the dark. "What's the most you've ever sold at one time?"

She never batted an eyelash. "Fifteen boxes."

My heard did another little flip. I don't believe in coincidences. It's an occupational hazard. "No kidding. When?"

"Last week. A man and a woman bought fifteen boxes. They wrote a check."

Out of the corner of my eye I saw a woman emerge from a parked car and walk in our direction. Her total focus was on me, but she spoke to the girl. "Do you need anything, Jenny?" she asked.

"More Mints and some Carmel Delights," the girl answered. "And would you take this twenty?" Jenny handed over the twenty I had just given her and the woman returned to her car.

"Is that your mother?" I asked.

Jenny nodded. "She stays with me every day while I sell cookies."

The mother returned with four boxes of cookies cradled in her arms. She eyed me warily as she put them in the cartons at Jenny's feet.

"What are you, the hidden supply line?"

The woman gave me a half smile and nodded. "It works better if people don't realize we have a full carload of cookies right here. That way they think they're buying the last Mint."

"This is quite a little entrepreneur you have here," I said.

"Jenny's a good kid, and she has a lot of spunk. I don't mind helping her. She's willing to help herself."

Jenny was no lightweight salesperson. She had just finished nailing a woman with a baby in her grocery cart for four packages of cookies. She gave her mother the ten.

There was a quiet space, with no customers coming or going. The sun had dipped behind the roof of the Coliseum, and it was suddenly chill. Jenny gave a shiver.

"How many boxes in a carton?" I asked.

"Twelve," Jenny answered.

"How would you like to sell two cartons all at once?"

"Really? You mean it? Plus the ones you already bought?"

"Sure. But it'll cost you. I'll need you to tell me everything you can remember about the man and woman who bought those fifteen boxes."

Jenny's mother stiffened. "Wait just a minute . . ."

I reached into my pocket and extracted my ID. "It's okay," I said. "I'm a cop, working a case. I really will buy the cookies, though, if you're willing to help me."

Jenny looked from me to her mother and back again. "Is it okay, Mom?"

Her mother shrugged. "I guess so. It's about time we left here anyway. It's starting to get cold."

Jenny packed up her supplies. I wrote the Girl Scouts a check for sixty bucks, and we transferred twenty-four assorted boxes of cookies from their trunk to the back seat of the Porsche. I made arrangements to meet them at Dick's for a milkshake and hamburger. My treat.

While Jenny mowed through her hamburger and fries, I chatted with her mother, Sue Griffith. Sue and Jenny's father were divorced. Sue had custody, and she and Jenny were living in a small apartment on Lower Queen Anne while Sue finished up her last year of law school. There was no question in my mind where Jenny got her gumption.

Showing great restraint, I waited until Jenny had slurped up the very last of a strawberry shake from the bottom of her cup before I turned on the questions. "Tell me about the man who bought the cookies," I said.

"It wasn't just a man. It was a man and a woman."

"Tell me about them."

She paused. "He was tall and black. He had a sort of purple shirt on. And high-topped shoes."

"And the woman?"

"She was black, too. Very pretty. She's the one who wrote the check."

"What was she wearing, did you notice?"

"One of those big funny sweatshirts. You know, the long kind."

"Funny? What do you mean, funny?"

"It had an arrow on it that pointed. It said *Baby*."

I had seen a sweatshirt just like that recently. At Darwin Ridley's house, on the back of his widow, who never went to his games, not even statewide tournaments.

"What color was her shirt?" I asked.

"Pink," Jenny told me decisively. "Bright pink."

It was all I could do to sit still. "What time was it, do you remember?"

"Sure. It was just before we left. Mom brings me over as soon as I get home from school and have a snack. We're at the store by about four-thirty or five, and we stay for a couple of hours. That way I catch people on their way home from work."

"So what time would you say, six-thirty, seven?"

She nodded. "About that."

"Jenny," I said. "If I showed you a picture of those people, would you recognize them?"

Jenny nodded. "They were nice. The nice ones are easy to remember."

Across the table from me, Sue was looking more and more apprehensive. "What's all this about?" she asked. "This isn't that case that was on the news today, I hope."

"I'm afraid so."

"I don't think I want Jenny mixed up in this."

"Jenny's already mixed up in it," I said quietly. "Aside from his basketball team, your daughter may have been one of the last people to see Darwin Ridley alive."

Jenny had watched the exchange between her mother and me like someone watching a Ping-Pong game. "Who's Darwin Ridley?" she asked.

"I believe he's the man you sold all those cookies to," I told her.

"And now he's dead?" Her question was totally matter-of-fact.

"Somebody killed him. Late Friday night or Saturday morning."

Kids have an uncanny way of going for the jugular. "Was it the woman in the pink shirt? Did she kill him?"

I've suspected for years that kids watch too much television. That question corked it for me, convinced me I was right. The problem was, it was closer to the truth than I was willing to let on. I already knew Joanna Ridley was a liar. I wondered if she was something worse.

"It's not likely it was his wife," I said, waffling for Jenny's benefit. "At this point it could be almost anybody. We don't know."

"I hope she didn't do it," Jenny said thoughtfully. "I felt sorry for her."

"What do you mean?"

"The man was in a hurry. He seemed angry. He kept looking at his watch and saying he had to go. She said he should go, that she'd pay for the cookies and leave them in his trunk."

"Did she?"

Jenny nodded, big-eyed. "I helped her carry them to the car. She started crying."

"Crying? Are you sure?"

"Yes, I'm sure." Jenny sounded offended that her veracity had been called into question.

"What happened then?"

"After she put the cookies in one car, she got in another one."

"What kind?"

"Brown-and-white car, I think."

"And did she leave right away?"

"No. She sat there for a long time, leaning on the steering wheel, crying. She finally drove away."

I turned to Jenny's mother. "Did you see any of this?" I asked.

She shook her head. "I must have been in the car, studying. When Jenny needs something, she whistles."

"What about the check?" I asked.

Sue answered that question. "I turned it in to the cookie mother yesterday. She said she had to make a deposit this morning."

I made a note of the cookie mother's name and number. For good measure, I had Jenny go over the story one more time while I took detailed notes. "Is this going to help?" Jenny asked when we finished and I had closed my notebook.

"I certainly hope so," I said.

"And can I tell the kids at school that I'm helping solve a murder?" she asked.

"Don't tell them yet," I told her. "I'll let you know when it's okay to say something."

Jenny looked at me seriously. "Can girls be detectives when they grow up?"

"You bet they can," I told her. "You'll grow up to be anything you want to be. I'd put money on it."

Sue Griffith got up. Jenny did, too. "We'd better be going," Sue said.

"Thanks for buying all those cookies," Jenny said. "But if you run out, I'll still be selling next week. The sale lasts for three weeks."

Jenny Griffith was evidently born with selling in her blood. I had a Porsche full of Girl Scout cookies to prove it.

I never did remember to buy the coffee. The coffee or the MacNaughton's, either.

I called Peters as soon as I got home. "Guess what?" I said.

"I give up."

"Joanna Ridley was at the Coliseum on Friday."

"I thought she didn't like basketball."

"We've got a Girl Scout who says someone who looked like Joanna Ridley paid for the cookies we found in his trunk. By check."

"She wrote a check?"

"That's right."

"So what do we do now, Coach?" Peters asked.

"I'd say we take a real serious look at the Widow Ridley and find out what makes her tick."

"Starting with United Airlines?"

"That's as good a place to start as any."

"How about the neighbors?"

"Them, too."

Peters hesitated. "What would she have to gain, insurance maybe?"

"It wouldn't be the first time," I replied.

"I've never dealt with a pregnant murder suspect before. The very idea runs against the grain."

"Murder's against the grain," I reminded him. "Pregnancy's no more a legal defense for murder than Twinkies are."

Peters hung up then, but I could tell it still bothered him. To tell the truth, it bothered me. Joanna Ridley bothered me. I recalled her house, the way she had looked when she answered the door, her reactions when she finally learned what I was there for. I would have sworn she wasn't play-acting, but as I get older, the things I'm sure of become fewer.

I kept coming back to the bottom line. Joanna Ridley had lied to us, more than once. In the world of murder and mayhem, liars are losers. And they're usually guilty.

Just thinking about the next day made me weary. I stripped off my clothes and crawled into bed. I wasn't quite asleep when the phone rang.

"How's it going, J. P.?"

"Maxwell Cole, you son of a bitch! It's late. Leave me alone. I've got a job to do. I don't need you on my ass."

"Look, J. P., here I am calling you up to lend a little assistance, and you give me the brush off."

"What kind of assistance?"

"You ever heard of FURY?"

"What is this, a joke?"

"No joke. Have you ever heard of it?"

"Well, I've heard of Plymouth Furies and 'hell hath no fury.' Which is it?"

"It's an acronym, F-U-R-Y. The initials stand for Faithful United to Rescue You."

"To rescue me? From what?"

"J. P., I'm telling you, this is no joke. These people are serious. They're having their first convention in town this week. They're up at the Tower Inn on Aurora."

"So what are they rescuing? Get to the point, Max."

"They're white supremacists. I interviewed their president today. No kidding. They want blacks to go back where they came from."

"Jesus Christ, Max. What does all this have to do with me? I need my beauty sleep."

"They said it's possible one of their members knocked off Darwin Ridley."

"Send me his name and number. I'll track him down in the morning."

"J. P. . . ."

"Get off it, Max. You know how this works. Some kooky splinter group claims responsibility for a crime and manufactures a whole armload of free publicity. Don't fall for it. And don't complicate my life. I've got plenty to do without chasing after phony suspects who are playing the media for a bunch of fools."

"Are you saying . . ." he began.

"If the shoe fits!"

With that, I hung up. The phone began ringing again within seconds, but I ignored it. It rang twenty times or so before it finally stopped.

Within minutes, I was sound asleep and dreaming about Girl Scout cookies.

CHAPTER 10

There's only one thing to do with that many Girl Scout cookies—take them to the office and share the wealth. So I drove to the Public Safety Building and parked the Porsche in the bargain basement garage at the foot of Columbia. I've noticed that my 928 commands a fair amount of respect from parking garage attendants.

This one held the door open for me as I got out. Then I crawled back inside and dredged out the two cartons of cookies. When the kid handed me my parking ticket, I gave him a box of cookies.

"Hey, thanks," he said, grinning.

"Just handle my baby with care," I told him.

"We always do," he replied.

I was halfway up the block when I heard squealing tires as he jockeyed the Porsche into a parking place. There was no accompanying sound of crumpling metal, so I didn't worry about it.

Peters glanced up from his newspaper as I put the cookies on my desk. "Want one?" I asked.

"Are you kidding? That much sugar will kill you, Beau. What are you doing, peddling them for one of your neighbors?"

"Peddling, hell! I'm giving this stuff away, all in the line of duty."

"Don't tell me you bought that many cookies last night when you were talking to that little girl about the Ridleys."

"She's a terrific salesman."

"And you're an easy mark."

For the remainder of the morning, while Peters and I valiantly worked at running a check on Joanna Ridley and tried to dredge a copy of the check out of a combination of Girl Scout and bank bureaucracy, our two desks became the social hub of the department. Word of free cookies spread like wildfire, and everyone from Vice to Property managed to stop by with a cup of coffee. Including Captain Lawrence Powell.

He wasn't above taking a cookie or two before he lit into us. "Whenever you two finish socializing, how about stopping by my office for a little chat."

Larry Powell's glass-enclosed, supposedly private office offers all the privacy of a fishbowl, which is what we call it. It isn't soundproofed, either. You don't have to be a lip-reader to know everything that's going on behind Powell's closed door.

"You're out of line, Beau," he said. "Dr. Baker has sent a formal complaint to the chief."

"That jerk," I said.

"Detective Beaumont, this is serious. Just because you can literally buy and sell city blocks in this town doesn't give you the right to run roughshod over elected public officials."

"Look, Larry, we're not talking net worth here. Baker demanded information before I had it. Then he pitched a fit because I wouldn't give it to him."

"This is a sensitive case, Beau. If you're going to go off half-cocked, I'll pull you two off it and give it to someone who isn't as hotheaded."

"It wouldn't be such a sensitive case, as you put it, if Peters and I hadn't figured out who he was. Darwin Ridley was just an unidentified corpse by a garbage dumpster until we got hold of him, remember?"

"We're making progress," Peters put in helpfully, hoping to defuse the situation a little.

Powell turned from me to Peters. "You are?"

"We've been working one possibility all morning."

"Well, get on with it, then, but don't step on any more toes. You got that?" Powell had worked himself into a real temper tantrum.

"You bet! I've got it all right." I steamed out of the fishbowl with Peters right behind me. Making a detour past our cubicle, I grabbed up our jackets, tossed Peters his, and shrugged my way into mine.

"Where are we going?" Peters asked.

"Out!" I snapped.

It took a while for the attendant to free my Porsche. It had been buried among a group of all-day cars as opposed to short-term ones. Once out of the garage, I hauled ass through Pioneer Square, driving south.

"I asked you before, where are we going?"

"Any objections to letting Joanna Ridley know we know she's a lying sack of shit?"

"None from me."

"Good. That's where we're going."

"Do you think it'll work?" he asked.

"She's no pro. She's not even a particularly good liar. It won't take much to push her over the edge, just a little nudge, especially in her condition."

Peters nodded in agreement.

By the time we got off the freeway, fast driving had pretty well boiled the venom out of my gut. It wasn't the first time I'd heard sly references to the fact that having money had somehow spoiled J. P. Beaumont. Money doesn't automatically make you an asshole. Or a prima donna, either. Damn Doc Baker anyway.

We drove across Beacon Hill, one of the glacial ridges that separates Puget Sound from Lake Washington. When we stopped in front of Joanna Ridley's house, there were no cars there at all. I was disappointed. I had geared myself up for a confrontation. Now it looked as though it wasn't going to happen.

We had turned around and were heading back to the department when we met Joanna Ridley's Mustang GT halfway down the block. She was alone in the car.

"We're in luck," I said.

I made a U-turn and parked in the driveway behind the Mustang. When we stepped onto Joanna's front porch, she greeted us with what could hardly be called a cordial welcome. "What do you want?"

"We need to talk."

She stood looking up at us questioningly, one hand resting on the small of her back as though it was bothering her. "What about?"

"About last Friday."

"I've told you everything I know."

"No, you didn't, Joanna. You didn't tell us you had gone to the Coliseum and talked to your husband. In fact, you told us you never went near his games."

Defiance crept across her face. "So I went there to talk to him. What difference does that make?"

"Why did you lie to us? You said the last time you saw him was at breakfast."

She dropped her gaze. With eyes averted, Joanna turned to the front door. She unlocked it, opened it, and went inside, leaving us standing on the porch. Peters and I exchanged glances, unsure whether or not we were expected to follow.

"After you," Peters said.

We found Joanna Ridley sitting on the couch. Her face was set, full lips compressed into a thin line, but there was no sign of tears. Peters sidled into a chair facing her, while I sat next to her on the couch.

"How did you find out?" she said, her voice barely above a whisper.

"It doesn't matter. The point is, we know you were there. We have a witness who saw you there. You signed a piece of paper."

She looked at me for a long minute. "The cookies," she said. "I forgot about the cookies. I wrote a check."

Putting her hand to her mouth, she started to laugh, the semihysterical giggle of one whose life has been strung so tight that the ends are beginning to unravel. The giggle evolved into hysterical weeping before she finally quieted and took a deep, shuddering breath.

"I don't know why I'm laughing. I went to tell him I wanted a divorce, and I didn't even do that right," she said finally. "I ended up paying for all those damn cookies."

"You didn't mention a divorce to us before."

"I didn't tell anyone. Why tell? If Darwin was dead, what did it matter?"

"But it could have some bearing on how he died, Mrs. Ridley. Do you mind if I ask why you wanted a divorce?"

"Mind? Yes, I mind."

"But we need to know," Peters insisted. "It could be important."

She sat silently for what seemed like a long time, looking first at Peters then at me. At last she shook her head. "Darwin was screwing around," she whispered. Once more Joanna Ridley began to cry.

Suddenly, I felt old and jaded. It didn't seem like that big a deal. Husbands screw around all the time. And wives put up with it or not, divorce them or not. And life goes on. In most cases.

Darwin Ridley had not survived his indiscretion, however. I wondered if we might not be treading on very thin Miranda ice. We had not read Joanna Ridley her rights. I was beginning to think maybe we should have.

Peters and I waited patiently, neither of us saying a word. Eventually, she quieted, got control of herself.

"Does it have to come out? About the divorce, I mean."

I did my best to reassure her. "We'll try. If it has nothing to do with the murder itself, then there's no reason for it to go any further than this room."

She got up and walked away from us. She stood by a window, pulling the curtain to one side to look out. I knew what she was doing—distancing herself from us while she waged some ferocious internal war. Finally, she turned to face us.

"I guess I could just as well tell you," she said softly. "You'll probably find out anyway. I had a phone call that afternoon, about three-thirty or a quarter to four. From a man. He said I'd better keep that mother-fucking son of a bitch away from his daughter."

"Talking about Darwin?"

She nodded.

"That's all he said?"

"No, he said I could tell that black bastard that his daughter wouldn't be at the Coliseum to meet him, that she wouldn't be at the game, and that if Darwin even so much as spoke to her again, he was a dead man."

Stopping, Joanna looked at me, her eyes hollow. "That's the other reason I went to the Coliseum. To warn him."

"I don't suppose the caller left his name and number," I said.

Joanna shook her head. "This came yesterday." Like a sleepwalker, she rose, crossed the room into the little study, opened a desk drawer, and extracted a large manila envelope, which she brought back to me. Her name and address were typed neatly on the outside. There was no return address in the upper left-hand corner. The postmark was illegible.

When I opened it, a single photograph fell out.

At first glance, it seemed to be a picture of a man embracing a woman in what appeared to be a motel room. Closer examination revealed the man to be Darwin Ridley, but the woman wasn't a woman at all. She was a girl. A blonde girl. She was still wearing a bra, but the camera had caught her in the act of slipping out of her skirt. A short, gored, two-toned skirt.

A cheerleader's skirt.

I shook my head and handed the picture over to Peters. He looked at it and dropped the picture on the coffee table like it was too hot to handle.

Captain Powell's sensitive case had just turned into Maxwell Cole's dynamite. I wondered briefly if it was too late to get the captain to put two other detectives on the case instead of us. I didn't think I wanted to be anywhere within range when this particular shit started hitting the fan.

I looked at Joanna Ridley then, standing there with her pregnant silhouette framed against the curtained window, with the muted sunlight filtering through her backlit hair. She was a picture of totally vulnerable, abject despair.

And in that instant, I knew what she was feeling.

She had lost the man she loved, and now even her memories of him were being shredded and torn from her. I knew all too well that sense of absolute loss.

I got up and went to her. Somebody needed to do it, and Peters wasn't going to. He didn't understand what was happening. I reached out for her and held her. She fell against my chest, letting my arms support her, keep her from slipping to the floor. Everything that stood between us, every conceivable barrier, disintegrated as I cradled her against me.

"Did you kill him, Joanna?" I asked, murmuring the question through her hair.

"No, I didn't."

From that moment on, I never doubted for a minute that she was telling the truth.

CHAPTER 11

▽

By the time Joanna drew away from me and I led her from the window back to the couch, Peters was ready to go straight up and turn left. He was there to investigate a homicide, not to offer emotional support and comfort to a bereaved widow, one he considered to be a prime suspect. I couldn't have explained to him what had just happened. I couldn't explain it to myself.

With an impatient frown that was far more exasperation than concentration, he picked up the picture once more and examined it closely. His brows knit.

"Can you tell which cheerleader it is?" I asked him. After all, Peters had been the one who had spent the afternoon interviewing the Mercer Island cheerleaders the day before.

He shook his head. "Not for sure." He glanced at Joanna, who was gradually pulling herself together. "Do you know?" he asked Joanna.

"No." Her voice was flat, her face devoid of expression.

Peters, reluctant to give up that line of questioning, took another tack. "Your husband never mentioned any of the cheerleaders to you by name?"

"Never."

Peters passed me the picture again. I examined it more carefully this time, looking at it less for its shock value than as an integral part of the puzzle that marked the end of Darwin Ridley's life.

I studied the background of the picture. Definitely a motel, and not a particularly classy one at that. The picture had evidently been taken through a window from outside the room. I don't know a lot about cameras, but I recognized this was no Kodak Instamatic. The clarity of detail, the finite focusing even through glass said the picture had been taken with top-flight equipment. Scrutinizing the background of the picture, I wondered if someone in the crime lab could blow the photo up large enough to read the checkout information in a framed holder on the room door behind the fondly embracing twosome.

"Could we take the picture, Joanna? It would help if we knew where and when this was taken. And by whom."

All the fight had been taken out of her, all her strength. She nodded in agreement.

"Did you have separate checking accounts?" Peters asked suddenly. "Checking accounts or charge cards, either one?"

"No." Joanna looked genuinely puzzled. "Why?"

"He had to pay for motel rooms some way or other. Do you mind if I look through his desk?"

"Go ahead."

Peters went to the little study, leaving Joanna and me alone. "Had you been planning to divorce your husband before the phone call?" I asked.

Joanna shot a darting look in my direction. "We were having a baby," she replied, leaving me to draw my own conclusions.

"But you believed the man who called you. Instantly. Even before he sent you the photograph."

"It wasn't the first time," she said quietly.

"Another cheerleader?" I asked.

"I don't know. I don't care. Maybe the same one. It doesn't matter. The marriage counselor said Darwin was going through a mid-life crisis, that he'd get over it eventually if I was patient."

A part of me objected to the term mid-life crisis. It's a handy rationalization that covers a multitude of sins. I've used it myself on occasions, some of them not very defensible. "Counselor?" I asked.

"We went to the counselor together, last year, a lady family therapist. I could tell something was wrong, but I didn't know what it was. All I knew was that I wanted to stay married. Being married was important to me."

"And in the course of counseling you found out your husband was having an affair." It's an old story.

She nodded. "He promised he'd break it off. He said it was over, and I believed him."

"And you decided to have a baby to celebrate," I added.

"We both wanted one," she said. "We had been trying for years. It was an accident that I turned up pregnant right then. Besides," she added, "I thought a baby would bring us closer together."

The look on her face, far more than what she said, told me exactly how badly Joanna Ridley had been taken in by the old saw that babies fix bad marriages. It certainly hadn't worked in this case. My heart went out to the lady who would be raising her child alone.

Sometimes, life isn't fair. Make that usually.

The doorbell rang, and Joanna hurried to answer it. Meanwhile, Peters returned from his examination of the desk. "Nothing there," he said.

Joanna ushered a heavy-set woman into the room. She was evidently a neighbor. In one hand she held a huge pot that contained an aromatic stew of some kind. In her other hand she carried a napkin-covered plate heaped high with some kind of baked goods. She glared at us, making it clear that we were unwelcome interlopers.

"You have anything to eat today, Joanna, honey?" she asked, still glowering at us, but speaking to Joanna.

"No, I . . ." Joanna trailed off.

"Now you listen to Fannie Mae, girl. You got to keep up your strength, for you and that baby. I'll just put this food in the kitchen." She bustled out of the room. Joanna returned to the couch.

"What did you do after you left the Coliseum?" Peters asked as soon as she sat back down.

Joanna regarded him coolly. "I drove to Portland," she replied.

"Portland, Oregon? Why?"

"To see my father."

"And did you?"

Joanna's eyes never strayed from Peters' face. "No. I drove past the house, but I didn't go in."

"Wait a minute. Let me get this straight. You left the Coliseum after talking to your husband, drove all the way to Portland to talk to your father, and then didn't go in to see him once you got there?"

"That's right."

"Why not?"

"Because I changed my mind. I realized I'd never go through with it, the divorce, I mean."

If I had been trying to sell Peters Fuller Brushes right then, I would have known I'd blown the sale. He lay his finger next to his nose, the palm of his hand covering his mouth. He wasn't buying Joanna's story. Not any of it.

"What time did you get back?" I asked, stepping into the conversation.

"Midnight. Maybe later."

"Did you see anyone along the way? Someone who would be able to say that they saw you there during that time?"

She shrugged. "I stopped for gas in Vancouver, but I don't know if anyone there would remember me."

"What kind of station, Joanna?" I prompted. "Can you remember?"

"A Texaco. On Mill Plain Road."

"How did you pay? Credit card? Cash?"

"Credit card. I think I used my VISA."

"Could you give us that number?"

Joanna retrieved her purse from a table near the front door where she had left it when she first entered the house. As we had talked, there had been sounds of activity in the kitchen. Now Fannie Mae reappeared, carrying a tray of coffee cups, a pot of coffee, and a plate of homemade biscuits. Joanna dictated the number to Peters while I helped myself to coffee, biscuits, and honey. Naturally, Peters abstained. Health-food nuts piss me off sometimes.

Within minutes several other visitors showed up, and it seemed best for us to leave. I wasn't looking forward to being alone with Peters. I figured he'd land on me with all fours. I wasn't wrong.

"You've really done it this time!"

"Done what?" I made a stab at playing innocent.

"Jesus, Beau. We never even read her her rights."

"We didn't need to. She didn't do it."

"What? How can you be so sure?"

"Instinct, Peters. Pure gut instinct."

"I can quote you chapter and verse when your instincts haven't been absolutely, one hundred percent accurate."

I could, too, but I didn't tell Peters that. Instead, I said, "Ridley was too big. With the morphine, he would have been all dead weight. She couldn't have strung him up, certainly not in her condition."

"She could have had help."

"She didn't."

Peters wasn't about to give up his pet suspect. "What about her father? The two of them could have done it together. She said she got back around midnight. The coroner said he died about two A.M. Portland doesn't give her an alibi, if you ask me."

I thought about Joanna's father, the kindly, stoop-shouldered old man who had let us in the house the day before. "No way," I said. "It's got to be somebody else."

We let it go at that. Neither of us was going to change the other's mind.

Before leaving Joanna's house, we had decided to stop by Mercer Island High School in hopes of determining the identity of Darwin Ridley's cheerleader. With that in mind, I turned off Rainier Avenue onto an on-ramp for I-90. Unfortunately, I had been too busy talking to notice that traffic on the ramp was stopped cold, three car lengths from the entrance.

Unable to go forward or back, we spent the next hour stuck in traffic while workers building the new floating bridge across Lake Washington escorted traffic through the construction, one snail-paced lane at a time.

We should have phoned first. We got to the school about twelve-fifteen, only to discover that Candace Wynn wasn't there. Her mother was gravely ill, and Mrs. Wynn had taken the day off.

Ned Browning's clerk wasn't exactly cordial, but she was somewhat more helpful than she had been the previous day. She gave us Mrs. Wynn's telephone number in Seattle. We tried calling before we left the school, but there was no answer.

Back in the car, we started toward Seattle. Thinking the other bridge might be faster, we avoided I-90 and circled around through Bellevue. Unfortunately, a lot of other people had the same idea, including two drivers who managed to smack into one another head-on in the middle of the Evergreen Point span. It wasn't a serious accident, but it was enough to tie us up in traffic for another hour, along with several thousand other hapless souls.

It was a flawless spring day, without a cloud in the sky, with Lake Washington glassy and smooth beneath us, and with Mt. Rainier a snow-covered vision to our left. Unfortunately, Peters was still ripped about Joanna Ridley, and I was pissed about the traffic, so we weren't particularly good company, and we didn't spend that hour admiring the scenery.

We finally got back to the department around two. I took Joanna's photograph and envelope down to the crime lab to see if they could lift prints or magnify the photo enough to read the print in the notice on the motel room door. Meanwhile, Peters settled down in our cubicle to try to track down Candace Wynn. By the time I got back to the fifth floor, he had reached her and made arrangements for us to meet her at a Greek restaurant in Fremont in half an hour.

Fremont is a Seattle neighborhood where aging hippies who've grown up and gone relatively straight try to sell goods and services to whatever brand of flower children is currently in vogue. Costas Opa, a Greek restaurant right across from the Fremont Bridge, is quite a bit more upscale than some of its funky neighbors. It was late afternoon by then. The place was long on tables and short on customers when we got there.

We sat at a corner window table where we could see traffic coming in all directions. Across the street, Seattle's favorite piece of public art was still wearing the green two days after St. Patrick's day. *Waiting For The Interurban* is a homey piece of statuary made up of seven life-size figures, including a dog, whose face is rumored to bear a remarkable resemblance to one of the sculptor's sworn enemies. They stand under what seems to be a train station platform, waiting for an old Seattle/Tacoma commuter that has long since quit running.

Throughout the year, concerned citizens and frustrated artists make additions and corrections by adding seasonal touches to the statues' costumes. That day, they all wore emerald green full-length scarves.

I expected Candace Wynn to drive up in her red pickup. Instead, she arrived on foot, walking the wrong way up a one-way street. The Fremont

Bridge, a drawbridge, was open. Candace darted through stopped vehicles to cross the street to the restaurant.

Her outfit wasn't well suited for visiting invalid relatives. She wore frayed jeans, a ragged sweatshirt, and holey tennis shoes. Sitting down, she ordered coffee.

"I'm in the process of moving," she explained, glancing down at her clothes. "The house is a mess, or I'd have invited you there."

"You live around here?" Peters asked.

She pointed north toward the Ship Canal. "Up there a few blocks, in an old watchman's quarters. View's not much, but I couldn't beat the rent. I'm moving back home, though, at the end of the month."

"Back home with your mother?"

She nodded.

"How is your mother?" I asked. "I understand she's very ill." Sometimes it surprises me when the niceties my own mother drilled into my head surface unconsciously in polite company.

Candace Wynn's freckled face grew serious. "So, so," she said. "It comes and goes. She's got cancer. She's back in the hospital right now. I'll be home to help her when she gets out. I was up with her all last night and couldn't face going to school this morning. Once I woke up, though, I decided to tackle packing. It was too nice a day to waste."

I had to agree with her there. If you've ever spent time with a cancer patient, you should know better than to squander a perfect day being miserable over little things like stalled traffic.

Somehow I had forgotten. I had spent the day blind to blossoming cherry trees and newly leafing trees. It took Andi Wynn's casual remark to bring me up short, to make me remember.

We had yet to ask her a single question, but already I was prepared to mark the interview down as an unqualified success. Whether or not she identified Mercer Island's precociously amorous cheerleader.

CHAPTER 12

After the waiter set down her coffee, Candace Wynn took one demure sip and then looked expectantly from Peters to me and back again. "You said you needed to talk to me."

I gave Peters the old take-it-away high sign. After all, Candace Wynn knew Peters somewhat better than she knew me. Besides, Peters' earnest, engaging manner encouraged people to spill their guts. I had seen it happen.

"That's right; we do," Peters said. "How long have you been at Mercer Island?"

"Ten years."

"All that time as counselor?"

"No. I've only been in the counseling department for the last year and a half. Before that, I taught math."

"And what about the cheerleaders?"

"I've had them the whole time. I was a cheerleader at Washington State in Pullman." She stopped and gave Peters an inquiring look. "I thought this was going to be about Darwin."

"It is, really, in a roundabout way," Peters said. "You told us yesterday that you were a friend of his. How good a friend, Mrs. Wynn?"

"Andi," she reminded him. She shrugged. "Fairly good friends. When I started teaching there, a bunch of us used to play crazy eights in the teachers' lounge in the morning—Coach Altman, Darwin, and a couple of others. You get to be friends that way.

"Playing cards?"

"That's right. And in the afternoons, some of us would stop by the Roanoke and play a few games of pool."

"Including Darwin Ridley and yourself?" Peters asked.

Andi nodded. "Yes."

"Did you know anything about his personal life?" Peters continued.

"Some, but not very much."

"Have you ever met his wife, Joanna?"

"No. I never even saw her. She didn't come to school, and she never showed up at any of the faculty functions, at least not any of the ones I went to."

"And she never came to the Roanoke?"

"No."

"Did you know she's pregnant?"

Andi looked at Peters. She seemed a little surprised. "Is she? I didn't know. That's too bad," she said.

Peters nodded in agreement. "Yes, it is. Did Darwin ever indicate to you that his marriage was in trouble?"

Andi Wynn sipped her coffee and considered the question before she answered. "I remember him mentioning that they were going for marriage counseling. That was some time back. A year ago, maybe a year and a half. He never said anything more about it. Whatever the problem was, they must have straightened it out."

I was growing restless, sitting on the sidelines. "Tell us about your cheerleading squad," I said.

"The cheerleaders? What about them?"

"Give us an idea of who they are, what they're like."

"They're mostly juniors and seniors . . ." she began. Then she stopped and looked at Peters. "You talked to most of them yesterday. What more do you need to know?"

"Most?" Peters focused in on the important issue. "I only met most of them? Where were the others?"

"Two were missing. One was home sick. She has mono. The other quit, transferred to a different school."

Peters had gotten out his notebook and flipped through several pages. "What are their names?" he asked, his pen poised above the paper.

"Those who weren't there yesterday?" Peters nodded in reply. "Amy Kendrick and Bambi Barker."

"Bambi? As in Walt Disney?"

"That's right."

"Which one has mono?" Peters asked.

"Amy."

"So Bambi transferred to another school," I said. "Recently?"

"Monday of this week."

"What is she, a junior?"

Andi Wynn shook her head. "A senior."

"And she's transferring this late in her last year? What's her problem? Flunking out? Having trouble with grades?"

"No, nothing like that. Her father just up and shipped her off to a private school in Portland, a boarding school."

"Which one?" Peters asked, still holding his pen.

Andi frowned. "St. Agnes of the Hills. I think that's the name of it."

Peters wrote it down. "Do you have any idea why she was sent away?" he asked.

"Not really. Her father's Tex Barker, though."

Peters dropped his pen on the table. The name meant nothing to me, but I saw the spark of recognition flash in Peters' eyes. "Wheeler-Dealer Barker?"

"That's the one."

I was tired of sitting on my hands. "Who the hell is Wheeler-Dealer Barker?"

"Beau here doesn't watch TV, Andi," Peters explained with a smile. Andi Wynn smiled back.

"Okay, you two. Stop making fun of me. Who's this Barker character?"

"He runs Tex Barker Ford in Bellevue," Peters told me. "His commercials are reputed to be some of the worst in the country."

"That bad?"

Peters and Andi nodded in unison. "Somebody gives out awards for the worst television commercials. It's like Mr. Blackwell's worst-dressed list. Barker won one last year, hands down."

"What else do you know about him?" I asked. Because of Peters' voracious reading, he always seemed to know something about practically everything. Wheeler-Dealer Barker was no exception.

"He came up here from Texas four, maybe five, years ago and bought up a failing Ford dealership on auto row in Bellevue. Within months, he had moved it from the bottom of the heap to one of the top dealerships."

"So the commercials haven't hurt him."

"Are you kidding? He's like that character with his dog Spot, one of those guys people love to hate, but they do business with him right and left. I understand he's made offers on two more dealerships, one in Lynnwood and the other down in Burien."

"And he lives on Mercer Island?" I asked, turning once more to Candace Wynn. "How did the daughter of someone like that fit in on Mercer Island?"

"Bambi landed in the in-crowd and stayed there. She never had any problem."

The picture Joanna Ridley had handed me passed through my mind. Bambi Barker had problems, all right, I thought to myself. Lots of them. They just didn't show. "When did you find out Bambi was being transferred?" I asked.

"She was at school Friday morning. I saw her. Then, right about noon, her father came to pick her up. I didn't see it, but I understand there was quite a scene in the office. Yesterday, her mother officially checked her out of school. You know, got the withdrawal forms signed, turned in her books, cleaned out her lockers, that kind of thing."

"Did you talk to her, the mother?"

Andi nodded. "Briefly. Tried to anyway. I tried to explain how tough it would be for Bambi to change schools this close to graduation, but she said it was too late, that they had taken Bambi down to Portland over the weekend."

"And this school . . ." Peters paused and consulted his notes. "St. Agnes of the Hills, you said. Where is it?"

"Somewhere in Beaverton, I guess." Andi paused, thoughtfully. "I still don't understand. What exactly does all this have to do with Darwin? I thought he was the main reason you wanted to talk to me."

I took the plunge. Peters would have walked around it all day. "Did you ever hear any rumors about Bambi Barker and Darwin Ridley?" It was the most delicate way I could think of to phrase a most indelicate question.

For a moment or two Andi Wynn looked at me as though she didn't quite grasp what I was saying. "Rumors?" she asked. "What kind of rumors?"

Peters cleared his throat. "We've been informed by a reliable source that there's a possibility that Bambi and Darwin Ridley were having an affair."

Shock waves registered on Andi's face. "That's a lie!"

"It's not a lie, unfortunately," I said. "We've seen proof. We just didn't know who the girl was. Now we do."

Candace Wynn drew herself up sharply and looked me right in the eye. "You don't expect me to believe that, do you? Darwin Ridley was a fine man. His memory deserves to be treated with respect."

"Andi, it's not a matter of disrespect . . ." I began, but she didn't wait long enough to hear me out. Instead, Candace Wynn angrily shoved her chair back from the table, rattling the silverware and glasses on the table next to us. She bounded to her feet.

"I won't listen to this! Not a word of it!" With that, she turned on her heel and stamped out of the restaurant.

"Nice going, Beau," Peters said. "What do you do for an encore?"

I watched Candace Wynn storm across the street and out of sight behind a wall of buildings. I shrugged. "After all, she's the cheerleading advisor. If she'd been doing her job right, maybe she would have noticed something funny was going on."

Peters leaped to Candace Wynn's defense. "You expect her to be psychic? Ridley wasn't exactly advertising the fact that he was screwing around. His wife didn't know about it. The girl's parents apparently didn't know. Why should a teacher? From the sound of it, she's got her hands full with a dying mother."

I have to confess, I didn't have a pat answer for that question. Why should Candace Wynn have known? I said nothing, and my mind went wandering down another track.

"What else do you know about this what's-his-name, Wheeler-Dealer? Would he really mail a copy of that picture to Joanna? A picture of his own daughter? I'm a father. It doesn't sound to me like something a father would do, not even a shitty father."

Peters agreed and offered an alternate suggestion. "Maybe somebody else sent pictures to both of them."

I gave that idea some thought. It seemed somewhat more plausible. "But who?" I asked.

Peters shrugged. "Your guess is as good as mine. What now?"

"We'd better drag our butts down to Portland and talk to Bambi Barker."

"Today?" Peters asked in surprise, glancing at his watch. It was already well after three.

"Why not today? If we left right now, we could just beat the traffic out of town. Besides, we wouldn't have to cross any bridges."

Peters shook his head. "It would be midnight before we got back. I don't like to come home that late. Heather and Tracie still get upset if I'm not home before they go to bed."

After the divorce, Peters' two girls had spent some time in a flaky religious commune with their equally flaky mother. With the help of my attorney, Ralph Ames, we had managed to get them back home and in Peters' custody late the previous fall. Kids are pretty resilient, but the two girls still hadn't adjusted to all the abrupt changes that had disrupted their young lives. They were still basically insecure. So was Peters.

"Why don't I drive down by myself, then?" I suggested. "It's no big deal for me to come home late. Nobody's there waiting. Besides, it's important that we talk to Bambi before her dear old dad has any idea we know what's been going on."

"You've got yourself a deal," Peters told me. "You drive to Portland, and I'll handle the paperwork."

Talk about getting the best of the bargain! I headed for my apartment. No way was I going to drive one of the departmental crates to Portland when my bright red Porsche was longing for the open road.

By four, I was cruising down Interstate 5, headed south. Once I passed the worst of the Seattle/Tacoma traffic, I set the cruise control to a sedate sixty-two. Red Porsches draw radar guns like shit draws flies. Sergeant Watkins had given me a long lecture in community relations on the occasion of my second speeding ticket. I had slowed down some since then.

As I drove, I was conscious of springtime blossoming around me. Spindly blackberry clumps were green with a thin covering of new leaves. Here and there, hillsides were graced with farmhouses surrounded by blooming fruit trees.

Between Seattle and Portland, I-5 bypasses dozens of little western Washington towns—Lacy, Maytown, Tenino, Kelso—places travelers never see in actual life. They're nothing more than signs on the freeway and names and dots in a road atlas. Nevertheless, bits and pieces of small-town life leaked into my consciousness. There was the ever-present message from an eccentric Centralia dairy farmer whose private billboard still wanted to get us out of the UN, and the new chain link fence surrounding the juvenile detention center in Chehalis that said we don't want our town contaminated by these kids. Further south, another billboard proclaimed the Winlock Egg Days.

I had never attended an egg festival. Or wanted to.

The day was flawlessly clear and bright. To the left across the freeway, Mount Rainier majestically reflected back fragile spring sunlight. It was too dark to catch sight of the shattered, still-steaming profile of Mount St. Helens.

I savored every moment of that drive south, from the thick papermill-flavored air of Longview to the cheerful lights on the grain elevator at Kalama. With every mile, the case receded into the far reaches of my mind. For those three quiet hours, I forgot about Darwin and Joanna Ridley, about Bambi Barker and her father, Wheeler-Dealer.

As a homicide cop, that's a luxury I don't give myself very often, but Candace Wynn and her mother had brought back memories of my own mother and her painful death. It had pulled me up short and forced me to recognize exactly how precious life is, had shocked me out of the trap of drifting through life without tasting or noticing.

I owed Candace Wynn a debt of gratitude. Sometime I'd have to call her up and thank her.

CHAPTER 13

St. Agnes of the Hills School sits well back from the road in the middle of Beaverton. It boasts an expanse of beautifully manicured, discreetly lit grounds sandwiched between business parks and new and used car lots. It was late evening when I drove up the circular driveway and parked in front of the building. Spotlights showed off the golden bricks and arches of a graceful Spanish facade on the front of the building.

In the darkness, one front window of the building glowed industriously. I climbed the circular stairway and tried the heavy, double door. It opened into a highly polished, tiled vestibule. Directly ahead, the doors to a plain chapel stood open, but the room itself was deserted. To one side of the vestibule, the fluorescent glow of a light revealed a tiny receptionist's cubbyhole. There was, however, no receptionist in sight. From a room beyond that room, through a half-opened door, I heard the hollow clacking of an old manual typewriter.

I paused in the doorway of the second room. A woman in a prim white blouse with a short blue-and-white wimple on her head sat with her profile to the door, leaning over a typewriter in absolute concentration, her fingers flying. She was a bony woman with a hawkish nose. Wisps of gray hair strayed out from under her headpiece.

She was typing at a small, movable typing table. The large wooden desk beside her was polished to a high gloss and devoid of any clutter. An equally polished brass nameplate on the desk pronounced "Sister Marie Regina O'Dea" in a way that said the lady brooked no nonsense.

As the unchurched son of a fallen-away Presbyterian, what I knew about Catholic nuns could be stacked on the head of a proverbial pin. My previous knowledge was limited to the convent scenes in *The Sound of Music,* which was, for many years, my daughter's favorite movie. The sum of my stereotypes went little beyond the schoolboy rumors that roly-poly equals pleasant and angular equals mean, and ugly girls become nuns when nobody makes them a better offer.

Looking at Sister Marie Regina's narrow face, I wondered if anybody had ever made her an offer of any kind.

I stood quietly, watching her type. The woman had no idea I was there. She typed copy from a neat stack of handwritten pages. When she reached the bottom of a page, she stopped, moved the top sheet to the bottom of the stack, straightened the pile with a sharp, decisive thwack on the table, and put them down neatly again.

When she stopped to change pages the second time, I decided to go ahead and interrupt her. "Excuse me, but I'm looking for the lady in charge, Sister Marie Regina, I believe," I said, nodding toward the polished brass nameplate.

Startled, she jumped, her hand knocking the stack of papers to the floor. Without a word to me, she bent down, retrieved the papers, and straightened them completely before she ever officially acknowledged my existence.

"Yes," she replied crossly, eventually, her tone saying she welcomed me about as much as someone welcomes the twenty-four-hour flu. And that was before she knew who I was or what I wanted. "What can I do for you?"

"For starters, could you tell me where to find Sister Marie Regina?"

"I'm Sister Marie Regina."

"Good. My name is J. P. Beaumont. I'm a detective with Seattle P.D. I'd like to speak to one of your students."

I held out my ID for her to look at, but her shrewd eyes never left my face, nor did she reach out to take the proffered identification.

"Which one?" she asked coldly. She knew which student I wanted, and I knew she knew. I went along with it, though, playing dumb just for the hell of it.

"A new student," I said innocuously. "One who's only been here a few days."

Sister Marie Regina O'Dea rose from the typing desk and walked to a tall, brown leather chair behind the polished wooden desk. With slow, deliberate movements, she picked up a blue blazer that was hanging there and put it on. She buttoned the front buttons with a flourish, like someone donning a full suit of Christian soldier armor.

When she spoke, her voice was crisp and peremptory. "Detective Beaumont, I'm sure you understand that the young woman you mentioned is here because she's undergone a severe emotional upheaval. Her family has no wish for her to be disturbed by you or by anyone else."

I matched my tone to hers. Two can play Winning by Intimidation. It's more fun that way.

"Sister Marie Regina, I'm here because I'm conducting a homicide investigation. Bambi Barker is a material witness. I'm afraid her family's wishes have nothing whatsoever to do with it."

She smiled, a brittle smile calculated to be totally unnerving. I'm sure it struck terror in the hearts of recalcitrant fifteen-year-olds. "If you're from Seattle P.D., aren't you somewhat outside your jurisdiction?"

Unfortunately for Sister Marie Regina, I'm a hell of a long way past fifteen. "Concealing material evidence to a capital crime is somewhat out of yours as well, wouldn't you say, Sister?"

She sat down in the high-backed chair and leaned back, clasping her hands in front of her. She regarded me thoughtfully. I don't believe Sister Marie Regina was accustomed to counterattacks.

"Exactly what is it you want, Detective Beaumont?"

"I want to talk to Bambi Barker."

"That's impossible."

"Why?"

I refused to budge under the weight of her level stare. For several long moments we remained locked in visual combat before I took the offensive and attacked her sense of order. I took a straight-backed chair from its place near the wall, moved it to a position in front of her desk, turned it around so the back faced her, and sat astride it with my arms resting on the back of the chair.

"What kind of financial arrangements are necessary to get a girl transferred into St. Agnes over a weekend three months before she's supposed to graduate?"

Sister Marie Regina didn't answer. She didn't flinch, either, but I continued in the same vein.

"Enough to maybe buy a personal computer to replace that ancient typewriter?" I asked. "Or what about a new car? Didn't I see a new Ford Taurus sitting out front, a silver station wagon with temporary plates?"

She blinked then, and I rushed forward into the breach. "I could make a real case in the papers that the car was a bribe, you know. Payment in advance for keeping the girl away from our investigation."

"But that's not true," she blurted. "It was only to get her admitted . . ." Sister Marie Regina stopped abruptly, clenching her narrow jaws.

"You know that, Sister. And maybe I know that, but that's not how it's going to read in *The Oregonian*."

"You wouldn't."

"Oh yes I would. I wouldn't hesitate a minute. I want to talk to that girl, and I want to talk to her tonight. Now."

Sister Marie Regina wasn't used to being outmaneuvered. She stared wordlessly at me for a long time before she reached for a phone, picked it up, and dialed a two-digit number. She tapped her finger anxiously on the phone while she waited for it to be answered.

"Would you please have Sister Eunice bring the new student to my office?" There was a pause. "Yes, I mean now," she added crossly. "Tell her to get dressed."

She got up from her chair, smoothed her jacket, and walked to the door. Sister Marie Regina was a fairly tall woman in exceedingly sensible shoes whose crepe soles squeaked on the glossy surface of the tile floor. "Follow me, please."

With her stiff blue skirt rustling against her nylons, she led me out of her office and down a long hall with a series of unmarked doors lining either side. Toward the end, she stopped, opened a door, and showed me into a tiny room.

"These are our visiting rooms," she announced curtly. "Sister Eunice will bring Miss Barker here shortly." With that she went out, closing the door behind her.

The room was actually a sitting room in the old-fashioned-parlor sense of the word. The furnishings consisted of two dainty, ladylike chairs, a loveseat, and a couch—all of it suitably uncomfortable. A matched set of end tables and a coffee table completed the room's furnishings.

The only light came from an old hanging glass fixture that hung down in the middle of the room. Every flat surface was supplied with identical boxes of industrial strength tissue. Evidently, tears, lots of them, were not unexpected phenomena in St. Agnes' visiting rooms.

Having met Sister Marie Regina O'Dea, I could understand the need for tears, especially if the other nuns turned out to be anything like their stiff-backed leader.

I tried both chairs and the loveseat before I settled uneasily on the couch. It seemed to me the couch had been purposely designed to be unsuitable for human male anatomy. Despite the couch's discomfort, however, I nodded off briefly before the door opened again.

I sat up with a start. At first, in the dim light, I thought Sister Marie Regina had returned. Instead, a woman who looked very much like the headmistress ushered Bambi Barker into the room.

The sister held out her hand to me. Her grip was cool and firm. "I'm Sister Eunice," she said. "And this is Miss Barker."

From the moment I saw her, I could almost understand Tex Barker's desire to lock his daughter in a convent. Maybe even a bank vault. She was a voluptuous little twit. My mother would have called her a floozy. Even in the ill-fitting plaid schoolgirl uniform she wore, her well-built figure showed through plain as day. Her long blonde hair was cut short around her face in the latest heavy-metal style, and she wore plenty of makeup. I was a little surprised the nuns let her get away with that.

Bambi Barker had evidently been crying. Her eyes were red-rimmed, her nose was shiny, and enough mascara had run down her face to make two long, ink black rivulets.

Sister Eunice motioned Bambi Barker onto one of the dainty chairs and seated herself primly on the other.

"Excuse me, Sister," I said, "but I'd like to speak to Miss Barker alone."

"That's not possible," Sister Eunice replied firmly, folding her hands in her lap and settling in. "As senior proctor, I am required to be in attendance when any of my girls speak to an unaccompanied male."

"But, Sister . . ." I objected.

"Now see here, Detective Beaumont." She smiled evenly, showing a set of dentures. She straightened her skirt carefully. "I was instructed not to interfere, but this is the only way you'll be able to talk to her."

She turned to Bambi, reached out, and patted the girl's knee reassuringly. "It's all right, Bambi. I'll stay here with you. All you need to do is tell this man the truth."

Keeping her head ducked into her shoulders, Bambi Barker peered up at me, her full lips gathered in a sullen pout. It was difficult to know where to begin. I hadn't anticipated asking intimate questions of a randy teenager in the presence of a straitlaced, aging nun.

"Did they tell you why I wanted to talk to you, Miss Barker?" I asked.

She shook her head, keeping her eyes averted.

"You've heard about Coach Ridley, haven't you?"

Her head jerked up as if someone had pulled a string. "What about him?"

"He's dead," I answered. "He died sometime Saturday morning."

For a moment her eyes widened in horror, then she shook her head, her blonde mane shifting from side to side. "You're kidding, right?"

"No, Bambi. I'm not kidding. He's dead. I'm here investigating his murder."

With no warning, Bambi Barker slipped soundlessly from the chair to the floor like a marionette with severed strings. Sister Eunice reached out and succeeded in breaking her fall.

"Oh, no," Bambi sobbed over and over as Sister Eunice caught her and rocked her against a flat, unyielding breast. "It can't be."

I slipped to the floor as well, lifting Bambi's chin so I could look into the shocked blue depths of her eyes. "What can't be, Bambi?" I asked. "Tell me."

She twisted away from my hand and once again buried her face against Sister Eunice. "Oh, Daddy," I heard her sob. "How could you!"

How could he indeed?

CHAPTER 14

Sister Eunice spent the next half hour on her knees on the floor of that visiting room, pasting the pieces of Bambi Barker back together and forever putting an end to my lean/mean stereotyping of Catholic nuns. Sister Eunice may have been every bit as angular as Sister Marie Regina, but she was anything but heartless. She held Bambi close, rocking her gently like a baby and murmuring small words of comfort in her ear.

There was nothing for me to do but sit and wait for the storm of emotion to blow over. Sister Eunice must have gotten tired of my just hanging around, because finally she ordered me out of the room, sending me on a mission to bring back a glass of water. When I returned, Sister Eunice had engineered Bambi back onto a chair.

"Here now," she urged soothingly, taking the glass from my hand and holding it to Bambi's lips. "Try some of this."

Bambi took a small sip, choked, and pushed the glass away. "I'm all right."

"Are you sure?" Sister Eunice asked.

"I'm sure," Bambi mumbled.

It was time to start, but I approached Bambi warily. "I have to ask you some questions, Miss Barker."

She nodded numbly, without looking up. "So ask."

"Do you know anything about what happened to Darwin Ridley?"

Bambi Barker raised her head then and looked at me. "It was just a game," she said.

"A game?" I asked, not comprehending. "What do you mean, a game?"

"A game, a contest."

I felt really lost. "I don't understand what you're talking about. What was a contest?"

She shot a quick glance in the direction of Sister Eunice, who sat with her hands clasped in her lap, nodding encouragingly. "Don't pay any attention to me, Bambi," Sister Eunice said. "You go right ahead and tell the man what he needs to know."

Bambi took a deep breath and looked back at me. "Each year the cheerleaders have a contest to see . . ." She paused and looked at Sister Eunice again.

"To see what?" I urged impatiently.

"To see who can get one of the teachers in bed. It's, you know, a tradition."

My jaw must have dropped about three feet. At first I didn't think I'd heard her right. But I had. A tradition! The last time I had heard the word tradition, Bob Payson was telling me about the basketball team and Girl Scout cookies. So while the boys were worrying about nice little civilized traditions of the tea and crumpet variety, the cheerleaders were busy balling their favorite teacher. Jesus!

My mother once told me that girls are born knowing what it takes boys fifteen years to figure out. About then I figured fifteen years wasn't nearly long enough.

"The same teacher?" I asked, finding my voice. "Or a different one each year?"

She shrugged. "Sometimes the same. Usually not."

"Somebody keeps track from year to year?"

She nodded. "It's in one of the lockers in the girls' dressing room. Written on the ceiling. But it was just a game. Nothing like this ever . . ." She broke off and was quiet.

"Now let me get this straight. Each year somebody on the cheerleading squad seduces one of the teachers, and then you write his name down on a list?"

She nodded.

"Was there a prize for this game?"

"At the beginning of the year, everybody puts fifty dollars into a pot. When the winner brings proof, she gets the money."

"Proof? What do you mean, proof?"

"I mean, like you couldn't just say you did it, you know? You had to have proof. A picture, a tape, or something."

Fifteen years? Hell, forty-three years wasn't enough. I glanced at Sister Eunice. She continued sitting with her hands serenely clasped, her eyes never leaving Bambi's face. Maybe living in a convent with high school kids had taught Sister Eunice a whole lot more about the world than I had given her credit for.

It was all I could do to keep from grabbing Bambi Barker by the shoulders and shaking her until the braces flew off her teeth. "I take it you won this year?" I asked dryly.

"Yes." When she answered, her voice dropped almost to a whisper. My question had brought back the reality of the consequences of that nasty little game, as well as a little reticence.

"And the proof?"

"A picture. One of my friends took it."

"So how did your father get it?"

"I don't know, I swear to God."

"And who sent one to Joanna Ridley? Your father?"

"Maybe. I don't know. I've never seen him so mad. He was crazy."

"When did he find out?"

"Friday. Friday morning. He came to school to get me. I thought he was going to kill me right there in the car."

"He threatened you?"

"He hit me." One hand strayed to her lip as if in unconscious remembrance of that slap across the face. Tears appeared in the corners of her eyes. Deftly, Sister Eunice reached out and wiped them away with a lacy handkerchief.

"Did he threaten Mr. Ridley?"

"I think so."

"You think?"

"He said he was going to do something, but I didn't know what it was. It sounded bad."

"Do you remember what it was?"

She rubbed her eyes and more mascara flaked off and landed on her face. "It was something like . . . It ended with *ate*. Something *ate*."

You don't have to work *The New York Times* crossword puzzle every day to be able to figure that one out.

"Castrate?" I asked. "Was that it?"

She nodded. "That's it. What does it mean?"

"Cut his balls off," I growled. I was in no mood to pull any punches or mince any words for Bambi Barker. She didn't deserve it, but I was aware of an uncomfortable shifting in Sister Eunice's otherwise tranquil presence.

Bambi Barker gulped and swallowed hard.

"That didn't happen," I added. "If that's what you're worried about. Somebody just strung Darwin Ridley up on the end of a rope."

Bambi dissolved into tears once again. When Sister Eunice reached out as if to comfort her, I stopped her hand. The nun looked me in the face for a long moment, then nodded in acquiescence and allowed her hand to drop back into her lap.

Suddenly, I realized Sister Eunice and I were coconspirators in the process. She wasn't merely observing. Sister Eunice was actively helping. What her motives were wasn't clear to me at the time, although it occurred to me that maybe she was bent on saving Bambi Barker's immortal soul.

We waited together until Bambi's sobbing quieted and eventually died away altogether. Only then did Sister Eunice reach out again, this time to take Bambi's hand. "Is it possible that your father did this terrible thing?" she asked.

You could have knocked me over with a feather. I don't suppose genteel Catholic nuns routinely conduct homicide interrogations, but Sister Eunice was a down-home killer at asking questions. She put the screws to Bambi directly, holding her eyes in an unblinking gaze, offering the girl no opportunity to look away or avoid the issue.

"He could have," Bambi whispered finally.

"All right, then," Sister Eunice said. Her voice was calm and firm. "You must tell Detective Beaumont here everything you know that could possibly be helpful."

"But I don't know for sure," Bambi protested.

"Tell us exactly what went on Friday," Sister Eunice urged quietly.

"After I left school?"

"Where did you go, home?"

Bambi nodded. "We went to the house. Mom was home, waiting."

That prompted a question from me. "Your mother knew about it, before you got there?"

"Everybody knew about it. There was a huge hassle, and Dad locked me in my room."

"How long were you there?"

"Until Saturday morning. Then they woke me up and told me to pack because I was coming here."

"They both brought you down?" I asked.

"We had to bring two cars. Mom drove one. They left it here." Bambi Barker's pout returned.

"For you?"

"No. It was, you know, like a gift to the school."

I get a little ego hit every time one of my hunches turns out to be correct, even when it's not particularly important. It's good for my overall batting average. Sister Marie Regina O'Dea's shiny new Taurus station wagon bribe gave me a little rush of satisfaction.

I said, "How nice. So they drove you down and checked you in. I take it you weren't especially thrilled to come here."

Bambi glanced in Sister Eunice's direction. "I didn't have a choice."

"Why not?"

"He said he'd disown me."

"Would he?"

"He did Faline."

"Who's that?"

"She used to be my sister."

Faline. Bambi. Obviously somebody in the Barker family was a Walt Disney fan. "Used to be your sister?" I asked. "What do you mean by that?"

"He threw her out three years ago. No one's heard from her since."

"Why did they send you here? Why this school?"

"My mother's sister is a member of the Order of St. Agnes in Texas. She's the one who suggested it."

I changed the subject abruptly, hoping to throw her off guard. "Tell me about Coach Ridley."

"What about him?"

"How long had it been going on, between the two of you?"

"There was nothing going on, really. I, like, pretended, but it was just a game. I already told you."

"But when did it happen?"

"You mean when did we take the picture?" I nodded, and she shrugged. "Only last week."

"Where?"

"It's a place up on Aurora, in Seattle. A motel."

"How come he didn't see the flash?"

"Molly was outside, using her dad's camera. It doesn't need a flash."

I didn't have nerve enough to look at Sister Eunice right then. I probably could have, though. She deals with teenage kids all the time. She's probably used to it. Me, I'm just a homicide cop. Right then, homicide seemed a hell of a lot more straightforward. The whole scenario of Darwin Ridley being led like a lamb to the slaughter because of some stupid adolescent game shocked me, offended me.

And I thought I'd seen everything.

"Who's Molly?" I asked.

"A friend of mine. My best friend. Molly Blackburn."

"Also a cheerleader?"

Bambi nodded. "She lives right up the street from us. Will she get in trouble, too?"

I made a note of Molly Blackburn's name and address. Molly Blackburn, the budding photographer. Or maybe Molly Blackburn, the budding blackmailer—whichever.

"I can't say one way or the other," I told her.

It was almost midnight when Sister Eunice led Bambi Barker back to her room. Bambi had started down the hall when Sister Eunice poked her head back in the door of the visiting room and asked me to wait long enough for her to return.

When she did, she ushered me out of the visiting room and down the long, empty corridor to a tiny kitchen and lounge. There she poured me a cup of acrid coffee that tasted like it had been in the pot for three weeks.

"Will you be returning to Seattle tonight, Detective Beaumont?" she asked.

I scratched my head and glanced at the movable cat's-eye clock above an equally dated turquoise refrigerator. It was well after eleven. We had spent a long, long evening with Bambi Barker. "It's late, but I suppose so."

"And you're a man of honor?" she asked.

"What do you mean?"

"I mean, you won't be talking to *The Oregonian* before you leave Portland, will you?"

"I told Sister Marie Regina that as long as you helped me, I'd keep my mouth shut."

Sister Eunice looked enormously relieved. "Good," she said. "I'm very happy to hear it."

So much for Bambi Barker's immortal soul. Sister Eunice had become my ally for far more worldly reasons than to keep Bambi's soul safe from hell and damnation. She had done it to keep Sister Marie Regina's Taurus station wagon off the editorial page. Situational ethics in action.

I took the rest of the coffee to drink in the car, remembering the old Bible verse about judging not and being without sin and all that jazz. After all, I had fired the first shot. And I couldn't argue with the results. I had gotten what I wanted from Bambi Barker.

As I started the Porsche, I realized how hungry I was. When I reached downtown Portland, I stopped off at a little joint on S. W. First, a place called the Veritable Quandary. I remembered it from the mid-seventies as a little tavern where they made great roast beef sandwiches and you could play pick up chess while you ate. Unfortunately, the eighties had caught up with it. The easygoing tavern atmosphere had evolved into a fullscale bar scene. The chess boards and magazines had long since disappeared. The sandwich was good, though, and it helped counteract Sister Eunice's bitter coffee.

It was only as I sat there in solitary silence, chewing on my roast beef, that I realized I had never asked Bambi Barker how much her prize was for screwing Darwin Ridley. On second thought, I was probably better off not knowing.

Thinking about it spoiled my appetite. I didn't finish the sandwich.

CHAPTER 15

There was a lot to think about on the way home. Bambi Barker had shaken me. I couldn't help wondering how I would have felt if I had discovered that my own daughter, Kelly, had been pulling something like that when she was in high school. Would I have taken the time to find out that the girls had been playing the teacher for a fool, or would I have jumped to the opposite conclusion?

There could be little doubt of the answer to that one. J. P. Beaumont has been known to jump to conclusions on occasion. Somebody by the name of Wheeler-Dealer Barker could very well suffer from the same malady.

In fact, the more I thought about it, the more I figured there was a better-than-even-money chance that Bambi's old man had jumped to his own erroneous and lethal conclusions. We needed to know his whereabouts on Friday night and Saturday morning, while Bambi was locked in her room at home and her mother was standing guard.

Knowing of Molly Blackburn's existence helped answer one puzzling question. The idea that a father would have mailed out such a compromising picture of his own daughter had never made sense to me. I couldn't imagine any father doing such a thing, not even in the heat of anger. I had gone along with that suggestion when no other possibilities had presented themselves, but it made far more sense that the picture might have been part of a blackmail scheme, a complicated, two-sided deal aimed at wresting money from both families involved, the Barkers and the Ridleys.

It seemed likely that a copy of the picture had arrived at the Barker home sometime Friday morning. That was probably what had tipped off old Wheeler-Dealer. Joanna's had arrived days later. That was somewhat puzzling. Why the delay? If you're going to blackmail two different sets of people, why not do it simultaneously? Or maybe they had been mailed at the same time and the postal service had screwed up.

My questions defied any attempt to find answers, but they served to fill up the long straight stretches of interstate. There was hardly any traffic on the freeway at that time of night. Just me and a bunch of eighteen-wheelers tearing up the road. I made it back to Seattle in a good deal less time than the three hours it should have taken.

I dropped into bed the minute I got to my apartment. It was three A.M. when I turned out the light and fell asleep.

Fifteen minutes later the phone rang, jarring me out of a sound sleep. "Please stay on the line," a tinny, computerized female voice told me. Within moments, Ralph Ames' voice sputtered into the receiver. He sounded like somebody had just kicked him awake, too.

"What do you want?" he demanded in a groggy grumble.

"What do you mean, 'What do I want'? You called me, remember?"

"Oh, I must have forgotten to turn that damn thing off when I went to bed."

"What damn thing?" I wasn't playing with a full deck in this conversation.

"My automatic redialer."

An automatic redialer! Ralph Ames' ongoing love affair with gadgets was gradually becoming clear to me. If my phone had been ringing off and on all night, it was probably quite clear to Ida Newell, my next-door neighbor, as well.

"That's just great," I fumed. "I went to bed fifteen minutes ago, Ralph. What's so goddamned important that you woke us both up?"

"Your closing on Belltown Terrace. It's reset for Friday, three-thirty. Can you make it?"

I took a deep breath. "Sometimes you really piss me off. It's three o'clock in the morning. You expect me to have a calendar in my hand?"

"If you had an answering machine . . ."

"I don't want an answering machine." I rummaged through the nightstand drawer for pen and paper and wrote down the time and place for the real estate closing. "There," I said. "Is that all? Mind if I get some sleep now?"

"Be my guest," Ames replied, then hung up.

A scant three hours later, the phone rang again. Once more I shook the fog out of my head. Eventually, I recognized Al Lindstrom's voice. Big Al, as we call him, is another detective on the homicide squad. He generally works the night shift.

"What do you mean calling me at this hour?" I'm crabby when I don't get my beauty sleep.

"Don't get your sweat hot, Beau. I've got someone on the line. She wants to talk to you. Real bad."

"Look, Al. I've barely gotten into bed. Can't you take a message?"

"She wants to talk to you *now*."

"Jesus H. Christ. Who is it? Can't you get her name and number? I'll call her back as soon as I get to the office."

"Just a minute. I'll ask." While he was off the line, I tried, with limited success, to rub my eyes open and unscramble my brain.

Eventually, Al returned to the line. "Says her name's Joanna Ridley. Says you can't call her. She wants to meet you in half an hour at the tennis courts in Seward Park."

"I'm still in bed, Al. I can't meet her in half an hour. Tell her I'll call her later."

"It's too late."

"Why?"

"She hung up."

"Shit!" I rolled out of bed. "Thanks a whole hell of a lot," I growled.

"Don't chew my ass," Al returned. "I'm just doing my job."

He slammed the phone down in my ear. I grabbed my nightstand telephone book and located Joanna's number, but when I finally dialed it, the line was busy. I tried several more times, but the line remained busy, leaving me to conclude that Joanna was serious about my not calling her back. She had evidently left the phone off the hook.

I gave my pillow a reluctant farewell pat and headed for the shower. Exactly eleven minutes later, the Porsche and I shot out through the building garage entrance onto Lenora.

Morning fog was thick as velvet as I drove up Boren and out Rainier Avenue. At six twenty-five traffic coming into the city was already picking up, but I was driving against it. I wondered as I drove why Joanna had refused to see me at her house, and why she had picked such an early hour in a deserted city park for our meeting.

Seward Park sits on a point that juts out into Lake Washington. On a clear day, Mount Rainier sits majestically above the water, framed on either side by the house-covered ridges of South Seattle and Mercer Island. That particular morning, however, there was no hint that a mountain lay hidden out there. Invisible behind the fog, it lurked in a blanket of silence that was broken only by the occasional huffing of an early morning jogger.

I saw Joanna Ridley's Mustang right away, tucked into a parking place against the tennis court fence. The driver of the Mustang, however, was nowhere in sight. Parking the Porsche next to Joanna's car, I set out looking for her.

Blooming dogwood and daffodils lined the park's entrance. I walked along a hedge of *Photinia*, it's new growth crimson above the older green leaves. The startling spring colors stood out in sharp relief against the shifting gray fog. The grass was heavy with dew, sponging down beneath my feet as I walked along the breakwater.

The park seemed a lonely, desolate place for a new widow. The idea of suicide fleetingly crossed my mind. I wondered if Joanna had decided to end her own life. The thought had no more than entered my mind, however, when I spotted her near the water.

Wearing a huge sweater, she stood on the rock breakwater, profiled against the gray of both the fog and water behind her. A light breeze blowing off the lake pressed the sweater's soft material around the bulge in her middle, accentuating her pregnant figure. Unaware of my approach, she peered down from her perch at something in the water below her, something I couldn't see. When I finally got close enough to look below the breakwater, I found she was watching a flock of hungry ducks out bumming for handouts.

"You wanted to see me?" I asked.

Without warning, she whirled and sprang at me, clenching both fists as she did so. She moved so fast I was surprised she didn't lose her footing on the slippery, wet grass. Just in time I realized she was bringing a haymaker up from her knees, putting the full force of her body behind it. If she had landed that blow, it would have sent me flying.

My reflexes may not be what they used to be, but they were still good enough to save my bacon. I dodged back, away from her doubled fist, which whizzed past my face within an inch of my nose. She came scrambling after me, her face a mask of hard, cold fury.

I had seen a similar version of that look once, that night in the Dog House after we left the medical examiner's office. That look was mild compared to this. Right then, Joanna Ridley appeared to be entirely capable of murder.

"It's about time you got here, you son of a bitch!"

I had expected our encounter to begin on a somewhat more cordial note. After all, I wasn't even late. I stepped back again, just to be on the safe side, staying well out of reach.

"What the hell's going on, Joanna? What's wrong?"

Her right hand shot toward the pocket of the voluminous sweater. My first thought was that she was going for a gun.

Once burned, twice shy. The last time I got burned by a lady with a gun, I came within inches of checking out for good.

With adrenaline pumping from every pore, I bounded forward and grabbed her wrists, pinning them to her sides before she had a chance to draw. Like a desperate, captive bird she struggled to escape my grasp. We must have stood like that for half a minute or so before I realized that what she had in the pocket of her sweater was nothing more than a rolled-up section of newspaper.

She was still pulling against me with all her might when I let go of her wrists. She fell away from me toward the breakwater and would have fallen backward into the lake if I hadn't caught her. We fell to the ground together in a tumbled heap.

The fall knocked the wind out of her. For a moment she was silent, her dark eyes staring up at me in mute rage. When she caught her breath, she screamed. "Get away from me, you bastard, Get away!"

"Are you all right? Are you hurt?" I tried to break through her anger, but she didn't hear me. She kept right on screaming.

Suddenly, I was lifted off the ground. Someone grabbed me by the back of my shirt the way a mother dog grabs a puppy to carry it. Except puppies don't wear ties with knots that block their windpipes. I dangled in midair, coughing and choking.

From behind me, I heard someone say, "Hey, lady. This guy botherin' you?"

Joanna Ridley didn't answer him. I swung around, trying to break his hold, but the guy had arms like a gorilla. I couldn't lay a hand on him. I was about to black out when he dropped me to the ground like a sack of potatoes. I lay there for a moment, stunned and gasping, trying to force air back into my lungs. When I looked up, a giant of a man was gently helping Joanna to her feet.

"I'm a police officer," I sputtered. I reached for my ID, but my pocket was empty. The leather case had evidently fallen out in the course of the struggle.

"Yeah, and I'm Sylvester Stallone," he returned. Joanna Ridley was on her feet and mercifully quiet. "You all right, lady?" he asked. "You want somebody to take you home?"

I crawled around on my hands and knees in the grass, searching for my ID. Finally, I located it, resting against a rock, just below where Joanna and I had fallen. I clambered to my feet and staggered over to where they stood. At six three, I'm no piker when it comes to size, but this guy made me look like a midget. Muscles bulged under his oversized T-shirt and rippled down his legs from under the skimpy running shorts he wore.

I tried to show him my ID, but he brushed me aside. "Get away from her before I call the cops."

"God damn it, I *am* a cop. Detective J. P. Beaumont, Seattle P.D. Homicide."

"No shit? Since when do cops go around beating up pregnant ladies in parks?"

I wouldn't have convinced him, not in a million years, but right then Joanna Ridley stopped her silent sobbing and, surprisingly, spoke in my defense. "It's all right. I fell down. He caught me."

The man bent down and looked her full in the face. "You sure, now? I can throw his ass in the water if you want. You say the word and I'll drown this sucker."

"No. Really. It's all right."

He stepped away then, reluctantly, looking from one of us to the other as if trying to figure out what was really going on. "Okay, then, if you say so." Without another word, he turned on his heel and jogged away from us, running shoes squeaking on the wet grass.

Warily, I approached Joanna. "What's wrong? Tell me."

Once again, she reached into the pocket. When her hand emerged, she was holding the newspaper. She was under control now, but her eyes still struck sparks of fury as she slapped the newspaper into my outstretched hand.

"I thought you said you'd keep it quiet."

"Keep what quiet?"

"About what happened. I thought I could trust you, but you took it straight to the newspaper."

"Joanna, what are you talking about?"

"The picture."

"My God, is the picture in here?" Dismayed, I unrolled the newspaper.

"It just as well could be," Joanna replied grimly.

I scanned down the page, the front page of the last section of the newspaper. The local news section. There on the bottom, four columns wide, was Maxwell Cole's crime column, "City Beat." The headline said it all:

"Sex Plus Race Equals Murder."

I scanned through the article quickly, while Joanna Ridley watched my face. When I finished reading, I looked up at her. I was sickened. There could be no doubt from the article that Maxwell Cole had indeed seen the photograph of Darwin Ridley and Bambi Barker. All of Seattle could just as well have seen it. The article left little to the imagination. The only thing it didn't mention was Bambi Barker's name. Knowing Maxwell Cole, I figured Wheeler-Dealer's money and position in the community had something to do with that.

I took Joanna Ridley by the arm and led her to her car.

"Where are you going?" she asked as she half-trotted to keep up with me.

"To find Maxwell Cole," I told her. "If I don't kill him first, you can have a crack at him."

CHAPTER 16

I put Joanna Ridley in her car and told her to go on home, that I'd call her as soon as I knew anything.

As she started the Mustang, I motioned for her to roll down the window. "Don't forget to put your phone back on the hook," I told her. She gave me a half-hearted wave and drove away.

I started the Porsche and rammed it into gear. My first instinct was to find Maxwell Cole, beat the crap out of him, and find out who the big mouth was, either in the crime lab or in Seattle P.D. Somebody had leaked the information.

I drove straight to the *Post-Intelligencer*'s new digs down on Elliott, overlooking Puget Sound. Eight o'clock found me standing in front of a needle-nosed receptionist who told me Maxwell Cole wasn't expected in before ten. I should have known a slug like Cole wouldn't be up at the crack of dawn.

Rather than hang around the newspaper and cool my heels, I went down to the Public Safety Building. I stopped at the second floor and stormed into the crime lab.

Don Yamamoto, head of the Washington State Patrol's crime lab, is a criminalist of the first water. He's one of those second-generation Japanese who, as a kid, was incarcerated along with his parents in a relocation camp during World War II. He spent all his spare time during the years they were locked up reading the only book available to him—a Webster's unabridged dictionary—and he came out of the camp with a far better education than he probably would have gotten otherwise.

He's a smart guy, smart and personable both, well respected by those who work for and with him. The receptionist waved me past without bothering to give me an official escort. As usual, the door to Yamamoto's office stood open. I knocked on the frame.

"Hey, Beau, how's it going?" he asked, looking up from a stack of paperwork on his desk.

"Not well," I answered. "We've got troubles." I laid it on the line to him. He listened without comment. When I finished, he sat back in his chair, folding his arms behind his head.

"I think you're wrong, Beau. That story didn't come from this office. None of my people go running off at the mouth."

He got up and led the way to the evidence room. He stopped at the doorway long enough to examine the log. "Only two people actually handled that photograph," he said. "One was Janice Morraine, and the other is Tom Welch. Either of those sound like people who'd be messing around with the likes of Maxwell Cole?"

I shook my head. I knew them both fairly well. I had to agree with their chief's assessment.

"So how did Max get the story?"

"Why don't you go straight to the horse's mouth and ask him that question?" Don suggested.

"I tried that. He wasn't in."

"So try again."

I turned on my heels and walked out of his office. Standing in the elevator lobby waiting for the door to open, I was surprised when the door *behind* me opened. Don Yamamoto followed me into the corridor. "But you'll let me know if you find out something I need to know, right?" he asked.

Don Yamamoto trusted his people implicitly. Up to a point.

I chuckled. "Yes," I answered. "I'll let you know."

It was eight-forty when I reached Peters' and my cubicle on the fifth floor. Peters glanced meaningfully at his watch. Having a partner can be worse than having to punch a time clock. Time clocks don't expect explanations.

"Get off it," I told him before he had a chance to open his mouth. "I got back from Portland at three this morning, and I've been up working since six, so don't give me any shit."

"My, my, we are touchy this morning," Peters said with a grin. "So tell me what you learned in Portland."

I did. All of it. By the time I finished telling him about the cheerleading squad's nasty little rite of passage, he wasn't nearly as cheerful as he had been. In fact, he was probably wondering about the advisability of having daughters.

"I talked to all those girls," he said. "They seemed like nice, straight, clean-cut kids."

"You can't tell a book by its cover, remember?"

"Right, so what do we do? Tackle Wheeler-Dealer? Go have a heart-to-heart talk with Molly Blackburn? Read the writing in the locker?"

I got up and glanced over the top of the cubicle walls to the clock at the end of the room. It was five to ten. "All of the above," I told him, "but not necessarily in that order. We're starting with Maxwell Cole, bless his pointed little head."

We dropped the Porsche off at my place and took a departmental crate to the P.I. It turned out Maxwell Cole's pointed head was nowhere within striking distance. The same scrawny receptionist gave me an icy smile and told me Mr. Cole was out on an assignment. She had no idea when he'd be back. Lucky for him.

We left there and drove to Mercer Island, figuring we'd make a brief visit to Wheeler-Dealer Barker's home on our way to his dealership in Bellevue. The address jotted in Peters' notebook led us to a stately white colonial on a lot that seemed to be several sizes too small. A multinote chime playing "The Yellow Rose of Texas" announced our arrival. A plain, small-boned woman wearing a long honey-colored robe came to the door.

Her mousy blonde hair was still damp from a shower, and her face was devoid of makeup. Her nose was shiny, her eyes red-rimmed. This was a lady who had been having a good cry in the privacy of her own home. She looked up at us anxiously.

"Are you Mrs. Barker?" I asked. "Mrs. Tex Barker?" I held out my identification so she could read it.

"I'm Madeline Barker," she returned.

"May we come in?"

She stepped away from the door uncertainly before finally motioning us inside. We entered a large, well-appointed vestibule, complete with a huge bouquet of fragrant spring flowers.

"What is it?" she asked.

I think I had expected Mrs. Wheeler-Dealer Barker to speak with a thick southern drawl. I would have thought she'd offer us coffee with chicory and maybe a mess of grits or black-eyed peas. I was dismayed to discover that all trace of her origins had been eradicated from Madeline's manner of speech. Grits and chicory were nowhere in evidence.

"It's about your husband," I told her. "Your husband and your daughter."

I said nothing more. A mixture of distress and confusion washed over Madeline Barker's face. Reflexively, she clenched her fists tightly and shoved them deep into the pockets of her robe.

"What about them?" she asked, her voice cracking as she struggled to maintain an outward show of calm.

"Would you mind telling us exactly what went on here Friday afternoon?"

She turned her back on us then and walked as far as the doorway into the next room. Stopping abruptly, she leaned against the wall for support, her breath coming in short panicky gasps.

Peters moved toward her. He spoke in a gently reassuring manner. "We're trying to resolve a homicide, Mrs. Barker. Darwin Ridley's. As I'm sure you know, your daughter was involved to some degree. We need to find out exactly . . ."

Madeline Barker suddenly found her voice and swung around to face us. "You don't think . . . Bambi couldn't have done it. She was here, in her room, all night. She never went out."

"We're aware of that. You see, we've already talked to your daughter."

"Oh," she said. "Then what are you doing here? Why are you still asking questions?"

"Was your husband here all night, too?" I asked.

She paled suddenly and retreated farther into the living room, instantly creating a larger physical buffer zone between my question and her.

"What do you mean?" she demanded. "You think Tex had something to do with it?"

"If you'd just answer the question, Mrs. Barker. Was your husband here in the house with you all night or was he gone part of the time?"

Madeline Barker pulled herself stiffly erect. "I won't answer that," she said. "I don't have to."

There are times when no answer speaks volumes. This was one of those times. Tex "Wheeler-Dealer" Barker had not been home all night the night Darwin Ridley died, of that we could be certain. That gave Barker two of the necessary ingredients for murder—motive and opportunity. When had he left the house and what time had he returned? Those were questions in need of answering. For right then we seemed to have taken a giant step toward getting some answers.

Peters did what he could to soothe Madeline Barker's ruffled feathers. "You're absolutely right, Mrs. Barker. You don't have to answer that question if you don't want to," he told her reassuringly.

The questioning process, conducted in pairs, is a subtle game. Peters and I had learned to play it well, using one another as foils or fall guys with equal ease. The slight nod he gave me said we were shifting to Good Cop/Bad Cop, and I was the bad guy.

"Could you tell us about the picture, then, Mrs. Barker?" I asked.

"Picture?"

"You know which picture, Mrs. Barker. We've seen it, and I'm sure you have, too."

I've learned over the years that if someone doesn't want to talk about one thing, you give them an opportunity to talk about something else. They fall all over themselves spilling their guts. Madeline Barker was happy to oblige.

She made no further attempt to pretend she didn't know what we were talking about. "It came in the mail," she admitted. "About ten o'clock that morning."

"Here? To the house?"

She nodded. "It was addressed to both of us, so I opened it. I couldn't believe my eyes. Bambi's always been such a good girl."

"Was there anything else in the envelope besides the picture?" I asked. "A note maybe? A demand for money?"

"No. Nothing. Just the picture. That awful picture."

"Where is it now?" Peters inquired.

"It's gone," she replied.

"Gone?"

"Tex told me to get rid of it. I burned it."

"And the envelope?"

"That, too. In the kitchen sink. I ran the ashes down the garbage disposal. That's what it was," she added. "Garbage."

"Let's go back to when you opened the envelope," I put in. "What happened then?"

Madeline Barker took a deep breath. "I was so upset, I didn't know what to do. So I called Tex. At work."

"And what did he do?"

"He came right home."

"To look at the picture?"

"Yes."

"And then what?"

"He went to school to get Bambi. To bring her home."

"He was angry?"

"Angry! He was crazy. Bambi wasn't like Faline. Bambi was never a problem. She was always a good student, always popular, easy to get along with. And then this. I was afraid Tex would have a heart attack over it. He already has high blood pressure, you know."

"What happened when he brought her here?"

"There was a fight, a terrible fight. She said she was going to the game no matter what we said, that we couldn't stop her."

"And that's when he locked her in her room?"

Madeline nodded, then turned an appraising look on me. For the first time I think she realized that we had already heard the story once from Bambi, that we were simply verifying information we already knew.

"Who came up with the idea of sending her to Portland?" I asked.

"I did," Madeline answered firmly. "We've fallen away from the church, but I wanted her away from that man. I wanted her out of town. I called my sister. She's in a convent in Texas. She helped us arrange it."

We didn't stay much longer after that. Madeline Barker had told us as much as she could, or at least as much as she would. There was no need to pressure her any more than we already had.

Once back in the car, Peters turned on the engine, then paused with his hand on the gearshift. "She still thinks Darwin Ridley seduced her daughter." Neither one of us had bothered to mention that it was the other way around.

I shrugged. "It won't be long before she finds out differently, especially with the likes of Maxwell Cole hanging around."

Peters drove us away from the Barker house. "That raises another question, doesn't it?"

"What does?"

"The picture. Why wasn't there a note? That bothers me. Blackmail requires communication—two-way communication. According to what Joanna Ridley told us, there wasn't a note with her picture, either. How can it be blackmail?"

"How should I know? These are a bunch of school kids. Maybe they don't know all the ropes yet. They're just talented amateurs trying to break into the big time."

"They've broken into it, all right," Peters commented grimly. "Murder's pretty big time."

I allowed as how that was true.

CHAPTER 17

Peters drove us to Wheeler-Dealer Barker's Bellevue Ford, which sits on a sprawling piece of real estate smack in the middle of Bellevue's auto row. The place was actually a total contradiction, a state-of-the-art auto dealership made up to look like an old-time, flagstone ranch house. The lot was lined with log-rail fences, and the salespeople were all decked out in cowboy boots and ten-gallon hats.

Obviously, Tex Barker had brought along the spirit of the Lone Star state as well as his name when he migrated to Washington.

The lady at the receptionist's desk wore a blue gingham outfit that would have been a lot more at home in a square dance convention than in an office. "Can I help you find someone?" she asked in the thick drawl I had expected from Madeline Barker.

"We're looking for Mr. Barker."

"He's on the phone just now, if you care to wait. Can I get you coffee, tea?"

"No, nothing. We're fine."

The waiting area had two genuine brown leather sofas with wheel spokes in the armrests. I hadn't seen one of those since the mid-fifties. I didn't know anybody still made them. The ashtray had a dead scorpion encased in it. I thought those were museum pieces as well.

"You've never seen any of his commercials?" Peters asked as we waited in the showroom full of cars.

"Never," I replied.

"It's interesting," Peters added.

"What is?"

"Now that I've met his wife. He's always offering to throw her in with the deal, if what they've got isn't good enough."

"Are you serious?" I thought about Madeline Barker. She didn't seem like someone who would enjoy that sort of thing, especially living among some of the more rarefied Mercer Island types. With a husband and a father like that, she and Bambi both must have had a lot to live down.

Not one but three hungry salesmen came by to pitch cars to us while we sat there. It was clear this was the good-ol'-boy, let's-go-out-and-kick-tires school of automobile salesmanship. They were particularly interested in pitching a T-bird Turbo Coupe that they all insisted was a "hot little number." I couldn't help wishing we had been driving my Porsche instead of the department's lukewarm Dodge.

Eventually, a door opened and Old Wheeler-Dealer himself sauntered out of his private office onto the showroom floor. He was a tall, handsome man in an aging cowboy way. He wore a dove gray western-style Ultrasuede jacket with a complex pattern embroidered on the front of the shoulders in flashy silver thread and a silver and turquoise bolo tie. His huge ten-gallon hat with its snakeskin band was tipped back on his head. I'm no fashion expert, but I guessed the alligator boots were of the real, rather than imitation, variety.

"How'do, boys. Understand y'all are waitin' for me?" Peters and I nodded. "Interested in one of our fine automobiles, here? We've got some sweet deals, I'll tell you, some really sweet deals."

"We're with Seattle P.D.," I said, handing him my identification. "Homicide. We're investigating Darwin Ridley's murder."

"What's that got to do with me?" Barker stuck out his chin and thrust my ID back into my hand.

"Plenty," I told him. "Do you mind if we ask you a few questions?"

"Mind? I most certainly do. I got a business to run here. I can't waste my time answerin' no-account questions." He turned and started back into his office. I reached out and grasped the sleeve of his jacket.

"We've talked to Bambi," I said.

He turned and swung around toward me. "You what?"

"I said, we talked to Bambi. Down in Portland."

"Why, you worthless creep. I'll beat the holy shit out of you." He took a wild swing at me, but Peters caught his fist while it was still in transit. It was the second time that day someone had swung at me and missed. My nose was grateful. So were my front teeth.

"I think we'd be better off discussing this privately, Mr. Barker," Peters suggested.

Barker shook Peters' restraining hand off his arm. "Oh you do, do you? What makes you think I want to talk to you in private or otherwise?"

"It's not a matter of wanting," I told him evenly. "We've seen the picture," I added.

A look of barely controlled fury crossed Tex Barker's face. "Oh" was all he said. He turned away and stalked into his office. Peters and I exchanged glances before we followed him. He stopped at the door, let us into the room, then snarled at the gingham-clad receptionist outside, "I'm not to be disturbed!"

He slammed the door and pushed his way past us into his small but sumptuous office, taking a seat behind a large, imposing desk. He made no suggestion that we be seated. We sat uninvited.

"Bambi had nothin' to do with that man's death," he declared, speaking slowly, attempting to keep his voice carefully modulated, making a visible effort to maintain control. Despite his efforts, the words virtually exploded into the room as they left his lips.

"Did you see Darwin Ridley last Friday?" I asked. "Did you talk to him after you saw the picture that came in the mail that morning?"

He glared at me. "I did not!"

I knew he was lying. I can't say for sure how I knew. I just did. Maybe it was the momentary flicker in his eyes. "Where were you Friday night, Mr. Barker?"

"Home."

I shook my head. "No. Not all night. Someone came to the Coliseum and spoke to Darwin Ridley just at the end of halftime. Were you that person?"

Tex Barker's eyes narrowed ever so slightly. "And what if I was?" he demanded. "What if I stopped by long enough to tell that son of a bitch that if I ever caught him near my daughter again I'd cut his black balls off?"

"Did you?" I asked.

He slammed his fist on the desk, sending a coffee cup skittering dangerously close to the edge. "No, sir, God damn it! I didn't. Never got a chance. Some SOB beat me to it. It ain't often somebody catches Wheeler-Dealer flat-footed, but someone sure as hell outdrew me on this one."

"So you're saying you'd have killed him yourself if you'd had the chance?"

"Damn right."

Peters had been observing this exchange from the sidelines. "What did you say to him when you saw him?"

"That he was a dead mother if I ever caught him within fifty miles of Bambi."

"I'd be willing to bet that wasn't news to him."

A self-satisfied grimace touched the corners of Barker's mouth. "No it wasn't. He'd gotten my message."

"What message? From his wife?"

Barker nodded. "That's right."

"And when did you tell him that?"

"Just at the end of halftime. I caught up with him after the team went on the floor."

"Let me get this straight," I said. "You came to the Coliseum, tracked him down during halftime, and told him that if he ever came near your daughter again, you'd kill him. Where'd you go after that?"

"Home."

"Straight home?"

Barker shrugged noncommittally.

"What time did you get there?"

"Ten. Eleven. I don't know, don't remember. I didn't look at the clock."

"I'd suggest you try to remember, Mr. Barker," I warned him. "We're dealing with homicide here. You have motive and you have opportunity. Within hours of the time of the victim's death you threatened to kill him. If I were you, I'd go looking for an alibi. Someone besides your wife," I added.

Barker glared back at me. "I don't need no fuckin' alibi. If I'd killed the son of a bitch, I'd be down at police headquarters braggin' about it."

That could have been the truth. Wheeler-Dealer didn't strike me as a man who would hide his light under a bushel, even if that light happened to be murder.

We were there a while longer. When we left and were making our way back to the car, Peters asked, "What do you think?"

"I don't think it was him."

Peters sounded shocked. "You don't? Why not?"

"His ego's all bound up in this. He's pissed because someone beat him out of getting even. Believe me, had he done it, he'd be yelling it to high heaven.'

"Beau, he's suckering you. That's exactly what he wants us to believe."

"We'll see," I said. "What say we drive over to the school and check out the names in the locker?"

"Sure? Why not?"

It was early afternoon when we got to Mercer Island High School. The clerk told us that the principal, Ned Browning, was busy. We asked for Candace Wynn instead. She was sitting at a desk in the counseling office, poring over a yellow sheet covered with writing. She stood up as we entered.

"Are you here about the memorial service?" she asked.

"Memorial service?"

"For Darwin. Tomorrow evening, after the funeral. Mr. Browning asked me to be in charge of planning it. The funeral is going to be small and private. We thought there should be something here at school for the kids. Something official."

"I'm sure that's a good idea, Mrs. Wynn, but that's not why we're here."

"What, then?"

"Do you have keys to the lockers in the girls' locker room?"

"Pardon me?"

"I had a long talk with Bambi Barker in Portland last night," I said. "There's something on one of the locker ceilings we need to see."

Andi Wynn frowned. "I could probably get a master key," she said doubtfully, "but I'm not sure I should. Did you talk to Mr. Browning about this? Shouldn't you have a search warrant or something?"

Peters sighed. "We probably should, but we're not searching for evidence per se. It's a matter of our simply corroborating something Bambi told us. I can assure you, we won't be looking for anything but that one thing."

Andi Wynn sat quietly, considering what Peters had said. Finally, she shrugged. "I don't suppose it would matter that much."

The three of us waited in her office chatting about inconsequentials until the final bell rang and school was dismissed. Then Andi left us to go to the office for the key. When she returned, she led us to the girls' locker room. While Andi stood to one side and waited, Peters and I spent twenty minutes opening lockers, glancing up at the top to see if anything was written there, and then closing them again, being careful to disturb nothing else in the process. We were almost finished when we opened locker number 211.

Peters was the one who saw the names written there. "Bingo! Holy shit! Look at this."

Peters isn't the excitable type. He stepped aside, and I moved quickly to the locker, craning my neck to see what was written there, scratched with a sharp object into the gray paint on the locker's metal top.

Just as Bambi had said, Darwin Ridley's name was the last one on the list, printed in awkwardly scrawled letters.

The name that caught my eye, though, was that of Ned Browning. The principal.

His name was on the list, too.

Twice.

CHAPTER 18

When I stepped away from the locker, Andi Wynn was looking uncertainly from Peters to me. "What is it?" she asked. "What did you find?"

"Look for yourself," I said.

She did. I watched her expression when she turned back to face us. "I don't understand."

"It's a trophy case," I told her. "The cheerleaders' trophy case."

"What does it mean?"

"It doesn't matter. Let's get out of here, Peters."

I welcomed the fresh air when we stepped back outside. I felt sick. Ned Browning, too. The one who had been so protective of his "young people." He, too, had fallen victim to the cheerleaders' hit list. More than once.

We were nearing the office when I rounded a corner and ran full tilt into Ned Browning himself. Ned Browning and Joanna Ridley.

Joanna looked surprised to see me. "What are you doing here?" she asked.

"Working. What about you?"

She nodded toward Ned Browning, who was carrying a large cardboard box. "Mr. Browning asked me to come get Darwin's things. They're hiring a replacement and he needs to use the desk."

Ned nodded. "It was most awkward, having to call, even before the funeral, but the board has moved forward and hired a replacement. He'll be here at school tomorrow. I felt Mrs. Ridley was the only one who should handle her husband's things."

"Did you find out anything?" Joanna asked.

More than we expected, I wanted to say, but I didn't. Instead, I reached for the box Ned had in his hands. "Would you like me to carry this to your car?"

She nodded, and Ned handed it over. It was fairly heavy. "I'll be getting back to my office," he said. He turned to Joanna and took her hand. "Thank you so much for stopping by. Will you be attending the memorial service tomorrow night?" he asked. "Mrs. Wynn here is in charge of planning it."

Joanna glanced in Andi's direction and shook her head. "I don't know. I doubt it. It'll depend on how I feel after the funeral. I appreciate what you're doing, but I may be too tired."

Ned nodded sympathetically. "I understand completely. It would be nice if you could. It would mean a great deal to the students, but of course your physical well-being must come first."

He took Joanna's hand and pressed it firmly. "You take care now, Mrs. Ridley. We'll hope to see you tomorrow. Let me know if there's anything else I can do."

Ned Browning scurried away toward his office, the little shit. I wanted him out of my sight. I turned to Peters. "I'll help get this loaded into Joanna's car and be right back."

We left Andi Wynn and Peters standing together in the breezeway. "Where did it come from?" Joanna asked.

"What?"

"The picture. I thought you were going to find out how the man at the newspaper got it."

"Oh, that." Maxwell Cole's column seemed eons away. "No," I told her. "I haven't been able to locate him yet."

"Oh," Joanna said. She sounded disappointed.

Her Mustang was parked in the school lot. She led the way to the trunk and unlocked it. The cover bounced open. A large tin-plated container, the kind restaurants use to hold fifty pounds of lard, sat in the middle of an otherwise empty trunk.

Joanna looked at it and frowned. "What's that doing here?" she asked. "What is it?"

"It looks like my flour container. But what would it be doing in my car?"

I put down the box. "I don't know," I said. "Let me take a look."

As soon as I cracked the lid on the container, before I even looked inside, I was sorry. The stench was overpowering. Fools rush in where angels fear to tread. I lifted the lid anyway.

Coiled at the top was a length of rope. Under it, through the center of the rope was what appeared to be a man's shirt. A maroon man's shirt, dusted with flour.

For a moment, Joanna had recoiled, driven away by the overwhelming odor of human excrement. Despite the smell, she came forward again to peer warily inside the container. She saw the shirt at the same time I did.

"That's his shirt," she whispered.

I shoved the lid back shut. "Are you sure?"

She nodded, holding her hand to her mouth. "That was his favorite, his game shirt. He always wore it."

"That day, too?"

She nodded. "It's either his shirt or one just like it."

I examined the outside of the container. A fine film of white powder lingered on the outside and on the top. I took a tiny swipe at the bottom edge with my finger and touched it to my tongue. It was indeed flour.

"And this looks like your flour container?"

"I'm sure of it. I keep it in the storeroom out in the carport. There's a smaller one, a canister in the house. When I need to refill it, I get the flour from this one."

"And you have no idea how long this has been in your trunk?"

"No."

I closed the lid of the trunk. "Open the car door," I ordered. "We'll put the box in the back."

Unquestioningly, Joanna did as she was bidden. She unlocked the rider's door and held up the front seat while I shoved the box in. When I turned back toward her, she was trembling visibly, despite the fact that a warm afternoon sun was shining on her.

"Wait here," I said. "We'll go somewhere where we can talk."

I left her there and went in search of Peters. I found him and Candace Wynn standing right where we'd left them. They were laughing and talking.

"I'm going to be gone for a while," I told Peters abruptly.

Puzzled, he looked at me. "Want me to go along?" he asked.

I shook my head. "No need. I'll be back in half an hour or so."

To this day, I'm not sure why I didn't have Peters come along with us. Joanna's Mustang was small, but there would have been room enough for the three of us.

Peters shrugged. "Okay. Suit yourself. I'll wait here. Besides, I should get the camera from the car and take some pictures of that list. Even if it's not admissible, doesn't mean it isn't usable."

I nodded in agreement. Leaving them, I hustled back to Joanna Ridley. She was still standing beside the Mustang, where I'd left her, as if glued to the spot. She jumped like a startled deer when I returned.

"Would you like me to drive?"

Wordlessly, she handed me her keys. I helped her into the car and shut the door. I got in and put the key in the ignition.

Joanna seemed dazed, unable to grasp what had happened. "Why are those things in my trunk?"

"That's what we're going to find out," I told her. I started the car and backed it out of the parking place. The only restaurant I knew on Mercer Island was a Denny's down near I-90. I fought my way through the maze of highway construction and found the restaurant on only the second try. For most of the drive, Joanna sat next to me in stricken silence.

Once in Denny's, we went to a booth in the far corner of the room and ordered coffee. "Tell me again where you kept the flour container," I demanded.

"In the storeroom at the end of the carport."

"Locked or unlocked?"

"Locked. Always."

"When was the last you saw it?"

"I don't know. A couple of weeks, I guess. I don't keep track."

"And you haven't noticed if the storeroom has been unlocked at any time?"

"No."

"When were you out there last?"

She shrugged. "Sometime last week."

"And the flour container was there?"

"As far as I know, but I don't remember for sure." She paused. "What are you going to do?"

"Take the container to the crime lab. See what they can find out."

"Why was it there?"

"In your car?"

She nodded.

"Someone wanted it found there."

"So you'd think I killed him?"

"Yes."

"Do you?"

"No."

There was another long pause. The waitress came and refilled both our coffee cups. While she did it, Joanna's eyes never left my face.

"Is that smart?"

"For me not to suspect you? Probably not, but I don't just the same."

"Thank you."

I was sitting looking at her, but my random access memory went straying back to Monday night, the first night I had seen her, when I brought her back from the medical examiner's office. The light in the carport had been turned off. Was that when the flour container disappeared?

I leaned forward in my chair. "Joanna, do you remember when we left your house that night to go to the medical examiner's office? Do you remember if you turned off the light in the carport before we drove away?"

She frowned and shook her head. "I don't remember at all. I might have, but I doubt it."

"Did you notice that when we came back the light wasn't on?"

"No."

"Where's the switch for the light in the carport?"

"There are two of them. One by the back door and one by the front."

"Both inside?"

"Yes."

I downed the rest of my coffee and stood up. "Come on.'

"Where are we going?"

"We're going to drop the container off at the crime lab and make arrangements for them to send someone out to your house to dust it for prints."

"You think the killer was there, in my house?"

"I'm willing to bet on it."

"But how did he get in? How did he open my car without my knowing it?"

"Your husband had keys to your car, didn't he?"

She nodded.

"And the killer had Darwin's keys."

She stood up, too. "All right," she said.

"I'm making arrangements for someone to put new locks on all your doors, both on the house and the car."

Joanna looked puzzled. "Why?"

"If he got in once," I said grimly, "he could do it again."

I had no intention of unloading the container from Joanna's car into ours to take it to the crime lab. Janice Morraine, my friend at the crime lab, tells me evidence is like pie dough—fragile. The less handling the better.

It was rush hour by the time we were back in traffic. I-90 westbound was reduced to a single lane going into the city. It took us twenty minutes to get off the access road and onto the freeway. Rush hour is a helluva funny word for it. We spent most of the next hour parked on the bridge. I would make a poor commuter. I don't have the patience for it anymore.

Joanna was subdued as we drove. "The funeral's tomorrow," she said finally. "Will you be there?"

"What time?"

"Four," she replied.

"I don't know if I'll make it," I said. "What about the memorial service at school. Will you be going to that?"

"No. I don't think I could face those kids. Not after what happened."

I didn't blame her for that. I would have felt the same way. "If I were you, I don't think I could, either," I told her.

The entire cheerleading squad would probably be there.

Except for one. Bambi Barker.

CHAPTER 19

Joanna Ridley dropped me back at Mercer Island High School a little after seven. It wasn't quite dusk. The only car visible in the school lot was our departmental Dodge. A note from Peters was stuck under the windshield wiper. "See the custodian."

I went looking for one. It took a while, but I finally found him polishing a long hallway with a machine that sounded like a Boeing 747 preparing for takeoff. I shouted to him a couple of times before he heard me and shut off the noise.

"I'm supposed to talk to you."

"Your name Beaumont?" he asked. I nodded, and he reached in his pocket and extracted the keys to the car in the parking lot. "Your partner said you should pick him up at the Roanoke."

It didn't make sense to me. If Peters had gotten a ride all the way to the Roanoke in Seattle, why hadn't he asked Andi Wynn to drop him off at the department so he could have picked up his own car? I was operating on too little sleep to want to play cab driver, but I grudgingly convinced myself it had been thoughtful of him to leave the car. At least that way I'd have access to transportation back downtown.

None too graciously, I thanked the custodian for his help and set off for Seattle. Something big must have been happening at Seattle Center that night. Traffic was backed up on both the bridge and I-5. I finally got to the Roanoke Exit on the freeway and made my way to the restaurant by the same name on Eastlake at the bottom of the hill.

Andi Wynn's red pickup wasn't outside, and when I went into the bar, there was no trace of Peters and Andi inside, either.

"Can I help you?" the bartender asked.

"I'm looking for some friends of mine. Both of them have red hair. A man, thirty-five, six two. A woman about the same age. Both pretty good-looking. They were driving a red pickup."

"Nobody like that's been in here tonight," the bartender reported. "Been pretty slow as a matter of fact."

"How long have you been here? Maybe they left before you came on duty."

The bartender shook his head. "I came to work at three o'clock this afternoon."

I scratched my head. "I'm sure he said the Roanoke," I mumbled aloud to myself.

"Which one?" the bartender asked.

"Which one? You mean there's more than one?"

"Sure. This is the Roanoke Exit. There's the Roanoke Inn over on Mercer Island."

"I'll be a son of a bitch! You got a phone I can use?"

He pointed to a pay phone by the restroom. "Don't feel like the Lone Ranger," he said. "The number's written on the top of the phone, right under the coin deposit. It happens all the time."

Sure enough, the name Roanoke Inn and its number were taped just under the coin deposit. Knowing that I had lots of company didn't make me feel any better. I shoved a quarter into the phone and dialed the number. When someone answered, I had to shout to be heard over the background racket.

"I'm looking for someone named Peters," I repeated for the fourth time.

"You say Peters? Okay, hang on." My ear rattled as the telephone receiver was tossed onto some hard surface. The paging system at the Roanoke was hardly upscale. "Hey," whoever had answered the phone shouted above the din, "anybody here named Peters? You got a phone call."

I waited. Eventually, the phone was picked back up. "He's coming," someone said, then promptly dropped the receiver again.

"Hey, Beau!" Peters' voice came across like Cheerful Charlie. "Where you been? We've been waitin'."

It didn't sound like Peters. "Andi and I just had spaghetti. It's great. Want us to order you some?"

Spaghetti? Vegetarian, no-red-meat Peters pushing spaghetti? I figured I was hearing things. "Are you feeling all right?" I asked.

"Me?" Peters laughed. "Never better. Where the hell are you, buddy? It's late."

Peters is always accusing me of being a downtown isolationist, of not knowing anything about what's on the other side of I-5, of regarding the suburbs as a vast wasteland. I wasn't about to 'fess up to my mistake.

"I've been delayed," I muttered. "I'll be there in a little while."

It was actually quite a bit longer than a little while. I drove and cussed and took one wrong turn after another. The thing I've learned about Mercer Island is that no address is straightforward. The Roanoke Inn is an in-crowd joke, set off in the dingleberries at the end of a road that winds through a seemingly residential area. By the time I got there, it was almost nine o'clock. I was ready to wring Peters' neck.

The building itself is actually an old house, complete with a white-railed front porch. Inside, it was wall-to-wall people. The decorations, from the plastic scenic lamp shades with holes burned in them to the ancient juke box blaring modern, incomprehensible rock, were straight out of the forties and fifties. I had the feeling this wasn't stuff assembled by some yuppies trying to make a "fifties statement." This place was authentic. It had always been like that.

In one corner came a steady jackhammer racket that was actually a low-tech popcorn popper. I finally spotted Peters and Andi Wynn, seated cozily on one side of a booth at the far end of the room. A pitcher of beer and two glasses sat in front of them. Peters, with his arm draped casually around Andi's shoulder, was laughing uproariously.

I had known Peters for almost two years. I had never heard him laugh like that, with his head thrown back and mirth shaking his whole body. He had always kept himself on a tight rein. It was so good to see him having a good time that I forgot about being pissed, about it being late, and about my getting lost.

I walked up to the booth and slid into the seat across from them. "All right, you two. What's so funny?"

Peters managed to pull himself together. He wiped tears from his eyes. "Hi, Beau. She is." He ruffled Andi Wynn's short auburn hair. "I swear to God, this is the funniest woman I ever met."

Andi Wynn ducked her head and gave me a shy smile. "He's lying," she said. "I'm perfectly serious."

That set him off again. While he was convulsed once more, Andi signaled for the bartender. "Want a beer?"

I looked at Peters, trying to assess if he was smashed or just having one hell of a good time. "No thanks," I said. "Somebody in this crowd better stay sober enough to drive."

The bartender fought his way over to us. I ordered coffee and, at Peters' insistence, a plate of the special Thursday night Roanoke spaghetti. The spaghetti was all right, but not great enough to justify Peters' rave review. I wondered once more exactly how much beer he had swallowed.

"What's going on?" Peters asked, getting serious finally. "It took you long enough."

"We found something in Joanna's car," I said. "I took it down to the crime lab."

Peters frowned. "What was it?"

I didn't feel comfortable discussing the case in front of Andi Wynn. "Just some stuff," I told him offhandedly. "Maybe it's important, maybe not."

Peters reached for the pitcher, glanced at me, and saw me watching him. "I went off duty at five o'clock," he said in answer to my unspoken comment. Leaning back, he refilled both his and Andi's glasses from the pitcher.

"We waited a long time. It got late and hungry out. We finally decided to come here. What do you think? It's a great place, isn't it?"

I wouldn't have called it great. It was nothing but a local tavern in the "Cheers" tradition, with its share of run-down booths, dingy posters, peeling paint, and loyal customers planted on concave barstools.

"I was telling Ron that we used to come here after school," Andi said. "Darwin, me, and some of the others."

When she called him Ron, it threw me for a minute. I tended to forget that Peters had a first name. And it surprised me, too, that in the time since I'd left them to go with Joanna Ridley, Peters and Andi had moved from formal address to a first-name basis. I felt like I'd missed out on something important.

"Is that right? When was that?" I asked, practically shouting over the noise of a new song blaring from the jukebox.

"Last year," she answered.

I swallowed the food without chewing it, gulped down the coffee, and rushed them out the door. Andi's pickup was parked outside. I got in to drive the Dodge while Peters walked Andi to her truck, opened the door for her, and gave her a quick goodnight kiss. Andi started her engine and drove away. Peters returned to our car looking lighter than air.

That kiss bugged me. I distinctly remembered Ned Browning calling her Mrs. Wynn, not Miss Wynn. What the hell was Peters thinking of?

I climbed Peters' frame about it as soon as he got in the car. "Isn't she Sadie, Sadie married lady?" I asked.

"Divorced," Peters said. And that was all he said. No explanation. Not even a lame excuse.

I stewed in my own juices over that for a while before I tackled him on the larger issue of the Roanoke Inn. "It's a good thing you left the car where it was when you decided to go drinking. We'd have one hell of a time explaining what we were doing hanging out in a tavern in a departmental vehicle at this time of night."

"Wait a minute. Who's the guy who was telling me just the other day that I needed to lighten up a little, to stop being such a stickler for going by the book?"

"I didn't mean you should overreact," I told him.

I took Peters to his own place in Kirkland rather than dropping him downtown to drive his Datsun back to the east side. I didn't know how much beer he had drunk, and I wasn't willing to risk it.

When I told him I was taking him home, he gave a noncommittal shrug. "I'm not drunk, Beau, but if it'll make you feel better, do it."

On the way to his house I told him about the contents of Joanna Ridley's trunk. "The rope was coiled on top?" he asked.

"Yes."

"And she could tell looking through the rope that those were the clothes he wore the day he died?"

"That's right."

"Doesn't it strike you as odd?"

"Why should it?"

"It seems to me that one way of knowing what's inside a closed container is to be the one who put it there."

"Joanna Ridley didn't do it," I replied.

He didn't talk to me much after that. I couldn't tell what was going on, if he was mad because I thought he was too smashed to drive home or if he was pissed because I wasn't buying his suspicions about Joanna Ridley.

As we drove into his driveway, I said, "I'll come get you in the morning if you like."

"Don't bother." His tone was gruff. "I'll catch a bus downtown. This is only the suburbs, Beau. Despite what some people think, it isn't the end of the earth."

He got out and slammed his door without bothering to thank me for the ride. I was too tired to worry about what ailed Peters. My three hours of sleep had long since fallen by the wayside. I needed to fall into bed and get some sleep.

It's hell getting old.

CHAPTER 20

My alarm went off at seven, and the phone went off exactly one minute later. It was Ames, chipper and cheerful Ames, calling me from Arizona and wondering whether or not I would pick him up at the airport at one that afternoon. I blundered my way halfway through the conversation before I remembered the real estate closing for Belltown Terrace was scheduled for three-thirty.

"Shit! I never wrote it down in my calendar."

"Wrote what down? What's the matter, Beau?"

"The closing. It's scheduled for the same time as Darwin Ridley's funeral."

"Do you have to go?"

"I ought to, but maybe I could ask Peters. He shouldn't mind."

"Good. After the closing, we need to go see the decorator, too. He's been calling me here in Phoenix. Says he can never catch you."

"Look, Ralph, I don't spend my time sitting around waiting for the phone to ring."

"You should get a machine, an answering machine with remote capability."

"Will you lay off that answering machine stuff? I'm not buying one, and that's final."

"Okay, okay. See you at one."

Even riding the bus from Kirkland, Peters beat me to the office. His unvarying promptness bugged the hell out of me at times, particularly since, no matter what, I was always running behind schedule. He was seated at his desk with his nose buried in a file folder. He was obviously scanning through the material, looking for one particular item.

"What are you up to?" I asked, walking past him to get to my desk.

"Here it is," he said. He dropped the file folder, grabbed his pen, and copied some bit of information from the folder into his pocket notebook.

"Here's what?" I asked. I confess I was less interested in what he was looking for than I was with whether or not there was coffee in the pot on the table behind Margie's desk. There was—a full, freshly made pot.

"Rimbaugh. That's his name."

"Whose name? Peters, for godsake, will you tell me what you're talking about?"

"Remember Monday afternoon? We talked to all those old duffers who are part-time security guards down at Seattle Center? Dave Rimbaugh is one of them. He was assigned to the locker rooms."

"So?"

"So I've got this next-door neighbor who works for Channel Thirteen. In the advertising department. I called him last night after I got home and asked him if he could locate a picture of Wheeler-Dealer Barker for us. He called just a few minutes ago. Said he'd found one and when did we want to come by to pick it up."

"Why go to the trouble? What's the point? We already know Barker was there. He told us so."

"Sure he did. He said he was there at halftime, but what if he was there later, too? Maybe he came back or, better yet, maybe he never left."

Picking up my empty coffee cup, I sauntered over to the coffee table mulling Peters' hypothesis. It was possible, I supposed, but it didn't seem plausible. I came back with coffee and set my cup down on the desk.

"Well?" Peters asked.

I shook my head. "I don't think so. Barker isn't our man."

"Why not?"

"Gut instinct."

Just that quick, Peters got his back up. "Right. Sure it is. You know, Beau, sometimes I get tired of working with the Grand Old Man of Homicide. You're not always on the money. I think Barker's it, and I'm willing to invest some shoe leather in proving it. You coming or not?"

He didn't leave a whole lot of room for discussion. We got a car from the garage, a tired Chevette without as much zing to it as the Dodge we'd driven the day before—no zip and a hell of a lot less leg room. I wonder sometimes if the ratings would be the same if the guys on "Miami Vice" drove Chevettes.

We stopped by Channel 13's downtown office. The receptionist cheerfully handed over a manila envelope with Peters' name scrawled on the front. Inside was an eight-by-ten glossy of Tex Barker himself, without the cowboy hat and grinning from ear to ear. There were several other pictures as well, eight-by-tens of people I didn't recognize.

Peters shuffled through them, looked at me, and grinned. "See there? What we've got here is an instant montage."

One of the realities of police work these days is that you never get to show witnesses just the person you want them to see. You always have to show a group of pictures and hope they pick out the right one. Going by the book can be a royal pain in the ass. I gave Peters credit for taking care of it in advance.

Dave Rimbaugh's address was off in the wilds of Lake City, about a twenty-minute drive from downtown Seattle. Peters drove. As we made our way up the freeway, Peters glanced in my direction. "Tell me again about the stuff you found in the back of Joanna Ridley's car. You said it was her flour container?"

"That's right. Out of the storeroom at the end of her carport."

"They're dusting it for prints?"

"The container and the trunk for certain. They said yesterday they're going to try to work out a deal with the county to run the contents past the county's YAG to see if they can raise anything there."

"YAG? What the hell's a YAG?"

"Their new laser printfinder. Janice Morraine was telling me about it. They use it to raise prints on all kinds of unlikely surfaces—cement, rumpled tin foil."

"Off rope and clothing, too?"

"Not too likely, but possible. She said there's a remote chance. I've also called for a tech to go over Joanna Ridley's house for prints."

"Any idea when the container was placed in the car or any sign of forced entry?"

I shook my head. "The killer had Darwin's keys, remember? House keys and car keys, both."

"I had forgotten," Peters said thoughtfully.

"She's going to have all her locks changed today, just in case."

Peters nodded. "That's probably wise." ·

We were both quiet for a moment. It was as good a time as any to bring up my scheduling conflict between the real estate closing and Darwin Ridley's funeral.

"By the way," I said casually, "Ralph Ames is flying in this afternoon. I pick him up at the airport at one. We're supposed to close on Belltown Terrace at three-thirty this afternoon. Do you think you could handle Ridley's funeral by yourself?"

I more than half-expected an objection, for Peters to say that he needed to be home with his kids. It's an excuse that packs a whole lot of weight with me. Had he used it, I probably would have knuckled under, given Ames my power of attorney, and had him stand in for me at the closing.

Instead, Peters surprised me. "Sure, no problem. What about the memorial service after the funeral? Want me to handle that, too?"

"That would be great."

Dave Rimbaugh's house was a snug nineteen-thirties bungalow dwarfed by the evergreen trees that had grown up around it. The woman who came to the door was almost as wide as the door itself. Her pug nose and the rolling jowls of her face made her look like a bulldog. A near-sighted bulldog wearing thick glasses.

"Davey," she called over her shoulder. "Hon, there's somebody here to see you."

"Davey" wasn't a day under seventy. He was a spry old man, as lean as his wife was fat. They were a living rendition of the old Jack Sprat routine. His face lit up all over when Peters showed his ID and told him who we were and what we wanted.

"See there, Francie. I told you I talked to a real detective on the phone, and you thought I was pulling your leg." He led us into the living room. Every available flat surface in the room was full of glass and ceramic elephants of every size and description. Dave Rimbaugh noticed me looking at them.

"We've been collecting them for fifty-six years now," he said proudly. "There's more in the dining room. Would you like to see those?"

"No, thanks," I told him quickly, stopping him before he could hurry into the next room. "I can see you've got an outstanding collection, but we'd better get to work. Business before pleasure, you know."

"Good." Rimbaugh nodded appreciatively. "Don't like to waste the tax-payer's money, right?"

"Right," I said, sitting down on the wing-backed chair he offered me, while Peters sank into the old-fashioned, flower-patterned couch.

Rimbaugh rubbed his hands together in anticipation. "Now then, what can I do for you boys?"

Peters grimaced visibly at the term "boys." It was clear "Davey" Rimbaugh regarded us as a couple of young whippersnappers. Doing his best to conceal his annoyance, Peters reached into a file folder and pulled out the fanfold of photographs. He offered them to our host.

"Take a look at these, Mr. Rimbaugh. See if there's anyone here you recognize, anyone you may have seen at the Coliseum last Friday night."

Dave Rimbaugh only had to glance through the pictures once before he pounced on Wheeler-Dealer's smiling countenance. "Him," he said decisively. "That's him. He was there."

Unable to contain her curiosity, Francie Rimbaugh got up from the couch and came over to her husband's chair. She stood behind him like she'd been planted there, leaning over his shoulder so she, too, could look at the picture in his hand.

"Why, forevermore!" she exclaimed. "I know him. Isn't that the man on the television, the one on the late movies? I think he sells cars. Or maybe furniture."

Dave Rimbaugh held the picture up to the light. "Why, Francie, I do believe you're right. He looked familiar at the time, but I just couldn't place him."

He patted his wife's rump affectionately and pulled her close to him. "Francie here, now she's the one with the memory for faces," he said. "Faces and names both."

"Do you remember when you saw this man?" Peters asked. "It's important that we know exactly when he was there."

Dave Rimbaugh leaned back in his chair and closed his eyes, frowning with the effort of concentration. "All I remember is, I was drinking a cup of coffee at the time. Almost spilled it all over me when he rushed past. Said there was an emergency of some kind. Didn't ask him what, just let him go through."

"So what time was it?" Peters prodded. "Halftime? Later than that?"

"I don't know if it was halftime or not. They play a whole bunch of games each day during the tournament. Let's see. Wait a minute, I had only two cups of coffee that night. That was all that was left in the pot when I filled the thermos. When he almost knocked me down, I remember thinking it's a good thing it's almost time to go home, 'cause there isn't any coffee left."

I could see Peters was losing patience with trying to pull usable information out of the old man's ramblings. "What time did you get off work?" I asked.

"Nine o'clock," he said. "Isn't that right, Francie? I was home by ten, wasn't I?"

She nodded. "That's right. We watched the early late movie together before we went to bed. The old one with Gary Cooper in it."

"And how close was that second cup of coffee to the time you came home?"

"It was just before. Sure, that's right. Must have been right around eight." Rimbaugh looked at us triumphantly.

"You're sure you didn't see him after that?" Peters asked.

"Nope. Not that I remember."

Peters sighed and rose. I followed.

"Does that help?" Rimbaugh asked.

"I hope so," Peters replied. "We'll be back in touch."

Once outside, we held a quick conference. "What do you think?" Peters asked.

I shrugged. "Eight o'clock sounds like halftime to me."

"But he could have come back later, without Rimbaugh seeing him."

That, too, was a distinct possibility. As distinct a possibility as anything I'd come up with. There was no way to tell for sure.

So much for being the Grand Old Man of Homicide.

CHAPTER 21

Peters went back to the Public Safety Building. During my lunch hour, I took the Porsche and drove down to Sea-Tac to pick up Ralph Ames.

Ralph was a dapper-looking guy, an attorney's attorney. He had a low-key look about him that said he knew what he was doing. I probably never would have gotten to know him if I hadn't inherited him from Anne Corley. It took a while to get to know the man under his air of quiet reserve, but once I did, he turned out to be one hell of a nice guy.

At the airport that day, when I went to pick him up, he had an uncharacteristic shit-eating grin on his face that worried me some, but not enough for me to do anything about it.

There was just time to grab him from the arriving-passenger level, hightail it back to town, and have him drop me at the department. He took my Porsche back to my place while Peters and I drove to Mercer Island High School, where we planned to have a chat with Molly Blackburn.

Ned Browning was most reluctant to call Molly out of class so we could talk to her. I have to admit that knowing the principal's name appeared not once but twice in the trophy list in the girls' locker room gave me a whole new perspective on his outward show of high principles and middle-class morality.

"Detective Beaumont, I'm not at all sure I should let you talk to one of my students without her parents' express knowledge and permission."

I wasn't feeling particularly tolerant toward that officious little worm. In fact, I became downright belligerent. "We don't have time to screw around, Mr. Browning. We need to see that girl today. Now."

"Certainly, you don't think one of my students had something to do with the murder!" There was just the right tone of shocked consternation in Ned Browning's voice. He should have been an actor instead of a high school principal. He gave an award-winning performance.

"Your students know a hell of a lot about a lot of things they shouldn't."

I let it go at that. There was no outward, visible sign that he understood the ramifications of what I said, yet I knew my seemingly casual remark had hit home. Finally, he reached for his phone and called for a student page to bring Molly Blackburn to his office.

Molly waltzed into the room like she owned the place. I recognized her as the blonde who had been pitching such a fit, literally bawling her eyes out, the day Peters and I had interviewed all those kids. Talk about acting!

"You wanted to see me, Mr. Browning?" she asked brightly.

"These gentlemen do," he replied. "You remember them, don't you, Molly?"

Molly looked at Peters and me. When she recognized us, she stepped back a full step. "Y-yes," she stammered uncertainly.

"Good. They've asked to speak to you. Mr. Howell is out today, so you may use his office. I have scheduled a parent conference in just a few minutes. Unfortunately, I won't be able to join you. This way, please."

Unfortunately? Hell! It was a good thing he had another meeting. No way would I have let that son of a bitch join us for Molly Blackburn's interview.

He led us to an adjoining office. Molly's entrance into that room was far different from the one she had made into the principal's office. She lagged behind us like an errant puppy who's just crapped all over the new rug and who knows he's going to get it.

We knew, and she knew we knew. As soon as the door closed behind Ned Browning, I whirled on her and let Molly Blackburn have it with both barrels.

"What's the matter? Did Bambi call to warn you?"

Her eyes widened. She was still standing in the doorway. She groped blindly for a chair and eased her way into it. "Yes," she whispered.

"So you know why we're here?"

She shook her head. "No, not really." Her face was white. She was scared to death, and I wanted her to stay that way.

"Are you the one who was trying to blackmail the Ridley's and the Barkers?"

"Wh-what?" she stammered. Under pressure, she seemed to be having a great deal of trouble making her voice and mouth work in unison.

"You're the one with the fancy camera, aren't you? The one who took the "proof" shot of your friend Bambi and Darwin Ridley?"

She licked her lip nervously, swallowed, and nodded. Barely. Almost imperceptibly.

"So where's the negative?"

"I don't know," she whispered.

"Don't know! What do you mean, you don't know?"

"It's gone. Someone took it."

"When?" I demanded. "Where was it?"

"I had it with me. I had all the negatives from that roll of film in my book bag. I didn't dare leave them at home. Sometimes my parents go through my things."

"So you carried them around with you. When did you notice they were gone?"

"Friday afternoon. After Mr. Barker came to school to get Bambi. I looked for them then, but they weren't there."

"And how long had the negatives been in your purse?"

"Not my purse. My book bag. I brought the picture to school on Monday. That was the day . . ." She broke off.

"Let me guess. That's the day you scratched Darwin Ridley's name in the locker."

"How did you know that?"

"It doesn't take a Philadelphia lawyer to figure it out," I told her. "So sometime between Monday and Friday, the negatives disappeared," I continued. "What happened to the original picture? Where is it?"

"It's gone, too. We burned it when we wrote down the name."

"Too bad you didn't burn the negative as well."

"Why? I don't understand."

I wanted her to understand. I wanted her to feel the responsibility for Darwin Ridley's death right down to the soles of her feet. "Because," I growled, "it found its way into the wrong hands. That's why Darwin Ridley was murdered."

Molly's eyes flooded with tears. "No! It's not true. It can't be!" She glanced in Peters' direction as if seeking help, reassurance. None was forthcoming. Peters had remained absolutely silent throughout the proceedings.

Now he folded his arms uncompromisingly across his chest. "It's true," he said quietly.

Molly doubled over, sobbing hysterically into her lap. Neither Peters nor I offered her the smallest bit of comfort. I felt nothing but profound disgust. Finally, she quit crying on her own.

"What's going to happen to me?" she asked, looking up red-eyed and frightened.

"That depends on you, doesn't it. Are you going to help us or not?"

She nodded. "I'll help."

"All right. Try to think back to when the negatives could have disappeared. Can you remember any times when the bag was left unattended?"

"No. I always have it with me." She motioned toward a shiny green bag on the floor. "See?"

"Did anyone else know the negatives were there? Did you tell any of your friends?"

"No. Not even Bambi. Nobody knew."

"And what were the negatives in? One of those envelopes from a fast photo-developing place?"

"No. A plain white envelope. I developed them myself. At home."

"It must be nice to be so talented," I commented sarcastically. "Do your parents have any idea what you've been doing?"

"Don't tell them. Please. They'd kill me."

I had been sitting behind the assistant principal's desk. I got up then and walked to the window. "They probably wouldn't," I said. "But I don't think I'd blame them if they did." I turned to Peters. "Do you have any other questions?"

He shook his head. "Not right now. You've pretty well covered it."

I looked back at Molly. She was staring at me, eyes wide and frightened. "Get out of here," I ordered. "You make me sick." She scurried out of the room as fast as she could go.

"You were pretty tough on her," Peters remarked after the door closed.

"Not nearly as tough as I should have been."

Glancing down at my watch, I realized it was after two, and I didn't have the location for my closing. "I'd better call Ames and find out where I'm supposed to be and when. If we're going to be stuck in traffic, it might be nice if we were at least going in the right direction."

I picked up the assistant principal's phone and dialed my own number. It rang twice. When a woman's voice answered, I hung up, convinced I had dialed a wrong number. I tried again. That time my line was busy.

Peters stood up. "While you're playing with the phone, I need to go check on something." He walked out of the office, and I tried dialing one more time. This time, when the woman's voice answered, I stayed on the line to listen. The recorded voice was soft and sultry.

"Hello, my name is Susan. Beau is unable to come to the phone right now, but he doesn't want to miss your call. Please leave your name, number, time of day, and a brief message at the sound of the tone, and Beau will call you back just as soon as he can. Thanks for calling. Bye-bye." Then there was a beep.

"What the fuck!"

I held the receiver away from my mouth and ear and looked at it like it was some strange apparition I'd never seen before. I felt like somebody had just clunked me over the head with a baseball bat. What the hell was an answering machine doing on my phone?

Just then, I heard Ames' voice, shouting at me from the receiver. "Hey, Beau. Is that you? Are you there? What do you think? Do you like it?"

"Ralph Ames, you son of a bitch. No, I don't like it. I told you before, I don't want an answering machine."

"Come on, Beau. It's great. In three days you'll love it. It's a present, an early housewarming present."

"You jerk! When I get home, I'll tear it out of the wall and wrap it around your neck!" I slammed down the phone just as Peters came back into the room. He was grinning, but he wiped the look off his face the minute he saw me.

"Hey, Beau. What's up?"

"That damn Ames went and installed a stupid answering machine in my house while my back was turned, without even asking me."

"So? It's probably a good idea. You're not the easiest person in the world to catch. Where's the closing? Did you find out?"

I had been so disturbed by the answering machine that I had forgotten the reason I had called. Chagrined, I picked up the phone and redialed. The answering machine clicked on after the second ring. "Hello. My name is Susan . . ."

"Damn it, Ames!" I shouted into the phone. "I know you're there. If you can hear me, turn this goddamned thing off and talk to me."

The woman's voice was stifled. Ames' voice came on the line.

"Here I am, Beau. What do you need?"

"The closing. I know when it is, but I don't know where."

"Downtown in Columbia Center. Up on the seventieth floor. Ellis and Wheeler. It's getting pretty late. Want to meet me there? I can bring your car."

"Fine," I answered curtly. "See you there." I hung up again.

"You don't have to be such a hard-ass about it," Peters chided me as I stood up to leave. "I'm sure Ames thought he was helping you out. There are times I'd like to have one of those gadgets myself."

"Great," I grumbled. "I've got a terrific idea. We'll unplug it from my house and plug it back in in yours."

Peters smiled. "When are you going to give up and accept the inevitable? Automation and microchips are here to stay."

"Not in my house they aren't," I replied, then stalked from the room with Peters right behind me.

I'm one of those people they'll have to pull kicking and screaming into the twenty-first century, if I live to be that old.

I have no intention of going quietly.

Chapter 22

On Friday afternoon, traffic in Seattle is a nightmare. We made it back across the bridge with barely enough time for Peters to make it to Darwin Ridley's funeral at the Mount Baker Baptist Church. Peters dropped me off at a bus stop on Rainier Avenue South. I grabbed a Metro bus jammed with rowdy school kids for a snail's-pace ride downtown. If I were into jogging and physical fitness, I probably could have beaten the bus on foot.

Once downtown however, Columbia Center isn't hard to find. It's the tallest building west of the Mississippi, to say nothing of being the tallest building in Seattle. The lobby is a maze, however, and it took a while to locate the proper bank of elevators for an ear-popping ride to the seventieth floor.

Stepping out of the elevator, the carpet beneath my feet was so new and thick that it caught the soles of my shoes and sent me flying. I came within inches of tumbling into the lap of a startled, brunette receptionist, who managed to scramble out of the way.

There's nothing like making a suave and elegant grand entrance.

"J. P. Beaumont," I said archly, once I was upright again, hoping somehow to regain my shattered dignity. "I'm supposed to meet Ralph Ames here."

It didn't work. Dignity was irretrievable. The receptionist had to stifle a giggle before she answered me. "Mr. Ames is already inside," she said. "This way, please."

Rising, she turned and led me down a short, book-lined hallway. As she looked away, the corners of her mouth continued to crinkle in a vain attempt to keep a straight face.

At the end of the hallway we came to another desk. There, the receptionist handed me off to another sweet young thing, a blonde with incredibly long eyelashes and matching legs. It was clear the personnel manager in that office had an eye for beauty. I wondered if these ladies had any office skills, or if good looks constituted their sole qualification for employment.

"Mr. Rogers told me to show you right in," the blonde said. She opened a door into a spacious office with a spectacular view of Seattle's humming waterfront on Elliott Bay. In one corner of the room sat Ralph Ames and another man hunched over a conference table piled high with a formidable stack of legal documents.

"So there you are," Ames said, glancing up as I entered the room. "It's about time you got here. I'd like to introduce Dale Rogers. He's representing the syndicate. This whole transaction is complicated by the fact that you're both buyer and seller."

Ames has a penchant for understatement. The process of buying my new condominium was actually far more than complicated. It was downright mystifying.

Months before, acting on Ames' suggestion that I'd best do some investing with my recent inheritance, I had joined with a group of other investors to syndicate the purchase of a new, luxury condominium high rise in downtown Seattle. Now, operating as an individual, I was purchasing an individual condominium unit from the syndicate.

Ames and the other attorney busily passed papers back and forth, both of them telling me where and when to sign. Between times, when my signature was not required, I sat and examined the contrast between the panoramic view of water and mountains through the window and the impossibly ugly but obviously original oil painting on the opposite wall. I couldn't help but speculate about how much this exercise in penmanship was costing me on a per-minute basis, and how many square inches of that painting I personally had paid for.

In less time and for more money that I had thought possible, I was signed, sealed, and delivered as the legal owner of my new home at Second and Broad. Ralph Ames literally beamed as I scrawled one final signature on the dotted line.

"Good for you, Beau. It's a great move."

Dale Rogers nodded in agreement. "That's right, Mr. Beaumont. As soon as the weather turns good, you'll have to have us all over for a barbecue. I understand there's a terrific barbecue on the recreation floor. My wife is dying to see the inside of that building."

"Sure thing," I said. My enthusiasm hardly matched theirs, however. I didn't feel much like a proud new home owner. I felt a lot more like a frustrated detective battling a case that was going nowhere fast, fighting the war of too much work and not enough sleep.

It was ten after five when we walked out of Columbia Center onto Fourth Avenue with a crush of nine-to-fivers eagerly abandoning work.

"Where's the car?" I asked.

"In the Four Seasons' parking garage," Ames answered. "But we've got one more appointment before we can pick it up."

I sighed and shook my head. I wanted to go home, have a drink, and put my feet up. "Who with now?"

"Michael Browder, the interior designer, remember? I told you about it on the phone. He's meeting us in the bar of the Four Seasons at five-thirty. Now that you've closed on the deal, he needs a go-ahead for the work. He told me the other day that you still haven't even looked at his preliminary drawings."

Bull's-eye! I had to admit Ames had me dead to rights. I had been actively avoiding Michael Browder, but I didn't care to confide in Ames that the main reason was that Michael Browder was gay. Ames had dropped that bit of information in passing one day. It didn't seem to make any difference to Ames, but it did to me.

I'm not homophobic, exactly, but I confess to being prejudiced. I don't like gays. I had never met one I liked. Or at least hadn't *knowingly* met one I liked.

Ames and I found a small corner table and ordered drinks. I sat back in my chair to watch the traffic, convinced I'd be able to pick out a wimp like Michael Browder the instant he sashayed into the room.

Wrong.

The man who, a few minutes later, stopped in front of our table and held out his hand was almost as tall as I am. Broad shoulders filled out a well-cut, immaculate, three-piece gray suit. He had neatly trimmed short brown hair. The solid handshake he offered me was accompanied by a ready smile.

"Mr. Beaumont?" he said to me with a polite nod in Ralph Ames' direction. "Michael Browder. Glad to meet you, finally."

No limp wrist. No lisp. No earrings.

Old prejudices die hard.

Settling comfortably back into a chair, Browder ordered a glass of Perrier. "Mr. Ames has been a big help," he continued. "He's given me as much information about you as he could, but it's very difficult to design a home for someone I don't know personally, Mr. Beaumont. I've been told, for instance, that you're sentimentally attached to an old recliner, but that's secondhand information. I told Mr. Ames that unless I talked to you, in person, I was leaving the project."

That didn't sound to me like much of a threat. I didn't care much one way or the other, and Michael Browder's speech didn't particularly endear him to me. In fact, I was downright insulted. On the one hand, he accused me of sentimentality. On the other, I was offended by what I viewed as his personal attack on my old recliner.

What he had said was true, as far as it went. I had indeed sent word through Ames that my recliner was going with me no matter what, and that it was moving to the new place as active-duty furniture, not as a relic destined for the storage unit in the basement.

"So do you have drawings along to show me or not?" I demanded impatiently.

Browder leaned down and opened a large leather portfolio he had placed beside his feet. By the time he had finished showing me the sketch of the living room, he had my undivided attention. By the second drawing, he had me in the palm of his hand. My previous experience with an interior designer had achieved somewhat mixed results. Michael Browder, however, without our ever having met in person, seemed to know me like a book.

The furnishings, the swatches of material, the colors, were all straightforward and attractive, functional and practical. They were the kinds of things I would have picked for myself, if I'd had either the brains or the time to do it. Throughout his presentation, Browder kept asking me pointed questions and making brief notes about color preferences, wood grains, and stains. His enthusiasm was contagious. By the time he was finished, I was pretty excited myself.

"So when do you start?" I asked.

"As soon as you say so," Browder replied.

"So start," I told him. "ASAP."

"And when can I pick up the recliner to have it recovered?"

I had been happy to see that he had included my recliner in his drawings for the den, but Browder had negotiated my consent to have the old war-horse reupholstered. It was a small concession on my part.

"You can pick it up whenever you want," I answered.

He nodded. "Good. What about now? I have my van along. We might as well get started."

Which is how we ended up caravanning over to the Royal Crest, all three of us. We went up to my apartment and straight into the living room, picked up the recliner, and hauled it downstairs in the elevator.

By then my opinion of Michael Browder had come a long way from my preconceived notion of what he'd be like, but once the recliner was loaded, he declined an invitation to come back up to the apartment for a drink.

"I've got to get home," he said.

It was a good thing. I was out of booze. Ames and I had to walk over to the liquor store at Sixth and Lenora for provisions before we could make drinks.

When I went into the kitchen to serve as bartender, I discovered the answering machine in a place of honor, sitting in state on the kitchen counter. In the intervening hours of paper signing and apartment designing, I had forgotten about the answering machine and how I had fully intended to wrap the electrical cord around Ralph Ames' neck.

Next to it on the counter sat not one, but two boxes of Girl Scout cookies. Mints.

Ames, from the doorway, saw me encounter the cookies and the machine. My dismay he read as a combination of pleasure and surprise. "I figured living in a secured highrise there's no way you'd have a chance to buy any Girl Scout cookies on your own," Ames said proudly. "I bought some at the airport and brought them along on the plane."

I didn't have the heart to tell him I had already single-handedly bought and given away a whole mountain of Girl Scout cookies. As far as the answering machine was concerned, it was easier to accept it with good grace than to be a pinhead about it.

Ames eagerly explained all the little bells and whistles on the machine, including the blinking light that both signaled and counted waiting messages and the battery-operated remote device that would allow me to retrieve my messages from all over the world. Great! I gritted my teeth into a semblance of a smile and kept my mouth shut.

We had one drink in my apartment, then walked over to Mama's Mexican Kitchen on Second and Bell for dinner. Despite the fact that he lives in Phoenix, Ames claims Mama's taquitos are the best he can get anywhere.

Myself, I'm partial to margaritas.

Mama's has those, too.

CHAPTER 23

I don't know why I bother having a clock in my bedroom. It isn't necessary. The phone usually wakes me up, even when I don't need to be up.

That's what happened that Saturday morning, a Saturday when I had planned to sleep late, stay home, and do nothing but work a week's worth of crossword puzzles. The best laid plans, someone once said. The phone rang at five after seven.

"Detective Beaumont?"

"Yes," I responded, fighting the surplus of tequila cobwebs in my brain and trying to place the woman's voice. No luck.

"This is Maxine, Maxine Edwards."

Maxine? I could have sworn I didn't know a single Maxine in the world. I still didn't have the foggiest idea who owned the insistent voice on the phone demanding that I wake up.

"Have you heard from Ron?"

I started to ask "Ron who?" when my brain finally kicked into gear. Maxine Edwards, the older woman Ames had hired to be Ron Peters' live-in housekeeper/babysitter.

"Not since yesterday. Why? Isn't he home?"

"No, he's not. He never came home at all. Heather and Tracie are upset." From her tone of voice, it was clear Peters' girls weren't the only ones who were upset. So was Maxine Edwards. "He called yesterday afternoon," she continued. "He said he was going to a funeral, that he'd be home late. That's the last I've heard from him."

I sat up in bed. The headache started pounding the moment I lifted my head off the pillow. "That doesn't sound like him."

"I know. That's what's got me worried."

"Where are the girls?"

"They're in watching cartoons. I didn't want them to know I was calling you. I told them you two were probably busy working and just didn't have time to call."

"We're not working," I said.

"I can't imagine him not calling," Mrs. Edwards continued. "For as long as I've been here, he's never done anything like this."

I had to agree it didn't sound like something Peters would pull, but then eating spaghetti didn't sound like him, either. My first thought was that Candace Wynn had something to do with Peters being AWOL, but I didn't mention that to Mrs. Edwards.

"Did he say if he was going anywhere after the funeral?" I asked.

"He said something about a memorial service afterward."

"That would be at the school. Don't worry. Let me do some checking. I'll call you with whatever I find out."

Bringing the bottle of aspirin from the bathroom with me, I ventured out into the living room. Ames was still on the Hide-A-Bed. He wasn't in any better shape than I was. "Who was that calling so early?" he groaned.

I went on into the kitchen to make coffee. "Mrs. Edwards," I told him. "Peters' babysitter. She's looking for him."

"He didn't come home?"

"No."

"Stayed out all night? That doesn't sound like him."

"That's what I told her."

When I went back into the living room, Ames was sitting on the side of the bed with the blanket wrapped around his shoulders, holding his head with both hands. I tossed him the aspirin bottle.

"Hung over?" I asked.

"A little," he admitted. He opened the bottle, shook out a couple of white pills, and popped them into his mouth. "What do you think happened?"

I shrugged. "Got lucky," I said. "He's probably screwing his brains out and is too busy to call Mrs. Edwards and ask for permission."

Ames chuckled at that. "I didn't know Ron had a girlfriend," he said.

"I wouldn't call her a girlfriend exactly. It's someone he just met this week. A teacher."

"What'd he do, start hanging out in singles' bars?"

"When would he have time for singles' bars? He met her at work."

"Really?"

"Where else? You don't find single women hanging out at Brownie meetings or in the grocery store."

"I heard otherwise," Ames commented. "Someone told me the best place for meeting singles is in the deli sections of supermarkets."

"I wouldn't know. I haven't tried it. Do you want coffee or not?"

"Please," Ames said.

Despite what I had told Mrs. Edwards, I didn't try calling anybody. Ames and I each drank a cup of coffee. I expected the phone to ring any minute. I figured Peters had ended up spending the night with Andi Wynn and had planned to sneak back into the house early before anyone woke up. He had probably reckoned without the Saturday morning cartoons, however, which start the minute "The Star-Spangled Banner" ends. Even kids who have to be dragged out of bed by the heels during the week manage to rise and shine in time for their Saturday morning favorites.

Two cups of coffee later I dialed Ron Peters' number again. Maxine Edwards answered. "Oh, it's you," she said, sounding disappointed when she recognized my voice. In the background, I heard a whining child.

"No, Heather, it's not your daddy," Mrs. Edwards scolded. "Now go away and let me talk to Detective Beaumont."

At that Heather pitched such a fit that eventually Mrs. Edwards gave in and put the girl on the line.

"Unca Beau," Heather said in her breathless, toothless six-year-old lisp. "Do you know where my daddy is?"

"No, Heather, I don't. But I can probably find him. Have you eaten breakfast?"

"Not yet."

"Well, you go eat. I'll make some phone calls."

"Do you think he's okay?"

"Of course he's okay. You just go eat your breakfast and do what Mrs. Edwards tells you, all right?"

"All right," she agreed reluctantly. It was clear Maxine Edwards had her hands full.

"Put Mrs. Edwards back on the phone," I ordered. In a moment the babysitter's voice came on the line. "I still haven't found out anything," I told her. "But I'll let you know as soon as I do."

When I hung up, I dialed the department. The motor pool told me Peters had turned his vehicle back in at nine the previous evening. That didn't help much.

I headed for the shower. "What are you going to do?" Ames asked me on my way past.

"Go and see if his car is still in the parking garage down on James."

"Wait for me. I'll go along."

It turned out the Datsun was there. It sat, waiting patiently, in a tiny parking place up on the second floor of the parking garage. So much for that. Wherever Peters was, he wasn't driving his own car.

I walked back down the ramp of the garage to where Ames waited in the Porsche.

"It's here," I told him.

"What does that mean?"

"I don't know."

"What are you going to do now?"

"Check in with the department and see if he stopped by his desk when he dropped off the car."

He hadn't. Or, if he had, he had left nothing showing on his desk that gave me a clue about his next destination. I paused long enough to try checking with a couple of night-shift detectives to see if they had seen Peters.

To begin with, you don't call guys who work night shift at ten o'clock in the morning unless you have a pretty damn good reason. I got my butt reamed out good by the first two detectives who told me in no uncertain terms that they hadn't seen anything and wouldn't tell me if they had and why the hell was I calling them at this ungodly hour of the morning.

The third one, a black guy named Andy Taylor, is one of the most easygoing people I've ever met. Nothing rattles him, not even being awakened out of a sound sleep.

"Ron Peters?" he asked once he was really awake. "Sure, I saw him last night. He came in around nine, maybe a little later."

"Was he alone?" I asked.

Andy laughed. "Are you kiddin'? He most certainly was not."

"He wasn't?"

"Hell no. Had some little ol' gal in tow. Looked like the two of them were havin' a great time."

"Auburn hair? Short?" I asked.

"You got it."

"And did Peters say if they were going anywhere in particular?"

Again Andy laughed. "He didn't say, but I sort of figured it out, if you know what I mean."

"Yes," I said. "I guess I do."

"How come you're checkin' on him, Beau? You afraid he's gettin' some and you're not?"

"Up yours, Taylor," I said, then hung up.

While I was using the phone at Peters' desk, Ames had been sitting at mine, listening with some interest to my side of the conversation. "So where's our little lost sheep?" he asked when I put the phone down.

"Being led around by his balls," I replied.

"Is that what you're going to tell Maxine Edwards?" I looked at Ames. He was grinning like a Cheshire cat.

"No, God damn it. That's not what I'm going to tell Mrs. Edwards."

"What then?"

"That he's working and he'll call as soon as he can."

I did just that, punching Peters' telephone number into the receiver like I was killing bugs. Mrs. Edwards answered after only one ring. She must have been sitting on top of the phone. "Hello."

"Hi, Mrs. Edwards. Beau here. I haven't located Peters yet, but I understand he's working. He'll call home as soon as he can."

"And I should just stay here with the kids?"

"Why not take them to a movie. It'll get their minds off their father."

"That's a good idea. Maybe I'll do just that."

As I stood up to leave, Ames handed me a yellow message sheet that he had plucked off my desk. "Did you see this?" he asked.

The message was from Don Yamamoto in the crime lab, asking me to call. I did. Naturally, on Saturday morning, Don himself wasn't in. The State Patrol answered and tried to give me the runaround. When I insisted, they agreed to have Don Yamamoto call me back.

"It's about the flour container," he said when we finally made the connection.

"What about it?"

"We got a good set of prints off Ridley's belt and also off the inside of the flour container. We're sending them to D.C. to see if we can get any kind of match."

"Great," I told him. "That's good news."

When I hung up the phone the second time, I told Ames what the crime lab had said as we marched out of the office.

Despite the good news from Yamamoto, I was still mad enough to chew nails. It was one thing if Peters wanted to get his rocks off with someone he had just met. I didn't have any quarrel with that. Peters' sex life was none of my concern, one way or the other. What burned me was that he had been so irresponsible about it. If not irresponsible, then certainly inconsiderate. Mrs. Edwards was upset. His kids were upset. So was I for that matter.

The least he could have done was call home, give some lame excuse or another, and *then* go screw his brains out. That way I wouldn't have been dragged out of a sound sleep and neither would Andy Taylor.

"So where are we going," Ames asked me once he caught up with me on the street. "Back to your place?"

"Not on your life. I'm not going to spend all day sitting there fielding phone calls for some wandering Romeo. And I'm not going to try calling his girlfriend's house, either."

"Why not?" Ames asked.

"Because I don't feel like it. Want to go whack a few golf balls around a golf course?"

Ames stopped in his tracks. "You really are pissed, aren't you? I've never once heard you threaten to play golf before."

"Nobody said anything about playing golf," I muttered. "I want to hit something. Hitting golf balls happens to be socially acceptable."

"As opposed to hitting someone over the head?" Ames asked. "Ron Peters in particular?"

"That's right."

"Golf it is," said Ames. "Lead the way."

CHAPTER 24

The Foster Golf Course in Tukwila was the only place a couple of rank amateurs could get a toehold and a tee time on a sunny Saturday afternoon in March. We chased balls for eighteen holes' worth and were more than happy to call it quits. Ames wanted a hamburger. Just to be mean, I dragged him to what used to be Harry and Honey's Dinky Diner, until Honey ran Harry off and removed his name from the establishment. We had cheap hamburgers before returning to my apartment late in the afternoon.

On the kitchen counter, the little red light on my new answering machine was blinking cheerfully, announcing a message. Grudgingly, I punched the play button and waited to see what would happen. The machine blinked again, then burped, whirred, and beeped.

"Beau, I just . . ." a voice began, followed by the dial tone and then an operator's voice announcing, "If you wish to place a call, please hang up and dial again. If you need help, hang up and dial your operator."

Ames came out of the bathroom and wandered into the kitchen just as I punched the play button again. "Who was it?" he asked.

"I don't know. I think it's Peters," I told him. "He sounded funny, though. Hang on a minute. I'm playing it again."

When I heard the message the second time, I was sure the caller was Peters, but once more he was cut off, practically in mid-word.

"That's all?" Ames asked. "Are there any other messages?"

"No, just this one."

I picked up the phone and dialed Peters' number in Kirkland. Tracie, Peters' older daughter, answered the phone instantly. Disappointment was evident in her voice when she realized I wasn't her father.

"Oh, hi, Uncle Beau. Is my daddy with you?" she asked.

"No, he's not."

"When will he be home?"

"I don't have any idea, sweetie. Let me talk to Mrs. Edwards."

"She's taking a nap. I'm taking care of Heather for her. Should I wake her up?"

"No, never mind. She's probably tired. I'll call back later." I hung up.

"He's still not there?" Ames asked.

"No, and that message on the machine has me worried."

Ames nodded. "Me, too. Mind playing it again?"

I did. It proved to be no different from the first two times we had heard it. The message simply ended in mid-sentence with no reason given.

"You're right. It sounds strange," Ames commented after the message had finished playing. "He seemed upset."

"That's what I thought, too. I've got a bad feeling about all this."

"Why not try the department once more," Ames suggested. "Maybe he showed up there while we were out playing golf."

I tried, but no such luck. No one had heard from him. For a long time I stood with the phone in my hand, my dialing finger poised above the numbers, wondering what I should do. There was a big part of me that wanted to go on living in a fool's paradise, believing that everything was hunky-dory, that Peters was just getting his rocks off with Andi Wynn and didn't care if the sun rose or set. But there was another part of me, the partner part of me, that said something was wrong. Dead wrong.

I finally dialed Sergeant Watkins at home. Watty has been around Homicide two years longer than I have. He's virtually unflappable. "What's up, Beau?" he asked when he knew who was on the phone.

As briefly as possible I summarized what I knew, that Peters had stayed out all night, that he had been fine when he dropped off the departmental vehicle at nine, that he had been seen on the fifth floor in the company of a young woman, and that he had left an abortive message on my answering machine at home.

"So what are you proposing?" Watty asked when I finished my recitation.

"File a missing persons report for starters," I said.

"Missing persons or sour grapes?" he asked.

"Watty, I'm serious about this. It's not like him to go off and not bother to call home."

"Now look here, Beau. Let's don't hit panic buttons. You know as well as I do how long it's been since Peters' wife took off. And you know, too, that he's had his hands full with those two kids of his. In other words, he hasn't been getting any. Give the guy a break."

"But Watty . . ."

"But Watty nothing. We don't accept missing persons reports for at least twenty-four hours. You told me yourself that Andy Taylor saw him at nine o'clock last night. Nine o'clock is still a good five hours away. If you go ahead and file a report, he'll probably show up and be pissed as hell that you're advertising his love life all over the department."

"But . . ." I tried again.

"No, and that's final."

Watty hung up and so did I.

"I take it he didn't think much of the idea," Ames observed mildly.

"Right."

I paced over to the window and stared down at the street below. It was Saturday and the area of the city around my building was like a deserted village. No cars moved on the street. No pedestrians wandered the sidewalks. Only a live bum kept company with the bronze one in the tiny park at the base of what I call the Darth Vader Building at Fourth and Lenora.

"So what are you going to do?" Ames asked. "Are we just going to sit around here and do nothing?"

"No, we're not," I replied. "I'm going to go to Candace Wynn's place, pry that worthless bastard out of the sack, and knock some sense into him. After that, I'll hold a gun to his head and make him call his kids."

Ames nodded. "Sounds reasonable to me," he said.

"Are you coming along, or not?" I asked.

Ames shook his head. "I think you'd better take me over to Kirkland and drop me off at Peters' house. You've got a bad feeling about it, and so do I. Somebody should be there with his kids, just in case."

One look at Ames' set expression told me his mind was made up. I shoved the paper with Andi Wynn's address into my pocket. "Good thinking," I agreed. "Let's get going." After I jotted down Candace Wynn's address from the file, Ames and I took off.

I didn't let any grass grow under my steel-belted radials as we raced across the Evergreen Point Bridge toward Kirkland. For a change there was hardly any traffic. The needle on the Porsche's speedometer hovered around seventy-five most of the way there. I screeched off the Seventieth Street exit on 405 and slid to a stop in front of Peters' modest suburban rambler.

I glanced at Ames. His ashen color told me we had made the trip in record time.

Heather and Tracie were out in the front yard tossing a frisbee back and forth. They dashed over to the car, pleased to see me and thrilled to see Ames. Ralph was the person who had bailed them out of their mother's religious commune in Broken Springs, Oregon. He is also one of the world's softest touches as far as little girls are concerned. They look on him as one step under Santa Claus and several cuts above the Tooth Fairy.

The two of them smothered him with hugs and kisses while he scrambled out of the Porsche.

"Call as soon as you can," he said, leaning back inside the car to speak to me. "I'll hold the fort here."

As I turned the car around in the driveway, he was walking up the sidewalk into the house with a brown-haired child dangling from each arm. Ames is my attorney, but he's also one hell of a good friend. He somehow manages to be in the right place at the right time, just when I need the help. No matter what was going on with Peters, Heather and Tracie couldn't have been in better hands.

Relieved, I flew back across the bridge. My mind was going a mile a minute, rehearsing my speech, the scathing words which would tell Detective Ron Peters in no uncertain terms that I thought he was an unmitigated asshole. In my mind's ear, I made a tub-thumping oration, covering the territory with pointed comments about rutting season and bitches in heat. In my practice run, Andi Wynn didn't get off scot-free, either. Not by a long shot!

The area west of the Fremont Bridge and north of the Ship Canal is a part of Seattle that hasn't quite come to grips with what it wants to be when it grows up. There's a dog food factory, a dry cleaning equipment repair shop, and a brand new movie studio sound stage. Added into the mix are Mom-and-Pop businesses and residential units in various stages of flux, from outright decay to unpretentious upscale.

Andi Wynn's address was actually on an alley between Leary and North Thirty-fifth, a few blocks north of the dog food factory. The fishy stench in the air told me what they were using for base material in the dog food that particular day.

I remembered Andi had told us that she lived in the watchman's quarters of an old building. The place turned out to be an old, ramshackle two-story job with a shiny metal exterior stairway and handrail leading up to a door on the second floor. An oil slick near the bottom of the stairs testified as to where Andi Wynn usually parked her pickup truck. Right then, though, the Chevy Luv was nowhere in sight.

I parked the Porsche in the pickup's parking place and bounded up the stairs. Halfway to the top, I tripped over my own feet and had to grab hold of the handrail to keep from falling. I caught my balance, barely. When I let go of the rail, my hand came away sticky.

The paint on the handrail wasn't wet, but it was fresh enough to be really tacky. The palm of my hand had silver paint stuck all over it.

"Shit!" I muttered, looking around for somewhere besides my clothes or the wall to wipe the mess off my hand. I turned and went back down the stairs. Partway down the alley, an open trash can sat with its cover missing. Whoever had painted the rail had used that particular can to dispose of painting debris, from old rags to newspapers. I grabbed one of the rags, mudded off my hand, and started back up the stairs.

Pausing where I had tripped, I examined the damage I'd done to the fresh paint. There, clearly visible beneath the fresh silver paint, was a scar. A deep blue scar.

I'm not sure how long I stood there like a dummy, gazing at the smudge in the paint. My eyes recorded the information accurately enough, but my mind refused to grasp what it meant.

Blue paint. What was it about blue paint?

When it finally hit me, it almost took my breath away. Flakes of paint, blue metal paint, had been found in Darwin Ridley's hair! And around the top end of the noose that had killed him.

"Jesus H. Christ!" I dashed on up the stairs and pounded on the door. "Police," I shouted. "Open up!"

There was no answer. I'd be damned if I was going to ass around looking for some judge to sign a search warrant, or call for a backup, either.

The first time I hit the door with my foot, it shuddered but didn't give way. The second time, the lock shattered under my shoe. With my drawn .38 in hand, I charged into the tiny apartment.

Nobody was home.

J. P. Beaumont rides to the rescue, and nobody's there. It's the story of my life.

CHAPTER 25

Cautiously, and without holstering my .38, I gave the place a thorough once-over. By the time I finished, I was beginning to worry about kicking down the door.

As nearly as I could tell, nothing seemed amiss in the apartment. There was no sign of any struggle. It looked like the bed had been slept in on both sides. I found nothing to indicate a hurried leave-taking. The closet was still full of clothes, and the dresser drawers contained neat stacks of female underwear.

Finally, I put my gun away, picked up the phone, and dialed Sergeant Watkins. At home. I figured I was going to get my ass chewed, and I wanted to get it over with as soon as possible.

Watty was particularly out of sorts when he came on the phone. It sounded like he was out of breath. I had a pretty fair idea what Saturday evening activity my phone call might have interrupted.

"I just broke into Candace Wynn's apartment," I told him without preamble. "Nobody's here."

"You what?" he demanded.

"You heard me. I broke into her apartment, hoping to find Peters. They're not here. Now I need some help."

"You're damn right about that! You need more than help. You need to have your goddamned head examined! You ever hear of a fucking search warrant? You ever hear of probable cause?"

"Watty, listen to me. That's what I'm trying to tell you. I've found something important. Remember the blue paint on the rope that killed Ridley and the chips of paint they found in his hair? I think I've found where it came from. I want a crime scene investigator from the crime lab over here on the double."

"Over where?" he asked. "To a place you've broken into without so much as a by-your-leave, to say nothing of a search warrant?"

"Did you hear what I said?"

"I heard you all right. Now you hear me. No way is someone coming over there until you have an airtight search warrant properly filled out, signed, sealed, and delivered. Understand?"

"But Watty," I objected. "It's Saturday night. Where am I going to find a judge at this hour?"

"That's your problem, buster. And you make damn sure it's a superior court judge's signature that's on that piece of paper. I don't want someone throwing it back in our faces later because it's just some lowbrow district court judge. You got that?"

"I don't want to leave here, though," I protested lamely. "What if they come back while I'm gone and find the door broken?"

"You pays your money, and you takes your choice," Watty told me. "You get your ass out of there and don't go back until you have that warrant in your hot little hand."

Watty was adamant. There was no talking him out of it. "All right, all right. I'll go get your fucking search warrant. But we're wasting time."

"You'll be wasting even more time if somebody files a breaking-and-entering or illegal-search complaint against you. Now, give me the address. I'll get somebody over there to watch it until you get back."

Grudgingly, I drove back down to the Public Safety Building, parked in a twenty-four-hour loading zone, and went upstairs to type out the proper form. When I finished typing, I grabbed the list of judges' home phone numbers and started letting my fingers do the walking. I didn't know it, but I was in for a marathon.

Fifteen no answers and three answering machines later, I finally spoke to a human being, a judge's wife, not a judge. She sounded more than a little dingy. According to her, all the judges she knew, including her husband, were in Olympia for a retirement banquet for one of the state supreme court justices. She would have been there herself, she assured me, but she was just getting over the shingles.

The lady must have been pretty lonely. She was so happy to have someone to talk to that she could have kept me on the phone for hours, giving me a detailed, blow-by-blow description of all her symptoms, but I was in a hurry. I cut her off in mid-diagnosis. "Where in Olympia?" I asked.

"I beg your pardon?"

"The banquet," I said, pulling her back on track. "Where is it?"

"Oh, at the Tyee," she answered. "At least I think that's what the invitation said. Since I wasn't going, I didn't pay that close attention."

I thanked her and hung up. Olympia is sixty miles or so south of Seattle.

Fortunately, the Porsche was still there when I went back outside. It hadn't been towed. It didn't even have a ticket plastered to its windshield. The parking enforcement officers must have been taking a coffee break. So was the State Patrol on I-5. I had clear sailing, and I drove like an absolute maniac—forty minutes flat from the time I left the Public Safety Building until I pulled into the parking lot at the Tyee.

I had driven the last twenty miles with my bladder about to burst, so my first priority was to find a restroom and take a leak. A dapper little guy in a suit and tie was having a hell of a time aiming. He was a little worse for wear, but I thought I recognized him.

"You wouldn't happen to be a judge from Seattle, would you?"

He grinned fuzzily. "That's right. Do I know you?"

He didn't then, but by the time he finished signing the search warrant, we were old pals. I grabbed the paper out of his hand and beat it back toward the car. I was back on the Fremont Bridge thirty-eight minutes later.

Happily, Sergeant Watkins hadn't been sitting around playing with himself in my absence. He had alerted the crime scene team and had worked out a treaty with King County for them to bring their laser printfinder along to the apartment. The King County Police crime scene van was parked in Candace Wynn's parking place.

Watty must have pulled out all the stops to conjure up that kind of interdepartmental cooperation on such short notice on a Saturday evening.

There was quite a crowd gathering between the alley and Leary Way. In the process of rounding up everybody we needed, Watty had inadvertently summoned the fourth estate. I found an unwelcome welcoming committee of reporters waiting for me behind the police barricade.

I parked the Porsche and started to make my way through the crowd. Somebody stopped me. "What's happening, Detective Beaumont?" a reporter asked, shoving a microphone in my face. "What's going on in there?"

Someone else recognized me. "Hey, Detective Beaumont, this another homicide? How many does that make this week? You guys going for some kind of record?"

Ignoring the cameras, I pushed on, wondering if there wasn't some other kind of work I could do that wouldn't put me in daily contact with the press.

When I finally reached the bottom of the stairway, I stopped to examine the motley crew Watty had assembled—two latent-evidence examiners from the crime lab, a beefy sheriff's department deputy packing what looked to be a large suitcase, a King County ID person, two night-shift homicide detectives from the department, and a uniformed S.P.D. officer. Each of them nodded to me in turn, but no one said anything.

Sergeant Watkins himself was waiting at the top of the stairs. He stood blocking the doorway, glaring down at me, arms crossed truculently across his chest. He looked like what he wanted was a good fight. "Give it to me," he demanded when I came up the stairs.

"Give you what?" I asked.

"The warrant, for chrissakes!" He held out his hand. I removed the warrant from my inside jacket pocket and slapped it into the palm of his hand. Holding it up to the dim glow of a street lamp half a block away, he studied it for a long time.

"All right," he said finally. "Break the door down."

For the first time, I looked at the door. Sure enough, while I had been driving up and down the freeway to and from Olympia, someone had jerry-rigged the door back together.

"How'd it get fixed?" I asked. "Did she come back home?"

"I fixed it, you asshole," Watty whispered through clenched teeth. "Now break this mother-fucker down, and make it look good. I want a picture of this on every goddamned television station in town."

I understood then why Sergeant Watkins was at the top of the steps and everyone else was waiting down below. Watty's nobody's fool. He was looking out for my ass, and his, too. It was all I could do to keep from laughing out loud as I kicked Candace Wynn's door in one more time. Once more with feeling. Take it from the top. J. P. Beaumont does "Miami Vice."

The only problem was, I kicked the door like it was really locked, like it hadn't been wrecked only hours before. I almost broke my neck when it caved in under my foot.

Once inside, Watty motioned the rest of the troops to join us. It turned out the suitcase contained King County's laser printfinder. The deputy, huffing, lugged the case up the stairs and put it down in the middle of Candace Wynn's living room.

The printfinder weighs around eighty pounds or so, and it works off a regular 110 volt plug-in. He fired it up, plugging it into an outlet right there in the room. The crime scene investigators dusted the various surfaces in the room with a fluorescent powder. Then, one of them donned a pair of goggles.

"Okay, you guys," the other said. "Here go the lights."

With that, he turned out all the lights in the room. We were plunged into darkness. The only illumination was the finger of light from the printfinder as it played over the glowing powder and the periodic flashes from a 35-mm camera as the other investigator snapped pictures.

I felt like a kid who had stumbled into a midnight session with a Ouija board. There was nothing to do but stand there with my hands in my pockets and wait as the investigator ran the lens in the end of a length of fiber optic cable over everything that wasn't readily movable and bagged up everything that was.

He picked up prints from everywhere—the table, the refrigerator, the bathroom counter and mirror, the couch and chair in the living room, all the while recording the prints on film for later examination. Not only did the laser pick up prints, it also located other bits of trace evidence—hairs and fiber fragments that would have been tough to find with the naked eye.

Finally, tired of doing nothing, the rest of the team went outside. The other homicide detectives gathered a series of paint scraping samples from the handrail on the stairs. I showed them which garbage can had held the painting debris I had discovered earlier in the evening when I had been looking for something to use to clean my hands.

Fascinated by the workings of the laser, I went back inside and followed the deputy around like a puppy. I was so intrigued with the process that I failed to notice when one of the crime lab boys came to the door and motioned Watty aside. Moments later, Watty switched on the lights.

"Hey, why'd you do that?" the laser operator griped.

"Can you take that thing outside?" Watty demanded. He looked more anxious, more upset, than I had ever seen him. His whole demeanor vibrated with unmistakable urgency.

"Now?"

Watty nodded.

"I guess we can finish up in here later," the tech grumbled. "But I'll have to get the van to fire up the generator. I thought we were going to be inside. Nobody told me we'd be working outside. I need a place to plug all this shit in."

"What's up?" I asked Watty as soon as they called the deputy back upstairs to carry the equipment down to the alley. "What did they find?"

"Come see for yourself," Watty said grimly.

I followed him outside and down the steps. The King County van had been moved farther down the alley and was parked next to the garbage can. The deputy was busy hauling out power cables to hook the laser up outside.

As we started away from them without acknowledging their presence, the members of the press put up a hell of a fuss.

"Ignore them," Watty ordered. I was only too happy to oblige.

We walked down the alley and gathered around the garbage can like a group of male witches around a mysterious caldron. Standing to one side, I watched as the laser operator lowered his cable into the can. The brilliant light illuminated only a tiny area at a time. Someone had removed the top layer of paint-sodden rags. I moved even closer to see what had been unearthed, what the light was focusing on.

It was a bottle, a tiny medicine bottle, the kind liquid narcotics are stored in before someone sucks them into a syringe.

I turned to Watty then. "Morphine?" I asked.

He nodded, saying nothing.

"Oh, shit!" I muttered. Sick with dread, I turned to walk away.

Just beyond the police barricade, a cameraman caught me walking back down the alley. As I passed him, I was aware of the red light from his videocam shining full on my face. It was then I realized I had never called Ames to let him know what was going on, and here I was, live, on the eleven o'clock news.

I wanted to grab the camera out of the man's hands and shove it down his throat. I didn't.

Excessive common sense is one of the few side benefits of advancing middle age.

Unfortunately, it's also a symptom of despair.

CHAPTER 26

We went back into Candace Wynn's apartment, eventually, after the deputy had used the laser to go over everything of interest in the garbage can. By then, Watty was as serious as hell. The morphine bottle was no joke. He watched over our shoulders while the crime scene team, the other two Seattle P.D. detectives, and I scoured the place inch by inch. We found a number of useful items, including the automobile license renewal form on Andi's Chevy Luv. Watty phoned the license number in to dispatch and told them to put out an APB on Candace Wynn.

I lost all track of time. Long after one in the morning somebody thought to reach down behind the couch cushions. There, stuck in the crack between the springs and the back of the couch, we discovered a small, dark, leather wallet. I recognized it at once.

"That's Peters'," I said.

Sure enough. Inside we found both his badge and his departmental ID. I felt like somebody had kicked me in the stomach.

Right up until then, I suppose I'd kept hoping I was wrong. Hoping that, despite the mounting evidence, Peters would show up and chew my butt for pushing panic buttons when he was just out knocking off a piece of ass. Finding his badge corked it for me. Cops don't get separated from their badges without a fight. Or without a reason.

When we finally left Candace Wynn's apartment, Watty and I took our separate vehicles and drove back downtown to the Public Safety Building. I went upstairs to write my report while a team from the crime lab night shift went to work as fast as they could on comparing the prints we'd found on the things in Joanna Ridley's trunk with the prints in Candace Wynn's apartment.

With every moment vital, it was frustrating to realize that the process, which would take several hours of manual labor, could have been done in a matter of seconds with a computerized fingerprint identification unit. The last request for one had been turned down cold by the state legislature.

When I finished my report, I stamped around the fifth floor, railing at anybody who would listen about goddamned stupid legislators who were penny wise and pound foolish.

In the meantime, another team downstairs had tackled the paint samples. It turns out that paint samples take a hell of a lot less time to compare than fingerprints. My friend, Janice Morraine, called me at my desk about three-thirty in the morning to let me know that the samples taken from Candace Wynn's porch matched those taken from Darwin Ridley's hair as well as those from the rope found in Joanna Ridley's trunk.

That one little chip of information told me who. It didn't tell me why or how. And it didn't give me a clue as to where she was right then.

I left the office about four. I had caught my second wind. Instead of driving home to my apartment, I headed for Kirkland. I needed to talk to Ames and tell him what we had found, to say nothing of what we hadn't. I also needed his calm assessment of the situation.

Much to my surprise, even at that late hour the lights were blazing in Peters' living room. I peered in the window of the door and caught a glimpse of Ames' head peeking over the back of a chair. His face was pointed at a snowy, otherwise blank television screen on the other side of the room.

A series of light taps on the window brought Ames scrambling to his feet. "Who is it?" He opened the door, then stood back, rubbing his eyes. "Oh, it's you," he mumbled. "Did you find anything?"

Ames led me into the kitchen, where we scrounged around for sandwich makings while I told him what I knew. He nodded as I talked.

"I watched the news at eleven," he commented somberly. "The reporters didn't have any idea what was going on, but I could tell it wasn't good."

"Did Heather and Tracie see it?" I asked.

He shook his head. "Mrs. Edwards finally talked them into bed about ten."

"Good."

Over a thick tuna sandwich, I finished the story, including all the minute details I could remember, from the paint samples and the morphine bottle to Peters' ID holder hidden in the couch.

Me and my big mouth.

When I ended my story, the room got quiet. It was then I heard the sound of a muted whimper coming from the other room.

Hurrying to the pocket door between the kitchen and the dining room, I slid it open. There, crouched on the floor, I discovered Tracie, her whole body shaken by partially muffled sobs.

"Tracie, what is it? What's the matter?"

I picked her up and held her against my chest. "You didn't find my daddy. You promised you would and you didn't."

I touched her brown hair, smoothing it away from her tearstained cheeks. "Shhh, sweetie," I whispered. "It's all right."

She pulled away and looked at me reproachfully. "It's not all right. He's dead," she declared. "I know he's dead."

"No, Tracie. Your daddy's not dead. He's lost, and we're going to find him. You wait and see."

"But what if he is," she insisted stubbornly. "That's what happens on TV. The bad guys and the good guys shoot each other. Usually, the bad guys die. But sometimes the good guys die, too."

Ames came over and gave Tracie's head a comforting pat. "This isn't TV, Tracie. Everything's going to be all right. You'll see."

"But what if?"

"Don't you worry. You go back to bed and let Uncle Beau and me handle it. It's late. Mrs. Edwards said you have to go to Sunday school in the morning."

"I don't want to go to Sunday school."

"Too bad." Ames reached out and took Tracie from my arms. She went without objection. He carried her out of the room and down the hall. When he returned to the kitchen, he was alone.

"Will she stay in bed?" I asked.

"We'll see," he answered.

"Goddamned television," I muttered.

Ames sat down across the kitchen table from me, a small, tight frown on his face. He rubbed his forehead wearily. "What would happen to the girls?" he asked.

"You mean if something happened to Peters?"

Ames nodded again. "Has he made any arrangements? Do you have any idea?"

I shrugged. "We've never talked about it."

"Somebody should have talked about it long before this," he said grimly. "And that somebody should have been me. It's my job."

"Come on now, Ralph. Don't blame yourself. We're all doing the best we can."

Unconvinced, Ames shook his head. "In a custody case like this, especially one where the mother is out of the country, I should have taken care of it."

I had come to Kirkland hoping Ames would make me feel better. Instead, he succeeded in doing just the reverse. The two of us sat there conferring miserably until fatigue finally caught up with us.

It was starting to get light outside when I bailed out and told him I had to get some sleep. Neither one of us went near Peters' bed. We rummaged around in a linen closet and found blankets and pillows. Ames took the couch. Stripped down to my T-shirt and shorts, I settled down on the floor.

I must have fallen asleep the instant my head touched the pillow. I was dead to the world when thirty-five pounds of kid did a belly flop onto my chest, knocking the wind out of me.

"Unca Beau, Unca Beau," Heather lisped. "Can I use the blanket, too?"

Unable to speak, I held up the blanket. A chilly, pajama-clad kid wormed her way into my arms, snuggling contentedly against my chest.

"Is Daddy still asleep?" she asked.

"I don't know, Heather. He's not here."

She sat up and looked at me accusingly. "He isn't? You said you were going to find him."

"I'm trying, but I haven't been able to yet."

"When will you?"

"I don't know. I can't say."

She got up and stood glaring scornfully down at me, both hands on her hips. "I want him home *now*," she announced. With that, she turned, flounced down the hallway without a backward glance, marched into her bedroom, and slammed the door.

"Sounds like 'Unca Beau' is in deep shit," Ames observed dryly from the couch.

I struggled clumsily off the floor with my bad back screaming at me. I'm too old to sleep on floors. " 'Unca Beau' is going to get the hell downtown and find out what the fuck is going on," I growled, throwing the wad of bedding onto a nearby chair.

I glanced at the couch, where Ames still lay with the blanket pulled up to his chin. "Are you coming or not?"

"Not. I'll stay here," he said. "I think it's best."

I had to agree. When I finally got moving, I discovered the hour or so of sleep had done me a world of good. I was awake and alert as I started toward the city. I drove with my mind racing off in a dozen different directions at once: Why? And how? And where? Those were the basic questions, but where was the most important.

Where could they be? With every passing hour, that question became more critical. I was convinced Peters was being held somewhere against his will. As time passed, Andi Wynn had to be getting more and more desperate. And dangerous.

Through a series of mental gymnastics I had managed to keep my mind from touching on the bottom-line question, the question I had fought to avoid all night long. But as I crossed the bridge to return to Seattle, the question asserted itself, surging full-blown to the surface: Was Detective Ron Peters still alive?

Yes, he was alive, I decided, feeling my grip tighten involuntarily on the steering wheel. He couldn't be dead. No way. Like Heather, I wanted him home and alive. Now.

Fighting for control, I took a deep breath. In the twenty-four hours since Mrs. Edwards had first called me, I had worked my way through a whole progression of feelings, from being pissed because Peters was out screwing his brains out to being worried sick that he was being held someplace with a gun to his head.

But once the idea of death caught hold of me, I couldn't shake it. It filled up the car until I could barely breathe.

The badge and ID told me Peters wasn't in control when he left Candace Wynn's apartment. The morphine bottle hinted at why. I suspected morphine had given Andi the edge both with Darwin Ridley and with Peters, providing a chemical handcuff every bit as effective as the metal variety.

And if Andi Wynn had indeed killed Darwin Ridley, then I had to believe she was capable of killing again. It was my job to find her, to stop her, before she had the chance.

Downtown Seattle was a ghost town at seven-fifteen on Sunday morning. I parked the Porsche in front of the Public Safety Building and hurried inside. There were only two people visible in the crime lab when I was led into the room. One of them was my friend, Janice Morraine. She reached into her lab coat pocket, removed a package of cigarettes, and nodded toward the door. "Let's go outside," she said.

As soon as we were out in the elevator lobby, she lit up. "Did you find Peters?" she asked, blowing a long plume of smoke toward the ceiling.

I shook my head. "Not yet. What's the scoop on the stuff we brought in?"

She shrugged. "We've got matches everywhere—the prints from Ridley's clothes, from the flour container, from the Fremont apartment, and from Joanna Ridley's house as well."

I felt the cold grip of fear in my gut. Looking at Janice's somber face, I could see she felt it, too.

"What does that say to you?" I asked.

"That the killer doesn't give a damn whether you catch him or not."

The knot in my gut got a little tighter, a little colder. I pushed the call button on the elevator.

"That's what I was afraid you'd say, but it's a her," I added.

Janice blew another plume of smoke and ground out the remains of her barely smoked cigarette in the sand-filled ashtray in the hall. "Good luck," she said softly.

I stepped into the elevator. "Thanks," I told her. "We'll need it."

When the elevator stopped on the fifth floor, I was almost run over by two detectives who charged through the open door. One of them grabbed me by the sleeve and dragged me back inside as the door slid shut.

"Hey, wait a minute. I wanted off."

"You'd better come with us," Big Al Lindstrom ordered.

"How come? What's up?"

"Somebody just spotted that missing Chevy Luv," he answered.

"No shit? Where?"

"Parked in front of Mercer Island High School. That's where we're going."

"Who's we?" I asked.

"Baxter here and me. You, too, if you want. Mercer Island Police say they have the place pretty well sealed off, but they called us to let us know."

Big Al and Baxter got off at the garage level. I had to ride down to the lobby and charge down the street half a block to where I had parked, but once I fired up the Porsche, there was no contest. I passed Big Al and Baxter on the bridge like they were standing still.

I'm not sure if it was because the Porsche was a better car or because Peters was my partner.

Actually, it was probably a little of both.

CHAPTER 27

We raced to the high school, only to find ourselves stuck behind a police barricade along with every body else.

The next hour and a half was an agonizing study of affirmative action in action. From a distance, I caught a glimpse of the new Mercer Island Chief of Police—a lady wearing a gray pin-striped suit and sensible shoes with a dress-for-success polka dot scarf knotted tightly around her neck. She had definitely taken charge of the situation.

When Marilyn Sykes, assistant police chief in Eugene, Oregon, was hired for the job on Mercer Island, there had been a good deal of grumbling in law enforcement circles. The general consensus was that, in this particular case, the best man for the job wasn't a woman. I hadn't paid a whole lot of attention to the debate since half the complainers said she was too tough and the other half claimed she was too soft. I figured the truth was probably somewhere in between.

Right then, though, watching the action from an impotent distance, my inclination was to dismiss Marilyn Sykes as a pushy broad, one who didn't have enough confidence in herself and her position to let any other cops within consulting distance, as though she was afraid our advice and suggestions might undercut her authority.

It's something I'll remember as one of the most frustrating times of my whole life. It was only an hour and a half, but it seemed much longer. I wanted to *do* something, to take some physical action, like knocking down the barricade and making an unauthorized run for the building.

Candace Wynn's pickup had been parked right in the middle of the high school lot, with no attempt to conceal it. Chief Sykes had sealed off the entire campus and was in the process of deploying her Emergency Response Team. Directing the operation from her car, she had the team secure one building at a time.

As a cop, I couldn't help but approve of her careful, deliberate planning. It was clear the safety of her team was uppermost in her mind. But I wasn't there as just a plain cop. I was there because Peters was my partner. Marilyn Sykes' deliberateness drove me crazy. I wanted action. I wanted to get on with it.

The interminable wait was made worse by the fact that our Seattle P.D. personnel were stuck far behind the lines, rubbing shoulders with reporters and photographers, all of them angling for an angle, all of them snapping eagerly toward any snippet of information. It was clear from the questions passing back and forth between them that the names of the missing officer and the missing teacher had not yet been released. I thanked Arlo Hamilton for that. At least Peters' girls wouldn't hear it from a reporter's lips first.

As the minutes ticked by and the tension continued to build, my fuse got shorter and shorter. Finally, I turned to Big Al, who was standing beside me. His face was grim, his hands jammed deep in his jacket pockets.

"God damn it!" I complained. "Why the hell doesn't she send 'em into the gym? I'd bet money they're in the girls' locker room."

Just then someone tapped me on the shoulder. I turned around and found myself eyeball to eyeball with Chief Marilyn Sykes herself. She was a fairly tall woman in her mid-forties, with sharp, hazel eyes and a tough, overbearing way about her.

"Are you Detective Beaumont?" she demanded.

I nodded. "I am."

"As I'm sure you realize, Detective Beaumont," she continued severely, "we've got a potentially dangerous situation here. What I don't need is a Monday-morning quarterback second-guessing my decisions, is that clear?"

Chastised, I gave the only possible response I could muster: "Yes, Ma'am."

She turned on her heel. "Come with me," she ordered over her shoulder.

I looked at Big Al, whose only consolation was a sheepish shrug of his shoulders. Without a word, I followed. She led me back to where her car was parked before she stopped and waited for me. By then, we were well out of earshot of all the reporters.

"The detective who's missing, Detective Peters. He's your partner?"

"Yes."

Turning away, she reached into her car and pulled out a hand-held walkie-talkie. She flicked a switch. "Come in, George. Have you cleared the way to the locker-room door yet?"

"Check," a voice crackled from the device in her hand. "Just now."

"All right. I've got someone here, Detective Beaumont from Seattle P.D., who thinks they're in that locker room. I'm sending him in with you."

I pulled my .38 from its holster and started scrambling out of her car. "Just a minute, Detective Beaumont," she snapped.

I stopped. Chief Sykes picked up a long roll of paper from the floor of the front seat. When she spread it out on the back seat, it was a detailed architectural drawing of the high school plant. With a slender, well-manicured finger, she traced a line from where we stood to the girls' locker room.

"This is the part we've secured," she said. "Don't go any other way, understand?"

"Right," I said.

"And no heroics. You want to see your partner alive, and so do we."

Once again she reached into the front seat. This time she brought out a bulletproof vest. "Put this on," she said. "Now get going."

I shrugged my way into the flak jacket and paused for just a moment before I bailed out of the car. Marilyn Sykes met my gaze without flinching. She was tough, all right, but not in the way her detractors meant. There was a soft spot, too. Not the kind of softness that translates into weakness, but a certain empathy that told me sometime in her past she, too, had lived with a partner in jeopardy, that she knew the terrible helplessness of doing nothing.

Someday, when we had time, Chief Marilyn Sykes and Detective J. P. Beaumont would have to sit down, have a drink, and talk about it. But not now.

"Thanks," I said, then took off.

I trotted through the buildings, careful not to deviate from the path she had laid out. My footsteps echoed through the silent walkways. I'm not prone to prayer, but I found myself muttering one as I ran. "Let him be safe, God. Please let him be safe."

A uniformed Mercer Island officer motioned me into the gym. "They're waiting for you by the door to the locker room," he whispered as I passed.

Waiting they were. Three officers, all wearing bulletproof vests, crouched against the wall on either side of the door. One of them motioned for me to join him. When I was in position behind him, he raised a bullhorn to his lips.

"Come on out, Mrs. Wynn. You're surrounded. Give yourself up."

There was no answer. The blank, silent door gave no hint of what was happening on the other side. We waited one endless minute. We waited two.

"Come on out, Mrs. Wynn. Come out before we have to come in after you."

Still there was nothing. No sound. Images of bloody carnage raced through my mind. Too many years on homicide had left my imagination with too much fuel for the fire. I pictured Peters lying face down in a pool of blood or dangling on the end of a rope with his head flopped limply to one side. In the silence I heard an imaginary hail of bullets slice into the door when we attempted to push it open.

"On the count of three, we're coming in. One . . . Two . . . Three . . ." One of the members of the team on the other side of the door reached out and tried to open it. Nothing happened. It was locked.

The leader, the man beside me, nodded to the guy on the other side. "Big Bertha it is."

The third man came forward carrying a hand-held battering ram. He popped the door twice before the lock crumbled. As the door swung open, the silence was deafening.

Crouching low, weapon in hand, I followed the leader into the darkened locker room. We switched on the lights. Inside, we wormed our way around first one bank of lockers and then another. The place was empty.

Peters wasn't in the locker room, and neither was Candace Wynn. They had been there, though. At least someone had.

The locker, the one with the list in it, the Mercer Island High School cheerleader trophy list, had been smashed to pieces by someone wielding a heavy object. I could make out only one or two letters from the battered piece of metal that had once been the inscribed ceiling.

"All clear in here, Chief," the leader said into his walkie-talkie. He put the microphone into his pocket, then walked up closer to the damaged locker.

"What do you suppose went on here?" he asked.

"Beats me," I told him. Quickly, I moved away to the other side of the room, out of casual conversation range but close enough to hear him give the all-clear to Chief Sykes via his walkie-talkie. I tried my best to become invisible. Just because Chief Sykes had been kind enough to include me in the operation didn't necessarily obligate me to full disclosure. I didn't want to tell them everything I knew. That locker list might somehow still be useful.

Marilyn Sykes strode into the locker room about that time. She glanced in my direction, then walked up to join the man by the locker. "Vandalism?" I heard her ask.

The man shrugged. "I give up. It's funny, but it looks like this is the only locker that was damaged." For a moment, Chief Sykes gazed at the mangled pile of sheet metal.

"Somebody went to a hell of a lot of trouble to destroy this one," she said. Then she turned to me. "What do you think, Detective Beaumont?" she asked.

Whether or not I wanted to be, she had pulled me back into the conversation. "Do you think this has anything to do with your partner's disappearance?"

By aiming her question directly at me, Chief Marilyn Sykes created an instant moral dilemma. I owed her, goddamnit! She had let me through the barricades onto her turf, and I owed her.

"I'd have the crime lab take a look at it if I were you," I suggested. That let me off the hook without my having to give up too much.

She nodded. "All right."

Wanting to get away quick, before she could ask me anything more, I turned and walked out of the locker room. Halfway down the walkway, I ran headlong into Ned Browning rushing toward the gym. "Hello there, Ned," I said.

He stopped cold when he saw me. He was uncharacteristically agitated. "Oh, yes, Detective . . . Detective . . . I'm sorry, I don't remember your name."

"Beaumont," I supplied. "Detective Beaumont."

"You'll have to excuse me. I understand there's been some difficulty in the gym. I'd been trying to get through, but they wouldn't let me until just now. Somebody called me at home when I came back from church."

"Church," I grunted with contempt. "That figures."

Browning started forward again, but I stopped him. "I'm going to want to talk to you, too," I said. "As soon as they finish with you."

"I don't have time, Detective Beaumont. My family is waiting for me. We're having guests."

"I don't give a shit if it's the pope himself, Ned. I want to talk to you alone. About the cheerleading squad, remember them? I'm sure you remember one or two of them fairly well."

An almost audible spark of recognition passed over his face. He paled and stepped back a pace or two. "What do you mean?"

"Don't play dumb. You know what I mean," I said menacingly. "I'll wait for you at Denny's, here on the island."

"All right," he said, crumbling. "I'll meet you as soon as I'm finished here."

You're finished, all right, pal, I thought to myself, but I didn't say it aloud. I didn't have to. And I wouldn't have to lift a finger to make it happen, either. Chief Marilyn Sykes and the Washington State Patrol's crime lab would take care of all those little details.

Meanwhile, while Ned Browning still thought there was a way he could wiggle off the hook, while he still thought there was a way to save his worthless ass and his career, I'd play him for all he was worth, see if I could wrangle any helpful information out of his scared little hide.

That's one thing I've learned over the years. If you have the slightest advantage, use it. And don't worry about it after you do.

Creeps don't have any scruples.

Cops can't afford them.

CHAPTER 28

When I walked back to the Porsche, old man trouble himself, Maxwell Cole, stood slouching against the door on the driver's side.

"Get away, Max. You'll scratch the paint," I told him.

He didn't move. "Hey, there, J. P. How's it going?"

"Get out of the way. I don't have time to screw around with you." Bodily, I shoved him aside far enough so I could put my key in the lock.

"I'll bet it is Peters, isn't it? That's the rumor, anyway," he said, grinning slyly under his handlebar mustache. "I mean, he's not here, and you are. Same thing happened last night, over in Fremont, or so I hear."

"Will you get the fuck out of my way?"

"And what's the teacher's name? Candace Wynn, isn't that it?"

"I'm not talking. Leave me alone, Max."

"I won't leave you alone. I want to know what's going on. Why won't they release any names? All Arlo Hamilton does is read prepared speeches that have nothing to do with what's going on. I want the scoop, J. P., the real scoop."

"You won't get it from me, asshole. Besides, it sounds to me like Hamilton is giving you guys just what you deserve."

"What do you mean?"

"What Arlo tells you is bullshit. What you write is bullshit. Sounds like an even trade to me."

Max took an angry step toward me, but thought better of it and stayed out of reach. He glared at me for a long moment before dropping his gaze, his eyes watery and pale behind the thick lenses of his glasses. "You're not going to tell me about Peters, then?"

"You're damn right."

I flung the Porsche's door open, bouncing it off Cole's ample hip for good measure. Just to make the point. He finally moved aside.

The problem with Max is that I'm so used to avoiding him that in the crush of worrying about Peters I had forgotten I needed to talk to him. Instead of starting the car, I got back out. Max moved away from me.

"You leave me alone, J. P."

"Where'd you get the picture, Max?"

"The picture? What picture?"

"The one you wrote about but didn't print. The one of Darwin Ridley and the cheerleader."

He smirked then. "You scratch my back, I'll scratch yours."

I didn't have time to mess around with him. I turned on my heel and got back in the car.

"All I want to know is if it's Peters or not."

"Fuck you, Max."

He looked offended. "I have other ways of confirming this, you know," he whined.

"So use 'em," I told him. "Be my guest, but you'd damn well better keep your facts straight, because I'll cram 'em down your throat if you don't!"

With that, I started the engine and laid down a layer of rubber squealing out of the parking lot.

I took a meandering route to the Mercer Island Denny's through the maze of interminable road construction that has screwed up traffic there for years. Surprisingly, lots of other people had evidently done the same thing.

The restaurant was busy, jammed with the after-church/Sunday-brunch crowd. I waited almost fifteen minutes before they finally cleared out the line and showed me to a table, a short-legged two-person booth in the center of the room.

During the few minutes I was there alone, I couldn't help reflecting. The last time I had been in the room I was with Peters and Andi Wynn together, that afternoon when we finished questioning the students. That time seemed years ago, not days. Since then, my life had been run through a Waring blender. Fatigue and worry weighed me down, threatening to suck me under and drown me.

Then Ned Browning entered. He rushed through the door and stopped abruptly by the cash register to look for me. Now, starting forward again, he slowed his pace, walking deliberately and with some outward show of dignity, but nothing masked the agitation that remained clearly visible on his face.

My transformation was instantaneous. Adrenaline surged through my system, pulling me out of my stupor, putting every nerve in my body on full alert. By the time he reached the booth, my mind was honed sharp. I was ready for him.

He held out his hand in greeting, but I ignored the empty gesture. Instead, I motioned for him to sit down opposite me. If he thought I had invited him over for a nice social chat, he was wrong. The sooner Ned Browning understood that, the better.

He paused and looked down at his hand, first comprehending and then assessing the message behind my refusal to shake hands. Maybe he had convinced himself that he had mistaken the meaning in what I had said about the cheerleaders.

My insult wasn't lost on him. Ned Browning was caught, and he knew it. Flushing violently to the roots of his receding hairline, he sat down.

"What do you want?" he asked in a hoarse, subdued whisper.

It was time for poker. Time to play bluff, raise, and draw. I happened to have a pretty good hand. "What did you use?" I asked obliquely for openers.

"I beg your pardon?" He frowned. He may have been as genuinely puzzled as he looked, or he may have been playing the game.

"What did you use to smash the locker, Ned? A sledge hammer? A brick? A rock?"

He drew back in his chair as though I'd slapped him squarely across the face. His unhealthy flush was replaced by an equally unhealthy pallor. "I don't know what you're talking about!"

"Yes, you do. You know very well."

He stood up. "I've got guests waiting at home. I didn't come here to play games."

I caught the sleeve of his jacket and compelled him back into the booth. "Fuck your guests," I snarled. "Believe me, this is no game."

His eyes darted warily around the room, checking to see who was within earshot, to see if there was anyone nearby who might know him or who had overheard my rude remark.

He made an attempt to retrieve his old stuffiness. "I don't think it's necessary to use that kind of language, Mr. Beaumont."

Once upon a time I had been briefly impressed by his outward show of high-toned values. That was no longer true. His high-toned values were a sham.

"Don't pull that bullshit on me. I'm not one of your students, Ned," I reminded him. "I'll talk to you any damn way I please."

His hands dropped to his lap, but not before I caught sight of a nervous tremor. An involuntary tic touched the muscle of his left jaw. A rush of gleeful satisfaction passed through me. I was definitely making progress. Visible progress.

Just then, our waitress appeared. "Can I get you something?" she asked.

"No, nothing for me," Browning murmured shakily.

"Toast," I said. "Whole wheat. And two eggs over easy." I nodded as the waitress offered and poured coffee. Browning refused that as well. When the waitress left, I picked up my spoon and began stirring my coffee with slow deliberation. Ned Browning was already nervous. Any delaying tactic, anything that would make him sit on his powder keg a little longer, would work in my favor.

Carefully, I put down the spoon, took a long sip of coffee, then leaned forward, thrusting my face toward his, invading the body space, the distance, he had created around himself.

"Let's get down to brass tacks, Ned. When did you find out about the list?"

"What list?" He was determined to play dumb. I was in no mood to tolerate it.

"The one with you on it, Ned. The pep squad score card. As I recall, your name is on it more than once."

In the previous few minutes, a little color had returned to his face. Now it drained away again, leaving him a pasty gray. That took the fun out of it for me, calling a halt to the game. I prefer someone who offers a little more of a challenge, a worthy adversary who fields the questions and makes me work for my answers. Ned Browning caved in so easily, I almost laughed out loud.

"You know about that?"

"Lots of people know about it. More than you'd expect. They also have a pretty good idea what it took to get on it."

"But . . ."

"When did you find out about it?" I insisted. "And how?"

"But she said . . ."

"Who said?"

"Candace. Mrs. Wynn."

"What did she say?"

"That if I destroyed the locker, no one would ever know."

"Right. And why do you suppose she told you that?"

"I don't have any idea."

"When did she tell you?"

"Saturday morning. She called me at home."

"What time?"

"It must have been around ten. I was out working in the yard when she called and asked me to meet her at school."

"And you did?"

"She said it was urgent, something I needed to know."

"Where did you meet? In the locker room?"

"No. In my office."

"All right, so after you met, what happened then?"

"She told me about the list. Said she'd just found out about it the night before, at Darwin Ridley's memorial service."

The little orange warning light in the back of my head started flashing. I had a vivid memory of Candace Wynn looking at the list in the locker after Peters and I found it. She had known about it for sure since then, and maybe even before that. Why had she lied to Browning about when she found out, and what had made it so urgent?

"So what happened?" I urged impatiently. "Go on."

"She said if anyone else found out about it, it would be awful for everyone. She thought the best idea would be to get rid of it, both for the girls' sakes and for the men as well."

"My, my, a concern for public relations. A little late for that, wouldn't you say?"

He frowned and said nothing. The waitress brought my food and set it in front of me. Browning stared miserably at my plate as though the very idea of food sickened him.

"So you got rid of it," I commented after the waitress walked away. "Pounded the locker to pieces. Right then or later?"

"Right then. She said she had a sledge hammer in the back of her pickup. I used that."

"You used it. She didn't? Did she go with you?"

"No. She waited in my office while I got the hammer from the truck and did it."

"Where was it?"

"The hammer? I just told you, in the back of her truck."

"Not the hammer. Where was the truck?"

"Parked in front of the school. Right where it is now."

"She hasn't moved it since then?"

"I can't tell for sure, but I don't think so. It looks to me like it's in the same place."

"Who left first and when?"

"I did. About eleven-thirty or so. She said she needed to pick up something from her office. She was still at the school when I drove away."

"And there was no one with her?"

"I didn't see anybody. There wasn't anyone in the truck when I got the hammer out or when I took it back, either. I didn't see anyone else on the grounds the whole time we were there."

"Any other cars parked in the area?"

"No, just her pickup and my Olds."

"How did she leave there, then?"

Browning shrugged. "I don't know."

I stirred my coffee again, trying to make sense of what he had told me. It didn't work. Finally, I said, "Candace Wynn worked for you for several years. Did you know anything about her personal life?"

Again he shrugged. "Nothing much. She was divorced. Her father died a year or so back. Her mother's been sick for several years."

"I remember seeing a bumper sticker on her truck. Something about sailing. Do you know anything about that?"

"She's supposed to be part owner of a boat over on Shilshole. I don't know the name of it or the names of any of the co-owners."

"And her mother's sick."

"She has cancer."

"I already knew that. Do you know where she is?"

"A hospital somewhere around here. A cancer unit, I believe."

"What's her mother's name? Any idea?"

"No."

I paused for a moment, wondering if there was any easier way to track down Candace Wynn's maiden name. "Is there a blank on the school district's employment form that calls for a maiden name?"

Browning shook his head. "No."

"What about the group insurance form? If she wasn't married and didn't have any children, she might have listed her mother as beneficiary."

"That's possible, but all that information is confidential. It's in the district office."

"Can you get it for me or not?"

"Not on a weekend. I could probably get it tomorrow morning. Why do you need it?"

"Because I've got to find Candace Wynn before she kills someone else," I said.

I pushed my plate aside, picked up the bill, and stood up. Ned Browning sat motionless, shocked by my words. He stared up at me. "Kills?" he repeated.

Obviously, none of the Mercer Island Police Force had chosen to clue him in on what was happening.

"And because tomorrow may be too late," I added.

I left him sitting there in Denny's, a man frozen in stunned silence. His past had just caught up with him, and his guests waiting at home were long forgotten.

As I started the car, I didn't feel sorry for Ned Browning. Whatever disgrace was coming to him wasn't undeserved. After all, he had been on the list twice, not once. Once was once, but twice was twice.

I did feel sorry for Mrs. Browning, however. She was probably a nice enough lady, one I would never meet even though I was changing her life forever. Whoever she was, wherever she was, her world, like Joanna Ridley's, was about to fly apart. She didn't have the foggiest idea it was coming, but J. P. Beaumont was sending trouble her way.

It was just as well we would never meet.

CHAPTER 29

The only thing to do was to find Candace Wynn's mother. Somehow.

I was sitting in my car with the engine running when I realized I was going off half-cocked. I waited until Ned Browning came out of the restaurant. Expecting me to be long gone, he turned like he'd been shot when I hailed him from the Porsche. He approached the car cautiously. "What now?" he asked.

"Do you have a picture of Candace Wynn?"

"No."

"Maybe not a separate picture, but wouldn't she be in a yearbook? Do you have any?"

He nodded. "I do have one of those, at school, in my office."

"Good. Let's go get it."

He started to object but thought better of it. He led the way back to the school, where a tow truck was just hooking on to Candace Wynn's Chevy. Avoiding the crowd in the parking lot, he took me into his office and handed me a copy of the current yearbook. Mrs. Wynn's picture was there, alongside her angelic crew of cheerleaders. There was another picture as well, a more formal one, in the faculty section of the book.

"Thanks," I said. "I'll bring it back."

"Don't bother," Ned Browning told me.

If I had been in his shoes, I wouldn't have wanted to keep a copy of that particular yearbook, either.

When I left him, he was standing in the middle of his office, looking at it the way someone looks when they're getting ready to pack up and move on. Ned Browning was a man who had worn out his welcome.

The next three hours were hard on me. They shouldn't have been, I suppose. After all, I'm a homicide detective. We're supposed to be tough, right?

But tracking through those hospitals, trying to locate Candace Wynn's mother, carried me back some twenty-odd years, back to my youth and to my own mother's final illness.

Maybe part of it is that you never get over your mother's death, no matter how long you live. Being in those polished corridors with their antiseptic odors and their stainless steel trays made it seem like yesterday, not half a lifetime ago.

Pain was all around. The patients had help for theirs, however fleeting the hazy comfort of drugs might be, but my heart went out to the empty-eyed visitors I found walking the halls, lingering in the rooms. There was no prescribed medication available to lessen their hurt.

I remembered only too well when I had stumbled blindly among them, holding tightly, stubbornly, to each grim crumb of hope. And then, eventually, the day had come when all hope was gone. I had resigned myself to my mother's loss, knowing the how. That was inevitable. But for three long years I had spent every resource at my disposal, delaying as long as possible the unpredictable when.

Walking the hospital halls that bright spring afternoon, knowing the difference between the budding promise outside and the burgeoning grief inside, I could relate to Candace Wynn just a little bit. Maybe, after fighting a losing war for far too long a time, she had cracked under the strain.

I started with the obvious, the Fred Hutchison Cancer Research Center on First Hill. A lady at the front desk cheerily told me they had a master list of all the cancer patients in Seattle, but without a name, she couldn't help me. She did, however, point me in the direction of the hospitals with known cancer units—Swedish, Providence, Cabrini, and Virginia Mason on Pill Hill—and later, University Hospital, Overlake, and Northgate.

I drove like a maniac from place to place, speeding on the way, leaving the Porsche in patient-loading zones with the hazard lights flashing when I went inside.

And all the while I was driving, I kept coming back to the same question: Why had Candace lied about the locker? Why had she pretended to have heard about it only the night before, and why had she encouraged Ned Browning to destroy it? She knew we knew about it. The list wasn't something that could simply be swept under the rug and forgotten. There was some reason for her telling Browning on that particular day in that particular place. I drove and wished I had the answer.

At each hospital, it wasn't a matter of waltzing up to the head nurse, showing her Candace Wynn's picture, and getting a straight answer.

Straight answers aren't to be had from either doctors or head nurses. They're usually too close to God to talk to mere mortals. I went looking for orderlies, for hospital volunteers, for candy stripers—little people who might feel some sense of importance in being asked to help.

And help me they did. They were happy to look at the picture of Candace Wynn, and over and over they shook their heads. No, they were sure no one like that had visited any of the patients who were in that hospital right then.

And with each shake of the head, with each negative answer, the icy knot in my gut got bigger. I wasn't getting any closer. A terrible clock was ticking in my head, telling me that time was running out. I tried to tell myself it was just from being in hospitals, from seeing so many people who were sick or dying or both. But that didn't help me shake it.

The lady at Fred Hutchison had given me a list of board-approved cancer units. I visited them one by one and came up empty-handed each time. By the time I reached the last one, I was pretty discouraged.

Instead of leaving the lights flashing, I searched around and found a real parking place in the lot outside Northgate General Hospital. I ignored the noisy horde of teenyboppers on their way to the latest teenybopper movie. They were having a great time, laughing and joking and shoving one another around. I wanted to tell them to shut up and pay attention, that there was a real world out there waiting for them.

Back in my car with yet another failure, I sat for a moment, resting my head on the steering wheel. I had struck out. Tired beyond bearing, I was determined to go on, if I could just figure out where I ought to go.

I tried to collect my thoughts. It was like corralling a herd of frightened, milling sheep. I kept after it, though, and gradually, as I sat there, order returned.

Going over every conversation with Candace Wynn, playing back each one in my mind, I picked out only those things she had told me about her mother. I remembered her saying she had visited her mother in the hospital during the third quarter of the game. That had to have been fairly late in the evening. After eight o'clock. Dave Rimbaugh had told us that much. To get to a hospital from Seattle Center before visiting hours ended, it must have been one fairly close at hand.

I got out of the car and walked back through the movie-going kids and into the waiting room at Northgate General Hospital. I walked up to the main desk.

"What's the closest hospital to Seattle Center?" I asked the young black receptionist. She turned to a much older lady sitting next to her.

"What do you think, Irene?"

Irene shrugged. "Group Health up at the end of Denny, or maybe Ballard Community."

I felt a faint surge of hope. Ballard Community wasn't that far from Seattle Center, and it wasn't that far from Fremont, where Candace Wynn lived, either. I charged out the door and back through the parking lot. When I started the Porsche and peeled out of the place, I left a few young high school bucks staring after me in open-mouthed envy.

Parking on N.W. Fifty-third, I dashed into the hospital and was directed to their medical/surgical floor, 5-E. There, I tackled a lady in a bright pink jacket pushing a cart full of paperback books and newspapers down the hall. Her name tag said Mrs. Rasmussen—a good, old-fashioned Scandinavian name.

"Excuse me," I said. "I'm with Seattle P.D. I'm trying to locate a patient."

She pointed down the hall. "If you'll just go down to the nurses' station, they have a list of all the patients there."

"No, you don't understand. I don't know the patient's name." I had conducted the same conversation over and over the whole afternoon. I opened the yearbook to where a piece of paper marked Candace Wynn's smiling picture. "This is her daughter."

Mrs. Rasmussen fumbled in the pocket of her pink jacket and brought out a pair of gold-framed glasses. She perched them on her nose and peered down at the picture. "Oh, her!" she said. The disgust in her voice was unmistakable.

"Her? You mean you recognize her?"

"You say you're from the police? Well, it's about time, that's all I have to say."

516 ▼ TRIAL BY FURY

"What do you mean? What are you talking about?"

"I was telling Betty just the other day that somebody should see to it that girl goes to jail."

"But why?" I was sure that if I ever got Mrs. Rasmussen on track, she was going to tell me everything I needed to know and then some.

"You know, some of the patients complain about their kids, that they do stuff behind their backs, give away their things, move into their houses whether they want them there or not. But I was there the day she made her mother agree to sell the house. It was awful. It made me sick. Mrs. Scarborough cried and cried about it afterward."

"That's her name? Mrs. Scarborough?"

"Yes. Elaine Scarborough. Second room on the left. The bed by the window." Mrs. Rasmussen took off her glasses and patted them back into her pocket. "That's not all, either."

"It isn't?"

"She kept saying that at home her daughter sometimes wouldn't let her have her pain medication."

"Did anyone do anything about it?"

"The doctor said he was sure the visiting nurses made certain that kind of thing didn't happen. But you should have seen how happy she was to be in a hospital so she could get medication when she needed it. She was in such pain! What kind of a monster would do a thing like that? I just can't understand it!"

Mrs. Rasmussen stood there glaring at me with one hand on her hip as though she expected me to come up with an instant explanation. What kind of monster indeed! There's no understanding that kind of human aberration.

A hefty nurse came rustling officiously down the hall. Mrs. Rasmussen beat a hasty retreat into the nearest doorway, saying a cheerful "Good afternoon" to whomever was inside.

Uncertainly, I paused in the hallway for a moment too long. The nurse, observing my indecisiveness, stopped beside me. "May I help you?"

"Yes. I wanted to see Mrs. Scarborough."

"Are you a family member?" the nurse inquired.

"No. Not really." I stopped short of pulling out my badge and identifying myself. It didn't make any difference.

"I'm sorry. Mrs. Scarborough is gravely ill. Her doctors have limited visitors to family members only, and even those are allowed to stay for just a few minutes at a time."

"But it's important . . ."

The nurse took my arm and guided me firmly back toward the elevator. "There is nothing more important than our patients' well-being," she said stiffly. "If the information you have for her is so important, then it would be best if you would contact one of the family members to deliver a message."

"Could you give me the names on the approved list?"

The nurse looked at me disapprovingly and shook her head. "Now if we really were a friend of the family, we'd know those names, wouldn't we."

Yes, we certainly would.

The elevator door opened, and I got on. The nurse made sure of it. I was surprised she didn't ride all the way down to the lobby and see me out onto the street. I would have made more of an issue out of it, but I figured having the family name was enough.

I made one stop before I left the building, at the pay phone in the lobby. A frayed Seattle phone book lay on the shelf under the phone. Unfortunately, there were six Scarboroughs listed. None of them said Elaine.

Rummaging through my pockets, I dredged out a collection of quarters. I dialed the first three numbers and asked for Elaine, only to be told no one by that name lived there. On the fourth call, Candace Wynn herself answered the phone. I recognized her voice.

"Hello?"

"Wrong number," I mumbled, disguising my voice as best I could. I hung up the phone, made a note of the address, and raced toward the hospital exit door, almost smashing into the glass when the electric door in the lobby didn't open quite fast enough to let me through.

Hospital doors aren't generally timed for people moving on foot at a dead run.

CHAPTER 30

It took exactly thirteen minutes to drive from Ballard Community Hospital to Thirtieth Avenue South and South Graham. Nobody stopped me for speeding. That's always the way. Where are all the traffic cops when you need one?

Had one pulled me over, I would have sent word to the department for help. As it was, I decided to go to the Scarborough house first, try to get some idea of the lay of the land, and then call the department for a backup.

Driving east after crossing Beacon Avenue, I spotted a small Mom-and-Pop grocery store with a pay phone hanging beside the ice machine outside. I figured I'd come back there to use the phone as soon as I knew what was coming down.

As plans go, it wasn't bad. Things just didn't work out that way.

At Graham and Thirtieth South, a towering electrical transmission line dissects Beacon Hill and cuts a huge green north and south swath through the city. The Scarborough address in the phone book was 6511 Thirtieth Avenue South.

The seriousness of my miscalculation became apparent the moment I saw the house. North of Graham, Thirtieth was a regular street with houses on one side facing the wide clearing under the power lines. On the south side, though, the 6500 block dead-ended in front of the only house on the block, 6511—the Scarborough house.

So much for sneaking around. So much for subtlety. Guard red Porsches are pretty goddamned hard to camouflage on dead-end streets when there's only one house on the block and the rest is nothing but wide open spaces.

Instead of turning right onto Thirtieth, I hung a left and drove north, ditching the Porsche three houses north of Graham behind a vagrant pickup truck sitting on jacks. I figured I had a better chance of getting close to the house unobserved if I moved on foot rather than in the car. All I needed to do was get close enough to have some idea of what was going on.

There wasn't much cover, even for someone on foot. The Beacon Hill transmission line was built in the twenties and thirties to bring power from the Skagit Valley power plants into the city. The right of way was purchased from farmers along the route. Later, the city grew up around the power line.

Directly under and for twenty-five or thirty yards on either side of the long line of metal towers, emerald green grass sprang to life. It looked as though the power line had driven every other living thing but the grass out of its path.

Here and there, looking down the line, a few houses remained, almost on the right of way itself. These were mostly remnants of the original farm houses, most of them still occupied and still in good repair.

The Scarborough house was one of those, a sleepy-looking relic from another era with a steeply pitched gray roof and a graceful white porch that stretched across the entire front of the house. Two matching bay windows, opening onto the porch, were carefully curtained so no one could see inside. To the right of the walkway leading up to the house stood a "For Sale" sign with a "Sold" sticker stuck across it.

I returned to Graham. Attempting to look casual, I sauntered east, hoping for a wider view of the house as it dropped behind me. A short distance up the street was a bus stop. I stopped under the sign and turned to look behind me.

I was far enough away that, for the first time, I could see the south side of the house. Parked next to it, almost totally concealed from the street, was the corner of a school bus. A van actually. A yellow team van.

As I stood watching, the front door swung open. Candace Wynn stepped outside, carrying a suitcase in either hand. With brisk, purposeful steps, she moved to the bus, opened a side door, and placed the suitcases inside.

Watching her, I had moved unconsciously into the middle of the street, drawn like a metal chip toward a powerful magnet. Too late I realized she was moving toward the door on the driver's side of the van. She vaulted into the driver's seat and slammed the door behind her. I heard the engine start and saw the backup lights come on.

Suddenly, behind me, squealing brakes and a blaring horn brought me to my senses as a car skidded to a stop a few feet from me. I scrambled out of the way only to dash into the path of another car. Blind to everything but the moving bus, I charged toward it.

It was only when the bus backed out and swung around to turn toward the street that I saw Candace Wynn wasn't alone in the vehicle. Peters sat slumped on the rider's side, his head slack and drooping against the window.

"Stop! Police!" I shouted, drawing my .38 from its shoulder holster. I saw Candace glance across Peters in my direction. Our eyes met briefly across the narrowing distance in a flash of recognition. She saw me, heard me, recognized me, but she didn't stop. She didn't even pause. Instead, the van leaped forward like a startled rabbit as she hit the accelerator. I saw, rather than heard, the side of Peters' head smack against the window.

What's the matter with him, I wondered. Is he asleep? Why doesn't he do something? "Peters!" I shouted, but there was no response.

I ran straight down Graham toward Thirtieth, hoping to intercept the van where the two streets met. As I charged forward, Candace must have read my mind. As she approached the intersection, she gave the steering wheel a sharp turn to the left. The van shuddered and arched off the rutted roadway, tottering clumsily onto the grass.

Good, I thought. She's losing it. But she didn't. Somehow she regained control. The van pulled onto Graham, skidding and sliding, a good ten feet in front of me. She gunned the motor and headed west. I put on one final burst of speed, but it was too little too late.

The Porsche, three houses up the street behind me, was too far away to be of any use. There was only one chance.

The drawn .38 was in my hand. I was tempted to use it. God was I tempted. But just then, just as I was ready to squeeze the trigger, another car met the van on the street. It was a station wagon loaded with people, two women with a bunch of kids.

I couldn't risk it, not even for Peters. I couldn't risk hitting a tire and sending the van spinning out of control to crash into innocent bystanders.

A second car stopped behind me with a screech of brakes. Horns blared. One driver rolled down his window. "What the hell's going on here?"

I rammed the .38 back into its holster and turned to race toward the Porsche in the same motion only to stumble over a little black kid on a tiny bicycle who had pedaled, unnoticed, up behind me.

"Hey, man, you a cop?" he demanded.

I sidestepped him without knocking him down and ran up the street with the kid trailing behind. When I reached the Porsche, I struggled to unlock the door, unable to fit the key in the lock.

"Hey, man," the kid repeated. "I axed if you was a cop. How come you don't answer me?"

Finally, the key slipped home. I glanced at the kid as I flung the door open. He wasn't more than five or six years old.

"Yes, I am," I answered. I fumbled in my pocket, located a loose business card with my name on it, and tossed it to him. Deftly, he plucked it out of the air.

"Do you know how to dial 9—1—1?" I asked.

He nodded, his black eyes huge and serious. "Sure."

"Call them," I ordered. "Tell them there's trouble. Serious trouble. I need help. My name's on that card."

The Porsche's engine roared to life. I wheeled the car around and drove into the confusion of cars still stopped to sort out the excitement. As I swung onto Graham, the boy was high-tailing it up the street on his bicycle, pumping furiously.

I'd have given anything for flashing lights about then, or for a siren that would have forced people out of my way. As it was, I had to make do with the horn, laying into it at every intersection, raging up behind people and sweeping them off the road in front of me.

As I fishtailed around a stopped car at the Beacon Avenue intersection, I caught sight of the lumbering van. It was far too unwieldy for the sports car rally speed and terrain. Half a mile ahead, it skidded into the wrong lane, around a sharp curve. I don't know how she did it, but Candace Wynn dragged it back onto the road. She could drive like hell, damn her.

As she disappeared behind the hill, I slammed the gas pedal to the floorboard and the Porsche shot forward. I was gaining on her. No way the van would be a match for my Porsche. No way.

I raced down Graham, swooping around the curve, over the top of the hill, and down the other side, with its second sharp curve. The traffic light at the bottom of the hill turned red as I approached. Despite my frenzied honking, cars on Swift Avenue moved sedately into the intersection.

One disinterested driver glanced in my direction as I tried to wave him out of my way. Another, a semidriver, flipped me a bird. I finally moved into the intersection all right, but only when my light turned green.

While I was stopped, I had looked up and down Swift, searching for her, but I saw no sign of the van. There was only one other direction she could go at that intersection, only one other choice—onto the freeway, heading north.

I shot across Swift and sliced down the on ramp. Far ahead, a glimpse of yellow school van disappeared around yet another curve, swerving frantically in and out of the otherwise leisurely flow of homeward-bound Sunday afternoon traffic.

I dodged from one lane to another. Where the hell was she going? Why did she have Peters in the car with her? My heart thumped in my throat as we came up the straightaway by the Rainier Brewery. I was closing on her fast, looking for ways I could cut her off, force her to the side of the road.

Just north of the brewery, I was right behind her, honking and motioning for her to pull over. Suddenly, without warning, she veered sharply to the right. With a crash of crumbling metal, the van smashed through the temporary guardrail on a closed exit ramp and bounced crazily over a railroad tie barrier.

I skidded to the shoulder. I couldn't follow her in the Porsche. It never would have cleared the railroad tie. Throwing myself out of the car, I tumbled over the shattered remains of the guardrail and raced up the ramp on foot.

Nobody clocked me, but I was moving, running like my life depended on it, wrestling the .38 out of its holster as I went. I knew how that exit ended. In a cliff. A sheer drop from thirty feet in the air over Airport Way.

I topped the rise. She must have thought the exit was one of the almost completed ones that would have swung her back onto Beacon Hill. At the last moment, she tried to stop. I saw the flash of brake lights, but it was too late. She was going too fast.

The van skidded crazily and then rammed into the two Jersey barriers, movable concrete barricades, at the end of the ramp.

I stopped in my tracks and watched in horror. For the smallest fraction of a second, I thought the barrier would hold. It didn't. The two pieces split apart like a breaking dam and fell away. Carried forward by momentum, the van nosed up for a split second, then disappeared from view.

An eternity passed before I heard the shattering crash as it hit the ground below. Riveted to the ground, frozen by disbelief, I heard a keening horn, the chilling sound of someone impaled on a steering wheel.

Sickened and desperate, I turned and ran back the way I had come. Within seconds, the wailing horn was joined by the faint sounds of approaching sirens. I recognized them at once. Medic One. The sirens did more than just clear traffic out of the way. They said help was coming. They said there was a chance.

"Hurry," I prayed under my breath. "Please hurry."

As I reached the Porsche, I saw two squad cars speeding south on the freeway, blue lights flashing. The boy on the bicycle had made the call. They were coming to help me.

Nice going, guys!

CHAPTER 31

It took three illegal turns to get off the freeway and reach the area on Airport Way where the van had fallen to earth. By the time I got there, someone had mercifully silenced the horn.

Naturally, a crowd had gathered, the usual bloodthirsty common citizens who don't get enough blood and gore on television, who have to come glimpse whatever grisly sight may be available, to see who's dead and who's dying. Revolted, I pushed my way through them. An uncommonly fat woman in a bloodied flowered muu-muu with a plastic orchid lei around her neck sat weeping on a curb. I bent over her, checking to make sure she was all right.

"Look at my car," she sobbed. "That thing fell out of the sky right on me. My poor car! I could have been killed. If someone had been in the back seat . . ."

I looked where she pointed. A few feet from the van sat the pretty much intact front end of an old Cadillac Seville. The rear end of the car, from the back seat on, had been smashed flat. All that remained behind the front door was a totally unrecognizable pile of rubble.

A few feet away lay the battered van, surrounded by hunks of shattered concrete. The van's engine had been shoved back to the second seat. It lay on its side like a stricken horse with a troop of medics and firemen scurrying around it.

My knees went weak. I felt sick to my stomach. The sweet stench of cooking grain from the brewery mixed with the odor of leaking gasoline and the metallic smell of blood. The concoction filled my nostrils, accelerating my heartbeat, triggering my gag reflex.

I attempted to stand up, hoping to get away from the smell and to escape the lady in the flowered dress, but she grabbed onto my arms, pulling herself up along with me. Once we were both upright, she clung to me desperately, repeating the same words over and over, as if repetition would make sense of the incomprehensible.

"It just fell out of the air. Can you imagine? It landed right on top of me."

Prying her fingers loose one by one, I broke away from her. "You stay here," I told her. "I'll send someone to check on you." I walked toward the wreck. A uniformed officer recognized me and waved me past a police barricade.

Just then a second Medic One unit arrived at the scene. A pair of medics hurried to the woman's side. I turned my full attention on the van.

Paramedics, inside and outside the vehicle, struggled to position their equipment, trying to reach the injured occupants of the van. I knew from experience that their job would be to stabilize the patients before any attempt was made to remove them from the vehicle, place them in ambulances, and transport them to hospitals.

Standing a little to one side, I waited. I didn't want to be part of the official entourage. I didn't want to ask or answer any questions. I was there as a person, a friend, not as a detective. The less anyone was aware of my presence, the better.

Dimly, I observed the gathering of reporters who showed up and demanded to know what was going on. Who was in the van? What school was it from? How had it happened? Were there any children involved?

Not directly, I thought. Only Heather and Tracie, whose father lay trapped in that twisted mass of metal. I thought of them then for the first time, of two girls waiting at home for me to bring them word of their father.

A paramedic crawled out of the vehicle and walked toward the lieutenant who was directing the rescue effort. In answer to the captain's question, the paramedic shook his head.

Dreading to hear the words and yet unable to stay away, I moved close enough to overhear what they were saying despite the roar of nearby fire truck engines.

"She's gone," the paramedic said. "What about the guy?"

"Lost a lot of blood," the lieutenant answered. "I don't know if we'll get him out in time or not."

I dropped back out of earshot, trying to make myself small and inconspicuous. I didn't want to hear more. The paramedic's words had confirmed my own worst fears. They didn't think Peters would make it.

I didn't, either.

I retreated to the curb and sat down a few feet away from where the woman in the flowered dress was being treated for cuts and bruises. I closed my eyes and buried my face in my hands. I kept telling myself that Seattle's Medic One was the best in the country, that if anyone could save Peters' life, they could. My feeble reassurances fell flat.

Peters was still trapped. How could they save his life if they couldn't even get him out of the van?

I forced myself to sit there. While the paramedics worked furiously to save Peters' life, they didn't need someone like me looking over their shoulders, getting in the way, and screwing up the works.

Detectives are ill-suited to doing nothing. It goes against their training and mind-set. Sitting there, staying out of the way, took tremendous effort, a conscious, separate act of will for every moment of inactivity. Watching the paramedics and the firemen on and in the van was like watching an anthill. Everyone seemed to be doing some mysterious specialized task without any observable direction or plan.

Then, suddenly, the anthill of activity changed. There was a new urgency as firemen moved forward, bringing with them the heavy metal shears they call the jaws of life. Without a wasted motion, they attacked the side of the van. Within minutes, they had cut a hole a yard wide in the heap of scrap metal. Leaning into the hole, they began to ease something out through it. They worked it out gradually, with maddening slowness, but also with incredible care.

Peters lay on a narrow wooden backboard with a cervical collar stabilizing his head and neck. Blood oozed from his legs, arms, and face. Carefully, they placed him on a waiting stretcher and wrapped his legs in what looked like a pressurized space suit, then carried him ever so gently toward a waiting medic unit. A trail of IVs dragged along behind them.

I was grateful to see that. The IVs meant Peters was still alive, at least right then.

As the medic unit moved away, its siren beginning a long rising wail, I was surprised to discover that darkness had fallen without my noticing. Floodlights had been brought in to light the scene so the paramedics and firemen could see to work. It was dark and cold and spitting rain. I had been so totally focused on the van that I had seen and felt none of it.

Chilled to the bone, I straightened my stiffened legs and walked to where the paramedics were busy reassembling and packing up their equipment. I buttonholed one I had seen crawl out of the van just before they brought Peters out.

"Is he going to make it?" I demanded.

"Who are you?" the paramedic returned without answering my question. "Do you know him?"

I nodded. "He's my partner."

"Do you know anything about his medical background? Allergies? Blood type?"

"No."

"We couldn't locate any identification. What's his name so I can call it ahead to Harborview."

"Peters," I said quietly. "Detective Ron Peters, Seattle P.D."

Just then a uniformed officer caught sight of me. "Beaumont! There you are. We were responding to your distress call when this happened. We heard you were here, but we couldn't find you."

I didn't tell him that I had been hiding out, that I hadn't wanted to be found. I shook my head. The paramedic I had been talking to moved toward me with an air of concern. I must have looked like hell.

"Are you all right?" he asked.

"I'm okay," I muttered.

A uniformed female patrol officer with an accident report form in her hand stepped forward and addressed the paramedics in general. "You found no ID of any kind? Any idea how the accident happened?"

"Nope." The paramedic pointed toward me. "He says the guy is a detective with Seattle P.D."

She turned to me, looking for verification. Sudden anger overwhelmed me, anger at myself mostly, but I focused it on her. She was handy. She was there.

"It wasn't an accident, stupid. Call Homicide. Get 'em down here right away."

I turned on my heel and stalked away. She followed, trotting to keep up.
"Who are you?" she demanded.

"I'm Detective Beaumont, Homicide, and that's Ron Peters, my partner, in that medic unit."

"You know that for sure?"

"Yes, I know it for sure! Now call Homicide like I told you."

"If you know something about this, I've got to talk to you," she snapped back.

She was right and I was wrong, but I kept walking. "They're taking him to the trauma unit at Harborview. If you need to talk to me, that's where I'll be."

My Porsche was parked at a crazy angle half on and half off the sidewalk. The flashers were still flashing. The woman followed me to the car and persisted in asking questions until I slammed the door in her face and drove off.

When I reached Harborview, Peters' empty medic unit sat under the emergency awning with its doors still open and its red lights flashing. The hospital's glass doors slid silently open and the two paramedics wheeled their stretcher back outside.

"Is he going to be all right?" I asked as they came past me.

"Who?" the one asked. "The guy we just brought in?"

"Yeah," I replied gruffly. "Him."

"Talk to the doctor. We're not allowed to answer any questions."

Talking to the doctor turned out to be far easier said than done. I waited for what seemed like hours. I didn't want to call Kirkland and talk to Ames until I had some idea of what to tell him, until I had some idea of what we were up against.

Word traveled through the law enforcement community on an invisible grapevine. The room gradually filled with people, cops keeping the vigil over one of their own. Captain Powell and Sergeant Watkins were two of the first to arrive. Shaking his head, the captain took hold of the top of my arm and gripped it tightly. He said nothing aloud. I felt the same way.

Margie, our clerk, came in a few minutes later, along with several other detectives from the fifth floor. It wasn't long before the officer from the scene showed up, still packing her blank report. Watty sent her away. I think we all figured there'd be plenty of time for filling out forms later.

At last a doctor emerged through swinging doors beside the nurses' station. A nurse directed him to me. He beckoned for me to follow him. I did. So did Watty and Captain Powell. He took us down a polished hallway to a tiny room. A conference room. A bad news room.

The doctor motioned us into chairs. "I understand Detective Peters is your partner?" the doctor said, turning to me.

I nodded.

"What about his family?"

"A couple of kids."

"How old?"

"Six and seven."

"No wife?"

"No." I took a deep breath. "Should someone go get the kids? Bring them to the hospital?"

The doctor shook his head. "No. He's in surgery now. It'll be several hours. If he makes it through that . . ." His voice trailed off.

"Look, doc. How bad is it?"

He looked me straight in the eye. "Bad," he said quietly. "His neck's broken. He has lost a tremendous amount of blood."

His words zinged around in my head like wildly ricocheting bullets. "But will he make it?" I demanded.

The doctor shrugged. "Maybe," he said. The doctor spoke quietly, but his words washed over me with the crushing roar of breaking surf.

Stunned, I rose from the chair. I couldn't breathe. I scrambled away from the doctor, from the brutal hopelessness of that maybe. I battled blindly for a way to escape that tiny, oppressive room before its walls caved in on me.

Powell caught me by the arm before I reached the door. "Beau, where are you going?"

"To Kirkland. To talk to his kids."

"I can send somebody else," Powell told me. "You don't have to do it."

"This is unfortunate," the doctor said. "Perhaps it would be better if someone else . . ."

I turned on him savagely. "Unfortunate?" I bellowed. "You call this unfortunate!"

Powell gripped my arm more tightly. "Hold it, Beau. Take it easy."

I glared at the doctor. "I'm going to Kirkland," I growled stiffly through clenched jaws. "Don't try to stop me."

I shook off Powell's restraining hand and strode from the room. They let me go.

When I pushed open the swinging door at the end of the hall, the waiting room was more jammed than it had been before. I recognized faces, but I spoke to no one. The room grew still when I appeared. Silently, the crowd stepped aside, opening a pathway to the outside door.

On the outskirts of the crowd, just inside the sliding glass door, I saw Maxwell Cole. He stepped in front of me as I tried to walk past.

"I just heard, J. P. Is Peters gonna be all right?" he asked.

I didn't answer. Couldn't have if I had tried.

Max gave me a clap on the shoulder as I went by him. "Too bad," I heard him mutter.

He made no attempt to follow me as I got into the car to drive away. Maybe Maxwell Cole was growing up.

Maybe I was, too.

Chapter 32

I started the engine in the Porsche. Instantly, a mantle of terrible weariness fell over me. It was as though all my strength had been sapped away, all the stamina had drained out of me and into the machine. Gripping the wheel, I felt my hands tremble. I was chilled, cold from the inside out.

It was well after ten. I understood why I had hit a wall of fatigue. The days preceding it, to say nothing of that day itself, had taken their toll.

Common sense ruled out hurrying to Peters' house to tell his girls. It was long past their bedtime. They were no doubt already in bed and fast asleep. Let them sleep. The bad news could wait.

I decided to go home, shower, and change clothes before driving to Kirkland. Mentally and physically, I needed it. Besides, a detour to my apartment gave me a little longer to consider what I'd say, what I'd tell Heather and Tracie when I woke them.

When I got to the Royal Crest, it was all I could do to stay awake and upright in the elevator. I staggered down the hallway, opened the door to my apartment, and almost fell over what I found there. My newly recovered recliner had been returned and placed just inside the door. How Browder had gotten it done that fast I couldn't imagine. But he had.

Unable to walk through the vestibule, I turned into the kitchen. There on the counter sat my new answering machine with its message light blinking furiously.

I counted the blinks, ten of them in all. Ames had told me that each blink indicated a separate message. I pressed rewind and play.

The first two were hang-ups.

The third was a voice I recognized as that of Michael Browder, my interior designer, telling me he was on his way to downtown Seattle. He was bringing the chair in hopes of dropping it off on his way.

The fourth call was Browder again, calling from the security phone downstairs this time, asking to be let into the building.

The fifth call was from the building manager, explaining that he was letting someone deliver a chair and that he hoped it was all right with me.

The sixth was someone calling to see if I was interested in carpet cleaning.

The seventh was from Ned Browning. He didn't say what day or time he was calling. He said he had just discovered that the keys to the Mercer Island team van were missing from his desk. Checking in the district garage, he had discovered that the van was gone as well. He had reported it missing, but did I think it possible that Candace Wynn had taken the keys from his desk while he was down in the locker room?

I stopped the answering machine and replayed Browning's message. Possible? It was more than possible. You could count on it. So that was why she had insisted on meeting Browning at school, why she had pretended to have just learned about the names in the locker the night before. She had lured Browning there so she could get the keys and steal the van.

But why? That still didn't give me the whole answer. Parts of it, yes, but not the whole story. Maybe she had known we were getting close and had wanted to use another vehicle in case we were already looking for her truck. But why a school van? Surely she must have known that by Monday at the latest someone would have noticed and reported it missing.

Unless, by then, she no longer cared whether she got caught. I remembered the fearless, single-minded way she had crashed through the barriers onto the exit ramp. Maybe she had reached a point where being caught was no longer the issue. Now, with Candace Wynn dead, hope faded that I would ever learn the answers to those questions.

I turned back to my answering machine to play the next message. The eighth one was from Joanna Ridley, asking me to call her as soon as I could. She left her number.

The ninth and tenth messages were both from Ames, looking for me, wondering what was going on, and had I learned anything.

The machine clicked off. I dialed Joanna's number, but there was no answer. I poured myself a tumbler full of MacNaughton's and dialed Peters' number in Kirkland. Ames answered on the second ring.

"It's Beau," I said.

"It's about time. Did you find him?"

"Yes."

"It sounds bad. Is it?"

"He's in the hospital, Ralph. The doctors don't know whether or not he'll make it . . ."

"And . . . ?" Ames prompted.

"Even if he does, he may be paralyzed. His neck's broken."

There was a stricken silence on the other end of the line.

"Are the girls in bed?" I asked eventually.

"Mrs. Edwards put them down a little while ago. I told them we'd wake them up if we heard any news."

"Don't get them up yet. Wait until I get there," I said. "I'm at home now. I need to shower. I'll come prepared to spend the night."

"Good," Ames said. "That sounds like a plan."

"I'll be there in about an hour," I told him. "Captain Powell was to give the hospital that number in case they need to reach us. Is there anything you need over there?" I asked as an afterthought.

"As a matter of fact, bring along some MacNaughton's."

"In addition to what's in my glass?"

"Bring me some that hasn't been used," he replied.

The shower helped some. At least it gave me enough energy to gather up a shaving kit and some clean clothes. I drove to Kirkland in the teeth of a roaring gale. Waves from Lake Washington lashed onto the bridge and across my windshield, mixing with sheets of rain and making it almost impossible to see the road ahead of me.

The storm's fury matched my own. J. P. Beaumont was in the process of beating himself up and doing one hell of a good job. What if I had called for help before I ever left Ballard? Was it possible that a patrol car could have reached the Scarborough house in time to keep Candace Wynn from getting away, from making it to the freeway? What could I have done differently so Peters' life wouldn't be hanging in the balance?

In the end, I couldn't ditch the singular conclusion that it was my fault. All my fault.

Ames met me at the door. He looked almost as worn and haggard as I felt. "Tell me," he commanded, taking the bottle of MacNaughton's from my hand and leading me into the kitchen.

Ames poured, and I talked. Off and on I tried Joanna Ridley's number, but there was still no answer. Between calls, I told Ames every detail of what had happened that day, down to the doctor's last words as I left the hospital. When I finished, Ames ran his hands through his hair, shaking his head.

"God what a mess! What are we going to do?"

"About what?"

"The kids."

"What do you mean? What'll happen to them?" I asked.

"That depends," Ames said quietly. "If Peters lives long enough to make his wishes known, he might have some say in it. Otherwise, with their mother out of the country, the state may very well step into the picture and decide what's best."

"You mean hand the girls over to Child Protective Services or to a foster home?"

"Precisely."

"Shit!" I had seen the grim results of some foster home arrangements. They weren't very pretty.

"Has Peters ever mentioned any plan to you? A relative of some kind. Grandparents maybe? An aunt?"

"No. Never."

Ames poured us both another drink. He looked at me appraisingly when he handed it to me. "What about you, Beau?"

"Me?" I echoed. I was thunderstruck.

"Yes, you. God knows you've got plenty of money. You could afford to take them on without any hardship."

"You're serious, aren't you!"

"Dead serious. We've got to have some kind of reasonable plan to offer Peters at the first available moment, before the state drops down on him and grabs Heather and Tracie away. And we've got to have something to tell the girls in the morning."

"But, Ames, I'm not married."

"Neither is Peters, remember? But you've raised kids before, two of them. And from what I've seen of them, you did a pretty commendable job of it. You could do it again."

"I've just bought a place downtown," I protested. "No grass. No yard. No swings."

"Children have grown up in cities for as long as there have been cities. Besides, if they don't like it, you can move somewhere else."

Ames was talking about my taking on Peters' kids with the kind of casual aplomb that comes from never having raised kids of his own. People talk that way about kids and puppies, about how cute they are and how little trouble, only when they've never pulled a six-year-old's baby tooth or housebroken an eight-week-old golden retriever.

Ames spoke with the full knowledge and benefit of never having been in the trenches. His naiveté was almost laughable, but he's one hell of a poker player. He had an unbeatable wild card—my sense of responsibility for what had happened. And the son of a bitch wasn't above using it.

"So what do we do?" I asked. He read my question correctly as total capitulation.

"I'll draw up a temporary custody agreement," he replied. "As soon as Peters is lucid enough for us to talk to him about it, we'll get it signed and notarized."

"Signed?" I asked.

"Witnessed," he corrected.

"And what if that's not possible? What if he never is lucid enough to agree to it?"

"We use the same agreement. It just costs more money to put it in force, that's all," Ames replied grimly.

I knew from experience that Ralph Ames had the moxie to grease the wheels of bureaucracy when the occasion required it.

It was one-thirty in the morning when we finally called it quits. The decision had long since been made to wait until morning to tell the girls. There was no sense in waking them up to tell them in the middle of the night.

For a long time after Ames went to bed, I lay awake on the floor mulling our conversation. Ames was right, of course. I was the only acceptable choice for taking care of Heather and Tracie. I had the most to offer. And the most to gain.

It was probably just a sign of fatigue, but by five-thirty, when I finally fell asleep, it was beginning to seem like a perfectly reasonable idea.

Heather bounded into my room an hour later. "Unca Beau," she squealed, climbing gleefully on top of me. "Did you find him? Did you?"

It was a rude awakening. Tracie, more reticent than her younger sister, hung back by the door. I motioned to her. With a kind of delicate dignity, she sat down beside me.

I swallowed hard before I answered Heather's question. "Yes, I did," I said slowly.

"Well, where is he, then? Why isn't he in his bed?" Heather's six-year-old inquisitiveness sought answers for only the most obvious questions.

"He's in the hospital, girls."

Tracie swung around and looked up at me. "He's hurt?"

"I'm afraid so."

"Will he die?"

"I don't know. Neither do the doctors."

"I don't want him to die," Heather wailed. "He can't. I won't let him."

Tracie continued to look up at me, her eyes wide and unblinking. "What will happen to us?" she asked.

Bless Ames for asking the question first, for coming up with a plan. "We talked about that last night," I assured them. "If your father approves, maybe you can stay with me for a while. Downtown."

"But you're moving."

"To a bigger place. There'd be more room."

My heart went out to Tracie. She was very young to be so old, to carry so much responsibility for what was happening around her.

Heather's sudden outburst quieted as suddenly as it had come. "Would we ride in a elevator?"

"Every day."

I reached over and tousled Tracie's long brown hair. "We'll take care of things, Tracie. Ames and Mrs. Edwards and I will do the worrying. You don't have to."

Tears welled in her big brown eyes. She turned around and launched herself at my neck, clinging to me like a burr.

I'm glad she didn't look up at me right then. I was busy wiping my own eyes.

CHAPTER 33

Ames had talked to Mrs. Edwards while I was telling Heather and Tracie. By the time we came out to the kitchen, the housekeeper, red-eyed but under control, was busy making breakfast. She dished out huge bowls of oatmeal. "You've got to eat and keep up your strength so your daddy won't have to worry about you," she said. Then she went over to the sink and ran water to cover her sniffles.

None of us ate the oatmeal.

I was pushing my chair back from the table when the phone rang. It was Margie, Peters' and my clerk from the department. She sounded pretty ragged, too.

"Sorry to bother you, Beau, but there's a message here I thought you should know about. It's been here since last night. From Harborview."

"From Harborview! Why didn't they call me here?" I demanded. "Powell was supposed to tell them."

"I don't know what happened, but here's the number."

I took it down and dialed it as soon as I heard the dial tone. "Emergency," a woman answered.

"My name is Beaumont. I had a message to call this number."

"One moment. Here it is. You're to call 545-1616."

My frustration level was rising. I dialed the next number. "Maternity," someone said.

"Maternity? Why am I calling Maternity?"

"I wouldn't know, sir. This is the maternity wing at University Hospital. Is someone in your family expecting a baby?"

"No, I can't imagine . . ."

"What is your name, sir? I may have a message here for you."

"Beaumont. J. P. Beaumont."

"That's right. Here it is. Hold on. It's early, but I can connect you."

Ames, who had heard the entire conversation, looked at me questioningly. I shrugged my shoulders. Why the hell would Maternity at University Hospital have a message for me?

"Hello." At first I didn't recognize the voice.

"This is J. P. Beaumont. I had a message to call."

"Oh, Beau. Thank you for calling."

"Joanna?"

". . . tried to get hold of you yesterday, but then my water broke, and they took me to the hospital."

I was so relieved it wasn't bad news about Peters that it was all I could do to make sense of what she was saying.

"You had the baby, then? What is it? A boy or a girl?"

She didn't answer. "I've got to talk to you. Right away. Can you come down here?"

"To University Hospital? Sure, I guess so." I held the phone away from my mouth and spoke to Ames. "She wants to see me."

"Go ahead. Mrs. Edwards and I will hold down the fort."

I drove to Harborview first. I went directly to the intensive-care-unit waiting room. Big Al Lindstrom, one of the night-shift homicide detectives, was sitting upright on a couch, his massive arms folded across his chest, apparently sound asleep. His eyes opened, though, as soon as I stepped into the room.

"Hi, there, Beau. Me and Manny are spelling one another. We'll be here all day."

I was glad to see him. "Any word?"

"It's touch and go. He's still heavily sedated. Understand you're looking after his kids." I nodded. "You handle that end of it. We'll take care of this."

"Thanks, Al." I didn't say anything more. I couldn't.

Leaving Harborview, I drove north to University Hospital. Joanna Ridley was in a private room at the end of the maternity wing. Her door stood partially open. I knocked on it softly.

"Come in."

I entered the room. Joanna was not in her bed. Wearing a white, gauzelike nightgown, she sat in a chair near the window, gazing across a still green, stormy Lake Washington.

"Hello, Joanna," I said quietly.

She didn't look up. "I read about your partner in the paper," she said. "Is he going to be all right?"

"His neck's broken," I told her. "If he lives, he'll probably be paralyzed."

"I'm sorry," Joanna murmured. She looked up at me. "I met her, you know. She had the nerve to stand right there and invite me to Darwin's memorial service." Her eyes filled with tears. "I'm glad she's dead," she added.

I stood there awkwardly, not knowing quite what to say. "Why did you want to see me?"

She pointed toward the closet. "There's a box over there, in my suitcase. Would you bring it here?"

The box was a shoe box, a red Nike basketball shoe box, size thirteen. I handed the box to her and she motioned for me to sit on the bed. She remained in the chair.

For a time after I handed it to her, she sat looking down at the box in her lap, her hands resting on the cover. When she finally raised her face to look at me, she met my gaze without wavering.

"I never knew it was the same woman," she said softly.

"Who was the same woman? I don't understand."

"Candace Wynn and Andi Scarborough. Darwin never wanted me near school. I thought that was just his way. It was one of those little peculiarities. I never questioned it. I never knew it was because of her."

"Joanna, I still don't understand."

"Darwin and Andi Scarborough went together in high school. Actually, they were in grade school when it started, back in those days when blacks and whites didn't mix at all, not socially. Their mothers broke it up, both of them. Darwin wrangled a scholarship to UCLA, a basketball scholarship. That's where I met him."

Slowly, the light began to dawn. "Darwin and Candace Wynn were childhood sweethearts?"

Joanna nodded. "I knew about her, at least I knew about a white girl named Andi Scarborough. His mother told me about her when Darwin and I were just going together. But I never knew her married name was Wynn. And I never knew she worked with him at school."

The lights came on. I began to fill in some of the blanks. "So they met years later and reestablished their relationship."

Joanna patted the box in her lap. "He kept her letters, locked in his desk at school. I found them yesterday when I started to sort through the big box the principal sent home."

"I'm sorry," I said.

She drew her chin up and squared her shoulders. "Don't be," she answered. "I'm glad I found them and read them. It makes it easier to go on. I didn't lose anything. It never existed."

A nurse poked her head in the door. She saw me sitting on the edge of the bed and frowned in disapproval. "You'll have to leave now. We're bringing the babies to nurse."

I started to my feet. Joanna caught my hand. "Don't go," she said.

The nurse glared at me. "Are you the baby's father? Fathers can stay."

"He's a father," Joanna said evasively. "I want him to stay."

The nurse clicked her tongue and shook her head, but eventually she gave in, led Joanna back to bed, helped her get ready for the baby, and then brought a tiny bundle into the room. I sat self-consciously on the chair by the window, unsure what to do or say.

I couldn't help remembering those first few tentative times when Karen had nursed Scott when neither of them had known what they were doing. That wasn't the case here.

When I glanced up at Joanna, she was leaning back against the bed looking down contentedly at the bundle nestled in her arms. "I've decided to name him Peter," she told me.

Without her having to explain, I knew why and was touched. It was a nice gesture toward Peters, one I hoped he'd appreciate someday.

"It's a good name," I said.

It was quiet in the room after that. The only sounds came from the lustily sucking infant. This part of parenthood made sense to me. It seemed straightforward and uncomplicated. Joanna Ridley made it look deceptively easy.

But still there was an undercurrent beneath her placid, motherly surface. I sensed there was more to the story, more she hadn't told me. I didn't know if now was a good time to ask her about it. Fools rush in where angels fear to tread.

"What was in the letters?" My question broke the long silence between us.

Joanna answered my question with one of her own. "Do you remember when Detective Peters asked me if Darwin had a separate checking account or credit cards?"

I nodded. "You told us no."

"I was wrong. There was a lot I didn't know, including an account at the credit union, a joint account with her, with Candace Wynn. I never saw the money. It was deducted from his paycheck before it ever came home, and he had all the statements sent to him at school. Between them they must have had quite a sum of money. Part of it came from Darwin, and part came from her. According to the letters, she had been systematically gutting her parents' estate for years. They used the money to buy a boat."

"A boat?"

"A sail boat. It was supposedly a partnership made up of several people. In actual fact, there were only two partners, Candace and Darwin. They planned to run away together until I found out something was going on. Then, even after she knew I was expecting a baby, she still kept talking about it in her letters, that eventually it would be just the two of them together."

Joanna paused and took a deep breath before she continued. "From the letters, it sounded like she understood about me, about the baby, but when she found out about the cheerleader, that Bambi whatever-her-name-was, she snapped."

The quote came unbidden to my mind. I repeated it aloud. " 'Hell hath no fury like a woman scorned.' Isn't that what they say?"

Joanna didn't answer me. I watched as she took the baby from one breast, held the child, patted his back until he burped, then gently moved him to the other breast. Once more I was struck by her beauty, by the sudden contrasts of black and white, skin and gown, sheet and blanket, mother and child. Sitting there in a splash of morning sunlight, Joanna Ridley was the epitome of every Madonna I had ever seen.

Beautiful and serene, yet she, too, had been scorned, betrayed. Where was her anger, her fury?

"What about you, Joanna?"

She looked up at me and gave me a wry grin. "I wasn't scorned, honey," she drawled with a thick, southern accent I had never heard her use before. "I was suckered. There's a big difference."

CHAPTER 34
EPILOGUE

The next few weeks were a blur. I camped out in Kirkland with the kids and Mrs. Edwards until school got out. I took a leave of absence so I could look after the kids and run back and forth to the hospital. The girls kept wanting to go see their dad, but he was far too sick for visitors. Peters' health remained precarious, and the doctors told us it would be months before he was entirely out of the woods.

Before Ames returned to Phoenix, we spent hours trying to second-guess what the long-term implications were, but other than sorting out the custody arrangement, we decided to hide and watch and not make any other plans until we had some clear direction from the doctors. Mostly, they weren't very informative, but they did hint that the fact that Peters had been unconscious at the time of the wreck was probably the only thing that kept him from being killed. The doctors vacillated between saying he'd never be able to live on his own again and voicing cautious hope that he might recover.

There were occasional times when Peters was fairly lucid. During one of those periods, I asked him if he remembered anything about his time with Candace Wynn. He said no. The doctors tell me that it's not unusual for a person who has suffered a traumatic injury to totally forget the events surrounding the injury.

Considering what I discovered, his amnesia was probably a good thing. Joanna let me read Candace Wynn's letters. In the last one, one written the Thursday before Darwin Ridley died, she raged about Bambi Barker. She had somehow gotten hold of Molly Blackburn's negative. Alternately threatening Darwin and pleading with him to run away with her, she ended the letter with the impassioned statement that if she couldn't have him, nobody would.

She must have gone over the edge then. From what the homicide detectives were able to piece together, she somehow convinced Darwin Ridley to come home with her, slipped him some of her mother's morphine, put a noose around his neck, and pushed him off the second-floor landing over her truck. All she had to do then was cut him down, hose him off, cover him up, and haul him away. The crime lab found bits of trace evidence in the truck that indicated she had used it to transport Ridley back to the dumpster where he was found. No one ever figured out for sure why she went to the trouble of stripping him, unless she used his clothes in a futile attempt to frame Joanna.

Eventually, Maxwell Cole came forward with the envelope and his copy of the Ridley/Bambi photo. The typeface on his envelope matched that on Joanna Ridley's envelope. It was also the same typeface on Candace Wynn's love letters to Darwin Ridley. The remains of the typewriter were found crushed in the wreckage of the van, along with a suitcase of small bills and Molly Blackburn's missing negatives. Peters' .38 was there, too.

Candace must have sent the pictures to the Barkers, Joanna, and the press, just as she had planted the evidence in Joanna Ridley's trunk in hopes of throwing us off the track.

She and Peters hit it off like a couple of star-struck kids. Maybe she was on the rebound. Maybe she liked playing with fire. Somehow, while he was at her apartment, Peters must have discovered something that alerted him, something that told him Candace was behind Ridley's death. Since she went to the trouble of painting the rail, he may have discovered the chafed place on the upright where the noose was tied off.

Whatever it was, when she overheard him trying to call me, she stopped him. That explained the cryptic message on my machine.

Ned Browning resigned on the first of April under a cloud of Chief Marilyn Sykes' making. His case won't come up for several months, but when it does, I doubt he'll be involved in the educational system anymore.

As for me, I'm beginning to get used to being a parent again. According to Ames, who just called from Phoenix, it's just like riding a bike. Once you learn how, you never forget.

He could be right about that.

ABOUT THE AUTHOR

J.A. JANCE is the bestselling author of eleven J.P. Beaumont mysteries, the Anthony Award-nominated *Hour of the Hunter*, and the Joanna Brady mystery series. She divides her time between Seattle, Washington, and Tucson, Arizona.